For You

Discover other titles by Kristen Ashley at:
www.kristenashley.net

Commune with Kristen at:
www.facebook.com/kristenashleybooks
Twitter: KristenAshley68

For You

KRISTEN ASHLEY

Copyright © 2014 by Kristen Ashley
First ebook edition: March 15, 2011
First print edition: January, 2015

ISBN: 069232366X
ISBN 13: 9780692323663

This book is dedicated to the town of Brownsburg, Indiana, USA. Home of the Bulldogs and a great place to grow up.

Acknowledgements

I wish to thank Stephanie Redman Smith, former Communications Officer for the Boone County, Indiana Sherriff's Department and Sgt. Steve Smith of the Lebanon, Indiana Police Department for their input and assistance while I was writing *For You*. Of course, I took some liberties but only cops and former dispatch officers will know which ones (I hope). Thank you both for working alongside me with this novel and helping me to make Colt's voice and the story more real and, for the most part, accurate.

One

ANGIE

Until that day, I'd made an art out of avoiding Alexander Colton. All my work would be for nothing, all because of Angie.

Poor, sweet, stupid, dead Angie.

⁓

Martin Fink and Christopher Renicki were the first two uniforms who responded to my call. I'd known Marty and Chris for ages. It was good they were partners. Chris was smart; Marty, not so much.

We were out in the alley, Chris doing crime scene stuff, Marty standing by me. A couple of squad cars with their lights silently flashing had pulled in on either side of the dumpster. Other uniforms had been dispatched to hold back the growing crowd and the crime scene tape was secured by the time Alec showed up.

He'd parked elsewhere and didn't come through the bar like I expected him to. He had keys to the bar, for one. For another, he knew the bar nearly as well as I did and not only because he spent a good deal of time sitting at the end of it, my brother standing inside the bar in front of him, both of them drinking beer and talking about shit I couldn't hear because I stayed well away.

Another surprise was he also didn't have his partner Sully with him.

I watched him as he walked up to Marty and me.

The detectives in town, not that there were many of them, wore ill-fitting, inexpensive suits or nice trousers and shirts with ties.

Not Alec.

Jeans, boots, wide leather belt, sports jacket that looked tailored for him (probably a present from Susie Shepherd) and a nice shirt.

Alec was a big guy even when he was a kid, just kept growing and growing. Dad used to say if he didn't stop his head would touch the clouds. Mom thought Alec and my brother Morrie were best friends because they were both the biggest kids in the class and it just grew from that. Morrie grew out as well as up, however. Alec just grew tall and broad but stayed lean. Alec was tight end to Morrie's offensive lineman during high school, and in all things life. Morrie did the grunt work and never got the glory. Alec knew how to block and was really good at it but every once in a while he got the chance to shine.

Alec's dark hair was too long but he'd always worn it too long, even as a kid. But he'd done it then because his mother was such a shit mother. She never remembered to get it cut. My mom finally ended up taking Alec to the barber when she took Morrie. Later he kept it long just because he was Alec. It curled around his ears and neck now and, as with everything Alec, it looked a little wild.

I stood there and watched silently as he made it to me and Marty, his eyes never leaving me. He didn't even look at Angie.

"Feb," he said on a short nod.

"Alec," I replied.

His eyes were a weird color; light brown with a hint of gold. His dad had the same eyes but his dad's eyes weren't exactly like Alec's. Alec's dad's eyes were mean.

Those eyes got hard as did his mouth when I called him Alec. They always did. Everyone called him Colt. *Everyone.* Even my mom and dad started calling him Colt after what happened years ago.

Only his folks and I called him Alec anymore, not that he talked to his folks since his dad was in prison for the second time and his mom was never sober and he never spoke to her. Not that I talked much to him either.

He hated it when I called him Alec but I didn't call him Alec to be a bitch or anything, just that he was Alec to me, he always had been.

"Colt," Chris said, calling his attention and Alec looked his way.

That was when he caught sight of Angie.

I looked at her too and wished I hadn't. I'd already seen enough, too much, so much I'd never forget.

I'd gone to high school with Angie. We'd been friends once upon a time, good friends. You could say we still were, but not good ones.

No, we weren't anything anymore because now she was dead.

Alec's midsection came into my vision and cut off sight of Angie. I lifted my eyes to Alec's face, which was still hard but now he was directing his hard look at Marty.

"Why's she out here?" he asked, sounding pissed-off.

"What?" Marty asked back, sounding as usual, confused.

"Jesus, Marty," Alec muttered, still sounding pissed and his eyes cut to me. "Go inside, Feb."

I stared at him and didn't move a muscle.

"Feb, inside," he repeated.

I still stared at him.

He took a step toward me and said low, "February."

My body jerked and I nodded. Inside would be good. Inside would be fucking awesome.

I went inside, headed directly to Morrie and my office—Mom and Dad's old office, the office Morrie and Alec and I practically grew up in—and coffee. I could still taste the vomit in the back of my mouth. I hadn't actually puked but it had threatened.

I was pouring a cup when Morrie came in.

Alec was big but my brother was enormous. He was also demonstrative.

He walked right up to me, took the coffee cup from my hand, plunked it down, yanked the coffeepot out of my other hand, slid it under the filter and then engulfed me in a hug.

I should have started crying then, I suppose. But I didn't.

"You okay, Feb?" Morrie asked, and I nodded, my cheek sliding against his big, barrel chest.

I wondered briefly why he was there. It wasn't his turn to open, it was mine.

My guess, Alec had called him.

"Sis," he whispered at my nod and I closed my eyes. He didn't call me "sis" very often anymore. Hadn't since we were kids. I missed it.

Still, no tears came.

"You want coffee?" I asked.

Morrie pulled away and gave me a look.

He didn't like what he saw, I knew it but he still said, "Yeah."

I made him a cup and we were taking sips when Alec filled the doorframe.

In the light I caught sight of the scar under his left eye. It was a little, puckered crescent moon, about the size of your thumbnail. I thought that was weird, it being that small, considering at the time it was made it bled a whole helluva lot.

As it did anytime I saw it, it made flashbacks flood my brain. Flashbacks of Alec, sixteen years old and sitting silent on the toilet seat in my mom and dad's bathroom and me, fourteen, standing there wiping the blood off his face with one of Mom's wet washcloths. Morrie coming in, giving me ice, me wrapping it up and holding it to the gaping cut under Alec's swelling eye. My dad walking in, taking in Alec, his bloodied face, his knuckles torn, bleeding and swollen, the way he held his body like if he moved it would be torture, and saying, "Police are going to your place, Colt, you're going with me. Jackie and the kids to the hospital."

That was the first time my father called him Colt. He never addressed him as anything else since.

"Jesus, what the fuck, Colt?" Morrie said upon seeing him. "Mom and Dad's bar? Seriously? Who the fuck would do that?"

Alec's gaze flicked to Morrie and he shook his head.

This was a good question, I thought. A dead body behind their bar? Crazy. My mom and dad were beloved in this town. So were their parents. So was Morrie.

Me? I wasn't sure. Maybe.

Or at least, I once had been.

"You called nine one one," Alec said, and I looked at him though I didn't quite meet his eyes.

"Yeah."

"You found her?" Alec asked.

"Yeah."

"What were you doing in the alley?"

I stared at him not seeing, then said, "Darryl."

"Fuck. Fuckin' Darryl," Morrie muttered, now he sounded pissed.

"Darryl?" Alec asked.

"He never takes out the trash at night. I tell him, every night. Guy's got nothin' between his ears," Morrie explained, telling the God's honest truth about Darryl and pulling a hand through his thick hank of blond hair. "Leaves it at the back door and forgets. First person in in the morning, usually me or Feb, take it out."

This wasn't exactly true. The first person in in the morning was usually me, not Morrie. Though, I had to admit, on occasion, namely my rare days off, it happened.

"You on last night?" Alec asked me, and I shook my head.

"Night off," I told him.

"I was on," Morrie put in.

Alec turned to Morrie. "Angie here?"

Morrie nodded. "Dude, she's always here."

This was true. Angie was a regular. She also regularly wore slut clothes and regularly got shitfaced and regularly picked up anyone who would fuck away whatever demons tortured her. Though obviously these efforts never lasted long because she was always back again, usually the next night. Angie wasn't hard on the eyes if you didn't look too close and see what her lifestyle was doing to her skin. There was no lack of choice for Angie.

"She go home with someone?" Alec asked Morrie.

Morrie moved his neck in that funny way he did when he was uncomfortable, like he was pulling at a too tight collar and tie, even though he was wearing a t-shirt with a zip-up hooded sweatshirt over it and his hand never moved.

Then he said, "Cory."

"Fuckin' hell," Alec muttered and he could say that again.

5

Cory's wife Bethany was pregnant with their third child. Bethany was also a screamer. And Bethany was going to have a shit fit. It wasn't the first time Cory strayed. Hell, Cory came on to me practically any time he got hammered enough to pull up the courage. It wasn't the first time he dipped his wick in Angie either. This also wasn't going to be the first time Bethany found out about Angie. Though it would be the first time Angie showed up the next morning dead in an alley and Cory would be involved in a murder investigation.

"You see anyone last night? Unfamiliar? Give you a bad feeling?" Alec asked Morrie and I knew this was brother-speak.

Alec would lay his career down on Morrie telling him he had a bad feeling about someone. Both of them could read people like books, something they could do forever. I'd never been able to lie successfully to either of them, not once, and I'd tried. It wasn't surprising Alec became a cop. It was natural-born even if on the face of it, considering his parents and, well, how he used to be, you wouldn't know it. It also wasn't surprising Morrie took over the bar. Even in our town—which wasn't huge but also wasn't small—the clientele was regular. Still, trouble could happen, especially when the races were on and anyone could wander in. You had to be able to weed the good from the bad so you could lock down the bad before shit happened.

"Nope, no one. Normal night at Jack and Jackie's," Morrie answered.

Alec looked at me. "Where's the trash?"

I again stared and repeated, "The trash?"

"You said you went out to the alley to take out the trash. Crime scene, far's I can see, is unaltered. Where's—?"

Alec stopped talking because I started moving. I wasn't thinking much of anything. I didn't even know why I was moving.

I plunked my coffee cup down, walked past Alec and went to the bar. The heavy panel was already up and over on its hinges where I guessed I'd put it when I went in to make the 911 call. I walked behind the bar and stared at the two huge bags of garbage that were sitting on the floor by the phone.

I hadn't even noticed I'd carried them back in and dropped them to make the call.

I turned around and saw Alec was standing close, his eyes on the trash.

"I just went to the door," I told his throat, seeing his neck twist, his chin dipping down to look at me but my eyes didn't move. "I just went to the door," I repeated then my head jerked, my ear going toward my shoulder and I felt a weird pain in the back of my neck at the sudden movement. "I just went to the door," I said again, for some stupid reason now whispering, "opened the door and saw her."

That's when I cried.

I didn't feel anything, didn't see anything, didn't hear anything, didn't taste the coffee in my mouth, just cried hard while my brain filled.

I saw her. I saw Angie and all her blood and all her exposed *parts*. Parts I should never see. Parts with skin, parts without, all of it, all of her, lying lifeless in the alley by the dumpster.

Then I heard Alec say, "I got her," and I realized his arms were around me.

I pulled away and stepped away. Distance with Alec, hell with *anyone*, but *especially* with Alec, was good.

I swiped at my eyes, controlling the tears, not looking at him. "I'm okay."

There was silence for a while but Morrie moved in close to me. I could feel his bulk filling the long space behind the bar.

"You gotta walk me through your morning," Alec said and I didn't want to but I lifted my eyes to his.

"What?"

"Walk me through your morning, Feb," Alec repeated.

"I came in to get ready to open—" I started.

"Your full morning," Alec interrupted.

I felt my mouth open, my lips parting. I could feel the sensation of skin separating from skin like it was the first time I'd ever done it when I knew I'd done it before. It just didn't feel like it then. It felt like the first time and it felt like my lips parted in slow motion.

I wished I'd brought my coffee with me.

"I woke up—"

"What time?"

I shook my head. "Normal time. Seven o'clock, seven thirty."

"You get up at seven thirty?" Morrie asked, like I had a screw loose.

"Yeah."

"Shit, Feb, we own a bar," Morrie stated. "How do you get up at seven thirty?"

"I don't know, I just do." And I did. Even if I lay my head down at three thirty in the morning, I woke up between seven and seven thirty. It was a curse.

"You woke up. What next?" Alec cut in giving Morrie a *shut up* look. I'd seen him do that a lot over the years. Usually Morrie didn't shut up. This time he did.

"I fed the cat—"

"Did you do it alone?" Alec asked.

I stared at him then said, "Feed the cat?"

He shook his head but it was a rough motion, jerky. "Wake up."

I sucked in breath, not wanting to answer the question, not wanting Alec to have that information, either answer I could give. But knowing I had to, I nodded.

He nodded his head, that motion was rough and jerky too. "What'd you do after you fed your cat?"

"I did yoga."

Alec's brows snapped together and now he was looking at me like I had a screw loose. "You do yoga?"

"Well…yeah."

He looked away muttering, "Christ."

I didn't know what was wrong with yoga but I didn't ask. I wanted this to be done. In fact, I wanted the day to be done, the year, I wanted it to be a year from now when all this would be faded and a whole lot less real.

"Like I was saying, I did yoga, took a shower and then walked to Meems'."

"Anyone see you walk to Meems'?" Alec asked.

"What's this about?" Morrie sounded like he was getting pissed.

"Just let me ask the questions. It'll be over and we can move on," Alec answered.

"Jessie," I cut in, still on a mission to get my story out so this could be over and we could move on. "I walked to her place and then Jessie walked with me to Meems'."

Jessie Rourke and Mimi VanderWal were my best friends, had been since high school.

"You and Jessie went to Meems', what next?" Alec asked.

"We hung out at Meems', had coffee, a muffin, shot the shit, the same as every day," I answered. And it was the same as every day, although sometimes Jessie didn't come with and it was just me and my journals, or a book or the paper, and my cup of coffee and muffin at Meems'.

I preferred when Jessie was there. Meems owned the joint and by the time I got there it was a crush so she didn't have time to gab. She had a plaque that said "reserved" that she put on my table, though everyone knew it was my table and no one ever sat there in the mornings but me. She didn't need the plaque, one of her kids carved into the table, "Feb's Spot, sit here and die." Meems' kids were a bit wild but they were funny.

"When'd you leave Meems'?" Alec asked.

I shrugged. "Ten o'clock, probably around there. Came straight here." Coming straight to J&J's wasn't far. It was two doors down from Mimi's Coffee House. "I opened up, started the coffee going and went to the back hall to take out the trash I knew was probably there. It was there. I opened the door, grabbed the bags and—"

I stopped and looked down at the garbage bags beside me. The rest didn't need to be said.

Alec's voice came at me. "You see anything else, Feb?"

I took in a breath because I needed it and I thought it was a big one but it felt shallow. My chest felt empty like I could breathe and breathe but there was not enough breath to fill it, never would be again and I looked at him.

"Anything else? Anyone in the alley when you went out?"

Morrie got closer to me, his arm sliding around my shoulders. "Jesus, Colt. What the fuck you sayin'?"

"She's warm," Alec answered, his words were clipped, short, bitten off like he didn't want to say them but he had to and he wanted them out of his mouth as fast as he could do it.

"Warm?" I asked.

I watched his teeth sink into his bottom lip. I knew why he did this. I'd seen him do it a lot in my life. He did it when he was seriously, *seriously* hacked off.

9

"The body," he said. "Angie."

"What?" Morrie asked.

"She's still warm," Alec answered. "She's not been dead long."

"Oh my God," I whispered. That empty feeling in my chest started burning. The vomit rolled back up my throat and I had to swallow it down.

"Are you fucking *shitting* me?" Morrie exploded.

"You see anything, Feb? Hear anything? Any movement? Anything?" Alec pushed. He wanted answers but he was going about it quiet, gentle.

"Jesus fucking Christ," Morrie cursed.

"Morrie, you aren't helping," Alec told him.

"Fuck that, Colt. My sister opened the door to a fresh murder scene!" Morrie bellowed. "You're sayin' the guy coulda been out there?"

I felt my muscles seize.

Alec either saw it or sensed it and his voice went scary when he said, "Morrie, for fuck's sake, you aren't fucking helping."

Morrie and Alec may have been best friends since kindergarten but they fought, a lot. It was never pretty and it could get physical. It hadn't happened in a while but, then again, nothing this big had happened in a while.

"I didn't see anything," I said quickly and I didn't. And, at that moment, I was glad I didn't.

I didn't want whoever did that to Angie to get away with it and, if I saw something, I wouldn't lie even though it would scare the shit out of me. But I didn't see anything and this was a relief.

I wasn't a bad person. But I wasn't a good person either. I didn't do good things like Alec did. I was just a normal person, I kept myself to myself. I also had been a bartender my whole adult life and grew up in a bar, not to mention I now part-ran one. So I kept other things to myself too. It was a job hazard. Everyone told you everything when they were hammered. Shit you did *not* want to know.

But I'd have done the right thing for Angie.

I just hoped Alec knew that.

He looked me direct in the eye and I let him. This went on awhile and was very uncomfortable. Not that I had anything to hide, just that these days anytime Alec stared me direct in the eye, it made me very uncomfortable. I'd been able to avoid it mostly for years, but now there it was.

"You're stayin' with me until Colt finds this fucker," Morrie told me and I broke eye contact with Alec to stare at my brother.

"I am not."

"You stay with him or you stay with me."

This came from Alec.

I transferred my stare to him, thrown for a moment because while I was perfecting the art of avoiding Alec, I pretty much figured he was returning the gesture.

"I'm not doing that either."

"Two choices, Feb," Morrie stated, his arm getting tight around my shoulders.

"I didn't *see* anything!" My voice was getting higher.

"Not takin' chances." Morrie didn't sound like he'd be easily swayed.

"This is ridiculous," I muttered, getting pissed.

I was a normal person and kept myself to myself, meaning I *liked* to keep myself to myself. Not have myself living with my brother and *definitely* not Alec.

"Ridiculous?" Alec said, his voice weirdly soft and compelling, drawing my attention to him and his face was hard again. He was angry, at *me*.

And I knew why.

I'd seen it, all the gruesome, bloody evidence of it in the alley.

"I'll stay with Morrie."

Morrie's arm gave my shoulders a squeeze.

Alec bit his lip again, still hacked off about something, what at that point I didn't know, but he kept staring at me, making me think it was me. Then he let go of his lip and clenched his teeth, making both of his jaws flex and I wondered if he was biting back words.

He succeeded if that was what he was doing since without saying anything, he nodded to me then to Morrie and he walked away.

⸻

Before Colt walked into his house, he knew Susie was there.

"Fuck," he muttered while entering.

He should have never given her his key. They'd been seeing each other off and on (mostly off) for three years and he'd managed to steer clear of doing it. He'd only done it because he needed someone to look after his dog when he went fishing with Morrie two weeks ago and Susie had begged him to do it. She'd never given the key back and he'd not had the time to ask for it or the patience to deal with the tantrum when he asked.

He ignored the fact that Susie was there and went directly to the kitchen, pulled a beer out of the fridge and used the edge of the counter to snap off the top.

He was halfway through downing it when Susie came in.

His chin came down as did his beer and he looked at her.

She'd been the town beauty since practically birth, homecoming queen, prom queen. Her father owned a variety of local stores and a shitload of property until he'd sold them all to big chains and land developers, making a mint and making his daughter, upon his death, the only multi-millionaire in town.

Susie Shepherd had been engaged twice, never married. Both men begged off, Colt knew, even though the story was spread that Susie had been the one to get cold feet.

After three years, Colt knew why they'd fled.

She was a beauty, she could be sweet when she had a mind to do it or she wanted something and she was a great lay, but she also could be a total bitch.

She was blonde, like February, but Susie's blonde hair wasn't thick and long and wild like February's. Even when February did whatever she had to do to make her hair almost sleek, it still flipped out at the ends, defying her, laying testimony to the deeper personality trait that February couldn't hide even though she tried.

Susie was also tall, like February. She just didn't have February's great tits and abundant hips and sweet ass. And, even though Susie's legs were long, they didn't seem to go on forever, like February's, like they could wrap around you twice to lock you close while you were fucking her.

And Susie just simply didn't have that look about her. That look February started to get when she was fourteen. That look that matured as she did. That look that promised she'd suck your cock, and get off on it.

12

That look that told you she'd sit on your face and fucking love it. That look that told you she'd let you do her doggie style, or any style, and she'd want more of it, beg you to do it harder. That look that said you could leave her on her belly in bed after you'd just fucked her, and she'd be totally okay with you going to meet the guys at the bar. Hell, she'd get up, clean up and come with you if she felt like it, but she'd have a mind to your space as long as you gave a mind to hers.

"You're late," Susie said, like she'd know what late was for him, which she fucking didn't.

"Angie Maroni was murdered this morning."

He heard her suck in breath and he wondered what world she lived in. Everyone else in town knew about Angie by noon.

Then again, Susie had never stepped foot over the threshold of J&J's Saloon as everyone in town over drinking age, and some of them under it, had. Susie shopped in Indianapolis, had her hair done there, met her friends there. She just lived here so she could pretend to be queen even though no one really liked her.

"How'd that happen?" Susie asked, and Colt saw Angie again in that alley. But even though he wanted to stop it, for the life of him he couldn't and he saw her with Feb's eyes.

It was a small town but it was close to a big city and two racetracks. Shit spread and, as a cop for over twenty years, a detective for over sixteen, he'd seen his fill of crime and definitely his fill of death.

But Angie, Christ, he could pick hundreds of deaths, even murders he'd prefer Feb to see.

"Knife," was all Colt would tell Susie.

He was close to ending it with her. He had been now for months; he'd just never got around to it. Still, he had no intention of telling her how Angie was murdered with a hatchet. She'd likely find out eventually if she started paying attention, but he wouldn't be the one to tell her.

She started to come closer, saying, "I'm sorry, Colt."

"Don't be sorry for me. It's Angie in the morgue."

Her lip started to curl up before she caught it. She knew that'd piss him off.

But he saw it and it pissed him off.

"Angie was a good woman."

She started to roll her eyes, again before she caught it.

That pissed him off more.

Susie saw it.

"She sleeps with anything that moves," Susie defended.

"I didn't say she wasn't a troubled woman. I said she was a good one."

"Maybe we shouldn't talk about your work," she suggested. "Get your mind off it."

Susie didn't want his mind off it. Susie didn't want to think about it or talk about it. She never did and she never gave a fuck if he did.

February would listen if he wanted to talk. She'd get him a beer or she'd pour him a Jack and Coke and she'd keep them coming. When he was done, she'd slide the tips of her fingers around his ear then curl them at his neck, her touch warm and steady and real and his mind would blank.

"All right, let's talk about Puck," Colt told Susie and her head jerked.

He hadn't wanted her to do it but she'd pushed it so he'd let her look after his dog Puck, a German shepherd. Puck, when Colt got home from fishing, surprisingly hadn't seemed the worse for wear under Susie's care. But the day after he got back, Puck's body had been found blocks down. Colt suspected he'd gotten out like he usually did when Susie would leave after Colt in the morning and she wouldn't fully close the door. This was something she'd done before; like Colt's house and what he kept in it didn't matter much to her. Puck, being a smart dog and liking it when he could run, nearly always got out when Susie didn't make certain the door was closed. Then again, it wasn't hard. He just had to pull it open further with his paw and go. Puck had been hit by a car or, by the looks of him when Colt found him, a fair fucking few of them.

Normally he'd take Puck with him when he went fishing but he and Morrie went to a new place that Morrie wanted to try and, at the cabin they rented, it was no pets allowed. Thus Susie getting the key.

Colt had loved that dog. He hadn't accused Susie, mainly because it served no purpose, especially considering the fact that she'd soon be out of his life. But he missed his damned dog and there was no denying it, he blamed her.

"Puck?"

"I'm not goin' fishin' again anytime soon and even if I did Puck's no longer here. You don't need my key."

Her eyes closed slowly, the lids taking their time on their descent like she was drawing the movement out, sucking more of his time.

She knew what he was saying.

She'd be stupid if she didn't. He hadn't taken her out in months, didn't spend the night at her place, didn't ask her to his, didn't call, barely touched her anymore, hadn't fucked her in that long and only slept with her the night before Puck died because she'd already been asleep in his bed when he got home. That had pissed him off too. He'd considered dragging her ass out of bed and sending her home or sleeping on the couch but he'd been too damned tired to bother with either.

The desperate play of her newfound desire to watch his dog meant she knew it was coming.

And now it was time.

When she opened her eyes he knew she was pissed and when Susie was pissed it was never pretty.

"February," she said.

"What?"

"It was all good, you and me, until February came back to town."

Jesus, not this again.

She was wrong. February had been back for two years, came back to help Morrie with the bar after Jack and Jackie finally retired and moved to Florida. He and Susie had been on a break then, one of many.

And everyone knew there was no fucking way Colt would get near February.

She'd made her choice but Colt had dealt with it. He'd told her but she didn't listen. It could have ended his career, could have landed him in prison, but he'd done it, for Morrie, for Jack and Jackie and especially for February.

It wasn't that he couldn't forgive her for what she did. It was that he couldn't trust her judgment. Because after he'd done what he'd done, she never let him back in, and that…

Well, that he couldn't forgive her for.

15

And obviously, since she'd tried to hack it for a while then given up, taken off for fifteen years and then steered clear of him the last two, he figured it was because she couldn't forgive herself.

No, his problem with Susie had nothing to do with February.

"This has nothing to do with Feb."

"Everything with you is wound up in February."

Colt wasn't going to have this discussion. It was late. He'd started the day with Angie's murder. Having Feb in his arms for the first time in twenty-two years only to have her pull right out of them. Spent some not-so-much fun time with Cory and his loud, screeching wife Bethany, who looked eighteen months pregnant rather than the six she was supposed to be. However she'd also given her husband an alibi, even though Colt knew Cory didn't have it in him to hack up Angie. And running up against bizarre dead end after dead end on a fresh case he had to crack, because this town had never seen a murder as brutal as Angie Maroni's and the whole fucking place was going to go berserk if word spread what happened to her.

Nope, he didn't have it in him to spar with Susie.

"Just give me my key, Sooz."

"I don't know why you're playing this game, Colt. You asked, she'd drop straight to her knees in front of that whole fucking bar and suck your dick."

All right, maybe he had it in him to spar with Susie.

"Watch your fucking mouth."

She tilted her head with her challenge. "Not wound up with February?"

She wanted it? He'd give it to her straight.

"Yeah, not wound up with February. That doesn't mean I wouldn't prefer her mouth around my cock. That I don't think of her when I'm fuckin' you. That I wouldn't mind comin' home to her and sharing my day, because she'd share it and you never gave a shit. But, like I've said a million times before, it's not gonna happen, I knew that a long time ago, so did Feb. It's done."

Her eyes went to slits while he spoke and she leaned in. "Don't give me that shit. It's never been done between you two."

"We've had this discussion before."

And they had, even before Feb came back to town. Susie never let it go, just like he suspected his ex-wife Melanie never let it go.

Unlike Melanie, it was likely Susie never let it go because he'd said February's name while he was fucking her the first time. But hell, he'd been drunk off his ass, which was the only way he'd have gotten involved with Susie in the first place.

Still, she was good in bed and she kept coming back for more so in the beginning, who was he to argue?

The next thirty months he had no excuses, except for most of them they'd been on a break.

"You're a fool," she spat.

"Just give me my goddamned key."

She walked to her purse which was on the kitchen counter. "You don't get it from her, you'll come back to me."

This, Colt thought, was doubtful. There wasn't a lot of choice in their small town, not any that wasn't already taken. Not that some of them didn't get in his space more often than not, just that he wouldn't fuck another man's woman. Still, even the rare times Susie could be sweet, which was whenever he ended it and she came crawling back, it wasn't worth this.

And it always ended like this even though she swore that it wouldn't. It wasn't always about Feb, but it was always ugly.

"You're right," he told her, wrapping his fist around his key which was dangling from her fingers. "I've been fool enough with you." He looked her in the eyes. "That's over."

He saw her face bleach of color and she flinched. Whatever he sounded like she must have took his meaning because he could even see the blow he'd struck to Daddy's Little Girl, who always got everything she wanted and who'd been working hard on getting him for three years and not succeeding. Instead, he'd been taking what he wanted from her and handing the rest back.

"She's welcome to you," Susie hissed, her eyes again slits, her pretty face gone bad.

She was full of shit. She'd call him the next day and apologize. She always did.

Colt wondered if he had time the next day to buy a new phone.

On that thought his phone rang and he turned away from Susie, put his beer on the counter, shoved his key into his front pocket and pulled his phone out of the back.

Susie was gone by the time he looked at the display, flipped it open and put it to his ear.

"Morrie."

"Dude, get over here. Right now."

Colt's blood turned to ice. Morrie sounded freaked.

"What?"

"I just opened the mail. Dude, just," Morrie blew out a breath, "Colt, man, just get over here."

"You at the bar?"

"Yep."

"Feb there?"

"Yep."

"She okay?"

"Far's I know."

"She see whatever you're talkin' about?"

"Nope."

"I'll be there in five."

Colt walked into J&J's.

It was late, it was a weeknight, but the place was packed.

Murder had a way of drawing people, Colt knew. Most everyone had that sick place in their head that was fascinated by violence. But he also knew this was more a show of support for Morrie and Feb and in small part, Angie.

A town could get ripped apart by tragedy, people turning on each other. But not his town.

Or, at least, he'd do what he could to stop it.

When he came in, Feb, behind the bar, slid her eyes to him and tilted her head in that delicate way she had before she looked away. The movement was tiny, just her jaw jutting out to the side, but the way she did it made a huge impact.

That's what she'd do for the last two years every time he'd come into the bar. It was the only thing she did anymore that reminded him of the way it used to be. When they were at high school and he'd walk by her class or she'd walk by his locker, her eyes would meet his—she always sought his gaze—and she'd tilt her head, lifting her jaw to the side, the movement spare, fluid, graceful.

There was nothing to it and everything to it. The other guys at school saw it and wanted it, but she only gave it to Colt.

Outside of Morrie, Jack and Jackie, back then February was the only good thing in his life.

And those jaw tilts, back then, were the best thing in it.

He used to smile at her and he'd barely catch it when she'd smile back because she always looked away while she smiled.

She was the best flirt he'd ever met, just with that fucking jaw tilt, and he'd never met better.

Now she didn't wait for his smile. Before he could do it, not that he would, she'd long since looked away.

Like she was doing now, nodding her head at a customer. Again the movement was slight and appealing and he felt his jaw grow hard at the sight.

He looked away but he couldn't stop himself from wishing she wouldn't dress like that. She didn't dress like Angie, not by a long shot, but Feb always had a way with clothes.

Tonight she was in a light pink, Harley-Davidson tee. A three-tiered Indian choker wrapped around her throat made of long, oblong, black beads with a silver medallion at the front; a signature piece she wore and she had several in different colors. More silver necklaces tangling under the choker. Long, silver hoops at her ears. Her smoothed out hair had enough time that night to grow a bit wild. And even though he couldn't see them he knew she wore faded jeans that weren't tight but they fit her too well and, probably, black motorcycle boots.

Since she'd been home, to his knowledge, she hadn't had a man. Not for lack of offers.

J&J's was the only bar within the city limits, right on Main Street. There were a few bars outside the limits, mostly hunters', fishers' or golfers' havens. There were restaurants that had bars. And there were several bars closer to the raceway, their clientele transient, mostly rough folk, drag, NASCAR and midget race groupies, going to those places because they were close and convenient to the campgrounds.

Over the years other bars had opened in the city limits and failed because everyone went to J&J's. The men went there more now that Feb was back. He knew the boys at work jacked off regularly thinking about her even (and especially) the married ones. He'd unfortunately heard all about it.

The chokers were the problem and the silver dangling around her neck. You could almost hear those necklaces jingling while you imagined fucking her or as she rolled in her sleep in your bed.

But mostly, it was the chokers. Something about them said something he suspected Feb didn't want them to say, maybe didn't even know they were saying, but they spoke to men all the same.

It was good she was home. No one would mess with Morrie and, if they were stupid enough, most had heard what Colt had done for her and absolutely no one would go there. Colt couldn't imagine, since he knew while she was away she'd lived the nomad's life tending bars in small towns all over the place, how she lived her life those fifteen years; beat the men back without Morrie and Colt having her back. Maybe she didn't and she just wasn't going to shit where she lived. Then again, maybe she'd learned her lesson.

It was no longer his business or his problem. Never would be again.

That was, unless someone made it his problem. He was still Colt and no matter what had happened, she was still February.

He saw Darryl tending the other end of the bar and he wanted a drink but he went directly to the small office in the back.

Morrie was sitting at the cluttered desk, his body hunched, his elbow on the desk, forehead in his hand.

This pose did not give Colt a good feeling.

Colt closed the door behind him and Morrie jumped.

"Fuck. Fuck. Fuckin' hell, I'm glad you're here," Morrie said, getting up and moving swiftly.

For a big man he was surprisingly fast and agile. This probably had something to do with the fact that they played one-on-one basketball together every Saturday or, when the weather was shit, they'd play racquetball. They'd both been athletes all their lives even though, when they were young, they'd intermittently get drunk, high and smoke. Still, they'd both always stayed obsessively fit.

For Colt, this was because he spent most of his youth watching his mother popping pills, chain-smoking cigarettes and sucking on a bottle of vodka. She didn't even bother pouring it, drank it straight out of the bottle, uncut. He never remembered a time when she wasn't zoned out or hammered, mostly both. She was thin as a rail, rarely ate and, even when she was young, her skin hung on her like old lady flesh.

His father wasn't much better. He didn't pop pills but he smoked weed and snorted coke when he had the money to buy it. He remained sober during the day when he had a job but at night he'd get hammered right along with Colt's Mom. Most of the time he didn't have a job so Colt's memories of his dad were pretty much filled with him less than sober.

For Morrie, he stayed fit because he'd been around Colt's mom and dad not to mention grew up in a bar.

Morrie picked up a Ziploc bag with a piece of lined paper in it and handed it to Colt.

"This came in the mail today, addressed to Feb," Morrie waved his hand at the paper. "I put it in that thing, the bag. I didn't want it to get tainted. Once I figured out what it was, I barely touched it." He jerked his head to the desk. Another bag containing an envelope was lying there. "Did the same with the envelope, it's here too."

It was good Morrie watched cop shows.

Colt looked at the paper. He hadn't seen paper like that in a long time. It was something you'd have at school. It seemed old, the writing faded. On the top in pencil, Feb's name was written.

He read the note, not understanding it. It sounded like teenage girl bullshit, a handwritten pissy fit. It even mentioned Kevin Kercher who'd gone to IU after high school and never came back, not even for reunions. Colt got to the bottom where the sender signed her name.

Angie.

"What the fuck?"

"*What the fuck is right!*" Morrie exploded. "Look at the back!"

Colt flipped the paper over and saw, again in pencil, this darker, newer, different handwriting, the words, *For you.*

Something heavy and disturbing settled in his gut. Something he didn't want there. It felt like it felt when he was a kid in his room, listening to his mom and dad fight. Knowing exactly when it would escalate by the change in their voices, being able to count it off to within seconds before he heard her head hit the wall or her cry of pain before her body hit the floor. He hadn't had that feeling in years, not in years. Not since he sat on that toilet seat with Feb wiping away the blood his father caused to flow from his face while Morrie got the ice and Jack and Jackie left their kids to take care of him, knowing they'd raised good kids who'd know what to do while they went about the business of rocking his world.

He wanted to open his own flesh and tear the heavy thing out. It didn't belong there. He'd worked for years making himself into a man who didn't carry that kind of weight around. Jack and Jackie had helped him get rid of it, and Morrie and Feb. He didn't want it back, not ever. But particularly not when it being there had to do with Feb.

He looked at Morrie. "Bring Feb in here."

"I don't want her seein' that."

"Bring her in here."

"Colt—"

"Morrie, this has to do with a homicide, bring her…the fuck…in here."

Morrie held his eyes for too long. So long, Colt thought the situation would deteriorate. He'd fought with Morrie, too many times, but the bad blood never lasted long.

But this was about February.

Finally, Morrie muttered, "Shit," and he walked out the door.

In his head Colt went over the crime scene.

Angie'd been done by the dumpster, murdered not dumped, right behind Jack and Jackie's bar.

Lab results weren't back, autopsy not finalized, but there'd been no apparent struggle. Her eyes were closed naturally which meant she was probably out but not bludgeoned. There were no head wounds. She had maybe been drugged when she'd been slaughtered, which was good. At least it was for Angie.

Bloody footprints leading away from the body, that much blood, what he did to her, the killer had to get messy. Footprints ended abruptly five feet away. He'd gotten into a car, his clothes and hands likely covered in Angie's blood, and drove away.

The hatchet was found not far from where the footprints ended. He'd tossed it aside. No prints on the hatchet, no DNA left at the scene that they could find, though, considering it was an often used alley, they were still sifting through all the shit they found.

But it appeared it was just the footprints and the hatchet and Angie's body. That's all he left.

And it had to be a he. No woman had the strength to hack those wounds, clean and precise, like he chopped wood for a living and knew what he was doing.

Unless she was a German shot-putter, it had to be a he.

Colt's thoughts shifted to Feb and Angie.

It hadn't escaped him as he went through his day they'd once been good friends.

Hell, even as recently as a few nights ago he'd watched Feb wander over to Angie's table and stand beside it, looking down at Angie, saying shit he couldn't hear but it made Angie laugh.

Angie didn't laugh much, never did unless she was flirting or unless Feb wandered over to her to shoot the shit with her to draw Angie out, to make her melancholy face alive again, even if for a few minutes.

But a long time ago, it used to be more.

When Angie and Feb were in junior high, Angie was at Jack and Jackie's nearly as much as Colt was. Jack and Jackie, and Morrie and Feb for that matter, collected strays. Jack and Jackie's house was always filled with kids and people for as long as Colt could remember. Angie's home wasn't much better than Colt's so, like Colt, but unfortunately for Angie only for a while, she'd been adopted.

Something had happened though, in their freshman year. Something that made Angie quit coming over.

Colt looked at the note.

Kevin Kercher happened.

Feb appeared in the doorframe and leaned a shoulder against it. She took him in but her eyes didn't meet his.

He had a sudden impulse to wrap his fist in her hair and make her look at him like she had that morning, like she used to do when they were partners in euchre. Or sitting across the dining room table one of the thousand times he'd been over at her house having dinner. Or when she was underneath him in the backseat of his car, her deep, brown eyes looking direct into his, nothing to hide, nothing to escape, nothing to fear.

Before this impulse could take hold, she lifted a hand and swiped back the hair from her face, pulling it away, holding it at the back of her head, exposing her ear and that silver hoop dangling from it.

There was something about that earring in her ear, the same something that said what the choker said. And Colt understood it then.

It highlighted the vulnerability of her body, enticed you to curl your hand around it, get your teeth near it, at a place where you could do your worst or you could do something altogether different.

Her voice came at him. "Morrie said you wanted to talk to me?"

Colt looked from her ear to her.

She'd changed clothes since that morning. Colt knew Morrie took her to her place to pack and move to Morrie's, Colt had checked in. She was now in her bartender clothes. Tips were probably better in those clothes rather than the light, shapeless cardigan she had on that morning. Though Feb could likely wring a good tip out of you with a glance if she had a mind to do it, no matter what she was wearing.

Still, she looked beat, drawn. Her shoulders were drooped, her eyes listless.

"Sit down, Feb."

She didn't argue, just dropped her hand, pushed away from the door and headed to the chair.

Colt walked to the door, closed it and moved back to her.

She tipped her head back to look at him, shoulders still sagging, her arms straight, her hands loosely clasped together resting between her slightly parted thighs. Angie's death had cut her deep, as it would anyone, particularly if you found her hacked up, bloody body. But it would especially cut up someone like Feb.

"I gotta show you something."

She nodded.

He handed her the Ziploc bag and she unclasped her hands and took it. He watched vertical lines form on the insides of each of her eyebrows as she scanned it. Her eyes moved down the paper then back up, then down again.

"I don't get..." The lines by her brows disappeared and her lips parted right before her head jerked back. "What—?"

"Do you know what that is?" Colt asked.

"Yes," she whispered then suddenly surged to her feet.

Her hand came out and grasped his shirt, her fist curling into it so tight he saw her knuckles were white, the skin mottled red all around. Her head was tipped down, looking at the note and her hand at his shirt was moving back and forth with force, taking his shirt with it as she beat his chest, not knowing she was doing it.

"Oh my God. Oh my God," she chanted, the hand holding the note was now shaking.

"Give me the note, Feb."

"Oh God."

"Hand me the note."

"Oh my God."

He took the note from her at the same time his hand covered hers at his chest, stopping the movement, holding it tight against his body.

Her eyes were glued to the note in his other hand.

"Look at me, February." She did as she was told, he saw her face was pale and he ordered carefully, "Tell me about the note."

"That note doesn't exist."

He lifted it and gave it a shake and didn't want to say what he had to say but he had to say it. "It's right here, Feb."

"I mean, I threw it away, like, *twenty-five years ago.*"

Fucking shit. Goddamn it all to hell.

That was what he was afraid she'd say.

"Tell me about the note," Colt repeated.

She shook her head sharply side to side—in denial, trying to focus, he didn't know. Her hand tightened further into his shirt, he felt it under his own hand and she leaned some of her weight against it, pressing her fist deeper into his flesh.

He waited, giving her time. She took it.

Then she told him, "We used to be good friends, you know that."

"I do."

"Angie used to come over all the time."

"I know."

"She liked Kevin."

He didn't know that but he wasn't surprised. Kevin was a good-looking guy; a lot of girls liked him. He was a year ahead of Colt, a senior when Feb and Angie were freshman. In their school, at that time, an impossible catch for Angie.

"He asked me out."

Colt felt that weight shift heavily in his gut.

"She was furious. She liked him, as in *really* liked him," Feb continued.

"You didn't go out with him," Colt stated this as fact, because he knew it was.

"Of course I didn't," Feb replied quickly.

And there it was. The web shot out and snared them both.

Of course she didn't because, at that time, Feb was his. Colt knew it. Feb knew it. Fucking Kevin fucking Kercher knew it, the fuck. Everyone knew it.

Her words kept strumming in his skull.

Of course I didn't. Of course I didn't.

Quick. Fierce. A statement of fact, just like his. If they were anything else but what they were now, if they were what they *should* have been, it would have been terse, dismissive, and that was what it sounded like. The faithful partner stating her commitment when she shouldn't have to. It was a given, fundamental. Their relationship formed on bedrock which would never budge, no matter what the temptation. It wasn't worth it if it threatened what they had, which was the world.

Colt fought against the web. He had to. It was his job and with Feb gone and after Melanie left him that was now his world.

"Do you remember this note?" he asked.

"Yes, but barely."

"You threw it away?"

"I guess so," she shook her head. "I don't know. Probably. It was twenty-five years ago."

"Think, Feb."

"I am, Alec!" she snapped. "But it was twenty-five years ago!"

Good Christ, he hated it when she called him Alec. He had no idea why she did it, she knew he hated it, but she did. She'd never called him Colt, even after that night when he'd told her that Alec was gone, that the name his parents gave him and called him was something he didn't want any claim to anymore. He wanted to be known as Colt, the name he and Morrie made up for him when they were six. The name he'd given himself. He'd begged her to stop calling him Alec, but she never did.

"Just take a minute and think," he urged, setting his anger aside.

She closed her eyes, tilting her chin away, pressing more of her weight into her hand at his chest, still not cognizant she was touching him there and he was touching her back or he knew she'd move away. Distance for Feb, since it all went down, was important. Not just with him, with everyone. But he'd noted, and it never failed to piss him off, *especially* with him.

She opened her eyes. "Mrs. Hobbs' class. Geometry. Second period." She shook her head but said, "We had that class together. She passed the note to me then. I think I threw it away."

It hit him and Colt remembered.

"You fought in the hall," he said.

Her eyes widened and she nodded. "Pushing match. Angie started it. Mrs. Hobbs broke it up. *Shit!*" Her head jerked to the side. "I totally forgot." She looked back at him. "Angie was crying and screaming but more crying. She was out of her mind. They sent her home."

"You were crying."

That's what he remembered. He'd seen her eyes red from the tears when she was at her locker. He'd walked her to class. He'd been late to his own. At lunch he'd told Morrie but Morrie had already heard about the fight from someone else. After school they'd made her sit through football practice so they could drive her home. Colt even remembered putting her in his car. She'd been silent. She'd never said why they fought. Feb could be like that, hold things to herself forever, a personality trait she had that was a nightmare he'd lived for way too long. It was just Angie was there one day and the next she wasn't. Feb had been devastated. Then Jessie's folks moved to town and Feb and Jessie hooked up, hooking Mimi with them, and Angie was a memory as it was with teenage girls.

"I still don't understand. Why's that note back now?" she asked.

He was now going to have to ask her the impossible and tear her up doing it.

"Do you remember anyone from school, anyone from that time, anyone…a teacher, a kid, a janitor, a regular at the bar, anyone, who seemed partial to you?"

The lines came back at her brows. "Partial to me?"

"Interested."

There it was. The impossible.

Everyone was interested in Feb, then and now. Everyone was interested in the family; Jack, Jackie, Morrie, Feb, their grandparents before they all passed. Susie Shepherd and her wealthy daddy may have been King and Princess of Diamonds in that town but Jack and Jackie Owens, their son Morrison and daughter February were King, Queen, Prince and Princess of Hearts.

Who knew? Feb may have dozens of sick fucks following her, taking pictures of her, stealing her notes, going through her trash, building shrines to her. Hell, Colt knew dozens who jacked off to her regularly.

His hand tightened on hers.

"Interested?" she asked.

"Unnaturally."

"Alec, what are you saying?"

Colt skirted around the issue. "Someone who would take a note you threw away. Someone who would keep it for twenty-five years. Someone who'd mail it to your family's bar. Feb, someone who was unnaturally interested in you."

Her whole body jerked, even her hand then it twisted on his shirt.

"No," she answered, sliding straight into the pit of denial.

"Think."

"What's this about?"

"Take time, Feb. Think."

"What's this about, Alec?"

He pried her hand from his shirt but gave it alternate purchase, forcing his thumb into her palm and curling his fingers around her hand at the same time he flipped the note and showed her the back.

28

Her hand went to her mouth cupping it, what was left of the color in her face draining clean away. He watched her sway and he used his hand in hers to push her back and down, forcing her into the chair. He let her hand go and put his to her neck, shoving her head between her knees.

"Breathe deep."

He listened to her suck in breath.

Colt crouched in front of her, keeping his hand at her neck.

After a while he asked, "You with me?"

She nodded and put pressure against his hand, lifting up just a little, her neck arching so she could look at him, her elbows going to her knees.

He kept his hand where it was.

"He killed her for me," she said, her voice hollow.

Colt shook his head. "You didn't ask him to kill her. He did it because he's not right in the head."

"We made up," she whispered. "Angie and me. It wasn't the same but we made up. We danced to Buster Poindexter's "Hot, Hot, Hot" at prom. You were there. Angie and me started the conga line."

He was there. He remembered that conga line. He remembered sitting in the back with Jason Templeton who was then a freshman at Notre Dame, both of them watching it and laughing their asses off. He remembered thinking he'd feel stupid, a sophomore at Purdue, coming home, taking his senior girlfriend to her prom. But he didn't feel stupid.

She'd had a blast. Feb always knew how to have a good time and Colt loved it when she did. He remembered the conga line flowing by their table and Feb had grinned at him at the same time she sang the words to the song at the top of her lungs. Then she twisted her neck and looked back at Angie who had her hands on Feb's waist. They'd laughed in each other's faces and then Feb, in the lead, always the one who started the party, wound the conga line away.

"I didn't want her dead, even back then, when we were fighting—"

"I know that."

She stared him in the eye for a brief moment before dropping her head. "I can't believe this."

"Feb, think." Colt brought the matter back to hand. "Anyone back then who took an interest in you, made you feel funny? Anyone that's still around now?"

29

She kept her head lowered and shook it, her long hair sliding across his hand, more of it falling forward around her face.

Christ, there was so much of it, he'd never seen so much hair, he'd never felt anything as soft.

He took his hand from her neck and she lifted her head. She looked at his fallen hand before her eyes found his. They were soft and lost for a moment, telling him only he could make her feel found and he almost touched her again, put his hand back where she needed it, before she straightened, ripping that look away from him.

He wanted it back, so much he felt that weight shift in his gut and the flash of anger at her for taking it away, keeping him out. Fuck, even now she wouldn't let him in.

He bit his lip, something he knew he did to control his anger. He had his father and mother in him, straight to his bones, and he held close to that control. He had to. Both of them could be ugly and violent, with words, with fists. Colt had it too. It came out twice without control, twice he'd nearly killed someone with his fists—one was his own father, the other Feb's husband.

"No," she answered. "No one."

"February—"

"I'll think, Alec. I'll think about it. I need some time. But I promise, I'll think and I'll let you know."

She was looking at him again, straight in the eye. She wasn't lying. She'd think. But right now this was too much…for anyone. Most people would lose it just from finding Angie's body. Feb was holding on.

His anger dissolved. It was no longer his place but he was proud of her.

"You've got my number?"

Those dents came back at her eyebrows and that lost look came back into her eyes before she masked it.

"Morrie's got it."

Colt straightened and dug in the back pocket of his jeans for his wallet. He pulled out a business card and handed it to her, flipping the wallet closed and shoving it back.

She stood, his card held in both hands by thumb and forefinger at both bottom edges, her head bent studying the print.

"I want you to have a care. Keep your cell on you all the time, keep it charged. Let people know where you're going and when you get there. Don't ever be alone. You feel something you don't like, see someone who makes you feel wrong, it doesn't matter they're innocent, you tell me, Feb." Her head came up and she looked at him. "Doesn't hurt them for me to ask a few questions, dig around." He watched her suck in her cheeks and he knew she was hesitating, Jack and Jackie's daughter, through and through. "This is serious. This is murder, Feb. This is about Angie."

She closed her eyes tight and looked away but not before he saw them get bright. Then she took in a breath and opened her eyes, the brightness gone. She'd locked onto her control. Looking back at him, she nodded.

Colt had one more piece of unpleasant business to deliver and he hated it, but he did it.

"Tomorrow, first thing, you need to write a list."

"A list?"

"Anyone who wronged you. Anyone you felt slighted by—"

"Alec—"

"Anyone someone not in the know might think did you harm or upset you."

Her eyes went bright again and her bottom lip quivered. "Alec—"

He hated to see her lip move like that, knowing her throat burned with the effort at fighting back the tears. But he had to be relentless, lives were at stake. "If this is about you, we need to lock it down."

"People are gonna—"

"Freak." Colt nodded. "But better they freak and stay breathin' than—"

"They'll hate me," she whispered.

"They won't. But if they do, they're stupid. This isn't about you. This is about a sick fuck who's out of his mind. They blame you, you're better off without them."

"Easy for you to say, people like you."

"People like you."

Something in her face shifted. He couldn't read it, it was there and gone. But whatever it was, it made that weight in his gut feel even heavier.

"Feb, I've no idea what this fuckin' guy is thinking, but I've gotta—"

31

She lifted her hand and waved it between them, the movement desperate. "I'll write a list."

It was on the tip of his tongue to say, *that's my girl.*

He didn't say it.

It was then the full realization dawned that this business was going to take its toll. On Feb, on him, likely on Morrie and undoubtedly on Jack and Jackie who, as soon as they heard what was going on, would be back. They were probably already on their way.

And the toll to be paid was not just because of Angie's murder and Feb's admirer, but because Colt and Feb had no choice but to be wound together again after years of being unraveled.

"Can I go back to the bar now?" she asked.

Colt nodded.

"You wanna talk to Morrie?"

Her question struck him like a blow, she knew him so well. And a thought he hadn't contemplated, hadn't allowed himself to contemplate for two years, came into his head.

How in *the fuck* could this woman who was laced into the fibers of his life be so fucking removed?

Colt nodded again.

Feb lifted her chin and without another word walked out the door.

When he lost sight of her, Colt's neck twisted and he bit his lip.

It was either that or tear the fucking office apart.

Two

PETE

I'd been up for two and a half hours by the time Morrie stumbled into the kitchen.

It had not been the most joyful two and a half hours I'd ever spent, drinking coffee and filtering through the silt of my life, trying to think of anyone that some unhinged psychopath might have decided done me wrong. Even if I did it after I'd done my yoga, which usually left me feeling mellow.

In that time, I'd also come to the conclusion that this new living situation was not going to work.

Delilah, Morrie's wife, had left him just over a year ago, taking the kids with her. It hadn't been long in coming but still Morrie, like any man, hadn't been paying attention. Her defection surprised him. He'd suffered her leaving like a blow. But after we'd taken over the bar, Delilah had changed.

Dee could tell it like it was but still, she used to be sweet as syrup, patient as a saint, a great mom, a good wife to Morrie, but she liked Morrie working construction. Out early, home early, at the dinner table with the family. Not out at noon, home after three in the morning, rarely seeing her or his kids.

She didn't get it about J&J's. Delilah didn't understand the importance of J&J's. Not even when Mom and Dad retired and I came back just because

Morrie wanted me to help him run the bar so the family wouldn't lose J&J's and also so the town wouldn't lose it.

Dee knew me. We were close even with the distance. She knew nothing would bring me home, except J&J's.

So Dee had their old house and Morrie had a new pad—an apartment, a new complex in town. So new, it was void of personality and I hated it. So did Morrie.

There were lots of things to hate about it but mostly I hated the trees. The trees that landscaped the outside were thin; the fluorescent tags from the garden store still on them, held up with sticks and wire to help them bear the brunt of winter and wind. The leaves in summer not throwing enough to make but a hint of shade. They'd probably be beautiful in about ten years, but now their existence screamed "New!" and something about it I did not like.

It seemed weird in my town because the rest of the town felt old, established, settled and safe. It wasn't that I didn't like change. I was used to change, a lot of it. It was just that I didn't like change in my town.

But there were three bedrooms and the all-important two baths. One bedroom for Morrie, one for his son, Bonham, the other for his daughter, Tuesday.

That was how much Dee had changed. Morrie had been named after Jim Morrison who our father idolized. I had been named after the month Valentine's Day fell in, Mom's favorite holiday and my middle name was Valentine, not to mention Mom said I was conceived on that day. Morrie had talked Dee (and she loved him so much it didn't take much effort) into keeping the family tradition, naming his son after John Bonham, since Morrie was a Led Zeppelin freak. He'd also talked Dee into naming their daughter Tuesday, which both of them swore was the day of the week she was conceived, which also happened to be Valentine's Day that year. Dee had barely made a peep naming her kids these crazy names.

Then again, Morrie and I never suffered from our names and Dee had loved my brother back then. Loved him enough to let him name their kids. Loved him so much she couldn't hack doing without him, seeing her family losing out to a bar.

All this meant I didn't sleep on their pull out couch in their TV room, which was what I did all those years when I came home. Sometimes, the times I didn't stay with Mom and Dad, doing the rotation, sharing my time between family members. I'd come home for Christmas or Thanksgiving or some other family event, like the kids' birthdays or Mom and Dad's 40th anniversary. Instead, all this meant I slept in Tuesday's single bed last night.

My bed at home was a queen. Some nights I slept like the dead. Other nights I moved.

Last night I moved and almost fell out of Tuesday's bed twice.

And my cat Wilson, unused to his new surroundings, steered clear.

I couldn't sleep without Wilson on my feet or, when I was moving, he slept somewhere close. Wilson was a cuddler. He liked my warmth and even when I shifted he didn't mind, he just shifted with me.

So I didn't sleep.

I hadn't slept well, not for years. But at least I slept some.

I needed to go home.

Morrie went straight to the coffeepot and poured himself a cup.

He didn't speak or look at me until he was well into his third sip.

Then he did. "See this arrangement is gonna work out great."

I loved my brother but he was such a fucking *man*.

He slept in his own bed, a big bed, in his own home. I slept in a foreign bed, a little bed, away from my home. But he got up and there was coffee brewed, coffee he didn't have to make, so it was all going to work out great.

"Morrie, this isn't going to work. Tuesday's bed…" He looked at me. "I don't sleep enough as it is."

"Colt's couch pulls out."

Oh fuck. No way. No way *in hell*.

"I'll move in with Jessie."

Jessie's husband was a chemist, he worked at Lilly and he got paid a shitload. They didn't have kids because that would cut into Jessie's affinity for having fun whenever the hell she wanted and doing whatever the hell she liked whenever the hell she felt like it. They had a three bedroom house. One bedroom Jessie had converted into a workout room. One had been decorated by some interior designer that Jessie hired when she'd got a wild hair up her ass. It had a double bed with a big, down comforter on it and lots of toss pillows and I knew Jessie put mints on the pillows when her mom and dad or her sister and her sister's husband would come to visit.

I could do mints while I was displaced because some creepy, sick psycho had fixed onto me and was murdering people I liked and sending me notes from high school and forcing me to spend time with Alec, time where he touched me.

"No offense but Jimbo is a dweeb and he doesn't own a .45," Morrie dismissed my suggestion by slightly insulting Jessie's husband who was, unfortunately, a dweeb but he also wasn't a pushover.

I changed the subject. "Please tell me you don't have a gun in your house with kids."

"I do. I'm an American. I know how to use it, my kids know to avoid it and it's locked in a safe anyway so they couldn't get it even if they wanted to make trouble."

I let it go and tried something else. "Al's not a dweeb and it's highly likely he owns a gun."

Meems' husband Al was anything but a dweeb. He'd been the center on the football team, on the line, right next to Morrie. Time had made him a little soft but it hadn't made him a slouch. And he was a hunter. I knew he had guns. And he loved me. I knew he'd blow the brains out of anyone who tried to hurt me or got near his wife and kids.

No, that wasn't true. Anyone got near his wife and kids, Al would not use his gun. He'd go in with his hands and rip them apart.

"They got no room for you, Feb. Theirs is a full house."

This was true. They had four kids and Al wasn't a chemist at Lilly. He worked on the highway crew. It was union, it paid well and the Coffee House was nothing to sneeze at because Meems could bake. Her muffins were orgasmic and her cookies and cakes were so good, you'd sell your soul to the devil if she made you do it just so you could have one. Still, they had four kids and Meems had a fondness for catalogue shopping. Bob, her postman, blamed her for the hernia he suffered last year and he wasn't joking.

"Colt works a lot. You wouldn't have to sleep on the pull out. He'd probably let you use his bed."

If Morrie was being funny, I wasn't laughing.

"If he's gone all the time, what purpose would it serve me staying there?"

I watched Morrie's face change, resistance drifting through it in a hard way, and I knew part of the bucketload of shit that sifted through my brain while I wasn't sleeping last night was going to come spilling out just then.

I wasn't wrong.

"We gotta talk about Colt."

I shook my head.

His coffee cup came down with a crash and I jumped back a foot. I looked down, seeing the mug had split right down the middle and coffee was all over the place, spreading, spilling down the side of the counter, dripping in a coffee waterfall to the floor.

I looked at my brother. "Holy shit, Morrie."

He turned and with an underarm throw he tossed the handle of the coffee mug, a jagged section of mug still attached to it, into the sink with such force it fractured again, bits flying out everywhere.

I didn't jump that time but I took a step back.

"Morrie—"

Morrie leaned forward. "You're gonna talk to me, February, talk to me right...fucking...now."

I lifted my hand in a conciliatory gesture but Morrie shook his head.

"You spill now or you spill when Mom and Dad get here. Your choice, but it's been too fucking long. We all let it go too long. We shoulda made you spill ages ago, before Pete—"

"Stop!" I shouted.

No one talked to me about Pete. No one.

Not Meems. Not Jessie. Not Mom and Dad.

Not even my brother, who I loved best of them all which was saying a whole helluva lot.

I thought that'd work. It had worked before many times. Everyone knew I couldn't talk about Pete.

But it didn't work. Morrie moved fast. Before I knew it he had his hand curled around my upper arm and he gave me a shake. It wasn't controlled, it was almost brutal and my head snapped back with the force of it.

My breath started coming fast but thin. Morrie got Dad's temper, which could flare out of control, though neither of them ever hurt anyone who didn't need to get hurt. I got Mom's, which also could flare out of control. But we were women and our hurt came from words rather than actions and those, unfortunately, lasted longer.

"What the fuck happened?" Morrie was in my face. "What made it go bad? What made you do what you did?"

"Let go of me Morrie."

"Answer me, Feb."

"*Let me go!*"

Another shake and my head snapped back. "*Answer me!*"

"*You're hurting me!*" I yelled.

"*I should knock some fuckin' sense into you!*" he yelled back.

I made a noise like I was going to vomit. It was involuntary and it sounded nasty. Then I wasn't breathing anymore, not even thin, useless breaths—nothing, no oxygen.

Morrie's face changed and he let me go, stepping back. He looked whipped, injured, the expression hideous on his face. The knowledge of what he'd done and what he'd said attacking him.

"Baby sister," he whispered but I shook my head.

He couldn't go back to beloved big brother now. Not after that. Not after that. No way. No fucking way.

"I'm moving in with Jessie," I announced, turning away.

"Feb, don't. You need to be protected. You need someone lookin' after you."

I turned back. "A couple of hours in, Morrie, fine job you made of it."

He flinched, his head jerking back with the weight of my blow. Just as I said, my anger came out in words and they hurt far worse than my arm was stinging just now.

I nodded my head to the bar that separated his kitchen from the dining area. On it, probably doused in coffee, was the list I spent most of the morning writing.

"Give that list to Alec. He wants it."

I left it at that. I had to. And I walked away to pack.

"You've got a nerve," Pete's Mom, LeeAnne, said in my ear.

"LeeAnne—"

"I'm not giving you his number, you bitch."

"This is important."

"Nothin's that important."

"Someone's dead."

LeeAnne fell silent and I lifted my gaze to Meems and Jessie who were both crunched into Meems' back office at the Coffee House. Both of them were watching me. Both of them looking pissed and harassed. Both of them knowing what this cost me. And both of them wishing they could pay the toll instead of me.

"Her name is Angie. Evidence came out last night that she was murdered because of something that happened between her and me. There's a possibility that anyone who..." Christ, how did I say this? LeeAnne was a bitch, the worst mother-in-law in history, but still, good manners prevented me from saying it straight out. "Anyway, anyone who didn't get along with me might be in danger."

"You're poison," LeeAnne spat. "Always were."

I didn't get that, even from LeeAnne. She was a bitch but she'd seen me in the hospital and she knew her son did that to me.

She knew it wasn't *me* who beat the shit out of Pete. It wasn't *me* who came home that fucking, shitty, awful night and attacked me far worse than any of the times before. Times which could be brushed away as too much drink or what Pete called "our passionate but volatile relationship" (I thought it wasn't much of the first and too much of the last). It wasn't *me* who tried to rape me, who I had to fight back, scared silly, losing the fight, only somehow to escape and drive over to Morrie's house.

It was just *me* who happened to pick a time when Alec was at Morrie's. And it was *me* who was battered, bloodied, my clothes torn, barely able to hold myself up, having performed a miracle by driving myself there in one piece at all. And it was *me* who Alec took one look at, turned to Morrie and said, "You see to her. I'll see to him." And it was *for* me that Alec drove straight to my house and nearly beat the life out of my husband.

"Please, LeeAnne, give me his number," I said.

"Still can't see right out of his left eye, my boy," she countered.

I didn't doubt this was true. Alec did a number on him. Detached retina, amongst other things.

It wasn't more than he deserved. He'd done a number on me. We were both in the hospital at the same time.

I got out earlier.

Pete got out and left town. He didn't press charges. This was likely due to Morrie, Dad and a variety of other townsfolk making this Pete's only option.

I wasn't going to say I was sorry.

I *was* sorry. Very sorry. So sorry it had seeped into my soul. But not sorry for Pete Hollister.

Having had a very long time to look back, Pete had always been an asshole. But he'd been a good-looking one. Not as good-looking as Alec but with Alec lost to me, Pete would do. And I needed someone. Someone to fill the hole Alec left. No, it wasn't a hole. It was a wound. I couldn't close the wound so I needed someone to numb the pain. Or take my mind off it. Pete did that. He was good at it. He delivered his own brand of pain in order to succeed wildly in this endeavor.

What I was sorry about was the fact that Alec hurt Pete and I knew he'd hate himself for doing it instead of hating me. And I was sorry that I put him in that position. It was the only one he had. He and Morrie had been looking after me so long they didn't know how to do anything different even if things had changed between Alec and me. And I was sorry that he saw me the way he did, beaten, not his February, never to be his February again. She was gone like he told me the Alec he was once was gone. Pete had beaten her out of me. I answered to my name but I didn't know who February was any longer. I'd spent nearly two decades trying to figure it out but never could. The only thing I knew was she wasn't the girl I used to be.

"LeeAnne, if you don't want to give me his number then just please call him and warn him—"

"I'll call. I'll tell him the bitch is back and he should brace. It was a dark day, the day he met you."

Then I heard her hang up.

I flipped my cell phone closed and curled my fingers around it.

"Well, that's done," I told Jessie and Meems. I was shaking.

I'd forgotten how much I hated LeeAnne. I'd always been so focused on how much I hated Pete that I forgot to hate his mother. But now I remembered.

I knew hate, even as a kid because I always hated Alec's parents.

Even as a kid, before I understood it and before it happened between him and me, I hated the way Alec's face looked when the call came, his mom telling my mom to bring him home (those times she remembered he was over at all). Or when his dad would come around to get him.

Then, when I grew older and I understood somewhere right and true inside me that he was mine, I hated them more when he'd get in a mood because of them. Because the town was talking about something they'd do that was crazy, like when his mom went drunk to the liquor store and fell into a display, making a bunch of bottles of rum fall over and crash to the ground and the police had dragged her in. Or when his dad showed up sauced at a football game and stood at the other team's bleachers and alternately bragged loudly about Alec or insulted their boys and he'd been jumped before some men from our side, some of the coaches and even some of the players, including Alec, had had to pull his dad out of the fray.

But that hate slipped away after that night when the police took his dad away and Social Services had told his mom he wasn't coming back and Dad and Morrie moved Alec into Morrie's room. Because after that night, he was safe, he was healing, he was finally home and I didn't have to hate anymore.

And for a while, those years when Alec finally was mine, I forgot what hate felt like.

Glory days.

"Feb—" Meems started.

I got up. "I need to get to the bar."

"Ain't no one gonna be bothered you take a coupla days off," Jessie told me.

"I'll go into hiding when the town finds out anyone who ever looked at me funny might be the next one to end up bloody and dead in an alley."

Jessie and Meems looked at each other before they both looked back at me.

"No one's gonna blame you for this, Feb," Meems told me.

"Right," I replied.

"Feb, everyone on some level is gonna understand you're feelin' exactly as you're feelin' right now," Jessie said.

"Maybe, after Alec catches this guy and the fear fades away. 'Til then…" I let that hang.

I'd been in a lot of small towns, sometimes spent only months in them, a couple, the towns that reminded me of home, I spent over a year. I knew how people thought. I knew how they could turn. I'd even seen it once and it hadn't been pretty. I hadn't even been involved and it still hurt to watch.

"Girl—" Meems started again.

"I need to get to the bar."

I moved and they stepped aside. They knew me. They knew when I meant what I said and when I meant business.

I gave a wave to Meems and Jessie walked beside me the short distance to J&J's.

"When're Jack and Jackie getting here?" Jessie asked.

Morrie had called them from the bar yesterday morning about two seconds after Alec had walked away. They were driving their RV up and were on the road by yesterday afternoon. Depending on how hell-bent Dad was to get here, they could arrive at any time. I figured Dad was probably pretty hell-bent and they could be crossing the town line as Jessie and my boots hit the sidewalk.

"Any time now."

"That'll be good," Jessie murmured as I opened the door to the bar.

I didn't agree with her.

Mom and Dad were going to feel the same pressure Morrie was feeling; the pressure to keep me safe. The pressure to keep me from feeling this weight hanging so heavy over my head, knowing, any time, without any control had by me, it could drop, crushing me underneath it. The pressure, which was there from Alec and me. The pressure they felt in the short time before I found Pete. The pressure they felt in the short time I remained home after Pete was gone. The pressure of wanting, with everything they were, for Alec and me to go back to what we had. Wanting it so much they'd be willing to *make* it happen. The pressure and disappointment of knowing they had no means of doing it.

Morrie's head (and everyone else's in the bar) came up to look at me when Jessie and I walked in.

I had no idea when the bomb would drop. Last night Morrie told me that Alec told him that Angie's note was going to remain under wraps and any chats he had with anyone I'd put on my list he'd do his best to keep under wraps too.

Alec was good at a lot of things. He'd been an All-State tight end. He'd gained a partial scholarship to Purdue. He'd graduated top of his class at the academy. He'd crawled out from under the stench of his parents and been a kid, and now a man, that people respected. He was good at being my brother's best friend, another son to my folks. He was a good cop. He'd even been a great boyfriend, the best, until he'd stopped being that.

But this was a small town. He wasn't *that* good.

Then again, the last person who wronged me breathed through a tube for a couple of days, courtesy of Alec, so who knew?

I split from Jessie who went straight to the bar. I went to the back, secured my purse in the office and went behind the bar.

My departure from Morrie's apartment meant he'd had to open up for once.

My longer-than-usual stay away, due to moving in with Jessie, having a shower there and getting ready to tackle the day there, then having to call Pete's bitch of a mom in Mimi's office meant I was in a lot later than usual.

When I hit the back of the bar, Morrie said, "Feb—"

"Save it." I didn't even look at him when I spoke. "You need to give me time."

That was all I was willing to say but I felt his relief because me asking for time meant him knowing I was holding a grudge, but also knowing I'd eventually let it go.

"I don't know about you but I need a drink. Meems' coffee is the bomb but it ain't gonna cut it right about now," Jessie announced.

Joe-Bob laughed at Jessie's comment.

Joe-Bob was a regular who planted his ass on the barstool by the front door at noon, opening time, every day and didn't pry his ass from that stool until closing time unless it was to take a leak or wander down to Frank's restaurant to eat a burger. Hell, he'd fallen asleep at that stool more times than I could count.

We left him to it. He paid his tab at the end of every month, though God only knew how he managed that. Things were rough for Morrie now that he was paying rent, helping Dee with the mortgage and paying child support. It was sad and it was wrong, but Joe-Bob was now beloved by Morrie. His tabs were helping to keep two roofs over Morrie's kids' heads.

I didn't laugh with Joe-bob, got Jessie a drink and then got down to work. I spent that time, like last night but more so today, trying not to think about Angie, about the note, about Alec, about whether my cat Wilson would make Jessie's husband Jimbo sneeze or about anything at all.

About an hour later, the door opened and Alec and his partner Sully walked in.

Unable and maybe unwilling to stop it, I felt my jaw move in a non-verbal greeting, the way it always did when I saw Alec. Always and forever. Since I could remember.

I used to do it because it made him smile at me, a smile I hadn't seen in years. A smile that others saw and it was handsome so I was sure they liked it, at least the girls.

But they didn't get it. They didn't get how precious it was. They didn't understand, it not being directed at them, what that smile could do. The power of it. It was like every time he smiled he'd opened a chest of treasure and said, "All this is yours."

Now I did it because it made his expression change. He didn't smile but there was something there, not treasure but precious all the same. It was nostalgic in that painful way nostalgia could be, but it was still precious and addictive, like a drug. I'd forget between times, but when he walked in, the craving would assault me, too much to fight. I was jonesing for it. So I went after it, lifting my jaw then his face would change and I'd allow myself half a beat to drink it in before I looked away.

Even after all that happened, today was no different.

Quick as I could, the second I got my Alec hit, I looked at Sully and understood why he wasn't around yesterday.

He looked like hell. Brimming eyes, red-rimmed nose and he was carrying a tatty tissue that had been overused.

"You need hot, honeyed water," I said to Sully when he hit the bar. Hot, honeyed water being what Mom used to make Morrie and I drink when we had a cold.

It probably had no medicinal effects at all except those wondrous ones only mothers could generate. Mothers who gave a shit about their kids and took care of them when they were sick like they were the most cherished things on earth and the world would not be right until her kid's cold went away. Mothers like my mom.

"I need hot, honeyed whisky," Sully told me with a smile.

I could do hot, honeyed whisky. I would have to run down to the corner store to pick up the honey but it was only six doors away.

"You on duty?" I asked.

He gave me a look. It wasn't a bad one. It wasn't pity or filled with blame. It was one filled with concern and a hint of understanding.

"Feels like, this case, with this cold, I'll be on duty until the day I die."

"I'm sorry, Sully."

"You apologize again I'll ask you over for dinner."

That made me laugh, the first time I'd done it in over twenty-four hours and it felt rusty in my throat.

Still, Sully's wife Lorraine was a shit cook. She was famous for it. Ever since she brought a half-dozen casseroles to the high school band's potluck fundraiser the first year they were married and gave food poisoning to half the band and some of the town.

The extra late afternoon bodies filling the room and the work and likely Alec being there made me feel suddenly hot.

I pulled off my sweater to strip down to the tank underneath as I replied, "I swear, I won't apologize again."

Sully's laughter was muffled by my sweater being over my ears.

Alec's comment was not, because the sweater was off by the time he said it.

"What happened to your arm?"

I dropped my hands, my sweater still in both of them, and looked at my arm. Morrie's fingerprints were clear as day, purple and blue and looking angry.

Fuck, but I always was an easy bruiser.

"Shit," Morrie muttered, eyes glued to my arm.

"Shit, what?" Alec asked, his gaze swinging to Morrie who looked just as guilty as he was.

"Alec," I said.

"Colt," Sully said.

"Shit, what?" Alec repeated, ignoring Sully and me, looking pissed.

No, looking murderous.

I'd seen him that way once. I was barely conscious then and it scared the shit out of me. I was fully conscious now and worried I was about to pee my pants.

"Alec, don't—" I tried.

Morrie tore his eyes from my arm and looked at his friend. "Colt—"

"Shit, what?" Alec cut him off, totally ignoring me. "You do that to her?"

Sully got close to him. "Colt."

"Please calm down. It was not a big deal," I tried again.

Alec ignored me again. "You put your hand on her?"

"Let's go to the back. Talk," Morrie suggested.

"That why she moved in with Jessie and Jimbo?" Alec asked.

Oh Lord.

I'd never lived in a city. Even when I was traveling, trying to find a way to get back to myself, I picked small towns. I did this because you were never faceless, not for long. You were never a number. When something happened to folk in small towns, the entire town felt it. Even if you didn't know someone, just knew of them, or a bit about them, you felt it when something happened. You sent a card. You gave them a smile when you saw them or someone who cared about them, a smile that said more than hello. People looked out for one another. You were friendly even to people you might not like just because it was the right thing to do and you'd likely see them again, maybe not the next day, but soon. And their kid would go to school with your kid. Or there would be a time when you knew you'd need their kindness or you'd give them yours.

But sometimes living in a small town sucked.

This was one of those times.

"Really, guys, this isn't the time—" Jessie entered the conversation and she was just as unsuccessful as Sully and I had been.

"Your job was to keep her safe," Alec told Morrie.

"Colt, trust me, we don't want to talk about this," Morrie said back.

"Jimbo can't keep her safe. He wouldn't have the first clue," Alec said.

"Excuse me," Jessie put in.

Alec's eyes cut to me. "You stay with Morrie or you stay with me."

"Alec," I said.

"Colt, man, you know that can't happen. You're primary on the investigation," Sully reminded him.

Alec was single-minded. Not moving his eyes from me, he'd made a decision. "Morrie fucked up, you stay with me."

"I'm not staying with you."

"You aren't staying with Jimbo and," his head dipped to my arm, "you aren't staying with Morrie."

"She's fine with us," Jessie said.

"She can't stay with you, man, you'd be yanked off the case," Sully told him.

Alec bit his lip then looked at Morrie. "Explain why you marked her."

"Like I said," Morrie was now getting pissed, "let's go in the back."

"Explain why she's standin' there with your mark on her after what she went through yesterday," Alec pushed, already pissed.

"Dude, as I said—"

"Explain why she lived through that asshole usin' his fists on her only to have her fucking *brother* mark her."

The bar—already on silent alert, everyone listening in and not hiding it—went wired.

Not me. I felt something else. Something far from pleasant. Something that made me feel sick.

Morrie's voice was vibrating when he warned, "Colt, don't compare me to Pete."

"You aren't explaining."

"What's goin' on here?" my dad said as my cell phone at my ass rang.

No one had noticed the door open. No one had noticed Mom and Dad walk in. No one.

Dad was looking between Morrie and Alec, his expression the same as it always was when he had to wade into one of their arguments or one of my arguments with Morrie.

Mom's eyes were on me.

I wasn't thinking. I should have said something, defused the situation. At least greeted my mom and dad who I hadn't seen since Christmas and it was now March. But instead I pulled the phone out of my back pocket, flipped it open and put it to my ear.

"Hello?"

I didn't even hear the words. The screeching was so loud there were barely words to be heard.

But even through the phone I could feel the fury, the anguish, the blame.

"Slow down," I said into the screeching. "What?"

"*Hacked!*" a voice I distractedly recognized as LeeAnne's shrieked a word in my ear that made my chest hollow out again. "*Hacked!*" she repeated.

"What?" I whispered.

"His landlord was at his *fucking* house when I called. He *fucking* picked up the phone. He *fucking* told me he was *fucking* hacked up with a *fucking* hatchet."

"Who?" I asked but I knew. I knew. IknewIknewIknewIknew.

"*Who?*" she squealed. "*Pete!*"

"Oh my God," I whispered, but the phone was sliding from my hand.

I didn't drop it, Alec was there taking it from me. Then he was talking in my phone. I heard my mom's voice, my dad's, Morrie's, Jessie's, Joe-Bob's, Sully's. I felt hands on me.

Then I ran fast to the women's toilets. Up came Meems' muffin and the coffee I had at her place. Then I wretched more. And more. Nothing coming out but my body wanted me to expel something else. Something it couldn't get rid of no matter how much I heaved. I felt the pain in my chest with the effort, the burning in the back of my throat, someone holding back my hair, me holding onto the toilet and heaving.

"Stop it, Feb," my mom said in my ear. She was close. I could feel the heat from her body.

"I've got to get it out," I gasped.

"Nothing else in there, honey."

"I've got to get it out."

Her cool hand wrapped around my hot forehead just like it did when I was a kid and I closed my eyes and focused on her touch.

I stopped heaving and sat back on my haunches.

"Go, Jessie. To the store. Toothbrush, toothpaste. Tell Morrie to bring some lemon-lime in here, a cold one. And a wet cloth."

I heard Jessie move but I didn't see her.

I saw a body by the dumpster, this time though it wasn't Angie's. It was Pete's.

I hated him. He hurt me, he nearly raped me, my husband, but it was true. He proved what I suspected, that men were no good. There were good men, like Alec, who were no good and there were shit men, like Pete, who were no good. That was all I knew. I'd wanted him to heal the wound but I knew, partway in it with him, he couldn't do that. Then I'd wanted him to numb the pain, but he'd only given me more, then taken away all that I had left.

But I didn't want him dead. Not any way but not *that* way.

"Feb, look at me. Look at your momma."

I didn't look at her, I asked, "What is it about me?"

"Honey, look at me."

I shook my head. "I don't understand."

Her hand came to my cheek and she tried to force me to look at her but I fought it, holding my neck still, clenching my teeth, staring at the wall.

"Honey—"

"Who's next?"

"February, you're scaring me," Mom said. "I need you to look at me."

Before I could do anything, even before I knew if I would, hands were under my armpits and I was hauled to my feet, pulled out of the stall, seeing my mom on her knees by the toilet, her head tipped back, her eyes on some point over my shoulder, some spot higher than me.

I twisted my neck and tilted my head back too, and saw Alec had hold of me.

"We need assistance here?" Sully asked, his voice nasally but the authority was still there.

I'd only ever heard that kind of authority from a cop. Teachers had a different kind. My dad, an even different kind. Mom, even different. Teachers, dads and moms, sometimes you listened, sometimes you didn't. But somehow you always listened to a cop.

"Maybe she needs to talk to someone," Mom said, getting up slowly but I didn't see her get to her feet.

I was jostled, brought around face to face with Alec.

"You need to talk to someone?" he asked, his body bent, his face in mine and I didn't know what his question was about so I didn't answer.

"Maybe she needs something to help her rest." This suggestion came from Morrie. "She doesn't sleep too good. Maybe we should take her to see Doc."

"You need something to help you rest?" Alec asked like Morrie was in another room talking to Alec in an earpiece and I couldn't hear my brother.

I didn't answer. I just stared at Alec, stared straight into his weird but beautiful gold-brown eyes.

His hands, both of them, came to the sides of my head. His palms, so big, so warm, were at my cheeks. His fingers, so long, so strong, were covering my hair. His face, a face I'd known as a boy and I'd watched grow into a man, was all I could see.

"February, talk to me."

I did.

But, "Alec," was all I could get out.

Then I fell forward and did a face plant in his chest. I grabbed onto his blazer and held on.

And for the second time in two days, I cried (essentially) in Alec's arms.

I heard Alec's phone ring but he didn't go for it. With my face plant, his fingers had slid through my hair and both his hands stayed where they were, curling around the back of my head, holding me to his chest.

I knew I should move away. I knew distance was paramount. But I couldn't. I was like a leech, latched onto him but instead of sucking blood, I was sucking strength.

I couldn't talk about Pete, not even now, not with anyone, especially not with Alec. But I wanted him to know I wasn't crying *for* Pete, I was just crying *about* Pete. No one deserved that, even though he was a dick, not even Pete.

But I couldn't tell Alec that, or anyone.

My crying stopped but I still held onto his jacket, my face in his chest, now because I was hiding.

Alec heard the tears subside and I felt pressure at his fingertips against my scalp.

"Can you talk to me now?"

I pulled away from his hands, let him go and stepped back.

We were alone in the bathroom.

I drew in a shaky breath and straightened my spine. Then I looked at him.

"I think seeing Doc would be good. Morrie's right, I don't sleep great."

"Why?"

"What?"

"Why don't you sleep great?"

I felt my head jerk and answered, "Because Tuesday's bed's small."

He shook his head. "You get up at seven o'clock when you don't need to, you gotta get home after three. You get three, four hours of sleep at night. That isn't good. Why don't you sleep?"

"I don't know. I've been working bars all my life, that's the way it's always been."

"No it isn't."

My midsection moved back like he punched me in the stomach.

He knew how I used to sleep. He'd slept over lots when we were kids. When we were teenagers all of us slept too late in the morning. It drove Mom wild but that's the way teenagers were. When he was at Purdue and Morrie would sneak me up there to spend the weekend with him, I'd sleep with him in his tiny bed in his dorm room, hiding from the RAs. We'd sleep in late and his roommate would scope out the bathroom, call the all-clear to Alec and he'd sneak me down when it was empty. Or when he'd moved to that apartment, he had three roommates but he commandeered the top floor, the attic room with the little three-quarter bathroom in the corner. The bed was a double in that room, much better. It had a desk, lots of floor space. I loved that room. I could pretend it was our place, our world and I did. That bed was perfect, just enough space so we weren't cramped, not enough that we didn't have to sleep close.

I used to sleep great, he knew that.

I used to sleep the sleep of someone who knew she was loved.

Now, I didn't.

"Feb, answer me."

"I don't know, all right?" I was sounding impatient. "Does it matter?"

"How long's this been going on?"

Apparently, it mattered to Alec.

"Long enough I'm used to it."

"It's not good."

"It isn't *now*. Now I need to close off my mind for a while, just for a while."

He watched me in a way that it felt like he was examining me. Whatever he saw, I could tell it troubled him at the same time it angered him.

Then he reached inside his blazer and brought out my phone. He handed it to me and I took it and then his hand went right to his back jeans pocket and he pulled out his own. When he flipped it open to look at it, his eyes grew hard at whatever he saw then he hit some buttons and put it to his ear.

I looked at him but he kept his gaze steady on the bathroom floor.

Finally he said, "Leslie? It's Colt. I need to pull a favor with Doc. He's gotta make time for Feb Owens. She's having trouble sleeping." He looked at me. "Yeah? Four? Good. Feb'll be there. Thanks." He flipped his phone shut. "You got an appointment with Doc at four."

"Thank you."

"Don't thank me. I'm not through with you."

My mouth filled with saliva and I swallowed it down. His face was back to hard, the way it got when I called him Alec, and I knew he was displeased.

He didn't make me wait to find out why.

"You're not gonna let me in, you've made that abundantly clear, but you gotta let someone in. You can't go on like this, it'll eat you alive. You're makin' your family watch, your friends, and it isn't right. It isn't *you*."

"Alec—"

"Shut your mouth."

I shut my mouth mainly because his tone was mean and he was scaring me, I felt the electricity of fear from head to toe. I'd never seen him act this way, not to me.

He'd been angry at me once, really angry, when I broke up with him. But even then he wasn't like he was now.

"Christ, Feb, talk to Doc, get some fuckin' help. You can't deal with this shit, with Angie, with—"

He stopped talking before he said Pete's name probably because I took an automatic step back. His gaze dropped to my feet and I saw his jaws flex. He was clenching his teeth.

Then he started talking again. "You can't deal with all this when you aren't dealing with whatever's been botherin' you since way before this shit started." I opened my mouth to talk but he leaned in and finished. "And no, don't try to kid me and for fuck's sake, don't kid yourself. It isn't about that asshole you married and what he did to you. Whatever's been botherin' you started way before that and we both know it, especially fuckin' *me*."

I felt winded at his words. The honesty at the same time Alec still sticking to his fucking lie. He'd never admitted it. He'd never copped to it. He'd acted like it was all me, like he'd done nothing wrong. He made me out to be the bad guy. I never accused him of it but he knew what he did and he never gave the barest hint of guilt or remorse. Now, even after all these years when I should have been over it, way over it, his words hit me on the fly and knocked the breath right out of me.

I still got out a whispered, "Alec—"

But I said no more, not that I had more to say, because he interrupted me.

"And for the *last* fuckin' time, stop calling me Alec." He got close, too close, and his head tipped down so he could stare at me. "You said you called me Alec because that's who I was to you. I'm not that anymore, whoever that was. I haven't been in a long time. So fuckin' stop calling me Alec."

He didn't give me the chance to reply. He turned and walked away. I stood in the bathroom in my tank top and jeans, holding my cell phone in my hand, staring at the door, feeling suddenly bone cold and thinking maybe he was right.

It was time to talk to Doc about what was bothering me.

And it was time to quit calling him Alec because, just then, what was left of my Alec was lost to me.

I'd been hanging onto it for a long time, with my jaw tilts, me calling him Alec.

But I knew it at that moment I couldn't hang on anymore.

He hadn't been Alec in a long time and I had to let him go.

Colt walked into J&J's late and saw Joe-Bob sitting at his stool, a couple bikers in the back. Colt had never seen them before, they were probably drifting through. The bikers were pulling on beers, playing pool. Angie's usual table was vacant, which it would be this time of night if she got lucky. Now seeing it empty made his fists clench.

Jack and Morrie were behind the bar. They were both looking at him after he completed his scan. They were also both moving down to the end of the bar where Colt always sat, around the curve so his back was to the door of the office, his vantage giving him a full view of the bar.

Colt slid onto a stool and Morrie asked, "Off duty?"

"Yeah."

Morrie twisted, bent then pulled three beer bottles out of a glass-fronted fridge. Jack moved to the shelves, grabbing the bourbon and three glasses.

Colt found his mind wandering to what he'd learned yesterday, the insignificant but unknown fact that Feb did yoga. That piece of information had slid into his brain half a dozen times in the last two days, pissing him off because he didn't know that about her. And it bothered him he didn't know. What bothered him more was that it bothered him at all.

Morrie uncapped the bottles, placing them on the bar with a dull thud. Jack put ice in the glasses then poured the bourbon, using the beverage gun to shoot a blast of Coke in Colt's before sliding the glasses around. The one that was cut went to Colt. The two straight shots, one went toward Morrie, Jack picked up the last and downed it in a gulp.

This was unusual. Jack liked his bourbon and was smart enough to sip it. He was also smart enough to play his cards close to his chest and almost always did. This act exposed his mood to anyone who knew him and it made that weight in Colt's gut shift disturbingly.

Colt nabbed the beer by its neck using two fingers and took a healthy pull.

"We good?" Morrie asked.

Colt's eyes moved around the bottle to his friend. He dropped the beer to the bar.

"Not really, but Feb's over it and Feb doesn't have much to do with me so I got no call to be pissed at you."

Morrie's lips thinned but he remained silent.

"We'll talk about that shit later. Tell us about Pete," Jack demanded and Colt turned to him.

Colt would have paid money, big money, not to be having this conversation. But he respected these men and they needed to know, so he did what was right even though it felt shit. And when he was done, he knew he'd feel even more shit.

Still, he let go of the beer and took a sip of bourbon before he started.

"Pete was done three days ago. Why no one told his mother, I don't know. He was the first that we know of."

Jack took a sharp breath into his nostrils.

Colt kept talking.

"We're exchanging information with St. Louis. Murder was mostly the same, 'cept Pete was awake when it happened and the killer did him at home and left him at home. He fought his attacker but the guy got a swipe to the back of Pete's neck, probably when he was running away. It incapacitated him but didn't kill him. He dragged Pete back to his bed and did the same as he did to Angie. Took off the clothes he was wearing, all of 'em, unlike Angie, and delivered blows to the groin, up through to the abdomen, near to the heart. The bed, the floor, the walls, covered in blood."

Jack and Morrie held his eyes, couldn't tear theirs away. Colt had seen that before, mortified fascination, hearing words that felt like acid going in your ears but you couldn't stop listening.

Colt went back to his beer and took a pull before he went on.

"Boys spent a lot of time at Angie's yesterday and today. Results are comin' in. Angie wasn't much of a housekeeper and she had a lot of visitors. We'll be siftin' through the shit we took from her house for a while. Got a couple of hits, guys she had who left DNA or prints and have records but they're unlikely. We're lookin' at them. Cory says he left her place around one o'clock. Said she was still pretty hammered when he left. Can't know, it's likely she doesn't take the time to make her bed, but it looks like she slept there and the killer took her from there. Though no forced entry. But her purse was there, her car keys, her car out front. Angie wasn't a walker. She went somewhere she'd take her car, even drunk. Toxicology came back. We're guessin' she'd dosed herself, probably needs to, way she lives her life, to get sleep. Had some over-the-counter sleep aids by the side of the bed, what amounts to four of them in her blood. Dose is usually two so she was either out our seriously groggy when he took her."

"Thank the Lord," Jack muttered.

Colt went on. He had a lot to say and he wanted to get it done. He wanted to get home. He wanted to sleep. He needed to be rested for whatever shit the next day would bring.

So he kept going.

"Killer left Angie's body exposed. He'd planned the show. Probably dressed her before he took her out but no bra, no underwear, no shoes. Pulled her top up to show her breasts, yanked her skirt up around her waist. No blows from the weapon except to her groin and abdomen."

Jack and Morrie remained silent. Then again there was nothing to say to these grim facts.

"Displaying the bodies the way he does, naked in Pete's case, exposed in Angie's, hacking into their privates, this is an effort at humiliation." Colt paused, the feeling of shit intensifying as he said, "A gift to Feb."

"Jesus fuckin' Christ," Morrie whispered.

"This has crossed state lines," Colt told them. "The Feds are movin' in. Already talked to them. Tomorrow morning got a meeting. Feds have called Quantico. The profilers are comin' from Virginia first thing."

"That's good, isn't it?" Morrie asked.

Colt had never worked with the Feds but he knew some guys who had, went to conferences, read shit about it. Sometimes they could be a pain in the ass. Most of the time, fresh eyes and that kind of experience were welcome.

Colt welcomed it.

"It's good," Colt said. "But I've already informed them of Feb and my history. I'll be takin' a step back."

"You need to be working this, son," Jack said, using the tone he always used with Colt. The tone he used with Morrie. The tone he used to use with Feb. That father's tone that Colt never heard from his own dad. The tone that said Jack believed in him, believed he could do what needed to be done, believed he'd do it right, believed no one could do it better.

"I don't take a step back myself, they'll push me back," Colt replied. "They don't care this is my town. They care about catchin' this guy and makin' him stay caught once they do. They don't need and won't tolerate anything that might jeopardize that." No response and Colt gave them both a look. "Sully will be the local primary and I'll still be workin' it."

"Least that's something," Jack remarked.

"We got more," Colt told them. "Chris canvassed. Surprisingly that time in the morning no one saw some guy hacking away at Angie. Still, Chris got two witnesses who report they saw a silver sedan. They didn't note the make and model. They thought it was an Audi or Mercedes, no license. They saw it pulling out of the alley around the time of the murder."

"That ain't much," Morrie said.

"Better 'n nothing," Jack replied.

Morrie nodded and looked at Colt. "If Pete was killed three days ago, and Feb got that note the day Angie died, did we miss something? What—?"

"Everyone knew what Pete did to February," Jack noted. "He had no reason to explain."

"Yeah, that's true. Still, the killer left a calling card in St. Louis," Colt told them.

Both men's eyes turned to him.

"St. Louis PD couldn't understand it, already knew they had someone who was seriously whacked in the head, but they didn't get the message until I told them," Colt said and Jack and Morrie stayed quiet so he gave them the news. "Bloody scene, carnage, but on Pete's nightstand was a pristine bouquet of flowers, no blood on them, set there after the mess was made." He paused, before he clipped out, "Tulips."

"*Fuck!*" Morrie hissed.

Tulips were Feb's favorite flowers. Colt used to buy them for her every birthday even though they cost some cake, finding tulips in October. Florist had to special order them. He bought them for her on Valentine's Day too. In her bedroom when she was a teenager, she had a big picture, white background, a spray of pink and white tulips in a vase displayed over her bed.

Colt kept speaking, giving them information to take their mind from the disturbing thoughts about how well this guy knew their daughter, their sister. It wouldn't take much to know Feb liked tulips, you just had to pay attention. But you also had to be close.

"Dead end on the flowers. He'd arranged them himself, bought the vase at Pottery Barn and fuck knows how many Pottery Barns are around the St. Louis area, not to mention he coulda gone to any mall between here and there. No prints on the vase. No stickers or residue left. He coulda got the flowers from anywhere, seein' as they're in season. Spring's here."

Colt used to buy her tulips in spring too, just because you could find them easy, they were all around and she liked them. To this day spring meant tulips to Colt and sometimes when he wasn't paying attention and didn't have control of the path of his thoughts, he'd see them, at a grocery store, in Janet's Flower Shop window, and think, *I'll pick those up for Feb*, before he could stop himself.

"Is Feb in danger?" Jack asked, and Colt looked at him.

Jack was trying to keep those cards close to his chest but the hold he had on them was far from steady.

"Can't say," Colt replied. "But the Feds, especially the profilers, they'll know more."

Jack nodded. He didn't like it, but he nodded.

Colt moved on to different business. "Sully and I went down Feb's list. Five names. We had the chat."

"They gonna keep quiet?" Morrie asked.

Colt thought about these visits. They were short and they were all the same, every one of them. The news was met with amusement, the upsets history, so slight they were barely remembered. Then Sully and Colt gave them more information and the amusement died and fear set in. He wasn't surprised at the end response. Two of them said the same exact words, "Poor Feb."

Not, "Oh my God," and not, "Poor Angie."

Angie was known. She managed to hold down her job but by most of the townsfolk she wasn't respected, she was tolerated. Some may have felt sorry for her but most simply didn't think about her and when they did, they didn't think much.

Feb, that was a different story.

"They'll keep it quiet, for how long? Don't know," Colt answered then he caught his friend's eyes. "You need to move back in with Delilah."

Morrie grinned. "Shit, tell me somethin' I *don't* know."

Colt shook his head. Morrie wasn't getting it.

"Far's I can tell February loves few people in this world. Jack, Jackie, Jessie, Meems, their families, your kids and *you*."

Morrie's grin faded.

Colt continued. "Angie and Feb had a stupid, teenage girl fight years ago and Angie bought it. You think Dee might not be on that list, this guy thinks he's takin' care of Feb's business, this guy thinks Dee hurt you and, through that, hurt Feb?"

Colt watched Morrie's entire frame grow tight.

"Talk to her, move back in with her, explain it," Colt pushed. "You need me to come with you, I'm there. She'll let you move in, least until this is over."

"You got time tonight?" Morrie asked.

"All the time you need," Colt answered.

"Let's go," Morrie said.

"Hang on two shakes," Jack said, his eyes on Colt. "This business is pressin', so I'll let you two go. That don't mean we don't got shit to talk about."

"Jack—" Colt started.

"I saw what I saw in that bathroom, Colt. We all did," Jack stated.

He could guess what Jack thought he saw.

What Colt saw and felt leaking into his shirt was Feb crying her eyes out at the death of some jackass that beat her to shit and tore the last bits of

February Owens away. Not that there was much left after whatever caused her to turn, but they were there. They'd come out once in a while.

After Pete was through with her, they vanished. Only the jaw tilt was left and rarely her laughter would be unguarded and you could almost hear the old Feb in it. But that was rarely and only happened when she was with Morrie's kids. Not with Morrie, her parents, even Jessie and Meems. Not that he'd seen and, he hated to admit it, but for two years and any time she was home the earlier fifteen, he'd been watching.

"Due respect, Jack, you think you saw what you wanted to see," Colt told him.

"Due respect, Colt, I saw what everyone saw. *You* experienced what you had to experience to hold yourself back," Jack returned.

That pissed him off.

"Not me holdin' back."

"You been holdin' back for twenty years."

"We aren't havin' this conversation," Colt declared.

"We are, just not now. You and Morrie got a daughter-in-law of mine to protect. See to that. We'll talk about this later."

Colt bit back his response. Jack meant too much to him to say what he wanted to say. They still weren't going to have this conversation, now, tomorrow, next week or ever.

Colt nodded anyway.

Jack nodded back.

"Let's go." Morrie was impatient.

Colt took another pull from his beer and slid off the barstool, repeating. "Let's go."

Three

PUCK

"I'm Agent Warren, FBI."

He was good-looking, Agent Warren, and he knew it.

He extended his hand to me and I took it. He probably had dozens of handshakes he'd practiced over the years. This one was firm but reassuring.

"This is Agent Rodman," Agent Warren motioned to the man at his side, yin to Agent Warren's yang.

Warren was mocha-skinned black, bald, his thick, long eyelashes declaring that he shaved his head rather than lost his hair, his tall frame was lean but not slight.

Rodman was white, showing signs that he needed to lay off the donuts, was obviously balding and didn't hide it and had the widest, most brilliantly gold wedding band I'd ever seen in my life.

Agent Rodman's handshake was just as firm and just as reassuring.

They were not my enemy. They were here to help.

This was good to know.

I saw movement out the corner of my eye and Colt and Sully were walking up. It cost me but I caught the jaw tilt before it even began.

"Colt," I said when he made it to me and Sully's body jerked at my word.

Colt didn't move, his expression revealed nothing. Even so, his eyes were locked on me in a weirdly intense way that made me fight back a squirm.

"Feb," Colt said back.

"Sully," I said to Sully, noting he looked a bit better and his voice, when it said my name, wasn't near as nasally.

"Feb."

Neither of them called me February, which I was surprised about. I thought in front of the FBI they'd want to appear official.

Then I realized I was not February to them in front of the agents. I was Feb. They knew me. I was one of their own, a citizen of their town but more than just some unknown someone they'd sworn to protect.

That was good to know too.

"You should know, Ms. Owens, that Lieutenant Colton has bowed out of the investigation," Agent Warren, clearly speaker for the FBI, put in smoothly.

This surprised me too but I didn't hide that surprise because underneath it was an irrational fear that was impossible to control.

Therefore I also didn't catch my response.

"Why?" My tone held clear accusation. I meant it to be and it was directed at the speaker for the FBI.

I watched Warren's dark brows draw together over his girlie eye-lashed eyes. "Lieutenant Colton explained you two have history."

I doubted Colt had explained that history thoroughly, but I also didn't care.

"He's a good cop."

"That's not in question," Warren stated.

"In fact, him stepping aside on his own proves your statement true," Rodman spoke for the first time.

I wasn't comprehending nor did I want to.

"He's a good cop," I repeated.

"Feb," Colt said, but I didn't look at him.

"He could prejudice the case," Warren told me.

"He wouldn't do that," I informed Warren.

"Maybe not but we can't take that chance and he doesn't want us to," Warren replied.

It was then I realized what I was saying, what I was doing and that I had no clue what I was talking about.

So finally, I shut up.

"Lieutenant Sullivan is local primary," Warren said. "Colton will be kept informed and will remain on the case in a consultative capacity."

He was giving me FBI-speak. In other words, I had no fucking clue what he was talking about with his "consultative capacity" bullshit and I couldn't ask him. Not now. Not in front of Colt. And not ever to anyone because if they told someone else how much I wanted to know and what that said about how much I wanted Colt on this case, they might jump to conclusions that weren't right.

I didn't like it much but I kept quiet.

"There are a few more people I want you to meet," Warren said. "Then I'm afraid we'll have to take a fair bit of your time this morning."

The FBI had taken over the conference room, which was a glass walled room to the side of the bottom floor.

The police station in town used to be the town library before they built a bigger library that was modern and situated closer to the schools. The station was an old, handsome brick building. They'd made the front of it look like an old time police department including two black light poles sitting on the wide cement railings at the bottom of the front steps on top of which were big, round, white lights with the word "Police" written on their fronts.

I'd taken Bonham and Tuesday on a tour years ago when I was home as they'd opened it to the public. I was curious as to where Colt worked even though I told myself I was doing it for Bonham who wanted to be like his Uncle Colt when he grew up.

There were cells and lockdown in the basement.

A vast open space on the first floor with files, a big counter facing the front door, some desks behind it, the conference room at the side, a few cubicles down the other side, offices at the back. In the back corner in a little, soundproof, windowed room was dispatch. Equipment down the middle of the room, two desks facing each other with an upright in between with knobs and dials. The dispatchers sat opposite each other with headphones on, like Connie McIntyre and Jo Frederick were doing now.

The top floor was what I heard Colt refer to as the bullpen, but it was officially known as the Investigations Unit, where the few detectives had their desks and where the interrogation rooms were. They had lockers up there, a big bathroom with some showers and they had a supply room up there too, where they kept guns and ammo, bulletproof vests, shit like that.

Sully came with the agents and me to the conference room but Colt didn't glance my way as he headed toward the stairs.

I met the profilers and I spent some time repeating a lot of what I already told Colt. Their questions were more thorough and they went over stuff often, shit I'd already answered then I answered it again, and again. I tried to remain patient and managed it mainly because Doc had given me some sleeping pills and I'd slept from nine o'clock last night to just after eight this morning when Mom woke me in Jessie's double bed (she'd spent the night on Jessie's pull out couch) and told me that Colt had called and the FBI wanted me at the station as soon as I could get there.

I hadn't had that much sleep in years. So long it felt like I lost days, not hours. Still, I got up, shook off the sleep in the shower and had a mild argument with Jessie, who thought I should dress up for the FBI and carted half of her burgeoning closet into the guest room in order to facilitate me doing this when I thought it was best, as always, to be just plain me.

I won.

The FBI asked about shit they didn't need to know, in my opinion, but I told them anyway. I didn't want them to think I had anything to hide and I didn't want them to think Colt did either. So I told them Colt and I were high school sweethearts, that he'd always been and still was like a member of the family. I didn't tell them why I ended it with Colt but I did tell them all about Pete, leaving it at the fact that Pete had done the right thing by skipping town but making it clear he came to this decision with a little help from family and friends.

On this point, I did not elaborate.

I also went through all my travels. Where I worked, how long I stayed, as best as I could. Fifteen years was a lot to remember. There were parts of my life that were burned on my brain. The first half of it and the last two years. The fifteen years I was traveling, not so much.

I found it vaguely odd, in the spare moments I had to think about it during their questioning, that I'd lived those fifteen years in a kind of fog. I thought I'd been trying to rediscover me but it seemed I'd spent that time existing and not on a path of discovery at all.

We were going over (again) the possible psychopath who'd been in my life for a long time, keeping tabs on me and working himself up to a murdering frenzy when I saw Colt coming down the stairs, his manner urgent, his eyes on the front door. My eyes followed his.

Mom and Dad were walking in, Dad carrying something in a Ziploc bag, holding it between thumb and forefinger like it was putrid.

Automatically I got up as my voice trailed off in mid-explanation that I had no freaking clue who was hacking away at people who'd shared my life.

I didn't notice all the agents and Sully's heads turning to look out the windows mainly because I was walking to the closed conference room door.

"Ms. Owens," Warren called but I ignored him and walked right out.

"What is it?" I asked across the room, Mom and Dad jumped and their heads swung to me.

Colt, who had his back to me, turned and he was now holding the bag.

The bag I saw would have been funny, say, in a TV show. The Ziploc bags I had at my house had big pink daises printed in a line across the front. But I knew the piece of paper wasn't funny even if it was in a Ziploc bag with daisies on it. It was less funny because I knew it came in the mail at my house, that's why it was in that bag. My parents had gone over to check my house. Mom told me they'd be doing it. And obviously they did.

I made it to them and Colt said, "Feb, go back in with the agents."

"What is it?"

"Feb—" Colt started, but I reached out fast and snatched the daisy bag out of his hand.

Then I retreated faster and turned my back to him.

I saw the words *I'm sorry I upset you about the dog...* before Colt reached around me and snatched the bag right back.

"I said, go back with the agents," he demanded, but I was looking at the note in his hand.

"Puck," I whispered to the note.

I'd been around his dog. He'd had Puck for years and even though a lot of the time he made himself scarce when I came home for visits, most of the times, since my family was the only family he had left and I came back for special occasions, he was around.

So was Puck.

65

When he wasn't on duty Colt took that dog with him nearly everywhere.

The last two years, Morrie and Dee, then just Morrie, would look after Puck when Colt went skiing in Colorado with Sully and Lorraine.

I liked Puck so when Colt went on vacation, I went to visit Morrie so I could be around Puck.

Puck was a great dog.

And Morrie had told me about Puck dying last week, right in the bar. Obviously, Morrie didn't know I liked Puck as much as I did because Morrie was shocked when I burst into tears right behind the bar, right for all to see before I realized what I was doing and walked back to the office to cry about Puck in belated private.

The psycho had seen me too.

"Does this have to do with the case?" I heard Warren ask.

"I'm guessin', yeah." I heard Colt answer.

"May I see?" Warren was being polite and I watched the note transfer hands.

But all I could think was that I killed Colt's dog. Lost women drinking away their lives in bars. Loser assholes probably tearing through women's lives in St. Louis. And now German shepherds who didn't do any living thing harm. Just gave unconditional love and cost a bit of money to keep in food and shots.

All of them gone, because of me.

"I'm sorry, Colton, but we need to show this to Ms. Owens," Warren said, and I turned to him, my movement stilted, like my joints needed oiling. "This will be upsetting," he informed me.

I gave him a look that screamed, *No kidding?* but I didn't speak. I just lifted my hand and took the note.

Typed out, it said:

I'm sorry I upset you about the dog. I didn't mean to. I thought you'd be happy that he hurt like he made you hurt. His has to be the worst.

It will be.

For you.

After I finished reading, for a second I went blind, the words erased from the paper and I saw nothing.

Then I turned to Agent Warren. "I need to make a statement on TV or something, tell him to stop. Tell him he's not helping me. Tell him this is not making me happy."

One of the profilers, went by the name of Nowakowski, said, "If you'd be willing to do that, we'll consider it, Ms. Owens, but right now we're unsure we want to alert the media to this."

"Then I need to send a message somehow." My voice was rising. "He thinks he's making me happy. I need to tell him to stop."

"Ms. Owens—" Nowakowski started.

"He's watching me. I started crying when my brother told me Puck died…in the bar I started crying. He's watching me. I need to be visible. What he's doing to Angie, Puck, I need to be visible. I need to show him he's not helping me, he's harming me."

The agents looked at each other and I felt a presence come close and I knew from experience it was my dad.

"I don't need to be here." My voice was rising as well as getting louder, sounding more hysterical. "I'm not helping here. I need to be out there." I pointed to the doors, my arm slamming into something solid. That something was Colt's chest, but I didn't stop. "I need to be where he can see me! I need him to see—"

"Girl, calm," Dad said, his hand coming up to curl on my shoulder.

I couldn't be calm if someone injected me. I'd killed Colt's dog.

I turned and tipped my head back. Day three, third crying jag I grabbed Colt by the lapels of his jacket and got up on my toes, feeling the tears dropping from my eyes, instant rivers of salt. So much water, I had my eyes open but I couldn't make him out. He was a total blur.

"I'm sorry. I'm so sorry. I'm so so sorry he hurt Puck. I'm so *fucking*—"

Colt's hand wrapped around the back of my neck, its steadiness and warmth coming as so much of a shock, I stopped speaking.

"February, it's okay." Colt's voice was quiet, just for me, only for me.

I shook my head. The movement unnatural and wrong, me alive and moving while all things around me were getting butchered. The tears still uncontrolled, my hands twisted in his jacket and I shook it. "It isn't."

And it wasn't. None of it was.

"Feb—" he began, but I lost it.

I lost it because it finally sunk in deep what my sick admirer considered his end game.

And the thought was intolerable.

Yanking Colt's jacket with a vicious pull, I slammed my fists back into his chest and screeched, *"He means to harm you!"*

Then I did it again and again, my repeated shrieks of those five words broken with sobs, my fists pummeling his chest, abusing his jacket, until his arms came around me, pulling me close, trapping my arms between our bodies.

My head was still tilted back and Colt was still blurry. Even imprisoned I was still hysterical.

"He means to harm you!"

"Do you have someone here who's qualified to sedate her?" Agent Warren asked and I tried to turn, tear out of Colt's arms to confront my new nemesis but Colt held me fast so just my neck twisted.

"I can't help if I'm sedated!" I shrieked.

"February, you need to calm down," Colt said firmly.

My head twisted back and I looked at him still sightless and weeping. "I killed your dog."

"You didn't have a thing to do with Puck dying."

"I killed your dog."

"She's hysterical," someone muttered.

My neck twisted toward the direction of the sound and I screamed blindly, "You would be too if you killed someone's dog!"

Colt's arms got so tight, my breath was forced out of my lungs and I heard him whisper the words, "Baby, stop it. You didn't kill my dog."

Baby, stop it.

Baby, stop it.

Baby, stop it.

The soft words bounced in my head, round and round, taking all my concentration. So much, I didn't have enough to remain standing and I gave Colt my weight, dropped my head and rested it on my hands, which were trapped against his chest.

Baby, stop it. You don't know what you're saying.

He'd said that years ago when I broke up with him.

Baby, stop it. You know the way it is between you and me.

He'd said that years ago too, when I told him he should act like a free agent when he went to Purdue and if he came back to me then we'd know it was meant to be.

He'd refused. He'd said he didn't want to be a free agent. He didn't want anyone, not anyone, but me.

Baby, stop it. Morrie gets it, your parents do too.

He'd said that years and years and years ago, after the first time he kissed me and I'd freaked out because I'd wanted that kiss so badly, and it was everything I'd wanted it to be, and it promised everything I needed it to promise, but I'd worried Morrie, Mom and Dad would get mad.

"I want him to be watching now," I said to my hands, the tears still coming but they were no longer loud and neither was my voice. My words, like his, were meant only for Colt. "I want him to see what he's doing to me."

Colt's arms got tight again. "He won't care, Feb. After all these years something started him on this path and he can't go back now. But you've got to be stronger than this, you've got to help Sully and the FBI and you've got to stand strong to the end." One of his arms came from around me and his hand went to the back of my neck, giving me a squeeze there and I tilted my head back to look at him, was able to get focused on him but still only blinking through tears. "And there'll be an end, I promise, February, and it won't end with the end of me. It will end with the end of what he's doing."

I nodded. Not because I believed, I was too scared to believe. I nodded because it was clear he believed.

"I'm sorry about Puck," I whispered and I knew it sounded stupid and like I hadn't gotten myself together but his hand at my neck gave me another squeeze.

"I know you are. I am too."

Colt knew it wasn't stupid. He knew I was just saying I was sorry as anyone would and as I hadn't at the time Puck died because I was avoiding him.

"This is over, you should get another dog," I advised.

His mouth moved. I didn't understand how but it wasn't anger. It was something else, something attractive, almost mesmerizing.

"I'll consider it."

I looked from his mouth direct into his eyes. "Good."

"Ms. Owens, if we can continue," Agent Warren said from behind me and Colt looked there before his gaze came back to me.

"You good?" Colt asked me.

No, I was not good. Any good left to me was stuck back in memories of the Glory Days. Or, sometimes, when Morrie would make me laugh or seeing how great his kids were turning out to be. Or biting into one of Meems' muffins or seeing her look at Al, even after all these years and four kids, like she wanted to rip his clothes off. Or watching Jessie's face get soft when Jimbo did something goofy like it was anything but goofy to Jessie.

For me, I'd lived my life for a while off other people being good.

But for the first time in a long time I was sick of living in a fog most of the time and sick of feeling shit the rest of it and I wanted good back too. But I wanted it for me.

"I'm good," I lied.

His hand and arm went away, I stood on my own two feet and I was concentrating so much on doing that, I didn't move away directly. I just tested my steadiness for a while before I tipped my head back, looked Colt in the eye, took a breath and then walked back to the conference room.

Someone got me a fresh coffee and everyone resumed their places.

"Now perhaps, Ms. Owens, in light of this new evidence," Agent Nowakowski carefully placed the daisy bag on the table, his voice was gentle but probing, "we should go back over your relationship with Lieutenant Colton."

His eyes were on me and he was examining me like Colt did yesterday and I figured, considering he did what he did for a living, there was a lot he could see.

Therefore, because this was important, not looking at Sully and hoping to God he'd keep his partner mouth shut even though I knew there was no way in hell he would, I said, "Alec Colton had been in my life since I was three to the time I was twenty. Not like my brother, something more. Everyone knew it, my family, our friends, everyone in town. Our breakup came as a surprise and still does to some, that's how big it was. I broke up with him and it doesn't matter why, I just did. He didn't break up with me. This guy, whoever he is, is not going to care about that. I went off the rails

70

after that and this guy, whoever he is, will know that like he knows everything else. And he'll blame Ale...Colt."

I took a sip of coffee, swallowed then took a deep breath and went on.

"It wasn't about high school sweethearts. Even when we *were* high school sweethearts, it was more. It was much more, more than many people have in their lives. Everyone knew that too. They also know, once I went off the rails, I never found my way back. Even after coming home. I suspect he wants to make Colt pay for that, even pay for taking me away when that wasn't Colt's fault either. So that's it, that's the story. There's no words to explain how big it was, what Colt and I had. Or how much it hurts when something that big in your life is swept away. Or how empty that place is that he once filled. Or how impossible it is to find something to fill it. But since everyone knew I drained myself empty, I suspect this guy knew too." I sat back and finished, "That's it."

Everyone was silent. I chanced a glance at Sully and he was looking at his knees.

"Lieutenant Colton was a lucky man," Agent Nowakowski said gently and my eyes moved to him. He was still studying me but now his eyes were as gentle as his voice.

"Make no mistake, sir," I replied, "Alec Colton was never lucky. He came into this world one of the most unlucky sons of bitches you've ever met and he's worked his ass off for everything he's ever had."

I had no clue how proud I sounded, nor how fierce, but out of the corner of my eye I saw Sully's head jerk up. But it was what Agent Nowakowski said next that kept my attention on him.

"February, the mistake is yours if you think that's true."

I heard a loud reverberating sound, like a tiny drop of moisture splashing against the bottom of a dry, cavernous pit.

I almost looked around to find the source of the noise until I realized I was the only one who heard it because it was coming from inside of me.

⌣‿⌐

Colt walked into J&J's. It was early but he was off duty. The Feds and Sully were still working but after the scene in the station his already minor "consultative capacity" became minuscule.

There was another reason he escaped the station and that was because Sully had told him, probably a dozen times that day, they needed to talk about "what Feb said in that room."

Seemed everyone wanted to discuss him and February: Susie, Jack, Morrie, Sully.

As for Sully, to be fair to Feb, Colt thought it was her choice if she wanted to share. He'd fucking well like to know what she said, make no mistake. But she should be the one to choose to tell him.

Walking into J&J's, he knew he was likely jumping straight out of the frying pan into the fire. But Feb had said she'd cried in the bar when she'd heard about Puck and that meant the killer was in the bar to see her crying. Therefore Colt was going to be in J&J's scrutinizing the crowd.

It was Friday night and J&J's, like always on Fridays, was packed. Darryl and Jack were working the bar, Feb and Ruthie, Morrie and Feb's only other employee outside Fritzi who came in every morning to mop and clean, were both out amongst the tables, dropping drinks.

Morrie was nowhere to be seen.

Feb glanced up, saw him and dipped her chin like he'd seen her do to hundreds of customers, saying hello, asking, nonverbally, "What can I get you?" or "You want another?"

Colt felt exactly as he felt that morning when she'd denied him the jaw tilt for the first time since he could remember. He felt like he felt when she called him Colt for the first time, something he'd repeatedly told her to do but something he found he fucking hated when she finally did it.

He felt like throwing something.

But instead he dipped his own chin and hid his response just as he kicked himself for being such an enormous jackass in the bathroom the day before. Finally losing it about her calling him Alec and taking away the only good thing they shared anymore.

Or so he thought.

After she denied him the jaw tilt that morning she threw a minor hissy fit about him being off the case. Colt had no idea if she was doing this because she thought the Feds were insulting him or if she wanted him working the case or both. He kept hearing her saying, "He's a good cop," over and over in his head and he liked the sound, too fucking much, but there was no denying he did.

And there was also no denying that her reaction to the possibility that he would get hurt, not to mention the death of his dog, had been spectacularly more mammoth than the tears she'd shed over her asshole ex-husband. They'd thought they'd need to sedate her. Hell, he'd thought it too. She was completely out of control.

But she'd let *him* calm her. Not her dad, or her mom, nor had she pulled herself together on her own. Colt had done it.

Feb could lose it. She had her mother's temper, which was volatile, though quiet. Making matters worse she was also emotional, again just like her mom. Both Feb and Jackie could descend into righteous indignation or inconsolable tears at the slightest provocation. Like Jack with Jackie, Colt had been the only one, back in the day, who could calm February.

And that day, he'd done it again.

And last, she wasn't avoiding his eyes anymore, or his touch. That morning, after her drama and him helping her to pull herself together, she'd stood in his arms and started a conversation about how he should get a new dog. When Warren interrupted the moment, Colt's hands itched to wring the man's neck. But when Colt finally let Feb go, she didn't step away, gain distance. She stood close then met his eyes before walking away.

He had no idea what any of this meant or if it meant anything at all and it was only her way of coping during a seriously shitty situation. He'd give her the lead and he'd wait.

What he wouldn't do was let Sully, Jack or Morrie piss all over it. If something good came of this mess, a détente between the two of them, he was going to take it and he wasn't going to let anyone piss on it.

No fucking way.

He slid onto his stool at the end of the bar and scanned the room.

"Off duty?" Jack asked and Colt nodded.

He heard the hiss of the cap coming off the beer, the thud of the bottle landing in front of him and he forgot until then how much he missed hearing Jack ask, "Off duty?" then the subsequent hiss and thud.

It sucked *why* the family was back together but he couldn't deny he was glad they were.

"Where's Morrie?" Colt asked, watching Feb talk to a table full of kids who looked too young to be sitting in a bar.

"Shoulda come in three hours ago, you missed World War Three." Jack's amused answer brought Colt's eyes to him.

"World War Three?" Colt asked the smiling Jack, not sure whether he was more surprised to see Jack smiling indulgently or to see that indulgent smile aimed at his daughter.

Jack had kept his mouth shut throughout the last two decades, but Colt knew Feb felt his condemnation. He knew it because she couldn't miss it, everyone saw it. Jack loved his daughter, always had, always would. They'd been close once, as fathers and daughters should be. Feb was Jack's little girl, not like Susie was a daddy's little girl.

What Jack and Feb had was special and it was beautiful.

But Jack took her breakup with Colt and her subsequent behavior, marriage and defection as a personal affront to the family he built. He'd accepted her and her decisions as that was Jack's way, but he didn't like them and he didn't pretend to. Colt had seen him smile at his daughter, laugh with her, but he hadn't seen that indulgent smile in twenty years.

Colt's gaze moved back to February who now had her tray tucked under her arm and she was scrutinizing one of the boys' driver's licenses. He watched as she said something then tipped her head his way. The boys all went pale in the dim lights of the bar and looked uncomfortably at him, some of them twisting in their chair to do it. Feb said something else and they quickly grabbed their jackets, the legs of their chairs scraping so desperately on the floor the noise could be heard over the music. Through their hurried departure Feb tapped the now-confiscated license against her palm, her eyes went to her father and she rolled them.

Colt stopped breathing.

Jack burst out laughing.

Feb used to roll her eyes all the time. The world was full of idiots doing idiot things that Feb thought worthy of an eye roll. Mostly the idiot things she did herself.

He'd always loved it that she could laugh at herself and all the trouble she got herself into because she was so fired up to suck all the life out of the world that she could get in her. She never blushed when she did something stupid or crazy or embarrassing. She'd just roll her eyes, throw her head back and laugh.

"I'm guessin' you won't shut us down, officer, since Feb didn't serve those young 'uns," Jack said, his voice vibrating with his chuckle. "Good you kids got so much practice flashin' your fake IDs and getting yourself into liquor stores, bars and trouble. Means Morrie and Feb can sniff 'em out from a mile away."

Colt was listening but he was watching Feb move to another table, her chin lifting, giving them a hello-what-can-I-get-cha.

"World War Three…" Jack said, capturing Colt's attention again and he turned to look at the man, "happened when Feb found out Morrie moved home. She doesn't know why, she thinks it's a trial reconciliation. Three hours ago she told Morrie to go home, help his now full-time workin' wife with dinner, help her with the dishes, help their kids with their homework and then to bed *then* he could come back here."

Colt thought this was good advice and Jack kept talking.

"Morrie told her his kids are ten and twelve years old and they don't need no help gettin' to bed and Dee's been doin' the dishes since she was a kid."

Colt thought this was a very stupid response and Jack kept right on going.

"Feb lost her mind, told him to stop bein' a jackass and get home to his family." Colt wished he'd seen that. "Morrie told her it was Friday and ain't no way he was leavin' this bar on a busy Friday night." Colt wished he'd been here to kick his friend up the ass. "Feb told him he had a choice, he could take care of his customers or he could keep his family."

When Jack stopped talking, Colt remarked, "No choice really."

"Yep," Jack grinned at him. "That's why Morrie ain't here." Jack's gaze sought his daughter and his voice was softer when he spoke again. "Ain't seen Feb act that way in too long." He didn't look at Colt when he finished. "Seems this situation has scared some life back in her. Ain't gonna thank the fucker for doin' it, but I'm glad all the same."

Colt remained silent but hid it behind a pull off his beer.

Jack took that time to turn his attention to Colt. "Seems to me there's advantage to be taken, son, and ain't no one in a hundred mile radius would blame you for takin' it."

Colt dropped the beer and opened his mouth but Jack threw up his hands in a gesture of surrender.

"That's all I'm sayin'. You're a man now, you play it as you see fit."

Before Colt could speak, Jack's eyes went over Colt's shoulder and he followed something around Colt's back.

Colt twisted and saw Feb heft up the hinged portion of bar and slide through, dropping it behind her.

Her eyes caught Colt's and before she turned away she said, "Hey."

Another new one.

She never said anything in greeting, not even "hey."

Then she turned away and walked down the bar. Colt's eyes followed her ass as she did it. Then they sliced to Jack who he caught grinning at him.

Jesus fucking Christ.

"Not smart, old man, gettin' your hopes up," Colt told him quietly.

"My age? Hope's about all I got left," Jack returned and headed down the bar.

Jack was so full of shit. The man had everything.

Colt nursed his beer and scanned the bar, cataloguing the customers, going through what he knew about them in his mind and understanding Feb's hesitation at pointing the finger at anyone. Most everyone there he knew. Most of those he knew his whole life.

There were a few drifters. Jack was a biker. He'd owned a hawg all the time Colt knew him. He had a "biker friendly" sign in the front window. He liked his Harley brethren to come in, take a load off, shoot a game of pool and drink a few rounds in his place.

Morrie and Feb continued the tradition.

Morrie owned a Fat Boy and Feb had more Harley-Davidson t-shirts than were probably carried in a single store. At the back, under the collar, if she lifted her hair up or, in the summer and the nights got too busy and she pulled it into a knot or ponytail on the top of her head, you'd see the story of her last fifteen years laid bare there. In a small decal under the collar,

Harley tees announced what store in what city and what state the tee came from. She'd been to Harley stores all over the country. Hell, she had several from the Harley golden triangle, Deadwood, Rapid City, and the grand-daddy of them all, Sturgis. She'd worn one the other night and tonight she had on a Sturgis Motorcycle Rally t-shirt, its army green fabric featuring a display of grinning skulls interlinked with flowers at the chest.

Her choker tonight had oblong brown beads.

She was four people down when she felt his eyes on her.

She lifted her head then pointed her chin at his beer. "You want another?"

This wasn't unusual. She may not have been exactly friendly for the last two years but she owned a bar, she'd brought him a beer.

"Yeah."

She came closer, grabbed a beer out of the fridge, stuck it in the bottle opener under the bar and yanked off the cap. She placed it in front of him and surprised him by lifting his old bottle and eyeing the swirling dregs in the bottom. Then, with practiced ease, she tossed it with a crash into the tall, thin, gray plastic glass recycling bin.

Her eyes came to his. "Jack chaser?"

This *was* unusual. She may have brought him a beer but she hadn't cleared the old one away and she *never* furthered the discourse in any way.

"Feelin' like keepin' my faculties tonight," he told her.

She nodded, her gaze sliding away. "Good call. Feds in town. Psycho on the loose. Faculties would be good."

Jesus. Who *was* this woman?

Before he could figure it out, she said, "Yell if you change your mind. Stayin' in Mom and Dad's RV with them tonight. You feel like gettin' a buzz on, Dad'll pour you in the back of my car."

She started to move away but he caught her by calling her name.

She turned back to him and he asked, "Why're you stayin' in the RV?"

She'd looked at him but again her eyes slid away though not before he saw them light in the dark.

"Jimbo's a bit allergic to cats. Woke up with his eyes matted shut, sneezin' like crazy." She looked back at him after she'd hid her humor at this piece of news and said, "Jessie wanted to kick Jimbo out but I explained that a psycho would probably not be afraid of two women wielding one of her many cans of hair spray and a lighter. Wilson and me are homeless for a while. Slummin' it in the RV."

Colt didn't find this funny.

"Jesus, Feb, just move in with me."

Feb's expression told him she did not find him funny either, though his intention wasn't to be funny.

"Colt—"

He cut her off. "There's no reason to fuckin' argue."

She took a step toward him and lowered her voice. "You're off the hook. Mom and Dad and me are movin' into Morrie's if things go okay with Dee and this reconciliation lasts longer than a night."

"You know how I feel about Jack but he's not a young man anymore."

"Maybe not but he's not stupid either. Something happens he'll know what to do."

"Not like a cop would know what to do."

Her head tilted with her question and her burgeoning impatience. "How much do you reckon I have to be worried?"

"None, you stay with me."

"Colt, you don't even *like* me. Why the fuck would I move in with you?"

"Who says I don't like you?"

She stepped back on a foot like he'd shoved her shoulders and her face carried an expression like he'd perpetrated a surprise attack.

"Feb—" Colt started.

"February! Woman, what's it take to get a drink around here?" Sheila Eisenhower shouted from the other end of the bar, standing by Joe-Bob who was staring at her with mild affront and it was highly likely she'd interrupted Joe-Bob's evening nap.

"I got her," Jack called, hustling down to the other end of the bar, leaving a stunned Tony Mancetti staring at the half-pulled mug of beer that Jack left sitting on the bar in order to rush to shut Sheila up and give Feb and Colt time to have their conversation.

"Brilliant, just brilliant," Feb muttered as she started toward Tony.

"Feb, we're not done talkin'," Colt stated, his tone short and clipped.

"We *so* are," Feb threw over her shoulder and hightailed it to Tony's beer.

Colt took an angry pull off his own beer mainly because the cool of the bottle soothed the itch he now had to wring Sheila Eisenhower's neck.

Feb didn't get near him for the next twenty minutes and Colt played the only card he had in his hand.

"Jack!" he called, and Jack jerked his head at Colt to tell him he'd heard him, finished the order he was filling for Ruthie and then walked to Colt.

"She can stay in the RV with you tonight but I want Feb and you and Jackie with me by tomorrow night."

"Son, your second bedroom is full of junk and Jackie and me slept on your pull out last Christmas. Hate to tell you this, boy, but it's lumpy."

"Pull the RV up outside but Feb's inside."

Jack pressed his lips together before he said, "Found out yesterday my girl's got a problem with insomnia and, I'll repeat, your pull out is lumpy."

"I won't pull it out when I'm sleepin' on it."

Jack's eyes grew wide. "You're givin' Feb your bed?"

"A man with a hatchet comes into the house I don't want Feb on the couch."

Jack threw him a look that Colt just caught before Jack turned away.

Colt had seen that look from Jack many times in his life. After football games. The four proms he took Jack's daughter to. After Colt graduated from Purdue. The first time Jack had seen him in a police uniform. The day they made him detective.

The weight he'd been carrying in his gut grew lighter.

Jack looked back at him. "She ain't gonna like it."

"She doesn't have much choice."

Jack grinned. "She comes with a cat."

This was not a pleasant prospect. Colt was not only a dog person, he didn't much like cats.

"It stays out of my way, I won't skin it."

Jack threw his head back and laughed so loud, February, bending to pick up a fallen towel from the ground all the way down the bar, twisted her head to look at them. She was too far away, the light too dim, Colt couldn't tell if her expression was anxious or angry.

Probably both.

"I'll have a word," Jack said, still chuckling.

"Have as many as you need but get her ass in my house."

Jack threw him another grin and Colt hated what he had to say next but part of his job was saying shit like this. He didn't like doing it at all but he really didn't like doing it with people he cared about.

"Don't get too comfortable with all this, Jack. The profilers profiled the guy. I want her at my house because she's not safe. You hear what I'm sayin' to you?"

Jack sobered instantly and leaned in.

"I hear you. You got more to say?"

He did so he said it.

"He's her age, probably went to school with us. Highly intelligent, organized and fixated. A sexual deviant. Likely he has a good job and is good at doin' it. It's probable she knows him. It's likely, with his level of intelligence, he doesn't think anyone's smart enough to catch him and he's good at hiding his perversion. He wants her attention. She goes off target, does anything he doesn't like, say, movin' in with me, his focus can shift from those who did her wrong to what he perceives as her doin' him wrong. This is a profile, not set in stone, but those guys are good at what they do and we'd be fools not to listen to what they say."

"Maybe she shouldn't move in with you."

"Maybe not, but you happy with any other place she could be?"

Jack read his meaning. Colt saw it written in turn on Jack's face.

"He's been fixated on her for over twenty years," Colt reminded him. "Something happened to set him off and it wasn't her comin' home. You hear anything, someone around her age, good job, good income, smart guy, who had something happen, say he got laid off, his wife left him, anything, you let me know and I'll let Sully know."

"His wife?"

"He's good at hiding his perversion, Jack. He's married, she wouldn't have a clue."

"Jesus."

"Get her ass in my house tomorrow night and sleep with one fuckin' eye open tonight."

"Don't think I'll be sleepin' at all, son."

"I wouldn't either."

"They gonna catch this fucker?"

"They'll catch him but only because they think he won't stop until he gets caught."

"She don't have that many enemies, Colt. Hell, she's only really got one and he's already dead."

"He'll make them up."

"Jesus."

Colt decided to finish it. "I know what you think this is, Jack, and it's not that. It's just me keepin' my family safe."

Jack turned fully to him and looked him straight in the eye. "Listen to what you say, son. What you just said tells me this is *exactly* what I think it is."

He gave Colt no chance to reply before he walked away and Colt found himself at the end of a bar that now both Jack and Feb were avoiding and he needed another beer.

Five minutes later, Darryl hefted up the hinged portion of bar and slid through.

"Get me a beer, will you, Darryl?"

"You got it, boss," Darryl replied, pulling out a beer, setting it in front of Colt and moving off without snapping off the non-twist cap.

Colt watched Darryl move away thinking they really should get rid of that guy. Two and two did not make anywhere near four for Darryl.

He reached over the bar, twisted to use the bottle opener underneath it and when he sat back down he saw Amy Harris making her way to him.

This sent a chill up his spine.

He'd known Amy for thirty years. She was between him and Feb in school.

She was very pretty and petite but had always been painfully shy. She got out of high school and got a job as a teller in the bank across the street from J&J's. She'd been in that job ever since, never moving up, never moving on. Even as pretty as she was, she'd never had a boyfriend that Colt knew of, not that he paid much attention to Amy. In fact, he rarely saw her, even though he'd lived in the same town as her for three decades. He'd see her at the grocery store, the post office, driving down the street, but not often.

He'd never seen her in J&J's.

She swung her head around, looked down the bar and Colt followed her eyes.

She was looking at February who was talking to a biker while she poured him a draft.

That chill slid round to cover his entire torso and locked in.

When he looked back at Amy, she was close.

"Anyone, um…sitting here, Colt?" she waved at the stool beside him, which was good because she was speaking so quietly he could barely hear her.

"Take a seat," he invited, and she hesitated before she did so.

Her eyes skittered back to February before she put her purse on the bar and folded her hands on it like if she didn't position them properly she was scared of what they'd do.

"How's things, Amy?"

He watched her body tense at his question and she turned her neck slowly to look at him.

"Not good," she said, again talking so quietly Colt barely heard her.

"Why's that?"

Her head jerked slightly and she closed her eyes before she opened them and whispered something he didn't catch.

"Come again?"

She cleared her throat and said louder, "Angie."

"Angie. Yeah," Colt replied, keeping his eyes on her, hers had moved to stare at her purse.

"I figured people would stay away," she said then lifted her hand and it fluttered weirdly in the air like a wounded bird before she dropped it to her purse again, wounded bird down. "From here." She glanced around the bar and her eyes moved to his again before she dropped them back to her bag and finished. "Guess I was wrong."

"Why'd you think they'd stay away?"

"Dunno. Just did. Angie."

"You know Angie?"

She shrugged and then her gaze moved to his chest. "She had an account at our bank. She always came to my station, every Friday after work." She shrugged again and looked back at her purse. "I was nice to her. Others could be…"

Her voice trailed away, the words left unspoken didn't need to be said.

Her body jumped suddenly and she said slightly louder, "Anyway, I thought I'd show Morrie and Feb my support, come to their bar, have a drink. But I guess everyone thought the same thing."

"This is what it's like every Friday."

Her eyes came to his and she didn't try to hide her surprise or inexperience. "Really?"

Colt couldn't help it. She was a harmless, shy hermit who wanted to do the right thing and it probably took everything she had to leave her cocoon of a world and come out to do it.

So he grinned at her and said, "Really."

Her eyes shot away from his face, they caught on something else and he watched her grow pale.

He followed her gaze and saw Feb halfway down the bar staring at the both of them looking like her body had been encased in ice.

But the expression on her face was raw. So raw it was difficult to witness.

"I shouldn't have come," Amy whispered, sounding urgent and hurried now, even scared, and Colt's head jerked to her.

"What?"

"Feb doesn't...they don't need me here. I'll just get home."

Before he could utter a syllable, she slid off her stool and wended her way through the crowd.

Colt forgot about her instantly and looked back at February.

She'd turned and was now standing, facing the shelves behind the bar, both of her hands were up, elbows cocked. She'd lifted up her hair, holding it high at the back of her head, the heavy fall of it was hiding her hands.

She wasn't moving.

Colt waited and she didn't reach for a bottle or a glass. She just stared at the shelves, inert.

"Feb, darlin', tequila," Jack called, not looking at his daughter.

Feb still didn't move.

"What the fuck?" Colt muttered as he watched her remain still.

Then he felt that chill that had evaporated at his torso come back and start clawing at his chest. He got up, pulled back the bar on its hinges, slid around, dropped it down and moved to Feb.

He had a hand on her elbow before her entire frame jerked, she dropped her arms and she turned to him.

"You okay?" he asked.

She stared unblinking at his face.

"Feb, I'm talkin' to you." His fingers were still wrapped around her elbow and he tightened them there.

"What?" she asked.

"You okay?"

She came out of her trance, dropped her chin and looked away at the same time she lifted her arm bent at the elbow and tried to twist out of his hold.

He tightened his fingers further.

She looked at his hand before her head came back up. "I'm fine."

"Somethin' spook you?"

"Cat walked over my grave."

"Cat walks over your grave, you shiver and get on with it, you don't freeze then lapse into a trance."

"I didn't lapse into a trance," she lied.

"Somethin' goin' on here?" Jack asked from close at Colt's back.

"Somethin' spooked Feb," Colt answered.

"Nothing spooked me," Feb lied again.

"Somethin' spooked her?" Jack knew Feb enough to know she was lying.

"Nothing spooked me!" Feb's voice was getting louder. "I just forgot what I was doin' for a minute."

"I thought a cat walked over your grave," Colt called her on her lie.

"That too," she returned.

"Which one is it, girl?" Jack asked.

Feb jerked her arm out of Colt's hold, took a step back but leaned forward, now totally loud and shouted, "Both of you, *back off!*"

Then she pushed through them, rushed to the end of the bar and threw the entry open on its hinges. It collapsed back onto the bar making a loud sound shaking the bar and taking Colt's beer down with it.

She ignored all this, threw open the door to the office and slammed it shut behind her.

Out of the side of his eye Colt saw Jack turn to him but he didn't take his gaze from the office door.

"You reckon she's spooked or bein' a woman?"

"Both," Colt answered and walked down the bar to the office.

He went in and closed the door behind him. Feb was standing at the desk, her profile to him. She'd again pulled the hair away from her face and had it held in a fist at the back of her head, exposing the line of her neck, more of her choker and her silver hoop earring.

"I said, back off," she told the desk.

"What spooked you?"

She didn't turn, didn't drop her arm, she just repeated, "Seriously, this is uncool and you know it. Back off."

He walked up to her and grabbed her arm, pulling it down. She turned to him, her eyes finding his.

"Was it Amy?" he asked.

There it was again. That raw look. Except in the office with the lighting better and her close it was considerably more difficult to witness. In fact, he knew he'd never fucking forget that look on her face.

"It was Amy," he said quietly, and she twisted her arm away from his hand, taking a step from him. So desperate to get away but trapped between his body and the desk, she bumped into it hard. It tilted and some papers slid off the cluttered top onto the floor.

They both ignored the papers.

"Talk to me, Feb."

"Did you talk to *her*?" she asked.

"What?"

"Did you explain the way it is?"

"Explain the way what is?"

"I didn't put her on my list, but I figured you'd talk to her."

That cold that was clawing at Colt's chest found purchase, tearing in, freezing his insides.

"Why would I talk to Amy Harris?"

Her brows came together, those lines forming at their edges this time deeper.

Accusation.

"I don't believe you," she whispered, and there it was, plain in her tone. Accusation.

"Maybe you wanna explain this," he suggested, treading carefully.

Something was happening here, something he did *not* get. Something that more than spooked her. Something that pained her and, whatever the fuck it was, it had to do with him and fucking Amy Harris.

She tore her eyes from his and shook her head.

"I don't need to explain it," she said to the desk.

"I'm thinkin' you do."

Her eyes came back. "Fuck you."

He wasn't concerned anymore, now he was getting pissed.

"What?"

"I said, *fuck you*." She leaned in on the last two words. "Talk to her, Colt. When you do, she'll know."

"Now I'm thinkin' *I* need to know."

She shook her head again, muttering, "Full of shit. So full of shit."

"February."

"Been the bad guy a long time, Colt, I'm used to it," she told him, making no fucking sense whatsoever. "You don't do the right thing and talk to her *you'll* be the bad guy. Yeah?"

With that, she pushed past him and, still in a huff, she snatched the door open and threw herself through it.

He wanted to go after her and he didn't care if there was a scene. J&J's was a bar, ripe for scenes. It'd seen its fair share.

But he was angry so he took a moment to find his control and this took a while.

Once he locked it down, a couple of things struck him.

Instinct told him whatever just happened didn't have to do with a hatchet murderer bent on inflicting bloody justice for the wrongs done to Feb.

Instinct told him whatever just happened had to do with the February Owens he loved becoming an altogether different February Owens.

He took in a deep, calming breath and sorted through his thoughts.

One thing he knew, if Feb wanted to hold something deep and not let it go, she was going to do it.

And whatever this was she had buried so deep, no one could dig it out.

So he'd have to find another way to dig it out.

Starting with Amy.

Four

BUTCH

I was sitting on my bed from last night, which had necessarily been converted to a table where Mom and Dad and I just had bacon, eggs and toast that Mom made on the RV's stove, when my cell rang.

It was sitting by my plate and I stared at it.

The front screen said "Colt Calling."

Colt had never called me before and I'd never called him. I'd successfully avoided programming Colt's number into my phone for two years as well as, I suspected, Colt doing the same with mine.

But there it was, his name on my phone. Not "unknown caller" but his name.

Somewhere along the line fucking Morrie had programmed fucking Colt into my fucking phone, the asshole.

And someone, probably fucking Morrie, had given Colt my number.

I snatched it up, flipped it open, put it to my ear and said, "Hello?"

"Your dad have a word with you?"

I looked at my dad sitting across from me then I looked at my plate then I looked out the window.

Then I blew out a sigh before I said, "Yeah."

"When're you gonna be over?"

I looked back to Dad. "It's Colt. He wants to know when we're gonna be at his place."

Dad looked at the narrow door behind him and turned back to me. "After my mornin' constitutional. I'm thinkin' thirty minutes." He lifted his hand, pounded his chest and let out a loud belch before he finished, "Maybe forty-five."

I closed my eyes. Dad's "mornin' constitutional" would occur in the room that also functioned as the RV's shower. Not to mention it would happen *in an RV* that was about as big as my bed at home, save about five square feet.

At least that knowledge made the pill that I had to move into Colt's house, and Colt's *bed*, a little easier to swallow.

"You hear that?" I said into the phone.

"Christ." He heard it. "Tell Jack to back into the drive at the side," Colt said to me.

"Gotcha."

"I'll be there when you get there."

"Can't wait," I lied, and I knew it sounded bitchy but what did I care?

"Feb."

I waited but he said no more. "What?" I prompted, eventually losing patience.

"Nothin'. Later."

"Later," I replied then flipped my phone shut.

It was nine o'clock and the morning had started bad. This was mainly due to the fact that I was still in a shitty mood after seeing Colt give Amy Harris one of his killer grins. And also because I was in a shitty mood because I reacted to it the way I did, giving too much away.

Then the morning got worse when Dad told me I was moving in with Colt. He told me this using the voice he used when he'd tell me things like I had to clean my room. Or I had to get my shit together and stop flunking chemistry. Or when I had to go over to Old Lady Baumgartner's house and vacuum and dust and clean out her cat's litter box because she was so old she couldn't do it anymore.

Of course, being the age I was now I figured I could ignore this voice.

Then Dad told me about the killer's profile. Then he and Mom gave me looks that showed precisely how worried they were.

I gave into moving into Colt's.

I didn't like it, but I gave into it. And even though I didn't like it, hearing the profile, there was no denying Colt's place, with him on his couch, his gun close and him knowing how to use it, was the safest place for me.

I used Dad's morning constitutional time to get my head together.

So shy, sweet, pretty Amy Harris, who was no less pretty after two decades, comes into J&J's for the first time in her life, doesn't order a drink (by the way), has a gab with Colt, which makes him smile at her and then scurries off.

So what?

It was a long time ago. A long, long time ago.

I needed to get over it.

Exhibit A was the fact that I'd lost half of my life to this shit. Drifting from town to town to try to escape it, but in the end, never letting it go and landing right back where I started. There were some good times in that drifting and there were some bad but there weren't many great times. None, in fact, that I could remember. And if I wasn't careful, the next half of my life wouldn't be much better.

Exhibit B was some guy was running over dogs and hacking up people because he was hanging onto some wacko delusion that he was connected to and doing this stuff for me. He probably had a crush or something, which he never let go and now, decades later, it came to this. Dead people and dogs in two states.

Therefore, evidence was pointing to the fact that I needed to get over it.

It was a long time ago, people had moved on but I was stuck in the past.

I needed to pull myself into the present, get past this latest nightmare and get a life.

So that's what I was going to do.

⟨⟶

Dad rolled up to Colt's house and I examined it out my window as he executed the four attempts he needed before he successfully backed the RV into Colt's side drive.

He did this into a drive that at the back end had a one car garage with a long, sturdy, sided overhang under which was a speedboat under a tarp.

I knew Colt had a speedboat. Morrie and the kids talked about it, I'd just never seen it. Sometimes Colt took Morrie and the kids (and used to be, Dee) to the lake in the summers. Both kids loved when their Uncle Colt would take them to the lake, they never shut up about it when they got back. They both knew how to water ski and they told me Colt went fast.

Colt, Morrie and I used to go with Mom and Dad to the lake. Dad didn't have a boat but he'd rent one. I'd never got up on skis even though I tried. Colt used to tease that I was lazy but really I preferred tubing. You were totally out of control when you were tubing. You just held on as hard as you could for as long as you could and enjoyed the thrill. I also liked just sitting in the boat and letting the wind whip my hair around my face and beat at my skin. No better feeling in the world than having the landscape slide by while the wind was in your hair, whether you were in a speedboat or on the back of a bike.

I looked away from the back of the RV and out the side window to Colt's house.

Colt had a crackerbox house in a crackerbox neighborhood that was so much better than Morrie's neighborhood it wasn't funny.

It wasn't because the houses were large and grand and beautiful. They weren't. They were small and one-storied but they'd been built in a time when houses needed to be put up cheap and space was all important so the houses were small but the yards were huge.

The neighborhood was better than Morrie's because these houses had been there awhile. There were no rules that said what color you could paint your house or where you could park your car or what you could put in your yard. People had built screened-in porches on the front and decks on the back. They'd built extensions. They'd put in flowerboxes on the front windows. They had playsets and round, above-ground pools in their backyards. They had custom-made wood plaques with flowers painted on them on the front of their houses that proudly announced the Jones's lived there (or whoever).

They had American flags hanging from slanted poles beside their front doors. Some didn't fly American flags but purple and white ones, with a bulldog emblazoned on it; the high school mascot. In those houses you knew they had a kid at school, probably an athlete or a cheerleader or the owners were alumni themselves or both. Others were gold and black Purdue flags or red and white IU flags. Others still were seasonal, orange, brown and gold leaf designs in fall, pastel flowers in spring, Easter eggs, Halloween witches, Christmas poinsettias or snowmen.

There were tons of trees planted willy-nilly, not in formation, not in a design some landscape architect sketched on a pad. And the trees were big and tall with wide trunks that grew so far out they'd cracked the sidewalks and full branches that, when they had leaves in a month or two, would throw so much shade during the hot, humid summer months, the entire neighborhood would feel like a cool breeze.

It was a great neighborhood and Colt's house was the house he bought for Melanie.

Colt married Melanie Seivers about five years after I left. Their divorce was final three years ago but she'd been gone a year before that.

She'd been in the year behind me in school—pretty, dark hair, dark eyes, sweet, quiet, a lot like Amy except Melanie was tall. I knew her in school and I knew her after it. She'd come over with Colt when I was there for family occasions.

You had to hand it to Melanie, even with me being what I used to be to Colt, she was always nice to me. Never made me feel funny, never made me feel like she felt funny around me. She was just a nice gal.

She couldn't get pregnant though, not Colt's faulty equipment, hers. She took it hard. Although my parents, Morrie nor Delilah ever talked much about it to me, when Mom called and said Melanie left Colt and they were getting divorced she finally talked about it, though not much.

"Some women…don't know, Feb…they just see no purpose in life without kids. Melanie was like that, just slipped through Colt's fingers no matter how he tried to grab hold. She gave him no choice, he had to let go."

I knew what she meant though not about the kids. He'd had another girl slip through his fingers who he'd tried to grab hold. I figured he knew when to stop trying.

Melanie had moved to another small town on the other side of the city. Not far, as the crow flies, but with the city in the way and having to navigate the highways and byways to get from here to there, she might as well have been in another state.

I didn't know what she was doing now without kids or Colt in her life. I did know I thought she was all kinds of crazy for leaving Colt. Colt was a man with all that entailed but even I wasn't fool enough to think, when you got down to it, he wasn't a good one.

Once Dad turned off the ignition to the RV, Wilson and I jumped out the side door. I had him in a kitty carrier in one hand, I had my bag in the other and I had my purse slung over my shoulder.

Colt had been standing in his front yard watching Dad trying to park from attempt two through attempt four. He walked up to me when Wilson and I jumped down from the RV. Without even looking at me he grabbed onto Wilson and then leaned around me and grabbed my bag and then he walked into the house.

I looked behind me to see Mom carrying Wilson's litter box. She jutted her chin to the door and I sucked in a breath, let it out and followed Colt into my new nightmare.

When I walked into the living room, the cat box was on the coffee table and Colt was crouched in front of it, opening the wire door.

I took this time to look around.

I was surprised to see Colt had pretty much erased Melanie unless she wasn't that into interior design. The place wasn't a bachelor pad by a long shot but it didn't have flowered wallpaper or wreathes made of twigs or little angel figurines (all of which I imagined were the way Melanie would decorate her and Colt's house).

There was a huge, double-wide frame on the wall. Colt's purple and white high school football jersey next to his Purdue jersey, both laid out careful and identical, same number on each, sixty-seven, his last name "Colton" across the shoulders. They were pinned to the mat, framed in a box frame on the wall. I hadn't seen it since he got it and sucked in a quiet breath just looking at it.

Dad had given that to him years ago for Christmas. Colt had liked it so much, after the wrapping fell away he took one look at it, one look at Dad and he left the room. I knew why. Men weren't good with displaying that kind of emotion. Dad got choked up too and hid it behind a cough. Mom just started crying. Morrie had followed Colt.

I shook off that memory because it included me getting choked up too at the time and I didn't want to do it now so I kept looking around.

In the room there was also a long, wide comfortable couch and armchair that I could tell wasn't exactly top-of-the-line but it was nothing to sneeze at either. Sturdy lamps with muted shades on top of dark wood end tables, framed photos here and there. I wasn't close enough to see what was in them but all of them were of people. It was a nice place.

Kitchen to the right, dining area in front of it over a bar. I could see the kitchen had been redone and well, though not recently. But it definitely wasn't original and someone had put some money into it and I was guessing that someone was Colt. I was also guessing that he did it for no-baby Melanie in the hopes that a kitchen would calm the baby craving which was something a man would do. Or, to be fair, something a caring man would do for a wife who was suffering an ailment he had no way to cure.

To the back, a double-wide opening that led to a den, which was where Colt spent his time, I guessed, mainly because it was where he kept his big, flat-screen TV (which *was* top-of-the line but it was my experience men didn't fuck around when it came to TVs). There were two big reclining chairs at angles to each other in front of the TV with a table between them, a stereo in the corner, loads of narrow CD shelves chock-full of discs around the stereo, neon beer signs that had been retired from the bar on the walls and a fancy pool table at the side. The den was not original to the house, an extension Colt or his predecessor put in. I was guessing on a cop's salary with that kitchen and the speedboat, the extension was there before Colt bought that house for Melanie.

To the left, a hall which I knew, because I'd been in plenty of houses like this, led to two bedrooms and a bath.

"You're here," Colt said and I looked from the doorway of the hall to him.

He'd come up from his crouch and grabbed my bag again. Wilson, my fluffy gray, had two kitty paws out of the box, two kitty paws in it. He was looking around, getting his new bearings and probably wishing he had opposable thumbs so he could hack me up, such was his current shitty life finding himself in four different houses in four different days, only one of them home.

I didn't have time to comfort my cat. Colt was showing what he meant by his words by disappearing down the hall.

I followed. He walked into the room at the end.

When I arrived I saw Melanie was gone from here too. Blue walls. Dark blue bedspread. Baby blue sheets. Over the bed a fantastic sepia print of the inside of Harry's Chocolate Shoppe, an old bar on the corner of the Purdue campus that Colt, Morrie and I spent a lot of time in. The shot was of the bar and its barback, devoid of people, just the wood, the stools, the shelves, the bottles, the mirror behind the bar, looking as old and cool as it was in real life.

I wanted that print, it was fucking fantastic.

But the bed was what captured my attention. It was *huge*. It had to be a California king.

Colt was a big guy but I reckon even he'd get lost in that bed. Definitely I would. I climbed into that behemoth they wouldn't find me for a month.

He dropped my bag on the bed and looked at me.

"Sheets changed, bathroom's through there." He jerked his chin and I saw that there was a master bath, another extension likely put in pre-Colt and Melanie, through an open door. "You can make yourself at home later. I got somethin' I need you to do."

I looked from the bathroom door to Colt but he was already moving out of the room. Again, I followed.

Mom and Dad were in by then. Mom was already in the kitchen making coffee. Dad had Wilson's empty case and was heading toward a side door in the kitchen, one that probably led to the garage behind the boat. Wilson was plucking his way across the carpet, sniffing, smelling Puck and not liking it. Except for Wilson and me, everyone was no stranger to this house. They were comfortable, at home, welcome, and something ugly slid through me that I tried unsuccessfully to ignore.

Colt stopped by the dining room table.

"Got my yearbooks out, need you to look through." He tapped the set of four large, hardbound, plastic covered books on the table and then he picked up a piece of paper and waved it once before setting it on top of the books. "This is a roster of Mrs. Hobbs's geometry class, second period, your freshman year. Look at these names, look at the books, think about anyone who might fit the profile we got yesterday. Not just names on this list, anyone." His eyes caught mine. "Your dad tell you about the profile?"

I nodded.

"Good. Look. Think. Call me." He was talking in clipped, short sentences and it occurred to me he wasn't wasting time with me. It also occurred to me this was because he was hacked off about something, likely my comment earlier that morning, or me walking out on him when he was being a total asshole last night or the fact I was in his house at all.

He turned to Mom. "Gotta get to work."

Mom came to the kitchen side of the bar, put her hands on it and said over it, "Why the hurry? I thought you were off the case."

"Body found early this morning just inside the city limits."

I drew in breath and it was so loud Colt turned back to me.

"Somethin' else, looks like a drug sale gone bad."

Mom shook her head. "I remember a time when we didn't have homicides and the only drug around was weed."

"City's stretchin', ten more years, it'll engulf us," Colt said. "City spreads, crime spreads."

This was the ugly truth. There used to be miles and miles of cornfields between us and the city. For fifteen years, each time I came home more of those fields were gobbled up by strip malls and housing complexes. We still were protected by a thin shield of farmland but it was weakening fast.

Colt's attention came back to me. "Scour these books, Feb. Don't go into J&J's until you're done. I'll expect a call by noon."

I opened my mouth to say something but he was again moving around the bar. He went into the kitchen and bent to kiss Mom's cheek. Dad came in from the side and Colt gave him a wave and then a "Later," and then he was gone.

"Where's he goin'?" Dad asked the door Colt closed behind him.

"Work. Some drug person was murdered last night," Mom answered, moving right to the cupboard where the mugs were, knowing exactly where to find them.

"Shit, I 'member a time when worst thing that happened around here was a bar fight at J&J's. Cops came, tossed the boys in a cell to dry out overnight and let their wives take 'em home the next mornin'." He went up to my mom and kissed the side of her neck. "We got out just in time, Jackie, darlin'."

Dad could say that again.

He and Mom got out just in time.

Though, bad news for me, when they got out, I got back in.

⟿

Mom was cleaning Colt's house. Dad was over at Dee and Morrie's doing something Dee needed done that Morrie never found time to do. I had my cell in my hand and I had to make the call.

I'd spent an hour going through the names on that list, looking at every face in Colt's yearbooks and reading what people wrote in it deciding, from what she wrote, that Jeanie Shumacher was a traitor (she pretended to be my friend!) and a slut (even though now she had three kids, taught Sunday school and used to be president of the PTA). And deciding from what Tina Blackstone wrote she was just a bitch. She'd always been after Colt. Even now she'd slither up to him at J&J's and give him her patented look, and although I was avoiding him, I always smiled to myself when I saw him shoot her down, time after time. And I noticed Amy Harris never wrote anything at all.

Nothing shot out at me. Most of the names on the list were people I didn't even remember and only barely remembered when I crossed-checked them with photos. A bunch of them were gone, didn't live in town or even Indy anymore. I looked, I thought, but nothing came to me.

Nothing but one guy.

I flipped my phone open, found Colt's name when I scrolled down and then I hit go.

"Feb," he said in my ear.

"Loren Smithfield," I said back.

"What?"

If we'd used the word back then, Loren Smithfield would have been known as a player. He was tall, dark blond with a bit of rust to his hair, good build but not an athlete.

No, Lore was the school flirt and definitely the school horn dog.

I had no idea how many girls he nailed. I just knew he nailed Jessie in her senior year of high school after sweet-talking her for the first three. She finally went out on a date with him and on date three, he got in her pants and took her virginity.

There was no date four and Jessie was heartbroken and humiliated even though she tried to hide it.

Loren tried to nail Meems. He tried to nail me. Hell, he tried to nail *everybody.*

He sat beside me in that Geometry class and he flirted with me outrageously, not something many boys did seeing as they all knew about Colt and me and seeing as, if Colt ever found out, everyone knew he'd mess them up. Loren flirted with me all through school, especially during that class and in our junior year when he sat beside me in Psych.

He was smart, really smart, got good grades but it was more. He was what my dad would call sharp. He was a quick thinker, good with words, thought things through three times as fast as anyone else, which made him an excellent flirt.

He had great handwriting and signed his name cool and weird. Creative. Taking his time, even at the top of tests, putting these rock 'n' roll flourishes on it that I always thought were super hip even though he always made me feel a bit funny.

"Loren Smithfield," I repeated to Colt.

"Feb, Lore doesn't fit the profile."

No, it was more that Colt didn't want him to. Lore was a drinking buddy of Colt and Morrie's. He didn't come in regular, say, every night, but he was in J&J's often enough, a few times a month. And when he was he was sitting beside Colt at the end of the bar, Morrie in front of them, all of them engaged in man conversation; some nods, some knowing grins, sometimes low, rough laughter.

"He sat beside me in Geometry class. He flirted with me all through school. He nailed everything that moved."

There was a hesitation then Colt said, "Lore's been married three times, three kids, two with the first wife, one with the last. He works for his dad's construction firm and he drives a Ford F150."

"So?"

"February, this guy we're after, he's got a desk job. Lore works with his hands. And this guy probably can't get it up, not unless he's doin' somethin' sick. Lore made those kids the old-fashioned way, not through a test tube. And you think Lore would be as successful as he is if he's into sick shit?"

I knew what Colt was saying. Lore had three wives because Lore had not changed. He still nailed everything that moved. He didn't search for his pieces out of town but did his thing right under everyone's noses. His wives, eventually getting sick of it, kicked his ass out.

I'd been around. I knew there were folks out there who liked their kink and sometimes that kink could get dirty and even creepy. But I didn't figure in this 'burg, which happened to be placed smack in the middle of the Bible Belt, that there would be that much choice of women who'd put up with dirty, creepy kink.

"And the witnesses saw a silver sedan exiting the alley, not a Ford F150," Colt continued.

"Loren isn't stupid, Colt. If he drove a woman into an alley in the morning hours in order to kill her, he wouldn't use his own truck. He'd rent a car."

"There somethin' I don't know about you and Lore?"

Colt's voice had turned funny—harder, abrasive. He was pissed about more than me pointing the finger at his buddy Lore.

But I had other things to worry about.

I couldn't say I liked Lore, I couldn't say I disliked him. He was a good guy mostly, funny, interesting. Still, I avoided him, for different reasons than I avoided Colt. Loren was persistent and I didn't want to give him the inkling he had a way in because if he had it, he'd never let it go.

This wasn't easy for me, pointing a finger at someone, even a jerk, which Loren definitely was. But we were talking murder.

"No, there's nothin' you don't know."

"Don't keep shit from me, Feb, not with this." His voice was still pissed, actually now it was *more* pissed.

"You think this is easy for me? Lore's got kids. Jessie slept with him in high school. Turns out it's him, Jessie'd be creeped out for years. Those kids—"

Colt interrupted me. "That all you got?"

I pulled my hair away from my face, holding at the back and stayed quiet.

Then I let my hair go and repeated softly, "This isn't easy for me, Colt. It's not only not easy, I don't like it." I paused and swallowed before I finished, "Not at all."

We were both quiet then.

Colt broke the silence and he didn't sound pissed anymore. "Go back over the list, Feb. There are three men on that list still in town or close to town who fit the profile. And they have silver cars."

I was a little surprised he knew that much and was that thorough. He knew what he was asking me to do that morning, he knew exactly.

"Who are they?" I asked.

"Not sayin', just look at the list."

"I thought you weren't working this case?"

"Not officially but that doesn't mean I'm gonna sit on my fuckin' hands when you're findin' dead bodies, cryin' in my arms and my dog's dead."

That made me go quiet again.

Colt wasn't quiet. "Feb, go back to the list."

"All right."

He didn't say anything for a while and for some reason I didn't let him go, just stood in his kitchen with him on the other end of my phone.

He again broke the silence by saying, "I'll talk to Sully. Someone'll look into Lore."

That didn't make me feel better at all but I was glad he trusted me on it.

"Okay," I agreed.

"Later."

"Later."

I flipped my phone shut and went back to the list.

She walked into J&J's when I was behind the bar.

It was late afternoon but it was Saturday and we had a decent crowd. Nothing overwhelming but enough to make me think people had not yet cottoned onto the situation, therefore avoiding J&J's and me like the plague.

I felt my neck get tight when I saw her.

Susie Shepherd.

I'd never liked her because she wasn't easy to like. Won every competition going, had so many tiaras she could convince herself she was queen of the world (and I suspected she did). She was also head cheerleader since she was a sophomore. It was unheard of for a sophomore to be head cheerleader. The top spot always went to a senior. But Susie's daddy made it so, meaning Susie had cheated girls out of the top spot for two years running. I was no cheerleader but I thought that was low.

Since then I kept in loose touch with Wyatt Taylor, sharing a drink with him every once in a while when I hung at J&J's while I was home. Wyatt had been in Colt and Morrie's crowd but he drifted away after school mainly because he got a Master's degree and a great job that meant a lot of travel, some of it even out of the country. Though they remained friendly, he wasn't exactly in with cops and construction workers.

Wyatt had dated Susie, fallen deep and asked her to marry him. Then she thought she'd nailed it and showed her true colors so he called it off. Told me he got a visit from her daddy and a trip to Hawaii if he kept his mouth shut about dumping her. He went to Hawaii. Still everyone knew he was the one who dumped her mostly because she was a bitch.

She sidled up to the bar, eyes on me and I was surprised, the way she was acting, that she hadn't put on rubber gloves and donned a contamination suit and mask. Beer and shots at J&J's was not Susie's style.

I'd often wondered how Colt got caught up with her but looking at her I no longer had to wonder. She was always beautiful, when she was young and now. A knockout.

However, considering all the shit that had come at me the last few days, I totally forgot about her. Now I was going to be sleeping in her boyfriend's bed.

This was not good.

Morrie was in the office, Dad was down the bar and Ruthie was casing the crowd, getting drink orders.

It was up to me mainly because she came right at me.

"Hey, Susie," I greeted, taking a step toward her as she slid on a stool with a look on her face that said she'd rather the stool was disinfected before she put her immaculate ass on it. "Get you a drink?"

I was trying to be casual. She knew all about me and everyone knew Colt wanted nothing to do with me. Furthermore, her boyfriend was a cop. He'd need to talk, let shit go and she, in my mind, was that source. She had to know the way it was.

"Diet," was all she said, and I turned, leaned, nabbed a glass off the back of the bar then twisted back, grabbed the beverage gun and dunked the glass in the ice bin. "Lots of ice." I dunked it again. "Add a lemon."

No "please," nothing. I was her minion. This was an order.

I could see she was still a bitch.

I pulled a lemon out of the tray and slid it onto the side of the glass. I even threw in two thin, red straws just to cap it off. That night I was going to be sleeping in her boyfriend's bed, she deserved more than one straw.

She took the glass, sucked on the straws and turned away. I saw Joe-Bob was watching her like he was a flightless chicken in a coop and a fox just dug under the wire.

Thankfully I was dismissed so I took off, going to office, telling Morrie I was going to re-stock the fridges then hightailing it to the back storeroom.

When I got out carrying a mixed box of beers, Morrie was behind the bar, his eyes on Susie (who was ignoring him) and his cell to his ear. Conversation in the bar was muted. People were waiting. They knew there was going to be a showdown, Susie was itching for it.

I ignored all this and got down to business with my box and the fridges, crouching low and rotating the new with the old.

It took five minutes from Morrie's call to Colt arriving at J&J's. I wanted to escape but I didn't want what my escaping would say to be said so I just slid the box down to the next fridge and kept right on restocking.

"Colt." I heard Susie say.

"What the fuck're you doin' here?" was Colt's not-so-friendly response.

This surprised me. I thought he'd ask her outside to go sit in his GMC or take her to the back office. That was Colt's style. Not confronting her in the bar.

"Having a drink," Susie replied.

"Bullshit."

"Now, Colt—"

"You want this, let's do it," Colt invited, and I kept right on rotating, pulling the old bottles out, setting them aside, putting the new bottles back, setting the old ones in front of them.

"You aren't answering your phone," Susie told him.

"I am. I'm just not doin' it when you call."

Oh Lord. Maybe she wasn't his girlfriend anymore, what did I know? Colt, nor Morrie, nor anyone kept me in Colt's romance loop.

"What'd I tell you?" Susie said, her voice now nasty. "Wound up with February. Three days it's been and she's already in your house."

Fuck, I just *knew* this was about me.

I decided that was my cue to escape. I stood up and closed the fridge with my foot, preparing to make good on my plan.

"Don't you move," Colt ordered, his voice hard.

My eyes went to him to see he was addressing me.

"What?" I asked.

"This is your place. It's not hers to make you feel uncomfortable in it," Colt said to me.

"Thinkin' you two should take this into the office." Dad was now there.

Susie ignored my dad. "Tina Blackstone called, said she saw you carrying her cat and her bag into your house."

I also forgot Tina Blackstone was Colt's neighbor and Susie's friend (though Susie probably didn't know that Tina tried it on with Colt on a variety of occasions). And I forgot Tina wasn't only a bitch, she was a busybody and she drained her ex dry, which meant she didn't have to work but part-time, which meant she had time to spy on Colt for Susie.

"And this is your business because…?" Colt asked.

"This is my business because I don't want to see you make a fool of yourself. Not even a week, Colt, and you're publicly gagging for it. It's sad."

I felt my head get light while visions exploded in it of my fist connecting with Susie's face.

I knew Morrie felt the same way because he suggested, "And I'm thinkin' that our soda's flat, Susie. Maybe you should go to Frank's, see if you like his soda better."

Susie ignored Morrie too. "So let's see if my guess is correct, Colt. Ask her. Ask her to get down on her knees and suck your cock. She'll be over that bar so fast—"

I moved in, so did Morrie and Dad and the whole place went quiet. Already listening, now they were doing it openly but Colt put his hand up, palm out toward me, never peeling his eyes from Susie's face, and for some reason me, Dad and Morrie froze.

"Daddy's gone Susie," Colt said in a voice that rang loud in the big, silent bar. "So you got only your money to protect you and since I don't give a shit about your money then I'll give it to you straight. I fucked you because I was drunk and actin' stupid and you reminded me of February. I kept doin' it because I could keep pretending that was true until you proved yourself to be the bitch you are and I couldn't ignore it anymore. Puttin' up with your shit wasn't worth getting off. I gave you too many chances to turn my mind to you and you never took a single one. So like I said three days ago, it's over. I'm done. You wanted a scene, there it is. You got it."

I was trying not to think of the fact that Colt just told me, my brother, my dad, his ex-girlfriend and around twenty citizens in our town he fucked Susie because he could pretend she was me. But it was impossible not to think about it because he did it. Right then, right there, right in front of me.

Susie leaned toward Colt. "You're a fool."

"Only one thinks that is you. Fuck, probably half the guys who've fucked you think of Feb when they're doin' it," Colt replied.

Morrie laughed at this. So did others, several of them, I just didn't see who they were because I couldn't tear my eyes off what was happening in front of me.

Susie had no ready retort because there was none to be had. She'd played out a faulty strategy and right then she knew it.

Finally, she tried another faulty strategy, false bravado and she hissed, "Don't think after this Alexander Colton, you can come crawling back to me."

"As ever, you got a creative memory, Sooz. Wasn't me who did the crawlin'. I figure, I asked, it'd be you who got down on your knees."

"Go to hell."

"You're in my space, means I'm already there."

Colt was good and I made a mental note not to get in verbal fisticuffs with him. Susie had made an art out of being a bitch. I was surprised he'd bested her. He'd wipe the floor with me.

She slid off her seat, hitching her bag on her shoulder and throwing a glare at Colt as she went.

I decided not to remind her she owed us for the soda. Colt had already rubbed enough salt in her wounds, we could do without the buck fifty.

She exited with her head held high and a flounce of her hair. Joe-Bob breathed an audible sigh of relief. All eyes in the bar swung to Colt and me.

"In the office," Colt clipped at me and then started walking toward the office.

I figured my best bet was to follow him so I did. I closed the door behind me and leaned my back against it. Normally distance from Colt was paramount, though lately this wasn't working for me. But after what just happened and what he'd said, distance was fundamental.

"Sully and me have managed to keep the town from talkin' about the notes, the Feds and your involvement with all that shit. People seein' you and me comin' in and out of this office, what happened at the station and Tina Blackstone's big fuckin' mouth, we got no control over. With all that's goin' on, you gonna be able to deal with this?"

Colt had evidently decided to ignore what he said to Susie, which I thought was a good play and I let him have it.

"Yeah," I told him.

"They're gonna jump to conclusions."

"They always do."

"I need to know you aren't gonna lose it."

"Lose it?"

"Lose it."

"What do you mean?" I asked.

"Go off half-cocked."

I stared at him then I repeated, "What do you mean?"

"You're not exactly known for havin' a level head, Feb. You got a lotta stress. Shit's gone down before and it didn't involve murdering psychos and bitches like Susie and you disappeared for fifteen years. Can't keep you safe if you haul ass."

Now I was losing my temper and that mental note I made not to get into verbal fisticuffs with Colt got lost somewhere in the flutterings of my brain.

"How did this get to be about me?"

He ignored my question. "I need your assurance you're gonna be able to ride this out."

"I can't believe this shit."

"Just promise me. It gets too much, you'll talk to Morrie, your mom, Jessie, Mimi, whoever the fuck and you don't just take off."

It was then I lost it. Covering the distance between us in three pissed-off steps, I got right in his face and when I spoke I did it *loud*.

"Colt, I was twenty-five and had just been beaten to shit and humiliated by my husband when I took off. Half the town feelin' sorry for me, the other half thinkin' I'm an idiot. I couldn't hold up my head. You have no clue how that feels but, let me tell you, it feels *shit*. You hear me?" I shouted. "I had nothin' to keep me tied here, so I left. Now I got ties. I got this bar. I got my respect for my brother. I promised him I'd pull my weight as a partner and that's what I'm gonna do and I don't fuckin' appreciate you insinuating I'd do anything different."

His voice got low and conciliatory when he spoke again but he didn't back down or move out of the space I'd taken.

"I appreciate that, Feb, but you gotta appreciate that I know you aren't exactly known for sharin' and they don't make a break in this case soon, this shit is only gonna get worse before it gets better."

"I'm not an idiot, Colt. I realize that."

"Then you can't think you're gonna go it alone. You try, you're gonna collapse under the weight of it or you're gonna feel that pressure and disappear."

"You don't know me well enough to say that."

His voice lost its conciliatory tone when he said, "You know I do."

"I'm not who I was, Colt."

"Fucking hell, Feb, I know that too. Been livin' that nightmare for a long fucking time."

"Poor you," I spat, so lost in my anger I didn't even begin to think what I was saying or if I should be saying it. "Try livin' *my* nightmare, you asshole."

It was his turn to get in my face. "You'd share it with me, I'd take that shot."

"Why are you doing that?" I shouted. "I don't need to share what you damn well know."

"That's your constant refrain, Feb. Is it sinkin' in yet that maybe I'm not lyin' and I have no fuckin' clue?"

"Not even for a second!"

"Christ," he bit off, but I was done and I took a step back.

"This is *so* over. Why we're still talkin' about it is beyond me."

"Maybe because it means something?"

"To who?"

"Fucking hell!" Now Colt was yelling. "You think two people don't give a shit about something would be shouting about it?"

I had no answer to that mainly because I had no intention of even thinking about that.

He read me and closed the distance I'd gained, getting back in my face. "There's a lot of people we both care about tied in this shit and now it's in their face. Again. We need to talk it out so we can finally shut it down and move...the fuck...on."

"I've moved on, Colt."

"Bullshit, Feb. You're stuck, same as me."

I turned away from him toward the door but he caught my arm and whirled me right back.

"We're not done."

"That's where you're wrong," I snapped and then told him what he already knew, "We are. We have been for twenty-two years."

I caught his flinch before I yanked my arm from his hand and walked right out the door. It was embarrassing knowing that everyone heard. Some of them pretending they didn't; others not bothering. But taking a page out of Susie's book, I kept my head held high and lifted my hand to slide it under my hair, pulling it off my neck and shoulders to let it fall down my back.

I went right behind the bar and asked, "You need another, Joe-Bob?"

"Always need another, Feb," Joe-Bob answered quietly, and I knew his eyes were gentle on me but I didn't meet them when I got him his beer.

I spent a lot of time with Joe-Bob. He was mostly a silent drinker, looked older probably than his years. Wife had left him, kids long gone. He didn't talk much when he got loused, he'd sometimes get in the mood to share but it was rare so I didn't know him all that well. Still, he was a fixture in my life and had been a while and seeing his eyes gentle on me I knew would undo me.

Colt wasn't through with me. I should have known he wouldn't be by the way he treated Susie.

As he walked down the bar toward the door, he said loud enough for everyone to hear, "See you at home, Feb."

Two could play that game.

"I'll be late," I called to his back. "Pull the covers back for me, baby."

He stopped with the door open in his hand, his eyes sliced to me and it was a wonder I didn't cower under his dark look, but he didn't hesitate before he openly gutted me. "Honey, you know I'd do anything for you."

The door closed him from sight and the bar was silent for a good four beats before the murmur of conversation jump-started my muscles.

Morrie slid close to me. "Feel like talkin' about Colt yet?"

"Fuck off, Morrie," I snapped.

"Didn't think so," Morrie muttered, but there was laughter in his voice and I just caught him exchanging a smile with Joe-Bob before they wiped their faces clean.

Then I got down to the business, under more than a dozen curious eyes, of wiping the bar top—every fucking inch so spotless it was sparkling.

Colt lay on his back in the dark on the couch with the light he left on for Feb outside shining through the blinds he closed at the windows. He'd discovered that sitting on his couch it felt just fine, but lying on it, not even the pull out, it was lumpy.

Feb's cat, who had given him a wide berth in the short time he was home before he settled on the couch, jumped up at Colt's feet. The animal rightly hesitated before he made his way up Colt's leg to his stomach then to his chest. He stood there for a moment before he lay down on his belly.

Colt wanted to shift the damn thing off him, but instead his fingers went to the cat's neck and he rubbed it behind its ears. The purring started immediately.

Trying to keep his blood pressure down, Colt didn't think of February and their fight that day.

In the attempt to do the same thing, he kept his thoughts off Susie and the idea that her behavior at J&J's might have scratched her name on a hit list.

Instead, he thought of Amy Harris.

He'd gone to the bank that morning only to find she'd called in sick. Dave Connolly, her manager, wasn't put out by this, he was worried. Dave told Colt that she'd been working there forever, before he was even hired there, and as long as he'd been there she'd only taken half a day off once, in order to go to her grandmother's funeral. She came in even if she had a cold or a headache and since she lived close, she was always the first one there when it snowed because she'd leave early and walk.

With no Amy to be had at the bank, Colt went to her house. Her car was in the drive and even though he saw movement at her draperies she didn't answer the door when he rang the bell. Not the first ring, or the second, or the third.

Colt was a cop in a small town. Years ago not much went down, speeding tickets, kids joyriding, a party at someone's place that got too rowdy, a fight at J&J's. Every once in a while there was a domestic disturbance. Sometimes folks would call with their concerns about how their neighbors were treating their kids.

Now there were more drugs, not just kids experimenting but adults flat out using. This meant more crime all around. He'd seen a lot, heard a lot, knew people did some shitty things to their neighbors, their partners, their kids, themselves.

Still, he didn't have the relentless experiences a city cop would have.

Regardless, that didn't mean he hadn't learned from what he saw and one of the first things you learned when you were a cop was to watch the way people behaved. Not what they said but what they did. The expressions on their faces, the tone of their voice. And always go with your gut.

And that ice-cold feeling Colt felt assaulting him last night came back when Amy disappeared after surprisingly showing at J&J's, essentially the scene of a crime, and behaving the way she did, especially when it came to Feb. His gut was telling him something about Amy wasn't right. He couldn't break down her door but he could dig and that's what he spent his afternoon doing after the incident with Susie and Feb.

He found Amy had good credit and was current on all her bills. She was close to paying off her house because, a lot of the time, she made double payments (which meant on a teller's salary she didn't have a whole helluva lot of other shit to spend her money on). And she never even had so much as a parking ticket.

Earlier that night, he called Dave Connolly at home and asked if he'd heard word from Amy, telling Dave she came around to J&J's last night, didn't look sick but was acting peculiar and he was checking up on her that day because he was concerned.

Dave, Colt discovered, needed to take management classes. As long as Colt knew him, he'd always been a talker. So even though she was an employee, with just a little coaxing, Dave didn't hesitate in talking about Amy.

Not that there was much to say outside of what he already told Colt at the bank. She was a dependable employee. He could count on one hand when her drawer came up not balanced at the end of the day. She was just social enough to be liked by her colleagues but not social enough to call any of them friends. And mostly she kept to herself.

"So shy, it's ridiculous. It's a miracle she can talk to the customers," Dave said. "Don't even know if she *has* any friends. Never talks about them or what she does on the weekend. Know she's close to her mom and dad but they live in Arizona now. Think she collects butterflies because all the girls get her shit with butterflies on it if they're her secret Santa or crap like that. Seriously, Colt, she's so fucking shy, I'm surprised she'd walk into J&J's

without getting hives." He hesitated before saying, "Damn shame. She's fine. Pretty little thing, everyone thinks so."

That sounded like Amy. He hadn't paid much attention but what he could remember, that was the way she was in school too.

It also sounded strange in a way Colt didn't fucking like when people were getting murdered and Feb and his necks were on the line.

And last, with no friends and no family close, it meant, unfortunately, he had no leads on Amy.

He heard the key in the door and he knew Feb was home.

The minute she entered, her cat deserted Colt and walked across the room, still purring.

He heard the rings on her hand sliding on the wall as she searched for the light switch and then the outside lights went out. Feb wore silver at her neck and ears, often at her wrists and she wore it on her hands too, always had on a variety of silver rings, could be a few fingers, could be almost all of them.

He wondered if she wore those rings to bed.

The purring escalated and moved and Colt knew Feb had picked up her cat and was on the move too.

She was in the hall when he heard her whisper to her cat, "Quiet, Mr. Purrsie Purrs. I know you're glad I'm home."

Jesus, she called her cat "Mr. Purrsie Purrs." Colt didn't know much about cats but he knew hers wasn't a stupid one and if the damn thing understood English and recognized this affront to his dignity, he'd scratch her eyes out.

She closed the door to the bedroom but the house hadn't been built out of high quality material, you could hear everything. Therefore he heard the toilet flush and the tap in the basin switch on and off, on and off, on and off, washing her hands, probably her face, brushing her teeth.

Then silence and he knew she'd climbed into his bed.

"Christ," he muttered in the dark.

His phone on the coffee table rang and vibrated, both loudly. He shifted and snatched it up, seeing Sully's name on the display before flipping it open and putting it to his ear.

"Sully."

"I wake you?"

"Nope."

Sully was quiet then he said, "Shit, Colt, we got another one."

Colt closed his eyes and sat up in the couch. "Talk to me."

"Guy's name is Butch Miller. From the history Feb gave yesterday, she'd worked at his bar years ago. Idaho Springs, Colorado. His body was found by his girlfriend. The minute it hit the system, it came up with big, honking ping. Warren and Rodman are already on a plane."

"God dammit," Colt swore. "I'm guessin' it's the same MO."

"Down to the letter to Pete's," Sully told him. "Including the tulips and the frickin' Pottery Barn vase. Means this guy did Pete, came up here, did Angie, spent the last two days takin' a road trip and did this Butch guy."

"Also means he knows her better than we expected, he's goin' after folks from the last seventeen years, not just folks in town," Colt replied.

"Yep."

"This is not good," Colt stated the obvious.

"This is not good," Sully repeated.

"Are you getting anywhere?"

"Lore's in town and has been without leaving, alibis for every move he makes. You know Lore, he's not much into bein' alone."

This wasn't a surprise. "What about the other three?"

"Two, we've had conversations with. They're unlikely. Denny Lowe, though, right now is prime suspect."

Colt thought about Denny Lowe.

Denny had lived in that town most of his life. Pipsqueak of a kid, no meat on him, always had greasy hair, grew up late, took a whole helluva lot of shit in the meantime and was teased viciously, mostly by Susie Shepherd and her gang.

But when he grew, he grew. Susie had graduated by then but everyone was shocked at how he'd turned out. Good-looking guy, not tall, average height, built lean but tough. He was painfully shy, like Amy, but once he came into his own, he seemed to shake it off. He wasn't the most popular kid in school but he wasn't a whackjob either. Sully's search into him showed he'd gone to Northwestern and got out doing something with computers, moved home, making a mint, lived on The Heritage in a big house off the golf course with a wife, no kids.

Colt didn't see him much, sometimes at Frank's having dinner with his wife, sometimes at the grocery store, again always with his wife, a couple of times at the liquor store, not with his wife.

He'd been in J&J's but he was nowhere near a regular. Colt hadn't seen him there in years. Definitely not since Feb got back.

Still, he fit the profile.

"Colt?" He heard Feb call.

He was looking at his lap and thinking about Denny Lowe and missed Feb coming out of his room. His head came up and he saw her dark silhouette in the hall.

Damn it all to hell, now he was going to have to tell her about this.

"Give me a second, Feb," he muttered, twisted and turned on the light behind him. He twisted back, saw her wearing nothing but a big t-shirt, her cat in her arms. He aimed his eyes at his lap so he wouldn't get another glimpse of her legs and said into the phone, "Why's Denny on your hook?"

"He's disappeared. His wife has too. No one answering the door and he's not been to work. They said he has the week off."

"So maybe he's on vacation."

"Maybe. His car sure as fuck is gone but no airlines have him or his wife on their reservations list. Family and friends don't know anything about a vacation. And you use your credit card on vacation. No transactions on hers or his. Funny thing, though, last coupla months Denny Lowe has been making hefty withdrawals from their joint account. Sum total, he withdrew fifteen G's."

That cold slithered around his chest and he asked, "Where's he got his account?"

"County Bank."

Shit, where Amy worked.

"Sounds like that hook's in deep," Colt remarked.

"Deep enough for you to talk to Feb about him," Sully said.

Fucking shit.

He lifted his head, found her eyes, noticed she'd leaned a shoulder against the wall and her cat was purring as she scratched his neck and said, "She's here. Just in from J&J's."

"After the scene at the station maybe you should get some bourbon in her before you do it." Sully was trying to make a joke.

Colt didn't feel like laughing. "Feb drinks rum."

"Right." Sully still thought it was funny. "Heard about today at J&J's, man. That shit's flying around town faster'n snot. I know you like that house, hope you two can live under the same roof without that roof blowin' clean off."

Colt was losing patience. "You wanna chat or you want me to talk to Feb?"

"Get the rum. Talk to Feb."

"Later."

Colt started to take the phone away from his ear but Sully's call stopped him.

"Colt?"

"Yeah."

"I know you don't wanna hear it but I'm gonna say it. Accordin' to Lorraine, you two were born to be together. And what I heard Feb say yesterday…" He let that hang, but before Colt could get in word one, Sully continued. "You don't sort your and her shit out, man, it'll be a tragedy."

"You done?" Colt asked.

"I'm done."

"I'll call you if there's something to report. Later."

"Later."

He flipped his phone shut and threw it on the coffee table. His eyes went to Feb and she was still leaning against the wall, holding her body like she was bracing.

"You still drink rum?" he asked her.

"Just tell me," she replied.

He threw back the blanket and got up, walking to the kitchen. He flipped on the lights and went to the cupboard where he kept his spirits. Dee drank rum like Feb, he knew he had a bottle and he was right. He pulled it down along with the Jack and grabbed some glasses.

"Colt, seriously," she said to his back.

"What do you cut it with?" he asked.

He heard her sigh then she said, "I'll get it."

He twisted to her. "You mix enough drinks. What do you cut it with?"

She stopped moving toward the fridge, stood still for a moment then headed to the opposite counter. He watched her lean against it but drop her cat.

"Diet," she finally answered.

He opened his fridge and couldn't stop himself from saying, "Holy fuck."

The fridge was brimming with food and beverage. It'd never been that full, not even when Melanie lived there and Melanie loved to cook.

"What?" Feb asked.

"Jackie's been here," Colt answered, grabbing a couple of cans of pop, diet for her then he put his back, thinking he'd prefer his bourbon cut only with ice.

He mixed her drink, poured his, dumped ice in, handed hers to her and stood close. She had her back to the counter; Colt had his side to it. She had her waist against it and he rested his hip beside her.

He watched her take a drink, her eyes on the floor.

"Don't know if I can soften this, February," he told her the God's honest truth.

"Don't try," she told the floor.

"He did someone you know in Colorado. Guy named Butch Miller."

Her head twisted around so fast the drink in her hand shook and the ice clinked against the sides.

"Colorado?" she asked quietly.

Colt nodded.

"Butch?" She was still being quiet.

Colt nodded again.

She took another drink, this time definitely a drink not a sip, and her eyes returned to the floor.

"This guy do you wrong?"

She licked her lips, kept studying the floor and nodded her head.

"What'd he do?"

"Doesn't matter."

"It does, Feb."

She twisted only her neck to look at him. She was losing it. He could see it plain on her face. "Yeah? Why?"

"It was private, between you two, we need to know. It was public, that's something else."

She held his eyes for a while before she looked away and muttered, "Fuck, that makes sense."

"What'd he do?"

She moved her neck in a circle then lifted a hand to pull the hair away from her face, holding it back behind her head. Fast and low, she said, "He owned the bar I worked at. We hooked up. It was good for a while then it turned bad. I took off after it did."

"How'd it turn bad?"

"He cheated on me."

"Were you exclusive?"

She dropped her hand but didn't lift her eyes. "I thought we were but apparently he didn't agree."

"Anyone know about this?"

"Me, Butch, the woman he was screwing."

"Anyone else?"

"No."

"You're sure?"

She looked at him then. "No, I'm not sure. Butch may have bragged about his escapades, she might have too. I didn't know who she was and didn't hang around long enough to chat. Just packed my shit and got out. What I saw, she looked like a snow bunny, probably a tourist or a city girl up the mountain with her lift ticket clipped to her parka. I was workin' the bar, came home because I felt like crap, and caught them in the act."

Jesus, and he thought his scene with Susie that day was bad. No comparison.

"You lived with him?"

Her eyes slid away but he caught the pain that sliced through her face. It wasn't raw but it wasn't easy to see either. "Just moved in the week before."

"Fuck, Feb."

She took a sip from her drink and said to the floor, "He was a handsome guy who owned a bar in a cool town. He knew how to have fun and liked to do it, obviously with anyone who struck his fancy." She shook her head. "Even though it felt shit he cheated on me…" She paused, took another drink, shook her head again then whispered, "Butch."

Colt lifted his hand to the back of her neck and pulled her to him. She didn't resist, just fell to the side, her shoulder hitting his chest and sliding along it until it was tucked under his pit and her temple hit his collarbone.

He kept his hand at her neck but tightened it.

He gave her a minute before he took his hand away but only to slide her hair out of his way so he could hold her there skin to skin. Again, she didn't resist, didn't move away, even standing in his kitchen, in the middle of the night, her wearing nothing but a t-shirt, Colt wearing nothing but a pair of shorts.

"You okay?" he asked.

"No."

He gave her neck a squeeze.

"I know, Feb," he said softly. "But you okay to keep talking?"

Her head came back and she looked at him. "More to say?"

"I gotta ask a few questions about Denny Lowe."

Those lines formed at her eyebrows again and she pulled away. He dropped his hand, took her glass, refreshed it and walked back to her, resuming his position.

She let him, didn't move away, just tipped her head back to look in his eyes.

"They're investigating Lowe," he told her. "You remember him?"

"I, yes, I…" she stopped and her head tipped to the side, "Denny had it rough, Colt. Susie was a bitch to him. But he pulled it out, got the last laugh. He was gorgeous when he graduated. Half the girls in my class had a crush on—"

She stopped talking suddenly, her face blanked of everything and she took a step to the side, sliding down the counter.

Then she turned to face him, put her hand to the counter and leaned into it heavily.

"What?" Colt asked but she didn't speak, so he moved into her and repeated, "Feb, what?"

She focused on him and said, "Freshman year, in lunch, during lunch…" She stopped and shook her head, looking to the side before she hissed, "*Fuck!*"

Colt slid his hand under her hair and curled his fingers around her neck again, putting pressure there for a different reason, to keep her attention on him. He got what he wanted, she looked back to him.

"February, tell me what."

She nodded but it was jerky. "Susie was going after him, her and some of the cheerleaders, a few jocks. God, I don't even remember who was there but I remember it was Susie doing most of the talking."

When she stopped speaking, Colt prompted, "What happened?"

"I waded in," she told him. "Me and Angie, but mostly me. I was always the one with the big mouth."

This was true.

"And?" he pressed.

"And nothing, that's it. I just walked over to them and told them to fuck off, leave him alone. I wasn't nice about it either. Susie had a few words for me but the jocks drifted away, probably because they knew you and Morrie wouldn't like it if they got into it with me. Once she realized she didn't have anyone at her back, Susie backed off too. Denny was long gone by then. He didn't do anything, say anything, just escaped as quickly as he could. I didn't even see him go since I was into it with Susie. He just vanished."

"That the only time you did that?"

She nodded.

"Denny ever say thanks, show gratitude, anything?"

"Nothing, I didn't know he knew I existed," she told him then her eyes, still on him, went far away and she went on. "I'd smile at him in the halls. I remember. I'd smile at him even when he was scrawny. But also when he filled out." She focused on Colt again and finished, "He never smiled back, looked right through me."

Colt had never been scrawny and he'd never been teased. Growing up he had his own hell to deal with but it wasn't that.

February had never been scrawny either and, because of him and Morrie, definitely never teased. She was a pretty little girl who grew into a very pretty teenager who grew up to be a very beautiful woman.

A pretty girl smiling at a shy, skinny, taunted kid with greasy hair, fuck, it must have felt like the clouds opened up and angels shined their light on him.

"Denny come into the bar very often?" Colt asked.

"I haven't seen him since I've been home," she answered and then said, "Colt, I don't think I've seen him since high school."

"Far as we can see, he fits the profile, Feb, and he's disappeared and he took fifteen K out of his bank before he did."

Feb dropped her head back and closed her eyes. "This can't be."

He gave her another squeeze at her neck to get her attention and he got it. She righted her head and looked at him again.

"All sorts of shit trips triggers," Colt said gently. "Maybe that tripped his."

"That's insane."

Colt couldn't help it, he smiled. "Honey, he's the guy, he's not acting exactly normal."

The skin around her eyes went soft as did her eyelids and her lips tilted up at the ends before she muttered, "This is true."

He'd never seen her face get soft like that, never seen that little smile, her look saying a lot, sharing humor but still holding something back. Fuck, but it was sexy as all hell.

She didn't move, didn't pull away from his hand when she kept talking. "I can see him knowing about Angie, he was in that class, he could take the note. And Pete," she didn't even hesitate in saying her ex's name, Colt was surprised to note, and she hadn't said Pete's name in Colt's presence since the day she showed up bloodied and broken on Morrie's doorstep, "everyone knew about him. But *Butch*?"

"It's him, there's a trail and we'll find it."

She studied him a moment before she nodded then her eyes drifted to his throat. "Will you do something for me, Colt?"

What he'd like to do was tell her to stop calling him Colt and call him Alec again but he didn't say that.

Instead he said, "What?"

Her hand came up and she grabbed his wrist, which was holding his bourbon. She lifted his hand with the glass up between their bodies and she rested her glass to his. She kept her head bent, her gaze on their drinks for a second before she looked at him.

"Angie was fucked up but she was a good person. Her parents were nearly as shitty as yours and she wasn't touched with a lot of love," Feb said softly then he felt her put pressure on her glass against his. "To Angie," she whispered then she took a drink.

Colt put pressure on her neck and she came a few inches closer before he took his own sip.

When they were done, she put her glass up between them again and taking her cue, he rested his against hers. Her eyes grew soft, this time in a different way, before she kept speaking.

"You had a great dog, Colt."

Fuck, she was killing him.

"I know," he whispered.

"To Puck," she whispered back and he felt his glass press into his hand before they both lifted them and drank again.

"This'll be harder," she told him, her glass again against his and her eyes again at his throat.

"Do it," he murmured.

She looked at him and said, "He was a dick, but he didn't deserve that," she pressed her glass against his. "To Pete."

Colt thought if Pete Hollister were ever to have a toast made to him that said it all, that was it. So he drank as did Feb and they resumed their positions.

"You didn't know him and he fucked me over but he was a fun guy who made me laugh." She pulled in a short breath and let it out on a shorter sigh. "To Butch."

On the last toast, Colt drained his glass dry, so did Feb and he put his on the counter, taking hers out of her hand and placing it beside his. Then he used his hand at her neck to pull her body to his and wrapped his arms around her.

She slid her arms around his waist.

Then she whispered into his chest, "See. Told you I'm not gonna leave."

"You're doin' great, baby."

Resistance he didn't know she was holding in her body drained away and she softened against him.

"Can I cry now?" she asked, but her voice said she was already doing it.

"Have at it."

Four days, four deaths, four times Feb cried in his arms.

He'd be the fool Susie accused him of being if he didn't admit he liked the feel of her right where she was.

But that didn't mean he wouldn't fucking jump for joy when this shit was over and at that moment he'd sell his soul so she'd never cry again.

When he heard the tears subside, he said, "Thank you."

"For what?" she asked his chest.

"For trusting me enough to give that to me instead of keepin' it in and lettin' it eat more of you away."

She gave a slight jerk in his arms, not resistance, surprise, before she settled back in.

Finally, she tilted her head back and he looked down at her but he didn't move his arms.

"I need to go to sleep," she said softly.

"You gonna be able to do that?"

"I'll take some of Doc's pills."

"That okay if you've been drinking?"

"I'll check the bottle."

Without another tactic left to him to delay, Colt let her go.

She started to the door but turned in its frame and looked back at him.

"I know it's heavy, Colt. Thanks for sharing the weight of it," she whispered then she walked with a hurried step, leaving him staring after her long after she disappeared down the hall.

Yes, she was fucking killing him.

Colt turned out the kitchen light, went to the couch, sat down, picked up the phone and called Sully.

Five

REPRIEVE

I got up feeling groggy. The pills worked great but they didn't know when to stop.

I threw the covers back off Colt's bed, rolled twice to make my way across the grand expanse to the side, threw my legs over, got up and dragged myself to Colt's bathroom.

I was so groggy, I was halfway through my morning routine before I realized Wilson wasn't sitting on the toilet seat watching me with blame in his eyes that said me brushing my teeth was not more important than him getting fed. Wilson was a cat and therefore could be aloof but he liked me and he didn't make any bones about showing it. When I was in a room, Wilson was in it too. He might not be laying on me or rubbing up against me purring, but he knew he was the man of the house and needed to keep me company so he didn't often leave me alone.

Therefore I went in search of my unusually absent cat deciding, even though Colt was super cool last night going so far as to toast Pete with me, still I'd kill him if he let my cat out only for Wilson to be murdered by a bi-species killing maniac.

I heard the meows the minute I fully swung open Colt's partially-opened bedroom door.

When I hit the doorway to the living room I saw Colt standing in the kitchen, a coffee cup in his hand, his back to me, his neck twisted, his eyes pointed down to the floor, which was the source of the meows.

In the depth and breadth of my vision I saw all of it, including some of the living room, the dining area, the kitchen and even out the kitchen window, which showed part of the speedboat, part of Dad and Mom's RV.

But all I really saw was Colt's back and it was a fucking great view. Nearly as good as his front view last night, shirtless, hair mussed and wearing shorts.

Damn, they needed to find this guy so I could get *the hell* out of there.

Colt turned when I hit the dining area and leveled his eyes on me.

"How do you get him to shut the fuck up?" he asked, his face cloudy.

Wilson meowed.

"You feed him," I replied, hitting the kitchen.

"Then for God's sake, feed him," Colt muttered, turning, backing up, leaning his hips against the counter and crossing an arm on his bare chest, his coffee still held up, his scowl still aimed at poor, defenseless Wilson.

I got down to the business of feeding Wilson. Wilson saw my movements, knew the drill and shut his kitty trap.

"Thank God," Colt muttered and I bit back a laugh but I couldn't bite back my smile. "You should name him something else," Colt told me.

"What's wrong with Wilson?" I asked Wilson's food.

"His name is Wilson?" Colt asked my back.

I looked over my shoulder at him and saw his brows were knitted.

"Yeah," I said, turning back to the food then moved to set it on the floor by Wilson's kitty water bowl that Mom put out yesterday.

"You called him something else last night," Colt said.

"I did?" I asked, going to the cupboard Mom took the mugs out of yesterday. I opened it to see in the divorce Melanie got the matching coffee mugs because none of Colt's matched.

I picked one when Colt informed me, "Yeah, you called him 'Mr. Purrsie Purrs.'"

I felt my neck get tight.

Oh Lord. That was my kitty speak. I only did that when Wilson and I were alone. Wilson loved it. Anytime I lapsed into kitty speak he came closer or if he was in another room he'd come running. But I let no one else hear my kitty speak. I thought Colt was sleeping or I'd never have done it. Obviously Colt wasn't sleeping. Shit.

I decided to make no comment.

"Feb?"

"Mm?" I mumbled to the coffeepot, pouring myself a cup and not turning.

"Feb."

"Yeah?" I asked, sliding to the side to open the fridge and grab the milk.

"February." Oh shit, I could hear his laughter in my name.

"What?"

"Honey, look at me."

I set the milk down next to my mug and turned to look at him. He was smiling.

"What's funny?" I asked.

"Mr. Purrsie Purrs is funny," Colt answered. He thought this was hilarious and I could tell it was taking everything for him not to laugh.

I rolled my eyes, muttered, "Whatever," and started to turn again when Colt murmured, "Baby," and when he did there was no humor in his tone at all.

At the timbre of his voice, I lifted my gaze to his and it felt like my head was moving in super slow motion.

But when our eyes met, things all of a sudden speeded up. Colt took one step forward in a lunge, his arm coming out and hooking me at the waist, then, when he stepped back, I went with him.

On the fly, I hit his body and my hands came up automatically to his chest to brace my fall. My hands were useless, his arms locked around me, his head came down on a slant and his mouth hit mine.

I wasn't prepared for it. I'd been in his arms a lot lately and it felt good, better than I remembered because it *was* better, to have him hold me, this man, this Colt, older, smarter, stronger, more experienced.

But I hadn't had his arms around me and his mouth on mine and my hands on the hard muscle of his bare chest and my bare legs tangled up with his while he was leaning against his kitchen counter, I was leaning against him and we were in his kitchen with me in my nightshirt.

123

I didn't even try to push away. I opened my mouth, inviting his tongue inside. It swept in and I felt the spasm between my legs, instant wet and ready, and I moaned into his mouth because it felt so damned good.

I went up on tiptoe, pressing my body to his. My hands slid up his chest, his shoulders, my fingers went into his hair holding him to me as his arm tightened around my waist, the other hand going up. I felt the weight of my hair lighten as he gathered a bunch in his palm and held it against the back of my head.

We went at it, wet and rough and desperate, and I wanted him so badly I had visions of pulling down my panties then his shorts then jumping up to wrap my legs around his hips and guiding him inside.

I didn't need foreplay. I just needed that kiss and Colt.

"Hey kids, we're goin' to Frank's for...*fuck*!"

I would have torn away, but although Colt's head came up, his arms got so tight I couldn't move an inch.

"Jack, get out of the way, what's the matter with...oh."

Dad, calling loud, probably thinking he was going to wake us, and coming up the rear and around grumbling at Dad, Mom.

Everyone stared at everyone else.

I didn't look at Colt but both Mom and Dad looked like they wanted to kick themselves while simultaneously looking like they just remembered it was their birthday and found out they'd won the lottery.

I had no idea what I looked like but testing Colt's strength with a cautious pull at his arms, which only grew all the more tight I knew he had no intention of letting me go. I made the decision not to fight it in this uncertain situation and I stayed where I was.

When no one said anything, I waded in. "I could do Frank's."

"We'll come back later," Mom said.

"You don't have to come back later," I told her, trying another tug at Colt's arms and finding them just as resistant so I gave up again. "You bought enough food to feed an army, we could do breakfast here."

"Why don't you come back?" Colt spoke and I could not only hear his voice, I felt it rumbling against me from crotch to chest and it felt far from bad.

"We'll come back," Dad said, backing out.

"We'll give you some time. An hour," Mom said, backing out with Dad.

"Jackie, an hour?" Dad muttered.

"More than an hour," Mom amended hurriedly.

"How 'bout we let them call us?" Dad suggested.

"Good idea," Mom muttered, and Dad with one arm extended to grab the door, Mom having disappeared, took one look at me and Colt, gave Colt a nod and then he shut the door.

I pulled back a lot harder against Colt's arms but those arms didn't budge.

I tipped my head back to look at him, putting steady pressure on his shoulders with my hands.

"Let me go."

"Why'd you name your cat Wilson?" he asked.

In my confusion at his inane and insane question, my steady pressure ceased.

"What?"

"Wilson. Weird name for a cat."

"Colt."

He grinned. "Better than Mr. Purrsie Purrs."

I put the pressure back on. "Colt."

His neck bent, dipping his face to mine, and he murmured, "Great kiss, baby."

The pressure ceased and I whispered, "Colt."

"I liked it."

"I think I need to move out," I announced.

He ignored me. "A lot."

"Maybe I'll move in with Joe-Bob. He was in Vietnam. Maybe he knows hand to hand combat."

"When you moaned in my mouth...*fuck*," Colt muttered, his arms giving me a squeeze.

"Will you stop talking about the kiss?" I squealed.

The grin came back but he said, "You aren't movin' out."

"I think it's best."

"You wouldn't know what was best for you if it smacked you on the ass."

125

"Colt."

"Though, I'll give it a try."

"Colt!" I shouted, giving his shoulders a shove and succeeding in gaining about three inches of space before his arms went tight again, hauling me right back.

"You wanna go to breakfast with your parents?" he asked.

What I wanted was to find a safe place in the world, one, little, safe place. I didn't care if it was a cardboard box in an alley in the scummiest section of New York City. If it was safe, with no murderers or bitchy exgirlfriends of the guy's bed I was sleeping in or ex-high school sweethearts who yelled at me and teased me about what I called my cat and who could kiss *way, way* better than he did twenty-two years ago, then I wanted to be in that box.

"You wanna know what I want?" I asked Colt.

His arms gave me a squeeze before one of his hands drifted into my hair and I felt him wrapping it around his fist.

"Yeah, I wanna know what you want."

Before I could stop it and even before I knew it was what I wanted, I said, "I want Dee and Morrie and the kids to come with us and, yeah, I wanna have breakfast with Mom and Dad at Frank's. The whole family, eating Frank's pancakes and drinking coffee and pretending life is normal."

His eyes moved over my face before he said quietly, "You want that, I can get you that."

"I want it," I said quietly back.

"You got it, baby."

Then he let me go, gently set me back a few inches with his hands at my waist, twisted, nabbed his phone from the counter, flipped it open, hit a button and about five seconds later, he said, "Morrie, get Dee and the kids together. February wants a family breakfast at Frank's. Meet us and Jack and Jackie there in an hour." His eyes came to me before he said, "Right. See you there. Later."

He flipped his phone shut and said, "Get a shower, Feb, or we'll be late."

Without anything else to do, I turned from Colt, finished making my coffee and I walked through Colt's crackerbox house that I liked too much, into his bedroom with the Harry's print I liked too much, past his bed that was big and comfortable and I liked it too much, into his bathroom that was just normal but it was still his so I liked it too much, and there I took a shower.

Sundays were golden days, always had been.

Years ago when we were younger, Mom and Dad didn't open the bar on Sunday. That meant that day was family day. Mom and Dad both home. Colt, Morrie and Dad used to sit in front of the TV watching football games and Mom and I would drift in and out. Mom would make nibbles for them out of cereal, nuts and pretzel sticks that she'd coated with some tangy, salty goo and baked. Or she'd make big bowls of popcorn that she poured real, melted butter on. At night she made us sit down to a big, family dinner, pot roast or meatloaf or fried chicken. After that we'd play a game, usually teams, boys versus girls. Or later we'd play cards, mostly euchre and Colt was always my partner.

When we got older, they opened the bar but for shortened hours, opening at three, closing at eleven. Morrie, Colt and I were usually out and about, hanging with friends or staying at home and watching videos or Colt and me would be up in my room necking.

I'd always loved Sundays but I hadn't had a really good one in a really long time.

That day Colt gave me a really good Sunday. Such a good Sunday, I could almost forgive him for what he did.

Frank's was a crush as it always was on Sunday mornings after church. We waited for a big table and it was worth the wait to have a stack of Frank's fluffy, blueberry, buttermilk pancakes smothered in whipped butter and warm syrup, a bottomless cup of his top-notch coffee and family all around being loud. I finagled a seat between Bonham and Tuesday so I could poke Tuesday in the side and make her giggle and grab Bonham's head and give him kisses so he would look at his dad and whine, "Dad! Auntie Feb keeps *kissing* me!"

Sometimes there were three conversations at once. Sometimes someone would capture everyone's attention. Sometimes someone would tell a story and everyone would laugh. Sometimes someone would just say something funny and everyone would laugh.

We all felt the glow of the day, even Dee. So much Dee did the unbelievable and walked down with us to J&J's to help us get ready to open.

Dee hung with me as I went about my business and I was guessing this was because she was unsure of letting Morrie back into her heart. I wanted her to let Morrie back into her heart but I didn't want to push so I let her trail me and showed her what I did.

She surprised me by seeming interested, paying attention and asking questions so I went a little overboard and showed her other things as well. When we opened, she sat beside Colt at his end of the bar, drinking diet, gabbing and laughing with Colt. The kids sat in the office, probably screwing everything up and I knew Morrie and I wouldn't be able to find anything for days.

Later, Meems called me to see what was up and I told her it was Sunday and everyone was hanging at J&J's. In twenty minutes, Meems and Al strolled in. Meems had a chat with Dee and then she and Dee led Tuesday and Bonham outside so Meems' Mom could take them and Meems' brood to her house to watch some new DVD Al bought and later, for dinner, she'd be serving them her famous homemade corndogs. I called Jessie to tell her the gang was all there and Jessie and Jimbo drifted in not long after.

The clientele on a Sunday were almost always only regulars. Usually lonely souls who didn't have anyone to spend their Sundays with but they didn't want to be alone. They'd sit in their chairs or on their stools, eyes usually glued to the TV over the bar, always ready to have a chat with you if you gave them a hint you were at their table or stool to ask for more than their order. And on a Sunday you always had time to chat about more than their order.

Dad, Mom, Morrie and me spent some of our time talking with customers—Mom and Dad more than Morrie and me as they had catching up to do. But most of the time we'd find ourselves over at Colt, Dee, Jimbo, Jessie, Meems and Al having a gab or a laugh.

I didn't think about Colt and my kiss. I decided to think about being with my family and friends and how good that felt without me holding onto shit and feeling mostly dead inside. How good it felt to laugh and feel it down straight in your belly. How good it felt to watch the face of someone you love get animated while they talked about something they thought was funny or something their kid did that was cute. How good it felt to be alive; unlike Angie, Pete and Butch who'd never have times like that again. How good it felt to realize this was precious and holding onto pain meant missing times like these even when they were right there for you, close enough to take hold.

Evening hit the bar and Al and Meems challenged Jimbo and Jessie to a round of pool. They'd been drinking steadily for hours and they were making more noise than we usually had on a Saturday night, and it could get seriously noisy on a Saturday night.

I was watching them when I saw Morrie come around the back of Dee's stool, lean in and kiss her neck. I also watched as a golden Sunday worked its magic and she tilted her head to give him better access instead of trying to move away.

My eyes slid to Colt who'd caught it too and his eyes had come to mine. We shared a smile and his hit me somewhere private, somewhere that had always been mine, somewhere that I'd never let anyone into, not even him decades ago. His smile just stormed right through the gates I had locked and settled in like it was going to stay awhile.

I looked away and thought it was high time for me to break my cardinal rule. I never drank on the job. If I was back of the bar, I was sober. Morrie didn't adhere to this tradition, though he never got sauced, just would have a beer every once in a while, usually when Colt or one of his other buddies dropped in. I made myself a rum and diet and brought it back to the end of the bar.

"You let Feb pick breakfast, *my* woman wants Reggie's pizza for dinner," Morrie announced to Colt before he slapped him on the back and said, "Dude, get your ass off the stool, come with me to order."

Reggie's was around the corner. Reggie was Irish, had a shock of red hair and scratched his beer belly when he laughed which was a lot, mostly at his own jokes. Even Irish, he made the best pizza in the county, bar none. You went there to order and if you were close enough, like we were, he sent his son, Toby to make the delivery.

Colt slid off his stool. I had my drink on the bar, my hand wrapped around it. Before Colt left, his eyes dropped to my hand, he reached out and grazed my knuckles with his fingertips. The touch was there and gone. I could have imagined it if I hadn't felt it zap straight through my system.

I stood there staring at my drink curled in my hand and I heard the front door close.

"Feb," Dee called and my head snapped up.

Her eyes were on me and she looked happy. I hadn't seen her that way in a while, her look erased the lingering effect of Colt's touch and I smiled at her.

"Thanks for giving my brother another chance." A cloud drifted across her happy face and I wished I'd never said anything. "Shit, Dee, sorry. I should keep my mouth—"

She cut me off. "What's happening with you and Colt?"

"Nothin'," I said quick as a flash. "He's helping me out, he's just being nice. It's an intense time. So intense, we've called, like, a truce or something."

"Don't know much about truces but I'm guessin', even if they call a truce, enemies don't touch each other's hands and they sure don't get caught by their parents making out in the kitchen."

Mom and/or Dad had a big mouth.

I turned fully to Dee. "Dee, honey, don't get any big ideas about this."

"You know, Melanie left because of you."

I felt my eyes grow round, actually felt them get big and I wondered if they were bugging out of my head.

"What?"

"She left, 'cause of you."

This couldn't be true. I didn't even *want* it to be true.

"She didn't. Mom told me she left because she couldn't have babies."

"Would *you* leave a man like Colt 'cause you couldn't have babies?"

I didn't answer that.

"Man looks like Colt?" she went on.

I took a sip of my drink.

"Man acts like Colt?"

I gave her a look and said quietly, "Dee, remember, I left—"

She shook her head. "When you left, Colt was still finding his way. I reckon you had reason but you held it to yourself. Fair play and no one has place to judge. In the end, when you two broke, the age he was? He was a man but we girls know he was mostly still a boy. But he's a man now. The kind of man you don't leave for stupid shit."

"Not being able to conceive isn't stupid," I defended Melanie.

"Nope, you're right. I didn't have Bonham and Tuesday, I don't know what I'd do. But Morrie stayed the man I married, livin' for me not livin' for the bar, he'd be enough for me for always."

"Morrie doesn't live for the bar."

Dee gave me a look and I couldn't say I blamed her. It'd feel that way to me, never seeing my husband because he was either sleeping or at the bar.

Morrie had played the field through high school and after. Never had a serious girlfriend, not once.

He'd met Dee years ago, she lived two towns over. They'd met after some football game when he'd been in his pads and jersey, walking back to the locker rooms after we'd beat her home team. They struck up a conversation that lasted about five minutes and he'd never forgotten her.

He met her again while she was at a friend of hers bachelorette party. Her girls had been doing the trawl, J&J's came up late, about six bars in. She'd been hammered and Morrie'd just been hanging at J&J's then, working construction. They'd struck up another conversation and he'd pitched a fit when she said she was leaving, getting into her girlfriend's car to go to another bar. It was part that he didn't want her to go, part that he didn't want her to get in a car with a drunk woman behind the wheel. Even just getting acquainted, they'd had a rip roarin' fight, Morrie won and he took her home. They were inseparable ever since—engaged within six months, married after just a year.

It was fair to say until we took over J&J's, he doted on her and she returned the favor, even after all these years and two kids.

But now Morrie took assuming the running of the family business seriously, maybe too seriously. She'd been lost in that and she didn't like it.

I could see her point.

"My babies are my world, but you got a good man?" Dee said. "Wouldn't be hard for you to make do."

"Mom said Colt and Melanie tried to make a go of it but Melanie—"

"Melanie wasn't Juliet."

I stared at her, silent, mainly because I didn't know what the fuck she was talking about.

Dee kept going. "Romeo and Juliet, say they didn't die but Juliet got pissed and took off. Everyone would know it was Romeo and Juliet, would always be Romeo and Juliet, even if later Romeo hooked up with Nancy. No one ever heard of Nancy, doesn't even sound right, Romeo and Nancy. Everyone knows Romeo's meant to be with Juliet. Even if Romeo loved Nancy, Nancy would always know she was never Juliet."

I didn't want Dee to compare Colt and me to star-crossed lovers who eventually died in each other's arms because, these days, that was way too damn close for comfort.

And I didn't want Dee to think like that at all about Colt and me and Melanie.

"Dee—"

"She lived her life with Colt in your shadow. She wanted a baby that bad to stake him to her, 'cause no way a woman could live her life knowin' she wasn't her other half's true other half. She had to find a way to *make* him stay and Colt would stay, no matter what, for family. She couldn't give him that and she couldn't live under that cloud, wonderin', each time you came home, when his head would turn."

I didn't want to be talking about this. We were treading on dangerous ground.

"He's a man, Dee, but he wouldn't step out on Melanie."

I said it even though I couldn't be certain it was true, not because of me but because Colt had a dick and that was, in my experience, the bottom-line truth of it for all men.

"Don't matter he wouldn't, she *thought* he would. She got out from under that cloud and I don't blame her. I don't know why she stepped under it in the first place. Made her miserable and she made Colt watch her fade away." I opened my mouth to say something but Dee waved her hand in my direction and continued. "I like Melanie, don't get me wrong, she's a good gal. But she didn't do right by him. He felt it, her leavin' him, and that was cruel. She wanted something she couldn't have, knew it and reached out and grabbed it anyway, but he paid the price."

Again, I knew was what she left unsaid and that unspoken word cut through me like a blade.

"Dee—"

"Everyone wants to see you two happy, Feb, together, apart, it don't matter. Just happy." She leaned in. "But neither of you are happy, girl, and we all know why. It's tearin' both of you apart and all of us right along with it."

"I love you, babe," I said quietly. "But with all the shit's that's going on, I don't need this."

"With all the shit that's goin' on, girl, you need this more than you ever did."

"There's things you don't know."

"Yeah, I know, but they happened *twenty years ago*, Feb."

"But—"

"Alexander Colton touched my hand, watched my ass while I moved, got that smile on his face when he saw me laugh, especially when I was going through all kinds of hell, I'd learn to get past whatever it was that happened twenty years ago and grab onto happiness."

I started to say something, I didn't know what, but I didn't get it out.

This was because I heard an angry, male voice shouting, "You *cunt!*"

My head came around and every fiber of my being froze when I watched Loren Smithfield stalk across the room.

"You...fucking...*cunt!*"

He was talking to me. I knew this because his eyes were on me, not to mention the fact that he was pointing at me.

"Lore, what the fuck?" Al asked loudly from the pool table, but his cue was at a slant at his side, held in his fist and he was starting to move closer.

Lore ignored Al. He had his target in his sights and not even Al was going to make him lose sight of that target. He made it to my end of the bar and smashed a fist into it, making a loud noise that caused me to jump. "Point the finger at me for killin' Angie! What the hell is *that?*"

Oh Lord. I didn't figure this was good.

"Lore, calm down, man," Jimbo said, moving in close as did Dad and, I was surprised to note (vaguely because I was scared out of my mind at the fury twisting Lore's face), Joe-Bob.

Dee sat frozen on her stool, her eyes locked on Lore, and Mom, Meems and Jessie stayed back.

So did I, holding my position by Dee with the bar a safety barrier between me and Lore's rage.

Lore jabbed a finger at me. "I got kids, they hear this shit…a job, a reputation, a life in this town, people think this shit about me, *you* think this shit about me. Jesus, you *bitch*!" He leaned in, his whole body a threat, still pointing at me. "I should hack *you* up, you crazy *cunt*!"

That was all he said because suddenly he wasn't there. Instead he was five feet back and still sailing, bumping into chairs, arms wheeling and Colt was stalking him silently, calmly, his movements slow and economical, his eyes on Lore like Lore was prey.

Lore gained control of his limbs, locked his eyes on Colt and took a stance that was defensive at the same time it was threatening. "Back off, Colt."

"You need to go somewhere and calm down, Lore," Colt advised, stopping, not taking a stance. Just standing there loose-limbed but looking alert and at the ready.

"Fuck that! She told you I killed Angie," Lore shouted.

"How'd you hear that?" Colt asked softly.

"Marty. We were havin' beers at Josh's place."

Colt shook his head in an unhappy way that I reckoned Marty just caught himself some trouble.

"She's helping with the investigation at my request," Colt told Lore.

"Yeah, and she fingered *me*!"

"February never said you did it."

"Yeah, if that's true why'd Chris come 'round yesterday, askin' my whereabouts?"

"Procedure."

"Bullshit."

"Chris came to you in plainclothes and asked you some questions, Lore. Don't you get why he did it like that?" Colt didn't wait for his answer and finished. "It's done, let it go."

"Fuck that, Colt, my kids hear about this—"

"They wouldn't of, if Marty had kept his fuckin' mouth shut and you'd kept your fuckin' cool and didn't come tearin' into this bar and makin' an ass of yourself. Now the whole town'll know and you got no one but yourself to blame."

"Yeah, and Feb."

Colt's body went from loose but alert to hostile.

"I'll repeat, Feb was acting on a request made by me."

"And I'll repeat, doin' that, she fingered me for hackin' up fuckin' Angie. Shit, I didn't even dip into that dirty twat. Who knows what she had swimmin' up there after the whole town had their dicks in her? And *I* get blamed for killin' her?"

"You're talkin' about an innocent woman who was brutally murdered."

"I'm talkin' about *Angie*."

Colt moved and therefore so did Lore. It wasn't exactly a surprise attack but still, Lore barely got a chance to throw up a defense before Colt had him flying through the air, one fist at his collar. Lore landed on his back on top of a table and Colt leaned over him.

"This'll get messy, you keep talkin' about Angie that way, and you'll be breathin' through a tube I *ever* hear you talk to Feb that way again."

This was not an idle threat and everyone in that bar knew it. Lore stared up at Colt and wisely kept his mouth shut.

Colt yanked him off the table by his collar and then with a shove sent him flying. Lore righted himself and went back on the defense. No threat this time, he was scared. I didn't blame him, with one hand Colt had sent him flying through the air.

"We ask a citizen to help with an investigation, we do it with purpose," Colt told him, his voice pure ice. "They think there'll be retribution, like you just dished out or worse, they'll hesitate or not help at all. Means we're fucked. I don't like to be fucked, Lore. I do the fuckin'. You got me?"

I heard Colt's ass ring but he ignored it as he faced down Lore.

After what took way too long, Lore mumbled, "I got you."

"Now go somewhere and calm the fuck down. You come back in here, you do it to have a drink and you have that drink after you apologize to Feb. We clear?"

Lore's gaze slid in my direction but it went right through me before he looked back at Colt.

"Clear," Lore said.

"You see Marty, give him fair warnin', he better avoid me for a while."

"Marty's fucked," Al muttered to Jimbo.

Lore stared at Colt for a while before he jerked his chin, his eyes moved to Dad and his expression turned hangdog as it hit him he might have just made enemies of Colt and my dad, not enemies you'd want to have especially since they were your friends and you liked them.

The circumstances were admittedly extreme but Lore realized then that he hadn't thought this through. The way he treated women, he didn't care about me. But his actions had shown disrespect to two men who deserved respect and no one in that bar—or any of the folk who would undoubtedly hear about this by morning—would give him an inch, not for a while. You didn't call Jack Owens's daughter a cunt no matter what she might have done. And you didn't get in Alexander Colton's face and make him lose control. Lore understood, just then, he'd given his own reputation a hit he wouldn't live down, not for a good long while.

Not to mention he made an ass of himself and got bested without even lifting a fist.

After dropping his head, Lore hit the exit with all due haste.

Colt's ass rang again and he cursed under his breath, his eyes locked on the closed door before he yanked out his phone, flipped it open and put it to his ear.

"Okay, is it me, or is anyone else having a problem with deciding whether to have a heart attack or an orgasm?" Meems asked.

"Orgasm," Jessie said instantly.

"Yep, same here," Dee put in.

"Fuck," Al muttered.

Jimbo shook his head but grinned at his wife.

"Well, that was a buzz kill," Morrie noted.

It was then I realized I was shaking.

"Got it, later," Colt said into his phone as he walked up to the bar, his eyes on me. He flipped his phone shut and shoved it in the back pocket of his jeans. "You okay?"

"Lore just called me the c-word," I told him.

"I know, you okay?"

"He said it more than once."

Colt bit his lip then let it go. "All right, but you okay?"

"He said it *loud*."

"Feb—"

"I'm okay."

"You sure?"

"I'm okay."

Or as okay as anyone could be who was called the c-word more than once.

"You're not gonna go half-cocked on me?" Colt asked.

I sighed before I repeated, "No, I'm okay."

"You're not gonna get a wild hair and haul ass?"

I rolled my eyes, leaned forward and said slowly, "Colt, I said, I'm oh… kay."

He grinned. "Last time you rolled your eyes at me, baby, I kissed you."

I sucked in breath, and if I wasn't mistaken so did Dee, Meems, Jessie *and* Joe-Bob.

I thought it best to quit speaking and just remain silent, maybe for the rest of my life.

Colt turned to Dad. "I got work, Jack, callout. I'm not done, you'll stay in the house with Feb?"

"Absolutely."

Colt looked at Dee. "Sorry to miss the pizza."

"I'm sorry too," Dee whispered, her eyeballs darting back and forth between me and Colt so fast it was a wonder she didn't give herself a seizure.

"We'll save you a slice," Morrie offered, slapping a hand on Colt's shoulder and giving it a squeeze at the same time he tugged it back and forth.

"I like it hot," Colt replied, aiming another grin at me. "Feb'n me'll order another one on her night off."

I sucked in breath again and considered throwing my drink at him but he said, "Later," and was walking out of target distance before I could put my thought into action.

As I glared at the door, Morrie walked around to the back of the bar and slid his arm around my shoulders, tugging me into his side.

"Family's here, Feb, friends, it's all good. You ready to talk about Colt yet?" Morrie asked.

I looked up at my brother. "Fuck off."

Al guffawed and I looked at him.

"You can fuck off too."

Al, Jimbo and Morrie burst out laughing.

I rolled my eyes, caught the roll, vowed I'd never roll my eyes again and belted back my drink.

Colt walked into his house to see Jack and Jackie planted in the den in the recliners, the TV on.

Jack's recliner was flat and his snoring was constant but muted.

Jackie turned to the door when he walked in and she gave him one of her warm welcoming smiles.

Jackie Owens had a lot of smiles, some of them were so big they split her face, making light shine out. This one wasn't as big but it was sweeter, speaking lots of words, most of which had to do with love and home.

When Colt turned to close the door, he saw Feb sitting on a stool in front of the kitchen bar on the dining area side. She had her hand flat on a book on the bar, in the other hand she had her fingers curled around a pen, one of her long legs dangling, the other bent up high and her heel was in the seat. She was wearing loose but short shorts, a cardigan and socks that were slouchy, looking too big on her feet. She had her torso twisted to him and she was giving him a scan with her eyes.

He closed and locked the door then turned again and headed to the kitchen, eyes on Feb as he went. She ducked and tilted her head, giving him the impression she was reading him from across the room. Then she turned, dropped the pen, picked up a ribbon, put it in her book and closed it. She hopped down from the stool and was in the kitchen doorway two steps before he got there.

"Bourbon or beer?" she said to him.

Yeah, she'd read him.

"Bourbon."

"Like last night?"

"Yeah."

She went to the cupboard and he turned and retraced his steps, walking out of the kitchen. He shrugged off his jacket, threw it on the back of the chair, pulled his badge off his belt and slid the shoulder holster down his arms, dropping both on the dining room table before he went back. By the time he got there, the Jack was on ice and she was fixing herself a rum and diet. She stopped what she was doing to hand him his glass and finished making her drink.

Then she turned, put the heels of her hands to the edge of the counter and hefted her ass up onto it, settling in and grabbing her glass. She was wearing a white, ribbed tank under her cardigan. It hugged her torso and didn't leave a lot to the imagination. Her choker was gone, so were her earrings, but the necklaces were tangled at her throat and she still had on her rings.

Her eyes came to him and they said, *tell me about it.*

Colt suspected she'd perfected that look, an occupational hazard. Though, he also suspected no one ever got that exact one. The looks she'd give customers would make them want to sit back, stay awhile and drink a lot. The look she was giving him told him she wanted to return the favor he'd done for her last night. He had a weight on his mind and she was willing to help him bear it.

He leaned a hip next to her knees and took a swallow of bourbon.

When he didn't speak, she said, "You got lots of work for a small town."

He nodded. "Someone's dumpin' bodies."

"Read about that in the papers."

"Yeah, Monica Merriweather was there tonight. Thinks she's Lois Lane," Colt said.

Monica Merriweather worked on the local paper. It was a weekly and mostly reported community news. Monica wrote practically every article. She was everywhere: high school games, church raffles, fundraising bridge tournaments. The woman didn't sleep much and when she did Colt thought she probably lay in bed with her camera around her neck.

"How many is it now?" Feb asked, and Colt took another drink of bourbon.

"Five in two months."

"That seems a lot."

Colt looked at February.

Susie never talked about his work. Melanie had a delicate constitution so Colt had learned to shield her from it. He'd had other women since Feb, between her and Melanie then between Melanie and Susie and during his breaks with Sooz. Some of them were steady. None of them were women with whom he felt compelled to share.

Feb was currently caught up in a shit storm of epic proportions and still, he thought she could handle it.

"It is. Same every time. They're done elsewhere, don't know where, bodies dumped remote, the woods, a creek, always when it's raining, evidence washed away. Never the same place but also not far from each other but somewhere they would easily be found."

"The one yesterday?"

"Yeah, yesterday and today. It's escalating."

"What are you thinking?"

"Don't know what to think. Working with the Indianapolis Metropolitan PD and they're scratchin' their heads too. Dump sites are clean, no footprints, no evidence, no witnesses. He goes in, does his business, gets out. All the victims are gang bangers, all black, none of them older then twenty-one, not big players. Bullet to the forehead. No signs of struggle. No marks on the body, wrists, ankles, they haven't been bound. It's like the killer took 'em by surprise, they were facin' him when it happened, saw it comin'. It came fast and he's a damn fine shot."

"Gang war?"

"Gang boys, they don't cart a body fifteen miles from the city into the sticks and dump it so it'll be found."

"Hate crime?" Feb asked.

"Maybe," Colt answered, though he didn't believe that. Racism was prevalent in their town, no denying it, but he doubted that was the motivation. If these boys had infiltrated the town, started recruiting, he could see it. But their territories were in the city, likely murdered there and transported. Someone had gone hunting.

Feb read him again. "Vigilante?"

She was quick.

"That'd be my guess."

"Is it gross?"

"What?"

Her voice dipped quiet. "The bodies. Is it gross?"

Something about that made him smile. "My opinion, dead bodies are gross all around, honey, even if it's your grandma laid in a casket. Dead bodies who've had a hole blown through the back of their heads, definitely."

The bottom half of her face scrunched up, wrinkling her nose, and he couldn't help but chuckle. He reached out and wrapped his hand around her knee, giving her a squeeze before letting her go.

"Gonna get this man to bed," Jackie announced, and Colt and Feb looked to their sides to see Jackie guiding a stumbling Jack to the side door using both her hands on him.

Jack emitted a rumble and muttered, "'Night kids."

Jackie gave them a smile and they disappeared through the door.

Colt stared at the door long after it closed then his eyes cut back to Feb when he felt her move in a fidget.

"This is getting to you," she said softly.

Colt nodded. "Most of those boys don't have a high life expectancy. They survive the street, they usually end up doin' time then gettin' out only to get caught and go back in again. Every once in a while one of 'em will get their shit together and pull themselves out. Any one of those boys we found could have been one of those who eventually got their shit together. What they do with their lives is no good but you never know when life will turn. Those boys didn't get the chance to have the epiphany that led them to gettin' their shit straight and I don't like it."

She put down her drink then her hand lifted high, toward his face. It hesitated and dropped down. He felt it settle at his neck, her fingers curling around and she leaned in. Slightly, but she came closer.

He'd been right. Feb touched him and his mind went blank.

"You should know, people sleep easier knowin' you do what you do," she told him and he shook his head. But she kept going, her hand tightening at his neck. "I don't mean generally, Colt. People sleep easier knowin' it's *you* doin' what you do."

Christ, he wanted to kiss her.

Before he could do it, she dropped her hand, hopped off the counter and gave him a smile that was a challenge.

"Bet I'd kick your ass at pool," she said.

Again before he could move or say a word, she grabbed her glass and walked out of the kitchen.

He watched her ass sway while she did it and then he poured himself more bourbon and followed her.

Colt came awake with a jolt. This was because Feb was shaking his shoulder.

He knifed double on the couch and stared at her silhouette in the dark.

"What?"

She leaned into him to reach around, the light flashed on and he blinked at the sudden brightness.

"My journals," she whispered.

She was crouched beside him at the couch wearing her big t-shirt and she surged to her feet, her hand going to her hair, yanking it from her face. Her movements were rough. She was agitated.

She kept talking. "A while ago, not long, weeks?" she asked, her voice high, strange, stressed. "I went home. Felt funny, I didn't know, just felt something weird."

That cold started curling around his chest. He threw back the blankets and stood up, his movements taking him close to her.

She tilted her head back to look at him and dropped her hair but her hand waved to the side, palm up, a gesture that seemed both scared and helpless and it made that cold slither closer.

"Why'd it feel weird?" Colt asked.

She shook her head but said, "My apartment just didn't feel right. It happened a couple of times actually. Didn't think, forgot all about it, thought I was bein' stupid. A woman, livin' alone, thinkin' stupid shit…" She shook her head again then said, quieter this time, that fear and vulnerability stark in her voice, "The thing was, one of those times, I found a journal on the floor of my closet."

The cold started clawing.

Since he could remember, Feb had diaries. She didn't hide when she wrote in them. When she was a kid and a teenager she'd be in Jack and Jackie's living room, her legs thrown over an armchair, her journal at her thighs, her pen scratching on the page. When she broke up with him, had her turn and he didn't understand why, he considered stealing one, reading it to find out why, but he knew that was a betrayal she'd never forgive. He'd hoped back then whatever had caused her to change would reverse and she'd come right back. But she never did and then it was too late.

She still did it, he knew. He'd been into Meems' to get coffee enough times to see she hadn't changed. She'd be at her regular table, the book in front of her, her head bent, one hand holding her hair away from her face at the back of her neck, the other hand writing on the page, her coffee cup in front of her, muffin remains on a plate. Hell, she'd even been at his kitchen bar writing in one that night.

"I'm guessing you don't keep your journals on the floor of your closet," Colt prompted when she said no more.

She shook her head again. "I've kept them all, starting from the diary Mom gave me when I was twelve, the little one with that lock on it you could break with your thumbnail." She licked her lips then said, "They're in a box at the top of my closet. I thought nothing of it, don't know why, it was weird but you don't think someone will…"

Her voice trailed away, her eyes drifted and he lifted an arm, put his hand behind her neck and gave it a squeeze to get her attention.

She focused on him and whispered, "Someone's been in my house, Colt."

"Let's go."

She didn't hesitate. She was down the hall double time. Feb took her clothes to the bathroom and he changed in the bedroom. He was in the living room, had his leather jacket on and his keys in his hand by the time she hit the room.

They went out to his GMC, climbed in and he drove them to her apartment.

He'd never been to her place but he knew where it was. She lived in an older complex, well-kept, tidy, rent was high, it was well-lit, there was good parking. The renters were young adults who had decent jobs who were starting out or old folks who moved there because their houses had gotten too much to take care of and they stayed there until they went into assisted living.

Feb had a ground floor door, pointed to the parking, exposed to the well-maintained grassy area in front, visible to the street and other apartments. There were some tall, full trees by the parking lot, planted smart to throw shade on the cars in summer, well-clipped shrubs hugged close to the building.

Someone walked up to her door, no way to hide.

Her hand shook as she tried to insert the key. Colt pulled the ring from her hand and let them in.

She hit a light and he was surprised to see it was a studio, not much space and it wasn't cozy. No television set, a stereo, big bed, yoga mat rolled up and leaning against a wall, framed photos all around but nothing else to decorate it.

She didn't spend time there, he realized, she was almost always at the bar. If not she was at Meems' or with Jessie. She didn't even have a couch, just a big, overstuffed armchair, ottoman in front of it with a table and standing lamp at its side, where she probably wrote in her journals and read.

She walked across the room and opened a door, pulling a string and the light went on. The studio was tidy, her closet was as well. A walk-in with shelves, clothes hung in an orderly way, organized carefully, jeans and pants in a section, shirts color coordinated, sweaters neatly folded and stacked on the shelves, shoes and boots arranged carefully.

She reached high, getting on her toes, and pulled down a box. She barely moved out of the closet before she dropped to her knees, the box in front of her and she stared inside.

Colt walked to her and looked down to see a bunch of mismatched books in a jumble in the box. Her head tipped back and he could see the tears glittering at the bottoms of her eyes.

"I was in a hurry, needed to get somewhere, I just threw the one that fell up into the box, thinking I'd go back and sort it and I forgot," she whispered. "I didn't even look."

He knew what she was saying. "How many are gone?"

She looked back into the box. "I keep them tidy. Don't know why, but I keep them tidy."

He crouched beside her and his hand went back to her neck.

"February, how many are gone?"

She shook her head, not looking at him.

"Feb."

She finally looked at him.

"I don't know, a lot."

Colt looked away and hissed, "*Fuck!*"

He moved his hand to her upper arm and pulled her up as he straightened. Then he put his hand right back to her neck, keeping her close, his fingers pressing deep, indicating she was not to move away as he yanked out his phone and called Sully.

"'Lo. Colt?" Sully said in his ear. Colt had woken him.

"I need you to get a team to Feb's place. Apartment number three, complex on Brown."

"Shit," Sully muttered, being a cop a long time the sleep was already gone from his voice on that word. "What?"

"Guy's been here. Took her journals."

Sully was quiet a moment then he said, "Well that explains that."

"Call the Feds. Get a team here."

"Done."

Colt flipped his phone shut and shoved it in his back pocket. Feb's neck was trembling under his hand.

"Honey."

She shook her head, kept shaking it, her body trembling but she held it loose, her hands dangling at her sides. She was lost, vulnerable. She'd been violated and she didn't know what to do with that knowledge.

He pulled her closer and her hands automatically came to his stomach. "Feb."

She tipped her head back. "He's been in my house."

145

"I know, baby."

"He's read my journals."

"Keep it together for me."

"He knows everything about me."

"Feb, keep it together."

She shook her head.

Then she closed her eyes tight and a tear slid out the corner of her left eye to trace wetness for an inch before it dropped off her cheekbone.

When she opened her eyes, she said, "Wilson was here. Wilson's friendly. He probably *touched* my cat."

"Feb, you gotta keep it together."

Her hands curled into his shirt and she sucked in breath.

"I wanna run, Colt," she whispered, now her voice was trembling.

"I know you do."

"I'm freaking scared."

"I know, baby."

"He was here," she whispered and then fell forward, planting her face in his chest and her fearful shaking turned to tearful shaking and Colt slid his arms around her.

Day fucking five, five fucking crying jags.

He wanted to *kill* this fucking guy.

"We need to get you out of here. I'm gonna take you back home," he told her.

She nodded, her face sliding against his chest and he wondered if she could breathe, she had it so tight against him.

He drew her away, led her out, secured the apartment and took her to his car.

They were almost home when she said, "I should have said something earlier. I feel like an idiot. I should have—"

"Don't do that, Feb."

She lapsed into silence.

Colt let her into his house and went right back out to the RV. He didn't fuck around but pounded on the door.

Jack, shirtless and wearing jeans, hair wild, eyes wilder, threw it open.

"You got your gun?" Colt asked.

He watched Jack's eyes slice to the house. He looked back at Colt, swallowed and nodded.

"Get it. Killer's been in her house, not lately, weeks ago. Team's headin' there now. I wanna be there while they work. You need to be inside with Feb."

Jack didn't say a word, disappeared, came back wearing boots, a t-shirt and he had his snub-nosed revolver in his hand.

When they hit the living room, Feb was on the couch, sitting on his blanket, her heels in the seat, her cat curled in her arms. She was staring, eyes vacant, at the wall.

Colt wanted to move to Feb but he turned to Jack.

"Get some of Doc's pills in her. Get her ass to bed. But you don't sleep."

Jack's eyes were glued to his daughter but he nodded.

Colt looked at Feb again to see her eyes were on him.

Again he wanted to move to her but instead he walked out the door.

He heard it lock before he was three steps into the yard.

"Sully!" Chris called and Colt, standing on Feb's front path with Sully, turned to see Chris in the doorway of Feb's apartment.

Sully hadn't fucked around and the boys weren't either, not with this case, not with it being about Feb. It looked like Sully had activated the entire task force that had been pulled together from all the departments in the county to work this case. There were enough of them to make enough noise that lights had come on. They were on show, folks watching from windows, some of them wrapped tight in robes with slippers on their feet coming out to watch openly.

Word was going to get out, people would speculate, their control over information was slipping. It would evaporate when, come dawn, they canvassed.

Both Sully and Colt walked to Chris.

Chris's eyes were on Sully, his face grim then he looked at Colt. "All right, Colt. We found somethin' and you gotta keep your shit together, man."

That cold that hadn't left his chest started biting.

"You don't…fuck, Sully," Chris said. "Should he even be here?"

"What'd you find?" Colt asked.

Chris didn't answer.

"He'll be all right," Sully assured Chris.

Chris shot Colt a look and stepped out of the doorframe. Sully and Colt entered. The boys were about their business, six of them. They looked up and then looked away.

On Feb's bed, which had been tossed, the mattress askew, there were three plastic bags, all three had white handkerchiefs in them, balled, looking crusty.

Cum rags.

Colt bit his lip and his hands curled into fists.

"Found them tucked between the headboard and box springs," Chris said. "She wouldn't find them even if she was changing the sheets."

Christ. Feb slept in a bed with some sick fuck's ejaculate tucked close.

"This is good, Colt," Sully said hurriedly. "DNA. We got DNA."

Colt stared at the bags.

He probably kneeled on the bed jacking off, thinking of her, looking at that framed photo of her on her bedside table. A photo of her in profile, her face filled with laughter, both Bonham and Tuesday caught in mid-wiggle in her arms. The kids were younger than now, maybe four and six. They looked like they were having a tickling fight.

"Colt, man, come back into the room. This is good."

"He jacked off on her bed."

"He's finally fucked up."

Colt looked at Sully. "You think that makes me feel better? Or maybe you think that'll make Feb feel better?"

"We're closer. You lose it, do somethin' stupid—"

That pissed him off and Colt felt his body get tight. "I'm not gonna do somethin' stupid, Sully. Fuck." Sully studied him and then nodded. Colt looked to Marty who was, in the small space, giving Colt a wide berth and turned to Chris. "You have a word with Marty, this doesn't get out."

"I know Marty fucked up tonight, man, but Lore'll get over it and the town will understand," Chris said.

"You have a word with Marty," Colt repeated. "I could report him and I should, what he did tonight. This leaks I'll have his fuckin' badge."

"Colt—"

Colt leaned in. "Have a fuckin' word."

Chris put his hands up. "I'll have a word."

Colt turned and walked out the door. Sully followed him. They stopped in the grass at the front of Feb's place.

"You're not doin' anything here but makin' yourself angry. Get home to Feb," Sully said.

Get home to Feb.

At that moment Colt didn't think anything would make him feel better, except February's hand at his neck. But, this scenario, it wasn't her job to comfort him.

Those words made him feel better. He didn't spare a second to think about why they did, not after all this time, all that had happened. He just knew in his bones they did.

Colt nodded to his partner, walked to his truck with his eyes to the ground, got in and went home to Feb.

Colt entered his house and saw Feb asleep on the couch under his blanket, Wilson curled at her feet, Jack sitting at the stool she'd been at earlier that night, his revolver on the bar in front of him, his hair wilder than before but not wilder than his eyes.

Colt walked to him, got close and said low, "I want you and Jackie in here tomorrow."

Jack kept his face expressionless and nodded.

"Make yourselves at home, you're gonna be here until this is over. Tell Jackie she has free rein what she wants to do with the shit in that bedroom."

"She'll be ecstatic," Jack said.

She would. Jackie was as tidy as Colt'd learned her daughter was tonight. Never happier than when she was cleaning except when she was throwing shit out, usually Jack's shit, which usually drove Jack up the wall. He was a hoarder.

Jack grabbed his revolver, got up, walked to the side door and Colt followed.

Jack turned at the door. "They find anything?"

"They're still lookin'."

"They find anything?" Jack repeated, needing something to hang onto before he got in bed beside his wife and put his head on a pillow.

Colt looked at him then said, "Caught a break. We got DNA."

"How's that?"

Colt remained silent.

"He leave hairs or somethin'?"

"Just leave it at that, Jack."

Jack stared a moment then surmised, "I don't wanna know."

"No, you don't."

"Which means I know."

Colt suspected he did.

Jack's eyes shifted to his daughter, his head lifting like a turtle, the muscles in his neck standing out before he looked back to Colt. "You keep her safe, you hear?"

Colt nodded. Jack opened the door and Colt stood in the frame watching until Jack disappeared in the RV and then watching longer.

Finally he shut and locked the door. Then he went through the entire house, every room, even the second bedroom, and checked doors and windows, making sure they were secure, blinds closed, Feb and him shut in tight.

As he did this his mind scanned the quiet, night streets he'd just driven through.

He'd taken his time getting home, cruising the blocks, round and round, looking for a silver Audi, which Denny Lowe drove. This wasn't the neighborhood for Audis, folks around here bought American made and he didn't find one. Only when dawn was kissing the horizon and he was far enough out that it'd be tough to get to Colt's on foot, Colt drove home.

When the house was secure, he went to his bedroom and pulled back the covers. She'd made the bed. He didn't bother except yesterday when he'd made it up for her.

Then he went to the couch and picked up Feb. She was out, dead weight, didn't even lift her arms to hold on. He carried her to his bed and set her in it. She rolled to her belly, lifted a leg and shoved her hand under her cheek on the pillow. Colt pulled the covers up to her shoulder.

Wilson jumped up and resumed his position at her feet, not picky about where he got his shuteye, just as long as Feb was there.

Colt found he was growing fond of that cat.

Colt took off his clothes, pulled on his shorts, unholstered his gun and put it and his phone by the bed, and even knowing there would be holy hell to pay in the morning, he crawled in beside her. He wasn't going to be far, not even as far as the couch.

Why he could handle a man traveling the country and hacking up people as some fanatical show of affection for Feb and he couldn't handle that same man breaking into her house, jacking off and leaving mementos, he didn't know. He didn't dwell. She wasn't going to be far away from him that night.

Once he'd moved in with Jack and Jackie, Colt used to be a heavy sleeper. But after Feb broke it off with him, he started moving in his sleep. He'd had a queen with Melanie and he was always waking her, never enough room. She said she liked it when he woke her. She tried to cuddle, which Colt didn't like much considering his body was active when it was unconscious. He'd bought the king after she left, plenty of room.

Now with Feb so far away, he felt the bed was way too damn big.

He shifted into the middle and pulled her close, not worried he'd wake her with his movements. He knew he'd get no sleep.

Her cat started purring for some ungodly reason. It was loud. Now Colt knew how Wilson got his nickname.

He listened to Wilson's purrs and Feb's deep breathing, and as the light filtered strong around the blinds, he fell asleep.

Fifteen minutes later, his phone rang and he woke up.

Six

MARIE

"Yeah?" I heard and my eyes blinked open.

When they did I could swear I saw the line of Colt's back, sloped because he was up on a forearm, the covers down to his waist. He had his phone to his ear.

I stared as he said, "Right, be there as soon as I can. Maybe an hour."

He flipped the phone shut and threw it on the nightstand.

Groggy, still partly asleep and fighting it, I got up on a forearm too.

"What are you doin' here?" I asked, though I kind of wondered what I was doing there too. I'd fallen asleep on the couch even though Dad tried to get me to go to bed. But I was spooked and regardless of the fact I was old enough to take care of myself and had been doing so with questionable success for a long time, I still didn't want to be far from my dad.

Colt turned to me and I noticed he looked wiped, his eyes shadowed and tired. I noticed this but I had bigger things on my fuzzy mind.

"Go back to sleep, baby," he said softly.

"What are you doin' here?" I asked again.

Wilson, realizing we were awake, decided it was breakfast time and we should be informed of that. He started up the bed toward me meowing.

"Feb, go back to sleep. I'll get Jack to come in."

Wilson made it to me and head butted my hand. I automatically started giving him scratches and the meowing mixed with loud purring.

But my mind was still on Colt who was *still* in bed with me.

"What are you doin' in this bed?"

He gave me a look before he threw the covers back and got out.

"I got work," he said, not answering my question. "I'll feed the cat."

He started to the door but I threw the covers back too and got quickly to my feet.

"You can't crawl into bed with me," I informed him.

He turned in the door. "February, we're not fightin' about this. Not only do I not have the time, I also don't have the energy or the inclination."

I was a dog with a bone. "You carried me to bed and got in it with me!"

My voice was rising. Colt ignored it and walked out the door.

Wilson, feeling this was a healthy indication he'd be getting breakfast soon, jumped off the bed I left him in and pranced out after him.

For my part, I stomped.

"Colt!" I snapped when I hit the hall.

He didn't reply.

By the time I hit the kitchen, he was reaching into the dish drainer to get the kitty bowl I'd washed last night.

"We need to talk about that kiss yesterday," I announced, not really wanting to talk about it but feeling, considering this morning's circumstances, that we needed to get things straight.

"We will," Colt agreed. "Not now," Colt evaded.

"Now."

He pulled open the top of the cat food tin but speared me with a glance. "Not now."

"Now."

He turned fully to me. Wilson noticed this delay and started meowing again.

"I got work," he repeated.

"You already said that."

"This conversation's gonna take time. I'm tellin' you I don't have that."

"Well, make it!"

He took one step to me and had his hand wrapped around the back of my neck so fast I didn't even get a breath in while he was doing it. It was then I felt a little bit of Lore's pain. I'd seen Colt move fast yesterday when

153

he took Lore down, I'd even seen him do it before he kissed me, but I still wasn't prepared for it.

He yanked me close and I almost didn't get my hands up to break my fall, but I did and they landed on his chest.

"I got home at dawn. I was in that bed with you for half an hour. I was in it because I'm not takin' any fuckin' chances. Someone who can get through a door can get through a window. They get through the window, they get me first. Now, do *you* get me?"

My mind blanked, my stomach curled sickeningly, and I stared at him.

"You found something last night," I whispered.

He let me go and turned back to the cat food.

"Colt."

Colt forked the food into the bowl. "We found something. When he visited, he spent time there."

"Oh my God."

I didn't know what this meant but the escalation in Colt's protection said it was no good. This wasn't about a madman invading my mind by stealing my thoughts written on a page. This was something that freaked him out and he was a cop. I didn't suspect much freaked him out.

He moved to put the food down for Wilson and Wilson settled down belly to the floor on all fours and stuck his face in it.

"What'd you find?"

He straightened and looked at me. "I'll know more this mornin'. They were still working when I left."

"What'd you find?"

"I gotta shower."

"Colt—" I started, but he was moving away.

I stared at the hall he disappeared into long after he disappeared. Even after I heard the shower go on in the master bath.

After a while it hit me that he was protecting me with more than him keeping close, close enough to sleep in his huge bed with me. He was protecting me by not sharing and I decided to wipe my mind clean.

Some folk, I suspected, would want to know.

I didn't want to know.

I knew enough and it was tearing at my insides. I could use a break.

By the time he came back out, hair wet, slicked back but still curling around his neck, dressed in jeans, boots, shirt, badge clipped to his belt, shoulder holster on, gun clipped in place, blazer bunched in his hand, I'd made coffee and toast. I'd also poured him some coffee and it was keeping warm in a travel mug.

He hit the kitchen, shrugging on his blazer. I was turned to him, one hand wrapped around his mug, the other hand holding up a plate with four slices of buttered toast.

"I made toast and coffee," I said.

He was looking at my hands but when I spoke his eyes came to my face. Something in them struck me funny, not in a bad way, in a good way. That look settled in beside his smile from yesterday, the one that was still lodged in that private place deep inside.

When I thought he'd stop moving toward me, he didn't and I had to jerk my arms to the sides to give him space and he took it. His hand came up and around the back of my head, fingers in my hair, fisting and tugging down. I made a surprised noise that came from deep in my throat when I had no choice but to tilt my head back before his mouth came down on mine.

This kiss wasn't hungry, wet and desperate. No tongues. It was hard, closed-mouthed and swift.

It still did a number on me and I felt a curl that I liked a lot between my legs.

He let me go, grabbed the mug and took the slice of toast off the top of the stack.

"We'll talk about that kiss later too," he said, turned and walked away. At the door he turned again and ordered, "Lock this after me. I'll send Jack in. You're not alone, Feb, ever. Not even in the storeroom at J&J's. Not even to walk down to Meems'. You move, you make sure you have a shadow. Yeah?"

I stood there still holding up the plate and nodded.

"Stay safe, baby," he said, the cop authority gone from his voice. This statement was quiet and sweet and it strolled right into that private place inside me, took its seat and sat back, intending like the others to stay awhile.

"You too," I replied and he left.

It took a while for me to pull myself together. The only reason I did was because the door was unlocked and I hated it but that scared the shit out of me.

I put down the plate, walked into the living room and locked the door. On the way back to the kitchen, the phone rang.

I hit the kitchen and reached out to the phone. It was an old-fashioned kitchen wall phone, yellow, boxy, with push buttons and a long, curly cord so you could wander the kitchen with it held in the crook of your neck while you were doing shit. I liked it mostly because I could imagine wandering Colt's kitchen with it held in the crook of my neck.

I put it to my ear and said, "Hello?"

No one spoke.

I felt a curl again. It was north, in my belly, and it wasn't pleasant.

"Hello?" I repeated, tentative this time.

"Um…hello, is Colt there?"

Oh shit, it was Melanie.

"Melanie?" I asked, though I didn't want to.

"February?" she asked back and I knew she didn't want to either.

Oh shit, shitshitshitshitshit.

"Uh…yeah. How's it going?" Oh my God, I hated this.

"Um…it's good. How're you?" She hated it too.

All I could think about was Romeo and Juliet and Nancy and I was going to give Dee what for the next time I saw her for putting that crap in my head.

"Things aren't great. You maybe didn't hear but I found Angie—" I was going into explanation mode. I didn't want her to get the wrong idea.

"I heard," Melanie cut me off then paused before she went on. "Poor Angie."

"Yeah."

"Is Colt there?" she repeated.

"No, he, um…left. You just missed him."

"I'll call his cell."

"Melanie—"

"It's not important anyway."

"Mel—"

"You take care, Feb."

"Mel—"

"See you."

Then she hung up. I closed my eyes tight and put the phone back in the receiver. I heard the key scrape the side door and Dad walked in.

"'Mornin' darlin'."

It worked for me that Dad didn't put the "good" in that greeting. It was not a good morning. It was just morning, or to be precise, it was a shit morning.

"'Mornin' Dad," I replied.

My cell rang about five minutes after Morrie, Dad and I opened J&J's. The display said "Colt calling."

I flipped it open and put it to my ear, "Hello?"

"Hey."

"Everything okay?"

"You know what I told you about last night?" he asked. "Before I wiped the floor with your ass at pool."

I was a good pool player. I'd worked in bars all my life, I had lots of practice. Still, Colt wasn't lying when he said he wiped my ass. It pissed me off but he did. It was embarrassing.

"You didn't wipe the floor with my ass," I lied.

"Honey, I *so* wiped the floor with your ass."

I rolled my eyes and said, "Whatever."

I heard his soft laughter and it struck me he was laughing and these days there wasn't much to laugh about.

"I remember about last night," I said.

"We got him."

I felt a weird sense of elation hit my gut and slither around in a happy way. It wasn't me working the case. It wasn't me going out and seeing dead bodies. But it was me hearing Colt's relief mixed with a hint of triumph. He'd got the bad guy and he was pleased.

"Who was it?"

"Calvin Johnson."

I could believe that, though I was still surprised. I knew Cal Johnson, had known him forever. He was opinionated and shared those opinions often and loudly. He also had a short fuse. He was a nice guy and I could say this because he'd always been nice to me, considering I wasn't a gang banger. But he had a definite sense of right and wrong and I didn't think it would take much to tip him over the edge of making something right even if he went about it wrong.

"I can see that," I told Colt.

"IMPD caught him last night. Fluke. Saw him loitering, older, white guy, rough, black neighborhood, he stood out. He was probably out hunting. They stopped for a chat, saw the gun on his belt, hauled him in. They found out he was from town and started questioning. He was uncooperative but he flipped for me."

"You got him to confess?"

"Yeah, started as a rage. His brother lives in LA, his great-niece was picked up by a gang for an initiation and they did a number on her. So much anger, didn't know what to do with it so he found a way to release it. But then he found he liked the way it felt, cleaning up the streets, so he kept doin' it."

Poor Cal. I'd heard about gang initiations. At his age, his great-niece must be in her early teens, if that. I was surprised I didn't know about his niece though. News traveled fast, bad news faster. Cal had kept it to himself, which wasn't smart. Meant he needed to get it out someway and he picked the wrong way.

"Still," Colt continued, "I think he was glad he was caught. He liked it and was starting to get off on it but he's got enough good in him to know it was wrong and the dark path he was on was gettin' darker. That's probably why he dumped the bodies so they could be found."

Catching Cal, Colt and the IMPD had saved the lives of some gang members, which I supposed was a good thing. He also stopped bodies being dumped in the town limits, which was definitely a good thing. He'd also stopped Cal turning his soul any blacker, which was also a good thing. Colt had scored and it was huge.

Because of that I couldn't stop myself from saying quietly, "Good job, babe."

He was silent a moment then he asked, "You at J&J's?"

"Yeah."

"Don't work tonight. We'll get Reggie's, take it home, drink beer and I'll give you a chance to salvage your pool reputation."

I knew he said this because he wanted to celebrate. What freaked me out was that he wanted to celebrate with me. Worse, that sounded like a kind of date except the "take it home" part, which made it sound like something else entirely.

"Colt—"

"I'll talk to Jack. He or Jackie can cover if you're on."

"Colt—"

"I'll pick you up at six."

Definitely a date-ish type statement.

"Listen to me, Colt—"

"Later, baby."

Then he hung up.

I was finding it hard to breathe. This wasn't because I was angry. This was because I wanted to eat pizza, drink beer and play pool in Colt's den with Colt. I also wanted other things too, if I was honest. I wanted them so much it was too much.

That wasn't what was making it hard to breathe.

What was making it hard to breathe was that I knew I could have them if I just reached out and took hold. And the excitement and anticipation of knowing that was unbelievably thrilling.

Letting go of the pain and deciding to live my life before it was too late meant something else was happening too. I was letting Colt back in, or he was pushing his way in, probably both. Golden Sundays and fucking fantastic kisses and a man going all out to protect you had a way of making that kind of shit happen. I didn't know if I was ready to take Dee's advice, forgive him, forget and move on.

Even after all of these years, even learning moment to moment these last few days what kind of man he'd turned out to be, I had to admit, I was still shit scared.

By three thirty I knew the news had broken or some of it anyway.

I knew this because, for a Monday afternoon, we had *way* more people in the bar than usual.

I knew it too because Morrie finally told me after I cornered him because he and Dad were getting called aside to have private conversations with patrons.

Firstly, everyone knew Colt and I had had scenes in this bar and at the station.

Secondly, everyone knew that one second Colt and I were circling each other and barely speaking, the next second we were having scenes in this bar and at the station and more, I was living with him.

Thirdly, not only had half my neighbors watched Colt and the boys going in and out of my apartment in the wee hours of the morning, but also Chris and Marty had canvassed, knocking on my neighbors' doors asking them if they saw anyone going into my house. They'd undoubtedly had their chats with Chris and Marty, gone back into their apartments and got right on the phone. Most of my neighbors were retired and this was gossip too juicy not to share.

Not to mention, Lore came in and did his thing, exposing me as someone who was assisting the investigation which didn't help matters.

Lastly, my cell never quit ringing. I'd never been more popular. Some—my closer friends—I picked up and gave them a kind of "I'm busy," "No Comment," "I'll call you later" malarkey. Others I didn't pick up at all.

The good news was no one was shying away from me or sending daggers at me with their eyes. They were coming into the bar and having drinks, not avoiding it. I felt mostly curiosity and some concern coming at me and I could handle that.

So the afternoon was crawling on and my drama was taking a new turn. I wondered if it lasted much longer if I'd eventually get used to it. I doubted it.

Morrie walked in with Bonham and Tuesday in tow. They raced to the office shouting, "Hey, Granddad! Hey, Auntie Feb," and disappeared behind the office door.

I'd been in the office that day and the kids had done a number on it. Nothing on the desk was where it'd been before and the computer was totally fucked up and had about fifty more applications than it had when they walked in yesterday. Still, I liked them being in the bar, which was where Morrie and I spent a lot of our childhood, and seeing as loved ones were close, it was a good place to be.

Morrie had his cell to his ear as he made his way behind the bar. "Yeah, Dee, I picked 'em up from school. Things are busy here. You mind comin' 'round after work to pick them up?"

He was close so, at his words, I punched him in the arm hard.

"Yow!" he shouted and I bugged my eyes out at him. "Nothin' Dee, darlin', just that Feb's in a mood." He chuckled and said, "That's it, babe. Later."

I was still glaring at him when he flipped his phone shut.

"What was that for?" he asked me.

"It was for tellin' Dee to come get the kids. She's tired. It's Monday. Mondays suck. She doesn't want to go out of her way to get the kids. And anyway, Dad's here, we're busy but he'd cover for you."

"Well, she'll want to come out of her way today," he replied.

"Yeah, why? Because your natural charisma will brighten her day?"

"No," he shot back. "Because I got reservations at Costa's tonight and she loves that place. We're gonna have a family dinner. It's a surprise."

I snapped my mouth shut, surprised and impressed. Morrie spoke the truth. Dee loved Costa's like crazy, the kids did too. Hell, I did too. Everyone loved Costa's. It was a great Greek restaurant one town over. It was where you went to celebrate things, birthdays, getting into the university you wanted, shit like that. Not just Monday night family night.

Morrie was going to score huge on this.

"Got anything else to say?" Morrie asked, and I didn't so I didn't say anything.

All of a sudden I heard Dad laugh and just as sudden his arms were around me and he was giving me a big hug. I hugged him back automatically. Then, when I got over my surprise that I was all of a sudden being hugged by my dad in the bar for no reason, I *felt* his hug and the feel of it almost made me cry.

Dad was a hugger, he was affectionate like Morrie, but I hadn't had a hug like that from my dad in a long...fucking...time.

That was when I really hugged him back.

"I love my girl," he whispered in my ear before he let me go.

I had tears in my eyes when I said to his back, "Love you too, Dad."

Morrie put his big mitt on the side of my head and gave it a shove.

I took a deep breath to control the tears and gave my brother a smile because with his head shove, he was saying he loved me too.

And somehow I felt like I'd come home. Not like when I got home two years ago to stay for good, or any of the times I'd come home to visit, but like I'd really, finally, come home.

The Terrible Trio showed up at quarter past five.

For me, this meant Jessie, Meems and Dee.

They ambled in, eyes on me and I knew I was in trouble.

Dee, I was expecting. The three of them together meant they'd planned this and it sent bad tidings.

"Hey, babe," Morrie called to Dee.

"Hey, hon," Dee replied. "Be with you in a sec. Gotta have a word with Feb before I take the kids home."

There it was. Trouble.

Morrie read Dee's tone. He read it and it made him do two things: grin and skedaddle.

Jessie, Meems and Dee bellied up to Colt's end of the bar and I approached.

"Get you gals a drink?" I asked.

"Not here for libations, girlie," Jessie answered.

I knew that. Shit.

"What's up?" I asked.

"Lindy, who heard it from Bobbie, who heard it from Lisa, who heard it from Ellie, who got it straight from the horse's mouth says you talked to Melanie this mornin'," Jessie told me.

My mind flew through the strategies available to deal with this situation. I settled on nonchalance. "Yeah, sure, she called this morning."

"And?" Meems prompted.

"And nothing. Colt was gone. He had work," I answered.

"And?" Jessie said this time.

"Nothin'," I replied.

"Girlie, your whatever-he-is's ex phones you, findin' you at his *house* first thing in the *mornin'*, you call your girlfriends so we can peck it over and so, when other people call us about it, we don't look like assholes because we're surprised," Jessie informed me.

"It wasn't a big deal," I informed her right back.

"It was, seein' as she was callin' Colt to ask him to dinner so she could see if he wanted to have another go," Dee told me.

"Another go at what?" I asked, then it hit me and I knew. I knew. Shit, I knew. I actually felt the blood draining out of my face before I whispered, "She said it wasn't important."

"She lied," Meems said.

"She ain't exactly gonna let you in on that," Jessie noted.

"Oh crap," I said, and then I leaned forward, put my elbows on the bar and my forehead in my hands.

I didn't need this shit, not for a variety of reasons. The obvious one being I had enough shit to deal with. The one that somehow seemed more pressing was that I didn't want Melanie to want Colt back because I didn't want to find out that Colt wanted Melanie back.

"February," Dee called.

"Give me a minute to think," I said to the bar.

"Well, let us in on this thinkin' 'cause maybe we can help," Jessie offered, and I straightened.

"How're you gonna do that?" I asked.

"Well, firstly, by telling you to pull your finger out about Colt and show him you're ready to try again," Meems stated.

"Actually, that's most of how we were gonna help," Dee put in.

"Great. That works. Thanks." My tone was pure sarcasm.

"Has he kissed you again?" Dee asked and I pressed my lips together.

"He kissed her," Meems muttered.

"They played pool too. Colt wiped the floor with her ass."

This came from my mother, who had planted herself by Dee and I hadn't even noticed.

Mom had, that day, been given free rein to clean out Colt's second bedroom. She called me at ten o'clock to inform me she'd talked Bud Anderson into delivering a brand new queen-sized mattress and box springs with a standard frame to Colt's house by three o'clock. She bragged to me for ten minutes about the bargain she got. I didn't dwell on why Mom was suddenly cleaning out and furnishing Colt's second bedroom. As I mentioned before, I had enough to deal with.

"How did you know about the pool?" I asked my mother.

"Colt told Morrie, Morrie told Jack, Jack told me," Mom answered.

Next time I ran away from home, I was going to a big city. The biggest. In China. Where not only were there billions of people, I didn't speak their language and they had good food.

"Colt wiped the floor with your ass?" Jessie was astounded. "You rock at pool."

"Maybe she was havin' trouble concentrating," Meems suggested.

"Colt leaning over a pool table, I'd have trouble concentrating," Dee remarked and they all dissolved into loud, girlie cackles.

I took this moment to pry my eyes off them and look around the bar.

Yep, just as I suspected, everyone was watching us.

Time to put things straight.

I leaned in and said low, "This is the deal. I got some whackjob murdering people because he thinks he's doin' me a favor. He stole my journals, which means he knows everything about me, all my private thoughts." They gasped through this new news. I ignored it and carried on. "Colt is being cool, way cool, cooler than he needs to be. I'm grateful. I don't know what that means and I don't know if I'm ready to explore it. I'm just takin' this one second at a time because that's all the strength I got left in me with this shit, which is relentless. I try to do more, I'll unravel."

They were all staring at me but I kept right on going.

"I need you all to help me keep it together. That means if there comes a time I want to share, I reserve the right to share even though I'm tellin' you right now, back the...fuck...off."

They all looked properly chastised, except Mom who looked weirdly proud. But I wasn't done so I kept talking.

"As for Melanie, she's a good woman. She doesn't deserve the shock she had this morning and she doesn't deserve us chewin' her up just about now. It'll play out as it plays out. This isn't 'may the best woman win' because neither of us deserves that and Colt doesn't either. These are lives were talkin' about. The lives of decent people and that means Melanie too. Yeah?"

They all looked at each other then they nodded to me.

I looked at Jessie. "And you can tell Ellie, Lisa, Bobbie and Lindy the same thing. Serious shit's at stake here and Colt needs to stay on target. He doesn't need more crap to deal with."

"All right, girlie," Jessie whispered.

"We were only tryin' to help," Meems said.

"I know you were," I told them. "And I appreciate that. But now you know how it is."

Before anyone could say anything else, Morrie came up to the girl posse.

"Hate to break this up, girls, but Delilah and me got a dinner reservation," Morrie announced.

Dee's face grew slack as she turned to him and asked, "We do?"

"Costa's, table for four and we better get our asses in gear. We're late, they won't save the table."

"Costa's," Dee whispered, her face no longer slack but brilliant and alive and I felt her look in my gut like a happy tickle.

Morrie slung his arm around her shoulders and scooted her off her stool. "My baby's favorite," he said. "Let's get the kids."

They wandered to the office and I smiled at Mom. Mom smiled back.

"Costa's. Yowza. Morrie's pullin' out the big guns," Meems commented.

"Sometimes, it's rare, but sometimes…men learn," Mom's voice was heavy with wisdom and experience as she slid off her own stool and made her way round to the back of the bar.

"I think I'll take a drink now," Jessie said to me.

"Not me, kids to feed," Meems told us. "Later lovelies." She blew kisses and then, ten seconds later, blew out the door.

I made Jessie's drink and was sitting it in front of her when my cell rang. I yanked it out and the display said "Colt calling." I flipped it open and put it to my ear.

"Hello?"

"Feb, honey, I'll be late but be there as soon as I can," Colt said.

"Colt—"

"Soon as I can. Later."

Then he hung up.

"Colt?" Jessie asked once I'd flipped my phone closed and slid it back in my jeans.

I sighed then said, "Yeah, he caught a bad guy and he wanted to celebrate with Reggie's, beer and pool at his house."

Jessie's lips compressed then slid to the side and stayed there. I watched her as seconds passed and her lips stayed put.

"Hurts, doesn't it?" I asked.

"What?"

"Keepin' your mouth shut for once."

Jessie grinned.

"Bitch," she whispered and didn't mean it.

"You're the bitch," I whispered back and didn't mean it.

Then I scanned the bar and saw I had customers who needed drinks.

At five to six, Colt met Sully on the lawn of Denny Lowe's house.

"Well, good news is, we know who's hacking people up in three different states. Bad news is, we got another body," Sully told Colt and Colt closed his eyes.

When he opened them, he said, "Talk to me."

"Marie Lowe, Denny's wife. Found by the cleaner this afternoon. Cleaner's Mexican and speaks about four words of English. Doesn't help matters that she's freaked."

"How bad is it?"

"Seein' as we reckon this was the first one and it started all this shit, he hadn't decided on his MO. Just hacked her to shit with an ax."

"Christ."

"Not much left to her. She didn't have some hair left and the wedding rings on her finger that you can see her wearin' in pictures around her

166

house, wouldn't know it was her. He went at it. Kept hacking long after she was gone. Looks rage-driven."

"We know why?"

"Nope. We'll start diggin'."

"We find out she's the first, whatever caused him to do her could be what sent him on this path."

Sully nodded.

"How long's she been dead?" Colt asked.

"Looks like a while, *smells* like a while, don't know for certain."

"How often does the cleaner come?"

"Don't know that either seein' as I don't speak Spanish and neither does anyone else."

"You got an interpreter coming?"

"Yeah, ETA," he looked at his watch, "maybe five, ten minutes."

Colt looked away, tearing his fingers through his hair and swore, "Fucking hell."

"Yeah, you're sayin' that now, wait until you get a look at the body."

Colt turned back to Sully and gave the front door a lift of his chin. Sully nodded and led the way. They grabbed cotton covers for their boots and plastic gloves and pulled them on before they went in.

Colt saw immediately that the place screamed money. He knew Denny was a computer programmer, designed some software that hospitals all over the country used and he made good money, but this place said more than that. Marie Lowe had good taste. It was sheer elegance.

Except, of course, the path of blood that stained the foyer and all the way up the wide, curling staircase that was accompanied by the sick smell of death.

Sully led Colt up the stairs while he talked. "Did her in the bedroom in bed, at least that fits the MO. Though he dragged her there, it started in the kitchen, blood all over the place."

"No one reported her missing?"

"While investigating him we found out she doesn't work. Don't know if she missed a nail appointment," Sully said. "She's not a local, no family close we know of but haven't looked into her much. Know she was forty years old. They been married a good long while, no kids. Maybe she met him at Northwestern."

They hit the bedroom but Colt saw it before he got there because the blood was all over the walls.

Definitely rage-driven.

"Holy fuck," he whispered when he saw what was left of Marie Lowe's body.

The Mexican cleaner was going to have nightmares for years.

He turned to Sully. "Get the interpreter to call the cleaner's family here. Talk to them about assistance. This is gonna fuck with her head for a while."

"Got it," Sully replied, and Colt walked fully into the room.

The boys were working the bed still taking photos. Andy Milligan, the coroner, already had the body bag spread out on the floor. How Andy was going to scoop up that mess and get it into a bag was beyond Colt, but he was fucking glad that wasn't his job.

Colt skirted the bed and saw a big, elaborately framed photograph on a bureau and he got close. Wedding picture. Denny and Marie, Marie smiling like it was the happiest day of her life. She looked young in the photo, maybe early twenties. She was pretty, blonde, dark brown eyes, tall, good figure that Colt could see even trussed up with all the material of her dress. Someone had spent some cake on the wedding if that dress and her flowers were anything to go by. Far's Colt knew Denny didn't come from money, though his dad didn't do bad as he was the local pharmacist, which meant probably Marie's family was loaded.

Colt's eyes moved to Denny in the photo.

Denny looked like he had a secret. He wasn't smiling near as wide, he didn't look relaxed and happy. He looked formal and stiff.

He'd settled for second best.

Colt hadn't noticed it when he'd seen them around in town because he didn't pay much mind to Marie Lowe, but she looked a fuck of a lot like Feb.

"I know," Sully muttered from beside him, reading his mind.

Colt turned to Sully keeping his body aimed away from the mess on the bed.

"Chris and Marty got witnesses at Feb's place," Colt stated because he knew this to be true. Chris had called him.

"Yeah, another fuck up," Sully replied. "I don't know, maybe he thought senior citizens take naps all the time instead of being nosy as shit, but got four folks who saw a man of his description go into Feb's house. One lady, name is June Wright, says she saw him twice and once, she reports, it looked like he was having trouble with his key. Or at least she thought so at the time. She thought he was Feb's boyfriend."

That comment made Colt's stomach give a sick churn.

"Picking the lock?" Colt asked.

"Probably. Don't know if you looked, her lock isn't great."

"Yeah, it isn't because she lives in a small town where this shit isn't supposed to happen. Most the population have locks like that."

"We better call Skipp, his hardware store is gonna get overrun."

"Already is," Chris said, getting close. "Day Angie died."

"Chris," Colt greeted him.

"Heya, Colt," Chris replied and looked at Sully. "Got somethin' interesting."

"That is?" Sully asked.

"This place has five frickin' fireplaces. All of them burn wood, not gas, not fake, real wood fire places."

Colt knew where this was going.

Chris continued. "They all got stacks of wood beside them, all of them, and a big row of wood down the back of the house, three rows deep. So much wood, shit, they'd need five years to get through it all. There's also a stump for choppin'. Looks like Denny Lowe chopped his own wood and it looks like he did it like a freakin' hobby. A hobby he liked, like, *a lot.*"

"This guy is whacked," Sully muttered.

"Yeah, choppin' wood as a hobby puts the icing on the cake of this guy bein' whacked," Chris said and jerked his head toward the bed.

Colt was thinking of a man who earned a better than modest living but chopped his own wood. He could have had the wood delivered but instead he had to have had full logs delivered.

This neighborhood, the cops would have heard about some fanatical log-chopping neighbor who was cutting down all the trees. Folks in this neighborhood didn't mind complaining. They paid big taxes and they felt they should get their money's worth. They called the cops if a neighbor's kid was playing his stereo too loud at three o'clock on a Saturday afternoon. Hell, it was a miracle they hadn't received a complaint about the noise made by Denny chopping wood all the time.

Most men chopped wood because they had to, not because they wanted to. Seemed to Colt, Denny Lowe had a lot of rage he'd been workin' out for some time.

"We need this place combed, someone needs to talk to the neighbors," Sully said to Chris. "You need reinforcements, let me know, we'll call 'em in. The Feds are heading back here and I've no doubt they'll get men on it too."

"Gotcha," Chris said on a nod and took off.

"Strainin' our resources, you on 'consultative capacity,' Marty havin' half a brain and needin' to pull the boys from the task force in every few hours. No cops on the street, we're gonna miss our quota this month of speedin' tickets," Sully joked.

Colt smiled at him. "This guy's gonna hit the history books, Sully. You'll have your own page on online encyclopedias."

Sully smiled back. "Better get Lorraine to take a decent picture of me."

Colt slapped him on the shoulder and gave it a squeeze. Then they walked out of the bedroom and made their way down the hall, avoiding the path of blood, and Sully stopped at the top of the stairs.

"How's Feb doin'?" he asked when Colt turned to him.

"She's holdin' it together."

"She's surprisin' me, and everyone, thought she'd flip and take off." He paused. "It's a good surprise."

"Yeah."

"She gonna be able to see it through?"

"She's got help."

Sully looked closely at him. "Yeah. She does." He took in a breath and said, "Listen, man, rumor is all over about this shit and you and Feb and now I heard from Lorraine that Melanie—"

"She called this morning."

Sully swayed back in surprise. "Fuck, really?"

Colt nodded.

"Colt...man, you should know the rumor—"

"Rumor's true. She called, wanted to have dinner, talk about things."

"You havin' dinner?" Sully asked quietly.

"Nope."

Sully's eyebrows went skyward. "That's it? 'Nope?'"

"That's it."

"Jesus."

"She shoulda called three years ago, Sully," Colt told him.

Sully gave him a look then grinned and said, "Feb."

Colt saw no reason to deny it and confirmed, "Feb."

Sully rocked back on his heels, still grinning but now grinning like a crazy fuck, he was so happy. "What chance you think you got?"

"Don't know. You'll have to wait and find out, just like me."

Colt wasted no more time. He was late as it was. He gave Sully a "Later," turned and jogged down the stairs.

Sully called after him, ribbing in his voice, "Spendin' the evening at your spot at J&J's?"

"Spendin' it at my house with Reggie's, beer, a pool cue and Feb," Colt called back, not looking up as he spoke, not giving a shit who heard. He hit the bottom, strode through the elegant foyer and right out the door.

Colt carried the six-pack to the front door, Feb carried Reggie's pizza box.

The minute they hit the room, they were assaulted by paint fumes.

"Oh shit," Feb muttered and Colt smiled.

He closed and locked the door behind them and when he turned, she was already headed toward the kitchen. He got there as she dropped the box on the counter. He put the beer in the fridge, grabbed her hand in his and tugged her out of the kitchen.

She tugged back while she said, "Colt."

Wilson hit the living room and let out a loud meow.

"Quiet pookie," Feb said to her cat.

"Pookie?" Colt asked over his shoulder, dragging her into the hall.

She gave him a look and asked, "You wanna tell me why—?"

She stopped talking when he halted at the door of the second bedroom and pulled her beside him. Then he reached in and turned on the light.

In the middle of the room was a mattress and box springs on a basic steel bed frame. The mattress and box springs had plastic on them. There was nothing else in the room and the walls had been given a basecoat.

"Guess you're getting a guest room," Feb noted.

Colt stared. The place had been chock-full of stuff, most of it he didn't even remember what it was. To have it cleared, a basecoat and new furniture, all in one day, was a miracle.

"Your mother doesn't fuck around," Colt remarked.

"I hope you didn't have anything in there that was precious."

Colt looked at her and said, "The only things precious in life breathe."

Colt watched as she stopped breathing and stared at him direct in the eye in that way she'd been doing lately. Her gaze filled with surprise and something more. Something welcoming. Something he hoped to hell was the invitation it seemed to be.

He still had her hand in his and he reached back into the room with his other one, turned out the light then guided her back to the kitchen where he let her go.

She went to the pizza box, he went to the beer.

"You got a choice, Feb. You can eat some Reggie's and then I can give you some shit news, or I can give you some shit news and then you can eat some Reggie's."

He turned from the fridge with two bottles in one hand and saw her drop the lid of the box back on the pizza, her neck twisted, eyes on him.

"Shit news, then Reggie's," she answered, her voice quiet but shaky. She was preparing.

He used the heel of his hand and the lip of the counter to snap off the caps on the beers and, when he turned to hand her hers, she was still staring at the counter.

"I wondered what all those marks were." She looked at Colt. "You need a bottle opener."

"Got one. It's over there." He pointed to a drawer across the kitchen. "Fridge is over here." He jerked a thumb to the fridge and he felt his words were all that needed to be said.

She walked to him, took her beer from his hand then walked to the drawer, rifled through it, pulled out a bottle opener and walked back to him. Reaching around him and up, she put the bottle opener on the top of the fridge and stepped away.

"Now it's up there," she said.

Colt did two things. He threw out an arm to hook around her waist, pulling her body to his and he burst out laughing.

Feb's body jerked against his arm and he tightened it. She went still and looked up at him. He quit laughing, gave her a look and then took a tug off his beer.

"Shit news," he said when he dropped his beer hand.

She took a tug off her beer, not taking her eyes from him.

"Marie Lowe, Denny's wife, was found murdered in her bed today." Feb closed her eyes but Colt kept talking, the faster he got this shit out the better. "She'd been dead awhile, days, maybe longer. She was probably his first."

Feb opened her eyes and said, "I had nothing against her. I didn't even know her."

"I reckon this was all his."

She nodded and asked, "Is there more?"

"Don't know a lot. They were just starting to investigate the scene when I got there. I went. I left. I came and got you. Nothin' I could do."

Her gaze drifted over his shoulder and she whispered, "Four."

"Feb?"

Her gaze came back and she said, "Four people and a dog."

Colt's arm grew tight again and he nodded.

"How long were they married?" she asked.

"Awhile," he answered.

"Why her?"

"Don't know. We'll know more tomorrow."

Her gaze drifted back over his shoulder.

"Marie Lowe," she said softly, trying the name out on her tongue and he didn't figure she liked how it tasted.

"Reggie's, baby," he said just as softly and her eyes came back to his again.

"Reggie's," she replied.

⟵⟶

That night Colt, who thought he knew most everything, learned a few things about February Owens.

For starters, first chance she got she took off her jewelry. She stood at his kitchen counter, her plate on the counter filled with Reggie slices, and lifted her hands, taking off the choker which Colt saw fastened with a snap. Then went the earrings. Then the bracelets. Last, the rings.

She set them on his kitchen counter, grabbed her plate and beer and wandered into the den. But Colt stood there for several beats staring at her tangle of jewelry sitting on his counter, laid there by Feb like she'd done it every night for years and a feeling swirled around his chest. He didn't get it just then, it would take him to later that night. All he knew was, it was far from cold.

Then he found out during their four games that she could play pool when she was concentrating. She beat him once, the other three games he took but he didn't whip her ass.

They were games that went slow because they were eating, drinking, talking and Feb was wandering around his house looking at the photos he had, some of them Melanie framed for him and left behind, none of them had Melanie in the picture but some of them had Feb. It was Melanie's way of saying she didn't feel Feb was a threat but Colt knew, deep down, she did.

Others were from Delilah who took photos all the time, on special occasions, during times at the lake or even when they weren't doing anything at all, just jacking around at her and Morrie's house, Colt's, Jack and Jackie's, at the park. Every birthday and Christmas, Dee'd have the best of them framed and she'd give them to him, always telling him she never knew how to shop for him. Colt always telling her the truth, she gave him what he wanted.

Others were from Jackie, not many. They were older photos when times were good between them all, but there were only a few. He knew

Jackie wanted him to remember the good times with Feb but she didn't want to cause him pain.

Feb surprised Colt by grabbing the frames or looking at them on the wall and reminiscing, sometimes she'd do it with a smile, sometimes she'd laugh. She didn't hold herself guarded. She acted like there was nothing to fear and nothing to hide.

It was her laugh that started him understanding what it was about her jewelry on his counter that made that feeling steal through his chest. It wasn't Feb's laughter from days gone by. It was coming more frequent now, it was different and Colt understood the change. It was a new kind of laughter because it was more experienced, worldly, husky, deeper, *womanly*. It wasn't the laughter of a girl who took a life filled with laughter for granted. It was the laughter of a woman who knew any laughter at all was a gift.

But it was their conversation about Darryl that made him finally comprehend his feelings about the jewelry.

He'd commented she should let Darryl go, saying straight out the man was a liability.

Feb lined up a shot, her torso bent over the table, her fine ass on display in her jeans. "Can't do that," she said and pocketed the three.

"Feb, I see him fuck up all the time. Folks even talk about it. You and Morrie gotta see it more than me."

She was roaming the table, eyes scanning for her next shot, and she said, "Sure. Still, can't do it."

Colt saw her shot the minute she honed in on it and prepared to line it up.

"February," he said before her full concentration needed to be at the table. "He's an ex-con and a—"

She straightened, put the bottom of her cue to the floor, her fist wrapped around it. She tucked it to her front and looked him direct in the eye.

"Yeah, Colt, he's an ex-con and sometimes idiot. Dad brought him in when no one else would take him."

Colt started to speak but Feb kept going.

"He's also an ex-con with a family he's tryin' to keep fed, a wife he's tryin' to keep from leavin'. He's an ex-con. Wouldn't find a job with anyone else, he didn't have us. If he found it, they wouldn't keep him. He's an ex-con tryin' to keep on the straight and narrow, somethin' would be difficult for him to do if we let him go and his life fell apart. He forgets to take out the trash, forgets orders halfway through, misplaces delivery notices he's signed for. But none of that's as important as a man who loves his family and wants a decent life."

Colt couldn't argue with that and he didn't. Feb knew the conversation was over, took her shot and didn't miss.

When she circled the table looking for her next one was when it hit him and he knew.

The kiss on Sunday morning he gave her wasn't about her rolling her eyes at him, reminding him how she used to be. The kiss that morning was the same. Colt climbing into bed with her last night and having pizza and beer with her now, the same.

He'd avoided the conversation they needed to have because he had no fucking clue why one day he'd known in a dark place in his soul there would be no February and Colt and he wasn't going to go back there, and the next day he was kissing her, flirting with her, giving her the family day she needed to keep her shit together.

Now he knew that feeling that stole around his chest at looking at her jewelry wasn't about going back to the February and Colt there used to be.

It was about finding the February and Colt there could be.

It was about that jewelry being there when he got up in the morning because she laid it there when she got home at night. It was about the woman she was now, not the girl she used to be. It was about a woman who'd make him toast and pour coffee in a travel mug when he needed to get to work. A woman who'd listen to his day and take his mind off it with a hand on his neck, a bourbon on ice, a constitution that could take the shit he saw every day and, after, challenging him to a game of pool. A woman who'd pay a man to work in her bar who fucked up just because she knew his life wouldn't be what he needed it to be if she didn't. And a woman whose best day was a day with her family and friends around her doing nothing but talking, laughing and being together.

He knew it was also about their history, the fact that the girl he once knew was in there, buried, maybe never to come out again but that didn't erase the history they shared and the fact that she was Feb.

But it was more about what was happening in the right here and now, who he was and who she'd become and the fact that he liked it.

And he knew, he played it right, he could take the advantage Jack said there was to be taken.

And he was going to take it.

After he beat her game four, she saw him stifle a yawn and her eyes got as soft as her voice when she asked, "How much sleep you get last night?"

He didn't lie. "'Bout three hours."

She took her cue to the rack on the wall and stowed it, saying, "You need your rest."

She wasn't wrong but he wanted that rest to come with her in his bed, those two silver necklaces she didn't take off jingling as she moved. The ones he suspected she never took off. They had delicate chains and from one dangled a chunky, oblong charm proclaiming her a "party doll." The other one a disc, not chunky, with a heart made out of hammered copper on it, a flower etched around the edges of the heart, the word on it contradicting her other charm, announcing the complexity of the woman wearing them. It said "peace" at the top of the heart.

Colt, however, suspected she let him get away with climbing into bed with her after she fell asleep when she had another load of shit dumped on her finding out Denny Lowe had been in her house, but she wouldn't allow it again when she was awake and had her faculties about her. And in order to play it right, he wasn't going to push it.

"You goin' to bed?" he asked and she eyed him, dubious about where he was going with his question.

"Gonna clean up the pizza and yeah, me and Wilson could use an early night."

"I'll change while you clean up," he told her and felt her eyes on him as he walked away.

He saw the bed made when he hit his bedroom. His clothes from last night, which he'd thrown on the floor, had disappeared. His shorts were in the laundry hamper. He got another pair and noticed her journal, pen beside it, on the nightstand. A book, the title he couldn't see, on top. Some tub of something next to it. He smiled to himself as that warm feeling swirled deeper through his chest.

She was in the kitchen when he walked out carrying the blanket and pillow that either Feb or Jackie put away in the hall closet.

She eyed the blanket and then her gaze came to him. He didn't see relief. He saw something else, not disappointment exactly, but close.

She'd turned out the lights in the den and now she left the kitchen, flipping that switch too.

"'Night, Colt," she murmured as he flicked the blanket over the couch. She didn't quite meet his eyes but she wasn't avoiding them for the same reasons she used to and he smiled to himself again.

"Nice night, Feb," he replied and her eyes jerked to his, a small movement indicating either embarrassment or the depth of some unknown emotion but it was there. It was solidified when she lifted her hand and tucked her hair behind her ear, self-conscious definitely and maybe even shy. It made the woman Feb was seem almost girlish and Colt liked that too.

She nodded. "Yeah, it was good." She looked away and finished, "Sleep well."

Colt settled in and Feb closed the door behind her. He listened to her going about her business but even when the noises stopped, the light didn't go out. Either she was reading or writing in her journal. He doubted it was the journal. She'd think twice about sharing her thoughts with the page now, thanks to Denny Lowe, the sick fuck.

Colt's mind went from Denny to Amy.

Instinct told Colt they were both caught up in this shit with Feb. How Amy factored into it, Colt didn't know and he couldn't imagine knowing the little he knew about her. But both Denny and Amy had disappeared, Denny for a murder spree, Amy into thin air.

That morning on his way to Indy, Colt had called Dave Connolly at the bank. Dave said Amy called in sick again and she sounded it. But, Dave told him, she did it through voicemail, left a message on Sunday, saying she was real bad and was going to see Doc on Monday. Colt had asked Dave if Amy had any particular friend at the bank, a customer she seemed to chat with more than others, a colleague she seemed partial to, even if it was just a might.

Dave's answer was chilling. He said she talked with Angie when she was in. Sometimes they'd chat for a good long while if they weren't busy.

Other than that, if Amy was close to anyone, it was Julie McCall.

Colt hadn't had time that day to stop by Amy's place, call Doc's to see if Amy came in or go to the bank to talk to Julie McCall, but he scratched it on his mental schedule to do first thing tomorrow.

On that thought, the light switched out in his bedroom.

Ten minutes later, he was still awake when his phone rang.

He picked it up, glanced at the display, flipped it open and put it to his ear. "Sully."

"Got the stressor," Sully said.

"What?"

"Marie Lowe's next door neighbor is also a close friend. She was freaked when she found out Marie was dead but, even freaked, Chris thought she acted like she wasn't really surprised. Chris called me in and it took a while, she waited for her husband to come home from the gym, he wasn't happy we were there. There were words. They had a private chat, but finally we convinced her to spill."

"What'd she spill?"

"Part of it we know, Denny Lowe's a sick fuck in the sex department. Couldn't get it up when they first got married, honeymoon was a disaster, by the way. She didn't fuck him before they got married. Makes a case for trying out the goods before you buy."

Colt clenched his teeth at Sully's innocent comment.

He'd never had sex with Feb even after all those years together. They'd done everything but the deed and he didn't let her take him in her mouth and he never took her with his. They slept together and screwed around all the time. He made her come with his fingers; she'd made him come with her hand. He'd had his mouth nearly everywhere on her, same with Feb on him.

But Colt had made the decision, a stupid one he thought after she broke it off, that he respected Jack too much to fuck his daughter before he put a ring on her finger.

Feb was a hot little piece even back then. She didn't like his decision but she respected it and gave into it.

This left him, essentially, a virgin at age twenty-two, something he didn't mind in the slightest when Feb was in his life, something that pissed him off royally when she waltzed out of it, went wild and started screwing everything that moved.

Sully took him from his thoughts by saying in his ear, "It came out later when Denny suggested they try things."

Sully stopped talking and Colt's body grew tight. "What things?"

"Marie didn't get it, not at the time, since they were livin' in Chicago. She wouldn't get it until about two years ago."

The warm feeling at his chest evaporated and that weight in his gut got heavier.

"What was it?"

"Role play, Colt. Prepare, my man…" Sully paused, giving Colt time. "He made her call him Alec and he called her February."

"Holy fuck," Colt whispered, forgetting the weight in his gut as he felt a shiver creep along his skin.

"Gets worse, man," Sully said quietly.

"Give it to me."

"Role play changed, got kinky, rough. Marie didn't like it but she did it because she loved him. Role play leaked out into life. There was a reason no one knows Marie Lowe and her best friend is her neighbor. He got to the point where he barely let her go out, not without him. Thinkin' about it, man, I'd see them around, but I never saw her by herself. Not even at the store."

Colt hadn't either.

"The neighbor, name's Carly," Sully went on, "said that Marie finally figured it out. Marie came over one day, an absolute mess, cryin' and car-ryin' on. Carly calmed her down and Marie said she had an appointment at the hair dresser but popped into Meems' to get a coffee. It was morning, Feb was there. You came in and before you left, you said something like, 'Hey, February, tell Morrie so and so,' and Feb said, 'Sure, Alec.' It freaked Carly out so much, because it freaked Marie out so much, she remembered what Marie told her word for word."

"That's because it's freaky, Sully," Colt spoke the truth.

"Well, yeah," Sully agreed. "This is where it gets scary, though these two couldn't have known it would."

"Go on."

"They decided to find out what the deal was with Denny, Feb and you. Carly said Marie was allowed to go out, get her hair done, manicures, stuff like that, shit Denny wouldn't want to do with her. Marie asked questions, so did Carly, they found out a lot about you two."

Colt wasn't surprised. Townsfolk talked, Colt knew that and no matter how many years slid by, Feb and Colt were always a favorite topic of conversation.

Sully continued. "They never understood it, or at least not what it had to do with Denny. Marie got fed up playing sleuth and told Carly she was gonna confront Denny with it. Find out. She was getting ready to leave. She was done with the rough sex, the games, him only gettin' hard if she called him your name. Him never saying hers when he was doin' her."

"So she confronted him and he went into a rage."

"That's what I figure."

"You find anything in the house?"

"Big house, lots to go through. No shrines to Feb, no pictures of her, nothin' that would link him to her, though they're still at it. And we don't know why he was withdrawing money which started a while ago, before he killed Marie. Andy thinks Marie's been dead over a week. We found out their cleaner was in Texas last week, visiting family. Denny must've forgot about her Monday visits."

"Denny probably didn't hire her or think about the house gettin' cleaned," Colt noted.

"Yeah," Sully said.

"That all you got?"

"Bit more, nothin' big. Marie was liked in the 'hood. Neighbors were upset, said she was sweet. Made good cookies. Always remembered their kids' birthdays and would get them cards and generous gift certificates. She went visiting a lot, considerin' her whole world was mostly that street. Denny, not so much. He'd attend a dinner party but mostly they said he was quiet and he wasn't popular. Always choppin' wood."

Colt could imagine.

"Anything else?" Colt asked.

"Her parents are comin' down, spendin' the night at the Holiday Inn by the highway," Sully answered. "We got an interview set up first thing

181

tomorrow. And Feds are at Denny's office as we speak. Took the head man away from his dinner table to go open up the offices. I'll know more tomorrow."

"What're they doin' about findin' this guy?"

"APB. Got his picture circulating, description, info about his car, had agents all over stop by different places Feb worked, asking questions, flashing his picture, leaving warnings. So far, nothin'. Nowakowski called, said it wouldn't hurt if Feb made another list."

Colt clenched his teeth again, not looking forward to asking Feb to do that.

"Got anything else for me tonight?"

"Nope, but I'll call you when I know more tomorrow."

"Thanks."

"How was Reggie's, beer and Feb?" Sully asked, his tone deceptively casual. Sharing serious information work voice gone, he now sounded nosy.

"You turn into a woman since I last saw you?" Colt asked back.

He heard Sully's chuckle before he said, "Just curious."

"Like I said, you'll know when I know."

"Shit, Lorraine's gonna be pissed. She told me to get something meaty."

"Tell Raine she's goin' empty-handed to the coffee klatch tomorrow."

"Like I said, she's gonna be pissed."

Colt didn't try to stop his smile.

"Later."

"Later."

Colt looked to the hall before he dropped his phone on the table and settled back, half expecting to see Feb standing there. But she wasn't probably because she took one of Doc's pills.

Therefore it was a surprise when, not a minute later, the door opened and he heard Feb's soft footfalls on the carpet in the dark.

He expected she was going to the kitchen for a glass of water or coming out to find out about the phone call.

She didn't do either.

She stopped, he reckoned, at the doorway to the hall and didn't move further.

He got up on both his elbows. "Feb?"

"Colt."

He waited. He didn't intend to share with her any of the shit Sully shared with him. And her new list could wait for the morning.

"Everything okay?" he asked.

"No."

"Trouble sleeping?"

She moved. He saw her silhouette come forward. She stopped by the side of the couch and he felt her eyes as she looked down at him.

"The phone call—"

"It's all good, February," he lied before he told the truth. "They're makin' progress."

She pulled in breath. Then she let it out.

Then she suddenly sat down on the couch by his hip.

"Feb—"

He saw her arm move and then he felt her hand land dead center on his chest.

"Colt," she said, her voice a voice he never heard from her before. Lower, so husky it was almost scratchy, communicating need.

He didn't know if he was reading her right and he didn't care. He'd deal with the consequences later if they were bad. If they were good, he wasn't missing the opportunity.

He pushed up to sitting, her hand sliding up his chest and he wrapped a hand around the back of her head. He pulled her mouth to his and felt her head tilt in his hand, preparing, ready.

Fucking brilliant.

The instant her lips hit his, they opened and he slid his tongue inside. As he felt his cock start to get hard at the mere taste of her, he felt her fingers curl around his neck, tight, holding on, just as she pressed her chest against his.

She wanted it, she'd come looking for it and she was going to get it.

He'd take her mouth on the couch but he was going to fuck her in his bed.

He broke free of her mouth and tossed back the blanket, throwing his legs over the side of the couch, straightening. She came up with him, turning toward him.

"Colt—" she started.

But he yanked her into his arms, his mouth came back down, hers opened back up and there it was. The need in her kiss, the same he expected she felt in his. So much, she moaned in his mouth, and just like the first time she did it, it felt fucking unbelievable.

His hands slid over her sweet ass then down. She knew what he wanted and put her hands on his shoulders, using them to deepen the momentum when she hopped up. He caught her ass in his hands and she circled his hips with her legs, his shoulders with her arms, both tight, holding on.

All of this happened without them breaking the kiss.

He turned and carried her to his bedroom and he wished the lights were on. He wanted to see her when he fucked her. But he wasn't going to waste the time to do it.

She was in just as much of a hurry. When they hit the room, she lifted her head, breaking contact with his mouth and took her arms from around his shoulders. Her hands going to her shirt, she yanked it over her head and tossed it aside.

Good Christ, she did something else like that, he was going to come like he did when he was eighteen and she jacked him off the first time, an endeavor that took her about sixty seconds.

He planted a knee in the bed then he planted her ass in it then he pulled away, hooking his fingers in her panties as he went. He yanked them down her legs and tossed them aside, again wishing he could see more than her dark form but he'd go with touch and taste...for now.

He didn't bother with his shorts and he didn't bother with kissing her again. He was impatient, he wanted a taste of her, he'd waited a long fucking time and that wait was finally over. Colt spread her legs with his hands at her inner thighs and put his mouth to her. She bucked against him and he heard her moan then he heard her necklaces jingle and he liked it so much, he growled against her.

Feb moaned again.

He wasn't gentle, he sucked her clit hard, buried his tongue in deep. He pulled her legs over his shoulders and she dug her heels in, using his back as leverage to rock herself against his mouth, her hands in his hair, holding him to her. So hot, so sweet, that need, it was fucking fantastic.

He was pleased to find she was just as desperate for it as he was. She came against his mouth within minutes and when she did he sucked her clit harder and her moans turned to gasps.

Colt disengaged, yanked off his shorts and came up over her, grabbing her by her pits and hauling her up the bed until her head hit the pillows. Feb was still climaxing when he took his cock in his hand and guided the tip inside. Then he surged forward and buried himself deep.

Yep.

Absolutely…fucking…fantastic.

"Alec," she breathed.

That was it. If he had any control, it was gone when she said his name. He fucked her as hard as he'd sucked her and she wrapped her legs around his hips, her arms around his back, one hand sliding up and into his hair, those fucking necklaces clinking, a little gasp coming every time he drove in deep.

He wrapped one arm around her head to hold her still so he could go deeper, put his other hand between them and found her again with his finger.

"No, too much," she whispered, her hips rearing.

"Fuck that, baby, you're coming with me."

"Alec, I've already—"

"Come with me, Feb," he coaxed. "Hurry baby."

Her breath caught, her hips moved with his and she let go.

"Too much," she whispered again, but she meant something different this time.

"That's it, honey, you're findin' it."

"Oh my God, Alec." Shock stark in her voice, shock mixed with hunger. She'd never had this before. "It's happening again. I'm gonna—"

She convulsed around his cock and it felt so fucking great he nearly forgot everything just feeling it. But he had the presence of mind to slam his mouth down on hers to capture the moans, doing so sending him over the edge and his world exploded.

When he came down he felt her clutching his cock inside her, the sweet ripple of it just as beautiful as her long legs still locked tight around him, her arms holding him, her fingers now sifting through his hair like she was memorizing the feel.

His fingers slid deeper between them and she made a low noise in his ear as they went. He was gliding, gently now, in and out of her. He slid his fingers around the root of his cock then against her, feeling her wetness, their connection, liking it, actually fucking loving it, before he pulled his hand away.

His face was in her neck, he moved and kissed the hinge of her jaw then moved again and he touched his lips to hers.

He looked at the angles of her shadowed face in the dark.

She kept him locked in her arms and legs.

"You okay?" he asked.

"Mm-hmm," she answered, her hand smoothing through his hair and around, her fingertips gliding across his jaw. "I'm sorry I called you Alec."

Colt gave a short laugh, pulled out and rolled, his arms going around her, bringing her with him. The covers were mussed from her being in bed. He moved his body and Feb's until he had the covers out from under and pulled them over, settling on his back, tucking her into his side.

She rested her head on his shoulder and her arm around his stomach.

"Don't be."

"What?"

"Don't be sorry you called me Alec."

"You don't like it."

"I'm findin' I don't mind."

He felt her muscles tighten and she said slowly, "Things have changed."

Damn straight they had.

His arm, wrapped around her waist, hand at the small of her back, dipped down so her ass was in his hand and he squeezed.

"You're Colt now," she whispered.

"Feb—"

"And um..." she started hurriedly, in a rush to get it out because he knew, if she didn't share now, she never would, "I *like* Colt."

Colt closed his eyes tight.

When he opened them and stared blindly into the dark, he said, "Make you a deal, honey."

"What's that?"

"You can call me Colt but, when I'm fuckin' you, you call me Alec."

He heard and felt her draw in breath. She held it a long time. Then she let it go and her body relaxed against his.

"In fact, any time you're in this bed, baby, you can call me Alec. I'm fuckin' you or not."

She settled deeper into him, murmuring, "Don't be an asshole…" She paused then finished, "Alec."

He laughed and her arm tightened around his stomach.

"Go to sleep, baby," he urged.

"Okay."

He listened to her breathe and he felt Wilson, who had wisely kept away for the last twenty minutes, jumped on the bed and settled. Colt felt the cat's weight against his foot, the one that Feb's feet were tangled with.

Wilson started purring.

February, surprisingly for an insomniac, became a dead weight against his side within minutes.

And Colt thought it had been a fuckuva long time, waiting for Feb to let him back in. But he decided it was well worth the wait because being in Feb was fucking spectacular.

Seven

AMY

I woke up in the same position I fell asleep. Colt's hand though, was no longer on my ass but resting heavy on my hip. Wilson was at our feet.

I knew that day it would be time to share. Not with Colt. With Jessie, Meems or Delilah.

Because I fucked up royally last night.

Last night, lying in Colt's bed, the night we shared replaying in my head, the night before, the phone calls that day, the kisses, the fact that this was all coming from Colt—just thinking about all of it turned me on. So much, I considered taking care of myself.

Before I could, his phone rang and I heard the murmur of his voice and I knew, I just knew, it was about me. It was about Colt taking care of me. Colt keeping me safe. Colt sleeping three hours and taking phone calls late in an all-out effort to end my nightmare.

So I waited for the call to end and I knew what I was going to do. I didn't come to the decision. I just knew I was going to do it. I didn't think about it because thinking about it would stop me from doing it and I didn't want anything to stop me.

It wasn't smart. It was stupid but I wanted it and I had the feeling Colt wanted it, I was going to give it to him and I'd worry about it later.

The same old stupid February.

So I did it.

Now there I was and it was all on the line, with family, with friends, with Colt.

I should have waited to see how it played out, what would happen after all of this shit was over.

But I didn't.

Same old stupid February.

I moved carefully, rolling away from him, deciding I needed yoga or tequila. Seeing as it was morning, I'd have to pick yoga. Though I would have preferred tequila.

My roll placed my back to him. I was nowhere near the other side of the bed when he caught me with an arm around my waist.

"Where you goin'?" His voice was gruff with sleep and it was at my ear because he'd pulled me back into his body.

"Feed Wilson," I told him.

His other arm slid under me. "Wilson can wait."

"Wilson doesn't like—"

I stopped speaking because his hands moved, one down my belly to between my legs, one up to cup my breast. Then his finger and thumb closed on my nipple and at the feel of it, so magnificent, I automatically pressed my ass into his groin and arched my back to push my breast into his hand.

"That's my girl," he whispered in my ear and kissed my neck and his words accompanied by his fingers worked sheer magic.

It didn't take long before I was riding his hand, my neck twisted, my face pressed in the pillows to stifle my moans.

"Give me your mouth, Feb," Colt demanded, and I didn't make him wait. Immediately, my neck twisted the other way.

He pushed up and kissed me and it was better than any kiss before, which was saying something. Better than any kiss from him, better than any kiss I'd ever had. It was the best.

His mouth broke from mine as my hips started jerking.

"That's it, take yourself there," he encouraged against my mouth.

"Alec."

"That's it baby."

My hips reared. I was close and getting desperate.

"Alec." His name sounded like a plea.

"You want my cock?"

"Yes," I whispered. I could feel it, hard, pressing against my ass and I knew what it felt like driving in deep and I wanted it more than breath.

"Tilt your ass, honey."

I did as I was told. He gave me what I wanted and slid inside, his hand between my legs still working me. His other hand slid up to my jaw, keeping my neck twisted. He was thrusting. I was gasping, closer, reaching for it.

Colt's gravelly words gave it to me. "Come around my cock, Feb."

Again, I did as I was told.

It had never been better. He was the best I ever had.

And last night was even better, coming twice, long, hard, in quick succession, unheard of, unbelievable, brilliant.

This time, more of the same, nothing like it. Soul shattering.

And I knew it wasn't just because it was great. I knew it was because it was Colt.

I came down and kept my ass offered to him as he continued thrusting, my hand moving down his arm, going between my legs, covering his, holding our hands together, feeling him driving in and out of me.

"You feel beautiful," I whispered and it was the truth.

"Baby," he growled.

My hand tightened on his. "Nothing like it, Alec. Nothing better than you."

He buried himself deep and groaned into my hair and I squeezed his hand even tighter.

He settled into my back, his hips moving gently like last night, gliding out an inch then coming back in, keeping the connection while giving me a sweet, intimate caress.

I liked it, too much. I was right, he felt beautiful.

I was so stupid.

"Next time," Colt said into the back of my hair, sounding sated yet weirdly disgruntled, "I'm gonna fuck you so I can see you when you come."

I wanted to be the smart February who declared there'd be no next time. But instead I was the stupid February who knew there would definitely be a next time, no matter what was at stake, even if what was at stake was everything.

"Babe, I need to feed Wilson," I whispered though Wilson was now gone and I couldn't hear him meowing, which was strange.

Colt's arms grew tight before they grew lax.

"I'm gonna sleep in." He moved and I knew it was to bend when he kissed my shoulder blade. "Wake me in an hour?"

It was a request so I said, "Sure."

He slid out of me, his arms giving me another squeeze as he did and when he let go I scooted off the bed.

I made the mistake of turning to look at him. Colt was up on a forearm, just a few inches, and his eyes were drifting over my body. I didn't know what he saw. I'd never been particularly modest, I didn't go around flaunting it, but with a lover I also didn't hide it.

With Colt, it was different. I wanted him to see what he wanted to see. I wasn't sixteen anymore, not even twenty, hell, not even thirty. He wasn't either but his body was fantastic, better than back then, bulkier, stronger. I wanted him to think the same thing and I couldn't be certain he did.

I rushed to my shirt and yanked it on. Then I did the same with my panties and I started to the door.

"Baby, come here," Colt called and I made another mistake and turned again.

He was fully up on a forearm, his hair messy, his face gentle.

I'd touched his hair last night and I'd forgotten how it felt, thick and soft, long enough for me to trail my fingers through it. I loved Colt's hair, always did.

Looking in his gentle eyes, feeling the specter of his hair sliding along my fingers, still feeling him inside me, feeling sweetly bruised between my legs and liking it, all of it, made my feet take me to him.

I planted a knee in the bed, leaning forward. I did this all without thinking about it. His soft call, his look, the memory of what we'd shared, it was like an invisible lasso, roping me in.

He reached out, his hand wrapped around the back of my head and he brought me down to kiss me, a sweet touch of tongues before his mouth disengaged and he moved back an inch.

"I'll be in the mood for more than toast when I get up," he told me.

"Gotcha," I replied, deciding that, if he wanted more than toast, he would get it. I'd make him a breakfast smorgasbord. I'd comb the woods for truffles on my hands and knees, nose to the forest floor if that's what he wanted.

He grinned and let me go.

And I fled the room but tried to do it looking like I wasn't.

An hour later I was back in the room.

It wasn't the first time I came back.

After feeding a surprisingly quiet Wilson (who seemed to be giving a mind to my parents, who were to my horror for some reason sleeping on the pull out couch in the living room, Dad snoring softly), I'd gone back to the room.

Colt had been asleep on his stomach, one knee lifted, one arm thrown out. He looked good in his sleep but he looked good all the time so I shouldn't have been surprised.

But there was something about him sleeping, not like it was when we were younger and I used to wake sometimes and watch him sleep for a while and remind myself of all the reasons I loved him before I went back into a doze. Now it seemed strange to see his energy shut down like it'd been switched off, because it was so much a part of him. Colt, who I'd known since he was five, was suddenly all new to me.

I'd taken my yoga clothes into the bathroom, brushed my teeth, washed my face and changed. Then I quietly left to make coffee, scan the contents of the fridge for ideas for Colt's breakfast smorgasbord and try to be quiet while doing breakfast prep work so as not to awaken my loved ones in the house. All of whom were there to keep me together, keep me safe, keep me strong.

But now it was time to wake Colt and I had no idea how to do it.

I sat on the bed and leaned deep. He was far away but I wanted to be at his front not his back so I could see him as he woke. I reached out a hand and slid my fingertips around his ear, something I'd do when he was agitated years ago. Pissed at something he heard his mom did. Anxious and trying not to show it when his dad killed those kids while drunk driving and got arrested, put on trial and thrown in prison. It always worked, my touch, and back then when I did it, it made me feel like I had magical powers.

His eyes opened at my touch and he half rolled.

"Sorry, babe, it's been an hour," I whispered and gave him a smile. "I'll make breakfast."

I pulled away and started to exit the bed when his arm came around my waist and I was flying back, surprised my body was out of control. My legs went flying in the air, my back hit his chest, my ass collided with his hip and then I slid as he twisted me around. My back landed on the bed and Colt's torso leaned into mine, my thighs over his hips, his mouth went to my neck and he kissed me there.

"Colt—"

His hand slid down my side and he lifted his head so his eyes could watch it move. "What's this?"

I looked down wondering if I spilled coffee on my top; it wouldn't have been the first time.

"What?"

"What you're wearing."

I looked back at his face. "Yoga outfit."

His eyes moved to mine. "I like it."

"Colt—"

"It's tight," he noted, his hand moving along the material at my ribs.

"Colt—"

His hand moved up and I drew in breath when he palmed my breast and his fingertips slid across the top edge of my yoga camisole. "Cleavage."

I couldn't help it, I smiled. "You act like you've never seen cleavage before."

"Seen it, even seen a hint of yours, baby. But never had you in my bed so I could see it close up."

He had, but just not recently.

"Colt—"

"And touch it."

I rolled my eyes.

"Nice," he finished.

His word gave me a curl between my legs.

Still, I said, "You have bad guys to pursue and I have to make you breakfast so you don't faint from malnutrition while doing it, so let me up."

He grinned at me. "Never fainted in my life, Feb."

"Well, let's not start today."

He didn't stop grinning when his head bent and he kissed me. It wasn't brief, a touch of the tongues, but deep and thorough and I liked it so much, I lifted my hand and slid it into his hair to lock his mouth to mine.

When he was done with my mouth, he pulled away, his eyes scanned my face and his expression got serious.

"We need to talk, Feb."

Shit. He was right. Still, I didn't want to talk, not then, not ever. I was willing to ride this out, see where it went, bear the consequences if it went bad. But I didn't want to talk about it.

"I'll make reservations at Costa's tonight," he went on.

"Costa's?" I whispered, forgetting I didn't want to talk.

As I mentioned, I loved Costa's and hadn't been there for years, not since Mom and Dad's 40th Wedding Anniversary.

His grin came back and he said, "Yeah."

"Morrie took Dee and the kids there last night."

"I know. Morrie isn't fucking around in his quest to take the 'trial' out of their trial reconciliation."

"I noticed," I replied but I was thinking about Colt and me at Costa's.

You didn't mess around when you went to Costa's. Anyone seeing us there would know it was a date or possibly think we were back together. And the last couple of days it seemed, even though it was weird, that Colt and I were dating. And last night it couldn't be denied, Colt and I had gotten back together.

And I liked that idea so much I didn't give a thought to the talk that would happen at Costa's.

Instead, I thought of something else.

I'd have to wear something other than jeans and a t-shirt or sweater or cardigan and I hadn't worn something other than that in so long I didn't even know what I owned that I could wear. And I didn't want to go to my place to find out.

Then it hit me.

Jessie.

Jessie would see me through this latest trauma. Jessie was a master shopper. Mimi could kick the shit out of a catalogue but Jessie knew every mall from here to Chicago like the back of her hand.

"Hello? February? Are you in the room?" Colt called and his face wasn't serious anymore when I focused on him.

"I need to call Jessie."

His eyebrows drew together. "Honey, how did Costa's and us talking bring you to Jessie?"

"I need something to wear."

His head jerked with surprise then his face grew soft and he kissed me again, rolling into me, his hands moving on me, he was taking this somewhere.

Before it got there, I broke my mouth from his and whispered, "Colt, the door's open and my parents are on the pull out."

His neck twisted and he looked at the door before his eyes returned to me. "Got a rule, baby. Jack and Jackie are in the house, you're in my room, you close the door. Yeah?"

He was being very bossy. Furthermore, you could hear everything in that house. The door could be closed and we could prop a mattress against it and Mom and Dad would be able to hear every word, every sound.

Still, without hesitation, I said, "Yeah."

He rolled again, over me and off the side, his hands firm on me and taking me with him to put me on my feet. Then he turned me around and slapped my ass.

"Make me breakfast," he ordered, and I threw him a look over my shoulder and wished I hadn't. I'd seen a lot of his body when he wandered around in his shorts but I hadn't seen it all. I wasn't wrong that it was great, even better than when he was a young athlete in his prime. Unbelievable.

"Honey, you gonna stare at my cock or you gonna make me breakfast?" Colt asked, I jumped and I could swear I felt my cheeks get warm. I was a forty-two year old woman. What was wrong with me?

"Right," I mumbled and got the hell out of there.

Dad was standing by the pull out, stretching and wearing his boxers and a wife beater. Mom was up on her ass, her back to the back of the couch, pulling her hair out of her face.

I pressed my lips together when both of their eyes came to me.

"Forgot this feelin'," Dad noted. "Draggin' your ass in the house after working 'til the mornin' hours."

"Me too," Mom replied throwing the covers back. "Bone tired."

"You owe us darlin'," Dad told me.

I was happy to owe Dad. Reggie's, beer and all that had happened with Colt last night and that morning would be worth whatever he wanted me to pay.

"Well take that times two because you'll probably need to do it again tonight," I said back and hit the kitchen.

I could have this conversation but I was on a mission. The shower was on in Colt's master bath and I didn't know how much time I had. Yesterday, Colt took no time at all getting ready. Today, he didn't have anything pressing but Colt didn't strike me as a man who primped. I could have only ten minutes.

"How's that?" Dad asked.

"Colt and I are going to Costa's," I answered.

Again the same old, stupid February. I should have kept my mouth shut.

"What?" Mom whispered and seeing as I was turning on the broiler of the oven, my head snapped up and around.

Mom was staring at me. Dad was staring down the hall.

I didn't know what they thought when they came in last night and saw the couch empty but whatever they thought didn't trouble them. Or maybe they were too tired to worry about it. Most likely they trusted Colt to take care of me.

Now, dawn was rising.

"I'll explain later. Colt's gotta get to work and I gotta make his frittata."

"Frittata?" Mom whispered again, and I sucked in breath at another display of my stupidity.

I was famous for my frittatas. When I was away, every time I came home Frittata Morning was always scratched on the schedule. Morrie, particularly, loved my frittatas. They were revered. They were like Christmas morning or a reservation at Costa's. They were a special occasion even though they were easy to make. Still, they were good, even I had to admit that.

"Mom, just…let me concentrate."

"Sure thing, honey."

I started the burner under the skillet that had pre-prepared raw, scissored bacon pieces in it, the eggs, chopped mushrooms and minced garlic would go in later. The shredded cheddar cheese I would toss on top before I slid it under the broiler.

I did this at the same time I started the toast. I was multitasking, on a mission. Why this was so important to me, I wasn't going to go there. It just was.

While I was cooking, Mom and Dad were taking turns in the hallway bathroom, Mom making the pull out, Dad pushing it back in, Mom returning the cushions.

I wasn't wrong. Colt didn't primp. Mom and Dad weren't even dressed when he came out, jeans, belt, boots, shirt, hair wet, badge on belt, blazer and shoulder holster in his hand. He threw them on the dining table and hit the kitchen as I was sliding the frittata under the broiler to finish it off.

I wondered how this would play out, me and Colt after our colossal shift having breakfast with Mom and Dad in attendance.

Colt didn't touch me as he went straight to the coffee and I tried not to be disappointed. Instead, I pulled out plates.

"Feb's giving us an impromptu Frittata Morning," Mom announced, hitting the kitchen and the coffeepot too, wearing her mom nightgown that was cotton and had cap sleeves, little flowers embroidered around the neck. It hit her at her knees and made her look like the mom she was.

"Yeah?" Colt answered and the far away way he said this made my eyes move from the cutlery drawer to him.

He was leaning against the kitchen counter, one fist wrapped around the handle of a coffee mug, this held up and forgotten. His other hand was out, his fingers poking at my jewelry. Something about him doing this, and the way he was, his neck twisted and bent, his eyes on my jewelry, his mind definitely elsewhere, made me stop and watch.

He pulled my choker free, carefully straightening it so it was flat on the countertop. He picked out my earrings, placing them together by the choker. Next came the rings, which he set in a row. He did this with what seemed like a strange reverence, fascinated by the process, his touch light on my jewelry and I felt it on each piece, as if his fingers were at my knuckles, my ears, my throat. It felt nice.

"Coffee, Jackie, I'm flaggin'," Dad said as he slid his boxer-clad ass onto one of Colt's stools.

I pulled myself together and dumped the cutlery by the plates, turning to grab the mountain of buttered toast I'd made and then turning back to place it up on the bar by Dad.

Mom gave Dad his coffee and I pulled the frittata out of the oven then switched it off. I grabbed a plate and a spatula to start serving.

"You ever have Feb's frittata, son?" I heard Dad ask Colt and I didn't look to see if he was still engrossed in my jewelry.

"Nope," Colt answered and his voice was no longer far away.

"In for a treat," Dad muttered and I slid Colt's piece on a plate, twisted and handed it to him.

"It's just essentially scrambled eggs," I said to Dad, not looking at Colt but feeling him take the plate.

"Yeah, scrambled eggs injected with a slice of fuckin' heaven," Dad replied.

I went back to serving up frittata and decided to change the subject.

"Dad, can you go by my place after the frittata and pick up my yoga mat?" I asked, still serving and handing Mom a plate, which she moved to set in front of Dad.

"Sure thing, darlin', after my mornin' constitutional."

I handed Mom her plate, grabbed my coffee and turned to Dad.

"After frittata, your constitutional, you goin' over to pick it up and coming back, me doing yoga and then getting a shower, I'll be late to open."

"Don't miss my constitutional, February," Dad said and this was true.

"You can have it when you get back," I told him and this was true too, though I doubted he'd go for it as nothing messed with his morning schedule. Not even a daughter who seriously needed the relaxation of yoga.

"Feb—"

"I'll get it," Colt said and my eyes went to him. Most of his frittata was gone, he had a forkful arrested halfway to his mouth and was looking at Dad. "There may be crime scene tape on the door and it's best I go in for it."

I forgot about that.

"Don't you have work?" I asked.

"Won't take fifteen minutes," Colt answered. "I'll get it, bring it back and then get to work."

I couldn't argue with that and didn't want to. It was nice of him and I was beginning to like the nice things he did for me. I'd been taking care of myself for a while, keeping myself to myself. I hadn't had that in a long time.

"Thanks," I said quietly and looked away.

"Jesus, darlin', you outdone yourself with this one," Dad proclaimed, mouth full.

"It's scrambled eggs, Dad."

"It's fuckin' beautiful, Feb."

"Whatever," I whispered, feeling embarrassed. This was, of course, the effect I was going for, for whatever reason, but getting it made me uncomfortable.

"Why aren't you havin' any?" Colt asked and my eyes went to him and then skittered over his shoulder.

"I don't eat before yoga," I informed him.

"Missin' out, baby," he said softly and my eyes skittered right back. I felt a warm heaviness hit me in three different places in my torso and I wondered if my camisole was holding up or if everyone could see my nipples had gotten hard.

They ate in silence and then Colt moved to take his plate to the sink. He turned, reaching around me to grab a slice of toast off the stack. He was behind me and I felt his hand hit the small of my back.

"Walk me to the door, Feb," he said in my ear.

I followed him to the dining table where he stopped, the toast in his teeth, to shrug on his holster and blazer then I followed him to the door.

He took a bite of the toast and as he chewed his other hand came to the top of my neck, under my jaw, his thumb jutting out to press under my chin and lift my face.

"Great mornin', baby," he whispered and that heady heaviness in my breasts and between my legs got headier. "Which means me askin' this is gonna suck."

"Oh shit," I said.

"Sully says Nowakowski wants you to make another list. The fifteen years you been away."

I pulled in breath through my nostrils then I let it go and nodded, which wasn't easy with his thumb at my chin.

"They'll need to know where to find 'em so if you know, even last known whereabouts, you add that to the list."

I nodded again.

He took in a breath before he said, "It'll help them to know what they did. They might be able to lock down a victimology, try to guess who's next. You'll need to record that too. Try and be thorough."

I didn't like doing this at all, but the last part I *really* didn't like.

"Give yourself some time, do it after yoga," Colt said. "You finish, you call me. Have someone walk it down to the station when you get into the bar."

I nodded again.

His face changed. I couldn't put my finger on how but, I swear to God, it seemed like he looked like he was proud of me.

"I'll call you when I get a reservation, tell you the time," he said.

I nodded yet again.

"'Tween then and now, honey, I suspect lots of shit is gonna go through your brain."

He wasn't wrong.

"Colt—"

He cut me off. "Ignore it."

I closed my eyes and opened them again when his lips touched mine.

He lifted his head an inch away and stated quietly, "This is good."

He wasn't wrong about that either.

"Promise me, whatever marches through that head of yours, you stick with me. Tonight we'll talk it out."

"Colt—"

"Don't say my name, give me your promise."

I sucked in breath, and when I let it out, I whispered, "I promise."

His thumb left my chin to trail along my cheek.

Then he said, "I'll be back soon as I can with your mat."

"Thanks."

"Later, baby."

"Later."

Then he let me go, unlocked the door and disappeared.

I turned to my parents and they were both openly watching me and more than likely had been openly watching Colt and me.

"Don't start," I warned.

"Got nothin' to say," Dad replied. "You know how we feel."

I did and that didn't help that feeling of fear that kept gnawing at my belly. Though it did make that feeling of happiness that was coating the region of my chest intensify more than a little bit.

"February," Mom called when I dropped my head to look at the floor as I walked to the kitchen.

I lifted my head to look at her.

"No matter what, we love you, you know that?"

My step stuttered but I recovered. Then I swallowed.

Then I said, "I know that."

"Now, can I have the last of the frittata?" Dad asked, eyeing my piece left in the skillet.

"Jack! That's for Feb," Mom scolded.

"She can make another one."

"Jack!"

I hit the kitchen, grabbed the skillet and tipped it over Dad's plate, sliding the last of the frittata onto his.

"We're even for last night," I said when I completed this task.

"What I saw at that door, girl, we already were," Dad replied.

Damn, but I was definitely stupid.

⌣⟶

Colt collected Feb's mat, took it to his house and took advantage of the fact that her father was in one bathroom, her mother in the other and she was alone.

Therefore, he spent some time necking with her pressed against the wall at the side of the front door. He did it until she moaned in his mouth and then he stopped, partly because he liked the idea of turning her on and then coming back to her later after she had time to let it stew. Mostly, because he liked her moaning in his mouth and if he didn't stop, he wouldn't have.

He wasn't going to think about what happened between him and Feb last night or that morning. He was going to wait and see where their conversation led tonight.

For his part, he was willing to set the past where it belonged and move on from there and he was going to do everything he could to get Feb to come around to his way of thinking.

He drove to the station, parking out back, going in the back door and up the back stairs. He checked in, checked his voicemail then he walked down the front and saw Sully in the conference room with what had to be Marie Lowe's parents.

He only gave them a glance, didn't want to get caught in what could seem like a stare. It wasn't right nor was it kind to stare at someone who'd just been tossed into the pit of grief.

He noted a lot in his glance.

He saw they were from money, which meant the house was likely not just Denny providing for his wife but his wife being a trust fund baby.

The father had finally given into age. He was letting himself go, had put on weight, didn't hold it even sitting down like he was comfortable with it in his flesh.

The mother hadn't given in. She'd had work done on her face, she was ten pounds underweight and she spent a goodly amount to keep her hair that healthy and blonde.

Their clothes were expensive and likely designer but they didn't shout it.

Marie's parents didn't have anyone to impress, the company they kept knew they were society. Even heading down to a small town on the news that their daughter had been murdered, they were put together well. Not because they gave a shit what anyone thought about them. It was habit, it was ingrained.

In his glance he also saw they were destroyed. They loved their daughter, it was clear to see and this had broken them. They weren't young anymore but they had life left in them and for the rest of it this break would never heal.

Denny Lowe had caused that and the second after Colt slid his gaze away from Marie's parents, he felt a swift rage burn through him, worse than anything he felt at what Denny did to Feb or Jack and Jackie, Morrie and him. When they caught that fucker, his family's fear and anguish would fade, time would heal their wounds. It'd leave a scar but it'd be a scar, a reminder, not an open, bleeding gash that would never close.

Only one thing Colt could do about his rage was what he intended to do.

He headed out the front door and started toward the bank. It was two blocks and still, normally he would have driven it. But he hadn't been to the gym since this business started and he found he had an abundance of energy. This shit wasn't happening, he'd be taking the day off and working out that energy in his bed with Feb. Unfortunately, this shit was happening.

Dave Connolly was in his office with some clients when Colt got there. Colt scanned the teller's stations and the name plates sitting on the high counters showed there were two Julies.

His scan also showed there was no Amy.

Colt gave Dave a chin lift and Dave gave Colt a "one minute" gesture with his hand. Colt nodded, headed back out, crossed the street and went to Mimi's to get a coffee. Mimi eyed him the minute he came in and so did half of the dozen patrons she had in line and at her tables.

"Hey, Colt."

"Meems."

Her eyes sparkled but then they usually did. Mimi VanderWal didn't often get in bad moods not since he could remember. This was likely the cause of Al's extreme devotion. Any man would count his lucky stars he woke up to that sparkle every day and went to bed beside it every night.

The sparkle turned playful and she asked loudly, "How's Feb?"

Colt shook his head but answered, "Doin' good."

"She wup your ass at pool last night?"

"She took a game."

"How many'd you have?"

"Four."

Her smile went huge. "From what I hear, that's four to you, one to her."

There it was, Mimi announcing to the entire place that after years of avoidance, Colt and Feb were now spending their time together playing pool. Most of them knew something was up, now Meems handed them another nuance.

It was time to put a lid on it. "Got work, Meems, can you get me an Americano?"

"Sure thing, you want a muffin?"

Colt decided to give her and his audience a bonus. "Nope, not hungry, had Feb's frittata this mornin'."

Mimi's eyes got wide. She knew exactly what Feb making a frittata instead of some eggs and toast meant and she hooted, "Oowee, a February Owens Frittata Morning! Don't tell Morrie, he'll be pissed."

Colt was done and his voice lowered when he said, "My coffee, Meems."

She grinned when she replied, "Gotcha."

When she finished his coffee and handed it to him, as usual he reached for his wallet.

And as usual she said, "Colt, like I always say, money's no good here. You serve and protect, I keep you caffeinated while you do it."

And as usual he dug in his wallet, took out several ones and shoved them in the tip jar.

But not as usual, when his fingers wrapped around the cardboard that surrounded the paper cup, Mimi didn't let go.

"Cheerin' for you, Colt," she said quietly, words meant for him not her customers. "Both you and Feb."

Then she let his cup go and turned away before he could say a word.

When Colt returned to the bank, Dave was free and he didn't hesitate in waving Colt into his glass-fronted office.

The minute Colt closed the door, Dave launched in, not sounding worried, sounding excited. Fuck, the man was nearly jumping up and down in his chair.

"Amy's no call-no show today."

Jesus, there it was. Amy was in thin air.

Colt, unlike Dave, *was* worried.

Seeing Angie Maroni and Marie Lowe and crime scene photos of Pete Hollister and Butch Miller would do that, considering instinct was telling him Amy was caught up in this shit. Colt barely knew her but he was learning about her and she lived her life protecting herself in a bubble of shyness. He found her hacked, he had no idea why, but it'd cut him deep.

He hid his reaction and took in Dave.

Some folk wanted nothing to do with cops or crime or crime investigation. Some did it when they had to but it was obvious they'd prefer their life had not veered down a course that would take them to a place they were involved. Some, like Dave, got off on it, their lives so small they welcomed any involvement in something bigger even if it had to do with hacked up bodies. Dave had no idea what this was about and he didn't care. He was willing to play his role in this drama no matter what it was and he was going to play it to the full.

"Julie McCall in today?" Colt asked.

"Sure, she's in," Dave answered, ever helpful.

"Sorry to trouble your business, Dave. I know you're busy but you got a place where I can talk to Julie in private?"

Dave did what Colt expected he'd do. He jumped up and rounded his desk, bobbing his head. He didn't care if his customers had to wait in line for a teller. He just cared that his life, which was mostly the same every day and he was too lazy to do shit about it to make it better, was suddenly filled with something more important, no matter he didn't know what that something was.

"Conference room," Dave motioned to a big windowed room in the corner of the bank.

"Private, Dave."

Dave's eyes got big. "Oh! Yeah, right." He thought about it and Colt clenched his teeth, thinking the guy was half moron. He had to know the bank like the back of his hand. "Staff room!" Dave announced. "Basement. No windows."

Jesus, this guy was annoying him. Unfortunately, he also needed him.

Dave led Colt to the windowless, vacant room and said he'd be right back with Julie. He didn't lie. Five minutes later, Dave walked in with one of the two Julie tellers.

"I'll leave you to it," Dave said with extreme consideration and closed the door behind him.

Julie McCall eyed him up the way a lot of women did, interest and appreciation clear on her face and she was sure to take in his ring finger. He'd had that kind of thing all his life, even when everyone knew his mother and father were drunk and no good and even when everyone knew that he was taken by Feb or, later, Melanie.

He wasn't interested in Julie McCall and there were a lot of reasons why. Most of them obvious, but they also included the fact that she was unattractive and he knew she thought the opposite.

She was lean and fit, not from being an athlete, from working out way too much to keep thin, going well past the good look of healthy to hit gaunt. She probably felt disgust for anyone overweight and had no problem saying it or showing it, mostly with her eyes, he was guessing. She was the kind to be able stare at anyone she thought inferior, do it openly and do it in a way that made them feel low.

Her hair was two shades too blonde, looking false and not suiting her coloring. It was arranged in a style too young for her years and, unlike some women whose youthful personality let them not only get away with this kind of thing but it was appealing, it made her look desperate.

Colt found, even though he hadn't spoken a word to her or she to him, he didn't like her and he couldn't have been more surprised that Amy apparently did.

"How can I help you?" she asked, solicitous and even a bit suggestive. She had all day if he wanted to take it.

"I'm Lieutenant Alec Colton."

She smiled and it was wincingly shrewd. "I know who you are."

Definitely suggestive and he didn't like that she knew who he was when he didn't know her. But then again, most everyone in town knew him. It came with his history and with the job. The last mainly because any time Monica Merriweather reported on a case he was working, she made certain his picture was included with the article in the paper.

He motioned to the table. "If you don't mind, Ms. McCall, I'd like to ask a few questions about Amy Harris."

Her eyebrows shot up. She might have thought a lot of things about him wanting to talk to her but pathologically shy Amy wasn't one of them.

"Amy?"

"Yes, Amy." He waited until she sat and he sat close to her, not because he wanted to but because playing her game would get him what he needed. "You want coffee?" he asked, his glance moving to the staff coffeepot in the corner.

"Nah, that coffee's terrible. I always wait." She eyed his cup. "I usually go to Mimi's on break."

Shared tastes. She was telling him, they had something in common.

He took a sip from his coffee before stating, "Amy's no call-no show today."

"Yeah, weird," Julie said.

"Dave says you two are close."

"Wouldn't say anyone was close to Amy but, yeah, we have a laugh every once in a while, me more than any of the other girls." She was reconsidering her casual friendship with Amy, pleased that it finally bought her something she liked.

Colt caught his lip curl and kept going. "You speak to her recently?"

"Not since we left work Friday night."

"She seem to be acting different lately?"

"How 'different?'"

"Anything."

She shook her head. "Nope, except she took that Maroni woman dying pretty hard."

"Yeah?" Colt prompted.

Julie's head tipped to the side, trying to read him, get a lock on what this was about. "Yeah. She was always nice to her. The rest of us..." She paused, her face showing her disgust as if a visit from Angie at her station tainted her in some way. "We did her business and got her to move on." She leaned in and whispered, "Skank City."

Colt tried to ignore the feel of his blood heating and went on. "They friends? You know, outside the bank."

"Not that I know of. Amy went to high school with her. Told us all she was nice, always was, she just had a tough life. But Amy's nice to everyone, much as she could be, seein' as she's screamin' shy."

"She say anything about Angie?" Colt asked.

"She wound up in this murder business?"

Fuck. He didn't want his investigating Amy to get around. He wasn't worried about the town. He was worried about Feb finding out.

"Nope, it's just she came into J&J's and she and I had a chat. She seemed distraught, I'm checkin' up on her." He forced a smile. "Occupational extra, got a worry about one of my citizens, I can do something about it."

He was talking out his ass. He just hoped she wouldn't know that.

She didn't know it. She probably spent her evenings watching *Survivor* or *Amazing Race* and rooting for the biggest asshole in both, not watching cop shows.

"Only thing I know is, she was cut up about Angie Maroni," Julie said. "Then again, anyone would be, knowin' that person for a while and them endin' up murdered."

Dead fucking end.

New direction.

It was a risk. Word about Marie was undoubtedly making the rounds. Word about Denny would be close on its heels. Soon, Julie McCall would link their chat to the murders and she'd talk, he had no doubt, and he didn't have the inclination to make any deal she would open to him to stop her mouth from running.

People were dying so he had no fucking choice.

"Do you know Denny Lowe?" he asked.

Another eyebrow raise then, "Um…yeah, sure. He's a customer."

"He come in a lot?"

"Sometimes Saturdays. He works."

"He seem partial to Amy's station?"

She shook her head, now confused. "Not really." She was thinking, trying to recall. "Actually, thinkin' about it, can't remember him ever goin' to her station at all." She focused on him again, "Though I can't be sure."

"They ever talk? She ever mention him?"

She kept shaking her head.

Christ, she was all he had and she was giving him nothing.

"'Cept…" she started.

"Yeah?" Colt prompted.

"Amy had a bit of a flip out not long ago. It was on a Saturday and it was when he came in."

Colt felt a spiral of exhilaration in his gut.

"What kind of a flip out?"

She waved her hand. "Well, Amy wasn't prone to flip outs and it wasn't a big one. She just said she needed a break early and took it but that's not her style. When she came back, she looked like she'd been crying. Didn't have to do with Mr. Lowe, though. I just remember that he was in when it happened. And I only remember because he took a big withdrawal and that doesn't happen often. Most folks can get their money from the cash machine, have to come to a station to withdraw that kind of dough and it's still unusual. Usually folks come to us to deposit, move money around, check balances, ask about or pay on their line of credit or mortgage. Stuff like that. You always remember a big withdrawal."

Colt reckoned you did, especially when you didn't have thousands of dollars in your own account which he guessed she didn't considering she wasn't wearing wedding rings but she was wearing clothes that were too expensive on a teller's salary. Envy and curiosity about how the other half lived likely baked those memories into your brain.

"You did his withdrawal?" Colt asked.

"That day, yeah."

"He talk about what it was for? Takin' a vacation? Buyin' somethin' special?"

She shook her head.

"He seem to have a preference in tellers?"

"Nope, there's just one line, folks come up to whichever one of us is open. Only Angie Maroni waited for Amy."

"That day, you know why Amy was cryin'?"

Julie shrugged. "Sure, I asked after work if she was okay. She said it was just that she was thinkin' about her boy."

It took everything Colt had not to jerk back at this news and that cold circled his chest, tight and vicious.

"Her boy?"

"Yeah, she had a kid, years ago. Put him up for adoption. She thinks about him a lot, she told me, but she doesn't get upset. She just got upset that day. Somethin' struck her and she got sad wonderin' where he was."

Colt didn't reply.

Amy Harris had a child. He had no idea.

And she'd got upset about it when Denny walked in, probably not a coincidence.

She was petite but nicely rounded. Very pretty but dark-haired. She had dark brown eyes. That and her curves were the only thing she shared with Feb. Feb was tall, blonde and her curves were more attractive considering the length of her frame and the way she held herself.

Denny Lowe wouldn't get it up for Amy Harris.

Unless while he was doing it, he was doing something else that would get him off.

Fucking hell.

Poor Amy.

"You would," Julie said, taking Colt from his thoughts. "You know, think about the kid you gave up. It's natural."

"She tell you about the kid's dad?"

"Yeah." Julie was now a font of information. "She knew him but she never told him about the kid. I wasn't around but she told me she took a sabbatical from work so no one would see her showin' and came back after it was all done."

"Why didn't she tell the dad? Weren't they together?"

"Nope, she said it was a one night stand, if you can believe that of Amy, which I couldn't at first. Thought she was jerking me around when she told me, tryin' to seem more interesting. But you could tell it was genuine. Said she didn't want him to know or anyone to know it was him. She was pro-tectin' him from something, I reckoned. Thought maybe he was married but didn't ask. She wasn't big on talkin' about it and didn't for years. Most of the girls, though, know now, even though none of us were around when Amy started here and it all went down."

This was, Colt knew, because Julie McCall had told them, the bitch.

Colt focused as Julie continued.

"Only some of the bank officers were around back then but only because, between most of 'em, they own the bank," she finished.

Colt leaned forward in order to pull out his wallet, which took him closer to her. Instead of leaning back as anyone would, she leaned forward too and he just caught another lip curl.

He sat back, flipped out his wallet and gave her a card.

"You hear from Amy, you can tell her I want to talk to her, see she's all right. Or you could just call me."

She'd call him, she heard from Amy or, he reckoned, even if she didn't.

She took the card and smiled, back to suggestive. "Sure, Lieutenant Colton."

He stood, pushing his wallet in his back pocket and grabbing his coffee. "Thank you, Ms. McCall."

He didn't offer his hand. He should have but he had what he wanted from her and he doubted there was any more to be had. Now she needed to know the limits to his friendliness.

She didn't take the hint. "Call me Julie."

He wasn't going to have the opportunity to call her anything and he found this a relief.

He just smiled and threw his arm toward the door, inviting her to precede him. Interview over.

She walked in front of him deliberately slow, drawing out her time with him and likely away from her job. She moved and he knew she wanted him to watch her ass while she was doing it. He did and almost laughed. He'd been watching Feb's ass move around her bar for the last two years and Julie McCall?

No fucking comparison.

At the top of the stairs he thanked her again, turned and gave Dave a nod. Dave was in his office with customers he was now ignoring as his eyes were glued to Colt. Before he could give his customers excuses and hightail it to Colt, Colt gave him a wave and took off.

He walked to Amy's and thought about her pregnant, having a baby and giving it up for adoption. He had no idea when this happened but he'd find out. She was working at the bank so it was after high school, maybe while Denny Lowe was in Northwestern or even later, when Denny married Marie. Like most kids whose parents didn't leave town, Colt remembered Denny came back during summer breaks and for visits before he moved home with Marie. It could have happened anytime.

There were lots of reasons women gave up kids but Amy didn't seem the type, not if she'd be crying about it years later. She was shy but she was sweet, responsible, close to her kin, she'd likely make a good mom. Something made her give up her kid and Colt worried it was something not good for Amy.

If it was because of what he worried it was, Denny had raped her or courted her and then forced rough, weird sex on her, then what this had to do with Feb and Feb's reaction to Colt being around Amy, Colt had no fucking clue.

Except if Denny called Amy February and demanded she call him Alec in return. He could see how that'd freak Amy enough to stay quiet a long while. Enough to take some time to get the courage to come forward, head to the bar, get ready to share then lose your courage when the time was right and get the fuck out of Dodge.

Still, none of this explained Feb's extreme response to seeing Amy with Colt.

He made it to Amy's to see her car still in her drive. He knocked then waited then knocked again. And repeat. Nothing and no movement at her draperies this time. He stood around long enough, checking the quiet neighborhood and letting the quiet neighborhood have the opportunity to see him again at her front door. He scanned the windows of the houses he could see, looking to see if some nose was watching just so he'd have another lead. He'd take anything. He stood around long enough for someone to come out, go to their car or come to him and ask him if he needed something.

Nothing.

So he went hunting, knocked on a few doors, both sides of her house and across the street.

No one home.

He gave up, and as he walked back to the station, his cell rang. He yanked it out of his pocket and the display said "February calling."

When Morrie gave him her number and he'd programmed it into his phone several days ago, he'd been uncertain how he felt about doing it. There was no uncertainty about how he felt about it being there now.

He flipped it open and put it to his ear. "Feb."

"List is ready. Mom's bringing it down to the station once we get to the bar."

She hated doing it he could hear it in her voice.

That's why he made his voice soft when he replied, "Okay, honey."

"You call Costa's?"

He could see she was rabid for Costa's but then again Feb liked to eat, always did. He'd noted in the last two years she still did the amount of times he saw her, Morrie, Ruthie or Darryl take off with orders and they got Reggie's or take out from Frank's or a delivery came from Shanghai Salon. You didn't get the kind of curves she had, curves he'd now seen naked and touched with his hands, from eating salads. The vision of her sliding off his bed to stand naked at its side this morning was pleasantly seared to the backs of his eyeballs and he hoped to God that burn never healed.

"Not yet."

"They get busy on a Tuesday."

They were busy every day.

"Baby, I'll call."

"They give you a song and dance about being booked, throw your police detective weight around," she advised.

He bit back his laugh and smiled into the phone. "We don't tend to do that."

"Colt, you get called out to see dead bodies for a living, you gotta get somethin' good outta that badge."

"We'll get a reservation," he told her and they would. Costa's was in another town but Stavros Costa knew Jack and Jackie from way back, Feb, Morrie and Colt too. They'd all been going there together for years. Feb's birthdays, Colt and Feb's first official date, when Colt made All-State the first time and the second, when they took sectionals, when they took regionals, the time Jackie won five hundred dollars in the lottery. Stavros knew all about Feb and Colt. If Colt called and said he and Feb were coming in for dinner, Stavros would build a table for them with his bare hands if he had to.

"All right," Feb said.

"How's your head?" Colt asked.

"My head?" Feb asked back.

"Yeah, you exhausted yet at how busy it's been in there?"

She was silent a second. Then he heard her soft, husky laughter and he felt that laughter slide through his gut straight to his dick. "Nope, not yet."

"Good."

"Gotta jump in the shower."

Now that was a pleasant thought to leave him with. He'd have to find a way to thank her.

"All right, later."

"Later."

He was walking down the sidewalk, the station in his sights, when he saw Sully walking Marie Lowe's parents to a car parked on the street. He shook the mother's hand and clapped the father lightly on the back. Sully was uncomfortable with their grief and didn't try to hide it.

There was an art to dealing with victims. You needed to show empathy while at the same time displaying professionalism. You had to say *your pain means something to me* and *I'm going to do something about it* at the same time.

Dealing with victims was the hardest part of the job, it didn't matter if their car stereo was stolen or their daughter was hacked to goo with a hatchet. They all got that lost look in their eye, their belief in the good of the world shaken. Difference was, you had your car stereo stolen, you got another one and moved on. No way to replace a daughter.

He waited for Sully at the foot of the steps and had to wait awhile because Sully watched long after their car drove away. What Colt saw in his glance of Marie's parents had sent a surge of rage through him. Sully had spent a morning visiting with them in that pit of grief, and even though he could walk out and they were there for eternity, it always took you a while to shake off the feeling of that place.

Sully caught his eye when he turned toward the station.

"You all right, Sul?" Colt asked when he got close.

"No." Sully's gaze moved away. "Denny Lowe is a goddamned cock sucking motherfucker who I'm glad's gonna burn in hell."

There you go. That pretty much said it all.

"Wanna walk down to Meems' and get a coffee?"

"I wanna hunt down Denny Lowe with a hatchet," Sully said then sighed and looked at Colt's hand. "You already got a Meems."

"It's empty."

Sully nodded. "Don't think even Meems' ginormous chocolate chip cookies would make me feel better but it's worth a try."

They walked to Mimi's and she didn't try to rib him. She took one look at Sully and was all business.

They got their order, Colt shoved more money in the tip jar and they sat at Feb's table which was in a corner, wall to one side, back to another short wall that led to an opening that allowed staff to get around the glass-fronted counter, space all around for ordering customers to stand and wait for the coffees, no table close. Feb chose it, he knew now, to build that invisible wall around, keeping out townsfolk she thought had lost respect for her. That table worked for him and Sully to keep their conversation quiet, though the morning rush was long gone and only a guy with a laptop and a mug at the table by the front window was company.

He put his coffee mug down and saw etched into the table, "Feb's Spot, sit here and die."

Meems' kids were terrors.

Still, how Feb thought the town had lost respect for her was beyond him. She may have shocked some, disappointed others, but that was a long time ago and she'd always be Feb. The woman who took her time to make Angie laugh, who told Sully she'd make him hot, honeyed whisky to soothe his cold and meant it, who kept Darryl employed when he was more burden than boon. That part of Feb had never changed and nothing she did back then could erase all that.

It was something to add to their list of things to talk about, after they got what was going on between them straight, but close after. He didn't like that she thought it and it was time to disabuse her of that notion.

"You get anything?" Colt asked after Sully had two big bites of his cookie. Colt had had several of those since Meems opened and it might be wrong, but Meems' baking helped brighten any shitty day, no matter why it was shitty. She was that good.

"Marie's Dad, Mr. Todd, liked the guy. He's feeling like a schmuck. Thought Denny was 'sharp as a tack.' Said so. Was pleased his daughter found a man who wouldn't lean on her for money but pull his own weight. They're loaded, you know," Sully said.

Colt nodded, he knew.

"Mrs. Todd didn't say much around about this time, didn't want to make her husband feel more a schmuck but, glances he gave her, guilty ones, made me think they'd chatted in the past and she disagreed."

"They give you anything else?"

Sully shook his head. "Tried to get the mother talkin' but don't think she had much to say. I'm guessin' her daughter didn't tell her that her husband liked rough sex and made her call him by another man's name. Still, they were close, easy to see, doted on Marie. They have another daughter. She and her husband are flyin' in from Houston. They're off to the airport to pick them up now."

"Get anything from the house?"

"Nothin'."

"The office?"

"Nope, clean. No files on his computer tracking Feb or you or any sick shit. Though his boss is stunned. Loved the guy. Said he was a genius. Said Denny got head hunted two, three times a year but was loyal to the company. Said Denny could be makin' double, even triple, but he never left. Thought it was because he liked his job. Had no idea it was because Denny wanted to be close to anything Feb."

That turned Colt's stomach but he shook it off and kept questioning.

"Colleagues?"

"The Feds are hittin' them this mornin' as we speak."

"More from the neighbors, any other friends?"

Sully shook his head.

"Anything else? He use a credit card? Called family, a friend, anyone been in touch with him since he did Marie?"

Sully took a drink from his coffee and another bite of his cookie. He did this while studying Colt.

Then he swallowed and said, "Nothin' so far. We're askin' though. But apparently, he's vanished."

Colt sat back in the chair Feb always sat in and looked out the window, taking a drink from his own mug.

"Colt," Sully called his attention back to him. "I know this is frustrating but we'll get this guy. He's fucked up, he'll fuck up again."

Colt knew he didn't have to remind Sully but he did it all the same. "He fucked his wife pretending he was me and pretending she was February."

"I could see that'd make you impatient for us to find him."

"What makes me impatient to find him is, he gets word Feb's in my bed, he's likely to get gripped by another rage and anyone could get in his way."

Sully changed the subject. "You been in that bed with Feb?"

Colt didn't answer his question.

Instead he changed the subject himself. "You know Amy Harris?"

Sully's wife was a local. She was two years ahead of Colt at school. Sully was from a small town about forty-five minutes away. He'd made the sacrifice, pulled up roots and made his life close to Lorraine's people. He did this because she had two living parents, three brothers and a sister, all who still lived in town. Sully only had a sister and she lived in Maine. Lorraine's way of thinking was, considering her family was close, and she was close to them, her town roots went deeper than his. Sully's way of thinking was he'd give Lorraine anything she wanted, part because he loved her and part because she could be a serious nag.

He shook his head. "Nope."

"She works at County Bank."

"Lorraine and me do our banking at State."

Colt lowered his voice. "I need you to mobilize the Lorraine gossip tree but I need you to do it without Feb, Jessie Rourke, Mimi VanderWal, Delilah or Jackie Owens gettin' wind of it."

Sully leaned forward. "What's this about?"

"Gut," Colt told him. "Amy Harris walked into J&J's a couple nights ago. She'd lived in this town all her life and never been there. She eyed Feb in a way I didn't like. She acted funny, we had a conversation that didn't sit well and walked right back out. Then she disappeared."

"Disappeared?"

"Never took a day off work that her boss remembers and now she's had three, today, no call-no show. No one's seen or heard from her and she isn't answering her door."

"What the fuck?"

"Found out she had a baby, 'while ago. Don't know whose as she's not a girl who gets around. At all," Colt told him.

"This somethin' to do with Feb or is it somethin' to do with Lowe?"

"Gut says, both."

"How's that?"

"Don't know that either but I was surprised to hear she had a kid. We weren't close but that was still news. Colleague reports she had a breakdown, took off from her station, early break so she could have a cryin' jag, thinkin' about her boy, which was way out of her standard practice. But she had it after Lowe came in to make a withdrawal."

Sully shivered and it was visible.

"You think he raped her?"

Colt shook his head. "No clue. I think she came in to tell me something or, way she was eyein' Feb, her. I think it's no coincidence she did it after Angie got murdered. I think it scared the shit out of her. And I think she lost her courage and didn't do it. I want to know what that something was because what I do know is, after she did that, she disappeared."

"What you want Raine to do about it?"

"I wanna know anything there is to know about Amy Harris."

"Without any of Feb and her gang findin' out Raine and her gang are askin'?"

"Without Feb or any of her gang findin' out *I'm* askin'."

Sully grinned. "Colt, man, you know, you're gonna have to buy her girls with somethin'."

Colt grinned back, "Sully, you're so full of shit. Raine isn't half as curious about the state of affairs as you are."

"What?" Sully threw out a hand. "You're my partner."

Colt shook his head but said, "Tell Raine Feb made a frittata for breakfast this morning."

Sully slammed his palm down on the table and gave a shout.

"Damn, man, you must be the *master*. Morrie tells me only thing better than Feb's frittatas is being touched by the hand of God."

Colt took another drink of coffee.

"They that good?" Sully pushed.

Colt thought of the best breakfast he'd ever had in his life. Jackie was no slouch in the kitchen, Melanie loved to cook gourmet crap and was always trying out a new recipe, and Frank's specialty was breakfast and his restaurant was known throughout Indiana as a place you needed to have breakfast before you died.

Feb's frittata beat all of them.

Colt's voice was low again when he replied, "Best I ever had."

Sully read his meaning and Colt realized it was a good idea to share. He'd helped his partner shake off the shadow of grief and remember life could be good.

Sully shoved the rest of his cookie in his mouth and took a slug of coffee right through it.

"I got a serial murderer to find," he told Colt, still chewing and then turned his head to call to Mimi. "Meems, sweetheart, you got a to go cup?"

Colt got a seven o'clock reservation at Costa's and called Feb to tell her he'd pick her up at the bar at six thirty.

He also called Doc to ask him if Amy came around to see him the day before. Or, more to the point, he called Doc's receptionist Leslie, who was old as dirt but had been sweet on Colt from the minute Colt's mother swayed in, drunk off her ass, yanking Colt, who was six and who'd burned his hand on the stove trying to make soup, behind her.

Colt owed a lot of people in that town for their kindness when he was living his hell. It was part of why he earned his badge.

Leslie told him no Amy even though she shouldn't have done it. She would have done anything he asked. Not because she was sweet on him, because she trusted whatever he was doing, it was the right thing.

An hour later, Colt got a surprise when Doc called him direct.

"What's this I hear you callin' 'bout Amy, son?" Doc asked.

Colt stifled his surprise and replied, "Concern, Doc. She's been missin' a few days and she's no call-no show at work. Not her style."

"Since when the po-lice investigate no call-no show?" Doc asked an excellent question.

Doc was a good old boy and sounded like a hick. He did this because he wanted his patients to talk to him about what ailed them, body and mind, so he could do something to help. They wouldn't do that if they held him up on the pedestal where most put doctors just because of their schooling. Doc broke down those barriers by affecting a personality that said *I'm one of you.* He was smarter than hell and should have retired years ago, but the town wouldn't stand for it. He'd be shoving thermometers under sick kids' tongues until the day he keeled over and died.

"Since it's Amy Harris. She doesn't have kin close, no friends to speak of and this is well out of character," Colt answered.

Doc was silent.

Then he said quietly, "Let this be, son."

That cold hit his chest and it went into deep freeze.

"Let what be, Doc?"

"Just let it be. I hear you and Feb're finally patchin' things up. No sense diggin' up the dead dog. It's dead. That's all you need to know."

"Doc, this could be tied to a murder investigation. You know something, you aren't doin' right not sharin'."

Now Doc was surprised. "What murder investigation?"

"We're guessin', and it's a good guess, that Denny Lowe killed his wife, Feb's ex, Pete Hollister, Angie Maroni and a man named Butch Miller."

"*Hoo,*" Doc's shock was audible. It came out of him like someone punched him in the gut.

Colt ignored the noise and thought about Amy.

Amy would go to Doc. Doc would have done her pregnancy test. He likely arranged for her care and even the adoption. Doc was a pillar of that community and he was for a reason. He wasn't just a doctor, he was much more.

"You know somethin' about Amy and Denny, we gotta know," Colt told him.

"Knew Marie, heard 'bout her this mornin'. Cryin' shame, she was a nice woman," Doc noted then asked, "Denny?"

"Evidence is pointing to him."

"Hard to believe, son."

"You don't know what I know," Colt told him. "You got somethin' for me?"

"No, Colt, I don't. Not on Denny and I would tell you, you know I would. Amy, I'm just sayin', you best leave that alone. She's a good girl."

"She connected to Denny?"

"Not that I know of. Would shock me deep I heard she was."

"Then why would you need to tell me she's a good girl?"

"Because, no matter what, it's plain old true."

The old man was hiding something.

"Doc."

"All I'm gonna say."

"Doc—"

"Colt," Doc said firmly, quietly, and in a way that made the cold inch tighter. Let it alone. Hear me, son?"

"I can't. I'll take it as read you'll keep this between you and me, but this shit with Denny is tied to me, it's tied to Feb and we're not talkin' in good ways. You seen a lot of sick in your life but I'll bet you your pension you haven't seen sick like this." He heard Doc take in a sharp hiss of breath but talked through it. "Feb's in danger and I am too. If Amy's in danger, she needs protection and she needs it now. Hell, Doc, she needed it last week and it's my job to see that she has it."

"I'll tell you, Colt, far's I know, Denny Lowe ain't tied to Amy. God's honest truth."

That meant whatever he was hiding, and he was hiding something, might be tied to Colt or Feb and he wasn't saying. Which meant it was.

"Doc, no matter how deep you bury that skeleton in your closet, somethin' always happens to make it rattle."

"You hear those bones rattlin', son, take my advice. You close the closet door."

Then Doc hung up.

Another dead end.

"Fucking shit," Colt cursed as he put down his phone.

"Looks like your day's turnin' out good as mine," Sully noted as he walked up.

Colt knew what Sully was talking about. Colleagues, neighbors and friends of Lowe were being interviewed everywhere. All they got was a few "We always thought he was a bit quiet," but nothing else. It was a shock even to his mom and dad, who still lived in town. Denny's mother was so cut up she'd had to be sedated by paramedics. No one had heard from him or seen him since the day Puck died, which the coroner told them was also the day he reckoned Marie died. They were coming up zero, which meant the only thing they had left was waiting for him to kill again.

He had no chance to reply to Sully, the phone on his desk rang again. He pulled it out of the receiver and put it to his ear.

"Lieutenant Colton," he answered.

"She's dead."

Colt knew the voice, even if it was a whisper. Julie McCall.

Fuck.

"What?"

"She's dead, Lieutenant. I'm standin' in her house and she's dead."

"Who?" Colt asked but he knew.

"Amy," she whispered and it surprised him, coming from that woman, but he heard tears in that one word.

"Exit the house immediately, Ms. McCall. Don't touch anything. Officers will be there shortly and I'll meet you out front."

"Okay."

"Don't touch anything," he repeated.

"I won't."

He hit a button on the phone and then hit the extension for dispatch. "Connie, get a unit out to Amy Harris's house, one six eight Rosemary Street. We got a four one nine."

"Four one nine," Connie repeated. "Sure thing, Colt," she finished and disconnected.

Sully was close when Colt put the phone down and grabbed his blazer off the back of his chair.

"Why you sendin' a unit to Amy Harris's house on a four one nine?"

Colt didn't look at him when he answered. He was on the move.

"Because she's dead."

Colt stood in Amy Harris's bedroom watching the boys cut her dead body down from the ceiling fan.

Hanged. Apparent suicide. No bruising. No marks. Hair tidy. Clothing tidy. House tidy, like she was preparing for company.

She had no shoes on. Chair on its side under her. No sign of struggle. No forced entry.

The coroner, Andy, told Colt his best guess: she died the day before, Monday.

Colt walked out of the room into Amy's living room and pulled the phone out of his back pocket. The display said it was ten past six. No Costa's tonight.

He opened it, scrolled down to Feb and hit go.

"Hello?"

"Baby, hate to tell you this but we can't do Costa's. I got work."

She was quiet a minute then she asked, "What kind of work?"

"Suicide."

He heard her gasp before she said, "Who?"

Colt had no intention of telling her that when they were on the phone. He hadn't had a lot of success controlling her temper or her emotions when he was in the same room with her. He was not going to make that attempt over the fucking phone.

"We'll talk about it when I get home from work."

"When's that gonna be?"

He heard the zip go on the body bag.

"Late."

"I'll give Mom and Dad a break and close tonight."

"They've only covered for you and Morrie one night."

"They're not as young as they used to be."

"I heard that!" Colt heard Jackie shout in the background.

He would have smiled normally, but he didn't feel like smiling just about now.

"Feb—"

"Colt, it's just..." she hesitated, uncomfortable, edgy, not sure if she should share. "I need to store up my markers for when we actually make it to Costa's."

There it was. Indication of a future.

That made him feel like smiling. He didn't smile but he did let it go.

"Is Morrie on with you tonight?"

"No, he's home havin' dinner with Dee and the kids."

"He comin' back?"

"I don't know."

"Call him, tell him he's comin' back."

"It's okay. Darryl's on."

"Honey, Darryl forgets what he's doin' in the middle of sharpening a pencil." He heard her soft laughter and went on. "Do me a favor, call Morrie. Minute Jack and Jackie prepare to leave, his ass is there."

"Okay."

"Can you call Stavros? Tell him we're not gonna make it."

"Sure."

"Sorry about Costa's."

"Beauty of Costa's," she told him, "it's always a promise, even the minute you leave."

Christ, he liked this new Feb.

"Later, baby."

Her voice was a whisper when she said, "Later, Alec."

That was another promise, one he liked better than the juiciest souvlaki and the sweetest baklava this side of the Mississippi.

He flipped his phone shut, tucked it in his back pocket, turned and called to Marty who was standing inside the front door. Marty jogged up to him.

"Do me a favor, go to your cruiser and call in a team. I want this place printed and combed."

Marty stared at him and asked, "For a suicide?"

Colt sighed instead of curling his hands into fists. "Just do it, Marty."

"Gotcha."

Colt walked out the door and to Julie McCall. He'd spoken to her briefly before entering and again coming out and asking her to stay. She was shaken up and crying when he arrived. She was still shaken up, but she'd reapplied her makeup since he'd last seen her.

"Ms. McCall, thanks for staying. I won't take a lot more of your time."

"I can't believe it, I just can't."

He nodded and asked, "This seem like something Amy would do?"

She shook her head. "No. No way. She was shy but she seemed...I don't know..." she searched for a word, "content, I guess."

She wasn't content the night she walked into J&J's. She also hadn't left a suicide note.

"You didn't happen to see a note when you walked in?"

She shook her head again. "No, I just, you know, you talked to me about her and her bein' no call-no show and all, I got worried. Then heard word about Marie Lowe and you talked about Mr. Lowe and well..." She trailed off then continued, "When she goes to visit her folks, I come and get her mail, turn lights on and off, that whole thing, so people won't know she's gone."

Colt nodded and she kept talking.

"I had her key. Keep it on my ring. It's hard to get them off so I didn't bother. She goes to see her folks regular, even during holidays, like the Fourth of July if they make a long weekend. I came straight after work, knocked on the door but she didn't answer. I thought, 'What the hey?' Right? I have a key, she won't mind."

Julie was right about one thing, Amy wouldn't mind.

"Place felt weird, silent, her car outside, she had to be there. So I had a look. That's when I found her and called you."

Death had a feel he knew. The place would definitely feel weird.

"I don't believe it," Julie said again, eyeing him and looking like she was trying hard to call up tears.

"Go home, Ms. McCall," he told her. "Call a friend, don't be alone tonight."

"Maybe I could...we could..." she paused. "Maybe later you'd want to meet for a drink? You know, toast to Amy?"

Was the woman seriously asking him out on a date after finding her friend had committed suicide?

It didn't matter. He'd toasted to enough dead people recently, it wasn't much fun then and it was with Feb. He sure as fuck wasn't going to do it with Julie McCall.

"I got work, Ms. McCall."

"Yeah, but...later?" she pushed.

"Ms. McCall—"

"It's just that…" She was searching and what she found was so lame it made him want to roll his eyes just like Feb. "I'm sad."

It was time to shut this down once and for all, and even though it wasn't exactly true, it also wasn't false so he said, "I appreciate this was difficult and I also appreciate the offer but, later, I'll be with my girlfriend."

Crash and burn. Her eyes screamed it, he knew, he'd seen it enough times. He had no problem with a woman being forward, he just had a problem with the ones who wouldn't take a hint.

Her eyes flitted away. "Yeah, okay."

"Call a friend," he advised. "Don't be alone tonight."

"Yeah, a friend."

"Drive safe," Colt finished and walked to his truck.

He opened the passenger side door then the glove compartment and found some plastic gloves. He closed the door, beeped the locks and snapped the gloves on while he walked back up to the house.

Colt was sitting at his desk, the station mostly quiet, and he was scanning the notes he'd written on a pad. He'd been writing and scanning them twenty minutes and nothing added up so he stopped scanning.

He picked up the phone and dialed the number he'd looked up half an hour ago.

It was late but Doc still answered, "Hello?"

"Doc, Colt."

"Son—"

"Doc, Amy's dead."

There was silence but Colt could feel the shock across the line.

"Murdered?" Doc whispered.

"Suicide."

"No," Doc breathed.

"You know I respect you, Doc, but I gotta ask. In light of this, you got anything more for me?"

"She leave a note?"

"No."

"Then I got nothin' more."

He did, the stubborn old jackass.

"All right, Doc."

"You call her parents?"

"That's my next call."

"Give me their number, son. I'll do it."

"I don't—"

"I know 'em, Colt. Not good hearin' this from anyone but I reckon it'd be better hearin' it from someone they know who took care of their daughter since before she could crawl."

Colt couldn't argue with that and he gave Doc their number.

He put the phone down at the same time Sully, sitting across from him at his desk, put his down.

Sully was grinning.

"Fuckin' A, Colt, DNA and some prints lifted from that shit we got from Feb's fit DNA and prints lifted from Denny's. We got him at her house."

Colt grinned back. "Great, Sully."

"Not done, my man. They also matched prints at Angie's."

Colt felt an electric pulse sear through his system. That news was more than great.

"Sure," Sully went on, "you could argue with the prints at Angie's, she had loads of visitors, probably why he was careless. He could have visited her anytime. But Feb's? He's fucked."

He was. Two plus two were equaling four, more than a coincidence. So much so, if the impossible happened and this shit went to trial, a jury would think that too. It was fucking brilliant.

"Anything from Pete and Butch?" Colt asked.

Sully shook his head but he was still grinning. He leaned back in his chair and lifted his arms to place both hands behind his head.

"Those scenes are clean but this is what I think," Sully started then leaned forward quickly, excited, ready to call it down and he put his elbows on his desk. "He goes to Feb's before all this shit, we don't know when, before Marie tips it with her confrontation. Does Feb routinely have her house fingerprinted? No. He doesn't reckon she'll ever find the cum rags 'less she moves and she might not even know what they are. Or, he's so sick, he might not even care or he might *want* her to find 'em."

Colt nodded and Sully went on.

"Then Marie tips it and he uses what he's learned from Feb's journals to go on his vengeance spree. From what we can tell, Puck's between Marie and Pete, probably still actin' on rage, maybe even lookin' for you, but findin' Puck. He's careful at Pete's but not so careful with Angie. Careful enough with the crime scene but, he lives in town, Angie's place he'd reckon was infected. Might even be he would think we wouldn't give two shits about Angie, bein' who she was. He's back to careful with Butch. After Marie, he's controlled with all of them, even Angie, perfecting the kill."

"The profilers get that list? Isolate a victimology?"

"They got it. They figure Angie was his way of announcing this to Feb, on a high from doin' Pete and decidin' it was time for her to learn she had a hero. But with that note about Puck, the warning about you and it bein' Butch and Pete who bit it, they're thinkin' his next target is a guy named Grant who lives in Sturgis."

Colt didn't want to know but he asked, "What'd he do?"

Sully didn't want to tell him but he said, "He worked a bar with her, assistant manager. Tried it on with her, wouldn't take no for an answer, got insistent. She liked the job, liked the town, wanted to stay awhile, she reported him. Grant didn't like it much and made his feelings known. Her manager made his feelings known by firin' Grant's ass. Guy left the job, not the town, kept harassin' her until she finally took off."

Colt again thought it was good Feb was home so he and Morrie had her back. He also wished he was the one who told this Grant asshole that there might be a serial killer with a hatchet after him, wreaking vengeance for all the wrongs done to Feb. He would have got a fair bit of satisfaction out of that.

"Grant bein' warned?" Colt asked.

"Agents headin' that way," Sully told him then asked, "You find any link between Amy Harris and Denny?"

Colt shook his head. He'd spent a goodly amount of time in her house and even more time talking to her neighbors. He found nothing in the house. The neighbors, all the same story. Shock at the suicide, she didn't seem that type of girl. They liked her as a neighbor. She was helpful, watching kids, dogs, cats, picking up mail while they were away. They knew her as sweet, nice, quiet and shy.

"Didn't even find any evidence she had a kid which means zilch on her having him adopted. Like it never happened," Colt told Sully.

"Maybe it didn't and she was tellin' tales."

"Weird tale to tell."

Sully nodded. "This is true." He gave Colt a look. "Could it be the world just didn't understand her and she'd had enough?"

In his sixteen years as detective he'd had five suicide callouts. In his career as a cop, he'd seen two more. Colt never understood murder, no matter what. Suicide was different. He didn't condone it but the seven he'd seen, what he learned after, he understood them.

Amy's, no.

"Doc's informin' her folks, I'll get to them when they get here."

Sully nodded. "Speakin' of here, why are you? You'll never earn another frittata from Feb sittin' behind your desk."

"She's closing tonight."

"Ah." Sully grinned. "Still, she's behind a bar, wearin' one of her chokers, no doubt, lookin' hot, definitely no doubt, and that bar's two blocks away. You walk out the front door, you're off duty. So, again, why you still here?"

"Good question," Colt said and stood up, grabbing his blazer.

He was on the move when Sully called out, "You still want me to activate the Lorraine gossip tree?"

Colt didn't turn, just lifted his hand in a wave that was a single flick of the wrist and called back, "Absolutely."

Colt hit J&J's and his eyes hit Feb.

Hers hit him and she gave him a jaw tilt.

Denny Lowe's psychotic vengeance, Cal Johnson's bleak retribution and Amy Harris's incomprehensible suicide and still, one jaw tilt from February and all was right in the world.

For the first time in twenty-two years after the jaw tilt, Feb didn't take her eyes off him. And for the first time in twenty-two years, he gave her a smile.

She caught it then bent her head, but he saw the smile that was directed at him but aimed at the floor. That smile was warm. It was knowing. It was everything it used to be at the same time it was a fuckuva lot more. He'd tasted her, he'd been inside her. She liked it enough to make him a frittata. Now her smile told him she also liked it enough to smile in a way that told him she wanted more.

Yes, all was right in the world.

He went to his stool and she followed him down the bar as he did.

He no sooner had his ass on it then she asked, "Off duty?"

"Yeah, honey."

"Beer, bourbon or both?"

"Beer."

She nodded and got him a beer.

He took a swig and she didn't move away.

"You okay?" she asked, and he saw her eyes on him when he dropped his arm.

"Been better."

"Was it someone you knew who killed themselves?"

"Yeah."

"Wanna talk about it?"

"Later."

She nodded and said softly, "All right, babe." She let it go and tilted her head to the side. "Had dinner?"

"Baby, it's nine thirty."

"So? Frank's kitchen's still open. I could send Darryl down with your order."

"I'd order a burger and he'd come back with a reuben."

"Yeah, but either burger or reuben, from Frank's, you got no complaint."

This was true.

"Get him to get me a reuben."

She grinned and asked, "That mean you want a burger?"

Colt nodded, Feb laughed and everyone in the bar watched the show. For once Colt didn't mind being their object of fascination. Fact was, hearing Feb laugh at that minute, after his day, he didn't fucking care, they could watch all they wanted.

She took off around the side of the bar, walking behind him. Colt itched to grab her but he didn't. In J&J's, she'd decide how what was going on between them was communicated.

Morrie came around him with a tray full of empties. "Hey, dude."

"Hey, Morrie."

"Any closer to the world bein' safe for my baby sister again?" Morrie asked, setting down the tray and throwing the bottles in the bin.

"Sully and the Feds scored some hits today."

"Awesome," Morrie smiled, transferring stacked glasses to the side of the sink under the bar.

Colt studied his friend.

Morrie was like his father when it came to Colt, always had been even before Jack. Morrie's belief in Colt went deep, to the molten center of the earth, made of something so strong, even that heat couldn't melt it, couldn't even bend it. Morrie knew Colt would make things right for Feb again even before things had changed between Colt and Morrie's sister. He knew Colt would work at it until he dropped and he believed that, even if the road to safety was paved with shit, Colt would make it to the end of that road, carrying Feb along with him.

Even though they'd disagreed and fought, Colt knew no better friend could be had.

He had no idea why God decided to place him, at birth, in hell only to lead him to salvation in kindergarten. Though he suspected if he hadn't experienced hell, he wouldn't have understood salvation. It might be fucked, but he felt grateful to God for showing him the way.

Colt swallowed the lump he felt in his throat and asked Morrie, "How's things with Delilah?"

"When I asked if I could skip the couch tonight when I got home, she hesitated at least thirty seconds before she said no," Morrie answered.

"Progress."

"Damn straight."

Feb came up beside him, close, wedging herself between Colt and the empty stool next to him. She leaned forward, forearms on the bar, her head turned to him.

"Burger, reuben or wildcard ham and swiss, comin' right up," she told him.

"I hate ham," Colt replied.

She threw her head back and laughed, loud and wild, exposing her throat, highlighting her choker, making Colt scan the bar to see they had a decent Tuesday night crowd. Maybe too decent for Feb to feel comfortable leaving Morrie and Darryl at the bar so he could take her home and fuck her brains out.

He also noticed, unusually slowly, with her choker she was wearing a fitted, white blouse, a long, straight figure-skimming jeans skirt, a pair of cowboy boots and her makeup was different, heavier, but instead of looking overdone, it made her eyes smoky and unbelievably sexy.

Dolled up for Costa's. And for Colt.

When she stopped laughing, her eyes came to his. "Frank uses that honey-baked ham, Colt, not the boiled stuff. You'll like it."

"I see Darryl's potential fuck ups come with the territory."

After his comment, her face assumed that look again; eyes soft, lids part lowered, lips tilted at the ends in that little, sexy smile, but this time he understood it. She wasn't giving him something, holding something back. She was giving him something fucking spectacular and she was promising just how much better it would be when she stopped holding back.

"Yeah," she said.

"I'll cope if it's ham," he told her.

She lifted up and turned her back to the bar. Reaching out a hand, she curled it around his neck.

"Promise, it isn't hard," she whispered, let him go and went back around the bar.

He was looking up at her when she'd touched him, which left him facing the room when she walked around him.

She might as well have grabbed his crotch and stuck her tongue down his throat. He even saw Lanie Gilbert pulling her cell phone out of her purse.

He didn't care about that either.

In all his years with Melanie, much as he loved her and he did love her, he never headed home knowing she would help him leave behind his day.

A couple of days with Feb and that was a given.

Colt turned from the bar to take a pull off his beer and watch Feb wash glasses in the bar sink.

Fifteen minutes later Darryl delivered Frank's famous fried tenderloin on a sesame seed bun and fries.

And Colt ate it without muttering a word while he watched Feb's shoulders shaking with silent laughter.

Colt was right.

February Owens was the kind of woman who'd sit on your face and fucking love it. She was the kind of woman who'd suck your cock and get off on it. She was also, he discovered, the kind of woman who'd do both at the same time, and come while doing it.

He didn't have the chance to try her on all fours because, the second time he made her come, he wanted to watch.

So he did.

After they were done, he took the time to use his cock to memorize her tight, wet pussy yet again at the same time using his tongue to taste the silver at her neck. He liked the sharp, cold, metallic tang of her silver mixed with the salty, warm taste of her skin. It was pure Feb, contradictory and addictive.

Then he pulled out, rolled off, turned out the light, settled on his back and tucked her into his side.

Regardless of the fact that he now had a newly painted guest bedroom with bed, dresser and a huge print of a fucking basket of flowers over the bed, Jack and Jackie had made it clear they didn't intend to be the third and fourth wheel while Feb and Colt were exploring their new situation. Colt brought Feb home early because the crowd got light and Morrie declared he and Darryl could handle it and they found the RV gone and a note saying they were moving into Morrie's apartment for the time being.

Colt could live with that. Morrie's place was far more secure than an RV.

"You tired, baby?" he asked.

"Mm," she answered and he had no fucking clue what that meant.

"You seem okay with all of this," he noted.

She tensed against him and he used his fingers to draw patterns on her hip, giving her time, waiting, feeling the tension drift away.

"I'm scared as shit," she finally whispered, again sharing instead of holding it in.

"Far's I know, Feb, only folk who can turn back the clock are in movies."

He listened to her take in a heavy breath.

Then she let it out and said, "That's true."

"Gotta live life lookin' ahead, you keep lookin' behind…" He let that hang and she nodded against his shoulder.

He decided to give it to her and see where she went with it. "I'll make it clear right now, honey. I like the idea of looking ahead at life with you."

"Colt—"

"I thought I was Alec in this bed," he meant to tease but she lifted up and looked at him in the dark.

"Yeah," she said softly. "But it was Colt just said that to me."

He felt that warmth spiral in his chest, wrapping his innards so tight, for ten full seconds he found it difficult to breathe.

Then she dropped her head and he felt her slide her nose along his jaw before she settled back into his side.

"You with me on this?" he asked.

Her arm around his stomach got tight. "I'm with you," she whispered.

He closed his eyes and his arm around her waist gave her a squeeze.

After a while she asked, "Was that our talk?"

"Most of it, yeah."

"Does that mean I don't get Costa's?"

Colt was tired, it was after midnight, there were always bad guys to catch and that was his job.

He still burst out laughing, turned to Feb and a while later he learned he was right about her letting him do her doggie style. He was right she'd want more of it. And he was right she'd beg him to fuck her harder.

And she got off on that too.

Eight

COLT

I realized my mistake the minute I hit the kitchen the next morning. I shot my wad too early with the frittata.

I should have saved it for something special. Our first week anniversary at least.

Not the first morning after.

Now I didn't know what to make Colt for breakfast. Especially not after a night where he gave me three more Colt-induced orgasms. *Three*. I didn't have to help at all, not even guidance with my hand or tilting my hips in a non-verbal cue or full-on verbal direction. Nothing.

The man knew what he was doing.

And a man who knew what he was doing deserved a good breakfast.

That man being Colt, looking like Colt, having a body like Colt's, keeping me safe at the same time he could make me laugh, deserved a *great* breakfast.

As I searched the fridge and cupboards, I saw Mom had shopped for Colt like she was fully stocking Julia Child's larder. I concocted a recipe and went for it when I heard the shower switch off.

As I cooked, I thought of the day before.

Yesterday had been my first fun day in a long time. After making that list, calling Colt and handing it off to Mom, suddenly I felt carefree. This was weird considering a psycho was on the loose, but it was true.

I had a bounce in my step and everyone could see it. Mom and Dad were obvious about being pleased as punch. Morrie eyed me all day, smiling slow and shaking his head knowing we didn't have to have that talk about Colt and glad of it. Even Joe-Bob took one look at me and grinned huge.

I called Jessie before I did my yoga and sent her on a mall trawl but gave her specific directions. It had to be an outfit February Owens would wear, not Jessie Rourke. It had to look like I cared, but wasn't trying too hard. And it had to be fit for a first date.

Jessie was beside herself with glee and called from practically every store she visited at the Fashion Mall at Keystone at the Crossing to tell me how her crusade was going. Then she came in the bar carrying a million bags and Mimi in tow. We went to the office and I tried them all on. Most of them were Jessie Rourke outfits (which meant she took them home with her). But she hit the nail on the head with the jeans skirt, boots and tight shirt. Perfect.

As we were doing this we giggled and gabbed and at the end I made up my face with makeup that I'd brought to work with me. It was like we were back in high school and didn't have a care in the world except getting that Shakespeare play read for English class or writing the report for Psych.

Until then I had no idea how much I was holding back, even with my friends, and letting go again felt so good, it was beautiful.

I also shared. Not much but I did. I had to. For some reason, it was bubbling up inside of me and I had to get it out.

The thing was, when I did and with how everyone was acting around me, I didn't feel like I was being stupid and I didn't feel scared. I felt like I was doing right, not by them, by me, by Colt, but in the end, letting them off the hook because they were worried about the both of us and wanted us to be happy.

And I had been right and Colt was right last night. We couldn't turn back the clock, go back and change things. We had life ahead of us. We needed to focus on that.

I just dropped the first slice of egged-up bread in the skillet when Colt hit the kitchen.

He didn't go directly to the coffeepot. Instead, he came directly to me and put a hand at my hip and his mouth to my neck. He kissed me there and I felt his head come up.

"French toast?" he asked, sounding surprised.

"Stuffed French toast," I corrected.

"You cook like this every morning?"

"No," I answered. "Only after I've had three orgasms I didn't have to give myself."

His arm shot around my belly to hold me tight to his long length at the same time he burst out laughing.

I dropped another slice of bread next to the first one and smiled but didn't laugh with him. If I laughed with him, I wouldn't be able to hear him doing it and it might take my mind off the feel of his body shaking with humor against mine.

I was unnecessarily scooting the bread around in the skillet when he stopped laughing and his arm gave me a squeeze.

"That happen a lot?" he asked. There was still humor in his voice, also a hint of curiosity and definitely an edge.

He shouldn't have asked, men shouldn't ask that shit. Still, I'd been gone a long time, and although we weren't living in the past anymore, that didn't mean we didn't have catching up to do.

"Hmm, let me see." I kept scooting the bread around. "That's happened zero times. The big goose egg."

His hand got tight on my waist and I twisted my neck to look at him.

His brows were raised. "Seriously?"

I tried not to get pissed. He was succeeding in both casually insulting me and being full of himself.

"Seriously," I replied. "Firstly, because there weren't that many guys I gave a shot. Secondly, because the ones I did either didn't have the talent or they didn't have the stamina."

He grinned. "Shoulda picked better, baby."

"I did all right in the end."

He burst out laughing again, gave my neck another kiss and let me go. *Then* he went to the coffeepot.

I flipped the toast while he poured.

"I'll have to pull back," he said, shoving the pot back in and turning to lean a hip on the counter beside the stove. "I don't, I'll put on fifty pounds."

I turned to look at him. "You don't get it, darlin'. I'm givin' you the energy so you can work it off."

He laughed again and moved away. I slid a piece of toast on a plate and started slathering it with cream cheese I'd beat up with powdered sugar, vanilla, slivered almonds and the zest of an orange.

"For the record February," Colt said to my back. "I've had bad. I've had good. A couple who were great."

I slid the second piece of toast on top and turned to him, curious myself even though I didn't want to be. He was sitting on the counter behind me and when my eyes hit his, he finished in a soft voice.

"Now, I've had the best."

I turned away quickly when I felt the heat rush my cheeks, ignoring the curl in my belly at his words that indicated what they meant to me. I dumped a pat of butter on top of the toast, slid it around while it melted and covered the whole thing with maple syrup that I'd nuked with a bit of orange juice mixed in. Then I turned to Colt again and handed him the plate.

"Now that we've established we're sexually compatible..." I started, reaching to the side to pull out the cutlery drawer and grab him a fork.

"Sexually compatible?" he asked.

I shoved the drawer back in and handed him his fork.

"*Extremely* sexually compatible," I amended.

He smiled and forked into his toast, muttering, "That's better."

I moved to lean a hip against his knee and asked, "What now?"

He took a huge man-bite of toast and said around it, "What now?"

"This."

His brows went up as he chewed.

"Us. Now. You and me," I explained.

He swallowed and asked, "We gotta plan this shit out?"

"Well...no, not exactly," I said as he forked in another bite.

I said that but I meant, *yes, definitely.*

Colt chewed, eyeing me like he knew what I meant wasn't what I said then swallowed again. "How 'bout we take this a day at a time, fix it so you don't have some whackjob on the loose wreaking havoc for you and then we'll see. Deal?"

That sounded like a plan.

I smiled at him. "Deal." I watched him fork up another piece and asked, "You gonna want another?"

"Yeah."

I made him more toast and then cleaned up after as he ate, liking his kitchen and moving around it while he was sitting on the counter eating food I cooked for him.

He finished, rinsed his dish and put it in the dishwasher while I was wiping down the counters. I tossed the sponge into the sink and dried my hands thinking he needed new dishtowels. Something yellow, bright and cheery.

"Feb, baby, got somethin' to tell you."

I turned to him and he moved into me. His face was serious and something about it made me brace. Bad news was coming and there were no longer thoughts of cheery, yellow dishtowels in my head even as he pulled the one I had out of my hands and threw it on the counter beside me.

He put both his hands to my neck, settling them where it met my shoulders, and he gave me a squeeze.

"Suicide last night," he said and stopped talking.

"Yeah?"

"It was someone you know."

Oh no. No. Nonononono.

"Who?" I whispered.

His hands gave me another squeeze before he pulled the earth right out from under me.

"Amy Harris."

For a second that lasted an hour, I couldn't think.

Then I asked, "What?"

"Amy Harris. She hanged herself Monday. Her friend found her yesterday."

Amy Harris. Shy, pretty, sweet Amy Harris. Shy, pretty, sweet Amy Harris who had, twenty-two years ago, taken everything from me.

Now I had it back and she hung herself.

"Oh my God," I whispered.

"Feb—"

My eyes lifted to Colt's. "It's because of me."

His brows snapped together just as his face grew strangely dark. "What?"

"Because of me," I repeated then lifted a hand and pointed at myself then at him then back at me while saying, "Because of me, you and me."

"Why would you say that?"

I felt my own brows snap together. "And why would you ask that?"

His hands gave me another squeeze. "Fuck, Feb, we're not goin' there again."

Then it dawned on me. Post-coital talk. Put the past behind us. Move forward. The whole while he knew Amy had offed herself.

I lifted my other hand and used both, pulling them up and separating them to rip his hands off my neck and I took a quick step back.

"You *prick!*" I screeched then turned on a foot and stomped out of the room.

He caught me in the living room with a hand on my arm, swinging me around to face him.

"Don't walk away from me," he clipped, edging toward angry.

"Fuck you!" I shouted, already beyond angry, twisting my arm from his grasp.

"What the fuck's the matter with you?"

I felt my eyes get wide. "Now?" I asked. "Now, Colt? Are you still gonna play this game *now?* Now that Amy's dead, dead because of you and me?"

"I don't know how you figure that, honey. Maybe you'd like to share."

Sarcasm.

I felt my head explode and it exploded by me screaming, "*You take the cake, Alexander Colton!* You take it and eat it and go about your merry fucking way! *A woman is dead!*"

"*I know that!*" he shouted back. "I saw 'em cuttin' her down!"

"And you're still playin' this game?"

"Gotta know the game before I can play it, Feb."

240

That's when I let it loose. "Sherry and Sheila Eisenhower's party, Colt. Cast your mind back. That was the night I caught you fucking Amy Harris!"

And after I said that, that's when I watched a change come over Colt. A change that was terrifying to witness. A change that froze every centimeter of his body. A change that told me I still had earth under my feet.

It had to be there because my world was about to rock.

⌒⟶

Colt stared at Feb, even heard her call his name, but his mind was somewhere else.

It was at Sherry and Sheila Eisenhower's party. A party he remembered clearly and at the same time didn't remember at all.

It was like a lot of parties he'd been to in high school, in college and, before Feb grew out of them or, more precisely, broke up with him, a little while after college.

Sherry and Sheila's folks were away. The girls got a couple six packs and asked their friends around. Their friends asked their friends who asked their friends. It was out of control within hours. A couple of people brought kegs. Some scored hard liquor. Others brought weed. Necking, fighting, laughing, puking, passing out, everything happened.

Colt remembered it because he woke up the day after alone in Sheila and Sherry's parent's bed. He didn't remember getting there. He'd been drunker than he'd ever been in his life, before or since. So drunk, he didn't remember a thing. He felt like an ass. It wasn't a high school party but he'd been one of the few who was of age and waking up in someone's parent's bed was high school shit.

He'd been clothed when he woke up though, he remembered that, and hungover. Nasty hangover, again the worst he'd had in his life, before or since.

He remembered it too because the next day, Feb, cold as ice, broke up with him. She didn't say why, she just said it was over. He felt such shit he remembered getting angry, but not much. She could get in a snit, though she'd never broken up with him. He knew he'd talk her around.

He never did and, shortly after, she went wild.

With sudden clarity he remembered Amy Harris was at that party standing removed at wall and talking to her friend, Colt couldn't recall the friend's name. He remembered seeing Amy there, being vaguely surprised, smiling at her and she smiled back.

He'd always smiled at her, he remembered, and even as shy as she was she always smiled back. Until after that party, now he was realizing, the rare times he'd see her, he'd smile but she didn't smile back, she just hurried away. He never thought a thing of it considering her disposition but now he feared he knew why she'd changed.

That night though, that was it. As far as he remembered, he didn't even speak to her.

And Denny Lowe was at that party too.

And Denny Lowe's father was a pharmacist.

He felt Feb's hand tug his and she called urgently, "Colt!"

His eyes focused on her.

His chest wasn't cold and his gut wasn't heavy. His whole body was frozen and he felt like he weighed a ton. Like if he tried to move a leg, he'd put his foot down and the earth would shake.

"I didn't fuck Amy Harris at that party," he said softly.

Feb was watching him. He saw distractedly that she wasn't angry anymore, she was something else.

"You did," she said softly back. "I saw you."

Christ. No.

Please, God, no.

"I didn't," he said.

"Colt, I saw you, you were moving on top of her and you were kissing."

He closed his eyes and shook his head, stepping away, pulling his hand from hers.

He thought back to the party.

It'd be easy to slip someone a mickey. So many people, so much booze, pot, it was a crush, a daze. He had no doubt he'd set his drink somewhere and went back to it later. Or handed his glass to someone who was offering to get him a refill.

Date rape drugs weren't prevalent back then but people had been finding ways to slip a mickey for over a hundred years, probably longer.

"Colt?"

He opened his eyes again. "You didn't see that, Feb."

"I did," she whispered.

"You're sure?"

"Colt, why are you acting this—?"

"Answer me," he clipped.

She nodded. "I was looking for you, asking around. Craig Lansdon told me—"

Colt's muscles got so tight he thought they'd snap.

"Craig Lansdon?"

He watched the color leak from her face. She remembered.

Craig Lansdon was Denny Lowe's best friend.

"No." She reeled back, her arm out, searching for purchase. Finding none, she kept going until her legs hit the couch and she stopped.

The whole time, her eyes stayed locked with his.

"I don't remember anything that night," Colt told her.

"You said that before," she whispered, the weight of understanding heavy in her voice.

"Because it's true."

She was still whispering and tears were shimmering in her eyes when she said, "They slipped you something."

"Amy too."

He watched as she visibly started shaking.

"Amy too," she nodded. "Amy too. Oh my God." Her hands went to her head, her fingers ripping into her hair, her palms resting against her forehead. "Amy," her eyes were glued to him, "I thought it was weird, even then, thinking..." She stopped. "You looked at me like you could see through me. Amy looked..."

She stopped talking, pulled her hands out of her hair and started running. He bolted after her and caught her in the hall but she fought him and he had to pin her against the wall to get her under control, his hands at her wrists, her hands pressed to the wall at the side of her head.

"*I asked Craig,*" she shouted in his face, "*where you were!* He said he saw you upstairs, I should go upstairs. I'll never forget it. He said to me, 'He's upstairs, Feb, saw Colt upstairs. Didn't look right, you should check on him.' He seemed *concerned*. That *dick*!"

"Feb—"

She struggled against his hold. "Sent me up after you. Him and Denny. Those fucking *dicks*!" She stopped struggling and stared at him. "Ruined my life. Broke my heart. *Tore me apart*!" she shrieked. "And you! And *Amy*!"

Amy.

Colt let her go and took a step away, a big one. He felt his shoulders hit the opposite wall.

Amy had had a child. She'd had *his* child.

"Holy fuck," he whispered.

"What?" Feb snapped.

"Holy fuck."

"Colt."

He lifted his head and looked at her. "Amy had a kid, put him up for adoption."

He watched Feb's head jerk back with such force, her hair flew around her shoulders at the same time he saw her body jolt.

"What?" she whispered, but he didn't hear her because that's when he lost control.

I watched as Colt stalked into the living room, straight to his gun holster on the dining room table.

I ran after him shouting, "*Colt!*"

"Call your father, get him to come over, lock up after me."

Frantic, I got between him and the door. I'd seen his face in the second before he headed to the living room and I'd seen that look on his face before.

He'd just figured out he'd been drugged against his will, violated someone at the same time he'd been violated and apparently had a child. No way was I letting him out of the house.

"Colt, stay with me," I begged, as he shrugged on the holster and reached for his jacket. "Let's talk this through."

"Outta my way Feb."

I was jockeying in front of him, hands up, eyes glued to him, trying to gauge which way he'd go to dodge me as he went toward the door.

He didn't try to dodge me, he came straight at me. My hands hit his chest and he pushed me back as he kept moving.

"Colt, where you goin'?" I asked.

"Craig Lansdon."

"No! Colt, no."

My back hit the door. He reached around me, put his hand to the lock and I heard it click. "Call your dad."

"Colt, don't."

Colt shoved me out of the way. I came right back, sliding between him and the partially opened door. I pushed against it with my back, closing it again before I wrapped both arms around him, holding tight.

"Stay with me," I pleaded.

"Got a kid. A boy."

I shook my head, fast and rough, not able to think about that just yet. "Stay with me, babe."

"He had a hand in it. He helped take you from me, do that to Amy, do that to me, he's gonna answer for it."

"Colt, calm down first. Let me call Dad."

"Get away, baby, before I set you away."

I squeezed him tight, hard as I could, got up on my toes so my face was close to his, and begged, "Don't do this."

He pulled back fast, out of my arms. Then he leaned down and put a shoulder to my belly. I was up over his shoulder and Colt was across the room in a flash. He dipped his shoulder, dropped me on the couch and before I got back up and was halfway across the room, he was out the door.

I followed him.

"*Colt, stop!*" I shouted, running across the yard.

He was in his truck and slamming the door. I hit it with both hands up, still on the run, then tried the handle. It was locked.

Colt started the truck. It roared to life, his foot heavy on the gas.

At the sound I jumped away from the truck. When he backed out of the drive, I turned tail and ran to the house, locked the door behind me and ran to my phone on the kitchen counter.

I called Morrie. It took me three goes to scroll down then up when I passed his name in my phonebook then down again, my hands were shaking so hard.

I put the cell to my ear.

"Whas' up?" Morrie asked. I'd woken him.

"Morrie, you gotta get to Craig Lansdon. I don't know where he is, but you gotta get to him. Call Sully. Colt's gonna hurt him."

"What?"

"Craig and Denny Lowe slipped him a mickey. I…it was…way back, at Sherry and Sheila's party. He…something happened. They slipped one to Amy Harris too. They had sex."

"*What?*"

"*It doesn't matter what!*" I shouted. "Denny or Craig or both of them drugged him and Amy. I caught them in the act. I thought it was something else but they were out of it."

"Holy shit."

"*Morrie!*" I screeched, out of my mind.

"I'll call Sully, sis, we'll find him. Just calm down."

"Stop him, Morrie," I begged.

"It'll be okay, baby sister. Promise."

Then he hung up.

Then I called Dad.

Then I heard Wilson meow at me. I looked down at my cat, who was looking up at me, uncertain of the state of affairs.

I scooped him up, walked to the couch, sat on it and held him to me, staring at the wall, seeing nothing, thinking of Colt saying he saw them cut Amy Harris down.

I was also thinking of Denny, ruining my life, ruining Colt's, taking everything from me, from both of us. He'd led me to Pete. He'd ripped me off the golden course of my life and shoved me down a dark path where I didn't want to be. I'd got lost, I'd wandered. It took me over two decades to find my way home.

And Amy? She had a kid, Colt's kid. A little boy. If Colt didn't remember, did she? Did she wonder why she was pregnant? Wonder if she'd been raped?

And Colt, all these years, he never knew, never knew what the fuck I was talking about. Because he didn't. And now he found this out and that, somewhere out there, he had a kid.

"Oh my God," I whispered and Wilson curled closer. "Oh my God."

⌒

I sat there on the couch cuddling Wilson and staring at the wall for a while.

Dad walked in and I knew it was him but I didn't look at him.

Mom walked in and I looked at her.

Then the tears started falling.

Wilson was gone and I was in her arms, the words pouring out of me through my hiccoughing breaths, coating my tongue with acid. Mom held me, tighter, tighter, swaying gently, cooing once in a while, whispering "honey," but for once Mom didn't help me. The tears didn't stop coming, or the hiccoughs, or the words.

"Honey, you need to calm down," she whispered, but I didn't. I couldn't.

I'd lost the beautiful life I'd been meant to lead. It had been torn from me but it was my fault that rip was never mended and I knew it. Stupid Feb, keeping it all in, holding grudges.

Worse, Colt was out there, madder than hell and I knew what he could be like when he got that mad. Everyone did. If he got to Craig before Morrie or Sully, the rest of Colt's life could be as bleak as his father's.

"I'll call Doc." I heard Dad mutter because they knew if Mom couldn't calm me then I was inconsolable and they were right. I was.

If I'd been coherent I would have been surprised at how fast Doc got there. One second he wasn't there, the next second Dad and Mom got me up off the couch and Dad and Doc guided me down the hall. They laid me in Colt's bed and I cried to Doc, whispering now, telling him all my secrets, all of Colt's, sharing way too late.

He injected me with something and it worked quickly. He sat next to me on the bed as the peace he gave me through a syringe stole over me. He pulled up the covers and slid the hair from my forehead.

"Like I said," he mumbled. "The dog was dead. Shoulda left him buried."

"Yeah," I mumbled back, a calming darkness creeping in around me. "Dog was dead, Doc. Denny killed it."

Then I was out.

⟝⟞

I woke up on my side, my legs curled up, Wilson in a ball in the crook of my hips.

I came out of it slowly as I lay listening, hearing the murmur of voices, knowing I wasn't alone in the house. Too many voices, all of them speaking low, but I knew there wouldn't be that many and the tone wouldn't be that calm if something bad had happened to Colt.

It was growing late, I knew from the feel of the day. I'd been out awhile. But I didn't get up. I lifted my hand, stroked my cat, and he started purring.

I had a lot of experience with animals. We'd had dogs and cats growing up. I'd learned a long time ago both canine and feline had one thing in common. They sensed a shit storm, they weren't the type to go running. They stuck close. The worse it got, the closer they stuck.

So I lay in bed for a long time, kept my head clear and pet my cat.

Then I got up, went to the bathroom, brushed my teeth, splashed water on my face, pulled a brush through my hair and went to my bag, changed the yoga gear I'd put on that morning to a pair of jeans, belt, t-shirt.

Then I sucked in breath, went to the bed, lifted Wilson in my arms and walked out of the room.

Al was sitting at the bar, Meems beside him. The smell of Mom's spaghetti sauce filled the air. She was at the pot stirring. Jessie had her head in the fridge.

I walked through the living room with Meems' eyes on me. I looked to the left and saw all four of her kids lounging in front of a muted television set.

"Hey, Auntie Feb!" Tyler called.

I dropped Wilson to his feet, waved at Tyler and smiled.

Kids, too, sensed shit storms and Tyler's returning smile was cautionary. That kid loved me, all Meems' kids did. This was because I spoiled the hell out of them and usually encouraged their bad behavior because it was never that bad and because Mimi and Al knew every kid had to have that one adult they trusted beyond anyone just in case life took them to a place where they'd need that trust and the wisdom only someone older could give. That was the brilliance of being the kidless best friend. You got all the good shit, never had to put up with the bad and the devotion that came from that was like a priceless treasure.

"Now Feb's up, does that mean we can turn up the volume on the TV?" Meems' oldest, Jeb, shouted.

"It's *Aunt* Feb, Jeb," Meems corrected, Jeb having decided he was now too old to call me "Aunt" and Meems having decided that she didn't agree, a battle that obviously still raged. "And no," Mimi finished.

"Aunt Feb, Jeb. Aunt Feb, Jeb," Maisie chanted, most likely in an attempt to simultaneously annoy her mother and brother, her favorite pastime and one at which she excelled.

Maisie was Meems and Al's third child, the long awaited daughter. First came Jeb then came Emmett then came Maisie. Meems had been so overjoyed she had a daughter she thought her luck had changed and broke her rule of only three kids (which meant breaking her rule of only two kids, she'd made the third attempt to get a girl) with the hopes of evening out the gender balance in the house. But along came Tyler.

Meems lucked out, though. Maisie was as much of a girl as you could get. So much so, even though Al, Jeb, Emmett and Tyler were about as boy as you could get, Maisie still helped Meems settle the balance of the house with the sheer amount of nail polish she had lying around. Not to mention her butterfly stickers, which were stuck to everything. And her hair barrettes and ponytail holders with sparkled ribbons attached to them, her glitter pens littering every surface, and her bobby pins with bees and ladybugs on them laid here there and everywhere. Meems' house looked like a little girl tornado swept through it. The odd GI Joe doll and baseball mitt didn't stand a chance.

"Shut up, Maze," Jeb snapped as I hit the kitchen.

"You shut up," Maisie retorted.

"No, you shut up."

"No, *you* shut up."

Good God, I'd had that same argument with Morrie about a million times when we were kids. If my life wasn't a certified disaster at that moment, I would have felt the beauty of a world that changed all around you in ways you couldn't control, but still stayed exactly the same in ways that were precious.

"Kids," Al said and at that one word, both kids shut up.

I looked at Mom who was still stirring but was now looking at me.

"Where's Colt?" I asked.

"You okay, sweetie?" she asked back.

I nodded and repeated, "Where's Colt?"

She drew breath into her nostrils and looked at her sauce before answering, "With Sully."

Something was wrong, she was holding back from me.

"Mom—"

"Girlie, let me get you a drink," Jessie suggested but Mom's head came up.

"No, not at least…" Mom paused and said, "Let me call Doc, see if it's okay Feb has alcohol after that injection."

"Good call," Jessie muttered as Mom hit the phone.

I looked around at everyone and asked again, "Where's Colt?"

"With Sully, lovely," Meems told me. "Like your mom said."

She was holding back too.

"He okay?" I asked.

"Sure?" Meems asked back. Jessie threw her a look, Al dropped his head and I knew she'd exposed something. I just didn't know what.

"Are you sure you're sure?"

As Mom started talking into the phone, Al waded in. "Feb, darlin', Colt's okay. Craig Lansdon is okay. Everyone's okay." There it was. They knew all about it. I couldn't dwell on that because Al kept talking. "Just that, Morrie got to him and Colt didn't feel like backin' down. We all know what happens when those two disagree on somethin' but it's all right now."

That meant Colt and Morrie got physical.

I closed my eyes and only opened them when Al said again, "February, it's all right now."

"Either of them get hurt?" I asked.

Al shook his head. "Morrie's gonna have a shiner. Colt's good. Morrie didn't want to hurt him, just contain him. So he didn't do the first and managed, when Sully showed, to do the last."

Mom hung up and announced, "Doc says no booze. Food. So let's get you some spaghetti."

I ignored Mom and asked, "When's Colt coming home?"

More shared glances, more cagey behavior and I felt a chill slide along my skin.

"What?" I pushed.

"Colt's gonna stay with Sully and Raine tonight, honey," Mom said, turning the burner on under the water. I could see the oil floating in wet bubbles on top and the thought of Mom's spaghetti, nearly as beloved as my frittata, made my stomach churn.

"Why?" I asked.

"Just needs some space, girlie," Jessie answered, head in a cupboard and she came out with a bag of potato chips. "You want an appetizer?" she asked, shaking the bag, which was the extent of Jessie's ability to provide appetizers unless she called a caterer. Jessie wasn't much of a cook.

I didn't want chips. I wanted Colt.

But I knew, I didn't act fast, I'd never have him. I knew, I didn't act fast, that same seed that was planted in my soul hours ago and was taking root and growing strong even as I slept my hysteria away, had been planted in his too. But he'd been conscious during that time. He had time to work with it, fertilize it, help it grow.

I looked at Al. "Al, will you take me to Sully's?"

Al looked at Mimi and, even edging toward frantic, this shocked me. Al was a man and by that I meant *a man*. He didn't often look to Meems to make a decision about what he was going to do or when he was going to do it.

But Al knew, he fucked up right now with this situation, he'd live with that fuck up for the rest of his life and the panic I was feeling increased.

"Honey, I'm not sure—" Mom started, but Meems nodded to her husband.

Al interrupted Mom by saying to me, "Sure, darlin'."

"Al—" Mom began again but I was on the move.

I went to Colt's room and pulled on socks then boots then a jeans jacket. Al was at the front door when I hit the living room and we were both out of the house before I gave in and looked around the room to measure their expressions. I didn't have a lot of courage in me. I was holding onto a thin thread of strength that was stretched tight and could easily snap. I needed to do this now or I was never going to do it and then, again, I'd lose everything. It hurt enough the first time, it'd destroy me now.

I climbed in the passenger seat of Al's truck, he started it up and we took off.

We rode in silence. Al wasn't much of a talker. He spoke when he needed to and said as much as had to be said, though Mimi told me and Jessie he was a sweet nothin's man. I loved knowing that about Al, though I'd never share it with him. My friend Mimi deserved sweet nothin's and Al deserved to have a woman who he'd want to give them to.

I wanted to talk though. I wanted to ask him, being who he was, how he was, a lot like Colt, how I should handle the situation I was about to walk into. I wanted advice on how to bring Colt back to me, knowing he'd used the hours I slept in drugged up unconscious to build a wedge between us. But I didn't reckon Al had the answers I needed.

I was all on my own with this one.

Al parked in front of Sully's house and Sully was out the door and half-way down the walk before I'd slammed the truck door. Lorraine appeared behind their storm door.

"Feb, sweetheart, I'm thinkin' this isn't a good idea," Sully said, coming at me, hands up, palms out.

I walked right by him. Sully was a man, a good one. He wouldn't do what he needed to do to stop me.

My obstacle, I knew, was Lorraine. She didn't want me in her house, she didn't want me near Colt, she'd be able to stop me.

I held my breath as I approached the house.

Lorraine reached to the handle, swung open the door, moved her body aside and held the door open for me.

"Thank you," I whispered as I slid by her, tears lodged in my throat.

"Work magic in there, honey," she whispered back.

I swallowed and went in.

Colt was in the living room, seated in the middle of the couch, forearms to his knees, a glass of Jack, uncut, not even with ice, held in one hand between his knees. The bottle was in front of him on the coffee table, mostly empty. Only his eyes hit me. Other than that, he didn't move.

Sully drank beer and on occasion would spring for a shot of single malt if he was in the mood. Lorraine wasn't a drinker at all. When she came to J&J's she ordered strawberry daiquiris which was mildly annoying, they were a pain in the ass to make. Still, she got loopy on them quick and Lorraine loopy was hilarious enough to be worth the pain it was to make a daiquiri.

That Jack Daniels was in the house for when Colt came around. I couldn't know how much he'd imbibed. He wasn't moving or speaking so even though I had years of practice being around people who were drinking, I didn't know what state of sober, or not, he was in.

What I did know was that Colt never drank his bourbon uncut. I knew Colt never drank vodka because both of his parents drank it and he also never drank his bourbon uncut. Usually, it was Coke he cut it with, if not, some water or ice. This was an effort to prove he wasn't like his folks, who drank their liquor straight, always and often. Colt drinking straight bourbon was not good.

Colt not moving or saying a word, worse.

I stopped far enough away he could see me, not close enough to push it.

And when I started, I didn't fuck around.

"I know you blame me," I told him.

He didn't move.

"I was there. I saw it. I coulda stopped it," I went on.

He gave me nothing even his golden eyes didn't flicker.

"Or I coulda said something after, so you'd understand, so Amy wouldn't have had to—"

He moved then, barely, his body locked and I reckoned this was to keep himself in control and I stopped talking.

He knew like I knew, I said something, even if it wasn't during the act but after, it would have saved a lot of hurt. Colt, being Colt, would have done something. Dad being Dad, and Mom being Mom, would have had his back. Amy wouldn't have suffered. She'd have had her son and Colt would have had him too. Colt, Dad and Mom would have made us all a family. Somehow they'd have made it work. They'd have made it work so

Colt and me would still have each other, Amy would have had us all and no one would be dead because it would have stopped Denny before the sick fully took hold.

I pulled in breath and whispered, "I have to live with that forever." My voice dipped even lower, the bitter guilt germinating from that seed stark in my tone before I repeated, "I have to live with that forever."

Colt still didn't move, didn't speak, didn't lift his glass to his lips or throw it against the wall. He just kept his eyes on me and the blame was clear.

"I was twenty," I continued, knowing it was weak but also knowing it was true. "She was everything I wasn't and you were...you were..." I couldn't find a word that said it all and what I used was just as weak but it'd have to do. "*Golden.*"

Even hearing the wonder I had of him heavy in that word, Colt gave me nothing.

"You could have had anyone you wanted, in this town, out of it, anywhere you went, anyone you wanted. Why'd you want me?" I asked and, not surprisingly, Colt didn't answer so I forged on. "She was sweet and quiet and shy. She was small and pretty and dark. I wasn't any of that. I was loud. I was wild. I did crazy shit," I explained. "That night I was drunk, I got home after seein' you two and my mind played tricks on me. Tricks it'd been playin' for a good long while." I shook my head, knowing it was stupid now but thinking it was real back then and said, "You wouldn't have sex with me."

There it was, finally his hand twitched, the bourbon sloshing in his glass.

That was all he gave me but it was something.

"I was getting worried, Colt," I whispered. "You seemed to want me but didn't want me. I didn't understand, even though you told me. You were a guy. I was willing to give it up, I made that clear. But you didn't wanna take it and that didn't make sense."

I watched but he gave me nothing more.

I kept going. "So, seeing you with Amy, being drunk and twenty and wanting you and not getting all of you, I know I was wrong now but then it seemed obvious to me." I hurried on, having to get it out. "I know it was stupid, I know that now, I didn't know it then, I couldn't. All I knew was you gave her something you wouldn't give me. How could I know that you'd both been drugged? That kind of shit never occurred to me."

I waited and Colt just watched me, unmoving.

There it was. That was it. It was done and pain burned through me so blistering, so deep, my body started shaking trying to hold myself standing.

But if we went our separate ways for good, he deserved to go his way knowing it all.

"Pete took my virginity," I told him, and I watched his head jerk, surprise flashed across his features before they settled into disbelief.

"I know," I went on, "what those guys said, I know all about it. I know everyone was talkin' about me. I'm not denyin' I went wild, got drunk, partied, smoked too much pot, fooled around. None of those guys got as far as you though. Not near as far. You probably don't believe me and why they said that shit, I don't know and I didn't care. I'd lost everything, my sole reason for being was tryin' to numb the pain and everyone thought the worst of me, what did it matter? Why fight it?"

I lifted a hand and pulled my hair away from my face, holding it at the back of my head, looking to the floor, talking to myself.

"And in the end, I gave it to Pete. Fuck. *Pete.* So goddamned stupid, I was always so goddamned stupid."

I dropped my hand and looked at him. He'd changed. I didn't know how but he had. Though I saw it, the change didn't register on me. I had my story to tell and I had to get out. I was done with it all. Colt was right, I couldn't hack it and I was going to haul ass. But I was going to do this first, he deserved that.

"Far as I knew, my first boyfriend cheated on me, any guy I kissed lied about me and my husband beat me. I know you know this but that time you saw me wasn't the only time he used his fists on me, it was just the worst," I informed him, not looking at him, my eyes having wandered over his shoulder. "Then I took off and kept myself to myself. I was lonely but I didn't care about that either. Lonely's a different kind of pain, it doesn't hurt as bad as heartbreak. I preferred it and embraced it 'cause I reckoned it was one or the other. It took me five years to find Butch and there was no one between him and Pete. I was workin' a bar in Georgetown and Butch came in. After that he came in as regular as he could for six months before he hired me at his bar. I worked there for two months before he got a date. We'd been together for four more before I let him fuck me and we'd been exclusive another six before I moved in with him. He was patient, worked at it hard and we had good times, but the minute he got it, he threw it away. I shoulda known he would but I fell for it, fell for him. Stupid, stupid February."

"Feb—" Colt said, but by then I was still looking over his shoulder, unfocused, unseeing, lost in my memories of a man dead because of me and memories of my life. All those memories dead too, also because of me.

"Liars, cheaters, beaters. Who needs that shit?" I asked the wall.

"Feb—" Colt repeated, but I talked right over him.

"After Butch, I was done. Met a guy, name's Reece, worked a bar I was at, a drifter like me. We kept in touch, even apart if we found we were close, we'd get together. He'd have women between times, not me, no one. Reece was safe, he made no promises and didn't mind I held everything back, preferred it that way. We both had one thing to give and we both took it. He cut through the lonely every once in a while, which was good because by the time we'd hook up, I'd need a break. He had a bike, would take me for rides." I closed my eyes, felt my lips form a half smile and finished on a whisper, "God, those rides…only times I ever felt free 'cause they were the only times I'd let me be me."

"Feb."

My eyes shot open because my name was said close and I saw why. Colt, glass gone, was standing right in front of me. He was looking at my face, not in my eyes, and I knew what he was seeing. I realized then I had started crying somewhere down the line, so lost in my stupid tale of woe, I didn't even know when.

That didn't matter either. Nothing mattered anymore.

"Denny wins," I whispered, my head tilted back, my eyes on Colt's and when I spoke his eyes came to mine. "He wanted every piece of me? He's got it. The fuck of it is…I helped him along the way."

Colt lifted his hand and slid his fingers to curl around the back of my neck.

"Baby—" he murmured.

I jerked away from his hand and stepped away. I couldn't take his touch. Not again. The memory of it was too sweet. So sweet it made my jaws lock. I turned, done sharing. I'd not share again. It hurt too much. I felt something close down inside of me as I took my first step to the door then, during the second one, it locked. Seemed strange I'd lock someplace that was empty inside me, nothing treasured to keep safe inside but I locked it all the same.

I didn't get the third step in.

Colt's arm hooked around my stomach and he hauled me back. I hit his body and his other arm came around me, holding strong, locking me close, no way to escape even if I fought it, which I didn't. I had nothing left in me.

His mouth was at my ear when he said, "Only way Denny could win is if we let him, baby."

I shook my head and said, "Colt, let me go. We both know we should have never started this again. We both know."

His arms grew tighter. "You walk away from me, you let him win."

"He's already won."

"He hasn't, Feb."

"He has and I helped. I got five lives on my soul, six, you count whatever happened to your son. No turning back the clock, right?"

His tight arms gave me a shake. "You aren't responsible for that, any of it."

"No?"

I felt his head shake. He was so close, his stubble caught at my hair. "None of it."

"I don't agree, and when I walked in here, you felt the same way."

One of his arms left my belly and came up to lock around my upper chest.

"I was pissed, baby."

I nodded. "Sure, now you feel bad, my sad story, you're over it. You get pissed next week, next month, then where will I be?"

"Feb—"

"Right back where I was ten minutes ago, Colt." I pressed against his arms. "Let me go."

"Feb—"

"That's not a life I'm willin' to lead."

"Feb—"

"Colt, let me go."

He gave me another shake, this one was rougher, almost a jerk and I knew he wanted my attention at the same time he was losing control. I stopped pressing and Colt started talking.

"Honey, I did that twenty-two years ago and doin' it again would mean me leading a life *I'm* not willin' to lead." He let my chest go but used my waist to whirl me to face him, his hands locked on either side of my neck, keeping me where I was and he dipped his face close to mine so he was all I could see. "You wanna play the blame game?" he asked. "We'll play."

This was said in a voice firm as steel and I braced because I'd heard that voice before. He talked to Susie like that, except this time there was no ugly, just hard.

Colt kept talking. "You walked away and I was such a jackass, I let you go. The hurt happened on both sides and we both acted stupid and gave into it. I knew I didn't do anything wrong but how hard did I try to convince you of that? You weren't who all those guys said you were bein', I knew it and I *still* believed it because I had to believe that new Feb was the one who broke up with me. We were both young, we were both stupid and we were both fucked over and we didn't know it." His fingers gave me a squeeze. "Now we *know* we're bein' fucked over and we let him do it again, we let him fuck us, we let him tear us apart, that's when we really let him win."

"Colt—"

"Only thing he wants is you," Colt said. "Maybe only thing he ever wanted in this world. You give yourself to me, he can't have it." His hands gave me another squeeze. "Like it right now or not, Feb, coupla days ago, you gave yourself back to me. You think I'm lettin' that go, think again because, baby, you're fucking *wrong*."

"Colt—"

"Hear me?"

"Colt—"

Another finger squeeze. "February, do you hear me?"

The tears came back. I felt them this time, pooling in my eyes and sliding down my cheeks with that sinister little tickle they always left in their wake.

I didn't touch him, get closer, nothing. Just looked in his eyes when I gave him the only thing I had left to give.

"Got a place inside me," I whispered. "Back then, way back then, I held it to me, don't know why, maybe because I thought you were holding something back from me, but I never let you in."

He dropped his forehead to mine and closed his eyes. "Honey—"

"You got in, Colt," I said and watched, super close, as his eyes opened and his hands tightened on my neck. No squeeze this time, they stayed tight and I could feel the pad of every finger pressing into my skin. "Few days ago, you got in. I didn't let you in, you just got in."

Finally I lifted my hands to his chest and bunched his shirt in my fingers.

"I wanna lock you there," I whispered, scared to death but sharing it all, hiding nothing, giving him everything, fighting the hitch in my voice that my tears were threatening. "Lock you up tight inside me, babe, and never let you out."

His hands came to my face and his lips came to mine. "Don't want out, Feb."

"You say that but you don't know what I mean." My mouth moved under his. "I won't let you out even if I make it so you want to leave."

"Baby, I'll never want to leave."

My hands twisted in his shirt. "Promise me."

He didn't promise me, not then, or more to the point, not with words.

He kissed me, his mouth opening over mine, mine doing the same under his, his tongue spiking inside, his fingers gliding into my hair, fisting. I felt pain in my scalp but it didn't register as I pressed into him, flattening my hands on his chest, caging them between us, caught up in a wordless promise that was the most beautiful thing I'd ever experienced, the most wondrous gift I'd ever been given in my life.

It was only after he lifted his head that he said the words he didn't need to say anymore.

"I promise, February."

I felt a weird, wonderful, warm whoosh flow through me. So much of it, whatever it was, I thought it had to start leaking out my pores, gushing right back out. Somehow, against the odds, my skin contained it and held it safe inside.

Once it settled, my hands glided up Colt's chest, his neck, and my fingers slid into his hair. I went up on my toes and I kissed him, giving him my own promise.

It was late when Colt closed the door behind Jimbo and Jessie, locked it and turned to the kitchen.

February and Jackie were in it, Feb drying a big stockpot with a kitchen towel, Jackie hand washing glasses and turning them upside down in the dish drainer.

At the sight something soothing slid through him, coating the rawness he'd felt all day. It didn't do much to take the pain away, the pain of knowing what was done to him, to Amy, to Feb, and the fact he had a son out there somewhere, but it helped, even just a little bit.

He knew that rawness would remain for a long time. He saw it in the eyes of a lot of people; rape victims who still had it stark on their faces months later while they sat on witness stands. Folks who'd been robbed who he'd see years later and he knew they now had dogs and alarms because that little sign was stuck in their yard warning those who might try again that they'd called Chip to install the system.

He couldn't handle that now, trying to figure out what would heal the hurt, turn it to a scar, keep him from picking at it. Whatever happened earlier that night—and the shit of it was he didn't help it by acting like a selfish ass—Feb was slipping through his fingers. She might have said she'd locked him tight but she was ready to bolt. Controlled panic was etched into her face and all along her frame and Colt had to put all his energy toward keeping his woman sane.

"Leave those to drip dry, baby girl," Jackie said when Feb put away the stockpot and reached for a glass.

"Don't like to face dishes in the morning," Feb muttered and Jackie's eyes moved to him.

He saw she was feeling what he was feeling but hers was double. All her energy was focused on keeping her daughter together and the same went for him. Two of her cubs got cornered under her watch and it tore at her.

Knowing Jackie was feeling that, Colt was struggling with his grip on justice, not knowing which was the better fate for Denny Lowe. Death riddled by bullets fired from the guns of an army of Feds or the rest of his life, rotting behind bars hopefully being gang raped at both ends.

It might make him sick but he decided instantly he preferred the last.

Colt shook his head at Jackie and she nodded. He wasn't quite sure what he'd communicated to her but he was sure, whatever it was, she trusted it.

He walked to the couch and sat down, needing more than anything to take a load off while Jackie announced, "Welp, cookin' for eleven people and cleanin' up after them done wore me out. I'm hittin' the hay."

Feb kept drying glasses and reaching up to place them in the cupboard as she said, "You gonna be able to sleep in the midst of garlic smells and lingering paint fumes, Mamma Jamma?"

There it was, another balm, Feb calling Jackie "Mamma Jamma," her nickname for her mother, something she used to say that also used to make him jealous, not having a mother he could nickname. Then his mother became Jackie and that jealousy slid clean away.

"So bushed, I could sleep while someone was painting around me," Jackie said back, leaned into her daughter and kissed her cheek. "Night, my sweet child."

Feb's voice was rough when she replied, "'Night, Mom."

Jackie came to Colt, who'd put his feet up on the coffee table, crossed at the ankles and was too exhausted to move as she walked to him.

She didn't mind. She just leaned down and put her hand to his face and kissed his opposite cheek.

"Sleep well, Jackie," he muttered while she did this, thinking she'd move away but she stayed leaned over him, her hand on his face but her head came up and her eyes went to his.

"You know, long time ago, I looked it up," she told him.

"What?" Colt asked.

"Your name," she told him, her voice soft, her eyes on his unwavering and he held his breath, knowing what was coming was going to strike deep, and he wasn't wrong.

"Alexander," she said. "Means warrior, defender. Colton, colt." She smiled. "Well, we all know a colt's got so much energy, always beautiful little things, strong, fast, all of 'em gonna grow up to be something magnificent."

"Jackie—" Colt murmured, forgetting about that rawness. Her words, in that moment, swept it away.

"Can't say much for your folks," she whispered. "But in their miserable lives they did one thing right. They made you and after they gave you to this world, they gave you a name that fits. Don't you think?"

He didn't answer her and she didn't wait for him to do it. She patted his face, straightened and walked quickly away.

Colt's eyes followed her and a memory hit him as they did.

He heard her voice coming at him from a long time ago. It wasn't soft. It wasn't a whisper. It wasn't like it was five seconds ago, filled with so much love, mixed with a mother's longing to take away a hurt she couldn't ease. It was filled with anger and determination.

He was sixteen and sitting on the side of an exam table in the ER. His nose was broken, a bandage across it, the cut under his eye stitched, his knuckles wrapped, his eye swollen shut. His father wasn't stronger than him, not at that time, hard living had worn the strength right out of him, and definitely not when he was as shitfaced as when he started it with Colt. But he was wily, he was mean and he didn't have a problem not fighting fair. Colt gave him a good thrashing, but his dad got his licks in for certain.

Feb was sitting beside him. She'd hooked one of her feet around his calf and she was swinging their legs together. She had his hand wrapped tight in hers, palm against palm, both of them resting on her thigh and he could feel the muscles flexing as she swung their legs together. Her moving their legs jarred his body and it hurt his busted ribs but he didn't say a word. He wouldn't have stopped her if he was in agony.

Morrie was standing across from them, his shoulder against the wall, his eyes looking out a window, his thoughts unpleasant.

Jack and Jackie were out in the hall with Hobart Norris, the Chief of Police back then. Jack's voice was a murmur, as was Hob's, as was Jackie's. But suddenly Jackie's voice grew louder.

"I don't care, Hob, you hear me? Social Services be damned. You go back to that station, you make your calls and you cut through your goddamned red tape."

"Jackie," Hob said, raising his voice too but trying to calm her.

"No, I see you don't hear me, so I'll explain. That boy in there's not goin' home to those two jackals. I been sending him back there for eleven years, each time it cut me to the quick. I also been talkin' to you 'til I'm blue in the face. I'm tellin' you, he's not goin' back there again. You tell me right now he has to go, I'll tell you right now I'll pack my kids and my husband in our goddamned car and you'll never see us again."

"I'll take it you mean Colt too when you talk about 'your kids,'" Hob stated.

"Damn right I do," Jackie returned, not missing a beat.

"Not a good idea to tell me your plan to kidnap Alec Colton, Jackie." Hob was trying to joke.

This was not a good idea. Colt knew it. Feb knew it. Morrie knew it. They knew it because they heard it, heard it through something they'd never heard before.

They heard Jackie Owens shout.

"A sixteen year old boy is black and blue in there, Hob, and you joke?"

Jackie had a temper, it was lethal but it was quiet. None of her kids ever heard her shout.

But those words bounced around the hall, around the room Colt, Feb and Morrie were in. Hell, they were probably heard throughout the hospital.

"Calm down, Jackie," Hob warned.

"I'll calm down when *my* boy puts his head down at night on a pillow under *my* roof!" Jackie shouted back.

That's when Jackie laid claim to Colt, at least in any official way. He might have felt like a cub wandering around, having never had a lioness who was there to protect him who was meant to keep him safe. But he wasn't one. Or he would be one no longer.

"He's not defenseless, woman." Hob was losing patience. "You should see what he did to his father."

"No, I shouldn't. I did, I'd get the itch to finish the job Colt started," Jackie shot back. Colt heard Morrie let out an amused snort and Feb squeezed his hand.

Hob tried a different tactic. "Jack, talk to your wife."

"Why? She's talkin' sense, far's I can see," Jack said.

"Jack—"

"Cut through the red tape," Jack interrupted.

"Impossible," Hob replied.

"Then tonight's your night to become a miracle worker," Jack returned.

At that moment Feb dropped her head to his shoulder and Colt forgot about his night when she did, wondering, if he was living with Jack and Jackie, how they'd feel if he asked their daughter on a date.

He didn't go home to his mother and father's, never stepped foot over their threshold again. He didn't know if Hob fixed it or Jack and Jackie just didn't bother following the rules and he never asked.

Jack took his friends Hal Woodrow and Phil Everly to Colt's house and he did it because both Hal and Phil were just as big and solid as Jack, they'd get no trouble. The three men packed up Colt's shit and brought it back to Jack's house.

Around about the time Colt was six and he was spending more nights at Morrie's than he was at his own home, they bought Morrie and Colt bunk beds. Colt and Morrie used to fight over who would sleep on top, so they separated the beds, put them both on the floor at opposite walls. Then Colt and Morrie used to fight by throwing pillows and toys at each other from bed to bed. This would turn into a game where they'd eventually laugh themselves sick and Jack would shout through the walls from his and Jackie's room, "Enough you two!" Then they'd hear Feb giggle from her room and Colt and Morrie would whisper to each other about all sorts of boy shit before they fell asleep.

Him moving officially into that room should have been no big thing. He'd had a bed in there for near as long as he had memories. Even so, his moving into that room was a big thing and everyone in the house knew it, most especially Colt.

He heard the cupboard close, his thoughts came back into the room and his head turned to see Feb running water over a sponge at the sink. He watched her turn off the water and wring out the sponge before she went to town on the counters and he was stunned when the rawness came back. Not that it was back, just that Jackie had managed to take it away so soon, even for a while. And also he was surprised that it didn't seem so fucking raw anymore.

"Come here, baby," he called, and Feb's head came up.

"I'll be there in a sec, just let me finish cleaning the counters."

She didn't need to clean the counters. She'd done it while Jackie was washing out the pot and skillet. He had no clue why she was doing it again.

"Feb, no one's gonna perform surgery on them. They're 'bout as clean as they can be."

"I like to wake up to a clean kitchen," she told him, still rubbing down the counters.

He let it lie. She liked a clean kitchen? Who was he to argue?

He let his head fall back to the couch and rubbed his face with his hands, thinking he'd never been so fucking tired in his whole fucking life. He left his hands where they were even after he heard the soft splat of the sponge hitting the sink and felt Feb getting close. He only dropped his hands and lifted his head when he felt her moving on top of him.

She straddled him, crotch to his crotch, knees and shins in the couch, ass to his thighs, her hands coming to rest where his head met his neck. Having Feb astride him, her hands on him, Colt found he suddenly wasn't the least bit tired anymore.

"I hate to ask," she said softly. "But you need to tell me about Craig, babe."

He knew he did. It fucking sucked and the fatigue slid right back because he knew he had to tell her and he might as well get it over with.

"How much do you know?" he asked.

"I know Morrie got to you and it got physical but everything was all right. That's all I know."

Colt nodded and put his hands to her hips then slid them back and over her ass. Liking them there, he left them where they were.

"Craig works for his dad's farm supply shop, out on 36," Colt told her. She nodded and he continued. "I was so out of it when I got there, didn't note it until later, but the minute he saw me come in, it was like he knew."

He watched her lips part slowly, like the skin didn't want to separate, before she said, "Really? How weird."

"Not weird when you know what I know."

"What do you know?"

He ran his hands down her ass then up her back and around her ribs, the sides of his thumbs brushing the undersides of her breasts. Colt just wanted to touch her, remind himself she was real, this Feb sitting astride him, gazing at him, her face gentle, her hands warm. But his cock jerked when her lips parted again, this time in a different way, just as her eyes grew soft. She liked his touch a lot and she didn't guard against showing it. Colt liked both knowing she liked it and that she wasn't afraid of showing it.

He moved his hands down to the tops of her thighs. He wanted to fuck her but he wanted to fuck her when he knew Jackie was asleep, Jack was still at the bar, he had this shit out and he never had to speak of it again. She looked at him like that again he'd fuck her on the couch.

Therefore, his hands stopped moving and he kept talking. "I got there, he took one look at me, put his hands up and said immediately, 'I'll tell you everything, Colt.' I didn't hear him, wanted to beat the shit out of him, that's all that was on my mind. He backed up, tryin' to calm me down. His dad got between us, another farmer, that's when Morrie got in, got me out. We were into it in the parking lot when Sully got there."

One of her hands moved from his neck to his jaw then it lifted and she smoothed one of his eyebrows. Then both of her hands dropped to his chest.

Through this she didn't say a word. She wanted it to help, he knew and it did, just not much.

When her hands settled, Colt kept talking. "Sully had called Chris and Chris got there fast. By this time I was calm enough to share what we'd figured out and Sully talked me into going with Chris to Frank's for coffee. I went and Morrie and Sully went in to talk to Craig. They came to Frank's after, relieved Chris and told me what they learned."

"What'd they learn?"

Colt shook his head. He still couldn't believe it. Even hearing it and repeating it, he couldn't believe it.

"Craig couldn't wait to talk," he told Feb. "They barely got him in the office before he split wide open. Sully said Craig called it 'livin' under a thundercloud.'"

Her head tilted and she muttered, "I don't get it."

"He isn't surprised about Denny, not in the slightest, Feb," he informed her and he watched understanding dawn as he continued. "Says he was gonna come into the station that day anyway. He'd heard about Denny, Marie, Amy, all the shit's been goin' down. He knew it'd come out and he didn't want that shit to stick to him."

"So, he was in on it."

Colt shook his head but answered, "Yes and no. He said he thought it was going to be a joke, Denny convinced him of it. Said Denny talked him into going with him and they broke into his dad's pharmacy and got some shit. Denny knew what he wanted, where to find it, had it all planned out. They were gonna play games at the party. He said he didn't know what Denny took or what it could do, not until after, but he reckoned Denny knew. Then Denny slipped the shit to me, Craig saw him do it and couldn't believe it. He freaked out because he knew if I found out I'd go ballistic. He just didn't expect he'd have to wait a couple of decades for it to happen."

She nodded and slid a hand up to where his neck met his shoulder, fingers digging into the muscle, massaging the tension there.

Her touch felt good and he finally felt the tension start to ebb as he kept going.

"Once I started to stagger, Craig figured either Denny gave me too much or that this game wasn't gonna be as fun as he thought. Denny told him the drug would make people high, make 'em do or say stupid shit and wouldn't last long. Denny told him it was all a lark and there were no side effects, folks would just laugh, it'd be a hoot. What he saw it did to me, Craig didn't like so Craig says he stepped in. So no one would see me and I wouldn't hurt myself, he says *he* took me upstairs and into Sherry and Sheila's folks' room."

The bitterness was clear in Feb's tone when she mumbled, "Nice of him."

Colt gave her thighs a squeeze. "Pissed as I was this mornin' Feb, I think he was tryin' to do right."

She shook her head, not yet willing to believe and Colt went on.

"Craig says he closed the door and later, when you asked him about me, he knew you'd take care of me so he told you where I was. Though he was a surprised when you came rocketing back down not five minutes after you went up. He knew by lookin' at you something was not right but he couldn't get to you to ask before you headed out."

"I got out of there fast," she whispered and Colt nodded.

She didn't need to say more. They'd been there, that was done.

Earlier that night without his asking, she'd laid herself bare for him, handed him her life, her loneliness, the pain Denny had caused. After wishing for years for Feb to let him in, he found listening to her, after she cut through his anger, he didn't want it anymore. Listening to her nearly made him come out of his skin. But he made himself listen because he knew she was offering him a gift. A gift he thought he needed, but realized when she gave it to him, he didn't want it even though it was a gift he felt honored that he received.

But they weren't ever going there again, not ever again. No matter what happened, what fights they slid into, what she feared, he wasn't going to throw that in her face because, no matter how she felt about herself, there was nothing to throw.

He didn't know about the lies, the betrayals, the blows he'd unwittingly landed when he didn't make love to her. He didn't know all that as the sickness that Denny planted years ago twisted in his gut that day. He didn't know he should have never made her go there in the first place. It'd been tough to guide her back out. She seemed so broken he feared he might not be able to do it. He sure as fuck wasn't going to take that chance again.

Colt lifted a hand, ran his fingers along her jaw and she twisted her neck, dipping her jaw to press against his fingers, accepting his unspoken apology or giving him her own. It didn't matter which, both worked.

He dropped his hand back to her thigh and kept speaking. "So he went upstairs to see what was the matter." Colt squeezed her thighs again before he said, "This is where it gets really ugly."

She lifted her other hand to his shoulder and started massaging there too as she said gently, "Tell me."

Colt didn't hesitate. This was the part he needed to get through and be done with, his own hell, a hell he didn't remember and didn't understand but he had it all the same. A hell Denny had led him to.

"Denny was in the hall outside the door, actin' weird. Craig wasn't dumb to the knowledge that Denny had a thing for you. Though he thought it was a crush, one that he was surprised after high school didn't go away. He's not a stupid guy and figured that's why Denny targeted me with the drugs. Says he tried to confront Denny in the hall but Denny wasn't listening to him. Denny was excited about somethin'."

Feb shook her head, a look of pain sliding into her face and settling there.

She stopped massaging his shoulders before she whispered, "Amy."

Colt nodded his head and tried not to let the heat prickling his skin take over. "Denny said he gave Amy 'just a little, enough to nudge her in the right direction.' Sully said those were the exact words, told me Craig said he'd never forget them. Said Denny looked like a crazy motherfucker uttering them and he knew he was when he found out Denny was playin' his game with Amy and me. I'm learnin' that Amy chooses her friends wrong and Denny was one of 'em. She'd spent some time with him and Craig and, for some reason, she shared with both of them that she had a crush on me."

The lines formed by Feb's eyebrows and her eyes went hazy trying to call up memories as she stated, "I don't remember them bein' friends."

"Me either but Craig says they were."

Her head tilted as she fought for recall and failed. "Well, it's not like I paid a lot of attention to them," she muttered before she focused on him and said, "Bet Denny didn't like hearing that from Amy."

Colt nodded his head, agreeing before he said, "Craig said Denny opened the door and by this time the deed was done. Amy wasn't blitzed, not like me, not according to Craig. She had enough of her shit together to pull the covers over us. Craig said she was rolled in a ball under the comforter, bawling like a baby and I was out cold."

"Colt," Feb whispered, squeezing his neck but Colt shook his head.

"I'm okay, baby."

"No, you're not."

She spoke the truth, he wasn't.

This shit seemed like a story to him. He didn't remember so it felt like he wasn't there. But the truth of the matter was, he *was* there, he was there and he was rendered helpless, likely acting on base instinct, God only knew, but in doing so he violated another person. The worst of it was, Amy wasn't out of it, not like Colt. She knew what was happening to her and that knowledge cut deep and his helplessness to stop it pissed him off deeper.

Colt pulled in breath. "You're right. I'm not."

She licked her lips then sucked them between her teeth before asking, "You wanna go on?"

"I don't, I won't," Colt answered.

Feb nodded, started massaging his shoulders again and he continued.

"Craig says Amy was hysterical. Part drunk, part high, babbling. Denny was laughing, thought it was all hilarious. Craig got pissed, pushed Denny out of the room down the hall. They had words and it hit Craig then that what Denny felt for you wasn't healthy. He had bigger worries though. Amy. Denny took off in a huff, Craig went back to Amy. When he did, she was dressed, pulling the covers over me, still crying, sayin' over and over again, 'It's all my fault, it's all my fault.' Craig got her out of there, in his car and drove her around until she passed out then took her home. Didn't want her mom and dad to see her high. Said her father was shocked. This wasn't somethin' Amy would do. But he asked Craig to carry her to her room because her father wasn't a big guy, wasn't strong, he couldn't do it. He says he felt like a shit because her father thanked him, even shook his hand, glad Craig had looked after his daughter. Told him he was a good friend."

"Oh Lord," Feb whispered. "I wonder if they thought...when Amy came up pregnant—"

"Craig wondered too," Colt cut her off. "Said that's when the thundercloud formed over him. You and me split. Amy got pregnant. She stopped speakin' to him for a time. Denny was off to Northwestern scot free, leavin' Craig here right under the bus. He kept his trap shut, hated it but did it because he thought Denny would implicate him, especially since he was in on stealing the stuff. Said Amy never said word one to him about it after and she and her parents remained friendly to him even though, on Amy's part, it was distant."

Feb's eyes wandered to the wall behind him and she said, "You know, don't think I ever saw Craig and Denny together after that."

"You wouldn't have. Craig said he confronted Denny one more time. Said, since he felt so much for you he should at least tell *you* what went down so you could fix it with me, but Denny told him to go fuck himself. Their friendship was over at that point but Craig never got the courage to act on his own and time goes fast, shit happens, eventually it was all too late."

Feb's eyes had come back to him while he spoke and she asked, "He willin' to testify to this?"

For the first time since the shit hit that morning, Colt smiled. His Feb was far from dumb.

"He says absolutely."

Her hands stopped massaging and she asked, "Do you think this'll go to court?"

Colt shook his head before dropping it back to the couch. His story was done and the exhaustion he felt from just talking seemed to seep into his bones. He slid his hands from her thighs, up her sides, one arm going around her waist, the other one up her back, her neck, into her hair. He pressed her down until she was flat against him, her forehead in his neck.

After he did this, he answered, "No way of knowin', Feb, how this'll turn out. If they'll bring him in or if he'll fight and get himself killed. Or, if they bring him in, if he'll confess. Just don't know."

"If it does, will I have to testify?" Before he could answer, her hand gripped his neck and she surprised Colt by saying, "Because, if it gets to that, I'm willing." Her hand squeezed his neck and she went on. "You can tell them that." She pressed against him at his chest, her forehead moving deeper into his neck. "I want it on record, I don't care where and if no one ever reads it, I want it on record what he did to us. I want to sit in a room and face him and tell him how he made me feel. I don't care if it doesn't penetrate that sick brain of his, I'm willin' to do it and I want the opportunity to tell him how much I hate him."

Colt was thinking that he might be wrong about Feb. Perhaps it wasn't panic etched in her face, her frame. Perhaps the severity of emotion she was keeping hold of just barely was something else. Perhaps February Owens was made of something he didn't expect. She'd been tested in the past and she'd failed. But that didn't mean she didn't learn from those failures.

She broke into his thoughts by asking, "You'll let them know?"

He nodded and said, "Yeah, honey, I'll let them know."

She gave his neck another squeeze and wriggled closer before she whispered, "Good."

Colt decided the time had come for them to move on to a more pleasant part of their evening and his arm at her waist dropped down so he could run his hand over her ass.

"All right, baby, I want my cock inside you but I'm wiped." He felt her tense against him as he kept talking, "So, seein' as you spent the whole day sleepin', I figure you're up for doin' all the work."

She lifted her head and looked at him. Her eyes were soft in that sexy way again and her lips were tipped up at the ends.

"Yeah," she said. "I'm up for that."

Colt lay on his back, his hand at Feb's breast, his other hand over hers between her legs, feeling her circle her own clit with her finger, watching her ride him and he knew she was close but she wasn't close enough. Watching her, feeling her, listening to her, he was closer and he was going to come before she did.

"Baby, hurry," he groaned and her head, tipped back, tilted forward, her hair slid into her face, around her shoulders, down her chest and her eyes, soft and turned on, focused on his.

Christ, just looking at her face when it was like that took him nearer the edge.

She leaned forward, putting her free hand to the bed, giving herself leverage to ram herself down harder on his cock, faster, and that was exactly what he didn't need. Fuck, now she was driving him over the edge and he was struggling to hold onto his control, to fight against her pull. He wanted her to come with him.

He rolled her nipple with his fingers and heard her moan, he liked the sound but he wanted it in his mouth.

"Feb—"

Her finger moved from her clit to become two fingers sliding around the root of his cock.

"God," she whispered. "That's you."

"It's me, baby."

She dropped down so her chest was against his, her mouth at his neck, her finger going back to circle her clit, this time faster, pressing deeper.

"I've got you back," she breathed against his neck.

"I'm right here."

"You're inside me."

"Feb—"

"Locked deep."

Fucking hell, she needed to fucking hurry. He was about to explode.

"Feb, honey—"

"Locked deep," she repeated on a whisper. He felt her pussy convulse around his cock just as she sucked in breath against his neck. He took his hand from her breast and grasped her hair, using it to pull her face out of his neck and bring it to him, her mouth opening over his and he absorbed her moan as he bucked his hips, buried himself deep and came right along with her.

After they came down, he pulled her hand out from between them and her weight collapsed on him as he circled her with his arms. She pressed her face back into his neck, slid the fingers of one hand into the hair at the side of his head and she ground her hips into his cock.

Her actions tore the words, "Fuck, baby," out of him because it felt so damned good.

"Locked deep," she whispered again and his arms tightened before his hands slid down to cup her ass.

Best place to be, Colt thought, locked deep in Feb. He was thinking figuratively because he knew it was true literally. She was a natural at this shit, considering she'd only had four lovers and apparently a number of long dry spells. Hell, she was so good, she could teach classes.

His mind turning to that, he decided when this was all over, there were a few men in the town he'd be having words with. Twenty-two years ago they spread lies about Feb. He'd see to it now the truth would come out.

She was still carrying around a reputation she didn't earn—not that anyone cared anymore except Feb—and Colt couldn't allow her to continue carrying that burden. In this mess that was a wrong Colt had the power to do something about and he intended to set it right.

Her fingers glided through his hair and she tilted her head to kiss the underside of his jaw, taking his mind from his thoughts.

"You go to sleep, darlin'," she encouraged.

His fingers tensed on her ass. "Not tired?" he asked.

She shook her head and he heard her hair brush the pillow, her necklaces clinking and felt her nose brush his neck, three things he automatically committed to memory.

"Feb—"

"It's okay, I'll watch you sleep."

He moved a hand from her ass to wrap it in her hair and lifted her head up with a gentle tug so he could look at her.

"Watch me sleep?" he asked, trying not to smile.

"Yeah," she said, her lips tipped up at the ends.

He lost the fight with his smile and remarked, "That'll be fascinating."

Her smile died and she told him, "I used to do it all the time. Watch you sleep, thinkin' how lucky I was, I had you."

Colt felt that warmth hit his chest with a force that knocked the wind out of him.

He didn't know that, she'd never told him. He was beginning to think he was uncertain about this new Feb who shared. If she kept sharing, she'd undo him.

"Now I can do it," she whispered, moving her face closer, "thinkin' how lucky I am havin' you back."

He couldn't take anymore.

Colt rolled her to her back, pulling out, losing their connection but covering her with his body as he ordered, "Shut up, Feb."

"What?" Her tone was confused but threaded with hurt.

"I said, shut up."

Her head twitched and her eyes slid away as she mumbled, "Sorry, I—"

His hand still in her hair twisted. "Don't say you're sorry." Her eyes slid back to his as he went on. "Got nothin' to be sorry for. And you got nothin' to feel lucky about."

"Alec—"

"One person lucky in this bed, baby, and that person's got a dick."

Her lips parted again as she stared at him silent.

"You know the life I was born into."

"Alec—"

"That life coulda taken me down a different road, but it led me to you."

"Alec—"

He heard a phone ringing, a cell, Feb's tone coming from the living room and he heard it so well he hoped to God Jackie was dead asleep because Feb was a moaner and when he was fucking her, she could get loud.

He ignored the noise and said to Feb, "Sucks, baby, what happened to us, what happened to you, what's *still* happenin' to you. But we're back on track and, make no mistake, it isn't you who's lucky, it's me who's the lucky one."

Her phone stopped ringing as she said, "Colt, it's me who—"

He dropped his head, kissed her quiet and when he lifted his head again, he said, "Stop sharin', Feb, can't take it."

He watched her eyes get big. "I thought you wanted me to share."

He smiled at her. "I'm thinkin' I was wrong."

"But—"

He touched his lips to hers again and teased, "You're too sweet, like candy, you keep goin', you'll rot my teeth."

He heard her phone start ringing again and he lifted his head to listen to it.

"Alec—"

Quickly and distractedly, he ordered, "Quiet, Feb."

"You're very bossy," she said on a mildly annoyed snap, one that said she didn't mean it but she also kind of did.

Her phone stopped ringing and he focused back on her.

"February—" he started to close the conversation down but her phone started ringing yet again and the warmth Feb injected into his chest evaporated. The cold taking over, he watched her head twitch as she finally heard her cell.

"Fuck," he cursed, pulling away from her and rolling off the bed.

He grabbed his jeans from the floor as she came up on an elbow, yanking the covers over her breasts. Her head tilted as she listened to her phone stop ringing then, seconds later, it started again. Her eyes sliced to his as he tugged on his jeans. He watched her face paling before she threw off the covers, twisted her legs over the side, got up and grabbed his shirt.

"Let me take care of this," he said to her as she shrugged his shirt on.

"Okay, but I'm coming with you."

"Feb—" he began as she bent forward to nab her panties but shot back up to lock eyes with him.

"I'm comin' with you."

At her tone Colt felt it prudent not to argue.

The phone stopped ringing and started again by the time she had her underwear on and three buttons done up at her chest. They hit the living room and she turned on a lamp. Her purse was on his coffee table, the cell on top stopped ringing only to start again.

He grabbed it, looked at the display and it said "Unknown caller."

Colt let it ring once more before he flipped it open and put it to his ear.

"Better be good, it's fuckin' midnight," he said into the phone.

He got silence back and he watched Feb watching him.

"Someone there?" Colt prompted.

Nothing.

"Don't piss me off," he warned and that's when he got it.

"She's not supposed to be there," a man's voice, vibrating with emotion, probably anger, said into his ear. Colt couldn't know for sure if it was Denny, if he'd ever actually spoken to the man it hadn't been in years. But he still knew it was Denny.

"Lowe?" he asked, waving his hand at Feb, motioning to the bedroom, hoping she'd understand what he meant. She nodded and ran down the hall.

"No," the man said.

"This isn't Denny Lowe?"

"No," the voice was getting agitated. "This is Lieutenant Alexander Colton."

Colt felt a chill shaft down his spine.

Fucking shit. This guy was *whacked*.

"You're wrong, seein' as I'm Alec Colton," Colt told him.

"No. No, you aren't. She isn't supposed to be there. Not without me."

Colt had absolutely no idea how to play this and he also didn't know if Feb was right now calling Sully.

He went with his gut, hoping Feb read his meaning and doing what he could to keep the sick bastard on the line. "She's Feb, Denny, you know she's meant to be with me."

"She's meant to be with *me*."

"How do you know she's here?"

"You can't have her, she's mine."

"Sorry, Denny, you're wrong. She's mine, always has been and you know it."

"You can't have her. She and I are meant to be together."

"How do you know she's with me, Denny?"

"*Stop callin' me Denny!*" he shouted as Feb hit the room, Colt's cell in her hand, her eyes on Colt.

"Denny, listen to me, you aren't doin' right by her. What you're doin', Feb doesn't want. You're tearin' her apart. Stop. Go to the nearest police station and turn yourself in."

"Gotta make her safe. It's my job. I'm the good guy. I'm the police. I gotta make her safe so no one can hurt her again."

"You aren't makin' her safe, Denny. You're hurting her, scaring her."

"She knows it's my job. She knows I'm doin' it all for her."

Colt tried something different. "How'd you get this number, Denny?"

"She gave it to me."

"She didn't. She hasn't seen you in years."

"I come in to the bar all the time."

"You do?"

"Yeah, I do. Sit at the end. She brings me beers. She watches me when she thinks I'm not lookin'."

Holy fuck, he had eyes in that bar.

"Denny, *I* do that. You haven't been in the bar since she's been home."

"I'm there all the time. Ask Morrie, he's seen me."

"No, Morrie has seen *me*, Denny. You aren't me," Colt told him. "Turn yourself in."

"Gotta make her safe so no one will hurt her again."

"Do the right thing, turn yourself in."

"Gotta make her safe."

"Are you in town? Is that how you know she's here?"

"Keep tabs on her, gotta keep her safe."

Jesus, who was this guy's eyes?

"Denny, don't make this worse for Feb, for you. I'm tellin' you, the best thing you can do is turn yourself in."

"Got two more then she'll be safe."

Colt heard the disconnect and hissed, "*Fuck!*"

Two more. One was him, the other a wildcard.

"Colt?" he heard Feb call and looked at her to see Jackie was now with her, Jackie's arm around Feb's waist, holding her daughter close.

"It was Denny," Colt confirmed and lifted his hand, indicating his phone. "You call Sully?"

Feb stepped away from her mother, came to him and handed him his phone, nodding. "Told him about the call, gave him my number."

Colt flipped her phone shut and his open. Scrolling to Sully, he hit the go button.

He listened to it ring once before Sully said, "Colt?"

"They get it?"

"Don't know, gotta keep this line open for the call back."

"I'll let you go but you gotta know, he's got eyes on the bar, Sul, and he knows she's with me now."

"Right."

"Send someone to the bar, do a sweep. It may be cameras."

"Your house?"

That chill shafted back up his spine. "My house too. I'll do the sweep tonight."

"Report in. Out."

Colt flipped the phone closed and looked at Feb. "Put some clothes on, baby."

"He's watching?" she whispered.

"Don't know. Put some clothes on."

She ran from the room.

"I'll make coffee," Jackie said and headed to the kitchen.

Colt followed Feb, he wanted to check the bedroom first and he wanted to do it wearing a t-shirt.

⌁

An hour later Colt sat on the couch, Feb curled into his side, her arm draped around his stomach, her legs bent and resting on his thigh. She was pressing in so close it felt like she wanted to graft herself to him.

Jackie was curled into the armchair angled at the side of the couch, her legs like her daughter's, resting on the arm of the chair, her eyes on Colt.

He had his arm wound around Feb's back, his hand resting lightly on her hip. He was trying to appear calm when he fucking wasn't.

He had his cell to his ear and he heard it ring once.

"Colt."

"House is clean, Sully."

"Bar isn't," Sully replied. "Two eyes so far, both pointed at the bar. They're still lookin' but they got some technical wizard who found the feed. They're tracin' it same time they're preparin' for a showdown."

"Give me more," Colt demanded when Sully stopped.

"Well the good news, it's amateur. Still brilliant but either dumb luck or lots of research. Probably got the instructions off the Internet. Means they're thinkin' he did it himself and maybe the equipment has a print."

"All right, what else?"

"Other good news is the feed has to be close. He isn't beaming it to the moon. If he's watchin', he's close too."

"Good."

"Okay, Colt, the *bad* news is, he knows Feb's there because he's got a camera on the street pointed at your house. They're now tracin' that feed too but we suspect it's goin' to the same place."

"So he's either close and watchin' or he's got an accomplice who's informing."

"That's right."

"He called her phone, Sully," Colt told him.

"Easy for him to find her number, seein' as he spent time in her house. Her number's on her phone bill. Called Chris, he said we got one of Lowe's prints off the big plastic folder she keeps her paperwork in, stowed in the closet on the shelf by her journals."

"Chris is a good man."

"Gotta watch it, Colt, he's after our jobs." Sully was joking but he wasn't wrong. Chris would make detective. He wanted it, he worked hard and he was fucking smart. So much so, he might even beat Colt's record to the badge.

"All right, got something more for you, Sully," Colt said, his fingers giving Feb a squeeze in an effort to give her strength before she heard what was going to come out of his mouth. "You need to give this to the Feds and their profilers. Guy's more whacked than we thought. He thinks he's me."

Colt heard both mother and daughter suck in breath but he only felt Feb's body get tight against his so he gave her another squeeze.

"He tell you that?"

"Identified himself as Lieutenant Alexander Colton."

He heard Feb's whispered "Oh my God," but kept on talking.

"Got jacked up when I called him Denny. Says he's the police and he's doin' all this to keep her safe."

"Jesus."

"Also said there were two more. I reckon he thinks one is me, the other..." he let that trail when Feb's head dropped to his shoulder.

"They didn't get time to triangulate the signal on the phone," Sully told him.

"Bad news."

"They're now monitorin' her phone, yours, your house phone and the bar."

Too little too late but who would imagine that fucking guy would actually call. Stupid move, he was getting messy and that could mean bad things. Though it could also mean good and Colt went with his last thought.

"We need to be in his face about this shit?" Colt asked. "Press a reaction?"

"I'm gonna get in his face," Jackie whispered her threat and Colt couldn't help it, he smiled into his phone. Jackie got a hold of him, hatchet or not, Denny Lowe didn't stand a chance. A lioness was lethal when her cubs were under threat.

"Well, unless he gets close and starts watchin' with his own eyes, that'll be difficult," Sully said. "They dismantled the cameras, all of them, even the one on the street. I'm learnin' the Feds *do not* fuck around and somehow they got an army to throw at this shit. Warren says taking the cameras offline is their own way of pressin' a reaction, pissin' him off, forcin' a move."

That was unfortunate. Colt liked the idea of standing in his open front door and kissing Feb good-bye before he went about his day. He'd take his time, he'd make it thorough, he'd get that moan in his mouth and he'd put his hands on her ass. He'd drive Denny Lowe over the next bend as Colt forced him to watch Colt stake claim to what was his, what Denny almost succeeded in taking away from him and what Colt got back. The man had a single synapse firing correctly in his brain, Colt wanted to obliterate it.

"Keep me posted," Colt told Sully.

"One other thing, man," Sully said hurriedly. "Feds want you to consider protective custody, for you and Feb."

Colt didn't like it, for him or Feb, meant her being pent up and him being disempowered. But he'd sure as fuck consider it.

"We'll talk, I'll let you know."

"Later, Colt."

"Later."

Colt flipped his phone shut and Feb lifted her head, opening her mouth to speak.

"One second, baby," he muttered on another squeeze at her hip.

He scrolled down his phone, found the number he was looking for, hit the button and put it to his ear.

"'Lo?" Chip said after ring four. Colt had woken him.

"Chip, it's Colt. Sorry to wake you but this is urgent."

"Everything okay?" Chip asked, trying to shake the sleep from his voice.

"I know it's late and I know your schedule's busy, but I need you to bump your other customers for a priority job, first thing in the mornin'."

"What job?"

"My house and I want a recon of J&J's. You think you need to, I want you to up the security there."

"This have to do with all the shit I been hearin'?" Chip asked.

"Exactly that."

"You and Feb safe?"

"Not by a long shot."

Chip didn't hesitate when he said, "Be there at seven."

"Later."

He flipped his phone shut and looked at Jackie then at Feb.

Feb was stuck in time. Colt knew it when she asked, "He thinks he's you?"

"He's whacked."

"I know that, but *he thinks he's you?*"

Colt smiled. He couldn't help it, her face was hilarious. His choices were either to smile, laugh or get up and put his fist through a wall.

"Okay, Feb, he's *seriously* whacked."

"Got that right," Jackie put in on a mumble.

He didn't want them to dwell, either of them, which meant shutting this down. You didn't talk about this shit in the dead of night when the demons could attack because you were vulnerable. You talked about this shit in the light of day when you had your defenses up and your mind could fight back.

"Time for bed," Colt announced, curling to get up and taking Feb with him.

"I couldn't sleep, no way I could sleep," Feb said, sliding both her arms around him when they got to their feet.

He looked down at her and smiled again. "All right, honey, then you can watch me doin' it."

Her head jerked, the cloud over her face cleared, she was fighting back the demons, just as her brows drew together and she said, "Okay, you're right, no more sharing. I give you the ammunition I'll never hear the end of it."

He curled his arms around her and gave her a squeeze, the smile never leaving his face. "You know I'm teasin', baby."

"I know and I like it now about as much as I liked it when I was eight and you and Morrie chased me around, waving frogs at me."

That memory was so hilarious—Feb screaming like a lunatic and running so fast her hair flew out straight behind her—Colt felt the memory simmer inside him and he couldn't stop himself from bursting out laughing. Jackie felt it too because she did the same.

"My girl, always hated frogs," Jackie stated when she'd controlled her hilarity.

"That's right, Mom." Feb leveled her irate eyes at her mother. "I'm a *girl* therefore I hate *frogs*. I'd get kicked out of the girl club if I didn't. Ask Maisie, she's got the rules memorized."

Jackie laughed again before her eyes moved to Colt. "February. Always been a scaredy cat. Can't even watch scary movies."

"Oh Lord," Feb mumbled.

"Gotta say, Jackie, it's probably good my woman can hold her shit together when a psycho is on the loose. Thinkin' that's more important than her bein' able to watch Freddy Krueger invading high school kids' dreams in a movie."

"Oh no," Feb whispered, her brows had separated but her eyes were now wide. "Now I'm thinkin' about Freddy Krueger."

Colt gave her another squeeze. "I'll keep you safe, honey."

"You can't!" she snapped. "He gets to you *in your dreams*!"

There it was again. It hit his gut like a rocket and Colt couldn't stop from laughing so hard that he couldn't hold his head up doing it so he bent his neck and shoved his face in the side of hers.

If someone had told Colt anytime during that day he'd laugh or smile or do them more than once, he'd have told you that you were fucking crazy.

But there it was. Owens magic.

Feb thought he was golden? He couldn't say he didn't like that she thought that.

But she and her mother were something else. Something that glimmered far brighter than gold. Something that made you believe there was a God but He didn't make miracles. He created beings and gave *them* the power to make miracles, miracles both great and small.

Nine

CHERYL

The doorbell jolted Colt awake. He looked to the clock, saw it was five to seven and slid out from under the dead weight of Feb that was pressed to his side.

Yanking on his jeans, t-shirt and grabbing his gun, he hit the hall then the living room and looked out the peephole to see Chip Judd standing on his front step.

He'd unlocked the door when Jack hit the room, his hair a mess, his jeans on, his chest bare and his hand curled around the butt of his revolver.

"It's Chip, Jack. It's cool, I called him."

"Chip?" Jack asked.

"Go back to bed, it's all good."

Jack studied him with sleepy intensity for several seconds before he spoke.

"Don't know what's good, you callin' the only boy in town who installs security systems and him bein' here first thing in the mornin'," Jack stated the obvious on a grumble then headed back down the hall, muttering, "Fuck."

Colt turned back to the door and opened it, nodding to Chip and stepping aside for him to enter but his eyes scanned the neighborhood. Chip's van was parked on the street, no Audi in sight, no other movement. Street was waking up. Half an hour it'd be alive, people heading to work. An hour after that, it would be napping again.

He closed the door, locked it and turned to Chip. Chip had his eyes on the lock Colt turned and then they came to Colt.

"You're standin' there holdin' a gun, big man, and you still turn the lock?"

"Man out there's hacking up people with a hatchet. He threatened me direct and Feb could turn his eye to her. Not leavin' the door open to that possibility, Chip."

Chip's face had drained to the color of his hair, which was nearly as white as an albino, before he muttered, "Fuckin' hell."

"Damn straight, now what can you do for me?" Colt asked.

Chip recovered his composure, dipped his head to the door and said, "First thing, get you a decent deadbolt. My experience? Two kinds of cops. Those with families who got so many damned locks their house is like Fort Knox and their wives got scoliosis from carryin' around their keying. Those without who don't spend enough time home to give a crap. You're obviously Cop Type Two. Gotta tell you Colt, that lock's a piece of shit."

Colt couldn't argue. His lock wasn't near as bad as Feb's but it was still a piece of shit.

"Put it in and a chain, all the doors. There's one at the side, one at the back. I'll need five sets of keys," Colt told him. Chip nodded and Colt went on. "What else?"

"We talkin' the basic model, the basic deluxe or the full-on deluxe?" Chip asked.

Security systems cost some cake, Colt knew, and this would be a hit. It was only six months ago he finished the last payment on Melanie's kitchen. Other than that, he studiously kept out of debt and saved as much as he could so when he quit the department his life could be a fair bit sweeter than a cop's pension would buy him.

He took a financial hit when Melanie left. She had a job and two incomes made their lives a fuckuva lot easier. Further, he let her clean out the house when she left. She let him keep both the house and the boat they bought together. Fair trade, to Colt's way of thinking. She got a job across the city and wasn't staying in town so she didn't need the house and he cared about that boat a whole lot more than any couch. Except, he had to dip into savings to furnish his house when she was gone.

Now he intended, soon as he could, to buy a bike. Jack had taught both Morrie and him how to ride years ago and both of them always liked doing it. So much, every once in a while Colt would rent a Harley and they'd spend the weekend riding.

But now he knew February felt free on the back of a bike and Colt wanted to give her that feeling as often as he could.

A security system would cut into that intention.

Then again, when this shit was over, he also intended to have a talk with Feb. A lot of the way she lived her life was going to change. Her living in a studio void of personality was one of them. Her spending a lot of time in his kitchen cooking him breakfast was another.

"Deluxe," he told Chip and he knew by Chip's response that Chip read his face while he was thinking.

"Good call, Colt," Chip replied. "I'll give equipment to you wholesale and discount the labor."

Colt shook his head and said, "No need."

Chip gave him a look then he laughed, loud and long and Colt could do nothing but watch because he thought his friend might have a screw loose.

"What?" he asked when Chip stopped laughing.

"Colt, my man, you called me at two in the mornin'. You think you didn't wake Josie with that shit?"

Oh fuck.

Chip's wife, Josie Judd, had been a friend of Feb, Jessie and Mimi's back in the day. She still was. Josie Judd was everyone's friend, sliding in and out of cliques like she was greased with shortening. Josie was a pleaser but it wasn't that. The woman was pathologically social.

Chip kept talking.

"She heard me say Feb's name and pestered me the minute I hung up the phone. She and her sister have been peckin' over you and Feb for donkey's years. Swear to God, they been drinkin' so much coffee and dreamin' up so many scenarios the last week, you'd think their brains would frazzle. They reckon this is a romance novel come alive. This bein' about you and

Feb, I don't give you deluxe and discount it, she finds out I charged you regular, she'd have my balls."

Josie might be social and a people pleaser but she was also a ball-buster, known throughout the town for all of the above. Colt reckoned the men in that town had a case to make Chip a saint the way he put up with Josie's energy, the endless round of parties she gave and dragged him to, all the times she said "yes" when Chip would end up doing all the work and the whip she used liberally on him.

Then again, the woman wasn't hard to look at, got her figure back within months after each of their three kids and Chip let it slip regularly that she gave world class head, liked doing it and did it often. He could have been full of shit, telling his tale so as not to appear weak, but Colt didn't see it that way. Chip smiled a lot and was one of the most mellow, adjusted people Colt had ever met. Getting great head from a woman who looked like Josie who was talented with her mouth could do that for a man. Colt figured, his own life wasn't totally fucked, he'd be about as mellow and adjusted as Chip right now and he was looking forward to that time.

But now he didn't have time to argue about what he'd pay and he wanted the system in without delay.

"All right, Chip, you do it discount, I'll get Feb to make you a frittata," Colt told him.

Chip whistled through his teeth. "Heard about her frittatas, big man." His brows went up. "You tellin' me you already earned one?"

Colt didn't respond and didn't have to, Chip grinned.

"Legend," Chip muttered before he said, "Got the keys to the bar? I'll swing by there, give it a look. It's been around awhile. Dad put it in and I wasn't on that job, probably could use some updating. Then I'll round up the boys and come back here."

Colt went to his keying, slid off the keys, gave them to Chip and told him the alarm code.

He opened the door and Chip hesitated in it. "Know I don't have to tell you this but keep her safe. Would suck, you two finally bein' back together only for one of you to end up hacked up with a hatchet."

"Yeah," was the only response Colt could come up with for that understatement.

Chip looked over his shoulder, his gaze hitting Feb's purse on the coffee table, before he again caught Colt's eye and he said low, "Pleased for you, Colt."

Then he took off.

Colt locked up after him and headed back to his room. It was likely the Feds found and raided Denny's spying on Feb lair and he wanted to get to the station to see what came of it.

He hit the room and saw Feb still asleep. He fell asleep before her so he didn't know when she finally dozed off. Still, he went to the bed, sat on the edge and pulled her hair off her neck before he put his hand to her hip, gave her a squeeze and bent to kiss her exposed neck. Then he touched his tongue to the chains tangled there.

She moved. He lifted his head and saw her open her eyes.

"You can go back to sleep, baby, just wanted you to know I'm gonna get a shower and head into the station. Your dad's here."

"Dad asleep?"

Colt reckoned he was and nodded.

"Mm," she murmured and lifted up to a hand.

"Feb, honey, go back to sleep."

"In a minute," she whispered, her hands coming to him, one arm wrapping around his back, the other hand sliding down his crotch over his jeans.

Her intention clear, it killed him when he had to say, "Baby, gotta get to the station."

Her face disappeared into his neck, her lips sliding up it and at his ear, her hand cupping his crotch, she said, "Lay back, Alec."

"Baby."

He felt her tongue touch his earlobe. He felt his cock start to grow hard and then he heard her whisper in his ear, "I want you in my mouth, Colt."

Colt figured he had a lot of work to do to erase the loneliness Feb had felt the last two decades of her life.

He might as well start now.

Colt was feeling unsurprisingly mellow and adjusted when he hit the bull-pen at the station.

However, considering the state of things, unfortunately for him this feeling wouldn't last long.

He saw Jo from dispatch heading toward the front stairs.

"Colt," she called when she'd stopped and turned to him. "Just put a message on your desk. They got a boy in interrogation room two. The Feds just started workin' him. Sully's watchin' and wants you with him, minute you get in."

"What boy?" Colt asked.

"Denny Lowe's eyes-on-the-prize boy," Jo answered.

Colt nodded, uncertain if he felt elation or dread and headed straight to the soundproof room next to interrogation two. He entered and saw Sully, Chris and Rodman watching through the one-way mirror as the profiler Nowakowski and Warren worked a young, skinny, mop-haired, pimple-faced, terrified-looking kid.

They all glanced at Colt when he entered but only Sully kept his eyes on him.

"Got him, Colt. Denny's officially fucked," Sully told him.

"Write down the email address you send the files to, Ryan, right here," Nowakowski's voice came through the speaker.

Colt closed the door and walked in, watching Nowakowski sliding a pad toward the boy, putting a pen on top.

Colt stopped beside Sully and saw Nowakowski was seated not across from the kid, beside him. The kid was at the middle of the table, Nowakowski at the side. Friendly, approachable, non-threatening. Warren was standing, shoulders against the wall by the door, head up, eyes looking down his nose at the boy, arms crossed on his chest. Unfriendly, official, a threat.

"I swear I didn't know," the kid said, his voice hitching, about to unman himself and trying like hell to stop it. "He said he was a cop. Had a badge and everything."

"We understand," Nowakowski told him, though Colt knew he didn't. He thought the kid was a dumb fuck which he probably was. Though for the life of him, Colt couldn't read that in anything Nowakowski was sending the kid. The guy was good.

"He said I was deputized, an official part of the operation," the kid said, his eyes on Nowakowski, disbelief at being duped on his face. "Said we needed to keep an eye on her all the time so we could keep her safe. She was under threat."

Yep, a dumb fuck, Colt thought as he watched Nowakowski nod with understanding and the kid picked up the pen and bent over the pad.

"Um, bad news, man," Sully mumbled to him, leaning close. "Lowe had eyes in Feb's apartment. We didn't find 'em. Feds did about an hour ago after we saw what all the monitors were picking up. Those were put in professional by Ryan here. Whiz kid, works at an electronic shop, does this shit as a hobby but also part side-business. Nanny cams. Shit like that. He's good, idiot savant. Chris did the sweep and he didn't pick them up. Feds said they'd have trouble findin' 'em if they didn't have the angles and a shitload more equipment and experience than a small town PD."

Rodman's eyes came to him and Colt kept his reaction to the news that Lowe and his lackey watched Feb in her apartment under control. It cost him but he didn't even bite his lip.

"He got cameras in my house I didn't find?" Colt asked.

"Nope. Just on the street."

"Where else?"

"Meems'. Boys are there now, yankin' 'em out."

Mimi was going to flip. Al was going to flip a fair bit harder.

"Someone sent to contain Al?"

"Did that myself before comin' in." Sully hesitated, his meaning clear before he said, "He's okay."

Which meant he wasn't at first until Sully talked him into being that way. Sully could work for the United Nations he was that good of a diplomat, which was the reason why Colt didn't do bodily harm to Craig Lansdon the day before.

"How's he gettin' around the security systems?" Colt asked.

Sully jerked his head toward the mirror. "Ryan here, dab hand at a lotta things, the little fuck. Unfortunately, he taught Lowe along the way."

"Why the fuck did he do that?" Colt asked.

"Lowe told him he was *you*. Had a badge and looked official. Lowe told him he'd be helpin' out the law if Ryan gave him some tutorin'."

"He half-idiot or something?"

"My experience, the smarter they are at one thing, the dumber they are with everything else. Ryan's the example that proves the rule."

"Will I get into trouble for this?" Ryan asked, calling their attention back to him and shoving the pad away, the email written on it, his eyes on the pad like it would come alive, jump up and take a bite out of him.

"Cooperate, Ryan, and we'll see what we can do," Nowakowski said and Colt's eyes shifted to the video equipment recording the interview, assessing if it was turned on and recording. Likely it was if the Feds, Sully or Chris set it up. Likely it wasn't if Marty had been there and done it. Colt figured Sully wouldn't let Marty anywhere near the equipment. They had learned that lesson the hard way.

"So," Nowakowski said, "just wanna go over what you said, make sure I got this right. Mr. Lowe hired you to disarm the alarms, assist in setting up the cameras and the feed. And he paid you to monitor them and email him recorded files."

"Yeah," Ryan replied. "He told me what he wanted and I set up face recognition software to get some of it. Most of the other stuff, I had to scan fast forward to get it."

"What'd he want?"

Ryan shifted uncomfortably in his chair.

Nowakowski read his discomfort and broke it down for him. "Let's start with the face recognition. Who was he watching?"

"The bar. The blonde and that guy when they were there together. The big guy. The other cop. He came in all the time. Sometimes to the coffee shop. Lieutenant Colt…I mean your guy, Mr. Lowe, said he was dirty."

Colt bit his lip then, he didn't give a fuck if Rodman saw it. Not only was Lowe impersonating him, he was also telling folks he was a dirty cop. That happened to him, fucking Rodman would bite his lip too. At least.

"Tall, dark hair, athletic build?" Nowakowski asked, and Warren's head turned toward the mirror. He knew Colt was watching.

"Yeah, him." Ryan nodded. "I didn't get it. What your guy wanted. They knew each other, the blonde and the big guy. You could see they knew each other. And he watched her ass, but fuck, *anyone'd* watch her ass. I watched her ass. She has a nice ass. Other than that, nothin'. Until recently."

"Recently?" Nowakowski asked.

"They'd disappear together in the office. We didn't put cameras there. Then they seemed unfriendly. Then real friendly. You know what I mean?" Ryan answered.

"You were watching February Owens and Lieutenant Alexander Colton, the real one, Ryan. He *is* a cop, but he isn't dirty," Warren put in. "You were surveilling a clean cop and his girlfriend."

Ryan wasn't such a dumb fuck as to be sitting in a room with two cops and find out he'd been watching another one and not know he was fucked. His face got even paler, the pimples coming out in bold relief and his hands clenched and unclenched on the table in front of him.

"I didn't know," Ryan said. "They barely used to speak."

"They've been havin' some problems," Warren shared. "They worked 'em out."

Ryan swung his head between Warren and Nowakowski. "He won't know, 'bout this, 'bout me? Will he? Witness safety and all that?"

Warren took an arm from his chest, pointed at the mirror and said, "He's watchin' you right now, Ryan."

"Oh fuck. Oh fuck." Ryan was squirming in his chair, not certain if he was allowed to get up but definitely certain he wanted to flee.

"Calm down, Ryan. We said he was a good cop. You cooperate, you got no problems with the real Lieutenant Colton," Nowakowski told both Ryan *and* Colt the way things would be. "Now, this has been goin' on for how long?"

"Six months, a bit more I think. Awhile," Ryan answered.

"Did Mr. Lowe ever come to watch the monitors?"

Ryan shook his head. "No, not ever. Just got the files."

"What else did you send him?" Warren asked and Ryan looked at Warren, then at the mirror. Then he turned to Nowakowski. "Will you ask him to leave? To stop watchin' me?"

"Think he's got a right to watch you a little while, Ryan, seein' as you been watchin' him and Ms. Owens. Don't you?" Warren asked. "Turnabout bein' fair play and all that shit."

Colt decided he was beginning to like Warren.

Ryan shook his head. "He won't...he won't—"

"What'd you send?" Nowakowski asked.

"But, he's watchin'," Ryan said.

"Ryan, tell us what you sent," Nowakowski pushed.

"He...you don't understand. He said he was a cop."

"Ryan, be smart now, all right? What did you send?" Nowakowski kept at him.

"I know it was weird!" Ryan flared, pushing his chair back several inches, enough to make Nowakowski sit back and go on alert and Warren to push from the wall. "But he said he was a cop! What do I know about cops?"

Warren took two steps forward and slapped a hand on the table, making Ryan jump before he barked, *"What'd you send?"*

"Her dressing!" Ryan shouted then shot to his feet, putting his hands to the sides of his head. "Dressing, undressing. That's all he wanted." Ryan's eyes went to the mirror for less than a second then they went to Nowakowski and he dropped his hands only to flick them out to the sides, twitchy. "Yeah, all right, I thought it was freaky! I'm not *that* stupid. If he didn't have the feeds from the coffee shop and the bar and want the footage of the big guy, I woulda known it was weird. But he wanted that too. I knew he was askin' for the extra because he was gettin' his rocks off but cops, they do that shit! Everyone knows that! And half the time he asked why there wasn't more and I lied and told him she changed in her bathroom. He wanted a camera in there but I didn't wanna see that shit and no reason for him to see it either, even if he was a cop. The big guy couldn't fit through a vent and whack her in the bathroom, for fuck's sake! So I put one in there but disconnected the feed and told him it malfunctioned. But sometimes he'd get very *fuckin'* perturbed when I lacked footage and he was a little bit freaky, dude. Seriously. So I'd send him some shit. Okay?" Ryan sat back down, elbows to the table, head back in his hands and he repeated, "I'd send him some shit. *Fuck.*"

"You get your rocks off, Ryan, like us cops, when you watched February Owens dress and undress?" Warren asked.

"No," Ryan mumbled to his lap.

Warren slapped his palm on the table and shouted, *"Don't lie to me!* You get your rocks off?"

Ryan bolted upright in his chair and yelled, "*No!*" Then his fists came down on the table. "Okay, at first, yeah, though I didn't jack off or anything. But then, even without sound, you could tell she was nice! You could see by the way she treated her cat and worked the bar. She smiled and it was real. People gravitate toward her. She's hot, sure, but after a while it was like spyin' on my big sister and it gave me the creeps." Ryan's gaze went back to the mirror and he said, "She's nice and you seem cool too. You made her laugh, she doesn't do that much. Glad you worked things out."

Five seconds before, Colt was using everything he had not to walk into that room and tear the little fuck's throat out. Just then, he started chuckling.

"Welp, you can sit easy, Colt, Ryan here's glad you worked things out with Feb," Chris muttered, laughter in his tone.

Before Colt could say anything, Nowakowski asked Ryan, "You see Mr. Lowe enter Ms. Owens's apartment?"

Ryan nodded. "Yeah, sure, he'd go in there. Said he was checkin' on things. Told me to shut down the cameras when he was in there."

Of course he would, Colt thought. Denny didn't mind Ryan watching Feb dress but he didn't want the little fuck to watch him jack off on her bed.

"You shut them down like he asked?" Nowakowski questioned.

"Yeah," Ryan answered.

Nowakowski tapped the pad with his finger. "Those files, Ryan, video files, those are big. Lieutenant Colton, he spend a long time in that bar?"

"Sometimes, sure," Ryan said, calming down at the change of topic but still on the alert.

"That's a lotta footage," Nowakowski remarked. "Those files would be large. You zip them or something?"

That's when Colt knew Nowakowski wasn't just good, he was sheer talent. There was something deeper. Nowakowski saw it and Colt didn't. Colt knew this because Ryan, already agitated, now was panicked clear as day.

"Sure," Ryan said, now for some reason lying through his teeth, trying to appear calm and failing. "Zipped 'em."

"Didn't burn DVDs? Hand 'em off to Mr. Lowe?" Nowakowski asked.

Ryan shook his head. "Saw Mr. Whoever during the deal, coupla times after then when we put in the cameras. Just email from then."

"So who'd you give the DVDs to?" Nowakowski asked and Ryan looked to the floor, the table, his hands, eye contact evaporated. "Ryan?" Nowakowski called.

"No DVDs, just emailed files."

"Take a lotta time to send those big files, even zipped. Most computers would time out."

"Got a high speed connection," Ryan said to his hands.

"Sure, you do. What about him? He confirm receipt of these big files?" Nowakowski asked.

Ryan shook his head. "No."

"So he wants this footage and he's cool with it bein' timed out? Seems weird, seein' as he'd get perturbed, you not sendin' enough of Ms. Owens," Nowakowski remarked.

"Maybe he has high speed too. He didn't complain about file crash."

Nowakowski turned the conversation. "You hear from him the last week or so?"

"Coupla times, yeah, after the big guy and the girl started to, you know, work things out, I guess. He was real interested in that and the street footage. Emailed, wanted me to make certain I rescanned the tapes, make sure I didn't miss anything. Her and him entering, leaving his house, when she'd chat with him at the bar, shit like that."

"So he's been in contact how many times in the last week?" Nowakowski pressed.

"Don't know, four, five, didn't hear from him a lot but started to hear from him more when the footage changed."

"You keep those emails?"

Ryan's head came up and a bit of belligerent swept into his face. "Yeah, they're on my machine that you seized."

Nowakowski, completely unperturbed, nodded. "Good. Now, who'd you hand the DVDs to?"

Belligerence gone, Ryan instantly was back to eye avoidance. "No DVDs."

"Who're you protectin', Ryan?" Warren, back at the wall, entered the interrogation.

"There aren't any DVDs," Ryan lied.

"All right." Nowakowski sat back, rested his elbows in his stomach and steepled his fingers. "Ryan, I want you to look at me."

Nowakowski waited patiently as Ryan plucked up the courage to lift his gaze and this took a while. He delivered the blow when he had Ryan's full attention.

"Mr. Dennis Lowe is wanted for the murders of four people. He hacked them up with a hatchet, the first victim, his wife, was almost unidentifiable, left a finger intact, the wedding ring he put on it telling us who she was. The other three he started at the groin and hacked up to the heart, near to splitting them in two. You gotta know about one of them since you had to see February Owens call the discovery of the body into the police and you watched Lieutenant Colton question her in the bar. Now, you can sit there, Ryan, and protect whoever you're protecting and become an accessory to multiple murders or you can tell us who you handed those DVDs."

Ryan's mouth was hanging open, jaw completely slack. So much Colt was surprised drool didn't slide from his lip.

Then he snapped it shut and rolled over immediately. "Candy Sheckle."

Nowakowski's eyes went to Warren but Warren was already leaving the room.

Then Nowakowski looked back at Ryan. "You know Candy?" Ryan nodded. "Tell me, Ryan."

"She's a girl."

"Guessin', with the name of Candy, she would be."

"She's a kind of…friend."

"Girlfriend?"

Ryan shook his head, heat hitting his face, making the pimples now nearly red. He wanted her to be, whoever Candy fucking Sheckle was, but he couldn't have her.

"No, just a friend."

"What kind of friend?"

"I help her out."

Nowakowski took his elbows from his stomach, unsteepled his fingers and sat forward.

"Ryan, I got all the time in the world. The problem is, Mr. Lowe has shared with us he's intending to kill two more people and *their* time is runnin' out. I'd appreciate it if you'd stop making this so hard so we can get on with our job and, maybe, save a couple of lives."

Ryan stared for a second then nodded. "She's a stripper. At Girls X."

He put up his hand and offered information Nowakowski didn't ask for but Ryan felt necessary to give.

"She's not like that. A lotta strippers, well, I don't know anyone other than Candy, and her real name isn't Candy. It's Cheryl. But anyway...people think strippers are skanks but she's not. She's real nice. She's got a kid and she wants him to grow up in a good neighborhood so she works real hard. She's um...she brought this Lowe guy to me. See, I used to help her out, go to the club, give her good tips and maybe a little on the side. But then she got hooked up with Lowe and, seein' as she's sweet, she told me to keep my money, she's got a boyfriend who takes care of her now and he's a good guy, a cop. So, you know, I was gonna talk to her when you let me go, but um...I'm thinkin' you should probably do it now."

"We should," Nowakowski affirmed, straight-faced and how he didn't laugh or even crack a smile Colt would never know. "So you gave her the DVDs?"

Ryan nodded then sat forward, eye contact back, earnest now. "Candy, she's gonna freak. She likes him, thinks he's a good guy, thinks we're doin' right. And really, stripper or not, she's nice. Seriously. Maybe you could be...um, gentle with her. Okay?"

"We'll take care of Candy, Ryan."

Colt looked at Sully and they both walked from the room.

"Bet you a thousand dollars Candy Sheckle's the spittin' image of Feb," Sully said as they headed down the hall to the bullpen.

"I'm puttin' a security system in today, Sul, not gonna take a foolish bet," Colt replied and caught Warren's eye as they got to the bullpen. "Name's Cheryl, not Candy," he told Warren who was on the phone.

"That would be Cheryl Sheckle," Warren said into the phone.

"Cheryl Sheckle, shit, her parents musta hated her," Sully muttered.

Colt stopped by his desk and leaned a hip against it. Sully stopped with him.

"Okay, Sully, breakin' this shit down, where the fuck are we now?" Colt asked. "Months before the murders, he's got a whole operation set up to spy on Feb and me. He's impersonating me, insinuated himself into two lives, both of which cost him big money. When did the withdrawals start?"

"Last coupla months."

"But he's been workin' this shit for six."

"I'll go back over the statements. See if other withdrawals increased."

"My advice?" Colt offered. "Get Marie's too. I reckon she had her own account, money from her parents. And talk to her neighbor again. See if Marie told her she was giving him money."

"Christ, you think he took his wife's money to keep his girl on the side and set up a Feb Watch?" Sully asked.

"I think he'd do anything," Colt answered. "He's a man without a moral compass, Sully. Drug me, okay, I'm a big guy, I can take it and get mine back if I have that inclination. Feb? She's got me, Morrie, Jack, Jackie, an army of support. Amy? Puck? Total innocents. Defenseless. He mowed through them and when he brought low Amy, Craig said the fucker *laughed*."

Sully got close and his voice got quiet. "Speakin' of that, I had a talk with Nowakowski before he went in. Explained a few things. He's considerin' helpin', if you ask, see if he can find a way to bypass some channels, you find out that adoption Amy fixed was closed."

Colt didn't want to talk about this, not now, and he didn't want Sully talking about it to anyone either.

"Sully—"

Sully lifted up his hand. "That's another night, another bottle of Jack, I know. Just sayin'."

Colt felt his blood start heating. "You think I should approach a twenty-one year old kid and let him know he's the product of...whatever the fuck?"

"I think you're my partner and a damn good friend and if you decide you want to find your boy, I'll do whatever I can to help. That's what I think, nothin' more, nothin' less."

"What I think is that enough of this shit is spreadin' around," Colt said. "Amy's dead and everyone knows her as a quiet, good woman. She doesn't need that coloring anybody's memory of her."

Sully shook his head. "That won't happen. Craig's promised to keep it quiet and you know anyone else who knows will. Including Nowakowski."

"All right, Sully. All I'm askin' is, you just keep it that way."

"To the grave," Sully promised, lifting his hand like he was taking an oath.

"Jesus, you're a pain in the ass," Colt told him and meant it. Sully could definitely be a pain in the ass.

"A pain in the ass that helped score multiple counts of unlawful entry on the sick fuck who's makin' your and Feb's life a livin' hell, not to mention whatever else we can pin on him through that shit." Sully grinned. "I'm thinkin' a nice shot of single malt from you, or two, and an invitation to sit in on Feb's next frittata."

"Feb'll make you a frittata every day for a year, you find this guy."

Sully kept grinning. "Once is enough. Every day's too much of a good thing."

He was wrong. He hadn't had her frittata.

Then again, if Colt had it every morning then when would he have her stuffed French toast?

Colt was walking back to the station from a very ticked off Mimi's with his muffin in a white bag and his Americano when his phone rang. He shifted the bag into the same hand as the coffee, yanked out his phone and saw the display said "February Calling."

He flipped it open one-handed and put it to his ear.

"Yeah, baby?"

"You owe me."

Her voice came at him, husky and still full of sleep. She'd called him first thing after waking up, her mind on what she did to him with her mouth. That knowledge and the sound of her voice hit him direct in the gut and scored straight down to his dick.

She was right, he did. He owed her big.

That was why he smiled into the phone, stopped at the foot of the steps to the station, dropped his bag and set his coffee on the stone balustrade.

"You just wake up?" Colt asked.

"Yeah, after you hit the shower, I slept clean through until Chip started banging away." She didn't sound pissed. She sounded slightly surprised, though he'd only hit the shower three hours ago.

"Sorry about that, honey. New locks. New alarm."

"That's okay," she said softly.

He took a sip of his coffee, waiting for her to say more. She didn't so he asked, "There a reason you're callin'?"

"Yeah, I'm running out of clothes. Is it okay if Dad or Morrie take me to my place to pick up more?"

Yes, it's fucking okay, he thought.

"Sure," he said then warned, "But honey, it was swept. It's probably gonna be a little less than your usual clean."

"Great," she muttered.

"Then again," Colt teased, wanting to take her mind off it, "most operating rooms are less than your usual clean."

"I like order," she replied. "Especially when my life is chaos."

"Bullshit, Feb," Colt kept teasing. "You're Jackie Owens's daughter. You like order all the fucking time."

"Something wrong with that?" she asked, now getting pissed. She always hated being teased, which meant he used to do it a lot because she was cute when she was pissed. That was, only when it was under his control.

"Nope, nothin' wrong with that," Colt answered.

She hesitated then called, "Colt?" like he wasn't on the phone with her but she was trying to catch his attention.

"I'm right here."

"Um…would you mind if I…" another pause then quickly, "clear a drawer and maybe…commandeer a few hangers?"

Fucking hell, she wanted to move her shit in and Colt felt that in his gut too.

"You know, so I don't have to live out of a bag?" she finished on a rush.

"Take as much room as you need," Colt paused too and then said, "And bring over as much shit as you want."

Feb was silent a moment before she said softly, "Okay, babe." Then she asked, "What's your day gonna bring?"

"So far, it's brought more dirt on Denny. I'll tell you about it tonight."

"They closer?" she asked.

"Closin' in."

"Thank God," she whispered then, her voice stronger, "Since I had an unscheduled day off yesterday, I need to be at the bar tonight. You wanna meet me there for dinner? Frank's. On me."

"You're on. Six o'clock."

"You want me to tell Darryl you want a tenderloin so you'll maybe get a burger?"

He smiled into the phone before he said, "Why don't we try a patty melt, see what that brings?"

He heard her laughter coming at him through the phone.

You made her laugh, she doesn't do that much.

He heard Ryan's words through Feb's laughter. Ryan was right, Feb didn't laugh much. Not for years and only genuinely with Bonham and Tuesday. She'd been doing it a lot more recently, mostly with him.

"Patty Melt Mystery Dinner it is," she cut into his thoughts after she stopped laughing. "Six o'clock. Shit!" she said suddenly, he heard the phone jostle and her far away shout. "Yeah, I'm up! Be out in a sec." Then she came back to him. "That's Dad, he says he wants to be briefed as to why Chip's here." She laughed softly again before saying, "Colt, babe, he actually used the word *briefed*." Colt laughed with her the second time before she finished hurriedly and distractedly. "Better go *brief* Dad. See you later. Love you, babe."

Colt froze and just managed to force out a "Later, baby," before Feb disconnected.

See you later. Love you, babe.

That was how she would end every phone conversation they had, which were daily when she wasn't up visiting on a weekend when she was at home and he was at Purdue.

See you later. Love you, babe.

He knew she'd been preoccupied when she said it, slipping back into a very old habit.

He also didn't fucking care.

He flipped his phone shut, shoved it in his back jeans pocket, grabbed his muffin and entered the station smiling.

⌒‿⌐

The phone on his desk rang. Colt picked it up, put it to his ear, looked at the name on the display on the desk set and said into the handset, "What's up, Kath?"

"Colt, Amy Harris's folks just walked in. I put them in the conference room."

Fuck.

He knew they'd arrived yesterday from Arizona to start making arrangements for the funeral. Yesterday, with Colt mostly out of commission, Sully had dealt with them, making an appointment for them to come and talk with Colt today at two o'clock.

Now it was today and it was fucking two o'clock.

"Do me a favor, ask them if they want coffee, get it for them if they do and I'll be down in a minute."

"No probs, Colt," she said and he put the phone down.

Kath was a civilian and she worked the front desk. She had a dickhead of a husband and five kids, all of them heathens. She did her best but, the dad they had, her kids acted out anyway, as often as they could and they were creative. When they advertised the job for the front desk, she applied for it, telling them it was a way to spend some time with her family since all of them, including her husband, sat in a cell on more than a rare occasion.

They gave her the job, mostly because she was a good woman, dependable, smart and, not including her husband, her family was a good family, deep down. They just had a lot of shit to get out and, until Kath grew a backbone and kicked her husband out on his ass, she needed all the help she could get.

Colt stood, pulled his blazer from his chair and shrugged it on. He was about to turn to the stairs when Sully walked up.

"Candy Sheckle's on her way in," Sully told him.

Colt's brows went up. "Of her own accord?"

"She had a shift at the club last night, just turned on her phone and, minute the Feds asked, she said she'd drop her kid off at her mom's and be right in."

"That's helpful," Colt remarked, surprised.

"Super-duper helpful," Sully returned, equally surprised.

"That'll be an interesting interview."

Sully smiled. "Can't fuckin' wait. You gonna watch?"

"Fuck yeah."

"See you there. I'll bring the popcorn."

Colt shook his head and went to the stairs.

The minute he saw Mr. and Mrs. Harris, seated but huddling together in the conference room, he knew why Craig had to carry Amy into the house, not to mention why Amy was petite. Her parents were both small. He didn't recall either of them but, if they were as quiet and reserved as their daughter, he doubted he ever saw them but in passing and probably wouldn't notice them.

"They didn't want coffee, Colt. The Mom drinks tea. You want me to run down to Mimi's?" Kath asked as he passed.

"You'd do that, it'd be appreciated," Colt replied, not taking his eyes from the Harrises.

"No trouble," Kath said and took off.

Mr. Harris caught his gaze while Colt made his way to the conference room. This would be difficult for more than the normal reasons. He had no intention of sharing. They didn't need to know their daughter went through what she went through. Still, he knew it and knowing it meant this was going to be far from easy.

He opened the door. Mrs. Harris twisted and looked up at him and Colt nodded to the both of them.

"Thank you for coming, Mrs. Harris. Mr. Harris."

Mr. Harris stood, reaching out and taking a big, yellow envelope from the table.

Without leading into it, he asked, "Can we talk privately, son?"

Colt looked at the envelope then to Mr. Harris who looked like hell then to Mrs. Harris who surprised him. She was gazing at him steady, straight in the eye. She looked sad but she also looked thoughtful and there was a softness to her eyes that Colt thought looked immensely kind.

Colt knew then that this was going to be more than an interview with grieving parents to ascertain if their daughter did, indeed, commit suicide so that he could file away her case, nice, neat and cozy.

This was going to be something he was going to like a lot less even than he expected. And he expected to fucking hate every second.

"This room is private, Mr. Harris. No one can—" Colt started.

"No eyes," Mrs. Harris cut in, her own eyes going to the windows.

Fuck.

"Of course," Colt said, turning to open the door and gesturing through it with his arm.

He led them up to interrogation room one, giving Sully a look and lifting his hand with his index finger extended to indicate he was taking interrogation one. Sully followed them with his eyes until he lost sight. Colt saw part of it and knew the other.

He opened the door to interrogation one and held it for the Harrises to walk through. He followed them and closed it behind him. Mr. Harris walked to the table. Mrs. Harris stood by the door.

Before he could speak, Mr. Harris put the envelope on the table and said, "We'll give you a moment of privacy to read this, Alexander."

Alexander.

Mr. Harris wasn't talking to Lieutenant Colton. He was establishing the fact that he was Colt's elder, he was doing it gently, but he was the authority figure in this scenario. But it wasn't authority he was communicating even though it wasn't Colt's daughter who hung herself. Mr. Harris was making a point of conveying he was there to provide support.

No, Colt wasn't going to fucking like this.

Colt was looking at Mr. Harris therefore it came as a surprise when he felt Mrs. Harris' fingers curl around his forearm. Colt's eyes went to her. She gave him a small, sad smile, squeezed his arm and then Mr. Harris touched her shoulder, gave Colt a nod. Colt moved away from the door and they left.

Colt walked to the envelope, feeling a bit of Ryan's pain. Whatever was inside could easily grow teeth and bite him.

There was nothing written on the front. The back was clasped but not sealed. Amy was long past keeping any secrets.

Colt opened the clasp and slid the papers out from inside, bent his head and read Amy Harris's suicide note.

Colt,

This is too late, I know, way too late. But I want you to know I'm sorry. I should have said it years ago but I didn't and you deserve to know why. You deserve to know everything.

I don't know how much you do know, or you remember, but I think it's not much from what I've heard and because, even after, when you saw me, you'd still smile at me. But this will explain things, I hope.

It was me who tore you and Feb apart. Me and Denny.

I didn't mean to be a part of it. I didn't even know I was. But, in the end, I had to be.

Denny knew I liked you. I told him a long time ago. A high school crush. We were good friends, Denny and I. I talked about you, he talked about Feb. He liked her a whole lot. Said she was special and they had a special friendship but it was secret. You couldn't know or, he said that Feb told him, you'd be angry. Now, I don't think this was true, but then I believed him.

It happened after that, though. You'd graduated from Purdue and we were all pretty much waiting for you two to get married. But Denny came home from Northwestern and talked to me and told me Feb had told him that things weren't going too good between you two. Feb was going to break up with you and it would soon be over. I guess I wasn't over my crush on you, in the end, the way things turned out. I guess that's why I did what I did. I keep trying to figure it out and that's what I've come up with.

Denny talked me into going to that party at the Eisenhowers. Do you remember it? I'm sure you do. Denny told me to "live a little." Normally, I wouldn't go but when I talked to Emily, she said it would be fun. She was always trying to get me to go out. So, we went.

I wish, Colt, so much over the years, you have to know, I wish I hadn't.

I saw you there, you and Feb, and it didn't seem Denny knew what he was talking about. You two seemed fine to me, like normal, like always.

Later that night, Denny brought me a drink, said I needed to "loosen up." I wasn't much of a drinker, never was. It hit me, what he brought me, real fast. I thought it was just a beer but I don't think it was. I couldn't know for sure, but, at the time, I just thought I was a lightweight, getting drunk on a few sips of beer.

Denny saw me going funny and told Emily he'd take care of me. What a laugh. Denny taking care of me. But I didn't know then and neither did Emily. We both thought he was my friend. Some friend.

He took me upstairs and said I should just lie down for a while. I don't remember it all, bits here and there. I felt so strange, like I wasn't me. I thought he was being nice, taking care of me, a good friend. Friends don't do what he did to me. They don't. But I wouldn't know that until later, when I learned Denny was not my friend at all.

At first, I didn't even know you were in the bed he put me in. And Colt, I swear, I promise and I swear, I don't know how it started. But, I think I started it. I wasn't thinking. I don't know what I was doing. I just started kissing you. You were there and you were Colt and I think I started kissing you. I was so drunk or whatever, it's all so fuzzy, you didn't kiss me back, or you did, I don't know. It didn't hit me until later that you weren't acting like you, you were acting like me. Like you were drunk or whatever. This is terrible and embarrassing but you have to know because I think I took advantage of you. We were moving around and somehow I got you on top of me and I liked it. I'm sorry, but I liked it. It's just the truth and you deserve to know the truth.

That's when Feb walked in.

I knew Denny was lying when I saw the look on her face. It was like she just learned someone she'd loved had died. Even being messed up, I'll never forget the look on her face.

Before I could say anything, she was gone and you were on top of me and I couldn't get you off. You'd passed out and you were so big, so heavy, I couldn't move you.

Then Denny was there, in the room, and I know he was in the room the whole time. He saw the whole thing. He was laughing, thought it was funny. I was trying to think straight, get you off me, get to Feb. I asked him to help me but he just kept laughing, saying, "Now it's over. Now it's over." He said it again and again. He sounded so happy. I knew he wasn't right then. I knew it. Really not right. But I didn't see it, couldn't think straight. Not until later, what he did to me and then, a lot later, what he did to Angie.

I got you off and I couldn't get untangled from the sheets, I was so muddled, and I just gave up and started crying. Craig was there then and he was so mad at Denny and I was lucky, for once, because Craig took care of me. He took care of you and me.

That was hard but this is harder because you have to know why I didn't say anything. Why I didn't tell you or Feb what happened.

The next day, my folks went to church and Denny came over. I felt sick, from what happened and from whatever he gave me and trying to figure out what I'd say to you and Feb. That's why I didn't go to church with them. But, even if I wasn't like that, I still couldn't have fought him. I did fight him, but I didn't win.

He hurt me, Colt. Right in the living room of my own home. He told me I couldn't tell you or Feb what happened. "Don't you fucking open your mouth," he said. I'll never forget it, those words, the way he said them. He wasn't a Denny I knew. But I told him I was going to tell you and he got mean, then meaner, then he hurt me, Colt. In the worst way. The very worst way.

Colt pulled in breath then sat down in a chair.

He didn't violate Amy and he didn't have a son.

He'd been right. Denny had raped her.

The first didn't make him feel better because he now knew the last.

He ran his fingers through his hair and then curved them around the back of his neck, squeezing tight, his eyes closed, the papers in his hand, Amy's words, written in pretty, neat handwriting. He wondered how many times she wrote and rewrote them. Or if she just poured it out and sent it to her parents.

The writing was too neat and he knew she'd practiced.

He bit his lip and pulled in another breath before he opened his eyes, slid the first sheet, which he'd read front and back, behind the other and started on the next page.

He left me and told me there was more of that if I opened my mouth. He knew, when I came up pregnant, that he did that to me. He sent me a note, put it in my mailbox and all it said was "Keep your mouth shut." I kept it and gave it to Mom and Dad with this letter. I don't know if it helps at all, but I'll ask them to give it you.

Colt, I didn't want that to happen to me again. That's why I didn't say anything. It wasn't until he hurt Angie, put her behind the bar, that I knew I had to do what was right. Don't ask me how I knew it was him, just that, I did.

But I went to the bar and I couldn't. The way Feb looked at me. I knew what she thought. And I couldn't hurt either of you anymore than I already did. And I didn't want him to hurt me.

So, by the time you get this, I will have made it so he can't hurt me but you'll know.

You can show this to Feb, I don't mind. Promise. You were sweet together and I like the idea that maybe I did a little something to make it all right between you two again. I'm just sorry I left it so late, too late for Angie but maybe not too late for you and Feb.

Please don't hate me, Colt. I couldn't stand that. I promise I wanted to do right.

And look into Denny. I can't say how I know that he did that to Angie except that I do. If he could do that to me, to you and to Feb, he could do that to Angie. He just could, Colt, trust me.

And one more thing and I'm sorry for this because I'm asking a favor I don't deserve to ask. But I had to do it, to protect him and I know you're a good man and you might not want to protect me but I figure you'll want to protect him.

I lied on the birth certificate. I said the father was Craig. I thought, if my boy ever came looking, that he should have a father he'd want to find, not Denny. If my boy comes looking, you have to talk to Craig. You have to tell him to keep my secret. You have to help protect my boy. I know it's a lot to ask, of you and of Craig, but I don't want him knowing, if he ever wants to find out, where he came from. Tell him Craig and me were young, but we were happy and we were in love. We weren't, but he was a good friend and he's a good man and every child should think they have a good dad and they came from love, don't you think?

My folks know what happened, they got their own letter and I know they'll stand by me. I just hope you and Craig will too. Will you do that for me? Please?

That's all there is to tell except to say I'm sorry. Really, so sorry. You don't know how much.

Amy

Colt read the last line again then again and he knew Amy was wrong. He knew how sorry she was. He'd seen her hanging from her ceiling fan. He knew just how sorry she was for something she fucking didn't do.

He slid the papers back into the envelope slowly and smoothed the clasp shut. Then he set it on the table and went to the door. He opened it to find the Harrises standing outside, Mrs. Harris holding a paper cup with a cardboard protector, the string from a teabag dangling.

"Would you come back in?" Colt asked.

They nodded and walked in, their eyes on the envelope.

"Please, sit."

"Are you okay, son?" Mr. Harris asked instead of sitting and Colt looked at him.

"No," he answered truthfully. "You had a beautiful, kind daughter who is no longer of this world and never did a thing wrong to anyone and definitely not to me. But she lived twenty-two years thinking she did. I'm not okay with that."

Mr. Harris's body grew taller, his shoulders straightening.

Mrs. Harris's body grew smaller, her shoulders sagging.

"We aren't either," Mrs. Harris whispered and Colt saw the tears trembling in her eyes.

"It helps, though," Mr. Harris said quietly, "to know you aren't either."

"Please, sit," Colt repeated.

Mrs. Harris didn't sit, she asked, "Will you tell February?"

Colt nodded. "Yes, I will. Soon as I can."

"Will she understand?" Mrs. Harris asked, her voice slightly higher, worried.

"She already does," Colt assured her. "We figured some of it out already. She's not okay with what was done to Amy either."

Mrs. Harris nodded, a tear slid down her cheek and she looked to her husband.

"We heard things, since we been back to town," Mr. Harris said. "Are they going to get him?"

"Yes," Colt said, knowing he shouldn't. Anything could happen. You didn't give assurances you couldn't stake claim to. But he said it all the same.

Mr. Harris gestured to the envelope. "Amy would want you to use that, if you need to." He opened his jacket and pulled another envelope out, this one smaller, white. "And this," Mr. Harris finished, putting the white envelope on top of the yellow one.

"When did you receive these?" Colt asked.

"The day Doc called," Mr. Harris answered, running an arm around his wife's waist and pulling her close. "We were out, didn't open the mail, not until after he called. We thought it could wait until we delivered it to you, face to face."

Colt nodded. Amy had planned her death precisely and he hated it that those plans were the last thing she carried out in this world. As he nodded, he heard Mrs. Harris's breath hitch.

"You need us anymore?" Mr. Harris asked, pulling his wife closer, wanting to get out of there.

"No, sir."

Mr. Harris nodded and led his wife to the door. Colt followed and watched the older man stop at the door then turn.

"Please don't talk to Craig 'less you have to."

Colt nodded.

"She'd want you at her funeral. Will you do that for her?"

Colt didn't miss a beat. "Feb and I'll be there."

"Mean a lot to Amy."

"We'll be there."

"Tomorrow, three o'clock. Service before. Markham and Sons."

"We'll be there," Colt repeated.

Mrs. Harris lifted her wet face to Colt and whispered, "You always were a good boy."

"And Amy always was a sweet girl," Colt returned. She nodded, fresh tears falling from her eyes, both her lips disappearing around her teeth.

Her husband bustled her out and Colt followed them close, like a guard, down the hall, through the bullpen with police and Feds studiously avoiding looking at the grieving couple, down the hall, through the front doors, down the stairs and to their rental car on the street.

Mr. Harris stopped, shook Colt's hand. When her husband moved away, Mrs. Harris got close, wrapped her fingers around his upper arm, leaned up high and Colt bent low so she could touch her cheek to his.

"Life lands blows you don't expect," she whispered against his cheek. "They wind you and there's some you never get your breath back. We didn't know, we asked, she never answered, but we suspected. Amy never got her breath back." She pulled her face away but stayed close and looked him in the eye. "Get your breath back, Alexander. Amy would want that for you."

"All my life, had good people looking after me," Colt promised her. "I get winded, I recover. Now, even with that, I'm breathing just fine, Mrs. Harris."

That last was a lie, but she didn't know that.

Though he wasn't lying, he'd recover.

She squeezed his arm, nodded again, let him go and turned away.

Colt watched the street long after their car disappeared.

Then he turned, took the front steps two at a time then the inside stairs the same.

"Colt!" Sully called, but Colt kept walking to interrogation one.

"Not now, Sully," he called back.

He hit interrogation one, grabbed the envelopes, headed out, dropped the white envelope on his desk and went back down the stairs at a jog. Then out of the station. When he hit the sidewalk, he was running.

He pulled open the door to J&J's and Feb, behind the bar, looked at him.

"Office," he said before she could do the jaw tilt.

He watched her head twitch as he covered the ground in less strides than it normally took him. As he went, she hurried down the bar. She hit the office barely a second after him. He took her arm, pulled her inside, slammed the door and then pushed her against it. He moved into her, fully invading her space, his arm with the hand holding the envelope went around her waist low, pulling her hips to his. His chest leaned deep, pressing her shoulders to the door. His other hand went to her jaw and he dipped his face close.

"I didn't violate Amy and I don't have a kid," he told her.

He watched her blink fast, twice.

"What?" she asked.

"What'd you see when you saw us?" he asked.

She shook her head, jerky, back to blinking.

"What?" she repeated.

His fingers tensed on her jaw, "Baby, what'd you see when you saw me and Amy?"

He knew by the look on her face she didn't want to relive it but she was also looking at his face. She read it and she did it, for him.

"You were under the covers, moving. You were on top of her. You were kissing. I could see her knees up, you were between her legs."

"Were we dressed?"

Her eyes grew dazed, unfocused, then she came back to him and she answered, "Yes. I think so, up top I could see, but you were under the covers. I didn't—"

He pulled slightly away and held the envelope between them.

"Read this, Feb. It's from Amy. Her parents gave it to me."

She stared at it like Ryan stared at the pad, like he suspected he'd looked at that envelope half an hour before.

He ran his fingers down her jaw before his hand fell away and he said, "It isn't easy to read, baby. Lowe raped her." She gasped. Her eyes flew from the envelope to him, he gave her a squeeze with his arm and went on. "It's ugly but it isn't surprising. I thought it'd hurt you any more than he

311

already has, I swear, Feb, I wouldn't let you touch it. But Amy wanted you to see it."

She stared at him for a while before she nodded and took the envelope, but Colt didn't make her read it on her own. His arm went around her and he pulled her lower body close until it touched his and he kept her there while her eyes slid back and forth across the page. She flipped the first paper then she moved to the next, flipping that too. Colt watched as she read and her eyes filled with tears, her bottom lip quivering, but she held them back.

When she was done, she tilted her head and whispered, "I'm so stupid."

He pulled the papers from her hand, turned and tossed them on the desk and came back to her. His arm still around her, his other hand going to her jaw, he dropped his forehead to hers.

"Don't go back there, Feb, that wasn't where I was taking you."

"I was drunk...I saw—"

He touched his mouth to hers to stop her words then said, "Baby, don't go back there. Stay here, with me. You're goin' where Denny's leading you, not me, not Amy." She pulled in breath, fought the train of her thoughts and nodded. "She wanted you to know." Feb nodded again. "She wouldn't want any more pain." Feb nodded yet again. "She'd want you to let it go."

"Yeah," she whispered.

"She gave all she could so we could let it go."

The tears slid down her cheeks and she repeated softly, "Yeah."

"The Harrises want us at her funeral."

She nodded again but her breath snagged.

"They need to see Amy didn't die for nothing."

"But she did," Feb whispered, her lips catching tears and her tongue slid out to clean them way.

"They need to think she didn't."

Feb nodded yet again. "We can give them that."

He pulled her in both of his arms. She stuffed her face in his neck and wrapped her arms around him, holding on tight.

"I hate him, Colt," she said into his neck, her voice thick, clogged, sounding choked.

"I know you do, honey."

She bunched his blazer in her fists at his back, yanking down on it hard before she sobbed, "God, I hate him."

He held her until she cried it out and pulled her face out of neck, tipping her head back to look at him. She let him go with one of her hands and wiped her face.

"You okay?" she asked.

"Will be, when this's over."

She nodded again and whispered, "Maybe wrong, seein' as it was the way it was with Denny raping her, but I'm glad you don't have to live thinkin' you did what I thought you did."

Colt helped her wipe her face before he said, "That isn't wrong, baby."

She dropped her forehead to his shoulder and sucked in a deep breath that expanded her whole body. Colt settled a hand around the back of her neck and when she let out her breath, she asked his chest, "We still on for Frank's?"

"Wouldn't miss it for anything."

Her breath hitched again and she said, "Missed too much already."

Colt closed his eyes before he opened them and ordered, "February, look at me."

She did what she was told and tipped her head back.

"Just as much a waste of time thinkin' about what life might have brought as it is thinkin' you can turn back the clock and change things."

She bit the side of her lip as her eyes slid to the side. Then she tilted her head and looked back at him. "But you've missed dozens of frittatas."

There she was. There was his girl.

"Just dozens?" he asked.

"You haven't had my homemade waffles yet. Or my Omelet á la Feb."

Colt smiled. "Damn, baby, look at me. I'm a forty-four year old man who's got a life of breakfast delights waiting for him."

She smiled back. It wasn't bright but it was something. "Don't think you don't have to earn them."

"I'll earn 'em."

She got up on her toes and touched her lips to his before looking him right in the eye.

"You better."

When Colt hit the top of the stairs at the station he went directly to his desk to drop the envelope on it but nearly stuttered a step when his head swung right and he saw her.

Sully was right. At a glance, Cheryl "Candy" Sheckle was the spitting image of February.

Closer inspection showed she was younger by at least a decade, maybe more and life hadn't been kind. It also showed her hair was dyed, not natural like Feb's. She'd had her breasts enhanced, they were larger than Feb's, didn't fit her frame, which was tall and attractive.

She didn't have Feb's style either but she was trying and this was likely because Lowe made her. She had a choker, not like Feb's or even close, but it was there. The tangle of silver was at her neck and wrists, rings, hoops in her ears. Feb selected her jewelry for a reason that was individual and it stamped her personality on her. This woman had hers selected for her and it was both not as high quality and she didn't carry it right. Her clothes were too tight but it was the t-shirt, jeans and boots. Again, not the same quality but near enough and she wore these, Colt suspected, because her man liked them, not because she did.

Her brown eyes caught sight of him and surprise flooded her face before she quickly averted her eyes and Colt felt his jaw get tight. She'd been given the same story as Ryan. She knew him and she knew him as a dirty cop.

Sully slid up to him as he dropped the envelope on his desk.

"Everything go all right with Amy's parents?" he asked.

"Good as it could, considering she sent her suicide notes to them and in them they learned their daughter had been raped by Denny Lowe."

Sully reared back a few inches before he breathed, "Fuck me."

Colt got closer and his voice dipped lower. "Kid's not mine. I didn't touch her, never had my clothes off, either did she. Kid's Denny's."

Sully's face got red before he said, "This guy's like a freakin' tornado, devastation in his wake." He looked at the envelope and back at Colt. "The note?"

"Yep, the one to me."

"Can we use it?"

"Parents've given permission."

"Feb know all this?"

"Just got back from the bar."

"How'd she take it?"

"Not good, but I learned I got waffles and omelets to look forward to. Though I gotta earn 'em so it ended on a high note."

Sully smiled and it wasn't with humor but something else. He didn't make Colt wait long to find out what that something else was.

"You remember that time we were in Winter Park, Lorraine went to bed and you and I decided to see a Colorado sunrise so we stayed up all night drinkin' and talkin'?" he asked then quickly added something that would give Colt an out if he didn't want to enter the conversation. "You were pretty hammered."

He *was* hammered. Enough to tell Sully everything about Feb, why he loved her and why it cut through the bone when he lost her. Not enough to forget he did it. It was after Melanie left, during the time he was pissed at her for giving up at the same time wondering if he unintentionally gave her some signal that she should.

"I remember."

"What you said, what Lorraine told me, I still didn't get it about February. Cold as ice to you. Everyone else, warm and sweet. All that mattered to me, she left and it scarred you." Sully was still smiling that smile when he said, "Waffles, omelets, a second chance in the middle of a shit storm and a girl who can stand strong through this crazy mess and go to work every day?" He shook his head. "Now, I think I'm gettin' it." His smile finally filled with humor. "Better thing though, now *you're* gettin' it."

Colt shook his head but he did it grinning. "Don't be rude, Sul."

"Gotta get you drunk, find out if she wears those chokers to bed," Sully joked.

"Now you're pissin' me off."

"Man, I'm just sayin', beware. *Everyone* wants to know that."

Before Colt could answer, he heard Nowakowski call, "Lieutenant Colton?"

He automatically looked to the right and saw Cheryl Sheckle glancing around, hope in her face, or expectation. Happy expectation. She thought her lover was close.

Colt hated to do it, but Nowakowski wouldn't have called his name unless he wanted to make his point, so he called back, "Yeah?"

Cheryl's body locked but her eyes sliced to him. Then the color fled from her face.

"Would you like to assist with this interview?" Nowakowski asked, tipping his head to Cheryl and Cheryl looked at Nowakowski then at Colt, face still white, now her hands were clenched.

What that fucking guy was playing at, Colt had no clue and he wished the asshole would have cued him.

"I'm thinkin' you got it," Colt answered wondering how this was, exactly, "taking care of Candy" as he promised Ryan he would do.

"Your call," Nowakowski lied. It wasn't Colt's call at all and he wondered what the bastard would have done if Colt had answered, "Yeah, sure."

Then Nowakowski motioned toward the hall that led to the interrogation rooms. "Ms. Sheckle, if you would?"

Her movements showed she was forcing them. She'd come in of her own accord thinking this was about the investigation of a dirty cop she was supposedly a part of. Now she wasn't so sure she wanted to be there. Still, she moved and Nowakowski and Warren followed her down the hall.

"Rodman says we're not allowed to eat popcorn during the interview. Might interfere with the equipment," Sully whispered as he and Sully followed Rodman into the hall.

Marty had brought in strombolis from Reggie's for lunch. Colt's was sitting like a weight in his gut. Popcorn would take him over the edge.

He didn't answer Sully as they walked into the room next to interrogation two.

Cheryl was already seated, her purse on the table by her side. Nowakowski had decided to sit across from her.

Warren, younger and far better looking than Nowakowski, was completely different than he was in the interview with Ryan. He was sitting at the side of the table. His pose was relaxed, the tutor there to help with prompts and provide support. Nowakowski was the professor who'd ask difficult questions on a test that if she failed she'd be fucked.

316

Nowakowski opened a folder and pulled out Denny and Marie's wedding photo, flipped it around and set it down in front of Cheryl. Already pale and visibly uncertain, the wedding photo was an act of cruelty. With one look at her face when she saw the photo, Colt knew she had no idea Denny was married, now or ever.

"Ms. Sheckle, do you know this man?"

Eyes glued to the photo, she swallowed then nodded.

"Who is he?"

"Lieutenant Alec Colton," she answered then went on hurriedly, her eyes lifting, "I mean, Alexander. His name is—"

"Lieutenant Alexander Colton was standing outside, Ms. Sheckle," Nowakowski interrupted her. "The tall man with the dark hair. Did you see him?"

She shook her head and looked at Warren then she leaned forward. "Okay," she started, her voice a loud whisper, "I don't know what you guys think but that man out there is no good. Okay? Alec told me he's dirty. You need to find Alec. Something's wrong."

"Alec was standing outside, Ms. Sheckle, would you like me to ask him to come in, show you his credentials?" Nowakowski asked.

"No!" she cried, leaning back but putting her hands, palms down, flat on the table. "No, you have to listen to me. Alec told me he's—"

Nowakowski leaned forward and tapped Denny's photo, his tone had changed. It was quiet, even gentle when he said, "Cheryl, can I call you Cheryl or would you prefer Candy?"

"Cheryl," she said swiftly.

"Cheryl, the man in this photo is a Mr. Dennis Lowe. He worked for a computer software company and he was married. He was impersonating a police officer, a real one by the name of Alexander Colton. He was doing this because he's obsessed with a woman named February—"

Nowakowski stopped talking because Cheryl Sheckle's body jerked violently and she let out a muted cry.

"Fuck, he called her February," Sully muttered.

"No," Cheryl whispered.

"He called you that didn't he?" Nowakowski asked.

She shook her head and whispered again, "No."

"He didn't call you that?"

She kept shaking her head. "He said it was because he met me in February. He said it was a nickname."

Warren shook his head then, "It isn't a nickname, Cheryl. It's a real person, her name is February Owens and he's been obsessed with her since they went to high school together."

Nowakowski didn't give her a break, didn't let it settle in, before he added, "She looks like you, Cheryl. You've seen her in the tapes, haven't you?" Nowakowski asked, pushing but still being gentle. "Have you seen her in the tapes? Doesn't she look like you?"

"He said he was a cop. He said—"

Warren leaned close. "He lied to you, Cheryl."

She closed her eyes tight, still shaking her head. "He was nice to me. He was nice. Men aren't…" She opened her eyes and whispered, "He was gentle with me. He said he loved me. He said we were born to be together."

"Alexander Colton, the man outside, the man you've seen in the tapes, he's February Owens's boyfriend. They have a history, Lieutenant Colton and Ms. Owens, a long one. *They* were born to be together, if you believe that kind of thing," Nowakowski told her.

She started shaking, her arms crossing on her chest, her hands rubbing her upper biceps. "Why—?"

"I'm sorry, Cheryl, but he used you to spy on the objects of his fascination. The man he wants to be, Lieutenant Colton, and the woman he wants to have, February Owens," Nowakowski informed her.

"Why would he do that?" she asked, but the pitch of her voice said not only didn't she want to know, any answer Nowakowski gave her she wouldn't believe.

"I don't know. I don't know why someone would do that," Nowakowski told her.

She kept rubbing her arms. "I have a kid, a son, he's good to him. Was teaching him football. Said he was All-State, he played for Purdue."

"Yes, that's true. Lieutenant Colton was All-State and he played for Purdue."

She shook her head, rubbing her arms up and down, her eyes filling with tears, spilling over, the wet tracking down her cheeks.

She looked at the photo and asked, "He's *married*?"

Layering of betrayals. Nowakowski didn't cool it she was going to get crushed underneath.

"He was, Cheryl," Nowakowski said and Warren turned to look at him. Nowakowski shook his head to Warren before he said to Cheryl, "Now, Cheryl, when was the last time you saw this man?" He tapped the photo. "Mr. Lowe."

She looked away then back. "Wednesday, not yesterday, last Wednesday."

Fucking hell, the day he murdered Angie.

"It was my day off," she continued. "He took me and Ethan to dinner. Said he wouldn't be back for a while. Had to go undercover on something. Asked if he could use my car, gave me his Audi. Even had it cleaned for me all the way through. The inside was still wet."

"Fucking hell. She drove here in his fucking car," Rodman murmured.

"What kind of car do you drive, Cheryl?" Warren asked.

"Toyota."

"Model, color?" Warren asked.

"Blue. Ethan likes blue. Um…Corolla."

"Year?" Warren kept at her and her eyes focused on him.

"Why are you asking me this?"

"Because we need to find him."

"Why? Because he impersonated a cop?" She flipped her hand out, her betrayal had settled, the anger was sweeping in after it. "He's obviously a dick but what's the big deal?"

"Please, Cheryl, just tell us the year of your car."

"Two thousand five, I think."

"Is it registered to you?"

"Yeah. Sure. Who else?"

Rodman turned and left the room.

"Has he had any contact with you since dinner that Wednesday?" Warren asked.

"Yeah, sure, of course, he calls me every day." Her voice was clipped now, her hands no longer rubbing her arms but grasping them. Protective. Anger was now settled and, quicker than Colt would have expected, bitter was moving in. She'd been fucked over before. A lot.

319

"The DVDs you were giving him, the ones from Ryan?" Warren asked and she stopped gripping her arms, her hands fell into her lap and she stared at him. "Are you still giving them to him?"

She shook her head, this time the shakes came short and fast. "Ryan's a good kid. He's a good kid."

"We've talked to Ryan, Cheryl. We know he's a good kid," Warren assured her. "Now, have you been sending the DVDs to Mr. Lowe?"

"Yes, yes. Fed Ex. He'd give me the addresses when he called and I'd send them. One a day since the one I handed him on Wednesday."

"Do you have those addresses?" Warren asked.

"Yes, the receipts, those little slips they tear off one for you. They're at home."

"Can we go to your home, Cheryl, get the receipts?"

She nodded. "Sure, but why? Who cares?"

"He's surveilling a police officer and his girlfriend. Unlawful entry to set up the cameras and—" Warren, started but she cut him off.

"Whatever," she said. Pulling her purse to her she dug in it and yanked out her keys. She was over it, done with Denny Lowe, ready to scrape him off and move on with her life, alone, without help, stripping to keep her kid fed. She tossed the keys on the table and she asked, "Am I gonna get my car back?"

"We'll do what we can, Cheryl," Warren said as Nowakowski nabbed the keys and exited the room. "Where was the last package you sent going to?"

Colt expected her to say Sturgis or Rapid City.

Instead she said, "Taos. It's someplace in New Mexico."

"Fuck," Colt hissed, reaching for his phone, he yanked it out and called Feb.

"Hey," she answered.

"Baby, who do you know in Taos, New Mexico?"

"What?"

"Who do you know in Taos, New Mexico?"

Her voice went guarded and she asked, "From the list?"

"Anyone, Feb. Do you know anyone in Taos or around there?"

"Yeah," she told him. "Reece is there."

Fucking *shit*.

Colt turned to the table behind him, pulling his pad and pen from his inside jacket pocket, he asked, "Reece his first name or his last?"

"Last."

"First name?"

"Graham."

"Got a number? An address?"

"Colt—"

"Number, Feb. Hurry, baby."

"Hang on…" she went away, probably checking her phonebook on her cell, and Colt flipped up the leather cover to his pad, put it on the table and bent over it, pen ready when she came back. "Five seven five, triple five, two zero zero two."

Colt took the numbers down and repeated them then asked, "Would he have one? An address? A place he gets mail?"

"Sure, he rents a place. Don't have his address on me, it's at home."

"Thanks honey, see you at six."

"Colt, is Reece in—?"

"At six, Feb. I have to go. Right now."

She hesitated then said, "Right. Six."

"Later, baby."

Her voice was shaking when she said, "Later, Colt."

Two days ago her shaking voice would scare the piss out of him. Now he knew she'd pull it together.

Colt flipped his phone closed and looked at Sully.

"Victimology is wrong," he said to Sully, pushing his phone in his pocket and tearing the paper off the pad. "He's not going after Grant because Grant never fucked her. He's going after anyone who fucked her."

"This Reece guy?"

"Was he on the list?"

"Nope."

Colt headed to the door, Sully trailing. "That's because he's an ex-lover and he never did anything to her."

"But he's wreaking vengeance for her," Sully said as they hit the hall. "He told us himself."

"He's wreaking *his* vengeance, not vengeance for her. Angie never did her wrong, not really."

"Why the fuck would he kill her then?" Sully asked.

"Who the fuck knows?" Colt answered and he stopped at Rodman who was hitting a button on his phone. "This is the next victim's phone number." He handed Rodman the paper. "Taos, New Mexico. Graham Reece. He'll be renting, not a long-term resident and likely workin' a bar."

"Sheckle's been sending gift packages," Rodman surmised, hitting buttons on the phone, the paper held up in front of him, his eyes scanning, multitasking.

"Only person Feb knows in New Mexico, they're close."

"He do her wrong?" Rodman asked.

"Nope, he just did her. Lowe wants to erase from the earth anyone who touched her," Colt answered.

"She needs to make a new list," Rodman said.

"She does, only name left on it would be mine."

Rodman blinked at him then mouthed, "Voicemail."

"I'll run a check, see if I can pull up an address or employment records on Reece," Sully said and hoofed it to his desk.

"Graham Reece," Rodman said into the phone, turning and starting to walk away. "This is Special Agent Maurice Rodman of the FBI. You're not in trouble and I need you to call this number the minute you get…"

Colt stood there alone in the bullpen, which was filled with activity all around, and he didn't have a fucking thing to do but wait.

An hour later Cheryl Sheckle sat in a chair across the room, her purse in her lap, her arms wrapped around it, her head turned to the side, her face set in stone.

She'd pulled her hair back in a ponytail and she'd taken off all her jewelry, every last piece. If she could, he knew she'd change her clothes, erase the Feb Impersonation that'd been forced on her, start finding the way back to herself.

Colt saved the file on Amy Harris he was finishing, got up and walked over to Cheryl. She didn't indicate in any way that she knew he was approaching except her body grew stiffer with his every step.

"Got a ride home?" he asked, standing over her. The Audi had been impounded.

"Mom's comin'." Short, precise, neither word she wanted to say.

"She gonna be a while?"

"Probably."

"Want coffee?"

She looked at him, tipping her head back, her eyes hitting his before she clipped, "No."

"Get up, Cheryl. There's a place a coupla blocks away from here. I'll buy you a coffee and you'll want a brownie from there, at least a cookie. You can call your mom and tell her to pick you up there."

"So, what? You're Mr. Nice Guy?" she snapped.

Colt shook his head and said, "Same guy done us both wrong. I thought least we could do since we share something like that, somethin' neither of us wanted to share and it was neither of our choice, we could share a great coffee and a fuckin' good brownie. That would be our choice and, trust me, it's worth the walk."

He saw her jaw work as she clenched her teeth through making a decision.

"Better'n sittin' around here," she finally mumbled as she stood, hitching the purse on her shoulder.

"Place's called Mimi's Coffee House," Colt said as he passed Sully who had his brows raised and his eyes on Colt. "Call your mom. Just a couple blocks up from the station."

Colt walked by her side as they made their way out of the station and down the sidewalk. She called her mother as they went and he listened as she drew out the conversation with her mom in order not to have to speak to him. She flipped the phone shut just as they hit the counter where a wide-eyed Mimi stood. Colt had already shaken his head to Meems in order to shut her up. He needed her ribbing him about February right then like he needed a hole in the head.

"Caramel latte, a large one, and one of those turtle brownies," Cheryl ordered.

Mimi nodded and smiled then she looked at Colt. "Regular for you, Colt?"

"Right, Meems."

"Take a load off, I'll bring 'em out," Mimi told them.

Colt led Cheryl to a table at the window not wanting her near Feb's place or the scratches that declared it so. Cheryl had enough to deal with, she didn't need to see that Feb belonged in a warm, welcoming coffee house with a proprietress who smiled and made orgasmic fucking brownies, though he suspected she already knew if she watched any of the tapes. But she didn't need to know the fact that Feb belonged in a place like this so much, her name was etched into the furniture.

Cheryl sat with a view to the street. Colt sat with a view to the door.

They were silent until after Mimi left their order on the table and walked away.

"I know you think I'm a moron," Cheryl told Colt, her mouth hard, her eyes though, now on him, held hurt.

"Trusting someone nice to you doesn't make you a moron. It makes the person who fucked you over an asshole," Colt replied.

She jerked her eyes from him and looked out the window.

"Feds talk to you about protection?" Colt asked. Cheryl didn't acknowledge his question so he went on. "Denny's behaving erratically, Cheryl. Be good for you to take your son and disappear for a while."

"Got a friend in Ohio, he doesn't know about her," she muttered, eyes at the window. "Already called her."

"Good," Colt said and leaned forward, took out his wallet, pulled out a card and slid it across the table to her before he put his wallet back and leaned back in his chair. Cheryl eyed his card but didn't touch it.

"You take that card, Cheryl," he said quietly and her eyes came to his but her body didn't turn to him. "You find another man, you call me. I'll run a check on him, see he's clean."

She rolled her eyes, not like Feb, not with humor at the foibles of the world, but with disgust, before she shook her head twice and said, "Right."

"Cheryl—"

She turned bodily to him and wrapped her arms around her chest, grabbing her biceps, protective again, but her voice was fuelled with acid. "I know what he did. *Denny.*" She spat out the name. "Killed folks. You think I'm gonna find another man? You're fuckin' crazy."

"I know it won't seem like it now but you'll find a time when you change your mind."

"Bullshit," she hissed, voice quiet but both furious and terrified, leaning toward him. "He's been around my kid! I been fuckin' a murderer!"

Colt leaned forward too and said, just as quiet but with no fury or terror, just force, "No, you thought you were fuckin' *me*."

"Makes it better?" she asked, brows going up, disbelief filling her face. She thought he was nuts.

"Yeah. It does."

"You that good?" Now she was sarcastic.

"No complaints, Cheryl," he told her honestly. "The thing is, I work hard to be a good cop, a good friend and that's what he was playin' at. *That's* what he showed you. *That's* what he wanted you to believe. You believed it, lick your wounds but let 'em heal and move on. When you do, you come to me and I'm tellin' you now, I'll do what I can to make sure you move on to the right guy."

"So, this a new service cops provide to gals like me?"

"No, this is somethin' I'd do for you because we both been fucked over by a sick fuck who threw you into hell and has been makin' me and my woman live in one for twenty-two years. Anyone finds out I offered it, much less did it, I'd be fucked. But still, I'm offerin' it to you. Throw away the card, I don't give a fuck. But it was me, someone fucked me over and another person showed me a kindness, I'd take it. I'm guessin' you don't get much kindness thrown at you. Ryan, me, not much else. Am I right?"

She looked away. He was right.

"Learn one thing from this, Cheryl," Colt advised. "Learn to see a kindness, a real one, when it's handed to you, and learn to take it."

She closed her eyes and twisted her neck, her face exposing pain before she opened her eyes and stared out the window again.

She wasn't giving him anything more.

Colt took a sip from his to go cup and called to Mimi, "Meems, wrap up a couple more of those brownies and a few cookies. Cheryl here has a kid."

"You betcha, Colt," Mimi called back.

Colt turned to Cheryl and started to stand, saying, "I'll leave you to your thoughts."

He was on his feet before he heard her ask, "Twenty-two years?"

He looked down at her to see she was still staring out the window. "Yeah."

She shook her head and the tears hit her eyes. The wall of hardness she'd built was flimsy, likely how Denny got in.

"You really All-State? Play at Purdue?" she asked, her eyes never leaving the window.

"Yeah."

"Why didn't you go pro?"

"Good enough for Purdue, not near good enough for pro."

"You want that?"

"Nope. I wanted to be a cop."

She tipped her head back to look at him and he noticed for the first time she was very pretty. Not because she looked like Feb, all on her own.

A tear slid down her cheek and she said, "I wanted to be a dancer. Looks like we both got what we wanted, hunh?"

The words had the edge of bitterness which coated an underlying sadness.

"Card works a second way, Cheryl," Colt said softly. "It works for kids who wanna learn to play football."

She closed her eyes and new tears slid down her face.

"Got a friend named Morrie who's got a boy, Bonham," Colt went on. "We toss a ball around a lot. Ethan would be welcome."

She nodded but looked away without a word.

"Feb would want to meet you," he pushed it, speaking quietly.

"Why?" she asked the window.

"Because she's a woman who's led a lonely life forced on her by a number of shitty guys and she's found her way through. She'd know what you're feelin' and she'd listen, or not, you don't feel like talkin'. She owns a bar, least she could do is make you a drink."

Cheryl put her hand to her ponytail, tugged it and said softly, "Right about now, I could use a drink."

"J&J's, two doors down, you can't miss it and you're welcome."

She said no more.

Mimi came up with a filled white bag and said to Colt, "I'll put it on your tab."

"Catch you on that tomorrow," Colt told her as she set the bag beside Cheryl's untouched brownie and quickly took off.

"Later, Cheryl," Colt said and turned to the door.

"Lieutenant Colton?" she called.

He stopped and looked at her. "Friends call me Colt."

She swallowed before she nodded and went on. "Colt." Then she whispered, "Thanks for not bein' an asshole."

He smiled at her. It wasn't the best compliment he'd ever had but, from Cheryl, it was likely one of the better ones she had to give.

Then he left.

At ten past six, Colt entered J&J's, looked to the bar, saw Feb and didn't get the jaw tilt.

She turned, walked down to his end and he met her there.

"Reece okay?"

Colt slid onto his stool. "Checked in, safe and sound and now on the alert for a hatchet murderer. Thinkin' about takin' a vacation."

She closed her eyes and whispered, "Thank God."

Colt fought back the jealousy her obvious emotion for this Reece guy caused. She didn't need that now. They'd talk about the fact that she'd need to phone Reece and let him know that contact would be minimal and friendly from here on in, but they'd talk about it later. And he'd share then that that contact would be very minimal and more cordial than friendly.

She opened her eyes and asked, "Off duty?"

"Yeah, baby. Beer."

She twisted, got him a beer and set it in front of him.

"So, you wanna guess what a patty melt got you?" she asked.

She was still wearing the relief on her face, shoving the last drama aside and letting the next snatch of the good life in before the shit hit again. She reached under the bar and pulled up two white, square Styrofoam containers.

"Ham and cheese?" Colt asked.

Feb shook her head.

"Oh fuck, another tenderloin?"

She smiled then flicked the latch and the Styrofoam flipped opened.

"Patty melt!" she announced then burst out laughing, so hard she flopped down beside the food, her arm bent on the bar, her head on it, her hair flying everywhere.

She was hysterical and he should have called her about Reece. Then again, he found out that Reece was safe ten minutes ago so he walked the news to the bar. He didn't know if that ten minutes would have stopped her from cracking up, but he was learning that he probably shouldn't have taken that chance.

He put his hand to the back of her neck and called, "February."

Her shoulders were shaking and she also shook her head.

"I'm all right," she told the bar then straightened. His hand fell away, she pulled her hair from her face and took in a breath before repeating, "I'm all right."

"Be a cryin' shame, honey, you miss me earnin' an omelet because you cracked up."

"An Omelet á la Feb," she corrected him.

"I can't say that," he told her.

"Why not?"

"I'm a man, Feb. I don't say shit like, 'á la' anything."

She started laughing again, luckily this time not hysterically, before she said, "I'm not gonna crack up, Colt."

"Promise me, baby."

She leaned toward him, putting her elbows on the bar and whispered, "I promise."

Colt leaned toward her, wrapped his hand around the back of her head, pulled her to him and kissed her.

When he pulled back, she asked, "So, how many folks are yanking out their cell phones just about now?"

Colt grinned at her and said, "Fuck 'em."

"Wanna move to China with me?"

"China?" he asked.

"Yeah, that's my next stop. Bet the Chinese won't care you kissed me in a bar."

"Soundin' good, baby."

"Now, you wanna know what I got for dinner?"

"Sure."

"Reuben."

"Sounds better than a patty melt."

"I ordered a ham and cheese."

Colt burst out laughing before he wrapped his hand behind her head and kissed her again.

"Trade ya," he said when he sat back.

"You're on," she smiled before she got herself a diet.

I should have known it wouldn't be an uneventful night because that wasn't happening much for me these days.

The bar for a Thursday was busy. This sucked, not because we couldn't use the money, we could always use the money. This sucked because it was so busy I didn't get a lot of time to stand at Colt's end of the bar talking to him. We'd been able to chat while we ate. But I wanted to know how he felt about his shitty day, take his pulse about Amy and her note and, mostly, I just wanted to stand at his end of the bar and talk to him. Being busy meant I couldn't do that, which sucked.

Morrie was home with Delilah, still working hard on taking the trial out of their trial reconciliation and when Colt got there I'd sent Mom and Dad home for a night of rest. It was Darryl, me and Ruthie with Colt playing my bodyguard. I didn't like this either, this meant Colt would have a long night of it, unless the crowd lightened and I could get him home. I could trust Ruthie to close if the crowd got light. Darryl, not so much.

It was when Stew and Aaron walked in that I knew there was going to be trouble.

I knew this because Stew was an asshole, always was, always would be. He'd brought trouble into that bar more than once when Mom and Dad were running it and also after Morrie and I had taken over. Stew was two years older than Colt and had been married once, for six months, which was all his woman could take. No other woman was dumb enough to try it for even that long.

Aaron, on the other hand, was a nice guy, in Colt's class at school. He was married, happily as far as I knew, and had two daughters he doted on. He and Stew hadn't been friends in high school or close after. How and when they hooked up, I didn't know. I just knew Stew could be trouble and Aaron was often along for the ride, mostly, it seemed, solely to yank Stew out of the trouble he caused. Why he put up with Stew was anyone's guess. I couldn't understand it but maybe, with home and hearth, wife and two girls, he needed to take a walk on the wild side, which was Stew, every once in a while. Personally, I would have picked something else.

I also knew there was going to be trouble because I felt it coming from Colt's end of the bar.

Colt looked for all the world like he was casually enjoying a beer at his best friend and reconciled girlfriend's bar. But everyone knew he was being vigilant. He clocked Stew the minute Stew walked in and the hostility coming from Colt was palpable.

At first I didn't get it. Except for the fact that everyone knew Stew was an asshole.

Then I got it.

Back in the day, Stew was the first person who spread the rumor that he'd nailed me. The only one in town who'd have balls enough to break the seal and court Colt's wrath. That was how much of an asshole he was. But, worse than that, he never touched me. I didn't like him back then either and I'd never even kissed him, nor would I, not even if I was trashed.

Also, Aaron did the same. It was later, after Stew, before they became friends and it was different. And it hurt because I actually liked him. The difference was, I got sauced and made out with Aaron mostly because I liked him. He seemed to be a good guy, nice looking and, with him, I had some hope. So at some party we hooked up and went at it, even though I didn't let him get his hands up my shirt. It only happened once and then Aaron called and asked me out. But by then I'd heard the rumor that he'd fucked me and I told him to take a hike. He told me he didn't spread it, which likely he didn't. It was likely we'd been seen necking and someone like Stew spread it. Then again, he didn't say it wasn't true either.

That last part was the part that hurt.

Those rumors spread far and wide and I knew Colt heard them, everyone did. I knew Colt heard them because after each new one, when he looked at me, he did it with less and less respect. Same as my dad. And Morrie. And everyone.

That part hurt more.

And I knew now, with Colt knowing the truth, with two men who lied about me hitting J&J's, the shit was going to hit the fan.

They came to the bar and Darryl cut me off to serve them. Darryl had been working at J&J's for five years. He'd moved his family to the 'Burg from a town about half an hour away to do it. A fresh start, mainly because it was the only job he could find after being let out of the joint. He wasn't cutting me off from Stew and Aaron because he knew about the history. He was doing it because he didn't like Stew and he didn't want me anywhere near him.

Darryl had done time twice, both for assault. He'd been to anger management classes so often they could name the program after him. Second time inside, though, he got a counselor he liked to talk to, someone he could trust and he let some shit go. Not all of it, but enough to get a lock on it and keep his cool.

Darryl might not have been the brightest bulb in the box, but that didn't mean he couldn't read people. You learned that in life, if you paid attention. You learned it in prison, if you wanted to stay healthy. And you learned it in a bar, if you wanted to stop trouble before it started. Therefore, Darryl had a lot of practice.

Darryl also wasn't dumb enough to know that Morrie and I put up with a lot of his shit. Then again, Morrie and I were smart enough to know that an ex-con who everyone knew had been locked down twice for assault and had the body of a human bulldog and the loyalty of a German shepherd made an excellent bar back. Not many who knew him would mess with Darryl and, given the opportunity, family or not, he'd seriously consider laying down his life for Mom, Dad, Morrie or me.

I left Darryl to it and went about my business, but kept an eye out.

I didn't have to wait. The minute Stew and Aaron paid, Stew took a look at me then his head swung to Colt. Then back to me. He didn't even hesitate before he wandered toward Colt and I had the distinct feeling his hearing about Colt and I was the reason he came in.

Aaron on the other hand *did* hesitate, as he should. I saw as the light dawned on him as to Stew's intentions and he started whispering to Stew. But Stew had his eyes on Colt, his face set, and I knew he wanted trouble.

Colt had his eyes on Stew and his face was set too, and I knew he was willing to give it to him.

I felt the whole bar tense, watching this and waiting for the showdown. Stew hit Colt's end of the bar, settling in, standing right next to Colt.

Stew barely got an elbow down and his head turned to Colt before Colt bellowed, "*February!*"

It was a bellow, it was loud and it carried.

I was surprised by this. Colt wasn't a man who bellowed. If Colt had a point to make, he did it quiet. Further, when he was with me and, although it pained me watching him all those years with Melanie, I knew he was gentle with his women. He could tease and be annoying in doing it and he had a temper, definitely. He would raise his voice if he got aggravated but there was never any danger there, not like what I felt from Pete when his temper would start to rear out of control. And I'd learned, watching Colt with Susie and feeling the hit of it myself, he could play dirty. But bellowing? Not his style.

Also I wasn't the type of woman to be summoned by a man. Not that I had many men to be summoned by but the last one I really had, Pete, taught me the valuable lesson that I should always be me. I might have lost hold of me for a while, but one thing was for certain after Pete, February Owens was not someone who was summoned.

However, looking toward the end of the bar, I had to be the February Owens that part-owned J&J's and didn't want trouble in her bar. I also had to be the Feb of the brand new and improved Feb and Colt, and for whatever reason—and whatever reason that was, it was important—my man wanted me.

Darryl looked at me but I went right to Colt, Stew watching me move, Colt not tearing his eyes from Stew, Aaron hanging back.

I stopped in front of Colt. "Yeah?"

"'Round here, baby," Colt said but he was still looking at Stew.

Shit, what'd he want from me?

"Colt—"

Colt's eyes finally came to me and one look at them I instantly scooted around, lifting the bar up on its hinges, sliding through the opening and dropping it behind me.

By the time I got there, Colt had turned. His heels were up on the stool's foot rail, legs bent, knees pointed toward the wall but his torso was twisted toward Stew. The minute I got near, his arm hooked around my waist and he pulled me between his legs.

Stew turned to watch, his forearm on the bar, his upper body leaning into it, his eyes on my breasts.

"Ain't that sweet?" he muttered.

"Stew—" Aaron started.

"Don't you think?" Stew cut him off by asking.

Colt didn't give Aaron a chance to answer.

"Which one of you wants to start?" Colt asked and this wasn't a conversation meant just for the four of us. Colt wasn't bellowing but he'd got folks' attention and he'd kept it. They were listening and he was talking clear enough for those close to hear.

"Start what?" Stew asked.

"Colt—" I began but got a waist squeeze that told me to shut up. I decided, seeing the set look on Colt's face, to shut up.

"Start apologizin'. For that shit you spread about Feb," Colt answered.

"What shit?" Stew asked but he knew. He just wanted trouble.

"Heard it from your own lips you fucked her. Heard it from hers you didn't. So I'm thinkin', since you lied about her, you'd wanna take this opportunity to apologize."

Yep, I was right about the trouble. But it was Colt wanting it and now I knew Stew would give it to him.

"She said I lied?" Stew's brows went up, giving trouble to Colt just as I suspected. "Hmm..." His eyes trailed me. "Maybe I did, maybe I dreamed it." He turned and leaned both elbows on the bar before he mumbled, "Great fuckin' dream. So great, felt real."

My body got tight. Stew was *such* an asshole.

"Stew—" Aaron began again.

Colt cut him off by saying to Aaron, "All right, you start."

"Feb knows I didn't say anything," Aaron said to Colt.

"Yeah, though I remember seein' you at Frank's and everyone congratulatin' you on your conquest, you didn't say anything to the contrary either," Colt returned and I hated with all my heart that Colt heard that shit.

I swung my gaze to Aaron and I knew it contained hurt and accusation. I knew this because I wanted it to.

Aaron took one look at me and shifted his feet.

Stew turned back to one arm on the bar and declared, right in front of me, "He nailed her."

"Colt, this is useless—" I started.

"Quiet, Feb," Colt murmured but to Stew he spoke louder. "So, you were there when Aaron fucked her?"

"*Everyone* fucked her, man." Stew looked at me. "Too bad you changed, woulda been nice, you bein' back, to—"

I interrupted him. "Stew, don't be an asshole."

"You like that?" Colt's eyes were still on Aaron. "Would you like it for your girls? To hear someone talk trash to one of your girls like that? Say some dumb fuck got it in his head to spread rumors, say your girls were easy, sweet pieces. Spread it around that they gave it away to anyone who wanted it?"

"Colt, it was a long time ago," Aaron said quietly.

"So, that'd be okay with you?" Colt pressed.

"Of course not," Aaron said then looked at me. "It was a fuckwad thing to do," he told me. "Stupid. I shoulda told folks they got the wrong end of the stick."

"So you *didn't* nail her?" Colt asked.

Aaron looked to his boots and mumbled, "No."

Colt looked at Stew. "But you did. Asshole like you, can't get a woman unless you pay for it, *you* tagged a sweet piece like Feb?"

Colt sounded incredulous and there was a snicker from somewhere close but I was too focused on what was happening to see who did it.

Stew had caught the insult. Forgetting or not caring that he was lying through his teeth about me and not willing to take that kind of hit to his manhood, he pushed away from the bar. "Fuck you, *Lieutenant* Colton. I don't gotta pay for it."

Colt leaned back a bit. "I don't know. I *heard* you did. Must be true."

Darryl slid around the bar to position himself at Colt's back.

"Shut your mouth, asshole, you didn't hear that," Stew clipped.

"I didn't?" Colt asked, feigning surprise. "Might just talk to a few folks about it, see if they heard the same thing. They heard it, it *has* to be true."

Stew straightened away from the bar and leaned slightly toward Colt. "That shit's not funny, motherfucker."

"No, guess it wouldn't be, havin' someone say shit about you others might believe," Colt said. "Then again, Angie Maroni was known for doin' everyone. Good woman, bad taste. Not so bad she'd give you a shot, though. Saw you my damned self, dozen times at least in this very bar, tryin' it on with her. Even Angie wouldn't give it up for you."

"I nailed Angie," Stew announced.

Colt's eyebrows shot up. "You did? Like you nailed Feb? In your dreams? Or was Angie real?"

I watched Stew's face, already set, grow rock hard and Aaron saw it too.

"Stew, let's go," Aaron said, his voice held urgency now.

"You think you own this town," Stew spat. "Cop. Untouchable."

"I'm off duty now, Stew, private citizen havin' a drink at my woman's bar."

"You're not untouchable."

"That sounds like a threat."

Darryl got closer. I sucked in breath. Colt waited.

He wanted it, wanted Stew to make the move. He was itching to wipe the floor with him. The bar waited with Colt, probably itching just as bad to watch him do it.

"Stew, come on, man, let's go," Aaron repeated.

"I should teach you a lesson," Stew said, and this was definitely a threat.

"I've always been a good student. Whatcha got for me?" Colt taunted.

Stew moved in closer. Colt let my waist go and then moved me aside. Darryl grabbed my upper arm and pulled me behind him.

That's when Morrie showed out of the blue with Dee behind him.

"What's goin' on?" Morrie asked, the shiner Colt gave him the day before having moved toward darker and uglier, which was what it'd do for another day or two before it started to fade. He was positioning Dee well away and getting close to Aaron.

"Stew here's gonna teach me a lesson," Colt said.

"'Bout what?" Morrie asked, his eyes never leaving Stew. He'd read the situation and he was on alert.

"Not sure, think it's about pickin' vulnerable women, spreadin' lies about 'em, sayin' you fucked 'em when you didn't. Stew here says he fucked Feb *and* Angie, when I know he didn't do either. Maybe it isn't a lesson, maybe he wants to convince me," Colt answered, not talking to Stew but not taking his eyes off him. Then he started to address Stew. "Angie, she can't speak for herself. But Feb, now February tells me you're a liar. What I want to know is, did you lie about my woman?"

Stew's eyes were moving from Colt, to Darryl, to Morrie not, I suspected, assessing the fact that he was fucked, but, I suspected, deciding which one to try to take on first.

"Colt, man, stand down. It was years ago and she wasn't your woman then," Aaron waded in, trying to play peacemaker.

Colt still didn't look away from Stew. "Honest to God, was there ever a time Feb wasn't my woman?"

"Yeah, when she was bonking me," Stew pushed it. "Then she was all mine."

Colt stood and got close. He had three inches on Stew but Stew didn't back down.

Morrie and Darryl got closer too.

Morrie spoke. "Colt, dude, this guy's not worth it."

Colt ignored Morrie and called to me, "Feb, you got anything to say?"

Damn, now he was dragging me into it.

"Like what?" I called back.

Colt didn't answer.

I watched the showdown for a few seconds and I decided I was done. It went without saying my life was shitty enough without Colt confronting every asshole that slid through it. Especially at my bar. I moved around Darryl and stood next to Morrie, close to Colt and Stew.

"Colt, Morrie's right. He isn't worth it."

"Did he fuck you?" Colt asked.

"Seriously?" I answered. "Pete was a dick but at least he was hot. You think I'd do this guy?"

"You hear that? She said she didn't do you," Colt said to Stew, leaning in closer. They were nearly nose to nose and Stew held his ground.

"Who'd you do?" Morrie asked, sounding curious and glancing at Aaron.

"We already established I didn't do Aaron. You missed that," I told Morrie.

"Did you do Willie Clapton?" Dee called. "He's hot and he said he did you."

"No, I didn't do Willie either. He might be hot but we made out and he's *not* a good kisser. I'm talkin' *bad*. I didn't wanna go there."

"Euw. Nothin' worse than a bad kisser," Dee noted.

"Willie's a bad kisser?" Morrie asked.

"Don't make me relive it," I said to Morrie.

"That bad?" Morrie asked. I made a face and Morrie whistled low before saying, "Sheds new light on Willie."

"Why're we talkin' about who Feb did?" Darryl asked.

"I think the point is Feb didn't do anyone," Colt said. "Am I right, Stew?"

Before Stew could answer, I offered helpfully, "I think the rumors got started because I necked a lot after I broke up with you," I told Colt. "Most of the time I was pretty drunk. Though I never made out with Stew, drunk or not."

"You didn't do anyone?" Morrie asked me, looking slightly shocked and I would have kicked him or at least punched his arm if the situation was a little less tense. However, the situation was very tense and I didn't want to be the one to send it over the edge.

"I did Pete," I answered.

"You were married to him," Morrie returned.

"Don't make me relive that either."

Aaron moved in closer and tagged Stew's shirt, giving it a tug before dropping his hand. "Come on, Stew. Let's just go."

Morrie was focused, however. "You just made out with all these guys?"

"Not all of them, for example, not Stew," I replied.

Stew's eyes moved to me and then he made his move to Colt, but verbally. He wanted Colt to start it, likely because if Colt did, he'd get in worse trouble than Stew, if it got ugly. There were a lot of eyes, a lot of witnesses. Stew started it, Colt could say he was defending himself. Colt started it, he would be fucked. Stew wasn't like Pete. He wouldn't back down and do the right thing with a little pressure from people. Pete did the right thing not because he was a good guy but because he was an outsider and he'd had a goodly taste of Colt's fury backed up by a goodly amount of pressure to get the fuck out of Dodge. Stew would push it and make things difficult for Colt at work. It was frowned on, cops getting in bar brawls and beating the shit out of guys who wronged their girlfriends, no matter who the dickheads were who did it and how much they deserved it.

So Stew made his move by repeating to me, "Bullshit, Feb. I nailed you."

Colt didn't miss a beat before telling him, "I know you didn't."

Stew's eyes went back to Colt. "And you know that how?"

"Because I *have* nailed her, and trust me, you had her once, you'd go back for more."

"Aw," Dee said. "That's kind of sweet."

I rolled my eyes.

Colt suddenly sat down.

Then he said, "Finish your beer, Stew, then I wanna see you in here again never. I never wanna see you in here again."

Stew stared at Colt, denied his altercation and with Colt unwilling to play, finding himself in a position that he was unable to escalate it. Though, he tried.

"Backin' down, Lieutenant Colton?" Stew taunted.

"Yep," Colt replied casually, turning toward his beer. "I gotta bust your lip, I might split my knuckle and I want free use of my fingers tonight."

That's when I rolled my eyes again at Dee who was grinning at me.

"Jesus, Colt, her brother's standin' right here," Morrie muttered, sounding only half-disgusted, the other half was amused. Noting the standoff was over he started to walk behind the bar, finishing, "You're off, Feb. Me and Dee are closin'."

This shocking announcement took my mind off the tense situation. "What?"

"Morrie's gonna show me how to use the cash register," Dee proclaimed, like Morrie was going to strap her into a spacecraft and take her on a tour of the stars. She was still grinning and following Morrie behind the bar.

"What?" I repeated to her back.

Dee turned and her face was awash in excitement. "And he's gonna teach me how to mix drinks."

"What?" I asked again.

"You good, boss?" Darryl asked Colt.

"Yeah, Darryl," Colt said, taking the final pull of his beer. Aaron had moved Stew a couple of feet away. The standoff was over. Colt backed off and sat down but everyone knew, even Stew, that Stew ended up the loser. We were all still the focal point of a lot of eyes but I wasn't paying attention, something more important was happening.

I followed Dee and Morrie behind the bar.

"Who's lookin' after the kids?" I asked.

"Mom and Dad came over, just to wind down a bit. They decided to spend the night. I'm spellin' you so you and Colt can get some shuteye," Morrie told me.

I turned to Dee and said, "But—"

"Family bar, family's workin' it," Morrie answered even though I spoke to Dee. It was then it hit me that Morrie looked happy, happier than he'd been in ages and Dee did too.

I felt my mouth drop open. Then I felt a happy tingle hit my chest. Then I thought I was going to start crying.

I had a feeling the trial was definitely gone from the trial reconciliation. And more than that, I had a feeling my brother worked a miracle. Because if Dee was coming in then Dee was going to be part of the bar, part of the family, and life was going to go the way it should go. With Colt in his seat and in my life and the family running the bar, *all* of my family.

"Do we have...?" I started, scared to say it out loud, like a pin would prick this fragile bubble of a dream if I spoke the words. But I took in a breath and then finished, "Somethin' to celebrate?"

I felt Colt's arm hook me around the waist and he pulled me from the back of the bar saying, "Yeah, honey. It's ten o'clock and we can be home by ten fifteen if you get your ass in gear. That's worth celebrating."

I pulled against Colt's hold but he kept tugging me toward the office.

"Morrie?" I called.

Morrie looked at me. Then he smiled. It was big, it was more than happy. He had his family back. Then I knew that a heavenly light, for that moment, was shining down on all of us.

"Go home, baby sister," he called back.

I smiled back at my big brother. Colt tugged me into the office and I moved my smile to him. He shared my smile as he lifted his hand to touch my jaw and my smile got even bigger. So big, it hurt my face, but I couldn't stop doing it and I didn't want to.

Then I grabbed my purse, shrugged on my jacket and went home with Colt.

We were home by ten fifteen.

⌇

"Alec," I gasped

"Say it again," Colt groaned.

"Alec," I repeated. "Harder, baby."

He gave me what I wanted and he gave it to me harder.

My shoulders were to the wall, my ass in his hands, my legs were wrapped around his hips, the fingers of one of my hands was gripped in his hair, the other hand was locked on his ass. Colt was on his knees and he was fucking me so hard I was certain the Harry's print was going to come crashing off the wall. And I didn't care.

"Give me your tit, Feb," he demanded, and I took my hand from his hair, cupped my breast and offered it to him.

Colt drove in deep but bowed his back, his lips latched around my nipple and he sucked in hard. I felt it from my nipple straight down between my legs, the path so sharp and true, I could have drawn the line down my own body.

"Yes," I breathed.

His mouth released me and he started driving inside me again, his lips moving to mine and my arm wrapped around his shoulders.

"You're gonna come, baby, I feel it, fuckin' love it, your pussy's ready."

He was so right.

It hit me. I clutched harder at his shoulders and my legs tightened around him in a spasm.

"That's it," he growled as the moan ripped from me, my head shot back, slamming against the wall next to the print, making it vibrate.

I was coming down when he hefted me up an inch and rammed in harder and so fucking deep, pulled out and rammed in again, staying put, his face went into my neck and he groaned against my skin.

It was when I felt his tongue tracing my necklaces, something he seemed to do a lot, something that I liked a lot, that I whispered into his hair, "You still owe me."

His tongue went away but I felt his lips smile against my skin as he started sliding slowly in and out of me. I loved it when he did that too, giving it to me soft after he fucked me hard, staying inside instead of pulling out and moving away. There was something about it, Colt keeping our connection and doing it like that. There was something that I couldn't put my finger on, but, whatever it was, it was beautiful.

"You forget, honey, that first time, I gave it to you with my mouth before I gave it to you with my cock." His head came up and he looked at me. "We're even."

Damn, he was right.

"Whatever," I muttered, and he smiled at me.

"You'll get my mouth back," he told me, still sliding in and out.

"When?" I asked.

"Jesus, Feb, you just came."

"What? I got a quota?"

He started laughing softly before he said, "Yeah, I gotta ration this so you don't kill me."

I put my lips to his but kept my eyes open when I whispered, "Beautiful death."

I watched close up as his smile died and something else came into his eyes the second before he kissed me. Then he pulled out, moved back, taking me with him, and put me in bed. Colt rolled to his back, tucking me into his side. He did an ab curl, pulling the covers over us. Then he reached to the light and turned it out.

One of my arms was trapped under me but my other hand was moving on him, lazy, light, his skin hot, hard, tight. I loved the feel of him. His arm was wrapped around me and he drew patterns on my hip with his fingers. I loved the feel of that too.

I tried not to think about how much of this I missed all those years I locked myself away. How much Denny stole from me, from us. But it was impossible.

Then again, if it had just been Colt and me, we would have had to learn this shit from scratch. I didn't know how many women he had and I didn't want to know. I just knew Melanie and Susie and I'd heard about a couple others. Sometimes a woman would come in the bar and her eyes would find him direct and I'd know somewhere that used to be ugly, she'd had him. Sometimes when they came in, his eyes would go to them and that same knowledge would shine through. He'd smile at them, not big, but it was there, or he'd dip his chin, and I knew it didn't end ugly but he ended it and the woman didn't want it to end. He was being gentle and gentlemanly, telling her she gave him good memories but keeping her back all the same.

I couldn't say how I knew all this was communicated but, being tied to him the way I was, I knew. I also couldn't say that happened often, but it happened enough and each time it was like a little dagger tip piercing my skin.

Though I was thinking, he hadn't had them, I wouldn't have what he had to give me now.

On the other hand, he could just be a natural at this kind of thing he was so good at it.

"How you feelin', honey?" Colt murmured and his voice rumbling in my ear, my body pressed against his, my fingertips skimming over his skin, all of that made my current thoughts tumble right away from me.

"Great," I whispered and those thoughts had fallen so far I realized I was. How I could be this happy about Colt and me and Morrie and Dee and that Mom and Dad were home, even after reading Amy's note and dealing with all this crap, I'd never know.

But I was.

Colt's hand flattened on my hip, slid down and his fingers pressed into my ass.

"Best ass in the county," he muttered, and I grinned.

"You do a lotta research into that?" I teased.

"Yep," he replied. My head came up to look at his shadowed face and he went on. "What can I say? I'm an ass man."

I couldn't help but laugh, so I did, but my hand slid up his chest to his neck and when I stopped laughing I asked quietly, "How you doin', babe?"

I watched the shadow of his head come up slightly from the pillow then it dropped down and he sighed. "I've had better days." His fingers pressed into my ass again before he finished, "Not many better nights."

I bent my head and kissed his collarbone before deciding to change the subject. "Am I gonna have to brace anytime some asshole from my past walks into the bar and you're there?"

"Nope," he said immediately. "Think tonight my point was made."

I stared at him and realized he was right. That bellow of my name, calling attention to us, getting the admission out of Aaron, casting doubt on Stew (good doubt, anyone who thought twice about it, which they probably didn't decades ago, would feel foolish for ever considering I'd give it to Stew), my and Morrie's conversation, all of it was perfectly played.

Not to mention, Colt and I were back together and as back together as you could get, kissing and sharing Frank's in the bar, me living with him. Two weeks ago everyone knew Colt wouldn't get near me and they thought this partially because they thought I'd run around. Truth was, I *was* always his woman and me running around, even broken up, was viewed as a betrayal (and girls were always looked down on if they had that reputation, earned or not). As ever about anything in a small town, but especially Colt and me, word would fly. Any guy who told their tale was probably going to look like a schmuck.

"You Superman?" I asked softly.

"How's that?"

"Leap buildings in a single bound, salvage girls' reputations in a second, that kind of thing?"

He was quiet for a while before he replied, "I can't leap buildings in a single bound, but I can make you come so hard you put a hole in my drywall."

"I didn't put a whole in your drywall."

"Glad that's Plexiglas on the print and I fixed it good, baby, or we'd be lyin' in a bed of glass."

"You're such an asshole," I said through my smile.

We both fell silent, me now thinking nothing but happy thoughts. I'd find out Colt wasn't thinking the same.

"You know, there wasn't a reputation to salvage."

This comment so surprised me, I lifted up my head and looked at him. "What?"

"People love you, February."

I shook my head and settled back down, but his hand squeezed my ass and he ordered, "Look at me, Feb."

"Colt—" I started but stopped when I got another squeeze.

"Baby, look at me."

I did as I was told.

"I told you about that kid we brought in, Ryan," Colt said.

Oh shit. I didn't want to think of all the shit he told me over Frank's that night, about the new people who Denny duped and sent straight into their own nightmares.

"Colt—"

"He said, watchin' you, he could tell you were nice. People gravitated to you. He wasn't wrong, Feb."

I shook my head and said, "It's late. Let's go to sleep."

Colt rolled into me, obviously not feeling like taking my hint to drop the subject. When he had me on my back and his dark shadow loomed over me, he kept talking.

"People love you."

"Stop it, Colt. We both know—"

"They do now and they always did."

"That isn't true," I whispered.

"It is."

"You didn't feel it," I told him.

"No, I reckon people were surprised, what went down, maybe disappointed, what they heard, and you felt that. But they never stopped lovin' you."

"Colt—"

His hand came to my jaw and tightened. "February, listen to me. You never stopped bein' you. It mighta been subdued but you were always the girl who looked out for the Angies and Darryls of the world. You were always an Owens, collectin' strays. You never changed that, no matter what they thought of the other."

"I don't think—"

His thumb slid over my lips. "Trust me, Feb. Now, they won't ever think of the other."

"That wasn't necessary," I said to his thumb and he laughed. It wasn't with humor. There was a bitter edge to it that pressed against my flesh.

"Not much about the wrongs done us I can put right. That's one so I did it. Fuckin' thrilled when that asshole walked in the bar tonight. Meant I didn't have to delay."

God, I loved him, always had, always would. I loved him so much, that feeling of fullness started to press against my skin from the inside and there was so much of it, I didn't think I could hold it all.

I wanted to tell him, I really did. I wanted to share, let him know. But this was new, just as it was old, and the idea terrified me.

So instead of *I love you*, I said, "Thank you."

"Don't thank me, honey. I believed it too. That's part of the wrong I made right tonight, lettin' people know I was just as much of an asshole believin' that shit as they were."

"You aren't an asshole," I defended.

"You called me one just five minutes ago," he teased.

"Oh, right," I muttered. "I forgot about that," I told him. "And I was jokin'."

"I know you were, Feb." Before I could say anything else, he kissed me then rolled us back so we resumed our positions and declared, "Now we can go to sleep."

"Oh, so *now* we can go to sleep, now that *you're* done talkin'?"

"Well…yeah."

"I was right."

"What?"

"Asshole."

A short laugh, this one *was* filled with humor.

Then, "Shut up and close your eyes, baby."

He was totally bossy.

Still, I did as I was told.

Wilson jumped up and curled his body mostly on our tangled feet, only partially on the bed, and I fell asleep.

A phone started ringing; I knew it was mine from the tone. It was my cell that sat next to Colt's on his nightstand, the one he put there, digging it out of my purse when we got home, preparing, just in case.

It jarred me awake, which jarred Wilson awake, but by the time I lifted my head to stare at it in sleepy horror, Colt was reaching toward the glaring light of the phone display that seemed to pierce right through the dark like a beacon of doom.

He brought it to his face as I got up on an elbow. He flipped it open and put it to his ear as I held my breath.

"Yeah?" There was a pause while I let out and pulled in just enough breath not to suffocate. "Yeah. She's right here."

Then in silence he held the phone out to me.

Knowing it wasn't who I thought it was because he wouldn't give it to me if it was, I took it. I looked at the display and saw who was on it. My breath went out of me again as I looked at the clock on Colt's nightstand. It was two in the morning, not unusual for the caller, but not acceptable anymore, though he didn't know it.

I saw Colt's shadow move, arm extended toward the light. Then I rolled up and over to sit on my ass, arm holding the covers to my chest as I lifted my knees and pressed my torso to my thighs.

Then I put my phone to my ear, the light went on and I blinked against the brightness as I said, "Hey, Reece."

There was nothing but silence for a while and I waited.

Then Reece said, "Expected it to happen eventually, darlin', but didn't expect it to hit me that hard the first time I heard a man answer your phone."

I closed my eyes tight and whispered, "Reece."

"No promises, beautiful, no expectations. That was the deal. You gave it to me."

"I know."

"Now I gotta find a way to give it to you."

"Reece—"

"Best way to find it right now is knowin' some jackass is out there carvin' up folks in your name and it's good for me to understand you got a man at your side."

"He's not carving them up, he's hacking them with a hatchet."

There was a smile in Reece's voice when he replied, "Whatever."

I felt Colt's hand hit the small of my back and then I felt his fingers run up the indentation of my spine and back down, the path short, the touch light but it was also steady. I knew it was weird in this situation but it made me feel better.

It helped that Wilson wandered up the bed and curled into a ball at my hip.

"You okay?" I asked.

"Headin' out tomorrow, goin' to ground until this guy is found."

"I'm sorry, Reece."

"Not your fault, darlin'."

"Still."

"Still nothin'. Could use a vacation anyway, haven't had a real one since we went to Tahoe."

Tahoe had been great. We went right before I came home and stayed a week. We rode there on the back of his bike and we splurged on a luxury rental. Gambled and rode during the day. Ate until we were stuffed. Fell in bed massively tipsy every night. It was a blast.

I'd seen him since as he used to be mine for those times I needed him. I took a two-week vacation the first year I was home, got in my car, told no one where I was going or who I was seeing. I hit a few places where I had friends, including spending two days with Reece in Sedona. Did the same the second year, catching him up in Taos, but that time I stayed four days.

Reece had come to visit me also, spending his time while I was at the bar catching up with friends he had close or visiting the Speedway and doing other tourist crap. He was careful not to infiltrate my life, like showing up at the bar, knowing, without me telling him, that wasn't his place to be.

When he was around I took some time off, not explaining why, and sometimes would go with him and show him around. Nights, if we spent the day apart, he was always there for me. I'd come home and he'd be in my bed. I'd wake him when I hit the bed, or, if he was out, I'd wake him with my hands or my mouth, something he didn't mind and I suspected he pretended to sleep just to get it.

Those days were over.

"You'll check in?" I asked.

"Sure."

"Frequently?"

"Yeah, darlin', but don't worry about me. It'll be okay. I can take care of myself and the Feds I talked to seem pretty fuckin' determined to find this guy."

"Yeah."

There was a hesitation before he said in a way I knew he was searching, "I'm guessin' I shouldn't call so late next time."

"Probably not."

Another moment of silence before he stopped fucking around and asked what he wanted to know, but he spoke in a voice that said he wished he didn't have to say his next words. "Hate to ask, beautiful, but gotta know. Your boy who answered the phone, this mean you'll not be callin' in a while?"

"Reece—" I started then couldn't say it.

When I stopped talking and said no more, Reece read me. We'd been in and out of each other's lives for a long time but we talked on the phone relatively frequently. He didn't know me through and through, but he knew me well enough.

"Fuck," he bit out. "Means you'll not be callin' at all."

"Reece."

"That hit me harder than I expected too."

"Reece—"

He cut me off. "Fucked up."

"Don't do that."

"Fucked up, I knew I had a good thing, threw it away. *Fuck!*"

"You didn't throw it away."

"How many times I watch you walk away from me, Feb? How many times you watch me?"

"Reece, don't."

"Too fuckin' many. Means I fucked up."

I pressed my torso deeper into my knees and whispered, "It wasn't meant to be, honey."

"I put an ounce of effort in it, I coulda made it meant to be."

I wasn't certain this was true, not now. Maybe years ago when I met him. He was a good guy and he never fucked me over. He was handsome. He was charming. He was smart. Always honest with me. When I had him, I had all of him. He made me laugh, not like I used to but he did it. He knew I loved the bike and he loved it too and taking me out on it. We fit together, were comfortable, would fall in with each other within seconds of being back. The sex wasn't great, like with Colt, but it was really good.

Now. No.

But I didn't tell him that and I didn't know if that was the right thing to do or the wrong thing.

"Sorry, Feb. You don't need this shit now, do you, beautiful? What is it, one o'clock?"

"Two."

"Fuck, sorry darlin'."

"Don't be."

"I'll call in."

"Thanks, Reece."

"Sleep tight, beautiful."

"Reece?" I called before he disconnected.

"Yeah, Feb?"

"You find another, don't watch her walk away," I said.

He laughed and it wasn't like he usually laughed. It was like Colt's bitter laughter earlier that night and it also pressed to my flesh like a blade, but it broke through and my blood beaded the edge.

Then he said, "Ain't another like you."

Then he disconnected. It took me a while to flip the phone closed and when I did my hand dropped to the mattress and I pressed my cheek to my knee.

I felt the phone slide out of my hand and the bed moving with Colt. I heard my phone hit the nightstand then the light went out. Then his hands were on me, pulling me back down, tucking me against his side, wrapping his arm around me, holding me close. I draped my arm around his stomach and I held him tight. Wilson settled into the small of my back, knowing with cat knowledge I needed his presence there, his warmth, all for me, not at our feet.

We were silent. There were no words for times like these.

At least I thought there weren't.

I thought that before Colt said, "What'd I say, baby? I'm the fuckin' lucky one in this bed, seein' as he watched you walk away, which meant you were free to make your way back to me."

That's when I started crying and Colt's other hand came to my hair, sifting through it, pulling it away from my face again and again before he curled his fingers around my neck and kept them there. I didn't know or care if it was cool to cry about another man while in my man's arms.

Lucky for me, Colt didn't seem to mind.

Ten

REECE

Colt's phone rang, I knew it from the tone and it jarred me awake. Keeping me at his side, he reached for it and I snuggled closer as he started talking.

"Colton." Pause. "Yeah, right." Pause. "Where?" Pause. "Got it. Gotta get someone in for Feb then I'll be there. Yeah. Later."

I lifted up to an elbow, pulled my hair out of my face and watched as he used his thumb on his phone, the light of the display illuminating his face.

"What is it?" I asked.

"Robbery," he answered, hit a button and put the phone to his ear.

I settled back into him, resting my head on his shoulder and draping my arm around his stomach, mumbling, "Bummer."

I was half asleep when he flipped his phone closed, moved and then I heard buttons being pressed.

I slid my cheek along his skin to look up at him as he put the phone to his ear.

"What?" I asked.

"Your dad's not pickin' up, phone's probably not close or he's out," Colt replied then he said, "Darryl?"

I got back up on my elbow and stared at him.

"Yeah, listen, I gotta go out on a call and Jack's not answering. Morrie closed and I know you're just in too, but they need a break from this business

351

and someone's gotta look after Feb. You think Phy would be cool with you comin' over and crashin' on my couch for a few hours?" Colt paused and I not only wondered what the answer would be but also when Darryl had been added onto Colt's Person Who I Trust to Protect Feb List.

Phylenda, Darryl's wife, was a good woman, a strong one and chock-full of attitude. She had to be. She knew anytime her man could fall off the wagon, do something stupid and, with a strike three, be gone for a good long time, so she'd be responsible for taking care of two kids who lived with the knowledge that their dad was in prison again. She knew this because she'd done it before.

She didn't come into the bar much because their kids were seven and nine and couldn't come with her. Not to mention she had a full-time job too and, with Darryl's hours, did most of the child rearing. And lastly, she didn't have people close to help out and she tended to keep herself to herself.

Though I saw her, just not often.

We closed the bar annually for a staff Christmas party where family was invited and we gave out bonuses to Darryl, Ruthie and Fritzi. At the Christmas party, as a grand finale, Morrie disappeared (Dad used to do this) and came out as Santa Claus and gave all their kids gifts, or, in Fritzi's case, her grandkids. We'd also close when we had our summer barbeque for close friends and the staff was always there. Dad did it for years and Morrie carried on the tradition.

Not to mention, I was one of the few people Phy would let watch her kids. Not that I did it often, sometimes when Darryl got his shit together and took her out and other times when she'd had enough and needed to go by herself to a movie.

I understood her and I liked her. She liked me back and there were not many of those kinds of folks on her list so I'd always felt honored by it. Still, I wasn't sure she'd want Darryl to get pulled into this shit.

"Thanks, Darryl, see you soon."

There it was. Phy didn't mind Darryl being pulled into this shit. Another indication about how they both felt about me.

"Hope the bar keeps this turnover," I said to Colt as he flipped shut what I saw now was my phone, likely because he didn't have Darryl programmed into his. "I'm thinkin' bonuses should be a lot bigger this year."

Colt didn't answer. He just curled up, taking me with him then he twisted and put me down on my back.

Then he touched his lips to mine and said, "Go back to sleep, Feb. I won't leave before Darryl gets here but, when I do, I'll be gone awhile."

My hand aimed at his neck. I had good aim luckily so my fingers curled around it before I whispered, "Okay."

He touched his lips to mine again then moved to pull away. I dropped my hand before he twisted back and looked down at me.

He didn't say anything so I asked, "What?"

"This happens a lot, honey. Crime doesn't occur just nine to five."

I felt what he was saying to me like each word wrapped around me, twining me in velvet lined rope.

He was telling me my future, what it'll be like, me being in his life.

God, I hoped that rope never dropped away.

"Bars aren't open just nine to five either, Alec," I said quietly.

I watched his shadowed head nod before he bent and gave me another kiss.

"We'll work it out," he murmured.

Then he exited the bed and I settled into it. It was just coming up to five in the morning and I was dog-tired but I still listened to him moving around, getting dressed, going into the living room. Wilson was following him around, I knew because Wilson was meowing. It was early for his breakfast but I knew Colt gave it to him because Wilson shut up. I also knew Colt gave it to him probably to shut him up.

I couldn't know for sure, but I think I fell asleep smiling.

Hours later I was standing at the counter on the kitchen side of Colt's bar, one of Meems' coffees half-drunk in front of me, the remains of one of her blueberry muffins to my side. I was wearing a pair of cutoff, faded jean shorts with a hem so frayed they should probably be tossed. But I'd had them so long I didn't have the heart to do it. I put on one of my older Harley tees, also faded, with my shorts and some slouchy socks. The mid-March weather had been a bit on the warmer side than usual but I still had on my socks because I always wore socks or slippers on my feet when I was in comfort mode.

Jessie was sitting on a stool opposite, next to Josie Judd, their own Meems' detritus in front of them. Chip, Josie's husband, and one of Chip's workers, Brad, were in the den positioning motion detectors in the corners.

Jessie had run into Josie at the Coffee House when she was on her way over and had stopped to pick up breakfast for her and me. Josie, being a friend, knowing her husband was working at Colt's house (and therefore being curious), hooked up with Jessie and came with her. We'd been nattering for half an hour while Chip and Brad put the finishing touches on Colt's new security system, playing double duty as bodyguards to me. When they got there, Darryl dragged his ass off the couch and went home.

Through the window I saw Colt head down the walk that ran the front of his house and I was watching the door when he came through it.

Jessie and Josie twisted on their stools and I straightened, pushing off my forearms, which I was resting on the counter. Colt got four, "Hey, Colts," and he returned the greetings. But I was giving him the jaw-tilt and not only did his eyes never leave me, he came directly to me.

I turned to him when he hit the kitchen and got close. Instead of smiling at me, he put a hand to the side of my neck and used it to pull me toward him and up. I went on my toes and he touched his mouth to mine. I heard, straight out, Josie's loud sigh and I nearly rolled my eyes but that might make Colt do more than a lip touch and I liked Josie, I didn't want her to expire from delight in Colt's dining area.

"You catch 'em?" I asked when he lifted his head.

"Baby, I just left the crime scene."

"So? I thought you were Superman."

He grinned and his grin communicated two things. One, he thought I was funny. Two, he was remembering our conversation last night. I felt warmth hit my cheeks and other more intimate places and found that two minutes before I was happy for all the company I had. Just then, I wished they'd all go away.

His fingers at my neck gave me a squeeze and he said, "Gotta hit the shower and get back to the station."

At the thought of Colt in the shower, Josie sighed again, this time louder.

He let me go, slid a glance across a grinning Jessie and a stars-in-her-eyes Josie and walked out of the kitchen and through the living room. Jessie, Josie and I watched him go. I was concentrating so hard on watching him move, I didn't note where their eyes were fixed. Personally, I was having trouble deciding where to put my own. Colt was a big guy and there was a lot to see, all of it good. He'd need to walk down a football field for you to have time to get it all in.

I turned, opened the cupboard, grabbed a mug and poured him some joe before following him with a "Be back in a sec," aimed at the girls.

When I hit the bedroom, Colt was standing by the bed and staring at the large pile of black clothes Jessie had brought over for me to go through in an effort to find something respectable to wear to Amy's funeral. Wilson was curled into a ball in the middle of the pile and he was ignoring Colt and me. It was morning naptime, which fed naturally into afternoon naptime, after which there was a short period of energy during the evening where sometimes he'd run around the house like a mad cat and others he'd just wander around meowing for no reason before it was time to bed down for the night.

"They're Jessie's," I told Colt, explaining the pile of clothes and handing him the mug of coffee.

"She movin' in too?" Colt asked, eyes still on the clothes, lifting the coffee to his lips, but I had stopped breathing.

What did he mean "too?"

Was I moving in? Did he *want* me to move in? Did *I* want to move in?

We'd been back together for four days. I thought that was pretty much the definition of "too soon." Then again, we'd known each other for thirty-nine years and that was undeniably the definition of "about fucking time."

"Feb," Colt called, and my body jolted before I focused on him.

"What?"

"You were starin' at me like I'd grown a second head."

"Um…" I started then decided to shy away from the subject. "I asked Jessie to bring them over. I only own bar clothes. I don't have anything to wear to the funeral."

"You looked nice in that jean skirt the other night."

"I can't wear a jean skirt to a funeral," I informed him, though I knew this was a wasted effort. Women shouldn't bother saying things to men about the intricate rules of clothing, such as what was appropriate to wear and when. It wasn't that men didn't listen. It was that they were genetically programmed not to process such statements. "And anyway, I bought that to go with you to Costa's. That's my Costa's with Colt skirt."

"You bought it to go to Costa's?"

"Well, *I* didn't. I sent Jessie on a mission."

I was not monitoring what I was saying. I was still freaking out about the "movin' in too" comment. If I was, I would have never told him I sent Jessie on a mission to buy an outfit for a date with him. It exposed too much.

He grinned again. This grin communicated two things too. One, he thought I was funny. Two, he knew I liked him, a lot, and he was feeling full of himself.

"Don't you need to take a shower?" I asked.

He kept grinning through the word "Yeah."

I motioned to the bathroom with my head before I started to turn, saying, "Well, there's crime to be fought, get a move on."

I didn't get to the door before he caught me, pulled me back into his body and bent his head to kiss my neck.

Then in my ear, he said, "I remember everything about you and I remember all the reasons why I loved you. Never could forget even when I tried." I sucked in breath, unprepared for this stealth attack, while he went on. "Who knows, baby? We had all that time together, I coulda got used to it, learned to take it for granted." His arms gave me a squeeze. "Now, that'll never happen."

I felt tears hit my eyes and there were a lot of things I wanted to do. Turn and kiss him. Wrap him in my arms so tight his body would be forced to absorb mine. Rip off his clothes and show him how much I loved him using my hands and my mouth. Or simply tell him I loved him, I had since the moment I set eyes on him, and I never stopped.

Instead of any of these, I warned, "Colt, it's eight forty-five and I haven't cried yet today. I got a funeral to go to this afternoon. Don't spoil my run early."

He ignored me.

"We'll settle this now," he said, and I braced because I didn't know what we were settling. It was a good idea to brace because what we were settling rocked my world. "Call your landlord today, tell 'im you're givin' up your lease. You gotta sublet for a while, fine."

"Colt—"

"Your dad, Morrie and I'll get your shit gradually. Spend some time today sorting it and mark the stuff priority that you need over here."

"Colt—"

"I don't give a shit where you put my stuff, what we've got double, what you decide to throw away."

Well, that would mean he'd have matching mugs. I'd traveled light for fifteen years but indulged on a killer set of stoneware when I moved home. It cost a whack and I wasn't home much to use it but I liked knowing I had it.

I didn't share this, I said, "Colt—"

"Just don't move the jerseys or the Harry's print."

"Colt—"

"And find some way to lose that fuckin' picture of flowers your mother put in the second bedroom."

"Colt—"

"It isn't me or you."

He obviously had been so focused on the picture he hadn't seen the be-flowered sheets and comforter Mom put on the bed or, clearly, the very ruffled dust ruffle. They weren't me or Colt either, by a long shot.

"Colt!"

"What?"

I turned in his arms and looked up at him. "Are you *telling* me to move in?"

"You got a problem with that?"

This was an excellent question. One to which the only answer was "no," yet even so, I couldn't utter that word.

Instead, I said, "Only people probably gonna use that room are Mom and Dad. She wants to sleep under flowers? What do we care?"

He smiled again and this smile only communicated one thing and that one thing made the tears prick my eyes again.

His voice was a lot less pushy and a lot more gentle when he said, "I gotta look at it every day."

"Then close the door."

His arms grew tighter, pulling me closer, before he whispered, "I'm gonna say this once and let it go."

Oh Lord, what now? He was relentless, I couldn't hack it.

"I missed you, February."

I was right. I couldn't hack it. The tears I was fighting back slid from my eyes and I felt my body start trembling in his arms.

"I'll take those tears this time, seein' as they're for me."

"Alec—" I whispered.

He talked over me, his gaze going from my cheeks to my eyes. "Today, you gotta worry about your funeral outfit, packin' your shit and one more thing."

What now?

He didn't make me wait. "Feds wanna put us in protective custody. They offered it the other night. I'm puttin' in the security system, which'll help with peace of mind. They protect us, it's a guarantee this shit goes away without us feelin' it. This isn't a decision I can make, you gotta make it, honey. You wanna go away and wait this out, I'll be with you. You wanna stay and live your life as normal as you can, I'll do what I can to protect you."

"Colt—"

"Take the day and tell me tonight."

As what was going on finally permeated, I tipped my head to the side and stopped crying before I asked, "Is this entire conversation gonna be one-sided or are you gonna let me speak?"

"I gotta get this out *and* get to the station. You speakin' means the first one will take longer, delayin' the second one."

There was my answer: this conversation was going to be one-sided.

I decided to communicate non-verbally, which I did, by glaring at him. He read it, it bothered him not even a little bit and I knew this because he smiled, gave me a squeeze and dropped his arms.

Then I found myself pissed that he'd just told me I was moving in with him, pretty much told me he still loved me, definitely told me he missed me and then he just let me go without kissing me.

"That's it?" I asked as he shrugged off his blazer and threw it on the bed.

He turned his head to look at me as he pulled the badge off his belt. "What's it?"

I looked at the ceiling and asked it, "Is it me, or was that just a momentous occasion?"

The ceiling had no answer but Colt chuckled and I glared at him again while he tossed his shoulder holster on his blazer.

"Did you ask Jessie to get a muffin for me?" he asked.

I blinked, stupefied at the change of subject.

"Yes," I replied and of course I did. I had no idea when he would be home but I knew he'd eventually be home and Jessie was going to Meems'. No one missed out on Mimi's muffins if they could help it. It was a crime against nature.

"Blueberry?" he asked.

Mimi made a lot of different muffins but the way she made her blueberry ones, with the crunchy sprinkles on top, made them the only way to go.

"Yeah," I said.

"Split it in half, baby, butter it and nuke it. I'll be out in a minute."

I watched, frozen, as he moved to collect the coffee cup he'd put on my nightstand before he'd grabbed me earlier. He took a sip, his golden eyes on me over the rim, then put it back down.

"Feb. Muffin?"

I came out of my deep freeze with a jerk and asked, "What am I? Your waitress?"

"Honey, last night, the least I earned was an omelet and you know it," he said as he started to unbutton his shirt. "This mornin', you can butter and nuke a muffin for me."

This was, unfortunately, true. My Omelet á la Feb was awesome. Though it was more that he earned a waffle. My waffles were killer. The orgasm last night he'd given me *while* holding me up and pinned against the wall—definitely waffle material. I could butter and nuke a muffin for him.

Even so, I turned to the door, muttering, "I'm rethinking breakfast payback."

I was two feet away from the door before his arm came around me again. I saw his other arm shoot out then I saw the door slam shut then I was turned and my body slammed against it. I lifted my chin to look at him and, a half a second later, Colt's mouth was on mine.

In the seconds I could think clearly before the kiss took all my concentration, I knew he'd been fucking with me. That kiss was wet, hard, long and involved a goodly deal of hand exploration, both his and mine (his, mostly at my ass, mine, the same on his ass). It was the kind of kiss you had to celebrate a momentous occasion. It was the kind of kiss you never forgot your whole life.

When he broke the connection of our mouths, he rested his forehead to mine and whispered, "I'll look forward to you making my house ours, Feb."

Then he let me go, leaving me against the door. He walked to the nightstand, grabbed his coffee and hit the bathroom, closing the door halfway.

I watched this whole thing, unable to move. I didn't know what I was feeling because I never felt it in my entire life. Never. Not when we were together before. Not anytime while I grew up in a happy house with a family I loved who looked out for me. Never. I wasn't even certain there was a word for it. But, like the kiss that came just before, I knew I'd ever forget standing there at Colt's bedroom door, feeling that startlingly miraculous feeling.

After I pulled myself together, wiped my face with my hands, turned, opened and walked out the door, I took a few deep breaths as I walked down the hall.

Jessie and Josie watched my progress but I was too busy freaking out at the same time trying to stop myself from doing cartwheels and maybe a few girlie, cheerleader jumps in the air with my arms straight up, waving imaginary pompoms to pay any attention to them.

"You were in there a lot longer than it took to hand Colt a mug of coffee," Jessie, always nosy, remarked.

I resumed my place at the counter about the same time my eyes hit hers, not together enough to remind myself that I usually kept myself to myself, even sometimes with friends, and I shared, "Colt's decided I'm moving in with him. I think he still loves me. He told me he missed me. The Feds have offered us protective custody and it's my decision if we go away while this all goes down."

Jessie stared at me, eyes wide for three beats then she said, "You weren't in there long enough for all *that*."

"Colt's focused. He has to get to the station."

"Are you moving in with him?" Josie asked and I looked at her.

"You didn't hear me. Colt's *decided* I'm moving in with him and he's focused. He didn't actually open it up for discussion."

"He *told* you to move in with him?" Jessie asked, her eyebrows so far up, half her forehead disappeared. It was clear by the look on her face she couldn't wrap her mind around this concept. I doubt Jimbo ever *told* Jessie to do anything. Then again, I also doubted Jimbo was up for the task of holding her by her ass with her back pressed against the wall while he fucked her, hard, until she had a mind-boggling orgasm.

"Pretty much," I said.

"I repeat, are you moving in with him?" Josie asked again.

I looked at Josie, so did Jessie. We all knew the history, too well. And anyway, we'd all just watched him walk through the living room. Half the women alive on earth who saw him walk through the living room wouldn't quibble if he told them to move in with him. He'd capped it with that kiss, which I wasn't going to share, that was Colt's and mine.

"He has a nice kitchen," I said by way of explanation and we all burst out laughing.

"Women," Brad muttered under his breath as he walked through the living room and we all turned to look at Brad.

He was probably twenty-three, twenty-four and he spent a lot of time at J&J's playing pool with his buddies intermingled with trying to score. He wasn't a bad looking guy, great body, not exactly tall, not short either, but very fit, though he needed some fashion direction. By my estimation, considering I didn't keep close tabs, he was half and half with the ladies, hit and miss. It wasn't that he struck out often. It was just that he'd do a lot better with practice.

He was nowhere near experienced enough to mutter the word "women" like that. However, I had learned from a lot of practice at keeping my mouth shut at the shit I heard at the bar to do exactly that. Keep my mouth shut.

Jessie never kept her mouth shut.

"Bradley Goins, learn quick, little man. You're in the abode of the master. You pay attention, you too can someday tell a hot chick she's gonna move in with you and she won't talk back."

Chip chuckled as he bent over his big toolbox. I shook my head. Brad mumbled, "Whatever."

Josie pulled her cell out of her purse, expertly flipped it open with one hand, hit a button and put it to her ear.

"Heidi? Get this. Listen." She held her phone toward the living room for a second, then put it back to her ear and asked, "You hear that?" She paused as my eyes slid to Jessie who was grinning so huge I thought her face would split in half. "No? Well that's a shower goin' and *in* that shower is Alec Colton and I'm in his livin' room." She paused again while I heard a loud squeal come from her phone. "Yeah, that's right, sister. I'm about two rooms away from a naked Alec Colton."

"Jesus," Chip muttered and Jessie and I started laughing.

"Yeah, you got it," Josie continued. "A naked and *wet* Alec Colton."

"Bet you forgot this part," Jessie said to me, still laughing.

"What part?"

"Every woman in town pantin' after your man."

I didn't forget it. I just forgot that feeling of not worrying about it. Once my brain led me to the path of worrying about it when Colt wouldn't have sex with me, it was all I could think of.

I scanned my emotions and tried to find a hint of anxiety. When I couldn't find it, I shrugged to Jessie and grabbed the white bag with Colt's muffin in it. I put the muffin on a plate, split it in half with a knife, smothered it in butter and set it in the microwave, ready to nuke when he came out of the shower.

"By the way," Josie said into her phone when I closed the door on the microwave, "I got it official, was right here when it went down. Colt and Feb are *baaaaaaaaaaaaack.*"

"Jesus, that shit'll be all over town in half an hour," Chip muttered again but, hearing Josie's happiness at relating this news, I felt something get tight in my chest.

It didn't feel bad because I knew Colt had been right. People never stopped liking me. Not Josie, her sister Heidi, her husband Chip, Joe-Bob,

Lorraine and the dozens upon dozens of people who didn't stop coming to the bar when it became mine or when trouble hit. People who didn't stop talking to me, smiling at me, laughing when I told a joke. People who were coming now to watch the Colt and Feb Show only partly because they were curious, but mostly because they cared, not just about Colt, but about me.

I hid the sudden emotion this knowledge welled up inside me behind a sip of my now-cold Meems' latte. It was a struggle to get the sip down, not because it didn't still taste good, but because I had a huge lump on my throat.

Josie got off the phone and Chip and Brad started testing sensors, beeping going on and off everywhere and I nearly missed the shower going off because of it. I still managed to time nuking the muffin just right and the microwave pinged about four seconds after Colt threw his holster and blazer on the dining room table under the watchful and varying degrees of lustful eyes of three women. Jessie's eyes were only a tad lustful, knowing it would never be and not bothered by that fact. Josie's eyes were more lustful, wondering how it would be. My eyes were probably seriously lustful, knowing how it was.

Unfortunately my family had good timing too and they hit the front door about the time I was sliding Colt's muffin from the microwave.

"Hey, Dad, Mamma Jamma, Morrie," I called as Morrie closed the door behind them and the security beeping went on and off again.

"Shit, I didn't get enough muffins," Jessie muttered.

"Chip, take a break," Dad ordered curtly instead of greeting us and I kept my eyes glued on him but felt Colt's head come around at Dad's words and tone.

"What's up?" Colt asked as I put the muffin plate down on the counter.

"Family meetin'," Dad replied.

Mom hit the kitchen and went straight to the mug cupboard and Morrie moved in behind Jessie.

"Maybe I should go," Josie mumbled.

"You're fine, sweetie," Mom said to Josie. Josie gave me a look to ascertain my agreement and I nodded though I wasn't sure I should have.

"Jack, I need to get to the station," Colt said, and Dad stopped dead center across the bar and leveled his eyes on Colt.

"Son," he said softly. "I said 'family meetin'.' Your work's important but there's nothin' more important than family."

Colt was behind me and I didn't see his response to this mainly because he moved in closer. I was standing at the counter, slightly twisted from it, my hand resting on it. Colt got in close and rested his weight into his hand, which he set so close to mine he was touching me. I figured, since he was settling in, he agreed with Dad.

"I'm thinkin'," Dad began, "since things are as they are, that this is good." He nodded to Colt and my hands on the counter. "That said, I'm not a big fan of you callin' boys out at the bar," he said to Colt.

Oh Lord, Dad was talking to Colt like he talked to Colt when Colt was fifteen. I hadn't heard him talk to Colt like that in donkey's years and I was not thinking this was good. In fact, I was thinking, since Colt wasn't anywhere near fifteen and definitely now was his own man, this was probably very bad.

"Jack, it was under my control," Colt replied.

"Lotta boys talked nonsense about Feb back in the day, you gonna call them all out?"

This statement shocked me. I watched Dad's face trying to determine if he thought it was nonsense now, or if he knew it was nonsense then. It came to me in a flash that he knew it was nonsense then and the respect he lost for me was not because he thought I was running around, but that I wasn't defending myself. Instead, I was allowing myself to get buried under it and then making more stupid decisions, like marrying Pete, getting messed up by him and then leaving, instead of sorting it out with Colt, losing all that was me along the way.

Dad, nor Mom, meddled, hardly ever. They advised, usually when you asked for it, but they let you go your own way, make your own mistakes and they hoped you learned from them. The past two decades must have been a living hell for them and maybe not just because of me and the path I chose, but also because of Colt and that he chose not to yank me off of it.

"They come to the bar and have a mind to mess with me or Feb, absolutely," Colt answered, his voice firm but slipping toward pissed. He didn't have time for this conversation but, even if he did, he still wouldn't have time for this conversation.

"Dad, only asshole who'd do that is Stew and Colt made things clear to Stew last night," Morrie put in.

Dad changed the subject and asked bluntly, "How solid are you two?"

I felt my head jerk then my muscles went stiff.

Things were getting more and more solid with Colt and that made me want to do cartwheels and cheerleader jumps but that was in my head. Out loud, in front of my family, Jessie, Josie, Chip and Brad, not to mention Colt, I did *not* want to be having this conversation.

Colt's hand came to my hip and he said, "Jack, due respect, let Feb and me work this out."

"Colt, due respect, you two are caught up in one *in*-tense situation. That situation is gonna go away, what I wanna know is, where will you two be after it's over?"

"Dad, please," I said.

"Like I said, Jack, we're workin' it out," Colt replied.

"And like I asked, Colt, how solid are you?"

"Jack—" Colt started.

"I watched two of the four people I love most in this world fall apart twenty years ago and I stood by while doin' it. This time, I'm askin', how solid are you?"

Colt's fingers gripped my hip hard and he declared, "Speakin for me, like a rock."

I closed my eyes tight, fighting back cartwheels and cheerleader jumps by pulling in breath.

"Feb," Dad called and I opened my eyes.

I hadn't even talked to Colt about this, now…

"Feb," Dad called again.

"Dad—"

"Feb—"

I stared at my father in the eyes and cut him off by repeating Colt's words. "Like a rock."

Dad smiled. I felt Colt's body touch mine as he came even closer behind me but I wasn't done.

"Which I would have liked to have told Colt without an audience, preferably at Costa's or, if not at some romantic locale, then at least one of the seconds we actually have alone, which are a fair few. So now, due respect and all that, you've pissed me off."

"I can handle that," Dad returned immediately, still smiling, moving forward, settling in between an also smiling Jessie and Josie and saying, "Jackie, need coffee, woman."

"Yeesh, I'm like a handmaid," Mom muttered but got Dad coffee. In Mom's actions I saw my future and it both scared and elated me. Colt gave my hip a squeeze just as his hand at the counter moved to fully cover mine.

This felt good, immeasurably good, but I wasn't done being mad and I kept myself stiff and gave my father the daughter death stare I'd been perfecting since my life began.

"Shut it down, February, and get over it. Meetin's not done," Dad said to me.

"What now? Got no more heartfelt declarations to give to the day," I returned.

"Then shut up and listen," Dad replied and I heard Colt laugh softly behind me, which made me grow all the stiffer regardless that he'd just declared we were solid as a rock which, normally, would be news worthy of etching into my journal with a gold-tipped pen.

I felt his lips at my ear before Colt asked, "Romantic locale?"

I rolled my eyes.

"Feb just rolled her eyes," Jessie told Colt helpfully and I transferred my death glare to her.

Colt's arm slid fully around my waist and I couldn't hear his laughter anymore but I sure could feel it.

"Maybe we're not solid," I announced to the room. "Maybe we're very, very shaky."

That's when I heard Colt's laughter come back.

"Earthquake!" I declared loudly, and it couldn't be missed, angrily. Regardless, Colt, and pretty much everyone else, burst out laughing.

"Feb, quit messin' around. Colt's gotta get to the station," Dad said after he quit laughing.

I decided not to inform my *father* that I wasn't messing around and instead felt slightly embarrassed but highly emotional and I didn't need that shit, definitely not facing a day with Amy's funeral looming and Denny out there wreaking havoc, but also not anytime.

Dad took a sip of coffee. Colt took his hand from mine on the counter, leaned into me to nab half of the muffin but kept his arm around me when his hand disappeared and I knew he was eating it. I kept up my grudge because I was good at it, known for it and, anyway, by my way of thinking, they all deserved it.

Dad started talking again. "Morrison and Delilah have worked things out. He's movin' back in and Jackie and me are movin' to his place for a while."

"You can have your pick," Josie told them. "Feb's apartment will be open, seein' as she's movin' in with Colt."

I felt Mom, Dad and Morrie's eyes hit me and Colt, all at the same time.

"Josie!" Chip snapped.

"What?" Josie snapped back with narrowed eyes. "Jackie said it was okay, me bein' in on the family meetin' and all."

"Shit, woman, that doesn't mean you can participate," Chip returned.

"You're movin' in with Colt?" Morrie asked me before Josie could reply, which was good, Josie could be a ball-buster. She was also not a woman who would be told what to do, not like Jessie, who knew the art of compromise (though, it should be said, Jessie knew it *existed*, she didn't utilize it much). Josie was so much not that kind of woman, she was a little bit scary. It was lucky she found Chip, who was as easygoing as they come. No matter that Josie was super pretty, not many men would put up with her being like that.

"Yes," I said sharply, deciding to officially tell Morrie later I was happy for him and Dee. "Now, can we move on?"

"You told Josie and Jessie?" Colt asked from behind me, giving me a squeeze to get my attention at the same time reaching for the second half of his muffin.

"Yes," I replied again.

"Baby, we decided, like, ten minutes ago."

I twisted my neck to look at him and said, "Correction, Colt, you *told* me to move in ten minutes ago."

He grinned through chewing and then, also through chewing, he said, "Yeah. Right." He swallowed and said, "Still, didn't 'spect you to announce it so soon." Then he took the last man-bite of his muffin, which was to say, shoving the rest of it in his mouth.

"I'm uncertain how this is moving the family meeting along so you can get to the station," I told him.

He chewed then swallowed again and said through another smile, "Just pleased you're so excited, honey."

"Do you have a hatchet?" I asked him.

"Got a mind to use it?" he asked back.

"Yeah," I said.

"Then, no," he said back.

"Kids, can we focus?" Mom asked, and I twisted back but also tried to pull out of Colt's arm. It tightened, which meant I failed so, instead I crossed my arms on my chest.

"Like I was sayin', we're movin' into Morrie's, a bit more room, Feb," Dad's eyes came to me then he went on. "'Cause Dee's gonna give notice today and try her hand at the bar. We're gonna be around to help at the bar and with the kids while she's gettin' on her feet."

This, I suspected from what happened last night and it also made me want to shout with glee. But, as I mentioned, I was good with a grudge so I kept my trap shut.

"It'd be good you could spell Feb too so she can get settled here and we can have some time together," Colt put in.

"Oh!" Jessie cried. "You two should take a vacation."

"Good idea," Mom said.

"Colt and Morrie just went fishin' and I'm fine without a vacation," I declared, then put in for good measure, "And I'm good with my schedule at work."

"You work more'n me anyway, Feb," Morrie spoke the truth. "With Dee helpin', we'll work somethin' out to make things more even and, in the meantime, you can take a breather."

"I like my hours," I asserted again.

"You'll have somethin' to fit in those hours now," Dad reminded me, another fact that made me quietly happy but I was damn well not going to show it.

368

"Hmm," I muttered and Colt gave me another squeeze.

"That settled?" Dad asked like he expected an answer rather than made his pronouncement and we were all supposed to fall in line, which was the way it always was and the way it always would be.

Of course, if I wasn't pissed and holding my grudge, this would have all made me pretty happy. I did like my hours but I liked them in a time when I could work them and pretend I wasn't working them so I wouldn't remember I was so damn lonely all the time. Now, I wouldn't know lonely if it bit me on the ass and, God knew, I could use a breather. Not to mention, the idea of a vacation with Colt sounded fucking awesome.

Then again, I'd be happier to wait until it was warmer and have that vacation somewhere we could take his boat.

I was not, of course, going to offer this piece of information to anyone at that present time, however.

"Walk me to the door," Colt said in my ear.

I decided to do what he didn't exactly ask seeing as I'd already acted uppity in front of Chip, who I didn't know all that well, and Brad, who I didn't know hardly at all, and my momma raised me right and she was right there besides. Jessie obviously didn't count because she was family and Josie was practically family so she also pretty much didn't count, but still.

Colt said his good-byes as he put on his holster and blazer and then he stopped at the door and turned to me.

At the door, he said, "You got until two thirty, when I come home to change and take you to the funeral, to get over your snit."

Snit? Did he say *snit*?

I felt my eyes narrow and my brow furrow and my foot itched to kick him.

He went on, totally ignoring my look. "'Til then, baby, get your studio sorted, yeah?"

"You do know that I'm letting you boss me around because we have an audience," I informed him.

He got closer and his voice dipped quiet, only for me to hear. "You're letting me boss you around because you know what I gave you last night, and the night before, and you probably got a good idea what I'll give you tonight."

Okay, so he was right, but I wasn't going to tell him so I stayed silent.

He got even closer, his face changed, something came over it, something that corresponded with the feeling I felt standing at his bedroom door not so long ago.

He put his hand to my neck and said even quieter, "And because we're solid."

I liked that look on his face, a face that had been a constant in my life in one way or another since I could remember. A face I'd seen many expressions glide through over the years. But I liked this one, a lot. Better than any other. So much I figured I'd never forget it either.

Even so, I was Feb and he was Colt, and we were now back to the way we were always meant to be so I told him, "We'll stay solid if you quit bossing me around."

He grinned, then he kissed me lightly before he said, "Nothin's gonna shake us, Feb. Not again." He gave me a squeeze before his grin changed to something else, the intensity slid from his expression and he whispered, "Really like those shorts, baby."

Then he took his hand from my neck, put it to my belly, pushed me back a foot, opened and walked out the door, shutting it behind him.

"Lock it, February!" he shouted from the outside.

"There's a million people in here!" I shouted back from the inside.

"Lock!" he shouted back to my shout.

I locked it then I watched through the window as Colt walked to his truck, got in, started it up, backed out of the drive and drove away and something about doing this made my "snit" melt away.

"Seriously?" Josie called from behind me. "Willie Clapton is a shit kisser?"

I turned to see Josie looking at me, Morrie grinning at me, Mom refilling her coffee cup, Dad with his head in the fridge and Jessie with her head tilted toward me, waiting for an answer.

I opened my mouth and the security beeps went off.

⌒⌒

That afternoon, somewhere around two thirty, Colt arrived in the doorway of his bathroom while I was standing at the mirror over his sink, finishing up roller drying my hair. His eyes hit me, did a slide from the top of my head, where I was holding a hank of hair pulled straight up, juicing it with heat, down my body, which was in a t-shirt of his I'd confiscated because it was huge, old, the lettering faded, and, most importantly, super soft, to my slouchy sock-clad feet.

Then his eyes came to mine and he said, "Baby, seriously?"

"What?" I asked, releasing my hair, which fell mostly in my face.

"You're not ready?"

"I'm borderline ready," I replied, pushing the hair out of my eyes.

"You're doin' your hair and wearin' a t-shirt," he told me like I wasn't aware of these facts.

"Give me a break. I've been busy," I said then promised, "I'll be ready in a jiffy."

His gaze lifted to my hair, where I was wrapping another huge hank around the roller brush, he sighed then disappeared from the doorway.

I looked at myself in the mirror.

I wasn't lying, I had been busy. After my morning drama, Dad, Mom and I went to my studio and Jessie went to the grocery store to pick up boxes. Dad righted the bed and furniture while Mom tidied and I prioritized my stuff. Jessie showed with the boxes and I packed in my clothes, my CDs and the stoneware for the first wave. One could argue the stoneware was not a priority, since Colt had plates and such. Still, I liked it, it cost a fortune so I should use it as much as I could and it'd go in his kitchen, so I decided it took precedence.

While Dad was taking the boxes to my car, a car he and Mom were using while in town since I didn't seem to be needing it, Mom, Jessie and I packed stuff for the second wave. We closed the boxes and stacked them by the door.

I realized while we were doing this that the third wave would be light and seeing this slightly shifted the feeling of contentment that was settling in my soul and a twitchy feeling slid in its place.

I didn't have much stuff, never had, and, at that moment I found it embarrassing that I'd lived as long as I had with so little to show for it. Even when I made my home with Pete for that short while, I hadn't accumulated much, probably knowing in the back of my mind somewhere that Pete and my arrangement would be temporary.

But all those years I lived light because it was easier to take off when the spirit moved me, which was often.

I hadn't known then and never thought about it, whether when I took off I was running from something or searching for it. I knew now I was hiding from it and "it" was the knowledge that I fucked up my life. I kept on the move so I couldn't settle into the understanding that the decisions I made, and kept making, weren't the right ones.

Now I was forty-two years old and never owned a home. I'd always rented furnished places and bought my first furniture—a bed, armchair and dinette set—two years before. I owned stoneware, some clothes, music, kitchen utensils, a box of journals, a yoga mat and some framed photos. My life didn't amount to much but a few boxes that could be carted across town in three trips.

I had a retirement fund, which I started feeding into five years ago. I also had a bunch of savings bonds and certificates of deposit, which I'd been buying for years and were now worth a fair bit, seeing as I didn't spend money on much. And I had a cat.

Other than that, nothing. I didn't have a house, a couch, a pool table and definitely not a boat.

As I was wondering how Colt would feel about how little I made of my life, we all carried the boxes into Colt's house.

This would obviously freak me out, but it should have been in a happy way. Instead, I started to get worried, and therefore, I let my guard down and made a mistake.

While unpacking the stoneware and Mom and Jessie rotated Colt's old stuff to a box to be taken to Goodwill, I told them that I thought Colt needed new dishtowels.

This wasn't a mistake for me, exactly, more for Dad. Without us finishing with the boxes, Jessie and Mom, both master shoppers, pressed Dad into taking us to the nearest mall where we bought dishtowels and, while we were at it, four new full sets of bath towels that were super thick and luxury soft to replace the ones Colt had in his bathrooms.

Jessie also guided us to her favorite shoe store under Dad's visibly growing annoyance, and we bought me a pair of black heels to wear to the funeral. I could almost, if I sat down carefully and didn't move too quickly, fit my ass and tits in her clothes. Shoes, no go. My feet were two sizes bigger than hers and I had nothing but a pair of black cowboy boots and black motorcycle boots and, of the two, I was going to go for the cowboy boots, but Jessie said they wouldn't do. Since we were there, Jessie also talked me into a pair of high-heeled boots she said would go better with my Costa's with Colt jean skirt and those boots were so hot, I knew she wasn't wrong.

Needless to say, we got home at a time where there was no way for me not to run late in preparations for the funeral.

I finished with my hair and was gunking it up with shit that cost a fortune but was worth every penny because it did wonders to my hair when I heard Mom and Dad call out their good-byes. I shouted mine back and wondered what they'd been doing while I was getting ready. I figured, knowing Mom, there weren't any boxes left and the new towels were probably in the wash in preparation to be used. Hell, by this time, they were probably in the dryer.

I walked into the bedroom and saw Colt's blazer was on the bed but the rest of the clothes he wore that day were on the floor. This might have irritated me normally, but since he was wearing a pair of suit trousers in dark gray, a tailored shirt in a gray only two shades lighter than the suit, had a tie hanging around his neck that was black but had a subtle pattern of lighter gray, blue and green, and he looked really good in all this, I didn't mention his clothes on the floor.

He looked at me, saw me staring at him unmoving, and said, "Feb, get a move on."

"Right," I replied, walking to the dresser where I'd commandeered two drawers, which meant serious reorganization since it was apparent that Colt had collected t-shirts since he was fourteen and never threw a single one away. After some time spent on this endeavor, I managed the task of fitting his t-shirts into two drawers rather than the four he used because, folded neatly rather than shoved in in bunches, they took a lot less room.

I pulled out undies and a bra and tugged on the panties under the t-shirt, then yanked off the tee, tossed it on the bed and put on my bra.

I was spritzing with perfume when Colt's hands hit my waist, slid in, crossed paths, and went up, one palming my breast, the other one wrapping around my side, his fingertips trailing along the bra line under my armpit.

I stopped moving except to shiver, mainly because I liked his hands on me and I felt it necessary to concentrate on that feeling.

"Is it sick you can make me hard before we go to a funeral?" he asked in my ear and showed me what he meant by pressing his hips into my ass.

I figured weddings and funerals put you in the mood. The first, because they were romantic and hopeful. The last, because they reminded you that life was short and you should spend as much of your time on the good stuff as you could while you had that time.

"I'm thinkin' it's natural," I told him. The flat of his palm did a circle against my nipple and it felt so good, without me willing it to do so, my head fell to his shoulder. Still, I said, "Colt, remember? We're runnin' late."

"Fuck," he muttered into my neck and let me go.

He walked to the bathroom while I started the process of getting dressed. I watched through the door as he stood in front of the mirror and did up the last buttons of his shirt at the collar then lifted up his chin and tied his tie. I had to quit watching because this seemed weird to me in a glorious way and it struck me just then that all those years, this was what I was hiding from. The knowledge that I'd lost a life where I could watch Colt casually getting dressed in the bathroom. I'd never needed a romantic fairytale of princes and castles because I always knew my prince was Colt and I didn't need a castle. I'd be satisfied anywhere, a crackerbox house or a cardboard box, just as long as Colt was there.

And, through those years, Colt wasn't there.

I shook off these thoughts in order to get dressed and had successfully smoothed on a pair of black hose, something I hadn't worn in so long I forgot how much I detested them *and* the act of putting them on, and shimmied into the pencil skirt of Jessie's I chose mainly because it fit, but barely, when Colt walked out of the bathroom. I was shrugging on the black satin blouse, which also fit snug, when Colt got close.

"Meet you in the living room," he said, and I nodded at him.

His eyes watched me doing up buttons for a while before he walked to the closet, nabbed his suit jacket and headed out the door.

I finished dressing and wondered how long it would be before my new spike heels would start killing my feet. I got my answer two seconds later when they started killing my feet. I put on my watch and a pair of diamond stud earrings that Reece bought me on what I thought at the time was a lark. I thought this because Reece made his usual show of acting like it was no big thing, even though they cost some serious cake. Now I knew it was a sign neither he nor I cottoned onto until it was too late.

I hit the living room and saw Colt, now wearing his suit jacket and looking even better than before, through the opening over the kitchen bar. His eyes were aimed at the counter but his head came up when he caught my movement and I nearly slid off the side of my heel when his gaze hit me.

"Ready," I announced and he grinned.

"I can see that."

I stopped in the living room but he didn't move nor did he take his eyes from me.

"We going or what?"

"Give me a minute, Feb. Don't get this view very often. In fact, never."

"It's just a skirt," I said.

"And heels."

"It's just a skirt and heels."

"A tight skirt."

"Jessie's smaller than me."

"And high heels."

"Colt—"

"Sexy-as-hell high heels."

I put my hands to my hips which made the blouse stretch tighter at my breasts and I knew Colt saw it because his eyes moved directly there.

"We're going to a funeral," I reminded him.

He looked at my face again but I could tell it cost him. "I take you to Costa's, you ditch the jean skirt and wear that."

"This is too fancy, even for Costa's."

"Don't care."

"If I eat wearin' this outfit, I'll explode out of it like the Hulk."

He liked this idea. I knew it because he smiled, slow and sexy.

In order to get a move on, I decided to throw him a bone. "I bought new boots for when we go to Costa's."

"Don't care about that either."

"You'll like them. They're high heels and, even bein' a girl, I think they're sexy."

"Costa's, tomorrow night," Colt said instantly and I couldn't help but smile.

"You'll never get a reservation at Costa's on a Saturday night."

"Watch me."

My smile got wider but I prompted, "Are we gonna go?"

His head tipped down to indicate the counter. "What's this?"

"What?" I asked.

"Looks like a pile of your mail."

"Mom, Dad, Jessie and I got a start on me movin' in. I grabbed my mail while I was there."

He looked down at the counter again and seemed to slip away to a place that he didn't like so I walked to the bar.

"Colt?"

His head came up and he said, "We haven't touched your mail, didn't fuckin' think of it. He could be communicatin' with you."

Although the specter of Denny was ever present, I still had managed to ignore it just enough to be able deal with it and I liked it that way. I peered over the bar at the stack of mail, which had a small parcel in it. I hadn't even sifted through it because I never got any good mail. I'd set it on the counter to go through when I had a bit of time. Now it seemed I was staring at a ticking bomb with a counter closing in on zero.

I looked back at Colt and asked quietly, "Can we deal with Amy first and that later?"

I needed him to say yes. I couldn't face Amy's parents and her funeral if I knew something from Denny came through the post. I could barely deal with it anyway.

"Yeah, baby," he said and relief filled me. "Let's go."

I nodded and we went to his truck. I had forgotten about the truck and if I hadn't I might have chosen a different outfit, something stretchy. As I stood in the passenger side door, my mind flew through strategies of how I was going to heft my ass into the seat without ripping the skirt at the seams.

"Feb, honey, get in," Colt said from where he was standing in the driver's side door watching me with mild irritation at another delay.

I looked at him and said, "I can't."

"Baby, we gotta—"

"No," I cut him off. "I mean, my skirt's too tight and my heels are too high, I can't—" I stopped talking when he shook his head and moved out of the driver's side door.

He approached me and bent, sliding an arm behind my knees, one at my waist, and he lifted me and put me in the seat. I held my breath while he did this for two reasons. One, it would hopefully suck in my flesh so the material wouldn't tear and two, because I didn't hold much hope it would suck in my flesh so the material wouldn't tear. Hope won and the material didn't tear.

"Thanks," I said when his arms slid away.

He was looking at me and grinning and I knew he thought I was a nut.

"Do I amuse you?" I asked.

"Yeah," he answered and then moved away.

He'd backed out and we were on the road when my mind went to places I didn't want it to go. Places that would torture me and places that made my pronouncement of Colt and me being solid as a rock a lie. I knew this shit with Denny, all we'd learned and all that we'd lost, would fuck with my head. I just didn't know how to fight it.

I was looking out the window, thinking of stuff I knew I should let go when I felt Colt's hand take mine. He laced our fingers together and pulled them to rest on his thigh.

"What's in your head?" he asked, and I looked at him.

"Nothin'," I lied.

"Bullshit," he replied. It wasn't mean, it was real, and I wondered if there would come a day when I was able to lie to him successfully and I doubted it.

"It's nothin'," I said again and his hand squeezed mine.

"Amy?" he asked.

"No." Even though it kind of was.

"The mail?"

"No." Even though it kind of was that too.

His hand squeezed mine again and he prompted, "Feb..."

I sighed. He wouldn't let it go and the days where I kept myself to myself were long gone and I realized then, they should have been long gone a long, long time ago.

So, I said, "It's just that…this is all a lot."

"I know it is, baby."

"It'll take a while to get used to it."

"I know."

"And get over what we've lost."

He gave me another hand squeeze and said, "Honey—"

"Colt, you don't really know me."

"I know you."

"Not really."

"I know you, Feb."

I looked out the passenger side window and tried to pull my hand from his but his grip just got tighter so I gave up.

Then I told him, "You got a good job, a home, a life. While I was gone, I didn't create any of that."

"So?"

I looked back at him. "So, doesn't say much for me."

"How's that?"

"It just doesn't."

He let my hand go but only so he could maneuver the truck into the parking lot behind the funeral home and pull into an open slot. Then he turned off the truck and turned to me.

When he did, he asked, "How do I make this better?"

Yes, he asked, straight out.

"What?"

"You're doin' your own head in, how do I stop that?"

I shook my head, not certain how to answer.

"I…I don't know," I stammered.

"You know it and you aren't gonna like me remindin' you of it, but twice this shit happened to me. You, dealin' with shit in your head and not sharin' and Melanie, dealin' with her own shit and not sharin'. Both of you let it eat you and both of you pulled away from me. Now, I'm not dickin' around with it again, tryin' to figure out a way in. So, I'm askin' the only person who can tell me, how do I stop this?"

"I don't think you can," I told him the truth even though it killed me to do it.

I watched him start to get pissed before he said, "So, you're sayin' I just watch it eat at you?"

"No, I'm sayin', only person who can stop it is me."

"What if you don't?"

"I—" I started but he turned his head away to look out the window.

"*Fuck,*" he hissed to the windscreen and I was right. He was *getting* pissed, but now he just plain *was* pissed.

"Colt—"

"We'll talk about it later."

"Colt—"

He looked at me again, clearly done with our conversation and I knew this with what he said next, "Do you need help gettin' out?"

I leaned forward, the skirt bit in but I ignored it and put my hand to his neck.

"Babe," I whispered, "it'd help me stop it if you don't give up on me."

I didn't know I had the answer until I gave it to him. He had no reply, he just stared at me and I had no idea what was going on in his brain. All I knew was, I upset him with my shit, which was just what it was, shit, and for then I needed to let it go. He was facing Amy's funeral too and he wanted to attend it just as much as I did, which meant not at all.

So I lifted my hand from his neck, ran my fingers around the curve of his ear before I settled them at his neck again to give him a squeeze.

Then I said, "I think I can hop down but it wouldn't hurt if you were there to spot me."

He closed his eyes, wet his bottom lip and when he opened his eyes again, they weren't pissed anymore. Instead, they were telling me without words he'd always be there to spot me.

I gave his neck a squeeze and whispered, "Love you, babe."

Without hesitation, his hand shot out and tagged me behind the neck, yanking me forward and testing the limits of the material of my outfit.

I didn't care because he kissed me. It was a hard kiss, closed-mouthed, but I liked it all the same. When he was done with my mouth, his lips went away but his hand slid into my hair, tilted my head down and he kissed my forehead before he pulled away.

"Let's get this done," he murmured. I nodded and Colt got out, rounded the hood, opened my door for me and I hopped out of the cab with his hands at my hips, spotting me.

Colt watched Feb work her magic the minute she hit the funeral home. Gone was whatever was eating her in the truck. She flipped on the February Owens light, the old one that he remembered so well and the new one that seemed to shine even brighter. It was a light that lit her from the inside out and she shone it on all around.

First was Craig Lansdon who was standing alone inside the door and caught their eyes the minute they walked in. Colt watched as Craig manned up immediately and headed to Feb and Colt, his eyes skittering between the two of them, knowing he needed to do what he did but not liking it all the same.

"Feb, I—" he started, but Feb moved into him, put her hand on his shoulder and cut him off.

"He played you, same as Colt, Amy and me."

"I shoulda—"

Feb interrupted him. "We were all young and stupid, Craig. None of us played it right."

He looked away, his jaw tensing. "Lotsa people are dead."

At that point Colt entered the conversation by asking, "And you coulda stopped that how?"

Craig looked back and replied, "I don't know, I knew him better'n anyone."

"He tell you, in a coupla decades, he was plannin' on headin' out on a killin' spree?" Colt asked.

Something about that struck Craig as funny, his lips moved, biting back a smile and he said, "We used to get pretty drunk but I 'spect I'd remember him sayin' somethin' like that."

Feb gave his shoulder a squeeze before she dropped her hand and moved into Colt, so close the side of her body hit his dead on and she stayed there.

Then she suggested, "How about we let that be all we give Denny Lowe during this occasion?" Craig nodded and Feb went on. "Or ever, Craig. How 'bout we let that be all we ever give Denny Lowe?"

The humor in Craig's eyes died, he swallowed and nodded again. Feb reached out and grabbed his hand, gave it a squeeze and smiled at him. Craig smiled back.

Colt put a hand to her waist and saw the Harrises, standing alone up by the closed casket, watching them.

Colt was pleased they'd chosen a closed casket. It was an occupational hazard that he'd seen more death than most and it was never pretty. He didn't get the idea of willfully exposing a dead body before burial. Dead was dead, it was unattractive, no matter who did the makeup or what outfit you chose and how much satin lined the casket. Colt thought viewing a dead body at a funeral home was one last but forced, indignity and he hated it.

"Baby, the Harrises," he murmured to Feb.

She looked up at him and tipped her head to the side before she looked back at Craig and said something, which stated her meaning clearly, "We'll see you in J&J's?"

"You bet," Craig replied quietly.

Colt gave him a nod, which Craig returned and they moved away through the milling, murmuring live bodies to the Harrises. While they did this, Feb caught people's eyes. Automatically and unknowingly assuming the mantle of Princess of Hearts, she smiled small and nodded, communicating like her mother, sharing understanding and peace with her eyes.

"Mr. and Mrs. Harris," Colt said as they arrived.

He shook Mr. Harris's hand, gave Mrs. Harris his cheek while Feb introduced herself and kissed them both on the cheek.

Then she moved into him, close again but she slid her arm around his waist and plastered herself to his side. Not done with her show to the Harrises that Amy didn't die in vain, she turned into him and rested her hand on his stomach. He reciprocated the gesture, sliding an arm along her waist.

Then Feb started talking in "we's."

"We're very sorry about Amy," she told them. "Truly."

Mrs. Harris was taking in Feb's hand at his stomach while Mr. Harris murmured, "Thank you."

"She...well, she was lovely," Feb went on. "And very sweet. We both liked her. It's...we just don't know what to say."

"Nothing to say during times like these, dear," Mrs. Harris replied.

"We want you to know, you and Amy, you're in our thoughts," Feb continued talking for the both of them as if they were a unit, one mind, one body, and Mrs. and Mr. Harris both nodded.

She caught sight of someone approaching and finished, "We'll leave you to your guests."

"Thank you for coming, Alexander, February," Mr. Harris said.

The return of Colt and Feb firmly established for the Harrises, Colt led Feb away.

When they were out of earshot, Colt asked, "You okay?"

"Feel stupid," she muttered. "What do you say?"

"What you said."

Her head tipped back to look up at him. She gazed at him a moment and then she smiled. It wasn't big, but it was enough and Colt decided, if they were still watching, he'd give the Harrises a bonus. He stopped Feb, bent his head and touched his mouth to hers. When he lifted his head, she curled into him and gave him a hug, a hug that wasn't for the Harrises. It was for Colt and Colt alone. He hated being there and he hated why he was there but he sure as fuck liked that hug.

Beyond them, standing by herself, Colt saw Julie McCall. She wasn't quick enough to avert her eyes before he saw her taking them in, avarice and hunger plain as day on her face.

Colt also saw an end to her days more bitter than even Amy's. Amy hadn't asked for her hand to be pulled away and reshuffled and couldn't do much with the cards she'd eventually been dealt. But Julie McCall kept calling for new cards instead of playing the ones she already had. Good or bad, she wanted more, not understanding she should raise, call or bluff, because the next hand was coming her way and it could be a hand where she won big. Instead, by asking for new cards, she kept giving it all away.

"Colt?" Feb called, and he saw she was looking up at him. He was still in her arms and she twisted her neck and looked over her shoulder to see Julie slide into a seat. "Who's that?"

"Friend of Amy's."

"You know her?"

"Yeah, she found Amy."

Feb studied Julie. "I've seen her around."

"Probably. She works at County Bank."

"Oh," Feb muttered then she looked at Colt and asked, "Do you want to say hey?"

"Nope."

Feb tilted her head to the side and opened her mouth to speak but Colt kept talking.

"She asked me out after she found Amy's body."

Feb's eyes grew twice their size, she leaned into him and whispered, "What?"

"No joke."

"She asked you out?"

"Yep."

"After she found Amy?"

"Not right after, she waited about half an hour."

Feb's mouth dropped open and she looked back at Julie. "Wow, Amy *really* didn't choose friends very good."

"Nope."

Feb's gaze came back to him. "What'd you say when she asked you out?"

"She asked if I'd meet her for a drink later and I said I'd be with my girlfriend."

Feb pressed her lips together but a brightness lit her eyes and Colt reckoned the lip press was to stop her from bursting out laughing.

Then she mumbled, "I shouldn't laugh, it's not nice, her gettin' shot down and all, not to mention we're at a funeral. But, for some reason, I think I'm gonna laugh."

Colt gave her a squeeze and advised, "It isn't nice and neither is she but save it, baby. You can laugh later."

Feb kept pressing her lips together but now she was nodding.

Her eyes went over his shoulder and she pulled partially away, keeping on arm around him, whispering, "Dave Connolly's headed our way."

Colt turned in her arm and saw Dave moving in their direction. He noted instantly that Dave had learned the lesson that the drama seemed exciting until it became real and people were dead. Dave looked crushed.

"Colt, Feb," Dave said when he hit them.

"Dave," Colt replied.

"You all right?" Feb asked.

"She worked for me," Dave told Feb like she didn't know. He looked at the casket and continued, "Amy." Then he looked back at them and finished, "What a waste."

Feb took a small step forward and grabbed his hand, giving it a little squeeze before she dropped it again.

"Never find someone like her to work a station," Dave muttered. "These days, folks don't have Amy's work ethic. They sneeze, they take three days off. Findin' someone will be a pain in the ass."

Feb pressed her lips together again and tipped her head back to look at Colt. Like Colt, she was uncertain how to react to someone who considered the loss of a human life a "waste" because it was an inconvenience to them.

Feb looked back to Dave and said, "Hopefully, you'll luck out."

"Yeah," Dave muttered, saw folks moving to seats, nodded to them with a small wave of his hand and said, "Later," before he headed toward Julie.

Feb exchanged another glance with him. It communicated volumes and Colt communicated back without words, instead he shook his head.

Then he guided Feb to a seat and whispered, "You gonna be able to sit down?"

"Just be prepared to offer me your jacket if this skirt gives way."

She took her time aiming her ass into the seat while she held her breath and Colt couldn't stop his smile even as he held back his own laughter. Once she accomplished this feat, he sat beside her and slid an arm around the back of her chair. She cautiously let her weight fall to the side until it hit him and she settled with her hand on his thigh.

The pastor headed to the podium but Colt's eyes caught on something and he looked to his left.

Mrs. Harris was turned in her seat. She didn't smile. She didn't nod. She didn't do anything, just looked at him and Feb. Then he watched her turn back when the pastor started talking and he wondered what was on her mind. Colt and Feb being back together was no balm to her soul, he knew. Nothing would be.

Colt's eyes moved to a casket containing the body of a woman who lived half a life. Pressed to his side was a breathing woman who'd done the same. Both, he figured, in one way or another, did this because of Denny.

He lifted his arm from the back of Feb's seat, curled his fingers around her shoulder and bent his head so his mouth was at her ear.

"Love you, baby," he whispered. Her head tilted back, her eyes caught his and then, with that February Owens light pouring out, she smiled.

Doc waited until after the funeral and everyone was walking to their cars from the graveside to make his approach.

Colt stopped Feb at the passenger side of the truck and waited for the old man to arrive.

"Colt, February," Doc said when he made it, his face showing this wasn't a friendly visit. He had something on his mind.

"Doc," Feb smiled at him and Doc smiled back. Then his eyes went to Colt.

"Let the dead dog alone, Doc," Colt told him. He felt Feb's body jerk in surprise at his side but he didn't look away from Doc.

"I see, you two together, you worked it out. And you two here, I figure you found it in your hearts—"

"Nothin' to find, Doc, let it lie."

Doc stared at him then he looked at Feb then back at Colt before he said, "Boy—"

"She told you it was me," Colt said.

Doc closed his eyes, opened them and said, "I know, man like you, even the man you were then, you'd—"

"She didn't do anything to me, Doc. Let it lie."

Doc got closer and his eyes slid to Feb and back to Colt and Colt knew what he was communicating.

Softly, he informed him, "The baby she had wasn't mine."

"Colt—"

"It wasn't mine, Doc, let it lie."

"She told me—"

"Let it lie."

"Boy, you know now, I know you do. No denyin' it, you got a son."

"The baby was Denny's."

Colt watched as Doc took a step back, his face showing surprise.

"I reckon," Colt went on, "she didn't wanna tell you because either she was in denial herself or, if she told you she'd been raped, she expected you'd try to get her to report it, something she didn't have the strength to see through. She picked me because she knew you'd let that slide and she picked Craig for the birth certificate because she wanted me and Feb to have no more harm. Now the bones are exposed Doc, let's all let them lie."

"I had no idea," Doc whispered, pain stark in his voice.

"She didn't want you to," Colt told him.

"I coulda helped her."

"We all could have, Doc. Like I said, let it lie."

"Rape?" Doc was still whispering but looking away, the pain now stark on his face.

Feb moved forward and gathered the old man in her arms and, to Colt's surprise, he let her. He was old, that much was obvious, but he never acted it. Now he looked like a hundred years of life had settled in his soul.

"You couldn't fix what you didn't know was broken," Feb said softly to him. "But you gave her the peace of mind she was askin' for at the time." She pulled back and looked at him before she asked, "And that's a good thing, right?"

"Never easy livin' with the knowledge that you could have done more, February."

"Nope, you're right," Feb replied. "So you'll have to live with the fact that you did what she asked, kept her secret, and, in a time when she was scared as hell, you gave her a little bit of feelin' safe."

Doc moved out of Feb's arms and lifted a hand to pat her shoulder but his mind was active behind his eyes, sifting through memories, trying to figure out what he missed, where he'd gone wrong and what more he could have done.

Colt decided to put a stop to it. "Denny Lowe started to wage war a while ago, Doc, with a lot of casualties along the way." Doc looked at him and Colt continued. "None of us even knew he was doin' it and comin' out victorious. Don't give him another victory, not standing yards from the grave of one he brought low. Amy wouldn't want that for the rest of us left standin'. In fact, she died so that we could all let it go."

Doc looked at him for a long time and he looked at him hard.

Then he said, "You were always a smart lil' bugger."

"Yeah, I think you mentioned that when I was about five and a fair few times since," Colt told him.

Doc kept looking at him then he turned to Feb. "How're you sleepin', February?"

Feb moved into Colt, slid her arm around his waist and put her head to his shoulder before she whispered, "Sleepin' good, Doc."

Doc took them both in and said, "Two weeks ago, you asked me, I'da said I never thought I'd see this end for you two."

"Drink it in," Colt suggested as he lifted his arm and curled it around Feb's shoulders.

The pall on the day was lifting because the funeral was over, he was taking Feb to a home she was moving her shit into and he thought it was highly likely he had something to do with her sleeping well. All was not well with the world, but at least it was better.

Feb leaned forward and whispered again, this time loudly, "He's very full of himself, Doc."

"A good woman gives him her love, that'll do that to a man, February," Doc whispered back, also loudly.

Feb's chin gave a startled jerk but Doc didn't give her time to let his compliment sink in. He lifted his hand and then let it fall before he turned and walked away.

Colt watched him and saw his shoulders were drooped, his gait was slow and Colt knew his thoughts were heavy. He'd always liked and admired the man but this feeling grew watching Doc shoulder a dead burden that wasn't really his. But, Colt thought, no good shepherd would let a member of his flock wander into danger without blaming himself for neglect, no matter if that flock was large and the lamb that wandered was acting out of his control.

Feb was watching him too as he got in his car, started it up and drove away.

She turned and looked up at him. "Do you think he'll be all right?"

Colt reckoned Doc, being Doc, carried more burdens than anyone Colt knew because Doc collected them. Death for Doc would be a gift because after, a man like him would be sitting right next to God.

"Yeah, he'll be okay," he answered Feb, tore his gaze from the road and looked down at his woman. "You need me to lift you into the truck again?"

She glanced around and then nodded. "But wait, like at the funeral home. I don't want anyone to see you doing it."

He wanted to hang out at a cemetery a lot less than he wanted to hang out and wait for all the cars to leave the funeral home, which was to say he didn't want to hang out at all.

Therefore he picked her up and she gave a small, muted scream, grabbed onto his shoulders. He opened the passenger side door and deposited her in the seat.

"Colt!" she hissed, her eyes darting around.

He put his hand to her knee, gave her a firm squeeze and her eyes shot to his.

"Baby, let's just get home."

The anger budding in her eyes died away before she whispered, "Okay."

Colt stepped back, slammed her door and headed to the driver's side.

Feb went directly to the stereo while Colt went directly to the alarm panel to stop the beeping.

"Can I put on a CD?" she asked as she hit the overflowing CD cabinets around the stereo, cabinets that had been overflowing before but now he saw CDs stacked on top and at the sides and he made a note to buy more cabinets when this shit was over.

"You can make that the last time you ask if you can do somethin' in this house," Colt replied when he successfully stopped the beeping.

She turned and stared at him before asking, "What if you aren't in a music mood?"

Colt started to the kitchen, shrugging off his jacket along the way, saying, "Feb, my ass is in a recliner, a game on or I'm watchin' a show, the stereo is off. Other than that, you got free rein with music."

She liked music, always did. When she was a teenager she drove Jack and Jackie up the wall, playing her music as loud as she did and as often as she did it. When she was in a car, you could always hear her coming. Even now, when she was forty-two, Colt heard her rock blaring from her car stereo speakers. She was known for it. And he'd seen her move her ass behind the bar when a song came on the jukebox that she liked. Hell, if he was honest, in the last two years he couldn't count the times he fought the urge to hit the box and select Mellencamp's "R.O.C.K. in the USA" or the Doobie Brothers' "Jesus Is Just Alright", two of a dozen songs he'd noticed she particularly liked, just so he could watch her move.

He swung his jacket over the back of a dining table chair when she announced, "There's somethin' you should know about me."

He turned his head to see she was still standing by the stereo watching him.

"Yeah?"

"I've taken to listening to Gregorian chants. I find it soothing."

Colt burst out laughing and went into the kitchen.

She was so full of shit.

"I'm serious," she called.

The girl he took to a Springsteen concert over twenty years ago, who screamed out every word to "Born to Run" and "Born in the USA" and the woman he'd seen not a month ago in her car with Jessie, both of their lips moving to Nickelback's "Something in Your Mouth" while the car windows shook with the sound did not listen to Gregorian chants.

"You feel like somethin' soothin', baby, go for it," he called back and stared at her mail.

He had to check in at the station and it was likely she'd want to get to the bar but they needed to get her mail out of the way before they did it.

He heard Fleetwood Mac's "Monday Morning" fill the room and he smiled. Gregorian chants his ass.

He'd pulled loose his tie so it was hanging around his neck, undone the top three buttons of his shirt and was sorting through what appeared to be mostly a big pile of junk mail when he heard her heels clicking on the tiles of the kitchen floor.

She had her hands to one of her ears and her eyes on the mail when she stopped beside him.

"Not feelin' in the mood to be soothed?" he teased.

"'Dreams' comes on after this song, then 'Rhiannon,'" Feb offered as explanation, setting her earring beside the mound of jewelry she left in the kitchen last night, and she went for the other one.

"*The Very Best of?*" Colt asked, watching her put the back on the earring and drop it next to the other.

"Yeah," she answered, picking up a flier for something, flipping it back to front without reading it, then setting it aside.

"Stevie Nicks, I reckon, is more soothing than Gregorian monks," Colt told her.

Her eyes came to his. "You called my bluff, babe. Now be a good sport."

He returned his attention to the mail but he did it smiling.

She reached into the pile and pulled out a small package, a bubble wrap envelope. Colt watched it slide across the counter before she lifted it up. In that time he saw the postal stamp and he dropped the catalogue he was setting aside and nabbed the package.

"Colt—"

He looked at the stamp, shut his eyes and bit his lip.

"Colt."

That time she said his name quieter and a tremor slid through it.

He opened his eyes and looked at her.

"Stamped Colorado," he told her and she looked down at the package. "You want me to open it?"

Her arms crossed her front and she grabbed her biceps, like Cheryl, protective. She did this never tearing her gaze from the package.

"Feb—"

"Open it," she whispered.

He did and he slid out of the bubble envelope something wrapped and taped carefully in layers of tissue. He tore it away, cautious to keep tissue around his fingers and he looked at a frame, which held a picture of Feb with a man he'd only seen dead in crime scene photos—tall, dark-haired, blue-eyed, good-looking.

They were standing behind a bar and she had her arms around his middle, her front pressed to his side. He had his arm around her shoulders, tight, keeping her close. She had her head tipped back, her long hair splayed along his arm and running down her back and her lips were pressed to the underside of his jaw but, even so, she was smiling. He was smiling too, big and broad, straight at the camera, a man who, by the expression on his face, had everything he'd ever need held tight in the curve of his arm.

Across the glass written in black marker were the words, *For you.*

Colt felt his stomach roil and his blood heat as he turned it upside down and put it on the counter.

When he looked at her, Feb was staring at it.

"You don't need to see that, baby," he said softly.

She shook her head but said, "I know what it is. Butch kept that frame on his nightstand. It was there before I moved in and I left it there when I hauled ass."

"February—"

Her eyes never moved when she cut him off, whispering, "He kept it."

"Feb—"

"He kept it," she repeated.

Colt slid his hand under her hair and wrapped it around the back of her neck, giving her a squeeze and her eyes lifted to his. Her face was bleak with pain and confusion.

"Baby," he muttered.

"Why'd he cheat on me if he'd keep it?"

"I don't know." And Colt didn't.

The man in that photo was holding Feb like he'd fight to the death before he let her go. Some men were weak, like Cory, Colt knew it, he'd seen it time and again. They loved their wives, their partners, but they still played around. Maybe they wondered if the grass was greener. Maybe they preferred the thrill of the chase or liked the excitement when a fuck was fresh and new. Maybe they wanted something their partner refused to give. Maybe they were just assholes. Though, the likes of Cory's wife Bethany were no Feb, still, maybe Butch was one of those, but Colt sure as fuck wasn't going to point that out to Feb.

She closed her eyes and turned her face away.

"This needs to go to the station, get processed," he told her.

She didn't open her eyes or turn to him when she said, "Okay."

He gave her neck a squeeze but she still didn't give him her attention.

"You want, baby, once it's processed, I'll get a copy made for you before it goes into evidence."

Her eyes came to him, her lips were parted and she just stared.

"You loved him," Colt said, it took a fuckuva lot out of him but he said it.

"Yes," she whispered and he knew that word took a fuckuva lot out of her too.

"You have that photo?" he asked.

"No."

"You want it?"

"Colt—"

He squeezed her neck again and repeated, "Do you want it?"

Those dents formed above her nose, by her brows, before she asked, "You don't mind?"

"Baby, he's a dead man." Her eyes closed again but she opened them when he used his hand at her neck to pull her closer. "I'm sorry, honey, that was harsh. The point is he was dead to you long before Denny killed him. He's no threat to me but he meant somethin' to you. You want the memory in that photo, you should have it."

Feb stared at him for what seemed a long time before she whispered, "I want it."

"Then you'll have it."

She nodded and swallowed, her eyes flicking down to the counter before coming back to his.

"Can you…" she started and stopped, sucked in breath and said, "Will you go through the rest of my mail? Open anything you want. I need to get out of these clothes and my feet are killin' me."

"You got it."

She pulled in another breath then fell forward, the top of her head hitting his chest and her hands coming to his waist. He felt her bunch his shirt there and listened to her take in more breaths, each one deeper than the last. He kept his hand at her neck while she fought for control. Then she pushed away and tipped her head back to look at him again.

"See, 'Dreams,'" she whispered the name of the song playing. "Soothing," she finished and then tilted her head back further, got close and kissed the underside of his jaw, like he saw her do to the man in the photo except without the smile.

She pushed away, walked away and Colt watched, doing a scan of his feelings after she kissed him like that, put her mouth on him the same way she'd done to another man.

He found he didn't feel jealous, resentful or angry.

He felt lucky.

"The picture came up clean," Sully said to Colt, sliding into his chair at his desk across from Colt's.

"No prints?"

"Wiped clean, nothin'."

Colt sat back in his chair and gave Sully his full attention.

"This shit gonna end soon, Sul?"

"It's all wrappin' up in a neat package tied with a bow, all we gotta do his catch this fucker," Sully told Colt. "You were right. Got the bank records and Marie made some withdrawals from her trust fund in Chicago. Total, twenty Gs since last February when Denny took on Cheryl. Talked to Carly, the neighbor. She said Marie told her Denny was askin' for money, Carly didn't know why because Marie didn't know why. Likely, this was part of Marie gettin' fed up and psyching herself up for the confrontation."

Colt nodded and Sully continued.

"Money adds up to what Ryan and Cheryl said he gave them, includin' equipment, gifts, shit like that. Incidental withdrawals from their joint account increased along the way. Nothin' big, a few hundred dollars here and there, but he was yanking money more often, 'specially the last six months."

"He pay Ryan and Cheryl in cash?"

"Always."

"The fifteen K?" Colt asked.

"Gave Cheryl five of it before he left to cover her Fed Ex deliveries and emergency expenses, Cheryl said."

"Five large is a lot for Fed Ex deliveries," Colt remarked.

"Big spender," Sully replied. "Cheryl said he was always generous."

Colt figured Cheryl wouldn't miss Denny but, the life she led, she couldn't help but miss his money.

"He couldn't have been plannin' a spree when he withdrew that money," Colt noted.

"No tellin' what he was plannin'."

This made Colt's blood run cold but he ignored it and carried on.

"He's in New Mexico, got a package there. Anything?"

"Zip. Guy's a ghost."

"We got the car he's drivin', photos of him out on the wire, we know where he is and who he's after. How the fuck can he be a ghost?"

"Colt—"

"Jesus, Sully, this shit's relentless. We got a boatload of evidence to nail this guy and we fuckin' know where he is and he's in the wind?"

"We have more on him, if you're interested." Colt didn't speak so Sully continued. "You asked me to activate the Lorraine gossip tree and we'll have to make a note to do that in future. Her women were a font of information. One of 'em, married to a bank officer, knew all about Amy, the baby, the adoption, everything, 'cept the rape and who the daddy was. Another knows Emily Hope."

"Emily Hope?"

"Yeah, she was Amy's best friend back in the day. She lives in Carmel now. She heard about Amy's death from the Lorraine gossip tree and she heard a helluva lot more from it too. She came in this mornin' before she went to the funeral."

Emily Hope. Hearing her name and associating it with Amy's friend, Colt remembered the name and the girl. He scanned his recent memories of the funeral and he tried to place the girl Amy used to spend time with there. He didn't know her back then but he had a thing for faces and he didn't recognize hers at the funeral.

"She's who I think she is, she wasn't at the funeral," Colt told Sully.

"Was she big as a house back in the day?"

Colt called her up and remembered her as being passably pretty and nowhere near fat. In fact, she was flat-chested, slim-hipped and almost had the body of a boy. A skinny boy.

"Nope."

"Bitch is huge now, Colt. *Huge.*"

"Sully."

"No, seriously, couldn't sit in a chair with arms. We had to bring her in one special. Enormous."

"All right, she's gained weight. What'd she say?"

"She said she always knew Denny was bad news, he always gave her a crap feelin'. She said she knew Denny raped Amy, told us without us askin'. Apparently, Emily was the only one she told and Amy swore her to secrecy. She said she hates Denny mainly because he raped Amy, obviously, but also because Amy, 'faded away,' her words, after the incident. They lost touch when Emily moved to Carmel, Amy doin' it, not returnin' calls or, if they made plans to meet up, Amy would cancel. Emily eventually quit tryin' and feels like shit now. She says she remembers the night Amy was drugged 'like it was yesterday,' her words again, and she's the one who brought it up. I didn't feed her nothin'. She remembers it because she just knew Denny slipped Amy somethin'. She's willin' to testify to the rape or anything we want her to testify to. Hell, she'd try to convince a jury she was there when he hacked away at Marie, she's so ready to testify. She's pretty pissed Amy's dead, probably feels some guilt. According to her, she has it figured out and her finger is pointed firmly in Denny's direction."

"Hearsay. She won't help much."

"Corroborate the note Amy wrote, should we need to use it."

This was true.

"Also got a hit on the Audi," Sully went on.

"Yeah?"

"Boys went over it, nothing there, totally clean, 'cept it was *so* clean they figured he'd had it done professional-like so they did the rounds. Hit on a valet service on the other side of Indianapolis, out of his way, not close to here, not close to Cheryl."

"Thinks to put us off the scent," Colt noted.

"Yeah, 'cept the Feds are persistent. They needed to, they'd check every professional car wash from here to Louisville, up to Chicago, over to Springfield and across to Cincinnati if they had to."

"So they found something?"

"Yeah, man. He'd done a job on it himself but, as you could imagine, they found blood and not a little of it. They remembered it and were freaked by it but he gave them the same ole with the whole, 'I'm Lieutenant Colton' business, flashed a badge and told them he'd been injured in the line of duty or some crap."

Colt felt his jaw grow tight before he stated, "That shit's gettin' old."

"I can imagine," Sully muttered, feeling his pain, then went on. "Identified him in a photo. Evidence is washed away but witness who cleaned is willin' to testify to what he saw, or, more to the point, cleaned."

"At least it's somethin'."

"We got more."

Colt looked at his friend and Sully continued.

"Feds had some expert compare the note Denny sent to Amy and some writing we found at his house and the writing on the back of the high school note from Angie to Feb. Denny wasn't bein' so careful years ago when he sent his threat to Amy after she fell pregnant. He wrote it out long hand. Expert says all the writing matched. They're sendin' the glass from the frame to be analyzed."

"He goes to trial, we're not tryin' him for rape, Sully."

"Just fittin' the puzzle pieces together and they're all formin' one picture." Colt just stared at him and Sully asked, "You want more?"

"You got it?"

"Yeah, or, Chris got it. He went to Skipp's, pickin' up somethin', who knows what. Chris is always workin' on his house. He saw that Skipp carries three different kinds of hatchets, two types of axes. One of the hatchets looks real familiar to Chris so he asks Skipp about the hatchets and Denny. Skipp, now this'll surprise you, the old fart, keeps everything. Every invoice for every nut and bolt he's sold since 1977 when he opened the shop. All organized, all at hand. Skipp remembers Denny, as you would, a man in expensive clothes buyin' a bunch of hatchets. He starts sortin' through his little file drawers and pulls out the invoices. Four different trips, Denny bought all three hatchets and both axes. One of those hatchets, same make as the one found in the alley by Angie's body. None of the remaining was found in the house."

"He took 'em with him."

"Did Miller with one of 'em, I reckon."

"Any way Skipp can trace the hatchet in evidence to his shop?" Colt asked.

Sully shook his head. "But, with all the rest of it, a defense attorney would have a helluva job passin' that off as coincidence, 'specially if the other four are recovered and that one's missin'."

This, fortunately, was true.

Sully took in breath through his nostrils and then said, "Now I got some bad news."

Colt slowly closed his eyes before he opened them and asked, "And that would be?"

"Monica Merriweather."

"Fuck," Colt clipped. He knew what was coming.

"She heard news of Pete, wasn't hard to put that together with Angie and then snoop around and find Butch. Not to mention Marie and rumor flyin' around. She came in today too, askin' questions. The Feds are pissed. They've kept the media from linking these cases and they don't want it out. The idea of some irritatin' woman who thinks she's Woodward *and* Bernstein and works for small town weekly paper breakin' this story has them in fits."

"You talk to her?"

Sully nodded but said, "She wants to talk to you."

Colt leaned back deep in his chair, pointed his face to the ceiling and put both his palms to his forehead.

Only person Sully couldn't sweet talk or swing to his way of thinking was Monica Merriweather. That was because, if she asked and was persistent enough, she could get to Colt and she liked getting to Colt. She also liked getting into his space and touching him a lot. When he first met her, he thought she was just a toucher. Later, when he saw her around other people, he noticed she saved that just for him.

Colt dropped his hands and looked at Sully. "You tell her I'm not workin' this case?"

"Seein' as you were first on the scene, I'm your partner and I am workin' this case, this is our town, but we still got a task force made up of boys from every department in the county, not to mention the frickin' Ef... Bee...Eye, I didn't share that morsel with her because she'd know somethin' was up if I did."

Christ, he hated it when Sully was smarter than him.

"Feds would appreciate it, you have a word with her," Sully said.

He had no choice and that pissed him off.

"I'll have a word with her," Colt replied.

"Got much on the robbery?" Sully asked.

"Got everything on it. Asshole didn't wear gloves, prints everywhere and he made a mess. He pinged huge when we ran his prints. Junkie from the city, what he's doin' out in the sticks is anyone's guess but riper pickin's, likely. Figure they got lucky on timing, the family had a redeye back up from vacationing in Florida. Big house, lotsa shit. He probably wouldn't have cared they were home or not and, if he's jonesin' and they confronted him, no tellin' what he'd do."

"You run him down?"

"Called into IMPD to check what they know about him and Drew and Sean headed into the city because Feb and I had to go to Amy's funeral. Drew reports, not surprisingly, he's not home. His woman says he disappears a lot."

"Bet he does."

"Drew and Sean also ran down a couple of his known hangouts but he's gone. He's scored and he's not sharin' so he's disappeared."

"Anything show up in pawn shops?"

"Not yet, least not the ones he's known to use."

"So I'm guessin' IMPD Vice know him."

"They say he asks for his favorite cell when they bring him in."

"Jesus," Sully muttered. "City's closin' in on us, Colt."

"Funny, that," Colt replied. "City's closin' in and the worst crime we ever had was one of our own against our own."

"Yeah," Sully said softly. "Funny."

Twenty minutes later, Colt walked into J&J's.

It was Friday night and the place was a crush. Everyone was on, Ruthie and Jackie working tables, Darryl clearing them, Morrie, Jack and Feb behind the bar.

The minute he walked in, Feb's eyes came to the door and he got the impression her eyes went to the door every time it opened that night, waiting for him. When she caught sight of him, he saw it, even in the dim light, her face got soft, her eyes especially, her lips tipped up at the ends and she did the jaw tilt.

That was new, her face getting soft like that. He liked it so he smiled at her, even though he would have smiled at her anyway.

Her eyes slid away and she smiled at the floor before she turned to the cash register.

He headed to his seat, which was as ever, empty and saw Lore sitting on the stool next to it.

He slid on his, Lore turned his head to him and asked, "We good?"

"You apologize to Feb?" Colt asked back.

"Yeah, and I bought her a shot."

"She drink it?"

"She gave it to Joe-Bob, but said, 'No offense, Lore, I'm workin'.' So I'm thinkin' she's good."

Colt's eyes found February and saw she was giving someone change.

"She's learnin' the art of forgiveness," Colt muttered to Lore.

"Lucky me," Lore muttered back as Feb headed their way.

"Hey, babe, off duty?" she asked when she arrived.

"Yeah, honey, beer tonight."

"Gotcha."

She got him a beer, opened it and instead of putting it on the bar in front of him, she handed it to him. He took it and then drew in a long pull.

"Ruthie's holdin' on you gettin' here to put our orders into Shanghai Salon," she told him when he put the bottle on the bar.

"We practicin' for when we move to China?" he asked. She smiled and he allowed himself a moment to enjoy sharing an inside joke with Feb. It'd been a long fucking time.

"You're movin' to China?" Lore asked and Feb burst out laughing.

Neither Feb nor Colt answered but they didn't have to. Tina Blackstone sidled by, eyes darting from Lore to Colt, opening herself to either one of them had a mind to slip in.

Colt looked away.

Lore muttered, "Catch ya later," and slid away.

"Honest to God, she's a nerve, comin' in to my bar," Feb said, and Colt looked at her to see her eyes following Tina.

"She pay for her drinks?" Colt asked, and Feb's eyes moved to him.

"Yeah."

"Good, then you can buy yourself more heels."

She grinned at him then said, "Find Ruthie, tell her your order. We're all hungry."

She started to move away but stopped and turned back at his call.

"You're hungry, baby, don't wait for me," Colt told her.

She tipped her head to the side and replied, "You said you'd be in."

"Yeah, but my schedule's always uncertain. You're hungry, get food. I'll sort myself out."

She leaned into her forearms on the bar and got close. "But, you're Colt. That means we'll wait, or at least I will." Then she leaned in further and touched her mouth to his before she pushed back and walked away.

Colt watched, his vision filled with the movement of Feb's ass, his mind filled with memories of her standing in his bathroom in nothing but his t-shirt, solving the mystery of how she smoothed out her hair. Both made him smile.

He found Ruthie and as he had Shanghai Salon's menu memorized much like practically every citizen in town, he gave her his order.

"You got it, Colt," Ruthie said and headed to the office to call in the order.

Colt returned to his beer and his stool and watched his family work their bar and the way they did it. You have a few drinks, you got the money to pay for them, you enjoy yourself but keep yourself in line, it was like you were at a party at their home: welcome and they hoped you'd stay awhile. Dee being there would make life complete. Colt was pleased she'd made that choice, taken that chance, and he hoped it worked out for her and Morrie.

On that thought, his phone rang. He pulled it out of the pocket of his suit jacket and looked at the display. A number came up he didn't recognize but he flipped it open and put it to his ear, covering his other ear with his hand.

"Colton."

There was a pause and then, "Um...Colt?"

Colt turned toward the wall to focus and he felt his gut get heavy. "Cheryl?"

"Yeah."

"You okay?"

"Yeah, I just..." she hesitated, "I don't know if you want to know this."

"Know what?"

"Just that..." another hesitation, "me and Ethan made it to Ohio okay. We're here. Ethan's sleepin'. He was excited all day. Thinks were on vacation."

Colt closed his eyes taking in a breath and opened them on an exhale, feeling that weight lighten.

"That's good," he said. "Feds know where you are?"

"Called 'em before I called you."

"You hangin' in there?" Colt asked.

"Could be better, seein' as my boss didn't take me hightailin' outta town with no notice too good and fired my ass."

"Cheryl—"

"It's okay. I hated that job anyway and hated my boss worse. I still got a shitload of that asshole's money and sold all that fuckin' silver he gave me, which, by the way, wasn't worth much. At least it was somethin' so I got a nest egg that'll last me and Ethan for a while."

Colt turned back to the bar and watched Jack laugh at something Joe-Bob said. Then his eyes slid to Feb and he watched her fill an order while she talked to her mom. Then he saw Morrie take some beer bottles from

Darryl and toss them in the bin, Darryl talking and Morrie grinning at whatever he was saying.

Then he thought of Morrie letting go his place, Feb letting go hers and Jack and Jackie off to Florida after Dee got settled in. Fridays and Saturdays, Darryl, Ruthie, Morrie and Feb always were working, on their feet and busy from five thirty until closing.

Then he thought about how he didn't want Feb on her feet and closing the bar day in and day out like she'd been doing for two years. It was then he acutely felt Dee's pain. If Colt was out of the house at some ungodly hour in the morning, which didn't happen often but happened enough, and Feb dragged in at three in the morning, they'd have a few hours of sleep together and most of the time he saw her would be sitting exactly where he was, watching her move around the back of the bar.

Therefore, he said to Cheryl, "You get back, you come to Feb's bar."

She hesitated before she asked, "Why?"

"I know some people who're good at takin' care of people and you're people."

"Colt—"

"You come, it could be me buyin' you a drink. It could be me talkin' my woman into givin' you a job. I'm not makin' any promises but there're far worse places you could be for either."

"I—"

"Either way, it won't take much of your time and it'll be worth it."

"But I—"

Colt cut her off. "In the meantime, I want you checkin' in."

"But—"

"Regular."

"To you or the Feds?"

"Both."

She hesitated again before she said, "All right."

"See you in J&J's."

"Yeah."

"Take care of that kid."

"Always."

"And yourself."

"Not so good at that."

"You're young, you'll learn." She didn't answer so Colt said, "Later."

"Colt?"

"Yeah?"

There was another hesitation before she said, "Thanks."

Then she disconnected.

"Who's that?" Feb asked and Colt, who was twisted to put his phone back in his suit jacket pocket, turned to see she was standing behind the bar right in front of him. He could tell by her face that she was preparing for whatever his answer would be, benign or malignant.

"Cheryl."

"Cheryl who?"

"Cheryl one of the names at the bottom of the list of people Denny Lowe fucked over."

"Oh," Feb muttered, her eyes gliding away, her thoughts unhappy. Malignant it was and it was lucky she prepared. "That Cheryl."

"She's safe in Ohio with her kid but her boss canned her for takin' an unscheduled vacation."

Feb's eyes shot back, her unhappy thoughts gone, new unhappy thoughts in their place. She leaned forward so close she had to put her forearms on the bar and she hissed, "But she's on the run from a *murderer.*"

"Don't know any but not sure men who run strip clubs worry about that shit. Think they worry more about losin' money."

Feb leaned back slightly and snapped, "Oh my God, that *sucks.*" Her eyes were on his and the feeling behind them, mostly anger, was intense. "She's got a kid! And she'd just been royally screwed! What a *dick.*" She shook her head and looked away, saying, "Poor Cheryl, she just needs this to deal with after learnin' about Denny."

Colt was finding it hard not to laugh but he didn't try not to smile.

"Good you feel that way, honey, since I essentially told her, she gets back and comes in, you'll give her a job."

Her gaze cut back to him then her brows drew together. She still looked pissed but he figured she wasn't pissed at some unknown strip club owner anymore.

Then she asked, "You did what?"

"Your monthly expenses are gonna change, movin' in with me. Morrie's overhead is gonna reduce significantly, bein' back home, and you need the help."

"Dee's gonna be comin' in."

"And Dee's gonna wanna work until three o'clock in the mornin' about as much as I'm gonna want *you* doin' it."

"Cheryl's got a kid, how's she gonna work until three?"

"Baby, she was a stripper."

He had her there. He knew it because she straightened, put her hands to her hips and stared at him without saying a word.

Then she found the words she wanted to say. "You gonna offer a job at J&J's to every stray that wanders your way?"

"Only the ones been fucked over by Denny Lowe."

He had her there too. Like it or not, Cheryl was in their club. A club they didn't ask to join but they were stuck together in it all the same.

Feb proved he had her when she asked, "She know how to make a drink?"

"She doesn't, reckon she can be taught, same as Dee."

"She got her shit together?"

"Does Darryl?"

Feb's eyes slid to Darryl then they hit the floor and she whispered, "Fuck me."

"That's later."

She looked at him and her face cracked. She didn't want to smile and she didn't want to laugh but she was having a hard time not doing either.

When she won her struggle against her humor, she declared, "I take her on, *then* you'll owe me."

"I'll pay."

She shook her head before she tipped it to his beer. "Ready for another?"

"When Shanghai gets here."

"All right, babe," she said and turned away and again Colt watched her ass when she did.

It was after they shared their food while sitting in the office and shooting the shit during Feb's break, all of which lasted less than twenty minutes.

It was after the crush hit the red zone, everyone in town buzzing and wanting to be out. Spring was there, weather was turning warmer, days were longer and dead bodies were being found. It was time, if you were alive, to be alive and get your ass to J&J's, have a drink, see your friends and neighbors and have a good time.

It was when Colt was feeling a fatigue he hadn't felt in a long time, with stress and broken sleep, all through riding an emotional roller coaster. He just wanted to go home and go to bed with Feb and, yes, with her damned cat draped on their feet.

It was when he thought this that he saw Feb slide through the crowd toward the jukebox. She found her song, put in a coin and pressed buttons. He'd seen her do that on occasion in the last two years. She did it more before, when she would be home visiting and wasn't working.

It was when she turned and headed toward a table where they were calling her name Colt decided he could stay awhile. If Feb was in the mood for some of her music, then Colt wasn't too tired to sit on a stool, drink his beer and watch her enjoy it.

It took five songs for Feb's to come on. She was behind the bar at the other end but Colt still knew it was hers. It wasn't what he was expecting, or anyone would expect. The music came loud because the box was set loud, but it wasn't rowdy Friday night bar music by a long shot.

The minute he heard the guitar his eyes went to her to see hers come to him. Then she dipped her chin, looking away while she tucked her hair behind her ear, bashful at showing her emotion.

And that's when Colt knew it wasn't Feb's song. It was the song Feb chose for him, or the song she chose to say the things she couldn't say.

A lump hit his throat, he looked down at his hand wrapped around his beer, which was sitting on the bar, and he paid attention to the lyrics to a song he'd heard time and again. Lyrics he knew and could likely recite if asked. Lyrics he'd never paid any real attention to in his life.

Staring at his beer, his hand tightening on the bottle, fighting that lump in his throat, he listened to Stevie Nicks singing "Landslide."

Colt'd always liked it. It was a great song. Listening to it then, he thought it was the most beautiful fucking song he'd ever heard in his whole fucking life.

He saw her hand wrap around his wrist the second Stevie quit singing and his head came up.

She leaned in close and whispered, "Go home, baby, get to bed. Someone'll drop me home later."

She didn't want to make a big deal of it, what she'd just given him, but her face was soft, her eyes especially, her lips tipped up at the ends, just slightly but it was all there. Nothing held back, everything she felt for him showing clear on her face.

He wanted to go home, he definitely wanted to go home, but only if he was taking Feb home.

But that wasn't the way she wanted to play it and she just handed him everything, he could give her this.

"Whoever brings you home walks you in," he ordered. She nodded and he said, "All the way in, Feb."

"Gotcha."

He lifted his beer and her hand fell away. He took one last pull and put it on the bar before he tagged her around the back of her head, leaned in and brought her mouth to his.

"Later, baby," he said against her mouth when he finished giving her his kiss.

"Later, Alec."

He pulled away but his hand slid through her hair to her cheek, taking hair with it but he didn't care and neither did she. She pressed her cheek into his hand as he ran his thumb along her cheekbone. Then his hand dropped away and he turned away before he did something asinine, like carry her out of the bar over his shoulder.

Calling his good-byes to a dozen people as he went, Colt exited J&J's, walked to the station, got in his truck and went home.

He saw Melanie's car parked out front as he turned into his street. He drew in an annoyed breath and decided his first order of business the next morning was putting in for vacation time. He'd just had time off but he didn't give a fuck. He'd take it unpaid if he had to.

He parked the truck in the drive, and by the time he slid out of it, she was walking across the yard toward him.

"Melly, it's ten thirty at night," he said when she was four feet away.

"Gotta talk, Colt."

Fucking hell.

"Mel, I'm wiped. Seriously."

She glanced at the house then to him and asked, "Feb livin' here?"

Fucking, *fucking* hell.

He looked into the night then at his ex-wife.

Melanie was everything Feb wasn't—dark-haired, quiet, thoughtful, patient. She didn't dance because she was worried people were watching and more worried about what they'd think. It took her weeks to come to a decision about anything, no matter how large or small because she didn't take risks, she treaded cautiously. He'd liked all that about her when he fell in love with her. He thought it was cute and it was. Until she took her time making the decision about leaving him, pulling away the whole time she took to make it. Then it wasn't fucking cute.

"Come into the house," he said. He didn't want to but he also didn't want to have this conversation at ten thirty at night in his yard.

He led the way, hearing Melanie's feet hit the turf as she walked beside him and partly behind him, something else she'd always done and something he never understood, why she'd never walk right beside him.

He unlocked the door and went to the security panel.

When he made the beeping stop, he walked to the lamp by the couch as she asked, "You have an alarm?"

"Yeah," he said, turning on the lamp.

In the light, she took him in, saying, "You're in a suit."

"Funeral today."

They both heard the meow and their eyes went to Wilson, who Colt could swear was standing in the doorway to the hall staring at Melanie with indictment in his eyes.

"You have a cat?" Melanie asked.

"Mel—"

She cut him off. "You hate cats."

Colt expelled a breath and Melanie's face crumpled as understanding dawned.

"It's *her* cat," she whispered.

He did not need this now. Actually, he didn't need this at all, but particularly not now.

With less patience than he would normally use with her, he reminded her, "You left me, Mel."

She closed her eyes and shook her head, small shakes, like she couldn't even commit to the decision to show that emotion. Then her eyes opened and she looked around the space, trying to find hints of Feb, evidence of a betrayal it wasn't hers to claim. They'd bought that house together, intending to use it to build a life, and she'd left him behind in it to live alone.

"You're here to say something," Colt prompted. "So say it."

Her eyes shot to his and he saw the sting his words caused. He'd always been tolerant with the quirks in her personality mostly because, in the beginning, he thought they were sweet. After that, he did it out of habit. She'd been gone a good while and he was out of the habit.

"She told everyone to stop talkin' about us," Melanie said.

"What?"

"Feb," she explained. "When people heard about...when I called...you know how people talk."

"I do."

"Well, she...Feb, told them to quit talkin' about us."

"You mean you," Colt said honestly, and Melanie sucked in her cheeks. "Feb told folks to stop talkin' about you."

She'd do that, Feb would. She might not tell folks to stop talking about her, or her and Colt, but she wouldn't stand and listen to folks talking about Melanie.

"I should have never said anything to Marla," Melanie stated quietly.

Marla Webster was Melanie's best friend and a pain in the ass. She had a big mouth, for one. For another, her mouth was loud, always nearly shouting even in a one-on-one conversation like she was talking to someone mostly deaf. Unfortunately, since she talked so damned much, you could never get a word in to tell her to quit yelling. One thing Colt didn't miss when Melanie left was Marla.

"I kept telling you, Melly, Marla's a pain in the ass."

Pain flashed through her face at the reminder of a time when Colt told her anything and the little patience Colt had left, he was losing.

She'd left him. He didn't ask her to leave, didn't fucking want her to leave, but she left. That decision was on her. What happened after was not her business. He couldn't say what would've gone down if this was happening and Melanie was in his life. The pull of Feb was so strong, he might have buckled and been drawn in by her. Then again, he'd loved his wife so he might not. But, all this shit was going down when he luckily didn't have a wife. And it was luck that he'd been free. He knew it in his bones and that might not say good things about him but he didn't give a shit.

Melanie's eyes came to his and he could see the tears threatening there.

"Is she living here?" she asked.

Colt told her the truth. "She's been stayin' here and, yeah, she's movin' in."

"So, if I asked—"

Colt shook his head. "Don't ask."

"But—"

"Don't ask, Mel."

And he knew it, he knew it then. He knew she'd been thinking about this since Feb came home, trying to make the decision of whether she should approach for reconciliation. Fretting over it for years and timing it too late.

But even if she'd come to him earlier, with Feb home he knew what his answer would have been even thinking he was finished with Feb. He knew it and Melanie knew it. If she stayed strong and true to him, there would have been no problem. But she hadn't and with Feb in town he wouldn't have taken her back to live under the cloud she brought. Those glances she always threw Feb's way. The times they'd all be together and he'd catch her studying him as if trying to read a hidden infidelity written on his soul. Why she was making this play now, he didn't have a clue and he didn't like it. It wasn't sweet, it wasn't cute. It was straight out selfish.

She nodded and looked to the floor, taking in a breath that hitched before she lifted her eyes to his again.

"Tell me one thing."

And he knew where she was going so he stopped her. "Don't ask that either."

"Colt—"

"We split and we did it amicably. You ask that shit, it'll piss me off."

She leaned forward and her voice went higher when she said, "I have to know."

Colt crossed his arms on his chest and leaned back, asking, "You think I'd fuck around on you?"

"She's Feb."

"We're not talkin' 'bout Feb now, we're talkin' about me, and you think I'd fuck around on you?"

She threw her arm out. "She's back in town and then," she snapped her fingers, "she's livin' in my house."

Okay, now he was pissed off.

"It's my house, Melanie, been my house and my house alone now for years."

"We bought it together."

"I remember. I also remember you leavin' me in it alone."

She hid her hurt behind burgeoning anger. "Well, it's a good thing for you now Feb's back I did that."

"You act like she drove into town yesterday. Feb's been back years."

"Yeah, you're right. So I guess I'm surprised it took this long."

"I'm not surprised, Mel. At this point, I'm kickin' myself in the ass for waitin' that long."

She reared back and clamped her mouth shut so hard he could hear her teeth crash together.

"This what you came to do?" Colt asked. "Piss me off?"

"No, of course not."

"Well, that's what you did."

She shook her head again and started, "I just…" then stopped, still shaking her head.

Colt turned, walking to the table, pulling off his suit jacket and hooking it on the back of a dining table chair then he turned back to her.

"Mel, there's been a string of homicides, two of 'em to be exact. A robbery last night. I been awake and on the go since before five and I'm fuckin' dog-tired."

She looked at him and her face went from upset to gentle with memories. "That used to happen a lot."

Colt didn't feel like reminiscing so when he spoke his words were short and clipped. "Still does. Never stopped."

She sucked in her cheeks again before she nodded. "I shouldn't have come."

No, she fucking shouldn't have.

"We done?" he asked and he'd used the wrong words. They stung too. He watched her flinch with the sudden, acute pain. It wasn't that he didn't care. It just wasn't his place to care anymore. He'd gotten used to that, he'd gotten over it and he'd moved on. She obviously hadn't. He had enough problems. He wasn't going to add hers to them.

"We're done," she said softly.

He walked to the door, opened it and held it for her.

She stopped and tilted her head back to look at him before she whispered, "It was nice of her…to try and stop people from talkin'."

"That's Feb," he said because it was.

She nodded again and said, "Take care, Colt. Sorry about…" she trailed off and made a gesture with her hand.

"You got a long drive, Melanie," he replied. "Be safe doin' it."

She watched his face a moment before she dropped her head and walked out the door. He stood in its frame and waited until she made her way across the yard, got in her car, started it up and drove away.

Then he closed and locked the door, went to his suit jacket, pulled out his phone, flipped it opened and called Feb. He didn't know if Tina Blackstone or anyone on his street was watching and he wasn't having that shit hit Feb's ears before he explained it.

"Hello?" she answered, the bar noise loud in the background.

"Baby, you got two minutes?"

"Everything okay?" The noises were changing behind her and he knew she was on the move.

"In the grand scheme of things, yeah. Just wanted you to know that Melanie was sittin' outside in her car when I got home. She wanted a few words, I gave them to her and she just left."

There was no response and then the bar noise significantly muted. She was in the office.

Then, she asked, "Melanie?"

"Yeah."

"She okay?"

"My guess? No."

Again no response before she asked, "*You* okay?"

"Be better around three when you crawl in bed with me."

His name was soft and sweet when she said it. "Colt."

He wanted to explore that soft and sweet but she couldn't and he didn't want to fall asleep halfway through doing it.

"I gotta hit it, honey, practically asleep on my feet."

"Okay."

"Later, baby."

"Later, Colt."

He flipped his phone shut, armed the alarm for windows and doors, took his gun and phone to the bedroom, got ready for bed and he fell asleep about five seconds after her cat, laying on his chest with Colt's hand scratching his ruff, started purring.

The alarm beeps jarred Colt awake and he laid in the dark listening to them, instantly alert, his hand moving toward his gun on the nightstand, trying to hear anything that came with the beeps, something that wasn't supposed to.

Then he heard, "Jesus, Feb, shut it off."

Morrie.

Then the alarm beeps came faster and louder.

"Fucking shit," Feb whispered loudly. "I got it wrong."

"Do it again," Morrie advised.

There was more beeping and then it stopped.

Colt's hand dropped and Wilson, who woke up too, got up from where he was curled into Colt's hip and jumped off the bed.

"You good?" Morrie asked.

"Yeah, thanks for walkin' me in," Feb whispered again.

"Gotta make certain my baby sister is safe," Morrie replied. Colt listened to silence for a while, the front door closing and then he heard more beeps, Feb pressing the buttons on the panel to rearm the alarm.

There was more silence then he heard Feb whispering yet again, "Whose belly is that? Is it Mr. Purrsie Purrs's belly?"

Christ, she was petting Wilson and calling him that idiotic nickname again. Poor fucking cat.

Colt smiled into the dark.

She hit the room and Colt heard the cat's purrs when she did. He didn't move as she dropped her cat, walked to the nightstand and he heard the soft thud of her cell hitting it then she went to the bureau and stopped. He heard her jewelry clinking as she placed it on the top and then he heard clothing rustle, more soft thuds as her boots hit the floor, all the while he watched her shadow moving and hopping around.

She nabbed something off the end of the bed and went to the bathroom, not turning on the light until the door was firmly closed. He heard the sink go on and off, on and off, washing her face, brushing her teeth. The light went off before she opened the door.

She moved the covers, pulling them back before her knee hit the bed. He was about to turn to her when he saw her shadow didn't move to lie down. She was on all fours, crawling in a direct line toward him.

Her hand went to the covers at his stomach then down then her mouth was on his stomach then that went down too.

"Feb—" he started.

"Hush," she whispered against his skin.

He heard her necklaces clink together as she wrapped her hand around his cock and he felt her tongue rolling around the tip.

Jesus, her sweet, wet tongue felt fucking *great*.

Blood rushed to his cock and he thought he might have made a world's record for getting hard.

"Feb—"

She slid him all the way in.

His hand went to her body which was now curled on the bed, her ass to her ankles, her stomach pressed to her thighs, him in her mouth while her other hand slid along the skin of his chest.

When he touched her, he was annoyed to find she'd left on her underwear and it felt like she had on his tee that she was wearing earlier that day. He slid his hand over the curve of her ass when her head started moving and he wasn't annoyed anymore. He was something else a whole lot different.

"Baby," he groaned.

As Feb worked his cock with her mouth, Colt hauled her lower body toward him. He had her underwear pulled over her ass and his hand between the legs she spread for him, she was rocking against his fingers and moaning around his cock, when her phone rang on the nightstand.

His hand froze and her head shot up.

"You have got to be *fucking shitting* me," Colt clipped and in that moment, he swore to God, if he saw Denny Lowe he'd rip the fuckwad's head off with his own hands.

Feb still had her hand wrapped around his cock but her head was turned to him and she whispered, "Colt—"

But he moved, yanking up her underwear. She let him go and he reached toward the light coming from her cell display, dragging himself up to sit once he grabbed it.

When he saw who was on the display, he changed his mind about whose head he was going to rip off.

His eyes went to her to see her shadow up on her knees and she looked like she was arranging her underwear.

He flipped open the phone, put it to his ear and growled, "This better fuckin' be good."

There was a moment of silence then, "I'm in the hospital with forty stitches in my fuckin' shoulder, closin' a fuckin' hatchet wound, that good enough?"

Colt felt his chest depress from the inside and he reached toward the lamp when his phone started ringing.

He ignored it, turned on the lamp and looked at Feb. She was on her knees but her ass had dropped to her calves and her face was white as a sheet.

"Talk to me," he said to Reece, not tearing his eyes from Feb.

"Bastard got away."

"God *dammit*!" Colt snarled.

"I'm in fuckin' Texas. Asshole tailed me, broke into my goddamned hotel room."

"You okay?"

"Did I not mention the forty fuckin' stitches?"

"Other than that, you okay?"

"I was on the move when he delivered the blow, thank fuck, or I'd not have a goddamned arm. But, yeah, other than that, I'm okay."

Colt's phone had stopped ringing but instantly it rang again and he looked at Feb, pointed to the phone and then held his palm out, telling her he wanted her to give it to him.

"The police with you?" he asked Reece as he watched Feb crawl over his body and then across the bed on her hands and knees to get his phone.

"Yeah, they're here. One just got off the phone, which is why I 'spect your phone's ringing."

Feb had come back and put his phone in his hand and he looked at the display.

Sully.

He let his phone go to voicemail and asked Reece, "What happened?"

"Didn't hear him workin' the lock but there's a streetlight just outside. It shone in bright when he got in the door, woke me up, thank Christ. I hauled ass outta bed and he came at me swinging. That's when he nailed me. I got a few licks in while yellin' blue bloody murder. Fucker's not a fighter. He's not wieldin' a hatchet, he's got nothin'. I got the hatchet away from him and he turned tail and ran. I went after him but he nearly ran me over with his goddamned car. Didn't think to grab my keys, seein' as some fuckwit was after me with a hatchet and I was bleedin' like piss."

"You call the cops?" Colt asked.

"Yeah, I called the cops," Reece answered like Colt had a screw loose.

"Cops go after him?"

"Got to the scene in less than ten minutes. Set up roadblocks, nothin'. He's vanished."

"Jesus Christ," Colt clipped.

"Feds want me in protective custody until they get him. I need to talk to Feb."

Colt looked at Feb to see she was deep breathing again, her eyes locked on him unblinking.

"Give me a second," Colt told Reece.

"What's your name?" Reece asked suddenly.

"Colton," Colt replied automatically.

Reece's voice changed from hacked off to soft. "All right, Colton, break it to her gentle."

Colt took the phone from his ear and put his palm over it.

"Baby, come closer." She immediately slid forward on her knees until those knees were pressed to his hip, her eyes still unblinking and fixed on him. Colt leaned into her and wrapped his hand around the back of her neck. "He's okay but Denny got to Reece tonight. Reece's got some stitches but he's okay. Denny got away."

He watched as she closed her eyes tight and turned her face away. She allowed herself about a half a second to have this reaction before she opened her eyes and looked at him again, lifting her hand palm up for the phone.

He handed it to her and she put it to her ear, her eyes dropping to the bed.

"Reece?" she waited. "Yeah," She paused and listened. "You okay?" She closed her eyes again and shook her head then opened them but didn't lift them. "I'm so sorry." Another pause and then quickly, "I know I don't have to—" She was obviously cut off and she waited a moment before she said, "Okay. Yeah. You can't check in?" She nodded, listened then said, "That makes sense. You'll call when this is done?" She listened again, more nodding then she whispered, "Okay, honey."

Colt fucking hated hearing her call another man "honey." She'd done it the night before too. He didn't like it then and he didn't like it now.

416

Then again, five minutes ago she had her mouth around his cock and he had his finger inside her and she was currently on her knees in his bed while wearing his t-shirt while Reece was in Texas, didn't have a prayer in the world with Feb and Colt doubted she'd ever given Reece something like "Landslide." If she had, the bastard would never in a million years watch her walk away. So Colt decided he had nothing to complain about.

"Stay safe, okay?" she asked, was quiet a moment and then her eyes moved to Colt before they went back to the bed. "Yeah, I'll be okay." She bit her lip before saying, "He's a cop, Reece. He knows what he's doin'." She went silent and then she smiled. "Yeah, a cop." She gave a soft laugh, listened then whispered, "He's a good man, honey, he'll take care of me."

Colt's fingers pressed into her neck and she looked at him.

"What?" she said into the phone then those dents came to the insides of her brows and her face went unfocused. "Um…okay, he's right here." She waited. "Yeah. You too. Later, honey." Then she held out the phone to Colt and said, "He wants a word."

Colt took the phone, gave her another squeeze with his fingers before he took his hand away.

"Yeah?" he said when he put the phone to his ear.

"Goes without sayin', cop or not, this motherfucker even *breathes* in her space, I'm holdin' *you* responsible."

"I can understand that," Colt said to him.

"That's good we understand each other."

"We do."

"You know what you got?" Reece asked, and Colt's eyes went to Feb on her knees, in his bed, in his t-shirt.

Shit yeah, he knew what he had.

"Yeah," he told Reece.

"Take care of it," Reece said then Colt heard the disconnect.

He flipped her phone closed and tossed it on the nightstand while Feb asked, "Everything all right?"

Colt looked at her. "He's worried about you."

"Well, *I* didn't have Denny Lowe and his hatchet in my bedroom tonight."

Thank Christ for that.

Colt decided it was time to have a certain conversation.

"We didn't talk about protective custody tonight, baby."

Her body gave a small jerk but after she recovered she held herself completely still.

"Feb?"

"Do you want us to go into protective custody?" she asked.

"It'd be smart."

She tilted her head to the side and he saw her eyes were active. She'd been thinking about this, a lot.

Her voice was quiet when she asked, "Doesn't it mean he wins, even a little bit, we go into hiding?"

"We're on top, he ends this in jail and we come out safe."

She looked away for a few seconds before she looked back to him and then came closer, putting her hands on his chest.

"Okay, listen to me, Alec, okay?" she asked, and he nodded, sliding his arms around her and pulling her closer as she went on. "I know this is gonna sound crazy but, he already took a lot of my life. We go away, we're together and we're breathin' but we're in limbo. Life's gonna go on but we won't really be livin' it."

"Honey—"

She lifted her hand and put her fingers to his lips before she whispered, "I wanna watch you get dressed in the bathroom. *Your* bathroom. I wanna make you breakfast in the kitchen. *Your* kitchen. I want you to come into the bar when you're off duty and I wanna get you a beer. I wanna fall asleep in your big bed with my cat on our feet. I want us to have the life we were meant to have. I want us to live the life we should have been living." She got closer and her voice dropped even quieter. "Baby, I don't want to miss another minute and it'd be even worse knownin' *he* took it away." Her hand slid from his mouth, down his jaw to his neck. "Is that crazy?"

No, it was far from crazy.

"It isn't crazy," he told her.

"Is it stupid?"

It wasn't crazy. The jury was out if it was stupid.

He didn't tell her that, instead, he said, "I'll keep you safe, Feb."

She nodded then ducked her head and pressed it into his neck. "I know you will. I'm countin' on it."

He pushed up until his back was to the wall and he pulled her close, into his lap, and she snuggled even closer, wrapping her arms around him.

"Gotta call Sully, baby."

She nodded against his neck.

He flipped his phone open and made the call.

"I'm halfway to your house." Sully used this statement as a greeting.

"I was on the phone with Reece."

"You know then."

"Yeah, they get anything at all?"

"They got a hatchet and an attempted homicide with a coherent witness who identified his attacker immediately, puttin' the last piece into the puzzle which'll nail this jackass to the wall."

"That'd make me feel better if he wasn't still out there."

"Half the east Texas police and probably every Fed in the Lone Star State are searchin' for him, Colt."

"Yeah, searchin'. Call me minute he's found."

"Gotcha," Sully said then he called, "Colt?"

"Yeah?"

"Without Reece as a target, he gets away, he'll be comin' after you."

"I know."

"Stay alert." The worry was clear in Sully's tone.

"You got it."

Colt flipped the phone shut and tossed it on the nightstand with Feb's.

He held her for a while and it seemed she liked the quiet and peace of it, left to her own thoughts, so he gave it to her. When he felt it was time, he started to move to the lamp but her hand moved down his stomach.

"Feb—"

"No, Alec," she said against his neck as her mouth traveled south. "He's gone now. Now it's just you and me and the life we were meant to have."

Then her body moved so her mouth could get where it wanted to go and Colt saw her curl herself between his legs then she sucked his cock while his hands held her hair away from her face so he could watch the show. Then, when he decided he wanted her pussy and not her mouth, he yanked her up, tore down her panties and planted her astride him. Then he watched her ride him while he fingered her clit until she came and then he watched her ride him more, until he couldn't watch because he came.

The light was out, he'd pulled the covers over them, she was pressed to his side, her leg thrown over his thigh and he could feel his wetness sliding out of her as she pushed in closer and Wilson hopped up and settled at their ankles.

"Love you, babe," she whispered into his chest.

He gave her a squeeze with his arm around her waist. "Love you too, Feb."

After a while, her weight grew heavier as did her breathing and he knew she was out.

He was hearing Stevie Nicks singing in his head when Colt fell asleep in the bed, in the house, with the woman at his side that life meant him to have.

After waiting for forty-four years, for the fifth night in a row, Alexander Colton was finally living the life he was meant to be living.

Eleven

UNIDENTIFIED

I woke up when Colt slid out from under me. I nabbed his pillow and pulled it to my chest, wrapping my arms around it.

Wilson followed him out of bed and started meowing. Then he followed him to the bathroom then he followed him down the hall then, after a minute or two, Wilson shut up.

I let Colt's pillow go, looked at the clock and saw it was after nine in the morning. I rolled when I heard Colt coming back down the hall and I got up on an elbow, pulling my hair out of my face to watch him walk into the room wearing nothing but boxers.

His eyes were on me and he came right at me, stopping briefly at the side of the bed to hook his thumbs into the boxers and yank them down. I got a good look. I liked what I saw but it didn't last long because he leaned in and pulled down the covers. A slight cold hit me before it was swept away when Colt put a knee to the bed right before he covered me with his body.

His hands went into the tee at my sides and his face disappeared into my neck where he said, "Mornin' baby."

This wasn't just a morning. This was a *good* morning. But I decided not to point that out because he probably knew it already.

I slid my hands across the skin of his back, turned my head and said into his hair, "Mornin'."

His hands were moving on me, his weight heavy, both felt unbelievably great as his lips slid up my neck to the hinge of my jaw where he said, "Fuckin' love Saturdays."

I smiled because he sounded content and also because I agreed with him. Only better day in the week than Saturday was Sunday and that was tomorrow. Something to look forward to and it'd been way too long since I'd had something to look forward to.

His hands went up the shirt, taking it with them then it was up further and he arched his back. I lifted my back from the bed as well as my arms over my head and the tee was swept away. He tossed it to the side and dropped his mouth to mine.

"Feel like waffles," he muttered against my mouth.

I knew what that meant.

Something else to look forward to.

One of my hands went up his neck and my fingers sifted into his hair before I replied, "Me too."

He grinned against my mouth then he took it in a deep kiss and, after, he did other things at other places on my body with his mouth. Then he was between my legs, lifting and spreading them wide and cocked with his hands behind my knees. He took me with his mouth, making me come. Then he moved up and over me, fucking me slow and sweet, then harder, then faster, then even harder, his hands on me, my hands on him, our mouths locked, tongues sparring, building it again for me, but now also for him, until I exploded the second time just moments before he lifted my knees high, rammed in deep and groaned.

After, when Colt was gliding gently in and out of me, his tongue tracing my necklaces, I was thinking I was pretty happy I'd packed the waffle iron with the stoneware.

Colt waited for his waffles because I did yoga.

Seeing as I'd had two orgasms, I didn't really need to do the yoga to relax and de-stress, but I did need to do it to practice and keep fit.

Colt sat at the bar on a stool wearing a pair of shorts and a tee, reading the paper and drinking coffee. I was in the den, my yoga mat down the length of the pool table, one of the scented candles that I brought over from my place burning and I had Norah Jones playing. I was trying to concentrate, clear my mind, focus on my positioning, my muscles, my breathing, deepening the poses, rooting myself to the floor for the balancing ones, but this was difficult. This was difficult partly because there was a lot of shit to think about so clearing my mind was a challenge. This was also difficult because, more times than most, when I caught Colt in my vision, he was watching me.

"Don't watch me," I ordered as I moved from triangle pose to downward-facing dog.

"Baby, your ass is in the air and you're wearin' tight clothes. Not watchin' you is impossible."

"You're breaking my concentration."

"With practice, you'll get used to me enjoyin' the show."

I rolled my eyes to the floor, which luckily Colt couldn't see.

"Next time, you're doin' this with me," I told him and he burst out laughing so I asked, "What?"

"I do yoga the day you play basketball."

Morrie and Colt had often tried to get me, Jessie, Meems or whatever girl Morrie was dating at the time to play basketball with them. It was supposed to be a low contact sport but the way they played it was not. I figured it was their way to look superior as well as bump into girls a lot. I didn't mind that. It was all the running and sweating and dribbling and *rules* that I minded.

No way I was going to play basketball. Ever.

"Enjoy the show," I invited, and dropped down into child's pose as I heard Colt chuckle.

Something about his chuckle, maybe the satisfaction I heard mixed with the humor, freed my mind. Everything left it and all I had was the scent of ocean in my nostrils, Norah in my ears, my mat under me and my muscles releasing.

I made Colt waffles. We ate them, both of us sitting on the counter. He helped me clean the kitchen, which I thought was nice until I realized he did this to delay taking a shower so he could do it with me.

The shower we had was nicer than him helping me clean the kitchen. A lot nicer.

We got ready for the day. This took Colt five minutes. It took me forty-five.

We went to my apartment and got another load, leaving behind nothing but my bed, nightstands, lamps, dinette set, table and armchair. While we were in the truck with the boxes on the way home, we discussed the rest of my belongings and how it was too bad Mom bought that bed from Bud because now we had an extra one. Still, Colt figured he had enough room in his garage to store it all until we could find homes for it. I'd called my landlord and he was happy I was jumping my lease by a few months. Our town was a popular location for city commuters and retirees looking for accommodation that took less than three hours to clean so he had a waiting list.

However, when we hauled the boxes into his house and went out to check the garage, we found Colt wasn't correct, mostly because Mom put all the shit from his second bedroom in the garage.

We stood staring at the stuff piled up in his garage, so much only a small amount of moving space was available.

"I'm not a big fan of scraping ice off my car," I commented, staring at all the crap in his garage and I felt his eyes come to me.

"Feb, for two years, you parked under a tree."

I was seeing that being a detective's girlfriend might not be as cool as I'd thought it would be, considering to be a detective you kinda had to be pretty sharp and you definitely couldn't let anyone pull anything over on you.

I looked up to him and replied, "Yeah, but I didn't *like* it. You got a garage, we should use it. The truck won't fit in here. My car will."

"It doesn't have an electric door opener."

"We'll put one in."

"Baby, I just put in an alarm."

Shit, he was saying he didn't have the money.

Denny Lowe was *such* an assface.

"I'll pay for it," I declared.

He gave me a Man Look, which communicated the fact that he wasn't a big fan of me paying for shit, seeing as I had a vagina and breasts. When we divvied up household responsibilities, his look foretold I'd get groceries, cleaning implements, clothing and linens with the odd knickknack or standing kitchen appliance thrown in. The garage was part of Man's World, not to be touched by female hands or updated with the woman's money.

Then he wisely decided to let that go and tried a different tactic. "The boat's gotta stay where it is."

I turned and looked out the little, high-up, square windows in his garage—which incidentally, seriously needed to be cleaned—to see the boat under the sided awning which would be a perfect fit for his truck so *he* didn't have to clear snow or ice.

My eyes moved back to Colt. "How 'bout we build a side thingie for the boat? You can park your truck where the boat is."

"Maybe I didn't mention that I got the full-on deluxe edition of an alarm," Colt noted.

I braved another Man Look. "I'll pay for the side thingie too."

I didn't get a Man Look because, instead, his brows snapped together before he asked, "You got that kinda cake?"

"I moved my belongings to your house in two trips, using two cars and a truck, Colt. I go to work in t-shirts. I got a low overhead," I pointed out. "Each month I have three CDs that mature in three different banks across the US of A."

"You cash in your CDs, you buy yourself a shitload of heels and a new car," he said, or more like, *decreed.*

It was then I asked the question I should not have asked. Not only was it my experience it was a useless effort to discuss clothes with men and therefore should be avoided. It was also my experience you should *never* discuss cars with men.

First, they knew more about cars than women, or more to the point, women if that woman happened to me. There were many men who even made cars a lifelong study but I, personally, couldn't care less. Second, because they knew more and *knew* they knew more, men usually acted annoyingly smug when any car discussion came up. That alone was reason to avoid car discussions. Third, they tended to be right, which was the biggest reason of all to avoid such discussions.

Even knowing all this, I asked, "What's wrong with my car?"

"Nothin', 'cept it was built during the Carter Administration."

Now he was pissing me off. I liked my car. Sure, it was old. Sure, it was small. Sure, it wasn't all that attractive. But it got me from point A to point B, it had a kickass stereo and it started up every time.

Well, most every time. It might need some coaxing on the really cold days.

"It was not," I defended my car.

"Does it have airbags?" he asked.

"No," I answered.

"Was it built in a time when there *were* airbags?" he asked.

"No," I answered, getting more pissed.

"You get into a collision, baby, your compact will fold like an accordion and you'll get stuck in that shit," he said, looking back to the pile of stuff in his garage and the tone with which he said his next words meant he'd come to a decision. "You need a sedan."

Visions of me in a staid sedan, which probably had a shit stereo, flooded my head. Then I realized Lorraine owned a sedan. So did Chris Renicki's wife, Faith. So did Drew Mangold's wife, Cindy.

And so had Melanie.

My neck started itching mainly because of the heat that was collecting there, which was mainly because I was moving from pissed to pissed *off*.

"We'll talk about this later," I said.

He nodded and threw an arm around my shoulders, guiding me out but he did so while saying, "Soon's this shit's over, we'll go to Ricky's, look at some four doors."

I decided to completely ignore the words "four doors" which made my head get light and I suspected if I uttered those words my hair would turn instantly blue.

Instead I focused on Ricky.

Ricky Silvestri owned six different car dealerships in the county, which meant Ricky had expanded the family business since I was growing up. His dad only owned four. Ricky was a born and bred car salesman and trained all of his employees in the art of sixty years of car salesmanship as passed down from father to son. If Colt and I walked into any one of his dealerships together, I would instantly become the invisible woman. If I walked in alone, they'd screw me three ways 'til Tuesday.

"I'm not getting a sedan," I said as he closed the door to the garage.

"I thought we were gonna talk about this later?" he asked, taking his arm from around me as he locked the garage.

"We were, until you brought Ricky into it."

"Ricky's a good man. He'll swing us a deal."

Colt and I clearly had different definitions of "a good man." I knew Ricky still played football with Morrie and Colt when they pulled together games every once in a while. I also knew Ricky could hold his liquor and be quiet while fishing. But, from bar talk with Molly Jefferson, who was Ricky's second wife, Theresa's best friend, I knew he didn't pay child support unless Theresa put out, or at the very least gave him a blowjob. Rumor had it Ricky took it hard when Theresa left him, seeing as he still loved her. Making matters worse, Theresa still loved Ricky, hence her putting out or giving head. Though she had little choice but to leave since he was screwing his secretary and everyone but Theresa knew it, until she found out.

Since I usually kept bar talk to myself, instead of sharing any of this with Colt, I said, "We're not talkin' *us* here, Colt, we're talkin' *you*. *I* don't want a new car."

"And *I'm* not gonna bust my ass so you and me can survive this Denny shit and then be called to the scene of an accident and watch them cuttin' your dead, mangled body outta that death trap you drive," he shot back.

Yet another indication that being a cop's girlfriend might not be as cool as I thought it would be.

I decided, since I was forty-two years old and the time had probably come, to try and be mature.

So I suggested, "All right, Colt, I'll look at cars with you, *not* sedans and *definitely* not four door sedans. But we'll have a look around if you consider helpin' me clear out this garage, we get an electric door opener and we build on a shelter for the boat."

His brows collided again and he asked, "How many CDs you say you have?"

"Nearly forty," I answered. "But I haven't mentioned the savings bonds."

His forehead cleared, he grinned and threw his arm around my shoulders again, leading me toward the house saying, "Shit, my girlfriend's loaded."

I thought about it and realized I kind of was. I wasn't a millionaire or anything but I reckoned I had enough money for a garage door opener, a shelter for the boat *and* to buy a new car; all of this free and clear. It would strike deep but it wouldn't wipe me clean. There was more than enough to hold back for a rainy day even if we took a killer vacation thrown on top.

So perhaps I hadn't accumulated nothing in my life and actually had something to bring to the table. I had another impulse to do a cheerleader, pompom jump but I squelched it mainly because Colt's heavy arm was weighing me down.

We went through the side door, hit the kitchen and I turned to Colt. "Play your cards right, baby, things could get exciting. You got a birthday comin' up."

And he did, it was at the end of April, next month.

His hand came up, fingers curling around the side of my neck and he brought me close.

"I already know what I want for my birthday and you already bought it," he told me.

"What's that?" I asked.

His head dipped so his face was close to mine. "You, in nothin' but those black heels bent over the pool table."

I sucked in breath as an internal shiver rippled through my body. Something like that would forever make playing pool with Colt a delicious experience. Therefore, something like that was too good to wait for his birthday.

I decided not to share this either as well as play it cool. "You don't want me to wrap it up? Get a lacy teddy or something? Garters? Stockings? That kinda shit?"

He grinned and put his mouth to mine.

"Knock yourself out," he said there before he kissed me.

When he lifted his head, let me go, turned me toward the living room and smacked my ass, muttering, "Gotta get to the park," was when I returned to thinking being a cop's girlfriend was going to be all right.

Delilah and I sat on swings at Arbuckle Acres park while Bonham and Tuesday mostly ran around screaming since Dee had confiscated their cell phones and told them in that lovingly exasperated voice that only moms could pull off to, "Go. Play. Be kids."

I personally didn't think ten and twelve year old kids should have cell phones and neither did Dee. Unfortunately Morrie had taken them to the mall about three weeks ago and Morrie, also not thinking kids that age should have cell phones, bought them anyway because they begged for them and he was a pushover.

The swings were a good place to be seeing as they pointed to the basketball court on which Morrie and Colt were playing one-on-one.

It was sunny and in the upper sixties. I had on a black tank with a big, embroidered butterfly at the chest and a black, belted cardigan that went over my ass, faded jeans with a rip in the right knee and my black motorcycle boots.

Colt had on a t-shirt, shorts and basketball shoes.

He was dripping with sweat, breathing heavily and grinning all the while taunting Morrie, who was also dripping with sweat, breathing even heavier and still had the shiner Colt gave him. Further, Morrie was scowling and he was losing.

"Why Morrie plays him, I'll never know. Can't remember the last time he took a game," Dee muttered, her eyes glued to the men, just like me.

Morrie was my brother and all, but in a clinical, detached, sister way, I noticed not for the first time my brother was good-looking and, like my dad, age was being kind to him. He was always a big, cuddly, handsome guy and all that remained. But he was also beginning to get that look that interesting men had. The kind of men you took one look at and you knew it would not be a waste of your time to sit down and have a beer with them, or two, or three.

Again, just like my dad.

In other words, Dee and I had a lot to glue our eyes to. In fact, it was a wonder Colt and Morrie, having their regular Saturday game, didn't draw a crowd.

I answered Dee's question, "Because he loves bein' anywhere and doin' anything with Colt, even if he's losin'."

She nodded because this was now and always had been an absolute fact.

"Dee," I called like she wasn't swinging right beside me.

"Yeah, hon," she replied.

"What made you decide to come work the bar?"

She quit swinging for just a beat before she started again and answered, "All of this stuff happenin', with that psycho and you and Colt and everythin', I just got to thinkin'."

"Yeah?" I prompted when she stopped talking.

"It's stuff I been thinkin' about awhile, just wouldn't let my head get around it because I got pissed off first and acted on it, kickin' Morrie out before I really ever talked to him. I was bein' stubborn, thinkin' I was savin' face. But, I reckon, your parents made a go of it with that bar all their lives and Morrie, Colt and you are the best people I know. They didn't have it any different than Morrie and me. They didn't even have a sister who was at the bar all the time, doin' most of the work. And they still made a go of it and raised three great kids besides. So, I thought, maybe I acted too quick and, with all this shit happening, I definitely thought life's too damned short."

I nodded. She was right. Life was too damned short. I was just glad that Dee didn't waste as much of it as me being stubborn and thinking I was saving face.

Then, her eyes still on the boys, she changed the subject and said, "Colt's so fast, almost a blur. You think he'll ever slow down?"

I watched my man move then jump, his arms up in the air, his wrists loose as he released the ball. It wasn't a whoosh, it rolled the rim about a quarter of the way around, but it still fell in.

To be kind to my brother, I didn't whoop, but I wanted to.

"You shoulda seen him play football, Dee," I told her. "Fast and strong. Never seen anything like it. When he had the ball, if he was going, he was so fast, no one could catch him, so strong, even if they did, they couldn't bring him down. If he bounced off another player, the crash the pads would make..." I trailed off as I heard them in my head like it was yesterday and all of a sudden memories flooded my brain.

Colt running down the field, one hand out, one arm tucked and holding the ball. Colt dipping his shoulder, landing a blow, blocking for his runner. Colt walking to the sideline, yanking at the snaps of his chin guard then pulling off his helmet, his hair wet with sweat and a mess, his face the picture of what my father called, "in the zone." The crash of the pads, the grunts of the players, the cheers from the stands.

I was proud to sit with Morrie, Dad and Mom at Colt's games at Ross-Ade Stadium at Purdue. It was cool watching Colt play college ball and it was a thrill seeing the name "Colton" on the back of his Boilermaker jersey.

But nothing was more exciting than high school football, not back in the day and not now. The whole town went to all the home games, even me, Morrie and Colt. All bundled up, drinking hot chocolate with a shared woolly blanket on our knees, I'd sit in the stands shoulder to shoulder with Jessie and Meems. I'd see Colt standing with Morrie and Lore and half a dozen other guys at the chain link fence around the track that surrounded the field. Most of the guys shot the shit and jacked around, only partially watching the game. Not Morrie and Colt. If the ball was in play, their eyes were on the field. Not reliving glory days. No. They were on sacred ground, communing with their brethren.

"Feb, hon, you there?" Delilah called, and I tore my eyes from Colt and Morrie and looked at my sister-in-law.

"Yeah, just…" I sighed then said, "Remembering stuff."

"Good stuff?" she asked quietly and it hit me then.

I *was* remembering good stuff and for the first time in a long time those memories didn't come with pain.

"Yeah," I said quietly back.

She scooted to the side in her swing and reached out a hand. I scooted toward her and took it.

"I like happy endings," she said, tightening her hand in mine, swinging her swing a bit back and forth, keeping her feet to the ground but coming up on her toes and then going back to her heels.

I squeezed her hand back, doing my own mini-swings, and said, "Me too."

We let go of each other's hands, lifted our feet, the chains we were suspended from swung us sideways into place and we looked back at our men.

431

After Colt wupped Morrie, he drove us home while I made a mental note to bring a towel to drape on his seat in the truck. He was drenched. I'd never seen so much sweat and I grew up essentially with three men.

Then for some insane reason, I shared this. "You need a towel for your seat."

"What?"

"You're sweaty. You need a towel for your seat."

"Feb, I own a truck," was his absurd reply.

"So?"

"You can sweat in a truck."

"Is that a rule?" I asked.

"Yeah," he answered. "You can sweat in a truck, certain vans and any car that was built before 1990. That's the rule. You know what you can't sweat in?"

I knew where this was heading so I stayed silent and looked out the side window.

He didn't let it go, which wasn't a surprise. Colt had never been one to let anything go. Back in the day we'd argue, mostly because Colt never let anything go but also because I never let anything out. It wasn't a good combination but we never argued mean. It was always about exasperation at each other's understood quirks but it was also always tethered to love. Half the time we'd end an argument laughing our asses off.

The only time he ever let anything go was when he let me go. Then again, that time it was a doozy what I wouldn't let out.

Therefore, not letting it go, Colt said, "A four door sedan."

"You can't sweat in a Volkswagen Beetle," I told him.

"You're not gettin' a Beetle."

"Why not?" I asked, looking back to him and sounding snippy because I liked Beetles.

"Because they're ridiculous."

"They are not."

"No Beetle, Feb."

"A convertible one?"

"Definitely not."

I felt my vision narrow mainly because my eyes narrowed.

"Why 'definitely not?'"

"'Cause, you got a roof, at least that's some barrier to the music blastin' outta your car four seasons in the year. You got a convertible, you'll get slapped with a moving noise violation."

I stared at him with what I suspected was horror. "Is there such a thing as a 'moving noise violation?'"

Colt didn't answer, which I didn't know whether to take as good or bad.

I decided to ask Sully, or more aptly, to ask Lorraine who would ask Sully, which would be more likely to get me a truthful answer.

Then I suggested, "How 'bout one of those new Minis?"

"How 'bout a Buick?"

I wasn't sure but it was almost like I tasted vomit in the back of my throat.

"A Buick?" I whispered.

"They're safe *and* they're American."

"Minis are English. The English are our allies."

"The new Mini is made by BMW which is German."

There it was, proof that he knew more about cars than me.

"Germans are our allies now too," I told him.

"How 'bout we talk about this later?" Colt suggested and I stayed quiet because I thought it was a good suggestion.

When we got home, Colt went straight to the shower. I went straight to the boxes.

I had time to get one unpacked, sheets and towels. My towels would go in his guest bathroom, which made our purchases yesterday towel overkill, something I decided I wouldn't tell Dad. My sheets would fit the bed in the second bedroom. They were feminine but far less flowery than the ones Mom bought. I therefore decided, when Mom and Dad left, to switch out the sheets and comforter in the second bedroom with mine and then put Mom's back on when she and Dad were in town.

I also decided to share this gesture with Colt, thinking it might bring me closer to a convertible Beetle, which was the kind of idea I'd never had. I'd never owned a new car or a nice one nor ever really considered such a purchase. Now that the idea was planted in my head, I couldn't stop thinking about it.

I was standing at the dining room table, staring at the half empty box with my journals in it, thoughts of Beetles swept away and thoughts of Denny clogging my brain, when Colt walked out.

I looked at him and saw his hair wet and curling around his neck. He had on what he'd worn earlier that morning, a long-sleeved, heathered blue Henley thermal, jeans, a great belt and boots. His eyes were on my journal box.

"I haven't written in my journal since—"

Colt's arm came up, his hand sliding under my hair and around the back of my neck, this action cutting off my words before he said, "I know."

I looked down at the box and muttered, "I don't think I ever will again."

His fingers gave me a squeeze and I looked at him.

"Isn't this whole exercise 'bout us livin' our lives the way we want to live 'em?" he asked.

"Yeah," I answered.

"So, you wanna write, write."

I looked down at the box again, seeing mostly my older journals there, ones I'd written in when I was a kid, a pre-teen. Also, some from the last fifteen years.

Once I finished one, I never cracked it open again. I gave it the garbage in my brain hoping to release it. I'd been doing it forever, but it was at that moment I realized that this never worked.

I stared in the box and whispered, "No. I don't need to give my thoughts to a page when I can give them to you."

His fingers tensed at my neck again. It wasn't a squeeze this time, or not one he meant to give. This movement was reflexive and intense. Then he used his hand to curl me to his body.

My arms went around him as his other arm wrapped around me. I put my cheek to his chest and plastered my body to his.

"How much chance I got of you takin' off a Saturday and spendin' the rest of it alone with me?" he asked the top of my hair.

I thought this was a great idea. However, I part-owned a bar and Saturdays were our busiest days, not to mention these days we were even busier than normal. Already I was way late. I usually worked early on Saturdays so Morrie could have his game with Colt. Luckily, since Mom and Dad were here, they could hold down the bar while we had a lazy day. I could play on the emotional trauma Colt and me were living through to get the whole day off but it wouldn't be right.

Again, I had to be mature and it sucked.

"Snowball in hell," I said to his chest, but I sounded as disappointed as I felt.

"That's what I thought," he replied before he kissed the top of my head and I tilted it back to look at him when he finished, "I gotta get to the station anyway."

"Can we get a Meems' before we go our separate ways?" I asked.

"You wanna cookie for lunch?" he asked.

"No," I answered. "Carrot cake."

He grinned but said, "Baby, I just played an hour of one-on-one. Carrot cake isn't gonna cut it."

"Mom bought enough deli meat and cheese to feed a battalion and we haven't touched it yet."

"You offerin' to make me a sandwich?"

"I'll make you two if you don't argue about a convertible Beetle."

His relaxed face became less relaxed.

I quickly offered an alternate choice, "Okay, I'll amend the deal. I'll make sandwiches if you take that journal box out to the garage and hide it in a place I won't see it for about twenty years."

I watched his face relax again before he said, "You're on."

He hefted up the box. I went to the kitchen.

My head was in the fridge and he was at the side door when I called, "So, ham and cheese?"

Colt stopped at the door, gave me a look and asked, "You want me to spank your ass?"

I considered this. Colt considered me as I did so. Then he laughed low and walked out the door.

I made him roast beef and swiss. I'd save the ham and cheese for when we both had a day off.

Colt and I walked into the bar. We both had our hands wrapped around the cardboard of a Meem's white, takeaway cup and I had cream cheese from the carrot cake I'd hoovered through at the Coffee House on my lip.

I knew this because when I entered the bar Morrie shouted, "You got a Meems's carrot cake and didn't bring one for me?"

Morrie liked Meems' carrot cake. It was his favorite. I didn't get him one because the piece I had was the last slice of the day. Even though my favorite goodie in Meems' inventory was her chocolate zucchini cake, I felt zero guilt about taking the last piece of carrot cake. Mainly because I had a psycho hacking up my ex-boyfriends and I was in a carrot cake mood. I figured the former meant I got dibs on the latter.

"It was the last piece," I told Morrie after I'd licked my lip clean and while I walked down the bar.

"She have any chocolate zucchini left?" Morrie asked astutely.

"Nope," I lied.

"Bullshit," Morrie muttered, and, as ever, I found it annoying I could never lie to my brother.

Colt followed me to the office where I stowed my purse in a drawer in the desk, sucked back the last of my Meems' and tossed it in the trash.

When I straightened, I said to him, "Next time I have frosting on my mouth, tell me, will you?"

His arm shot out, hooked around my waist and he hauled me forward. Then he bent his head and licked my lip where the icing was.

My fingers curled into his thermal and they did this in an effort for me to remain standing because Colt's tongue felt so nice it had a direct effect on the ability of my legs to keep me upright.

"Morrie ruined it," Colt said when he lifted his head. "I was savin' it for later."

"Yeah, and I was walkin' down the street with cream cheese on my lip," I returned.

"How much you care about that?" he asked and he sounded weirdly curious.

Because he sounded curious, my eyes slid to the side as I mulled over his question.

Then my eyes came back and I answered, "Not much."

He grinned.

I continued, "Then again, no one was on the street to see me and it's only two doors down."

"About fifteen cars passed us, baby."

"Yeah, but they don't count seein' as I didn't really notice them so in my head they don't actually exist."

He was still grinning when the door opened and Dad stood there. His expression was not good in a way that was *really* not good and both Colt and I got stiff simultaneously.

"Colt," Dad said. "Fuck, son, I'm sorry but I think you need to get out here."

"What?" Colt asked, and I watched Dad twist his neck, extending it in a way I'd seen before, not often but he did it when something happened he didn't like, something that upset him or something that worried him.

His eyes hit Colt and he said, "Your ma's here."

This was such a shock I felt my head move forward with a jerk as my eyes grew wide.

"His mother?" I asked.

Dad shook his head but said, "Yeah, darlin'." Then he looked at Colt. "She's askin' for you and Jackie's circlin'. Morrie and Dee're tryin' to get her to move on but she's resistant and it's workin' Jackie up. I can see it, she's gonna blow. We can't get rid of Mary and we're losin' hold on keepin' Jackie from goin' ballistic. Sorry, Colt, wouldn't ask you this if I didn't have to, you know that, but I need you to come deal with your mother."

I looked up at Colt and saw his face was blank but stony.

Although most things about Colt had been shielded from me by pretty much everyone, I knew a lot about what had happened with Ted and Mary Colton the last twenty-odd years. One of those things I knew was that Colt hadn't seen his mother in years and never spoke to her.

Colt had attended my wedding to Pete because he was that kind of person, responsible, doing the right thing, even though I hated him being there as much as it was obvious he hated it. He left the reception before we cut the cake.

I hadn't attended his wedding to Melanie even though Melanie sent me an invitation. This was because I was irresponsible and rarely did the right thing, but also because I was weak and I knew deep down there was no way I could handle it. I sent them a wedding gift from their registry that cost more than I could afford at the time. But I did it anyway, thinking I was making some kind of idiot point that was probably lost on them.

I'd also heard from Mom, who was furious about it, that Mary Colton had showed at the wedding. She'd been trashed out of her gourd and started to make a scene, blathering on, apparently (this I heard not from Mom but from Jessie) about how the wedding was a farce and Colt was meant to marry me.

She luckily didn't make it into the church. She did this outside and then Colt, Dad, Morrie and Sully got rid of her with Jimbo driving her home. Colt had somehow shielded Melanie from it and, as far as I knew, she never heard a word about it happening.

Even back then, thinking I had no right, when Mom called to tell me this happened, and Jessie augmented the information, the knowledge pissed me off to such an extreme that I was glad I wasn't there because I knew there was no telling what I'd do if I was.

Before Colt and I broke up, but long after he'd moved out of his mom and dad's house, Ted Colton hit two kids while drunk driving and killed them both.

Colt and I knew the kids. They were good kids, never got into trouble. The girl was named Jenny and she won the Spirit of Junior Miss at the Junior Miss Pageant the fall before. The boy was named Mike and he was an ace shortstop for the high school team. They'd been dating for ages and were on their way back from a late movie at the mall. They were seniors in high school, but I'd been in school with them both for two years before I graduated. Colt and I didn't know them well, but we knew them.

By this time, Colt was far removed from Ted and Mary Colton. In all eyes, he was a bona fide member of the Owens clan and had been long before he moved into our house. Therefore, no one even looked at him askance when this happened.

Still, Colt knew their blood ran in his veins and his dad killing two kids cut Colt to the quick. With me at his side, he attended both funerals and for weeks he slid into a darkness that I worried he'd never come out of. But he did when he applied to the Police Academy. He'd always known that was what he wanted for his future, but his father's mindless act of violence spurred Colt to doing it.

After the accident, Ted Colton was in pretty bad shape too, but he survived. Once he was healthy, he went to trial then he went to prison. Years later, he got out on parole and went back due to parole violation, which consisted of twice being hauled in for drunk and disorderly, once being pulled over for a DUI and then there was the small matter of him never showing at parole meetings.

When he did his time, he got out again only to go back in when he robbed a liquor store; not their money, a box of booze. The man behind the counter saw him, called the cops and instead of stopping, Ted led them on a fifteen minute high-speed chase through the streets of town that ended with Colt's Dad driving through someone's yard and into their living room. Luckily he caused no bodily harm, not even to himself. Stupidly, he got out of the car, drunk off his ass, resisted arrest and he did this with a knife. Making matters worse, he had borrowed his neighbor's car without their knowledge, which meant they were pretty pissed when they found out it was used during a burglary and wrecked during the ensuing chase. Therefore, they were happy to report it as stolen.

Ted Colton had always been a mean drunk but I'd never thought he was a stupid one.

Back to prison he went, where, as far as I knew, he was still rotting.

His mom, though, had moved to a trailer park in the next town and how she managed to keep her trailer and her vodka and pill habit when I'd never known her to work a day in my life, I had no clue. But I didn't doubt she did.

Dad turned to walk out the door and Colt and I followed. I did this quickly because Colt was moving fast. I caught up with him when we hit the bar, coming to his side and grabbing his hand. His eyes never left the woman who was standing at the bar but his fingers curled around my hand so tight I worried he'd break my bones. It took effort but I didn't make a peep at the pain.

The bar was nearly silent, no buzz of conversation, only the jukebox playing. It was usually set low for the day crowd. We turned it up at night.

I was shocked at the vision of Mary Colton. She didn't look like I always remembered her looking, unkempt, clothes wrinkled and sometimes not clean, skin sallow, hair in disarray. She looked clean, her hair cut and tidied. She had makeup on. She was wearing jeans and a sweater, both of them washed and well-kept, her jeans even looked ironed.

None of this hid the years of hard drinking and internal abuse her body had endured. She was too thin, her hair, although tidy, looked bristly and there were steel gray roots exposed at her part, the rest of it a fake dark brown that was obviously a home dye job in dire need of a refresh. Her face was lined, her skin sagging, her hands were thin and deeply veined, the knuckles seemed huge, the bones were visible, all of this making her hands look like claws.

My mom, not too far away and staring daggers at Mary, looked the picture of youth and vitality next to Colt's Mom. They were close to the same age but Mom looked thirty years younger.

Mary turned to watch us walk up to her. I saw her take us both in, her eyes dropping to our linked hands and then they closed, slowly, almost like she was suffering some kind of internal pain.

Then she opened her eyes and Colt stopped us three feet away.

"Alec," she said, her voice deep, rasping and unfeminine from years of chain smoking.

I felt my body give a jerk when I heard her call Colt that name and I swore, in his bed or out of it, I'd never call him that again. I finally understood why he hated it. Said by her, it was hideous.

"There something I can help you with, Ma?" Colt asked.

She hitched her purse up on her shoulder and shifted on her feet.

Then she said, "I been hearin' some things."

"Yeah?" Colt asked. Even though this was a prompt, the way he said it communicated that he didn't particularly want a response nor did he care what that would be.

She looked at me then tipped her head back to look at Colt and I noticed she'd shrunk, significantly. Both Ted and Mary had been tall, which was why Colt was tall. I stared at her, trying to see some beauty in her, wracking my brain to remember her when she was younger, to remember Colt's dad, trying to figure out how this person and her husband made a man like Colt, and I couldn't see it.

"I heard you sorted things with Feb," she said.

"I did," Colt replied, his answer short, not initiating further discussion.

"I'm glad," she told him but he didn't respond so she looked at me and said, "For both of you."

I didn't know what to say but I thought I should say something so I muttered, "Thank you, Mrs. Colton."

She nodded, I went quiet and Colt stayed silent.

"I heard other things too," she went on, looking back to Colt.

"Don't believe everything you hear," Colt told her and her brows twitched.

"You safe?" she asked.

"Yes," Colt lied instantly.

Her head moved to the side, almost like Dad's had done, her neck slowly twisting and extending. She knew he was lying.

Then she straightened her neck, took in a breath and announced, "Your father's gettin' outta prison."

"Good for him," Colt said but he didn't sound pleased. He sounded courteous in that way people were courteous when they were in a position where they were forced to be polite but they really couldn't care less.

"He's dried out, Alec. We both have. For good this time. We found the church," she told him.

"Good for you too." Colt's tone hadn't changed.

She bit her bottom lip, exposing her teeth, not like Colt did when he was angry. She was anxious and Colt wasn't giving her anything to go on.

Then she said, "I thought you might like to know, maybe you might like to—"

Mom cut her off by saying, "He wouldn't."

Mary turned to Mom, moving slowly still, cautious, uncertain and maybe even scared or perhaps shy, and she said quietly, "Jackie."

"You got a helluva nerve walkin' in here, Mary Colton," Mom told her and Dad moved closer to Mom.

"I'm tryin' to do right," Mary said to Mom.

Mom let out a short, breathy, angry laugh before she asked, "Do right?"

"Jackie," Colt murmured.

But Mary said over him, "Yeah, Jackie, do right."

"Well, you're forty-four years too late," Mom snapped.

"Jackie, darlin', let's you and me go to the office," Dad said.

"Not leavin' Colt in here with her," Mom said back.

"Jackie, he's—" Dad stopped talking because Mom gave him a look and it was the kind of look that would make anyone stop talking, even Dad. Then Dad's gaze shifted to Colt and Mom's shifted back to Mary.

I decided to wade in before Mom really let loose and I took a small step forward but didn't let go of Colt's hand.

"Mrs. Colton," I called, and she turned back to look at me. "It was nice of you to come by today and let us know about Mr. Colton. But how 'bout you go on home and you give Colt a chance to think about all this. You want, you can come with me to the office. I'll get your number. He wants to call, he'll get in touch. That sound okay?"

Colt's hand squeezed mine and I squeezed back. Through this Mary looked back and forth between Colt and me.

Then she said, "All right, Feb. That sounds fine."

I gestured behind me with my head and said, "Let's go."

I released Colt's hand but my eyes moved to his as I turned to the office. His face was still blank and stony, nothing there to read, giving nothing away. If he looked at his mother like that, it was a wonder she didn't run out the door.

I walked to the office and Mary followed me. Standing by the desk, looking awkward and out of place, her hand clamped around her purse strap and clenching it convulsively, she gave me her phone number while I wrote it on a pad on the desk.

When I was done writing the number, I straightened but saw she was looking at the closed door.

Then she turned back to me and, hand still clenching and unclenching her purse strap, she said in a rush, "I heard you were interviewed by the FBI. I heard your ex-husband was killed in St. Louis. I heard the police were at your apartment. I heard Chip Judd's been workin' at Alec's place, puttin' in a system. I heard a lotta things, February." Her eyes were getting bright and I could see the whites of her knuckles, she was clenching her purse strap so tight. "He lied to me out there, Alec did. You're not safe."

"We're fine, Mrs. Colton."

"You're not safe."

"We're fine."

She shook her head, the movements quick and erratic, then she stopped and said, "I done him wrong."

She was right about that, so I kept quiet.

"I know I did. I know. My boy," she whispered the last two words, did those head shakes again and her eyes got brighter. "He always…" she started then stopped then started again. "You were…you meant the world to…he and you…" More head shakes and then she said, "He got you back and you're not safe."

"We're just fine, Mrs. Colton."

The tears hit her eyes but didn't spill over, just shuddered at her lower lids, the overhead lights illuminating them so much they shone, and she stared at me, her eyes never leaving mine.

Then she whispered, "You're lyin' too."

I had no response because she was already turned and walking to the door. I followed her out and she walked to Colt. She didn't do it quickly. She did it hesitantly, guarded, like she was ready to bolt if he made a lunge.

"I hope you call, Alec," she told him and quickly looked at Mom, not wanting to give Colt the chance to respond, knowing if he did what he'd say she wouldn't like. Then she said softly, "I'm sorry, Jackie. You're right, I know, I have a nerve and I know you won't believe this but I was just worried about your girl and my boy."

Before Mom could speak, she scurried quickly out the door, still clutching her purse.

The minute the door closed, a murmur of conversation hit the bar and I looked up to Colt to see he was staring at the door.

I grabbed his hand and gave it a squeeze. "You okay?"

He looked down at me and gave my hand a tug, bringing me closer. "This happens from time to time."

"It does?"

"You okay, dude?" Morrie asked from behind the bar.

"Yeah, Morrie," Colt replied to my brother but his eyes were on my mother. I looked to her and she still appeared fit to be tied.

"She knows you got trouble, she even said it, and she still waltzes in here—" Mom groused.

"Jackie, darlin', leave it be," Dad cut her off.

"Jackie, you know this isn't a big deal," Colt told Mom but he was lying. If it wasn't a big deal, his hand would not nearly have broken mine. Twenty-eight years he'd been separated from his parents and that time had not diminished their power over his emotions.

Mom gave Colt a good long look, then her neck snapped around and she looked at Dee. "Delilah, make me a G and T and use a heavy hand."

"I've never done a G and T," Dee whispered to Morrie as Mom bellied up to the bar.

"Ain't hard, babe," Morrie said, turning toward the back wall filled with mirror-backed shelves of liquor and Dee's eyes came to Colt and me.

"I don't even know what a G and T is."

"Gin and tonic, Dee," I told her.

She nodded, lifted a hand and muttered, "Got it. I can do that, heavy hand," and she turned to Morrie.

I looked back at Colt and prompted, "This happens from time to time?"

His hand came to my hip and brought me even closer as he leaned his back into the bar. "Last few years, every once in a while. She's been tryin' to dry out."

This was news.

"Tryin'?" I asked.

"She falls off the wagon a lot." I nodded and he continued. "She'd come to the house."

I put my hand to his chest and whispered, "Sorry, babe."

"She usually needs money."

"You give it to her?"

"Did in the beginning, or Melanie did. Melanie left, I kept up a coupla times, then quit."

My eyes slid to the side. Mom was about five stools down, two of those taken by patrons who were pretending, badly, not to listen. But Mom also had Mom Hearing so I shifted to Colt's side, my back to Mom and the customers and whispered low, "Mom know about this?"

"Nope," Colt answered.

"She didn't ask for money this time."

"Nope."

I got closer. "You *really* okay?"

"Nope."

I dropped his hand, lifted mine, slid my fingers around his ear before they glided down to curl around his neck and I murmured, "Baby."

He bent his head so his face was closer to mine and he murmured back, "Better now."

God, I loved him.

To communicate this, I went up on my toes, touched my nose briefly to his and then rocked back.

"You gonna see your dad?" I asked.

"My dad's standin' in this room," Colt answered and my chest got tight, not in a bad way, just that I was glad he found a good replacement.

"Colt—"

"Ma's annoyin' but I can handle it. The man whose seed made me doesn't exist in my world."

"Colt—"

"Beat the shit outta Ma, beat me, killed two kids. He doesn't exist."

I gave his neck a squeeze and for his sake, let it go. "Okay, baby."

Colt looked to the door then back to me. "She loves you, you know."

"What?"

"Ma, even when I was with 'em and she was drunk, she used to talk about you all the time. Said you reminded her of her." I fought my lip curling but he caught it and his arms slid around me pulling me close. "She used to be somethin', Feb. Would get smashed and show me pictures. You wouldn't believe it unless you saw it but, honest to God, she used to be somethin'."

More evidence that I'd made the right decision to pull my shit together before it was too late.

I nodded and said, "This sucks, we were havin' a good day."

"Yeah," he agreed.

I smiled at him. "But day's not done and tomorrow's Sunday."

Colt smiled back and repeated, "Yeah."

"Don't worry about Costa's tonight. Come here, Dee's on, Jessie's watchin' the kids. We'll have family night at J&J's."

"Sounds good."

I pressed into him and said, "I'll pick a better song, one we can dance to."

"I don't dance, honey."

This was true, he didn't. He preferred to watch when I did it. I knew he could move though, because he would dance to a slow song. He was a great lead, his hips would sway, taking mine with them, and he had fantastic rhythm. If I'd had any experience at the time, I would have realized this prophesied good things to come.

Thinking about it, I said, "We'll put some music on when we get home."

He grinned and said, "Anything you want, baby, but when we dance at home, we'll be horizontal."

I grinned back and replied, "That works for me."

Colt went to the station to find out what was happening with the robbery investigation and I took over letting Dee shadow me at the bar. Making drinks and making change wasn't rocket science but we were relatively busy and when it got busy you had to have a good memory and be able to multitask.

I saw George Markham, the head honcho of Markham and Sons Funeral Home, walk in still wearing a suit from funeral duties. He slid in beside Joe-Bob, caught Dad's eye and Dad moved down to his end of the bar.

There were two funeral homes in town but most folk chose Markham and Sons. This was mostly because it was on the main drag. Therefore, if you had a funeral to host, you'd get maximum attention from people driving by, counting the mourners standing outside chatting or having a smoke.

The location of Markham and Sons allowed the all-important assessment of the post-mortem popularity of the deceased.

Amy was quiet but young and well-liked and just the young part would draw people out because that kind of tragedy had a way of doing that. She was a bank teller so a lot of people knew her even though they didn't really know her. When Colt and I walked through the milling crowd outside Amy's viewing, she had to hit three and a half out of five on the popularity scale. This was saying something considering Colt told me Amy had no real friends left when she died.

I knew George. He was the kind of man you knew in town because no one could escape spending some time at his business. I knew him but he rarely came into J&J's. He liked to golf and would drink at the clubhouse. Though, when Dad was running J&J's, George would come in from time to time to shoot the shit.

Therefore George being there, and looking like he was coming direct from a funeral, meant something was up.

I sidled down to George and Dee followed me. Dad felt us coming, started to turn and George and Joe-Bob's eyes came to us as we got close.

"Feb, darlin'," Dad said, "before the crowd hits for the night, maybe you should show Dee how to restock."

"I already know that," Dee replied, obviously wanting to know why George was there too. "Feb taught me last Sunday."

Dad looked at Dee, wanting to say something but biting his tongue.

I looked at George.

"Ain't no secret, Jack," George said to my dad.

"What's going on?" I asked.

Joe-Bob shifted on his chair. I saw it out of the corner of my eye but I kept my gaze on George.

"Got Angie at the home, had her for a while. Talked to her parents twice, they say they got no money for a funeral. I don't find someone who'll help, Angie'll be buried—"

"I'll pay," I said instantly, cutting him off and kissing that kickass vacation good-bye.

I knew why he was there. Firstly, Angie spent a lot of time in J&J's, but secondly, and more importantly, Dad had a way.

Years ago, the town had a little league team that was so good they made it to some championships that meant the entire team had to fly to Japan. Problem was half the kids on the team didn't have parents who could afford to send their kids to Japan to play baseball. Therefore Dad fleeced every customer out of a donation to help the kids go and gave a hefty donation himself besides. Same with Whitey West when he lost his insurance and couldn't afford his chemo treatments. Same with Michaela Bowman, who used to work at J&J's, when her juvenile delinquent son fell asleep in bed smoking pot and burned out half the inside of her house, luckily escaping before he got too injured himself, but insurance wouldn't pay so Dad collected.

"Feb," Dad said.

"Morrie and I'll kick in too," Dee said.

Dad turned his attention to her. "Delilah, darlin', you and Morrie got two mouths to feed."

"So?" Dee asked Dad.

"Don't got much but I could give you a little," Joe-Bob put in.

"What's this about?" Lanie Gilbert, a stool down from Joe-Bob, asked.

"Lookin' for money to help pay for Angie Maroni's burial," Dee informed her.

"I'm in," Lanie said and I stared at her. Lanie came into J&J's a lot, not to get trashed, mostly because she was social and liked the selections on the jukebox. Though I'd never seen her spend time with Angie, in fact, like most women, she gave Angie a wide berth.

Before any of them could have second thoughts, I asked George, "How you wanna play this?"

George glanced around and said, "Anyone wants to contribute, they just bring it down to the home and the boys and I'll sort it."

"What about her headstone?" Lanie asked.

"We'll figure somethin' out," George told her.

Lanie got up from her stool. "I'll come down, got my checkbook with me, and I'll look at some catalogues of headstones."

I had no idea if there was such a thing as headstone catalogues and I looked at Dee who was pressing her lips together. She caught my eye and shrugged her answer to my non-verbalized question.

"We'll get the word out, George," Dad said as George moved toward Lanie who was moving toward the door.

"'Preciate it, Jack," he said. "Angie, she was…" He trailed off then said, "No matter what, town should take care of their own."

"Yeah," Dad replied.

George nodded, gave a little wave and followed Lanie out the door.

George was so right. A town should take care of its own. And it would, Dad would see to that.

I looked at Dee and asked, "Bud draft is gettin' low. You wanna learn how to change out a keg?"

"Highlight of my day, hon," she replied, though this was a lie. We both knew her highlight of the day was watching Morrie play basketball, even if he lost. For me, watching Colt play was the bottom of three top highlights for my day. If we danced horizontal tonight, it'd be kicked down to four.

On that thought, I grinned at Dad then at Joe-Bob and then Dee and I changed out a keg.

As he walked from the bar down to the station, Colt's phone rang. He pulled it out of the back pocket of his jeans, looked at the display, flipped it open and put it to his ear.

"Yeah, Sully."

"You close to the station?"

"Walkin' there from J&J's now."

"Double time, man, Evelyn and Norman Lowe just showed with a big, ole box. We put 'em into interrogation one and we're gettin' 'em some coffee."

"I'll be there in two minutes."

"Good, but not waitin', man, want them fresh. I'm goin' in."

Colt flipped his phone shut and shoved it in his pocket. He was one hundred percent certain he did not want to know what was in the box that Denny Lowe's parents had brought to the station. He still hoofed it double time.

He hit the station and it was strangely quiet. This was because it was Saturday, a weekend, so the day would be relaxed. It'd get busy in the night.

This was also because a serial killer's parents were on the premises carrying with them a box and it was likely the observation room next to interrogation one was shoulder to shoulder.

Colt's eyes hit Connie through the windows in dispatch and she was watching him. She was talking into the microphone that curved around to her mouth but she also pointed to the ceiling, pumping her hand twice then she gave him a thumbs up.

Sully was already in with the Lowes.

Colt took the stairs two at a time, dumped the cup with the dregs of his Meems' in the trash and hit the observation room.

He was right, it was packed. Without a word, everyone shifted aside so he could have a bird's eye view.

"You understand this is difficult." Colt heard Norm Lowe say when he hit the one-way window.

Norm was standing behind and beside his wife's chair, his hand on her shoulder. Evelyn Lowe was seated, handkerchief sandwiched between both her hands and her face, her neck was bent, her shoulders shaking.

Looking at the man he hadn't seen in years, a memory struck Colt.

It was when Colt had been young, seven, maybe eight, and ill. Colt didn't get sick often but he was then. So sick he didn't go to school, which he'd always liked, even as a kid, it was an escape from home. He didn't even go over to Morrie's, which meant he had to be really sick because he always preferred to be at the Owens', not to mention he knew even then Jackie was a helluva lot better at taking care of a sick kid than Colt's Mom was.

In fact, he was so sick his mother braved the world she didn't often go out into unless it was to hit a liquor store and she took him to see Doc. Then later, with no one to watch him, even though she was half-snockered, she put him in her car and took him to Norm Lowe's pharmacy to pick up Colt's prescription.

Colt remembered Norm looking down at his mother from the raised station, the white shelves of medicine behind him, wearing a crisp white labcoat with his name embroidered in cursive with blue thread over the coat pocket, the filled prescription bag in his hand, the bag held back from Colt's mother, and saying, "Now, Mary, we both know this wouldn't be a good idea."

Colt remembered it clearly, like it happened the moment before, but until that second he'd buried it. He'd buried it because, that day long ago there were people in line behind his mother. Everyone knew Norm's meaning, refusing his mother Colt's medications. He was intimating that she'd take them herself. Even Colt knew it, at his age, and he'd been humiliated, mainly because Norm Lowe was probably right.

His mother didn't fight it. She grabbed Colt's hand, ducked her head and walked as straight a line as she could muster right out of the store. She took him back to Doc and Doc saw them right away. Handing her the prescription from his cabinet, Doc said to Colt's Mom, "Next time we'll remember this, Mary. You got somethin' you need for Alec, you'll get it direct from me."

Colt couldn't remember if his mother ever gave him the drugs and it was the only time he remembered ever needing any.

He did remember, years ago a new chain store pharmacy was put in at the edge of town and he'd talked Melanie into moving her prescriptions to the chain, though he never could understand why he wanted her to do this. Most of the folks on insurance or Medicare didn't have a choice but to go to the chain. If they did, they'd go to Norm just because he was a local.

Not Colt.

Since Colt was seven to the time that chain opened, he never stepped foot in Norm Lowe's pharmacy, partly because he had no need, partly because that buried memory kept him back.

Now, staring at him, Norm's back ramrod straight, his face looking carved from a rock, his wife a mess in front of him, his son on the road carrying out a violent rampage, Colt found he could call up no empathy for the man.

He would soon understand why.

"We'll give you some time," Sully, seated by Evelyn, said quietly.

Everyone waited for Evelyn to pull herself together and Colt watched as Norm squeezed her shoulder. Colt didn't know why but this gesture looked to him less like a show of support and more like a demand for his wife to get control. It was then Colt knew Norm Lowe was not the kind of man who would allow his wife to walk down the street with frosting on her lip. Not because of how this would reflect on her, but because of how it would reflect on him.

Evelyn nodded her head and lifted it, wiping the tears from her face and swiping under her nose.

"I'm sorry, Lieutenant Sullivan," she whispered.

"You okay to talk now, Mrs. Lowe?" Sully asked, and she nodded again but it wasn't her who talked.

"We found *that*," Norm announced, dipping his head toward the medium-sized box on the table beside two untouched Styrofoam cups of coffee, "in the house."

"And what is that, Mr. Lowe?" Sully asked, and Evelyn made a noise that sounded painful, a choked sob. A sob Norm ignored.

"Dennis asked his mother to hold some things at the house. She did. Never told me. I knew about *that*, well..." He let that hang and Colt watched Evelyn's face blank so much it was void. One second, she was tearful, the next, her face was a clear slate. She was so good, it only took a second. A defense mechanism, a practiced one. It was then Colt knew Evelyn Lowe lived under a tyrant.

As had Denny.

"I never looked in the box either," she said quietly. "I just thought it was stuff he and Marie couldn't hold in their house."

This earned her another shoulder squeeze from her husband as he reminded her at the same time telling Sully that his wife was an idiot and he himself had not one thing to do with that box or what was going on with his son. "They got five bedrooms in that house, Ehv."

"Yes, yes, I didn't think. Stupid of me," she said quickly.

"After we heard of the goings-on, Evelyn remembered the box," Norm stated and Colt thought his choice of the words "goings-on" to describe a killing spree was both interesting and sickening, more the last than the first, far more. "She pulled it out, opened it up and showed it to me. That was less than an hour ago. We brought it right here."

In other words, *my son is a psychopathic killer but I'm a decent citizen here to help.*

"May I look in the box?" Sully asked and Evelyn pressed her lips together. Norm nodded curtly.

Sully got up and pulled back the flaps to the box. The room went wired as he looked inside. He dipped in his hand and it didn't have to go very far. Colt could see from his vantage point the box was filled with photos and he knew what they showed. Colt had no reaction to this. It wasn't surprising and he was finding it was better to store up his reactions for shit that was worth it.

Sully pulled out only a handful. He managed to keep his expression neutral as he flipped through them. Then he put them down on the table and turned to the Lowes.

"That's a lotta pictures of Feb Owens and Alec Colton," he remarked.

"Box's full of 'em," Norm agreed amicably.

"Denny take these?" Sully asked.

"I've no idea," Norm answered.

Sully looked down at the box, dug his hand in and pulled out more from the middle. Flipping through them he said, "Looks like someone's been takin' pictures of Feb and Colt for years."

"Looks like," Norm replied.

"You have any idea why Denny would have these?"

Evelyn Lowe made a high-pitched sound in the back of her throat but Norm talked over her, saying, "No idea."

Sully looked to the woman. "Mrs. Lowe?"

She got another squeeze from her husband, therefore she repeated, "No idea."

Sully's face got tight and his eyes rested on Norm's hand on Evelyn's shoulder a brief moment before he looked at Denny's father.

"You think I could talk to your wife in private?"

"No. I. Do. *Not*," Norm answered, enunciating each word clearly, helpful citizen a memory in a flash.

"Norm," Evelyn whispered.

"We're not suspects in this situation," Norm told his wife.

"No one said you were," Sully put in.

It was then Norm drew the line in the sand, showing directly where he and his wife stood and the fact that their son stood on the other side and that was exactly how everyone, including the police, should view it.

He did this by saying, "And we won't be treated as such."

"I'm sorry if you feel I'm treatin' you that way," Sully sat back down, letting Norm have the dominant position. "Not my intention at all. Just tryin' to get to the bottom of things."

"We have no involvement in this," Norm stated firmly. "Dennis brought the box to the house. We kept it there for him not knowing what it contained. Evelyn says she thinks he brought it over just over a year ago."

When Feb was back in town. It could be he brought it over because Marie could discover the box and run into Feb or, for that matter, Colt. It was more likely he brought it over because he was making plans to set up even more thorough surveillance of Colt and Feb. With video, he didn't have to flip through photos nor did he have to court getting caught taking them.

"Can we keep the contents of this box for the investigation?" Sully asked politely.

"Why would we need it?" Norm asked back, happy to be rid of it.

"Thank you. We appreciate you bringing it down," Sully's tone had a finality to it.

"Shit," Sean, one of the newer detectives, said from beside Colt. "He's lettin' the mother off the hook."

"She's got somethin'," Mike Haines, another more experienced detective in the unit, muttered from the other side of Sean. "Sul won't let it go."

Norm helped his wife out of her seat and Sully rose from his.

As they turned to the door, Sully used a conversational tone that smacked so contradictorily against the words he said that they struck the room with a force that couldn't be ignored. "You have heard, of course, that Denny attacked another one of Feb Owens's friends last night. Blade of a hatchet cut into his shoulder. It took forty stitches to close him."

Sully was looking in the box. The Lowes were silent because, of course, they *hadn't* heard. And Sully continued as if in afterthought.

"Oh, and two unidentified bodies have been found, one man killed early this mornin' in Oklahoma, appears to be in a rage, not much left of him. The other's been dead awhile, just discovered this mornin' in Pueblo, Colorado. He's got a face left so they're siftin' through missing persons."

"What?" Colt whispered, not having heard this.

"News just came in 'bout ten minutes before the Lowes showed," Garrett "Merry" Merrick, another veteran detective, murmured.

Evelyn had frozen, Norm's face turned from rock to ice.

"'Course, odds are, we'll catch him as he's told us he's comin' up here to do the same to Colt. Still, we reckon he's pretty angry, seein' as he didn't get to dispatch his intended victim in Texas. So, we don't get hold of him beforehand, we suspect the bodies'll pile up from Oklahoma to here. Takes a coupla days to make that ride, you take time out to murder people. We figure couple more bodies at least. Maybe fathers, maybe brothers, maybe husbands." Sully shrugged like it didn't matter much to him. "You see it all in this job, gotta find a way to shut it down."

"Ehv, let's get you home," Norm said to his wife with false courtesy but he didn't take his glacial gaze from Sully. He knew the game Sully was playing.

Sully was throwing the photos back into the box and flipping back the flaps, muttering, "Helps, sometimes, knowin' what drives 'em. Not all the time, mind, but sometimes."

Colt's eyes went to Evelyn. She was cracking, plain to see.

Norm's hand was firm on his frozen wife's arm. He'd slipped up, bringing her to the station. She'd either demanded to come, which was unlikely, or she'd been so undone by the news, and thus so fragile, Norm didn't know what to do with her and he'd made the mistake of allowing her to come, thinking he could keep her under control.

Then again, a mother's love, even if her son had gone bad, was hard to control. Colt'd seen it over and over. Pete Hollister's mother was a prime example. That woman knew what her son did to Feb, putting Feb in the hospital, and she stood by Pete, badmouthing Feb along the way.

Sully knew this too and he was going to play it.

Norm saw his wife breaking and his voice was a warning when he said, "Evelyn."

"Also helps us," Sully cut in, "if we know, to figure a way to bring 'em in, you know, *safe* like. Get 'em help."

"You don't want to help my son," Norm accused, casting doubt on Sully, hoping Evelyn would rise to the bait.

Sully looked at him and asked good-naturedly, "You know me, sir?"

"I—" Norm started, but Sully cut him off.

Good-natured gone, colder than steel and firmer than concrete in its place, Sully said, "You don't know me, Mr. Lowe, so you can't say that about me."

"He was touched," Evelyn whispered and the observation room went electric.

"Evelyn," Norm snapped.

Sully turned fully to her, she had his complete attention. "Touched?"

"Touched."

"Evelyn!" Norm's voice was sharper and his hand on her arm gave her a quick but vicious shake.

"Mr. Lowe, due respect, but I'm thinkin' you shouldn't handle your woman like that in front of a cop," Sully warned quietly, but quiet or not, that steel was still in his tone.

Norm instantly dropped his wife's arm but declared, "We're leaving."

"When he was a little boy. Norman's brother," Evelyn said softly.

"Quiet now, Evelyn," Norm hissed at his wife, leaning toward her. "You don't know that."

She turned her head to him. Still talking softly, finding her way, uncertain of her footing and downright scared, she whispered, "I know it."

"You don't."

"Denny told me."

Norm threw out a dismissive hand. "I think it's clear by his behavior that Denny tellin' you anything can be taken with a grain of salt."

Still soft, Evelyn said, "Not then, not then, Norman."

"Ehv."

"He was five," she whispered and Colt closed his eyes.

"Jesus, sick, fuck, Christ," Sean muttered and Colt opened his eyes.

Evelyn looked back at Sully, squared her shoulders and sucked in oxygen through her nose, counting on it giving her strength. "Far as I reckon, it'd been happenin' since he was a baby."

"No, now it's Jesus, sick, fuck, Christ," Mike remarked.

"Evelyn, you be quiet, you hear?" Norman warned.

She didn't take her eyes off Sully when she replied, "Been bein' quiet a long time."

"No use dredgin' this up," Norm told her.

For some reason those words were Norm's mistake. Evelyn's body visibly locked but her eyes sliced to her husband.

"No use dredgin' it up." Her voice was still soft but it held an angry hiss. "No use takin' him to see a psychologist when he had those dreams, would draw those pictures. No use havin' him talk to someone when he killed our *dog*," Evelyn returned, building her backbone with every word.

456

"Holy fuck," Merry muttered.

"Classic case. Christ," Mike noted.

Norm looked at Sully and declared, "Denny didn't kill our dog."

"So, Sparky *fell* on a hatchet?" Evelyn asked, unpracticed sarcasm in her tone but still, it worked.

"Evelyn, I hardly think—" Norm started but Evelyn interrupted him.

She looked back to Sully and said on a rush, "Norm's brother liked babysitting. He did it for us a lot. *A lot.* Kept tellin' us to go to movies, out to dinner, have a *break* from our boy. Felix had no wife, no girlfriends, no interest, never did, but he liked babies, he liked little boys, he liked them *a lot.* Used to go to the park just to watch them. I'd take Denny on the weekend. He'd always be there to come with me. I thought it strange, thought he was a bit peculiar, but it was more than a bit peculiar."

"Denny told you he touched him?" Sully asked.

"Told me, yes, told me how too," Evelyn answered.

"Dennis couldn't know—" Norm started but stopped when Evelyn looked at him again.

"If he didn't know, if *you* didn't know, why'd you send Felix away?"

"He got a position out of state," Norm reminded her.

"*You* arranged for him to get a position out of state."

Norm dismissed his wife and looked at Sully. "This is ridiculous. Felix died of leukemia five years ago. He can't even speak for himself.

"And thank goodness. Thank goodness. Thank goodness for that," Evelyn said. It had built up for years and she'd been holding it back, or Norm had been crushing it down, but now she let it go. There was a force of feeling behind her words so strong it was a wonder her husband didn't go back on a foot. Hell, she'd been holding this back so long, it was actually a wonder she herself didn't implode.

"That's my brother you're talkin' about, Ehv."

"That's the man who drove our boy into madness, Norm."

Sully cut in. "You know how he links to Feb and Colt?"

"Yes," Evelyn said.

"Absolutely not," Norm said at the same time.

Evelyn turned to him. "We do." She looked back to Sully, "Or, *I* do."

Norm was losing it, his face getting red, his eyes already blistering hot, if she didn't find alternate accommodation that night, she'd catch it.

"Evelyn," he bit off.

She ignored him and kept looking at Sully, taking a deep breath, she said, "Sometimes he'd talk to me. Not much, sometimes. I wanted him to talk to someone else…" Her head twitched in her husband's direction, it wasn't much but her accusation was clear. "But we couldn't do that so I thought it would be good if Denny would talk to me."

"So he told you about Feb and Colt," Sully prompted.

"Once, each." She nodded and went on. "February stood up for him, something at school." Her eyes slid to the side, taking in her husband a moment then they went back to Sully. "Not long after, Alec Colton beat up his father and went to live with the Owenses."

"He say why this meant somethin' to him?" Sully asked.

"No, but I reckon in February's case, no one stood up for him, not in his whole life, and he had some demons he was battlin'. He didn't need the likes of Devon Shepherd's uppity daughter makin' his life a livin' hell at school."

"Colt?" Sully pressed.

"Hero worship, I guess. I suspect, beatin' up his dad like that and endin' up with the Owenses, Alec Colton did somethin' Denny wanted to do. Then, of course, there was the fact that Alec had Feb."

"I don't believe this," Norm muttered.

"You were hard on him," Evelyn told Norm.

"I'm his father!" Norm's voice was rising.

"You were *too* hard on him," Evelyn shot back.

"He was a difficult boy to raise," Norm returned.

"Yes, he was and there was a reason for that, wasn't there, Norm? A reason you ignored."

"He needed a firm hand."

"He needed understanding and professional help."

"Right," Norm blew out that one word dismissively.

"Right," she whispered back and then threw out her hand to indicate the room. "Look where you are. Can you still stand there and say, yet again, Denny didn't need professional help?"

"She's got a point there," Mike muttered.

"Will this help you?" Evelyn asked, now looking at Sully.

"Yes, Mrs. Lowe, it'll help a great deal," Sully answered.

She took in another breath through her nose and then she asked, "Will it help Denny?"

"Denny?" Sully asked back.

"You knowin' this, will it mean you'll understand, get him some help?"

There it was. A mother's love.

Even knowing this, Sully didn't understand. Colt knew that. But Sully didn't let on and said firmly, "Absolutely."

She nodded, sucked in more breath, lifted her head then asked, "Can I use your phone? I want to call my sister to come to pick me up."

"Thank God for that," Sean whispered. "The old man's itchin' to lay into her."

"What's this now?" Norm asked, not about to be denied the chance to pull her back down where he wanted her, right under his thumb.

Evelyn looked at him and stated, "I think I need some alone time."

"Hopefully, the next twenty years," Merry put in.

"You stay in here, Mrs. Lowe, we'll get you to a phone," Sully said quickly then turned to Norm. "Mr. Lowe, I'll show you out."

"But—" Norm began.

"This way," Sully pushed.

"My wife—"

"Needs some alone time." Sully's voice was back to steel and he used it and his body to guide Norm to the door.

Unwilling to lose face, Norm scowled at Evelyn but followed Sully. Evelyn lifted her hand and smoothed it across her hair, which was neatly pulled back into a bun. Her hand was shaking. Looking toward the floor, she sat down with her back to the door and to her husband.

Sully opened the door and Norm walked out.

The show over, people in the room were shifting, quietly moving out.

Mike moved toward Colt.

"More news in, Colt," he said. "Not just the bodies but the hatchet is also the same brand as what Skipp sold Denny and he ditched Cheryl

Sheckle's car. They don't know what he's drivin' but they found her car about three blocks away from this mornin's body."

Well at least they knew where he was headed even if they didn't know anymore what he was driving to get there.

"What news on the bodies?" Colt asked.

"This mornin', pure rage. Reports say the remains of the victim looked like Marie. They even had trouble figurin' out if it was a man or a woman."

"Christ," Colt muttered.

"The other body, done on the way from Idaho Springs to Taos. He was hacked like Angie, Pete and Butch, 'cept he got him by cavin' in the back of his head while he was runnin' on some path. Likely a surprise attack. They found the body off the path. It'd been there awhile and the animals had gotten to it. Still, enough of him left to match a photo. We suspect somethin' to come through soon."

"Six," Colt said, counting victims, or at least the dead human ones.

"That we know of," Mike replied, looking less than happy to say these words.

"What I wanna know is," Sean turned to them, jerking his head to the window, "don't these people pay attention? Cop shows? Movies? News? Fuck, their son is killin' dogs and drawin' unhealthy pictures and what? Nothin'? It's fuckin' textbook."

"Denial can be crippling," Merry, who'd also joined them, told Sean.

"Nope," Sean replied, tipping his head to the interrogation room. "She knew. Just think that guy's an assclown. Get my prescriptions there," Sean said. "At his place. Got allergies. Definitely feelin' a change comin' on."

"'Spect Norm Lowe'll lose a bit of business," Mike noted, and Colt's eyes went to the interrogation room.

Norm and Sully were gone. Evelyn was still sitting down but now staring at the box. Even unmoving, she looked like she was lost in a way she'd never be found. Then again, Evelyn Lowe had likely been lost a long time.

"Think it might be a good idea, Norm Lowe retires," Colt muttered.

"And moves," Mike added.

"You're up next," Merry noted carefully, his eyes on Colt. "You takin' precautions?"

Colt looked at him. "Yeah."

"Creepy shit, Colt," Mike remarked and Colt looked at Mike.

"Yeah," he repeated.

Mike grinned. "Still, even creepy, I could see it would make it easier for a man to handle, he goes home to the knowledge he can play a game of pool with February."

Sean grinned too. "Yeah, Feb playin' pool in your own den, wearin' that choker, a pair of her jeans. Fuck. That'd seriously make it easier."

Garrett Merrick didn't comment; he just smiled at Colt.

"Hear you only let her have a game," Mike noted and Colt was slightly annoyed, slightly impressed, that the gossip was so accurate. "Was me, I'd let her take 'em all."

"It isn't you," Colt reminded him and was extremely glad he was in the position to do it.

Mike's grin got bigger before he muttered, "Damn shame."

One good thing about the conversation was that it was different to the conversations he'd overheard since Feb came back to town. Feb being in his bed meant he wouldn't have to listen to the men discussing jacking off to her anymore and he had to admit that was a relief.

Of the many plusses of having her back in his life, that was one of them. A small one but in the current circumstances he was hanging on to all the positives he could get.

With a low wave to Sean, Merry and Mike, Colt exited the interrogation room and he managed to do it without again looking at the broken Evelyn Lowe.

And he did this because Sully was right. The job they had, the things they heard and saw, you had to find a way to shut it down.

Colt was closing down his computer, preparing to leave the station and get to his J&J's family night, a night where he suspected Feb would be in the mood for music, when Sully came up to his desk.

"Got a sec?" Sully asked.

Colt watched his screen go blank then he looked at Sully. "This gonna creep me out, piss me off or both?"

"Just fillin' you in."

Colt sat back and Sully took that as his cue to sit down at his desk opposite Colt.

"Colorado body identified. Man's name's Jayden Whelan. Wife reported him missin' four days ago. Got two kids and owned a roofin' business. On Sundays, he'd run trails. Left, didn't come back."

Colt twisted his head as he closed his eyes, trying not to think of two kids without a dad and a woman without her man living for days wondering where he was and now having to live a lifetime knowing he was never coming back. Colt tried not to think of this, to shut it down, and he failed.

When Colt opened his eyes, he was staring at the floor. He did this for a while before he looked back at Sully.

"Why the fuck's Lowe huntin' trails?"

"You ask me?" Sully answered. "It's 'cause Jayden Whelan was forty-one years old, he was six foot three, had dark brown hair, light brown eyes and pictures we got show he looked a fuckuva lot like you. I reckon somewhere along the line, Jayden caught Denny's eye and he likely followed him"

"That's not fillin' me in, Sully," Colt told him. "That's creepin' me out *and* pissin' me off."

Sully nodded understandingly but said, "Brace, man, we have no ID on today's victim but odds are, more of the same."

Colt didn't reply because there was nothing to say. Sully was probably right.

"The highways and byways between here and Oklahoma are crawlin' with Feds, cops and highway patrol. Everyone's got a picture, everyone's knows the mission. Be a miracle, Denny makin' it to town."

"He made it to Reece and he escaped him too," Colt pointed out.

"Yeah, he did," Sully agreed eyeing Colt closely. "You and Feb think about protective custody?"

What Colt was thinking at that moment was that the jury was no longer out on if it was stupid or not they didn't let the Feds take them in.

Still, for the life of him he couldn't bring himself to take away what February wanted, not only because of why she wanted it but because of what it was.

"Feb wants to live a normal life," Colt told him, and Sully took in breath, ready to say something, so Colt went on quietly. "I know, Sul. But she has her reasons and I have my reasons for givin' into those reasons."

"He gets through the heat, Colt—"

"Then we're prepared for him. We got a man in plainclothes in the bar all the time, patrols front and alley all day, all night, as often as possible. Feb and me are home at night, same for the house."

"Wanna park a guy outside," Sully said.

"You got the manpower, do it," Colt invited.

Sully gave him a hard look then said, "Feb's got her reasons, you got yours, but I'll say this once, even though I know you know it. We got a man out there in a rage. He's missed out on a target and he's been cut off cold turkey from his drug of choice, video of you and Feb. I spent about ten minutes, Colt, siftin' through that box of photos and he's been lurkin' in your and her life for years and neither of you knew it. No matter what I promised Evelyn Lowe, I don't see a happy end to this shit, not for Denny. What I want to avoid if *at all* possible is you or Feb gettin' caught in the crossfire."

"That's my goal too, Sully."

"Then talk to her again about protection."

Colt pulled in breath through his nose.

Then he promised, "I'll talk to her."

Sully's body relaxed into his chair but Colt didn't make his promise solely to make Sully feel better. He did it because his partner was right. He wanted Feb not to miss a second of the life they should be leading and he didn't want to miss it either. But the end was near. They could sacrifice a few days in order to keep themselves safe.

The phone rang on his desk. He saw the name come up on the display, leaned forward and pulled the handset out of the receiver.

"Yeah, Betsy?" he said into the phone.

Betsy worked front desk on weekends, some nights. Betsy retired early. She was Catholic and had approximately thirty children and grandchildren, all living in town. She took the job so she could still afford Christmas presents and because every single one of them thought her being retired meant she was designated nanny, chauffer, errand runner and maid. They were

463

wearing her out. Weekend shifts and three to elevens a couple of nights a week at the front desk was her refuge.

"I figure you been through the mill, Colt, so you know how sorry I am to tell you Monica Merriweather is here to see you."

Colt could picture Betsy at the front desk and Monica Merriweather standing right in front of her. Betsy would tell it like it was, even in front of Monica. Betsy might be a pushover for her family because she loved them but she'd learned to hold her own and was known as a woman who voiced her opinion. Further, she worked at a police station. Pushovers didn't last long at a police station.

"Tell her I'll be right down," Colt told Betsy.

"Other things I'd prefer to tell her but I'll tell her that," Betsy replied and then put down the phone.

"Monica," Colt told Sully.

Sully grinned and said, "Go get her, tiger."

Colt grabbed his blazer and shrugged it on while he took the stairs. When he saw Monica, his eyes never left her.

She had a bob of dyed red hair that didn't suit her coloring or the shape of her face. She was hitting middle age badly, was short and the last couple of years had put on a little pudge, mostly due to regular flybys at Mimi's and a summertime habit of stopping at Fulsham's Frozen Custard Stand.

Her position as top reporter for the *Gazette* gave her importance in town, people wanted her attention, wanted their name or event in print.

Monica had elevated that importance on her own and the last five years or so, her self-conceived power had led to her getting nosier than she should, even given her profession. Her decades of consistent but thwarted attempts to get on staff at the *Indianapolis Star* saw her writing turn gossipy and sometimes nasty, something which was not only unnecessary for a small town weekly, but also not popular. The real power she held, the power of the printed word, meant she could get away with it and people still showed her respect. They might have done it but behind her back she was widely disliked and, by some, even hated.

She'd never married, likely because she carried the triple curse of being unattractive, unlikeable and giving up the status of being a woman to be known only as a reporter.

"Colt," she said with a false ingratiating smile when he approached her.

He stopped well away and greeted, "Monica." And as he knew she would, she moved into his space so he quickly asked, "What can I do for you?"

She tipped her head to the side and said, "Figure Sully talked to you?"

"Yeah."

"Feds are here," she went on.

"Yeah," Colt agreed.

"Somethin' goin' on that the people should know about?" she asked.

She didn't want to do a service to the citizens of the town. She wanted a juicy story she could break and show the editors of *The Star*.

"Figure they know already what they should know," Colt told her.

"What I hear, there's more to it," Monica returned.

"Yeah? What'd you hear?" Colt asked and she grinned again and put her hand on his arm, touching him briefly then pulling away before he could.

"Now, wouldn't be good for me to tell you that, would it?" she asked.

Colt played dumb. "Why not?"

She just grinned again.

Colt wanted to be at the bar, not talking to Monica, so he got down to it. "My advice, Monica? You should leave this alone."

"That sounds interesting."

"At this point, it's far less interesting than you think," Colt lied.

She got closer and it took everything Colt had not to step back.

"What I hear, it's *very* interesting," she whispered.

Colt played a card. "You tell me what that is, maybe I could confirm or deny it. You don't, and you run with it now, you'd be all kinds of fool."

He gave her confidence a hit, she was unsure. She knew talk was talk and things could get embellished along the way. She moved too soon, no matter how miniscule, any dreams she had left of being at *The Star* would be lost. She tried to hide it but he saw it in her face.

Colt kept going, dangling the carrot. "You work with us on this, we give you an exclusive after it plays out."

"An exclusive to a weekly?" she asked, eyebrows up, disbelief in her tone.

"Town's paper, who else?" Colt returned, but she knew what he was saying. He wasn't offering the *Gazette* an exclusive. He was offering it to Monica.

She studied him before wheedling, "Worth my while to wait?"

Colt wasn't giving her that. "Sorry, Monica, you'll have to wait and see, just like us."

Her hand came back to his arm but this time she kept it there and again Colt fought the urge to pull away. "Colt, the Feds are here. There are four dead bodies in three states. Same MO."

"Not the same." That, at least, was the truth, or it was in Marie's case.

"Close enough," she returned.

"Monica, trust me, I'm givin' you good advice on this one."

"You're tryin' to gag the press."

That pissed Colt off. Sure, that's exactly what he was doing but he hadn't put up with her shit and played her game for years to have her call him on something she had to know was important.

His voice dipped lower when he said, "You pay attention, you'll see I'm tryin' to give you somethin'. You don't play, this ends, you got nothin'." Her interest was even more piqued, he saw that too.

"You want this, you gotta give me more," she pushed him, the greedy bitch.

"More than exclusive?" he asked.

"You gotta give me Cal Johnson."

"Old news, Monica, you reported on that this week."

"Not with an interview with the cop who got him to roll over."

Colt couldn't see it as news, just her way of taking his time, something she liked to do.

"No one's interested in that shit."

"Yeah, you're right," she said agreeably. "So, instead, I'll take you and Feb."

Colt swallowed a growl. She had that all along. She knew the murders were linked with him and Feb and she wanted it all.

She squeezed his arm, getting excited. "High school sweethearts, brought back together by murder and mayhem." She leaned in. "Hell, this could be a book."

"It's not gonna happen," Colt told her.

She squeezed his arm again. "That's my offer. I lay low until this busts and then you give me the *real* exclusive."

"You don't lay low, you don't get jack shit," he returned.

She dropped his arm, leaned back and grinned again, thinking she was calling his bluff. "I could live with that."

Colt shook his head but smiled, leaning back himself, calling hers. "Nope, Monica, run it and for the next forty years you'll kick yourself."

Her head jerked and her lips parted before she gave it away. "We're not talkin' *The Star* here, are we?"

Colt knew reporters would soon be crawling all over town. This shit was going to be big news and national and Monica wasn't wrong, it was worthy of a book and probably some hotshot would even make a movie out of it. If it had to be someone, might as well be one of their own. But even so, Colt had no intention of handing her him and Feb. And given the fact she'd made a lot of enemies in that town, folk wouldn't care Monica was one of their own. They'd talk to anyone about what they knew about Feb and Colt before they'd spill to Monica. She'd fucked herself.

Therefore Colt bit back a smile before he replied, "Book tours."

Greed suffused her face and her grin turned to a smile.

"Exclusive?" she pressed his promise.

"I'll talk to Sully." And he would talk to Sully and maybe Sully would give it to her, if he felt generous, but that was doubtful. Colt wasn't going to go after the Feds. They might talk, they might not. They wanted to seal their retirement by making their own deals, he wasn't going to hand them to Monica.

Luckily, she didn't think to pursue that.

"I'll be expecting your call to confirm," she said.

"Don't. I won't call. This is trust or we got nothin'." Sully might screw her, Colt knew, and he had no problem with that since he intended to do it himself.

"You think I'll leave with that?" she asked.

"Life is risk. What I'm tellin' you, this one is worth takin'."

She stared at him longer than was comfortable but Colt withstood it. Then she reached out and clutched his arm one more time before turning and walking away.

Colt had no idea if he'd contained her or not, but he hoped he did. It was Saturday. The *Gazette* didn't run until Wednesday. Denny would probably be caught by then, God willing. She shopped this to *The Star*, it was likely they'd screw her and hand it to someone on staff. They had far better resources than Monica and the *Gazette*. They wouldn't give her access to those, no way they'd work with her, and she likely knew it. She was fucked if she tipped it now.

"Need to call the janitor, mop up the slime trail she left," Betsy commented from beside him.

Colt turned and grinned at her. "Tell him to prepare, Bets, another coupla days we'll be drippin' with it."

"Can't wait," she muttered.

Colt laughed quietly then said, "Later."

She turned to him and her annoyance fled, light hitting her eyes before she said, "Have fun with Feb."

Colt shook his head, waved at Betsy, put Monica out of his mind and headed to the door, which would lead him to J&J's.

Colt sat on his stool, Jack and Morrie in front of him behind the bar, all of them sipping bourbon through their smiles.

Dee was at the middle of the bar with Jackie. Dee was catcalling, Jackie slamming her palms on the top of the bar like everyone else who sat or stood the length of it. The rest of the bar was clapping, whooping, whistling, stomping or some combination of the four.

All eyes were at the floor space in the middle of the bar where Feb was being swung around to Bob Seger's "Betty Lou's Gettin' Out Tonight" by none other than fucking Joe-Bob.

Colt had known Joe-Bob a good long while and he'd only ever seen the man sway to the bathroom, lurch out the door or stumble down the sidewalk.

Now he was moving like he did it for a living, he loved his job and he was damn good at it. Feb's hair was flying out everywhere and she was laughing out loud, trying to keep up with Joe-Bob as he twisted her, twirled her and spun her around. The old guy knew what he was doing and he was loving it just as much as Feb. His body jumping and jerking with the rhythm, totally in control of Feb and he was grinning like a fool, having the time of his life.

Seger was pulling out the stops and so was Joe-Bob just as Jack shouted loud, "That's my girl!"

Feb threw a bright smile their way before Joe-Bob gave her a jerk of the arm, whirled her in then sent her back out flying before he spun her with one hand over head, the other hand catching her hip to keep her going and going. Then he pulled her to a stop, yanked her in his arms and twirled them both round and round before stopping with Feb in his arms and he held on tight as the piano gave its final flourish. Feb held him back, cheek to cheek, giving him a big hug.

Jack had closed down the jukebox in order to play Seger's crowd pleasing "Nine Tonight Live" and Bob and the Silver Bullet Band went straight into "We've Got Tonight." Joe-Bob immediately began swaying with Feb in his arms as she held on tight.

Colt watched this for approximately half a second. He knew he should give Joe-Bob his moment, but Joe-Bob could have another moment another night. Tonight was Alexander Colton's night to slow dance with February Owens.

He put down his bourbon and headed toward the couple. As he moved, all eyes came to him. By this time, Colt was used to it, he couldn't give a fuck and he kept right on walking.

Joe-Bob saw him, lifted his chin then pushed Feb out for another, slower twirl, stopping her facing Colt then giving her a gentle shove in Colt's direction.

She didn't need any prompting. She moved into his arms with a small smile over her shoulder at Joe-Bob and a bigger one for Colt when she turned back to him. Colt slid his hands around her waist, crossing them at the back, resting them at opposite hips, gaining full-body contact. She curled both her arms around his shoulders, the fingers of one hand going into his hair as her hips found his rhythm. Colt bent his neck so his temple was pressed against her hair and she tilted her head so her cheek was pressed to his jaw.

They didn't speak, they just moved. Colt found himself marveling at the fact that she fit him so perfectly, fell into his rhythm like it was the most natural thing in the world, as if she was born to slow dance in his arms.

Then again, that had always been the way with Colt and Feb.

Always.

Her hand slid through his hair to curl around his neck. She tipped her head back and in his ear, whispered, "Since I was three, there's never been a day when I wasn't in love with you."

Colt didn't answer. He just closed his eyes, held her closer and kept swaying.

And he didn't stop, didn't let her go, not even when Seger started singing "Night Moves."

But he did let Darryl have her for "Rock and Roll Never Forgets" and Colt went back of the bar because Morrie was also now swinging Delilah around. Colt watched and saw that Darryl was nowhere near as good as Joe-Bob, but he was also no slouch. Morrie had always liked dancing to anything. He was a natural and it was obvious, with practice borne from time, Dee knew his moves. But Jack and Jackie had also joined them and it wasn't hard to see where Morrie and Feb got their talent. Jack and Jackie could fucking cut a rug.

Colt heard a call and saw that Ruthie was busy but Tony Mancetti was at the bar and had a bill folded lengthwise in his hand. Colt got Tony a beer, Ruthie got him change and Colt's eyes went back to the dancers in the middle of the floor just as Feb's laughter pierced the air in a direct trajectory, the sound stabbing him in the chest. It was painful, but it was a beautiful pain.

He'd been right the day before. Twenty-two years of her laughter, her smile, her body, her jewelry on his kitchen counter, he might have gotten used to it and moments like this would have been lost on him.

Now he knew that he'd never miss these moments and he'd always feel that beautiful pain because he'd always understand how precious they were.

They were in bed in the dark, Feb pressed to his side, Wilson draped over their ankles.

She was drawing mindless patterns on the skin of his chest, her hand moving slower and slower as her body settled into his.

"Feb," he called and wished he didn't have to do it.

"Yeah, babe?" Her voice was quiet, tired. It was past three in the morning and she'd worked and partied all night, both hard.

"Tomorrow, I want us to go into protective custody."

The weight of her body changed and he knew the relaxation of impending sleep had disappeared.

She lifted her head to look at his face in the dark. "I thought we—"

"Found out today that it's highly probable that Denny killed two more people." He heard her pull in breath through her nose and he continued. "No one you know, unless you know a man named Jayden Whelan."

He saw the shadow of her headshake in a "no."

"Random victims, baby. He's getting out of control and we're pretty sure he's headed up here."

"But—"

"Feb, they'll get him."

"But—"

"And I want you safe until they do."

"You can keep me safe."

"Yeah, I can, by talkin' you into protective custody."

She looked away then back and said, "I don't want him to have any more of my life."

"And I don't want him to have all of it."

"Colt."

He gave her a squeeze with the arm he had around her waist, lifted his other hand and hooked it around the back of her neck, bringing her face closer before he whispered, "Baby, I'm askin' you to do this for me. Will you do it for me?"

She hesitated only a second before she whispered back, "I'll do it for you."

No argument. There it was. That was his girl.

He brought her mouth to his for a short kiss and he let her go. She settled back in, head to his shoulder and started to draw her patterns on his chest. Colt stayed awake until her hand stopped and her weight became heavy against his side.

Then he fell asleep at about the time Chris Renicki, sitting in an unmarked car on the street one house down from Colt's, poured his second cup of coffee out of the thermos he'd brought.

Chris took a sip then glanced into the night surrounding Colt's neighborhood, doing a scan for about the fiftieth time since he got there, seeing nothing.

Twelve

I jerked awake thinking I heard my brother shouting the word "frittata."
I knew this wasn't the residue from a bad dream when I heard Colt
mutter, "I'm gonna fuckin' kill him," before he threw the covers aside,
knifed out of bed, grabbed his jeans from the floor, yanked them on and
stalked out of the room buttoning them.

Wilson trotted out after him, tail straight in the air.

Before Colt got to the front door, I heard Morrie shout, "Frittata!"
again and then there was loud knocking through the four beeps of Colt
disarming the doors and windows.

The knocking stopped and Colt said loudly, "Seriously?"

Then Morrie said, also loudly, "Dude, I missed the last one."

Then Tuesday shouted, "Hey, Uncle Colt!"

Then Bonham, so like his father, shouted, "Auntie Feb, frittata!"

Then a lot of noise as the kids ran inside, likely straight to the pool
table. Before I'd been to Colt's house I'd heard a lot about the pool table
from the kids. It was nearly as legendary as the boat. Colt having these two
things was more likely the reason Bonham wanted to be like his Uncle Colt
than the coolness of Colt being a cop.

Then I heard Dee saying, "Sorry, Colt, I tried to stop him."

I thought I heard Colt grumble something and I looked at the clock. It
was nine-oh-eight.

I rolled to my back, mumbling, "Fucking hell."

Firstly, I mumbled this because I was going into protective custody with Colt and I wanted to have a lazy Sunday morning in bed with him. His bed. *Our* bed. Secondly, I mumbled this because I was going into protective custody at all. Lastly, I mumbled this because I wanted to sleep more.

I was up on an elbow with the covers pulled over my chest when Colt stalked back in and announced, "Command performance, February."

By the look on his face I was guessing he was about as happy as I was to have early morning Sunday company.

"You wanna change your mind about that answer of you ownin' a hatchet?" I asked.

"Be cleaner usin' my gun," Colt returned, giving me the impression he was really thinking about this option even though I knew he wasn't really thinking about this option.

I smiled then said, "We gotta count on Tuesday and Bonham takin' care of us in our old age. You murder their father, I doubt that'll happen."

For some reason this was the wrong thing to say. I watched as Colt's face changed, pain slicing through it before it went blank.

I sat up fully in bed, still holding the covers to my chest, and called, "Colt?"

He shook his head, his face relaxed and he said softly, "Get up, baby."

"Colt."

He ignored me and went to the bathroom. I got out of bed, pulled on my underwear and Colt's tee and waited until I heard him brushing his teeth. Then I knocked on the bathroom door and came in at his call.

I walked to him at the basin and leaned a hip against the counter, watching him brush. His eyes didn't meet mine.

"What's on your mind?" I asked quietly when he spit the foam in the sink.

Colt avoided my question, turned on the tap in preparation to rinse and said, "I'll call Jack and Jackie. They won't want to miss a frittata and, they're here, we can tell them all at the same time we're goin' into custody."

I got closer as he bent at the waist and rinsed his mouth.

I put my hand to the skin of his back. "Okay, but Colt," I said low. "Something happened in there, baby. I saw it. Honey, tell me what's on your mind."

His head tipped back so he could look at himself in the mirror. He held his own gaze for several beats and I waited. He made me wait awhile before he straightened, turned, my hand dropped from his back and I held my breath at what I saw in his face when he finally caught my eyes.

"Woulda talked you into namin' a boy Jack, we had one. Jacqueline, we had a girl," he whispered, and I closed my eyes and swallowed back the pain.

He'd wanted kids and I did too. Even back in the day, both of us young, we'd talked about it. We didn't talk about it a lot but we talked about it enough that it was understood, when we made it official, we weren't going to waste time building a family.

Then he went through the heartbreak of Melanie not being able to conceive.

Now, with him forty-four and me forty-two and us just starting out again and needing time, it wasn't impossible but it also maybe wasn't smart for us to try to start a family at this juncture. If we tried and it didn't happen, we'd both just have more heartbreak and we'd had enough of that.

His hand came to the back of my neck, curling around, warm and reassuring and I loved it when he did that. Even now, when yet another thing Denny stole from us tore through our consciousness, his hand there felt good, it felt right and it made the pain hurt a whole lot less.

"Honey," he called, and I opened my eyes.

"You wouldn't have had to talk me into that," I told him and he grinned, not a happy grin or one filled with humor. It was a grin that broke my heart.

"Don't 'spect I would've," he said.

I moved closer and his hand at my neck gave me a squeeze as his other arm went around my waist. I put my palms on his bare chest and pressed my cheek there.

"You think there'll come a time when this shit quits hittin' us, stuff we missed, things he stole?"

"Yeah, baby," he said reassuringly, though I didn't quite believe him mainly because he didn't sound like he believed himself.

"You sure?"

Another squeeze at my neck. "Yeah."

I nodded, my cheek sliding against the warm skin of his chest.

"One thing..." I started and then my throat closed and I couldn't go on.

This time I got a squeeze from his arm at my waist before he prompted, "Baby?"

I cleared my throat and slid my hands around him, holding him around his waist too.

"One thing," I said into his chest. "One thing that's good, Colt, and that is, every day, for all these years, I thought of you, dozens of times a day. Every day. Every single *fucking* day."

"February," Colt whispered.

"Still do, except, now...it doesn't hurt anymore."

His hand at my neck went into my hair and gave it a tug. When my head went back, his face was already there and his mouth was on mine.

Colt tasted of toothpaste when he kissed me and I thought it was the best thing I ever tasted in my life.

"What's takin' so long?" Morrie bellowed. Colt's head came up and this time he *was* grinning with humor.

"Shut up, Morrie! We'll be out in a second," I shouted back, still holding Colt close.

"Get the lead out! I'm hungry!" Morrie was still bellowing and I heard Tuesday giggle.

My body melted further into Colt's. "He's a pain in the ass," I noted, but having Colt in my arms and my family in the other room, I went on. "Still, I love Sundays."

"Best day of the week," Colt replied.

I smiled before I agreed, "Absolutely."

"Baby?" he called like I wasn't in his arms.

"Yeah?"

"We got a lifetime of Sundays ahead of us," he reminded me.

I tipped my head to the side and I felt my smile change and the only word I could think to say to express how happy this idea made me was, "Yeah."

Then I decided Morrie could wait a bit longer, so could the Feds, so could protective custody, and I got up on my toes and kissed Colt in our bathroom.

⌒

Colt sat at his desk at the station, Sean in the chair by the desk, Sully across from him.

Colt was antsy but he needed to get this done.

February was at the bar. She'd wanted to go there, sort some things out, preparing, like Colt was now, to be away.

Marty, in plainclothes, was there playing bodyguard.

This was why Colt was antsy. Chris had done night duty, which was good. Colt could trust that Chris would stay alert all night. Marty, Colt couldn't trust and he wasn't happy leaving Feb at the bar even though Morrie was there, as was Darryl and, although they weren't yet open, Joe-Bob had already been let in and was in his seat. It wasn't exactly an army of protection, but Denny and a hatchet would have some troubles getting through four men to get to Feb.

But Colt had a bad feeling in his gut, he'd woken up with it and it hadn't gone away. And when he had this feeling, he didn't want to be away from Feb. Therefore, even with four men between her and the possibility of Denny showing, Colt was still antsy.

Warren and Rodman were waiting for Colt to lay his caseload on Sean before they handed Colt and February over to the US Marshalls to take to the safe house. They were antsy too. Visibly so. Time enough had lapsed for Denny to hit town and they wanted this done so they could focus on the hunt.

"You'll only be gone a day, two tops," Sean said, and Colt nodded, hoping Sean was right.

"Though, in that time, shouldn't be hard for you to track down our guy," Colt replied, talking about the stoned-out burglar. "He should have gone through his stash by now and is likely looking to score again."

Sean nodded back at Colt as three phones rang simultaneously and the vibe in the room suddenly went electric.

Colt tensed and his eyes sliced to Sully, who was watching him as he leaned toward his phone. Sully didn't get it to his ear before Colt heard footsteps coming up the stairs, fast.

He swiveled in his chair to see it was Betsy. She took one look at Colt, her face pale, her eyes filled with fear. That weight in Colt's gut turned solid as an anvil and Betsy said breathlessly, "Shots fired at J&J's."

"Quiet," Denny clipped.

I swallowed, turning around in my seat in the car to look at Melanie. I gave a shake of my head to the obviously petrified Melanie, who'd just been whining, making low keening noises around the gag in her mouth and doing this mainly because she was scared out of her brain.

"Sweetheart," Denny called, his voice soft and loving, and I knew he was talking to me.

I turned my eyes to him. I didn't want to, but I did.

Light brown hair, good haircut, blue eyes, decent build, probably a couple inches taller than me—he looked like Denny, but older.

And he was covered in blood. Joe-Bob's blood, Darryl's blood, maybe even Marty's blood.

And his blue eyes were wild. I'd never seen eyes like that and they scared me more than the blood, more than what I'd just seen at the bar because I knew he wasn't done.

I swallowed again and fought back the tears that were stinging the backs of my eyes and the scream that was lodged in my throat.

"You know, even when I was with her," Denny went on, jerking his head toward the backseat where Melanie was tied up and gagged, "I only wanted you."

"I know," I forced out, my voice sounding ragged, thinking it prudent to play his game and trying not to think of much else.

"It's only ever been you, February," Denny said.

"I know," I repeated and closed my eyes tight before I looked back out the windshield. Then I swallowed and called, "Alec?" and using Colt's name to address Denny made me feel like I had acid poured on my tongue.

"Yeah, sweetheart?" Denny answered.

I searched for the courage I needed and pulled it up. "Can we just let her go?"

"Sweetheart."

"I don't want her here."

"Oh," Denny replied, "I'll take care of her."

Melanie squeaked in terror and I closed my eyes tight again.

That's what I was afraid of.

There was a cruiser, lights still flashing, at the front of J&J's and more sirens could be heard in the distance when Colt ran toward the front door. Sean and Warren were at his heels, Sully and Rodman not far behind them.

He had his gun in his hand but before he hit the door it flew open and Adam, a uniform, shot out, his hand to the radio at his shoulder, his mouth turned there.

"Officer down, J&J's Saloon. I repeat, officer down, J&J's Saloon."

Adam didn't even look at Colt as he ran to the trunk of the cruiser to get the first aid kit.

Colt ran into the bar.

Joe-Bob was by the front door, slashed to shit, blood everywhere. Colt didn't even have to check to know he was dead.

He crushed down the rage that threatened to burn through him and saw Marty five feet away, on his back, covered in blood and looking either dead or, God willing, unconscious. Ellen, Adam's partner, was on her knees beside him. At one glance Colt saw Marty took at least three bullets into the vest he was luckily wearing. Unfortunately, he also took one in the neck.

"Feb?" Colt asked Ellen. She shook her head, that anvil twisted, scoring against the lining of his gut. "Marty?" Colt went on.

"Breathing," Ellen replied.

"Morrie?"

"Out back," Ellen said, holding a bar towel to Marty's neck and Colt ran to the back.

Darryl was on his ass in the alley, his face gray and pinched with pain, his back to the brick wall of the bar, blood spatters could be seen up his neck. Morrie was crouched beside him, his back to Colt, his body hiding Darryl's.

"Morrie," Colt called. Morrie twisted and Colt got a look at his friend and saw he was unharmed. Then he got a look at Darryl and skidded to a halt.

"*Fuck!*" Colt hissed and pulled his phone out of his back pocket.

"We need to get him to a hospital." Morrie's voice was soft and calm but it had an edge.

"Feb?" Colt replied, the phone to his ear and ringing.

"He got her. I'm sorry, boss. I—" Darryl started.

"Quiet, Darryl, just be still," Morrie hushed him and Colt's call connected.

"ETA on ambulances at J&J's?" Colt asked Jo in dispatch but he heard the sirens out front.

"Should be there, Colt," Jo replied.

"Darryl's in the back, the alley," Colt told her, looked over Darryl's injuries and continued, "Been hacked, also, what I can see, been shot."

"Got it, Colt," Jo said, but Colt was already flipping his phone shut.

He skirted Morrie, went around Darryl's legs and crouched at Darryl's other side.

"I need to know which way they went. You see that?" he asked Darryl.

"Right, out the alley," Darryl answered, his head tipping to the left, telling Colt where he'd last seen the car, his voice as pinched as his face.

"What was he drivin'?" Colt went on.

"White Ford Taurus. Didn't get a number, but it was an Oklahoma plate," Darryl answered.

Colt put his hand to Darryl's shoulder as the paramedics came running out the back door carrying their kit. He ignored them and said softly to Darryl, "Good."

"Came in the front but was parked in the back. He got Joe-Bob first," Darryl continued. "Crazy Joe-Bob went right at him, even though that guy came in swingin'. Then he started shootin', didn't hesitate, took down the cop before he even got his gun outta his holster," Darryl finished as Morrie moved away and the paramedics moved in.

"Just relax, Darryl," Colt urged.

"I told Feb to run. She did but he ran after her. He shot at me, hit me, but I tried—"

"Relax."

"Lieutenant, move away," the paramedic ordered, and Colt didn't hesitate. He moved.

By that time Warren and Rodman were in the alley as was Sully and Colt moved to them.

"White Taurus, Oklahoma plates, north out the alley," Colt said, pointing in the direction Darryl indicated and Warren opened his phone as did Sully.

"I was at Mimi's," Morrie whispered. "Feb wanted a latte. I was at Mimi's gettin' her a latte."

"Morrie, hold it together, man," Colt said.

"I was gettin' her a fuckin' latte."

"Morrie, keep it together."

Morrie twisted his neck, his hand coming to the collar of his t-shirt and he pulled himself together but his eyes went to Colt's and he said, "That asshole's got my sister."

Colt knew that. He knew it. He felt that knowledge weighing heavy in his gut.

"Melanie," Darryl said and everyone's eyes turned to him.

"What?" Colt asked, but it felt like something lethal had hold of his heart.

Darryl blinked then lifted his chin and said, "Feb went with him because he's also got Melanie."

Then Darryl slid to the side and lost consciousness.

"No, this isn't right, Alec," I said as Denny pushed Melanie onto Susie Shepherd's couch.

He had hold of Susie who was trembling from the top of her blonde head to the tips of her blood red painted toenails. She was trembling because, now that Melanie was on the couch, Denny wasn't just holding her bicep in his hand, he was also now holding his gun to her head.

"February, do as I said, sweetheart, tie her up," Denny commanded.

I shook my head. "Please, Alec, let's just go. You and me, let's just go."

Denny leaned forward and shouted, "Tie her, the fuck, *up!*"

I decided not to push it, moved forward, my eyes locking on Susie's before I walked around her. I used the rope Denny gave me and pulled her wrists behind her back.

"I don't know how to tie someone up," I said, winding the rope around her wrists. "Maybe you can hand me the gun and do it yourself."

"Quit fuckin' around, Feb."

"No really—"

"*Quit fuckin' around!*" Denny shouted again. Susie jumped under my hands and Melanie made a terrified noise from the couch. "I wanna get this done and get the fuck outta here."

"Okay, Alec," I whispered, scared, clueless, wondering if Colt or Sully or the Feds would ever think in a million years that Denny would take Melanie and me to Susie Shepherd's house.

I tied Susie up but I didn't do a good job with it mainly because I wasn't lying, I didn't know how to tie someone up. Also, I didn't want to do a good job.

"Done," I said, my hand going to Susie's forearm. I gave her a squeeze there, not knowing what I was saying, just wanting her to have something, to tell her we were all in this together, to tell her I would do what I could.

Denny yanked Susie forward and shoved her to sit on the couch next to Melanie.

I stood there, my mind going a million miles a minute. Should I lunge for the gun? Should I go for the ax he made me carry into the house? If I did, would he shoot me, or Melanie, or Susie?

Time.

I needed time.

"Why?" I asked Denny as he stared at the two terrified women on the couch.

"Gag her," Denny replied.

"What?" I asked.

"Gag her, Susie, the fuckin' bitch. Don't want her talkin'. Don't want her runnin' that sick mouth of hers."

I looked at Susie. She was scared stiff. She didn't have it in her to speak. "She won't talk," I told him.

Denny looked at me and said calmly, "I don't want to repeat myself again, sweetheart."

I shook my head, still trying to buy time for Melanie and Susie and for me. "I don't have anything to gag her with."

"Find something. I'm sure she has some fancy-ass scarves somewhere."

Was he serious? He was going to let me wander the house looking for a scarf?

I shot Susie and Melanie a look then muttered, "Be right back."

Then I ran from the room.

⌒⟶

Colt's phone rang in his hand. He didn't even look at the display before he flipped it open and put it to his ear.

"Colton," he said, his eyes on the gurney with Darryl strapped to it that was being wheeled into the bar, his mind on Feb and Melanie, his gut twisted in knots.

"Alec?"

It was his mother.

Fucking shit.

"Ma, I can't—"

"A man has Feb," she said on a rush and Colt felt ice water slide through his veins. "I'm in my car outside a big, fancy house on The Heritage. Street's called Vine. A man's got Feb and Melanie. He's also got a gun. He took them into the house."

"Vine?" Colt asked, but he knew. Denny, that sick fuck, he knew.

"Yeah, Alec, one three eight Vine."

Jesus, Susie's house.

He looked at Sully. "He's taken them to Susie's." His eyes went to Warren. "One three eight Vine. The Heritage. Susan Shepherd's house."

Warren, Rodman and Sully immediately turned and jogged away. Colt followed them. His strides long, his patience spent, he was fighting a fear that nearly immobilized him and Morrie was at his side.

"Ma, drive away," he told his mother.

"Feb's in that house with a man's got a gun," his mother told him.

"Drive away. Now."

"I knew you weren't safe so I been watchin' and I saw—"

After forty-four years, Colt finally had something to thank Mary Colton for.

"Drive away, Ma."

"Alec—"

"Do it. *Now*."

She hesitated then whispered, "Don't you get hurt."

"Please, Ma, just drive away."

"All right, Alec," she said. "I'll drive away."

"Ma?" Colt called before he heard her disconnect.

"Yes, son?"

Then Colt said something to his mother he'd never said in his life, or at least not saying it and meaning it, "Thanks."

I went to Susie's bedroom, straight to the phone by the side of her bed. I dialed 911. I had no idea how much time I had, Denny was crazy and he could do anything.

When I heard the voice in my ear, I whispered over it, my words hurried and hushed.

"This is February Owens. Denny Lowe has me, Melanie Colton and Susie Shepherd at Susie's house. He also has a gun and an ax. He's hurt people at J&J's Saloon. I can't talk anymore. I'm setting the phone down but not hanging up so you can't talk either. He can't hear you. I'm calling again on my cell in a few seconds, don't let the operator talk when the call comes through. I'm going to keep my cell with me and the line open. That's it. No more talking."

Then I set the cordless on its side by the base and shouted, "I don't know where she keeps her scarves, Alec! Ask Susie where she keeps her scarves!"

"Just look around!" Denny shouted back.

I pulled my cell out of my back pocket and didn't fuck around with scrolling to anyone's number. I dialed 911 and then yanked my t-shirt out of my jeans and slid the phone in, display down, between my belly and my belt. I pulled the t-shirt back over it and tucked it around the phone.

"Found one!" I shouted my lie, but started searching and luckily found Susie's scarves in the first drawer I pulled open.

I nabbed one and ran back to the living room, praying he hadn't started without me, but also that the 911 operator would keep quiet.

"You want me to gag her?" I asked loudly the minute I hit the room.

"Yeah, darlin'," Denny said, and I walked direct to Susie, my eyes sliding between her and Melanie, trying to tell them without words it was going to be okay and hoping I wasn't nonverbally lying.

"What next?" I asked Denny as I gagged Susie.

"Erase," Denny answered and I straightened and turned to him.

"What?"

"Erase," Denny repeated, moving toward me, taking me by the arm and pulling me back.

"Erase?" I asked. "What—?"

"Gonna erase everything, Feb. All of yours, all of mine." He lifted the gun and pointed it at Melanie as I stood and stared at him, frozen stiff with shock. "So we can get back to the way it's supposed to be, gonna erase it all."

He was going to shoot Melanie, I knew it, and he wasn't going to hesitate.

I didn't think. I just went for the gun. But I was too late.

He pulled the trigger when my hand hit his wrist and the gun exploded as the noise pounded against my ears and my heart stopped beating.

"He's got a gun," Morrie said, sitting beside Colt as Colt drove his truck to Susie's.

"Yeah," Colt replied.

"How'd he get a gun?" Morrie asked.

"Don't know," Colt answered.

Morrie was silent, staring out the windshield.

Then he said, "Joe-Bob—"

"Nope, not now, Morrie. Later."

Morrie was silent again and Colt concentrated on driving, thinking about time, how much had elapsed, what was Denny's intent, why he'd gone off target. He was supposed to be hunting for Colt, not Susie, not fucking Melanie. Melanie could barely handle giving herself a paper cut. She'd come undone being a hostage. Colt didn't know what this meant. He didn't know what it meant for Susie, Melanie or Feb. He didn't know how much time they had.

"A fuckin' latte," Morrie muttered.

"I need you to be cool, Morrie," Colt told him.

"If I hadn't—" Morrie started.

"If you hadn't, you'd be hacked or full of holes too," Colt told him.

"Better'n scared shitless he's got my sister."

Morrie was wrong. If he thought he was right, he just had to ask Jayden Whelan's wife.

"No, it isn't. Not when you got a wife and two kids at home," Colt said.

"I was buyin' a latte, Colt."

"You were doin' something your sister wanted you to do. You think Feb's happy about where Joe-Bob, Darryl and Marty are now? Do you think she'd want that for you? For Dee? For Bonham and Tuesday?" Morrie made a guttural noise and Colt went on. "Focus, Morrie. This ends today and you and me, we don't need to lose control and fuck it up."

Morrie paused then blew out a breath before he said, "Yeah."

"You with me?" Colt asked.

"Yeah."

Colt turned on Vine and he tried to take his own advice. He tried to keep control, be cool.

But all he could think was he promised Feb he'd keep her safe and, at that moment, she was far from safe.

"What the fuck you doin'?" Denny shouted, but I was staring at the bullet hole in the wall beside where Melanie's head used to be.

She'd fallen to the side, into Susie who had also leaned away. Both of them were crying behind their gags, which worked for me since neither of them was bleeding.

Denny pushed me away and stared at me. I had to think fast, I had to buy time.

"You shot at Melanie!" I yelled.

"I gotta erase—"

"Colt wouldn't shoot at Melanie!" I yelled over him. He went stock-still and his face went funny, not a good funny, a *bad* funny.

"What'd you say?" he asked quietly.

"I said Colt wouldn't shoot Melanie. And he wouldn't have hacked up Angie. Or Butch. Or even Pete. Colt's about good. He'd never hurt *anyone*. You're not supposed to hurt anyone!" I shouted.

"I'm not Colt," Denny told me. "I'm Alec."

I shook my head again, short, fast, all the while blinking. I didn't understand.

"You're Alec," I said to him.

"I'm Alec," Denny agreed.

"And Alec is Colt."

Denny shook his head then he grinned. This wasn't a good grin either. It, too, was a bad grin and it scared me to the depth of my soul.

"No, Feb. I'm Alec. I'm yours. Alec has always been yours. But Colt, he's different. He's wrong. He hurt you and, for that, he's gonna die."

Colt pulled in, parked, exited the truck and scanned the surroundings. There were four cruisers, which had lined up at angles to the house as well as Sully's unmarked car, Colt's truck and Warren and Rodman's black SUV.

"Go in low," Colt ordered Morrie who'd come around the back of the truck to Colt's side. Colt bent double himself, running nearly in a squat to Sully who was crouched behind a cruiser.

"What've we got?" Colt asked.

"The SWAT team's en route, they'll be at least another ten minutes," Sully answered.

This was not good. Ten minutes was a long time. Too long.

"Any visual?" Colt asked.

"Curtains just been pulled, he's seen us," Sully replied.

"Hard not to see," Morrie muttered and they heard more sirens in the distance so Morrie went on. "And hear."

"Fed's said go in hot."

Colt lifted up and looked at the house, curtains drawn, door closed, no visual. Then he crouched low behind the cruiser.

"You see Feb?" he asked Sully.

"Nope, just Denny."

"Fed's plan?"

"Talk him out."

"So, are they gonna do that tomorrow or just after they take a tea break?" Morrie asked, his eyes on the conferring Warren and Rodman that were crouched behind another vehicle, Warren on the phone.

"Denny's gone rogue, he's off plan. They don't know what to do with him. They're talkin' to Nowakowski," Sully said as he lifted up and looked through the passenger windows at the house before he went low again.

"What—?" Colt started but stopped, his muscles petrifying instantly when they heard gunfire inside the house.

"Oh my God. Oh my God," I chanted as Susie's eyes came to me, pain and fear etched in them.

Then she slumped to the side, blood oozing from her chest.

Melanie was whimpering. She'd thrown herself off the couch and was trying to crawl away, not an easy thing to do on your belly, in a panic, with your hands tied behind your back.

My first thought was to help her but Denny turned to Melanie, aimed the gun, and I had to move fast. I lunged at his arm and caught his wrist, jerking it upward when he fired.

"Stop shooting at them!" I screeched.

Denny threw me off again and glared at me. "Gotta get this done."

"We need to call an ambulance. You've shot Susie," I yelled.

"Shoulda started with her first. World could easily do without Susie Shepherd," Denny declared.

"That isn't your call," I snapped. "You're not God."

He tired of the conversation, looked over his shoulder at the windows and, with utter, yet bizarre, calm he announced, "We gotta hurry, cops are here."

And thank God, thank God for that.

"Give me the gun," I demanded, moving to him again, putting my hand to his wrist but he pushed me away.

"February, stop fuckin' around."

I shook my head. I needed to help Susie and this needed to end. She was alive, I could hear her groaning. Her head was to the armrest, her eyes on me, her hands still behind her back, blood coming out of her, staining her couch.

I couldn't let Susie Shepherd die on her own couch with her hands tied behind her back and the gag I'd tied around her mouth still in place. I couldn't. I had to do everything I could to stop it.

Denny rushed forward and pulled the slithering Melanie back several feet using her hair to do it. She cried her pain out from behind her gag and the sound of it, the sight of her head jerking back in that awful way, made my stomach roil.

"Stop it!" I screeched, going for Denny, but he pushed me off again, let Melanie go and turned his body and his gun on me.

"What the fuck's the matter with you?" he snapped.

What did I say? How did I play this? How did I buy the cops time to get in here and stop this madness? And why the fuck weren't they coming in?

I had no idea but I had to come up with something.

"Alec wouldn't do this. Not *my* Alec. He's good and gentle and kind. He doesn't shoot people and pull their hair," I told him.

"We can't go back to the way we're supposed to be if they aren't erased."

"We'll *never* go back to the way we're supposed to be if you don't stop this!" I shouted. "Let me take Susie out so they can get her help. Let Melanie go. And then, after we let them go, you and me, we'll start over."

"Can't do it unless it's erased."

"I'm tellin' you, Denny, we *won't* do it *if* you erase them!" I screamed.

He blinked and I knew I fucked up. I called him by his real name.

Before I could take it back, he lifted the gun and pulled the trigger.

⌒

Colt tore at Chris and Sean as Morrie did the same with Rodman and Sully.

"Shots fired, shots fired," someone said into their radio.

Three shots.

Three shots fired.

Three women who'd shared part of his life might have taken a bullet.

And in between that time, the only thing he could hold onto was the sound of Feb shouting.

But she wasn't shouting anymore.

"Stand down, Colt," Chris grunted as Colt pushed against his and Sean's weakening hold.

"He's got hostages, Colt. You can't go tearin' in there," Sean said.

Did he? Three shots. Three women. No further noise.

Did he still have hostages?

Colt shoved Chris aside and Sean shifted, planting his feet behind him and putting all his weight into Colt.

"Morrie, relax or I'll have you cuffed," Sully threatened Morrie who was struggling five feet away.

"My sister's in there," Morrie returned, like Colt, he was still fighting against the restraining hold.

Colt's eyes went to his friend and seeing Morrie, Colt suddenly stopped pushing and a strange calm settled over him.

He wasn't going to get anywhere like this. Not losing control and acting like a moron.

He'd have to find another way in and he had to get in. He had to see. He had to know if February was okay and he had to deal with Denny if she was, and more so, if she was not. He didn't care if he lost his badge. He didn't care if he carried on the Colton family tradition in prison. If Feb was gone, out of his life for good this time, he knew there was nothing left to care about.

He looked at Warren who was pulling a loudspeaker out of his SUV and Colt pushed away from Sean and walked to the agent.

"Send me in," he demanded to Warren.

"Patience, Lieutenant, we got this. Let us open a line of communication," Warren stated.

They didn't have this. Colt saw it in Warren's face, indecision. Shots were fired from a man who was known to favor a hatchet and, thus far, had taken no hostages. They had no idea what they were dealing with in that house.

"Three shots were fired," Colt told him. "We need to go in."

"Patience, Lieutenant. SWAT Team isn't here and Nowakowski feels he'll do your woman no harm."

"*Women*, Agent, Feb's not the only one in there."

"We're gonna try to talk him out."

"He wants me," Colt reminded Warren. "Send me in and I'll get the women out."

"Let us deal with this, Colton."

"We got ears," someone shouted and Colt's head turned to a cruiser where Eric, another of the town's uniforms was folding himself in the passenger seat. Everyone jogged to the cruiser but Colt pushed in close.

"Someone's called 911, not talkin', just opened the line," Eric whispered.

"Sweetheart," a man said over the radio.

"Stay away from me," Feb replied and Colt's neck twisted at the fear he could hear stark in her voice, even muted and scratchy over the radio. But even so, relief poured through him that she was speaking at all.

"Come here, February." the man demanded.

"You just shot at me!" Feb yelled.

"I'm sorry. I'm sorry, sweetheart…but you can't call me that."

"Don't get near me."

"Feb, I need you to listen to me."

"*She's hurt!*" Feb screamed, so loud they could hear it not only on the radio but rom the house and Colt's eyes opened. The dread in his gut had lifted, not much, because either Susie or Melanie had been hit, but Feb sounded strong and Colt looked toward the house.

"We start again here, we gotta start clean," the man said.

"By killing Melanie and Susie? Are you nuts?" Feb asked.

"Oh shit," someone close to Colt muttered but Colt could have said it himself. Denny Lowe *was* nuts and he didn't need Feb riling him.

"February…" the man said then he asked, "What's that?"

"What?" Feb asked back.

"Feb, what's that? In your shirt."

Fuck, she had the phone on her and Denny had seen it.

Feb wisely changed the subject. "You just shot at me. I want to go," she snapped. "I just want to *go*. And I'm taking Melanie and Susie with me."

"Lift up your shirt," Denny demanded.

"I'm going," Feb declared.

"You can't go. You're meant to be with me and to be with me we have to start clean. Now, what's in your fuckin' shirt?" The man's voice was getting agitated. They didn't have much time. Susie'd already suffered a gunshot wound, God knew the state of her. Melanie was likely up next. And Feb, Feb kept at him like this, Denny would do her too.

Feb stayed on target, keeping his focus off her phone. "Susie's bleeding, she needs help. You let her bleed to death on her own couch, I swear to God, we're through. *Over.* You hear me?"

Colt turned to Warren. "Talk to him or I go in," he demanded.

Warren turned to the house and lifted the speaker to his mouth.

"Dennis Lowe!" he called through the speaker and Colt went around the cruiser to the driver's side, opened the door, pulled the latch to the trunk then moved to the back of the cruiser, nabbed a vest and put it on while Warren continued. "Dennis Lowe, this is the FBI. We're outside and we know you're holding February Owens, Melanie Colton and Susan Shepherd. We know you've shot Susan. We don't want anyone else hurt. Put down your weapons and exit the house immediately. This will be your only warning."

Sully got close as Colt pressed down the Velcro. "Colt, man, what—?"

Colt didn't look at him. In fact, he ignored everyone, including the variety of voices shouting his name as he jogged to the house, pulling his gun out of the back waistband of his jeans.

"February, just please, come here," Denny pleaded.

My eyes went to Susie. Her eyes were closed. Either she was dead or unconscious. I'd successfully taken his mind off my phone but I knew I was running out of time.

"Let them go," I demanded to Denny.

"Why won't you *listen* to me?" he shouted.

"Maybe because you're shooting people and acting crazy!" I shouted back.

For some reason, his eyes went to the door then he lunged toward me.

I was too slow in making a move to avoid him. He caught my arm and pulled me back.

Then the door opened and Colt walked in, carrying a gun, calm as you please. Upon entry, he lifted his weapon, aiming dead on at Denny.

I stared at Colt as I felt the cold steel of the gun hit my temple.

Then Denny said, as if he was hosting a dinner party, "I'm glad you could make it."

⌐⟋

"Let her go," Colt ordered.

"Drop it," Denny Lowe demanded in return and he jerked Feb in his hold.

Colt's eyes went to the gun at his woman's head and his blood, already boiling, starting singing through his veins.

"I said, *drop it!*" Denny shouted.

"You won't hurt her, Lowe," Colt guessed and he was right.

Denny took the gun from Feb's temple, turned it on Colt and fired.

⌐⟋

I watched Colt's big, solid body jerk as the bullet hit his vest and I screamed.

Then I turned and threw my weight at Denny. Taking him off balance, we both went to the floor.

My hands circled his wrist, both of them grappling for the gun.

"Get them out, out, out, *out!*" I shouted at Colt, struggling with Denny.

"Feb, roll away," Colt demanded, his voice sounding funny, like he was winded as if he'd just run a race.

"Get them out!" I repeated.

"*Roll away!*" Colt bellowed, obviously getting his breath back.

It would seem I *was* the kind of woman who listened when a man bellowed because Colt did it twice and twice I did what he said. I rolled away, onto my back. When I did, Denny lifted the gun but Colt was standing over us. Colt fired and Denny grunted in pain before his gun hand fell.

"Get Melanie out," Colt told me as he kicked at Denny's hand and the gun went skidding across the room.

"Colt."

"Feb, *now!*"

I got to my feet and went to Melanie, pulling her to hers. She didn't waste time and, still whimpering, ran directly toward the door.

I didn't see if she made it, wasn't paying any attention because Denny had scooted back then he was up, unarmed but charging Colt. When he did, Colt south-pawed him, holding nothing back, his shoulder dipped, his torso twisting at the waist building momentum, he connected direct in the wound at Denny's shoulder.

The sound was sickening as Colt's fist struck the seeping flesh. Denny let out a rough howl of pain, fell back and then, like the crazy man he was, without hesitation, he charged Colt yet again, growling like an animal the whole way.

Colt planted his feet, lifted his now bloody left hand and caught Denny by the throat, his fingers curling under his chin and around his jaw. With what looked like little effort, he cocked his elbow and flung Denny away.

Any man in normal circumstances would be humiliated by the ease of Colt's defense. Colt was essentially fighting with one arm tied behind his back as he hadn't dropped his gun. But Denny just went reeling several feet, his good arm windmilling, before he righted himself.

"Lowe, it's over. Stop," Colt ordered, but Denny came right back at him.

Colt didn't touch him this time, he dodged him and Denny flew by.

"Get outta here," Colt ordered to me, sounding impatient, but his eyes never left Denny. He was focused but he knew I was there and not leaving.

Now Colt brought his gun up, his head cocked to the site and he aimed at Denny and I knew he was finished fucking around, even if Denny was no longer armed. Denny was bent double, one hand to his bleeding shoulder, the other hand dangling useless. His eyes, seething with palpable hate, were on Colt and he was panting like a dog.

I didn't do as Colt asked. I went to Susie and pulled her dead weight up. I managed to get behind her and grabbed her under her pits, trying to be careful and failing because I was panicked. I pulled her around, yanked her down and she thudded against the floor.

I was bent double, dragging her across the floor, still watching Colt and Denny as Denny grabbed the ax with his good hand. Not giving up, so insane he didn't know he'd lost or not caring. His right shoulder was bleeding, even if Colt didn't have a gun, he could do little harm with a gunshot wound and an ax in his left, non-dominant hand.

Then, suddenly, coming from everywhere, the room was filled with men.

"Drop it, Lowe," Sully demanded, but Denny raised the ax unsteadily in his left hand, his eyes on Colt, a half a dozen guns aimed at him.

I fell to my knees then back to my ass as someone else shouted for Denny to freeze. I pulled Susie into my body, between my legs, protectively wrapping my arms around her ribcage. I didn't know why I did this but I did.

And I didn't know why I did what I did next.

But I did.

"Don't, Denny, please, don't," I whispered.

Denny froze, everyone froze, but only Denny's eyes came to me.

I shook my head at him. "Please. For me?"

"We hafta be together," he told me.

God, he was totally fucking crazy.

My head was still shaking. "You don't stop, you'll get hurt."

"His has to be the worst," Denny declared, his eyes shifting to Colt and me, back and forth, back and forth, so fast, he was making me dizzy.

"It has been, Denny. I promise. It's been the worst, for both of us," I said and his eyes settled back on me. "When you took me away from him all those years ago, he's been living with twenty-two years of the worst. So have I."

"He hurt you."

"He never hurt me, Denny."

"He cheated on you with Amy," Denny told me. "I saw him, *you* saw him."

I tipped my head to the side before saying, "You know he didn't do that. You know."

"He did."

"No, he didn't."

"February—"

"You took away my life," I whispered.

His head jerked, his face grew slack for a second as if not comprehending then that crazy light lit in his eyes again and he said, "Don't you see? I'm tryin' to give it back. We had everything, Feb. You and me. We had it all. We were happy. So fuckin' happy, we laughed all the time. *You* laughed all the time. *I* made you laugh. I'm your Alec. You love me. You always did and now I've come back."

"You're not my Alec. You never made me laugh. Colt made me laugh and you took that away too. You're not Alec. You're not Colt. You're Denny."

"I'm your Alec."

"You're Denny," I repeated and went on. "And I've got it back, Denny, but I've lost a lot of it. You took it away. You tore it from me. Everything I had, everything I ever wanted, you took it all away. Happiness, laughter, family, babies, Alec, the real Alec, *my* Alec. You took it all away. Don't make this worse. Please, just don't. Put down the ax."

He shook his head. "I did all of this for you. *For you.* I coulda made you happy. I could still make you happy."

"It'd make me happy, you put down that ax."

"Feb—"

"Don't hurt anyone else for me, Denny. Not even yourself. Just put down the ax."

"You don't understand. Why don't you understand? Everyone knows, everyone knows it's Feb and Alec. It's always been Feb and Alec. It'll always be Feb and Alec. No one's loved you like me."

"You're right about that," I whispered. "No one's loved me like you."

He read my words wrong. He read them like permission, his eyes went back to Colt and I knew. I knew what I was trying wasn't going to work.

"No one'll ever love you like me," he murmured and it was a vow. "All I've ever done, all I ever was, was for you."

Then he lunged.

I closed my eyes and screamed, but I still could hear the gunfire all around me.

Thirteen

STAVROS

"What?"

"You heard me, Feb."

I looked at Doc, speechless.

Doc patted my knee and got up, saying, "You can put your clothes back on."

I didn't move.

Instead, I asked, "How?"

He was walking to the sink and he turned to me, brows lifted, face carefully blank but, if I could think at that moment, I would have sworn he was trying not to laugh, and he repeated, "How?"

I was back to speechless.

"Feb, I'm guessin' you know how."

"But—"

"Have you and Colt been using protection?" Doc asked.

"No…but—"

"Then *that's* how."

"I'm forty-two years old," I reminded him.

"You still have a period?"

"Well, not anymore."

He chuckled. I went back to staring. He turned back to the sink and washed his hands.

When he came around again, drying them, he said softly, "Get off my table, February, get dressed and go tell Colt you're pregnant."

Then he tossed the paper towel in the trash and walked out of the room.

"Hey, Kath," I said, walking in the front door of the police station.

"Hey, Feb," Kath said back, grinning huge.

Since she couldn't know I was pregnant and probably wouldn't be grinning huge at that knowledge, (like I was grinning on the inside), just maybe grinning, I asked, "What?"

"Well, let me see..." Kath said, then leaned forward when I made it to the front counter. "I gotta count 'em down. First, Bethany kicked Cory's ass out last night."

I leaned forward too and repeated, "What?"

"Walked right into Tina Blackstone's house, caught them in the act and threw a fit to end all fits."

I put both hands on the counter and leaned forward. "So *that's* what all that noise was about last night. Colt was so pissed, I had to get creative so he wouldn't go over there and wade in."

Kath nodded, still grinning. "Forgot, you and Colt live across the street from Tina." Then her face changed, it went dreamy before she said, "Creative with Colt, bet that was fun."

"It was," I affirmed with my own smile, because it really, seriously was. "Anyway," I went on, deciding to share my own gossip, "Bethany may be loud but, the shocker is, Tina's louder."

"That doesn't surprise me. She always struck me as someone with a big mouth," Kath noted.

"Yeah, a big mouth is one thing, a *loud* mouth another. Bethany could win awards and still Tina's *a lot* louder."

Kath laughed then one upped me. "Did you know Bethany went into labor right then and there?"

"No joke?" I breathed.

"No joke," Kath replied. "And, right after she had the baby, a little girl, by the way, she kicked his ass out. They hadn't even cut the umbilical cord. Rumor has it, he's moving in with Tina."

"Out of the frying pan, into the fire," I muttered, and Kath's grin got even wider. "Wonder how Tina'll take to Cory playin' around."

"You and Colt might want to consider soundproofing," Kath suggested and I figured that'd be a good idea. "But that's not it," Kath told me.

"What's it, then?" I asked.

"Colt fucked Monica Merriweather."

I blinked fast about a dozen times before I asked again, "What?"

"Yonks ago he told her he'd give her an exclusive on the whole..." She stopped talking, her expression changed and she waved her hand in the air in an effort to say words she didn't really have to say. "Then, he didn't."

"I know."

"She's pissed. She's been in, like, every day for the last two months since it went down. Gettin' in Colt's face, gettin' in everyone's face and gettin' nothin'. Colt's sealed up tight. Sully's sealed up tight. Everyone's sealed up tight. Monica is persona non grata even more than she *was* persona non grata and pretty much everyone hated her before. Now she's not gettin' anything not just on *that* thing but on *everything.* She's been locked out."

"I know that too, Kath." And I did, Colt told me all about it.

"Welp, did you know Monica and Colt had a showdown just two feet away from me not ten minutes ago? Apparently, that reporter from *The Star's* got a book comin' out and before it's even in the bookstores, he's sold the movie rights."

I knew what she was saying.

I couldn't say I was pleased there was going to be a movie made about the Denny mess and I was also not pleased there was going to be a book. But Colt warned me this was probably going to happen. We'd been through weeks of reporters hounding us anywhere they could get to us before they realized we weren't talking, Sully wasn't talking, the FBI weren't talking. They finally figured out they were only going to get the information released as a matter of course and then the next story came along and they lost interest.

What I could say was I was pleased that Monica wasn't going to make her career from it.

Colt had told me about her and since the day Denny came back to town she'd been a serious pain in the ass. Calling Colt, calling me, stopping by the bar, coming to the station, bothering me when I was at Mimi's. She'd written three articles about us and made some shit up and it wasn't nice shit. Colt lost his cool and talked to Eli Levinson. Eli was one year ahead of Colt at high school, the wide receiver on the football team who went to law school, opened up his practice in town, and Eli owed Colt a favor. Eli paid up by slapping Monica and *The Gazette* with a cease and desist which included a threat of litigation should they libel us any further. *The Gazette* had gladly printed a retraction and also just as gladly used that as an excuse to dump Monica's ass. We'd heard word they'd fired her yesterday.

Evidently she wasn't too happy about losing her job *and* her promised (and reneged) exclusive on the story of the year.

"Who won the showdown?" I asked Kath, even though I knew the answer.

Kath was talking through her laughter as she answered, "Seein' as Monica got physical and is currently in lockdown, I'd say Colt won."

My mind filled with visions of short, pudgy Monica going up against tall, lean Colt. I swallowed back a giggle and looked up the stairs.

"She got physical with a police officer?" I asked.

"In the end, three," Kath answered.

I swallowed more laughter before saying, "So, is he in a good mood or a bad mood?"

"Can't say. Monica's in lockdown, which is good, but she had her hands on him, which he never liked."

I felt my lip curl and said, "I don't blame him."

"Prefers your hands on him, I reckon." I heard from my side and I turned to see Marty standing there.

My eyes went to his neck, the scar still vivid, and I felt that familiar tightness in my throat just as I fought it back and forced a smile.

"Hey, Marty," I said softly, reaching out and touching my fingers to his hand. His hand twisted and he touched my fingers back before both our hands fell away. "I hear you're back in uniform."

"Yeah, a week. Thinkin' about takin' a vacation."

I laughed and Kath said, "You just had a month and a half off and then some."

"Yeah, through April showers. Now sun's out and I feel the need to go fishin'," Marty answered.

"Then what you doin' at the station on your day off?" Kath asked.

"Heard Monica's in lockdown so I came to take a picture." He lifted up a digital camera. "Wanna put one in the visor of all the cruisers, do my bit to keep morale up." He turned to me. "Wanna copy?"

I shook my head. "Thanks, but no. I've seen enough of Monica for a while."

"Reckon so," Marty replied and I gave him a smile that said more than the fact that I thought he was funny. It was the smile I'd given him in his hospital room and more than a dozen times besides. In fact, every time I went to his house, with Colt, with Mom and Dad, with Dee and the kids, all of those times bringing casseroles or Mimi's baked goods, all of them not ever going to be enough to say "thank you for taking a bullet to the neck in an effort to protect me."

After I gave him my smile, I turned to Kath.

"Okay if I go up?" I asked, my eyes going to the stairs before I looked back at her.

"Sure," she said.

I smiled at her, gave Marty's arm a squeeze and then headed up the stairs.

Colt was at his desk, his back to me, his hand holding a phone to his ear, and I got a tickle in my belly from both seeing him and from holding my secret.

He turned to me and I read right away he wasn't in a good mood. He tipped his head to the chair by his desk and I headed that way.

"You got until Friday, Ned." I heard Colt say as I sat down beside his desk and I knew he wasn't in a bad mood just because of Monica but because we'd hired Ned to build onto the garage and he was jacking us around getting it finished.

This was unusual. Ned was known to get his work done on time and on budget.

Then again, Ned's wife had chosen about two days into our job to do a runner with one of Ned's workmen, leaving Ned with two kids not yet in kindergarten and, therefore, Ned's mind was on other things.

"Yeah, I get it. I know you've hit the shit, but you said it'd take three weeks. We're workin' on week six and I got a driveway full of crap. Both Feb and I are parkin' our cars on the street and Feb's car's barely got its new plates," Colt told him, and I smiled to myself because my new car with new plates was a cute, little, blue, convertible Volkswagen Beetle.

I'd won that fight using my high-heeled black shoes, a lacy black teddy that Jessie and I picked up at Victoria's Secret and the pool table. My strategy worked. By the time I asked him, Colt couldn't say no.

That was well before his birthday. On his birthday, he got what he'd always had way back when. Mom's pork tenderloin with her famous mustard sauce followed by an angel food cake and the whole family packed around our dining table. Dee had given him a framed picture of me and Colt that she took at the bar. It showed Colt at his stool, his legs spread, me standing between them. I had one arm around his shoulders, my other hand on his chest and my lips were resting on his hair. He had his forehead on my shoulder. We were both in profile but you could see we were both laughing. I didn't remember why we were laughing, but I did remember how his laughter felt sounding against my body. It was a great present and at that moment that picture was sitting on his desk.

My present was good too. It involved lacy underwear and high heels again, this time red and it included garters and stockings with seams up the back.

I liked Dee's present best.

Colt liked my present better.

"Nope, Ned, don't buy that since Jackie's been watchin' your kids," Colt went on, paused then sighed and said, "Just get some focus and get it done. Yeah?" He listened for another second then said, "All right, later," and he put down the phone.

Without hesitating, he rolled to me, leaned in, nabbed me behind the neck and pulled me forward for a hard, longish, closed-mouthed kiss right in front of everyone in the bullpen.

Back in the day Colt had been affectionate. He held my hand. He sat close and put his arm around my chair. When he walked me to class, he either had his thumb hooked in the back belt loop of my jeans or his arm around my shoulders.

Now it was the same and then some. If I was close, he was close, kissing, touching, holding hands, nabbing me and pulling me in to touch his mouth to the necklaces at my neck, wrapping his fist in my hair to hold my head steady just so he could talk to me. No matter where we were or who was watching.

At first I figured this had to do with what happened that day, what he'd walked into at the bar, what he'd walked into at Susie's. But I thought it'd die down.

When it didn't, I decided it had to do with all that and all that came before it and the fact that Colt was making up for lost time.

I didn't mind this, not at all. I didn't care who was watching either and I was happy to make up for lost time and I'd be happy if it lasted the rest of my life.

"Whatcha doin' here, baby?" he asked when he let me go but he stayed leaned into my space so I stayed leaned into his.

"Came by to tell you I got a reservation at Costa's tonight," I told him, having decided Costa's was the perfect place to tell Colt, if it all went okay, he was going to be a father. We'd had three more reservations there since it went down with Denny, and because of his work, we'd had to cancel all three.

He smiled but asked, "I thought you were on tonight."

"Called Cheryl. She could use the extra shift."

Colt's smile got bigger. "What time?"

"Seven."

"I can do that."

"Colt?" I called and he leaned in closer.

"Right in front of you, honey."

"Please, don't miss this one," I whispered, his head tipped to the side and his gaze grew intense.

"All right," he whispered back, seeing I was going to say no more, not then, and letting me have it. "I won't miss it."

My fingers curled around his knee and I pushed. "Promise me."

His fingers went into the hair at the side of my head, his palm warm against my cheek when he replied, "Baby, I promise."

I pressed my cheek into his palm.

Then I smiled.

"What do you think?" I asked Phy as I came out of the dressing room.

"Danny! Quit it and come here!" She ignored me and the other patrons staring at her aghast as she shouted loudly to her son who was racing through the rails of clothes.

"I like it, Auntie Feb." April, Phy's daughter was giving me the once, twice and three times over.

"Thanks, baby," I said to April and looked at Phy. "Phy?"

Phy looked at me as Danny slunk toward her, his lip sticking out. "You look good in everything, Feb."

"Thanks, but 'good' isn't what I'm going for."

"It's too tight," Danny announced, arriving and stopping just outside his mother's reach to cross his arms on his little boy chest and glare at my dress.

I smiled at him. "Now *that's* what I'm going for."

Phy gave me a look that made me laugh softly and I went back into the dressing room and changed back into my jeans and tee.

I was thinking the dress was overkill considering in a few months I wouldn't be able to wear it. Furthermore, I was going to need a whole new wardrobe for a while. Money wasn't getting low but it was flowing out pretty damned fast.

I'd cashed in some CDs and some bonds, bought the car, the garage door opener and paid Ned. Colt and I had also pre-paid a cabin by a lake in Wisconsin for a week in June. He'd want to fish, I knew, and I'd want to do absolutely nothing but be with him, even if he was doing something as mind-numbingly boring as fishing. So that worked for both of us.

Colt and I, Dee and Morrie, Mom and Dad as well as a number of other citizens helped pay for Angie's funeral. It had been as nice as a funeral could be.

Mom and Dad had flat out paid for Joe-Bob's. His had been nicer, most of the town showed up, which meant most of the town shut down to do it. It was the biggest funeral I'd ever seen, standing room only at Markham and Sons. The few people left in town to drive by would have seen Joe-Bob went way past five on the funeral popularity scale, tipping the pointer straight to the unheard of ten.

After, Mom and Dad, Morrie and I threw a huge party at J&J's. We gave out tickets, first drink free, and Dad grilled bratwursts in the alley that Dee, Mom, Mimi, Jessie and Lorraine had cleaned up with Morrie, Jimbo, Al, Sully and Chris's help doing the heavy work. They'd festooned it with lights, balloons and streamers. It wasn't a place of death and kidnapping and blood anymore, but a happy place, a place to party. We'd partied and, as usual, the party had lasted all night.

I reckon Joe-Bob would have liked that.

With all that spending, it was lucky that it was summer and turnover at the bar always went up in summer.

But it was more. The races were on and we were now a place of interest, almost a tourist attraction. Folks coming into the bar to see where a serial killer made his final kill, to have a look at the woman who was his obsession. Some even took pictures of Joe-Bob's stool, a stool Morrie, on his own and not telling anyone, had taken away and reupholstered in black velvet, a big, black, satin ribbon attached across the seat, the sides of which were big, satin bows. Every day upon opening, Morrie or Darryl or me poured out a draft and rested the mug on the seat. It was a memorial of sorts.

It was also a stool no one but no one put their ass on anymore and never would.

Then there were some who even tried to take pictures of me.

Pictures of the stool pissed everyone off but we got used to it, as long as they bought a drink or two, we let it slide. When they tried to take a photo of me that was a different story. It pissed Morrie and Dad off when they tried it. It pissed Darryl off more. They pointed their camera or cell phone at me, they were shown the door, usually by Darryl. Sometimes, they were shown the door in a not very nice way, again usually by Darryl. A couple of times, it was so not nice, they called the cops. Unsurprisingly, any cop that showed up to that call arrived and they weren't in a very good mood when they did. Not at Darryl, at tourists doing stupid shit that fucked up their day. The cops didn't tend to spend a lot of time explaining their bad mood before they explained where the town line was and asked if the tourist wanted an escort there. The tourists usually declined their offer at an escort but took them up on the directions.

I hung up the dress, grabbed my bag, exited the dressing room and Phylenda, April, Danny and I walked to the cash register.

When I handed over my credit card, Phy asked, "You gonna let me in on your sudden need to have a fancy tight dress?"

I turned to her and didn't hesitate. "Yeah, I figure I better wear fancy tight dresses while I got the chance, seein' as, in a few months, I'll be big as a house."

Phy wasn't one to show her emotions, she didn't give much away. She'd learned to hold things close and not expose anything, give anyone a weapon they might use against her.

But Phy was changing. Nearly losing her man a different way and him being made into a hero by town's talk and his own actions had a way of doing that. Darryl did what he did and he showed his true self, maybe late, but he did it. She found herself in the position of having a man who she could be proud of and her kids having that kind of father. For years, Darryl'd been working hard to show her he was that man, but she couldn't ever trust it. He put his life on the line to save mine and that was different. She wasn't used to being able to hold her head up high, but I could tell she was getting used to it. I could also tell she liked it a lot.

Therefore, when she read my meaning, her eyes went wide then they grew wet.

"You're serious?"

"Doc told me today."

"How far along?"

"Ten weeks."

Phy blinked, I giggled, leaned close and whispered, "Yeah, I think it happened the first time we did it."

She whistled and said, "Shee-it, Colt's swimmers must be super-powered."

I didn't doubt that, practically everything about Colt seemed super-powered.

I signed the receipt, took the bag and we headed into the mall, making a bee-line toward Jessie's favorite shoe shop.

"I'm scared," I told Phy, my eyes on the kids who were wandering ahead of us aimlessly, taking in all they could around the mall, probably wondering what they could ask their mom to buy them that she wouldn't say no to.

"Why?" Phy asked and I looked at her.

"I'm not exactly twenty anymore."

"Women havin' babies later and later, seems to work for them."

I looked back at Danny and April. "Yeah, maybe so, but doesn't seem much works for me and Colt."

I jumped when Phy's arm went around my waist and I looked back to her. She wasn't open and she wasn't touchy either. But now she was close.

"Feb, that was then and this," she put her other hand to my belly, "is now."

I pressed my lips together and I felt my own eyes get wet.

She smiled at me as I breathed deep.

Then she dropped her hands, shouted at her kids and we turned into the shoe shop.

"What's the big to do?" Dee asked, arms crossed, eyes on me, much like Jessie and Meems (though their arms weren't crossed), all of us scrunched into Mimi's little office at the back of her coffee shop. "I gotta get back to the bar."

"Jeez, Dee, you act like that bar'll crumble to the ground, you're not in it," Jessie muttered and Dee swung her eyes to Jessie.

"Yeah, well, I love Darryl. We all love Darryl. We all know *why* we love Darryl. That don't mean Darryl can hold down the fort without a little help," Dee retorted, being generous with her words for, hero or not, once Darryl recovered and got back to work a couple of weeks ago, he had not, unsurprisingly, changed. "Ruthie's on vacation. Cheryl's not on until seven. Morrie's at home with the kids. Jackie's watchin' Ned's babies and Jack's in the office, payin' invoices. Not to mention, Feb's here, actin' weird and goin' shoppin' with Phy, of all people."

"Yeah," Jessie's eyes swung to me and they held accusation clear as day. "Why're you shoppin' with Phy?"

"She has the day off and she needs to get out of the house every once in a while," I told Jessie.

"But *I'm* your shopping buddy," Jessie told me. "Phy's your movie buddy."

Since the incident I had taken to spelling Phy's nursemaiding Darryl by taking her to the movies. When I did this, whoever was available, Mom, Dad, even Colt, watched over Danny and April and also Darryl.

"Today, Phy's my shopping buddy," I said to Jessie.

"Well, don't think I'm gonna be your movie buddy. I don't like goin' to the theater. You can't pause the movie if you all of a sudden find you want some Raisinettes," Jessie decreed.

"Can we get to the point of why Feb's asked us here at all?" Mimi put in.

"Yeah, I gotta get back," Dee repeated.

"You said that," Jessie told her.

"All right, guys," I cut in, "eyes on me." When they turned me, I went on. "You have to swear, I tell you this, you keep it a secret, no one, no husbands, no friends, no parents, no sisters, you tell no one, not until nine o'clock tomorrow morning. Got me?"

Their faces had all changed, gone curious and expectant. They were getting used to a February Owens who shared and I found they liked it a whole lot. Since they did, I also found I did it a whole lot more.

"Colt asked you to marry him," Mimi breathed her very wrong guess.

"Hallelujah!" Dee shouted before I could confirm or, more accurately, deny.

"I get to be Matron of Honor!" Jessie screeched.

Before I could say word one, Mimi turned to her and demanded to know, "Why do you get to be Matron of Honor?"

"I found her first," Jessie said to Mimi.

"So? You got to be *my* Matron of Honor and Feb got to be *your* Maid of Honor and that means *I* get to be *Feb's* Matron of Honor," Mimi returned.

"Guys," I tried to interrupt.

Jessie ignored me and said to Mimi, "Yeah, but I still found her first."

"What you're sayin' is, I'm forty-two years old and I'm gonna die not bein' *anyone's* Matron of Honor?" Mimi retorted.

"Guys," I repeated.

"It ain't all it's cracked up to be," Jessie told her.

"Yeah, so, why you want it so bad?" Meems shot back.

"Guys!" I shouted. "Colt didn't ask me to marry him. I'm pregnant!"

Everyone's gaze came to me then they froze.

"What'd you say?" Dee whispered.

"I'm ten weeks pregnant."

They all stared at me then Meems burst into tears, came forward and yanked me out of my chair and into her arms. Then I felt Jessie get close then Dee, everyone holding onto everyone and Jessie and Dee jumping up and down a bit.

I felt their jumps, their arms, their tears that were now coming through laughter and I suddenly wondered what Angie would have done, she'd lived to see this day. Angie, who knew how I felt about Colt before anyone because I'd confided it to her when we were eleven. Angie, who'd called me and patched things up the minute she heard Colt took me on our first date.

Angie's life may have worn her down before it was snuffed out, but I reckon this news would have lightened the load more than a little even if for just a short time. I didn't know what to do with that knowledge so, like a lot of shit, I set it aside until there came a quiet time where I could give it to Colt, he could give me a squeeze or a kiss or do something else that only he had the magical power to do, and the pain of it would melt away.

They pulled back but all of them kept a hand on me.

"Colt doesn't know?" Jessie asked.

I shook my head. "We're goin' to Costa's tonight."

"Perfect," Dee whispered, tears still shining in her eyes.

"Yeah," I whispered back, looking at Dee then at Jessie then at Meems. Feeling their touch light on me. Seeing the wet glistening on their cheeks, their smiles full of joy for me, for Colt, for our future, a future that was bright. I finished with, "Perfect."

"Thanks for doin' this," Colt said to Cheryl as they walked up the front walk to Ned's house.

"No worries," Cheryl replied, her eyes on the door.

She'd cut her hair shorter so it just brushed her shoulders. She also regularly wore mini-skirts and high-heeled shoes even working at the bar. Both were her style and both looked good on her. So good, Feb said that Cheryl told her tips at J&J's were better than her tips stripping. This probably had something to do with the fact that J&J's was busier than ever seeing as now it was infamously famous and also seeing that neither Feb nor Cheryl were hard to look at, which meant the standard clientele had upped substantially.

"How's Ethan gettin' on in his new school?" Colt asked.

So she didn't have to drive to town from Indy and also drive back in the dead of morning, Cheryl had moved into Morrie's apartment with Jack and Jackie, who spent most of their time at Morrie and Dee's or J&J's anyway, often looking after Ethan along the way.

"Likin' it, made some friends, has play dates, friends sleepin' over, sleepin' over at friends. He's at a play date now," she replied then her neck twisted and she pressed her lips together before she stopped on the front stoop and looked up at Colt. "Moms here know me as workin' at J&J's, not a strip club. Got no problem, their kid hangin' with someone whose mom works at J&J's. Back then...well, goes without sayin', a stripper's house isn't the popular choice for a play date."

"That's good," Colt said quietly.

"Yeah, it is," Cheryl said readily and looked him straight in the eye. "You ain't gonna like hearin' this but I gotta say it and I'll only say it once, yeah?"

Colt figured she was right; he wouldn't like hearing what she had to say.

He'd discovered that when Cheryl wasn't guarded, and even when she was, she was a straight talker. She was usually pretty cautious with this around Feb, Colt, Morrie, Dee, Ruthie, Jack, Jackie and Darryl, mostly because she liked them all and never guarded against showing that. But she didn't hesitate unleashing her straight talk on customers. Feb said it was a good trait to have working at a bar. But then again, Feb took one look at Cheryl, who'd come into the bar with her son Ethan, and a half second later

Feb planted Cheryl firmly under her wing just as Colt suspected she would. Colt figured Cheryl could do just about anything and Feb would accept it.

"Yeah?" Colt prompted, wanting to get it over with, whatever it was.

"He was a crazy, fucked up mess and he did awful shit but, in a way, he led me out of a trap I couldn't find my way out of and probably never would. I ain't grateful to him. I'm grateful to you. But that doesn't change the fact that he's what brought me here."

"You brought yourself here," Colt told her, not giving Denny an inch, no credit, not for any of the good shit that he'd been the undeniable catalyst for kicking off. That sick ass didn't deserve any and Colt was firmly of the belief that eventually, somehow, for everyone, even Cheryl, it would have all found its way to good without Denny. "You could have made a different decision."

She just looked at him and remarked, "Not real good at acceptin' gratitude, are you, Colt?"

Colt gave it back to her straight. "Not real good at talkin' about Denny Lowe."

She nodded in understanding. "Like I said, just this once, no more."

Before Colt could say anything else, Jackie opened the door.

"Get in here quick," Jackie said, pushing open the screen. "They're asleep, miracle I got them both down. We time it right, Colt, and I can be done and back before they wake up."

"It's cool, Jackie. Ethan was a handful, got up to more than three kids. I can handle it," Cheryl told her, pushing in.

Jackie gave Colt a look that spoke volumes about Ned's now motherless children and she showed Cheryl around the house, giving instructions as they went. They put their heads into the kids' room, and as all this was happening, Colt waited in the living room. When they came back, Jackie and Colt said good-bye to Cheryl and Colt led Jackie to his truck.

When they were on their way, Jackie took in a breath and asked, "You talk to Susie?"

Colt didn't want to think about Susie.

Darryl, Phy, Marty and Joe-Bob's kids had all handled what happened remarkably well, throwing no blame, which was good since only blame could be settled was on a dead man, so it was a waste of emotion.

Melanie had been a wreck, which wasn't a surprise. She was in counseling and Colt checked on her a couple of times a week, mostly because Feb nagged him to do so. Though if she hadn't, he still would have done it just maybe not as often. Melanie had been off work for a while but had finally gone back. She was pulling herself together, she was doing it slowly, which was her way, but at least she was doing it.

Susie, being Susie, hadn't handled it so well.

"I talked to her."

"She the one who gave it to that kid from *The Star*?" Jackie asked.

"Yeah," Colt answered.

Jackie sighed then said softly, "People work things out in different ways."

Jackie was wrong or, more likely, she was being generous. Susie wasn't working anything out. Susie was, as usual, being a bitch.

The only thing that surprised him was the stories printed in *The Star* laid out the truth about Feb and Colt as far as Susie knew it, but there was nothing ugly, nothing mean. Colt figured the way Feb had a lock on the unconscious Susie, clearly in shock, so much, after they took down Denny, they had a job of getting Feb to let her go, Susie absorbed something good from Feb. It was a fanciful notion, but since Susie didn't have many not ugly, not mean bones in her body, that was the only way he *could* figure it.

Jackie changed the subject and remarked, "Don't know why you aren't takin' Jack or Morrie." She looked from the road to Colt and said, "You know I like me a bike, honey, but pickin' a Harley is man's work."

"We aren't lookin' at bikes, Jackie," Colt told her then pulled into a spot on the street in front of Reinhart's Jewelry Store, stopped and turned off his truck.

She looked out her window to the store then she looked at Colt then back at the store.

He knew she'd cottoned on to the situation when she dropped her forehead to the window and whispered, "You shoulda brought Cheryl. My fingers are bigger than Feb's."

"Your taste's the exact same, though."

It was a lie. Jackie's taste was nothing like Feb's. She knew it and he knew it. Colt just wanted her there. He knew she knew that too and it took a beat, but he heard the hitch in her throat that meant tears and he put his hand to her back.

"Jackie, look at me."

She took her time but she turned to look at him, tears in her eyes but a shaky smile on her face.

"You know, I was honored, dancin' the mother's dance with you at your and Melanie's wedding," she whispered.

"Yeah, you told me then."

He could barely hear her when she said, "I'll like this one better."

Colt didn't say a word before she turned and was out the door and heading to the store.

This was partly because she moved fast.

This was mostly because he couldn't speak around the lump in his throat.

"All right, you got us both, what's this about, son?" Jack asked when Morrie closed the office door at J&J's.

Jack was in the desk chair. Morrie had his shoulders to the door. Colt had his shoulders to the wall.

Colt didn't mince words. "Just got back from Jackie helpin' me pick out Feb's engagement ring."

Morrie turned and slammed his palm against the wall, giving a whoop.

Jack dropped his head and stared in his lap.

Colt ignored Morrie and called, "Jack?"

"Out," Jack muttered.

"Dad?" Morrie called.

"Out," Jack repeated, and they both heard it.

Colt looked at Morrie to see Morrie was looking at him. Without another word, they walked out.

Ignoring the fact that they left Jack in the office crying, something they'd never seen in their life and something they were both pretty fucking happy they hadn't really seen then, Morrie asked Colt, "You want a beer?"

"Nope, got shit to do."

Morrie scooted behind the bar and Colt stopped at the side of it.

"You told Sully?" Morrie asked.

Colt's felt his brows draw together and annoyance hitting him. "Before I told you and Jack?"

"Just askin'," Morrie muttered.

"Shit, Morrie, seriously?"

"Already did best man duties at one of your weddings. I figure—"

One of his weddings?

"Don't fuck with me, Morrie," Colt warned.

"You two are close."

"Yeah, close enough for him to be in the wedding party. Shit, Morrie, you're gonna be my fuckin' brother-in-law."

Morrie's head jerked as this knowledge dawned on him then he grinned. "Yeah."

"And you've been my best friend since I was five."

Morrie's grin got bigger. "Yeah again."

"So don't fuck with me."

"Dude, be cool," Morrie said, still grinning.

Colt shook his head and rapped his knuckles on the bar, moving to leave. "Gotta go."

"Colt, wait," Morrie called. Colt stopped and turned to his friend. "I'm happy for you."

Colt nodded and smiled. "Thanks, man."

"I'm happier for her," Morrie said quietly and Colt felt his neck twist.

"Right."

"Thank you for bringin' her back."

"Morrie."

"I missed her, man."

"Morrie."

"Dad did too."

"Stop, Morrie."

"Dude, just sayin'—"

Colt cut him off and put an end to that particular conversation. "You're welcome."

Morrie nodded then declared, "If you don't play 'Mony Mony' at the reception, I'm boycotting."

Colt moved to leave, shaking his head again. "I'll make note of that."

"And 'Shout,'" Morrie yelled at Colt's back. Colt lifted a hand and flicked out his fingers. "And 'Livin' on a Prayer,'" Morrie went on and Colt stopped and turned to him.

"It's a wedding reception, Morrie, not a fuckin' '80s flashback."

Morrie's eyes swept the bar and when they hit Colt, he was grinning again.

Colt reckoned about fifty cell phones were now being dialed. He was still shaking his head when he walked out the front door and he didn't care that news was right then sweeping town, not at all.

Colt sat on the top of picnic table at Arbuckle Acres Park, his feet on the bench and he watched his mother walk up to him, as always, clutching her purse.

When she got close, he called, "Hey, Ma."

Her smile was small and hesitant, as always, when she replied, "Hey, Alec."

He watched as she sat on the bench by his feet, her eyes to the ground.

"How're you gettin' on?" he asked her and her head came up but her hand never quit clutching the strap on her purse.

"Where's Feb?" she asked back instead of answering.

"Don't know. She's been kind of busy."

Her eyes slid to look over his shoulder and she muttered, "She usually comes with you."

"I needed to talk to you alone today."

Her eyes slid back to his and then skidded over his shoulder.

"Everything okay?" she asked the sky over his shoulder.

"Everything's good."

"Feb okay?"

"Yeah."

"The family?"

"We're all fine, Ma."

She nodded then looked back at the ground. "Your dad's home."

"You told me that last time, Ma."

"He's doin' good, stayin' sober, just like me."

"Glad to hear it," Colt said, and he was. At least he was glad to hear it about her.

"He said he wants you to think about lettin' him come, next time you call."

Colt shook his head. "Ma—"

"Just think, Alec. Next time we talk then you can tell me, okay?"

Colt kept shaking his head. "Don't want you to get your hopes up."

She looked at him and said, "Talk to Feb about it."

"Ma—"

"Just promise me you'll talk to Feb, please, Alec?"

Colt looked at his mother. Two months ago, Mary Colton had helped to save three lives, one was precious to him and the other two, in one way or another, meaningful to him, though Melanie more so. There were a few very unlikely heroes in that town. Darryl was one of them, Mary Colton another. But both changed their earned reputations proving that deep down they had something that made those reputations false.

For that reason, he said, "I'll talk to Feb, but you should know, even if I do, the answer is unlikely to change."

"I know," she whispered and her eyes yet again slid away.

"I'm askin' her to marry me," Colt told her and her gaze shot right back.

She was still whispering when she asked, "What?"

"Tonight."

"Oh my God," she breathed and her hand came to his knee.

She hadn't touched him, not since they started to meet there at the park, almost always with Feb bringing coffees and treats from Mimi's or a packed lunch. It didn't matter to Feb that it wasn't 911 that pointed them to Susie's house, but Colt's mother, Feb would have come with him anyway if he wanted to meet his mother. But Colt did wonder if she'd bring coffees, baked goods or packed lunches if Mary Colton hadn't helped to save her life.

Though, he guessed she would.

Colt put his hand on his mother's at his knee, her body jerked and she tried to pull her hand away but his fingers curled around hers, holding it tight.

He caught her eyes and kept her gaze, speaking softly. "I don't want to hurt you but you gotta know, I'm dancin' the mother son dance with Jackie." She closed her eyes and he squeezed her hand until she opened them again then he continued. "But, you stay sober, I want you there. Not him, just you. Yeah?"

She nodded and he squeezed her hand again.

"Will you..." Her voice was choked. She cleared her throat and her hand jerked in his but he kept his hold firm. She pulled in breath through her nose and asked, "I don't...well, we both know I don't deserve that dance, but will you dance another dance with me?"

"Yeah," Colt replied without hesitation.

Her hand twitched in his and she repeated, "Yeah?"

"You stay sober, then, yeah."

"I'll stay sober, son," she promised.

"I reckon you will," he told her and again her hand twitched.

He'd never believed in her, never.

Then again, she'd never stayed sober this long and she'd never saved Feb's life, so he figured he owed her that.

She pressed her lips together, sucked in breath through her nostrils, keeping control but just barely. Then she nodded and she squeezed his hand.

"You need money?" Colt asked.

"We're good," she said quickly.

Colt tugged gently on her hand. "Ma, you need money?"

She pulled in another breath through her nose, shook her head, and said softly, "We're good, honey."

"Call me, you do."

"Okay."

"Maybe next time you can come over to the house, have dinner."

He watched her swallow then nod. "I'd like that."

He gave her one last squeeze and then let her hand go. Pushing up, he jumped off the table and she stood up.

As he walked beside her to her car, she asked, "Feb a good cook?"

"Yeah, though she mostly cooks breakfast. Dinner we usually have Frank's at the bar. Or Reggie's."

"Frank's a better cook than most everyone I know."

"That's the truth."

"And Reggie's is the best pizza I've had in my life and I used to live in Chicago so you know what that means."

"I do."

She stopped at the driver's side door and before she could do it, Colt leaned in and opened it for her.

She didn't get in. She tipped her head back and looked at him.

"You happy, Colt?"

He felt his body jerk and he blinked.

She'd never called him Colt.

He covered his surprise and the strangely welcome feeling he felt at her calling him by what he considered his true name by answering, "Yeah."

She nodded. "All a mother can ask." She put her hand on top of his, his was resting on top of the door, and she dipped her face, looking into the car and muttering under her breath, "Love you, son."

Then she quickly folded herself into the car, and without looking at him, grabbed the handle, slammed the door, started the car and pulled away. She was ten car lengths away before she got the courage to toot her horn.

When Colt heard it, he couldn't bite back his smile.

Colt opened the front door, entered and shouted over the loud music, "Baby, I'm home."

"Be right out!" He heard Feb's words coming down the hall.

Wilson trotted into the room, stopped, looked at Colt and let out a loud meow.

"Quiet, cat," he muttered and Wilson replied with a louder meow.

Colt shrugged off his blazer then his shoulder holster. He hooked the blazer around the back of a dining table chair, threw the holster on the table, unclipped his badge and threw that on it too.

He hit the kitchen and saw the remote for the stereo sitting by Feb's cell phone. He picked up the remote, pointed it into the den and turned down the music. Then he looked at her cell phone and was grateful for the music, seeing as she had twelve missed calls, all of them likely about them playing 'Livin' on a Prayer' at their wedding reception, a reception Feb didn't know about yet. Then Colt went to the cupboard with the cat treats and Wilson let out another loud meow.

Colt shook the treats into his palm then he threw one into the living room. Wilson watched it go until he lost sight then he ran after it. Colt couldn't see the cat but he heard another meow and he sent another treat sailing and heard Wilson's cat feet chasing after it.

This happened twice more before Feb's voice came from the hall again.

"You're making him fat."

She was right. This had come to be Colt and Wilson's habit when Colt got home and Wilson was getting fat. Feb had put a limit on three treats a night. Colt and Wilson ignored that limit and jacked it up to six. This was mostly because, if Colt didn't go to six, Wilson wouldn't shut up.

"He's fine," Colt said, his hand up about to throw another treat before Feb hit the room and he saw her.

She was wearing a skintight, dark purple dress and a pair of high-heeled, sexy sandals. Her makeup was heavier than normal and nearly as sexy as her shoes. Her hair was partially sleeked but it had more wave and volume than usual and it was far sexier than her shoes. Colt felt the vision of her score a path from his lungs, through his gut, straight to his dick.

He'd been right. She had something planned tonight and he sure as fuck wasn't letting her steal his goddamned thunder.

"That's quite a dress," he remarked when he could speak again, then Wilson meowed. He threw the cat treat and Wilson's paws could be heard scampering after it.

"That's enough treats," Feb replied, stopping opposite the dining table and putting her hands to her hips, which meant the material at her tits stretched tight and he felt that in his dick too.

He shook out another treat and sent it sailing.

"Colt!" Feb snapped

"Come here," Colt replied.

Her eyes went to the microwave and then back to his. "You're late. It's six forty-five. We've gotta go."

Colt put the lid back on the treats and set it on the counter before he repeated, "Come here, Feb."

She ignored him and said, "Can I drive?"

"No," Colt answered. "Come here."

She tipped her head to the side. "Why can't I drive?"

"Deal was you could have that car as long as I don't have to get in it. Remember?"

"That was a stupid deal," she muttered.

"You agreed to it."

"I was coerced," she shot back and this was true. She'd played him using her shoes, her hands, her mouth, her ass, her pussy, her lacy teddy and the pool table, and after she got what she wanted, he'd played her right back.

Her hands went from her hips to cross on her chest. "Come on, Colt, it's a new car. I like drivin' it."

"We're goin' somewhere, *anywhere*, I drive and I don't drive a fuckin' Beetle."

She rolled her eyes saying, "You're such a man."

This was true too, but Colt decided not to agree to something that was obvious.

"Feb, not gonna say it again," Colt warned her. "Come here."

He watched as her eyes locked on him and her body locked too.

Then she asked, "Why?"

"Just do it."

"Why?"

"Feb—" he started.

But she muttered, "Oh, all right," dropped her arms and walked to him in the kitchen. As she did so, he put his hand in his pocket, palmed the ring there and pulled his hand back out.

She stopped in front of him, tipped her head back and asked, "What?"

Colt leaned his hips back against the counter and looked at her.

There had been a time in his life when he knew without a doubt this moment would come. Then there was a time in his life when he knew without a doubt this moment would never come. The first he took for granted.

The second had cut so deep, it'd been raw for decades, and he'd had to learn, with some difficulty, to ignore it.

When he was twenty-two, he'd had thoughts of tulips and candlelight and even getting down on his knee.

Now that the time was there, he didn't mind that he was going to do it in a kitchen with his hips against the counter and Feb impatient to get to Costa's so she could do what he was just then going to do. He knew from the way she behaved at the station that she wanted to talk about marriage and he wasn't about to let her do it without his ring on her finger.

"You know I love you," he told her and her ear dipped to her shoulder just as her eyes went soft and her lips tipped up.

"Yeah," she whispered.

"Love you enough to let you get that damned car," he said and the softness went out of her face.

"I'm thinkin' the word 'let' when you're talkin' about me should be banished from this house," she declared and Colt grinned.

"Love you enough to let you spend your money on my garage."

"*Our* garage."

"Instead of heels."

"Colt, hello?" she called. "Black, red…" she pointed to her feet, "now matte silver."

"Matte silver?" Colt repeated, still grinning.

"The color of my shoes," she informed him and he looked down.

"Is that what that's called?"

"Like you care," she mumbled, and he looked back at her.

"You're right, I don't care."

She rolled her eyes and his hand shot out, nabbing her behind her neck and pulling her forward. She lost her balance and landed full-body against him, her hands at his waist, fingers curled into the material of his shirt there as his other arm snaked around her waist.

He wrapped his fist in her hair and tugged her head back. "Love it when you roll your eyes, baby," he whispered and her expression grew soft again.

"What's got into you tonight?" she whispered back, her eyes searching his face. "You're acting weird."

"I want it big," he answered and those dents formed at her brows again. "The biggest."

"Want what big?"

"Our wedding."

She closed her eyes and lifted her brows and when she opened them again, his right hand took her left and pulled it in front of them. He watched her eyes drop to their hands, but he didn't take his from hers so he could watch the wonder that stole into her features as he slid his ring on her finger.

When he'd seated the ring at the base, he repeated quietly, "The biggest."

"Colt," she whispered to their hands, her eyes on the diamond there.

"Food, a band, dancing, a shitload of flowers and you in a white dress," Colt told her, pressing her hand flat to his chest, and her eyes went to his as his arm curled back around her waist to hold her body close.

"Colt."

"We're ridin' away on a Harley, though."

"Colt."

"Honeymoon on a beach."

"Colt."

His head came down and he put his mouth to hers. "I'm gonna fuck you in the sand under the stars."

Both her hands curled around his neck, her fingers going into his hair and she whispered, "Colt."

"You gonna marry me, baby?"

She tipped her head so their foreheads were pressed together and she rubbed her nose along the side of his before she said, "Yeah."

His eyes dropped to her mouth and he muttered, "Good."

Before he could kiss her, she pulled her head away.

"Can I say something?" she asked.

"After I kiss you."

"No, before."

"What?"

"I just have one question to ask."

"The answer is yes."

Her lips tipped up, her face got that soft look yet again, and Colt's hand tightened automatically in her hair as his arm at her waist gave her a squeeze.

"That's good," she whispered.

"What's good?" he asked.

"That the answer is yes. 'Cause, see, I still wanna name our son Jack or, if it's a girl, our daughter Jacqueline."

Colt's body turned to stone, his mind blanked, his stomach dropped but his mouth moved to form one, quiet word. "What?"

"If the baby I'm carrying is a boy, I want to name him—"

Feb didn't get to finish because before she could, Colt yanked her even closer, took her mouth with his, and he kissed her.

The phone rang and Stavros Costa rushed to it.

"Costa's," he answered.

"Stavros, it's Colt."

Stavros looked down at his reservation book then up at the clock then he rolled his eyes, knowing what was coming.

"You're canceling," Stavros said into the phone. "Again," he finished.

"We're on our way."

"It's nine o'clock, you're two hours late."

"Coupla things came up."

"I gave your table away, Colt, an hour ago."

"Got another one?"

"Colt—"

Stavros heard Colt cut in. "February's wearin' my ring and carryin' my baby, Stavros." Stavros sucked in breath at this long awaited, very welcome, unbelievably happy news, and Colt finished. "Now, you got a table or what?"

Stavros grinned into the phone. "Don't got one, I'll build one."

He put down the phone on Alexander Colton's laughter.

The 'Burg Series continues with *At Peace*.

Made in the USA
Lexington, KY
27 January 2017